CHLOE'S MISTIGRI

a novel by

Thomas L Hall

NoCo Publishing

FORT COLLINS

NoCo Publishing, LLC

This book is a work of fiction. Any references to historical events, real people, or real places are used fictitiously. Other names, characters, places, and events are products of the author's imagination, and any resemblance to actual events or places or persons, living or dead, is entirely coincidental.

Chloe's Mistigri. Copyright © 2020, 2021 by Thomas L Hall. All Rights Reserved. Printed in the United States of America. No part of this book may be used or reproduced in any manner whatsoever without advanced written permission except in the case of brief quotations embodied in critical articles or reviews. For information, contact NoCo Publishing at www.nocopublishing.com.

NoCo Publishing and design are trademarks of NoCo Publishing, LLC.

For information about special discounts for bulk purchases, or to inquire about bringing the author to your virtual or live event, please see contact information at www.nocopublishing.com.

Book jacket art Copyright © 2020, 2021 by Thomas L Hall. All rights reserved. Cover design by Danielle Mazzella di Bosco. Image of the Flying Tigers, a photograph by Robert T. Smith, copyright usage by permission of his son, Brad Smith.

Map art Copyright © 2020, 2021 by Amanda Smith. All rights reserved.

10 9 8 7 6 5 4 3 2 1

Library of Congress Cataloging-in-Publication Data has been applied for.

Names: Hall, Thomas L
Title: Chloe's Mistigri / Thomas L Hall.
Description: Second NoCo Publishing hardcover edition. | Fort Collins : NoCo Publishing, 2021.
Identifiers: LCCN 2020919479 | ISBN 978-1-7357881-6-6 (hardcover)

BISAC: FICTION / Literary. | FICTION / Coming of Age. | FICTION / Historical / World War II. | FICTION / African American / Historical. | FICTION / Southern. | FICTION / Friendship.

ISBN 978-1-7357881-4-2 (ebook)

For

Pumpkin, Sweet Cheeks and Criquette

CHLOE'S MISTIGRI

CHAPTER	
	PROLOGUE
1	CRICKETS
2	LE MARDI GRAS
3	GREENVILLE
4	THE LEVEE
5	ST. LOUIS NO. 3
6	THE KING RANCH
7	MARIA AND MARIE
8	ASHES
9	LOUIS'S STAR
10	ON TOUR
11	IT AIN'T THE ALAMO
12	INTRODUCTIONS
13	THE MUSIC BOX CAFÉ
14	FUTURES
15	HOWARD AWAITS
16	THE RECRUITMENT
17	GOODBYE
18	THE JAGERSFONTEIN
19	THE LAGOON
20	THE OLD MAN'S SCHOOL
21	ORION
22	IT AIN'T SANTA CLAUS
23	CHRISTMAS IN BURMA
24	RELIEF
25	MISTIGRI
26	THE BIG APPLE
27	HAMILTON
28	REUNION
29	THE HUMP
30	THE RAJ
31	THE LAST RUN
32	EL HOTEL NATIONAL
33	THE LETTER
34	GONE FISHIN'
35	REMINISCENCE
36	TRADING RECIPES
37	THIRTY-TWO
38	SHINE

CHINA-BURMA-INDIA THEATER

mistigri (mistigris) [mistigri] *n.m.* **1** cat **2** jack of clubs, one-eyed jack **3** joker (in a deck of cards) <***Loc:*** IB, VM, Da84, Lv88>[1]

---

[1] "Mistigri." *Dictionary of Louisiana French, As Spoken in Cajun, Creole and American Indian Communities,* Albert Valdman, Senior Editor. Jackson, MS: University Press of Mississippi, 2010, p. 400.

PROLOGUE

APRIL 1934

He figured the water oak's split trunk was maybe eight feet at the base. Hard to say with the roots spreading like that. Up top, ten thousand blue-green leaves, refreshed from the rain, welcomed the noonday sun. PJ lay below, his head turned on the cool damp grass, playing a game with the light that slivered through the rustling leaves with each breezy gust to bounce off the ground. He counted the flashes that disappeared in an instant.

"Like them fireflies on the Alabama."

He climbed to his feet and circled the tree to where the Spanish moss hung low over the water's edge, taking measure of the long tapering branch that arched out over the coulee. It bowed some, then straightened again above the water.

"Looks like it's smilin'."

Last night's hard rain would do wonders for the fields east of town. That's what Frank said at breakfast. As for the coulee, it was churning, up a couple feet but still well below the banks. Sleep was cool last night for the first time since he arrived, but this noonday air was thick, hanging heavy like clothes forgotten on the line. He struggled his sticky T-shirt over his head and rolled up the thin, dingy cloth. Other than icy cold Dr. Pepper, he liked nothing better on a steaming hot day than cool shaded mud in his toes.

Shirtless PJ Benoit was a sight to behold. Washboard abdomen, chiseled arms swinging from broad shoulders that shaped a triangle over his tiny waist. He was a physical aberration, his body looking more like a featherweight boxer in his prime than a newly twelve-year-old boy all of four feet tall with a sprinkling of light freckles across his tanned schoolboy face.

Taking up the rope he'd found in Frank's car barn, he rewound it neat and pulled it over his cow-licked sandy hair. The coil hanging from his neck, he took two deep breaths and started to climb. "These trees are differ'nt." The live oaks he'd climbed back in Texas had crusty bark, hard on the knees. "This bark's *slipprey*."

He quickly reached the smile branch, which started a foot and a half thick before tapering to nothing well over the opposite bank. With the rope weighing heavy on his neck, he thought it best to scoot on his bottom rather than monkey-climb it. Out he went, down the scoop and back up and over the water's edge. Legs dangling over the rushing brown water below, he closed his eyes and envisioned pulling the rope taut, jumping back, swinging out. *Flying.*

A katydid interrupted the thought, to be joined by another, then another, and another. A full chorus quickly rose from the shade.

He raised the rope over a crooked grin, let out some eight feet and started wrapping the branch. He imagined the rope's path, swinging him like a pendulum. "This ain't wide water. Should scooch back some." Struggling himself backwards, the coil of rope on his thigh, he heard a scream.

***

She'd never heard katydids. The volume, the intensity of the chorus amazed her. The air was thick and pungent with honeysuckle, a new scent, too. Chloe approached the water's edge cautiously, sliding her scuffed Mary Janes along the slick wet ground. She'd never seen a snake outside a terrarium, and she didn't much care for them behind glass, either, so at the sight of this five-foot-long cottonmouth easing with the current down Coulee Galleque, she screamed, standing frozen in her white cotton dress, the one with tiny embroidered flowers stitched across the chest.

Spying the girl, PJ was struck by another memory from back in Alabama. Cookies with white icing. Rows of them cooling on his mama's red-and-white kitchen towel. "Looks like an angel cookie." He figured this angel to be about his age. Even from way up, he could tell she was pretty. He was about to finger whistle when he heard the boy's voice.

"Hey!"

Bright colors in plaid, moving up the path.

"Wha ta hell ya doan heah?"

He recognized the voice, having heard it for the first time just a week ago, his very first day at the school in Abbeville. Heard a lot more of it since then, too. It was the voice of Davey Johnson, youngest son of Bubba Johnson, the sheriff of Vermilion Parish. Davey Johnson was accompanied by his inseparable sidekicks, Bobby Talent and Jimmy Sweeney. At fourteen years old, both Bobby and Jimmy were a year younger than their leader.

Davey Johnson shouted again as he neared the girl, "I sayed, wha ta hell you doan heah?"

This aggressive intrusion coming so quickly after her initial shock from the snake disturbed her something awful, and she instinctively recoiled closer to edge of Coulee Galleque. The three white boys, all in dungarees and short sleeves, stepped forward. The tallest, in green and yellow plaid, continued.

"*Yeah?*"

Chloe was flummoxed. The tall one closed the distance between them, while his pals maneuvered to encircle her.

"You deaf oh somtin?" Davey shouted in her face. "I axe you a question."

"Yeah, he axe ya question," Jimmy Sweeney echoed, jabbing Chloe's shoulder hard.

"I was . . . just . . . walking here," she responded, timidly. "I . . . I saw a snake." She pointed at the coulee, composing herself as best she could. She raised her chin, "I was startled."

The boys looked at each other in silence, then burst out laughing.

"You startle, yeah?" Davey said, hands on his hips. He surveyed the water. "Well, wha ya doan heah hunten snake, huh? Ya know, dis heah's Ol Man Smit's prah-pha-tee. Yous trespassen. Look ta me like you come down heah to poach Ol Man Smit's watta snake."

Bobby and Jimmy chuckled.

Chloe was terribly confused. She knew English fairly well, but until this moment, had known nothing of coulees, water snakes, or even teenaged bullies. "Je ne c'est pas. I . . . I was walking here, looking, oui? I have only been here a short time, in this place."

Under the circumstances, she was gathering herself well. Just eleven years old, she'd spent most of those years in adult company. She could feel the threat of these boys, yet was at a loss for how to respond, how to interact. It was all foreign to her, literally so. She'd spent much of the last two months frightened and lonely, but never before had she felt so terribly alone.

"You new rown heah," Davey continued, as he looked the girl up and down. "I doan rememba seen you befoe. Buh I doan geh down to Coonsville too much."

The other boys cackled.

"An you looken foe snakes, huh?"

"No. No, I . . ."

"Well den. We hep yeh out." Spreading his hands out over the water like a preacher before a baptism, the tall boy continued, "Ya see, da big rain drive dem snake up outta deah holes in da banks. Now dat tings ah setten down, dey back in ta watta, jus swimmen long, looken foe a new hole." He faced the girl with a threatening smirk. "Ya know, we all like finden new holes, doan we, boys?"

Chloe gasped, her memory raising the stench of sweat, booze, and onions in her nose. She pictured the man's body facedown on the stained floor, blood trickling from his ear.

Davey Johnson circled the girl and poked her in the breastbone. "Ya like dem snakes so much, how bout ya go hep em out?"

With both fists, he clenched Chloe's dress at her chest and pushed her toward the bank. She lost her footing and stumbled backwards, pleading through a scream, "Non, s'il vous . . . non!"

With one last thrust, the Johnson boy shoved her over the edge. She grabbed at his arms, only to be swatted away, and tumbled headfirst, the lip of the bank scraped her skin from hip to calf as she slid over the edge. Arms flailing and terror in her eyes, she skidded six feet down to the waterline. Chloe couldn't swim.

She tumbled head over heels, and her shoulder exploded in pain when she broke through the water. Her face submerged in the murk, she cried out, and what she inhaled seared her lungs and filled her with panic before the torque from her submerging body drew her head above the waterline. Coughing and delirious, she thrashed her legs and an arm. Her other was tangled in something over her head, and it felt like it was on fire.

A tree root hanging off the bank had snagged the girl. Four feet in length, sun-bleached since its excavation by the Great Flood seven years earlier, the root was one of many, all running in parallel down to the water, which together, from the other side of the coulee, looked like a cage made from stiff frayed rope. Fortunately, and painfully, the root caught the crook of Chloe's left arm and broke her fall. Her body swayed in the current as the churning brown water grazed her chin and splashed her face.

She clawed at the dirt bank with her free hand. Both of her worn Mary Janes and a lacy white sock were gone. She could feel the cool, muddy slope with her toes. Dangling there from the root, she pumped her legs as though she was running, but it was too slippery to gain any hold. The shredded break of a large tree limb slammed into her ribs, and the relentless current twisted the debris across her side and back, tearing her dress and slicing her torso. To the grinning tormentors up on the bank, her screams sounded more like whimpers. Chloe was out of her head with fear and could do nothing to improve her position. Disoriented, she stopped clawing, stopped running, and hung there by a numb arm.

The bullies in plaid kept taunting the girl, unaware of the fourth boy, who had reached the ground just as Chloe tumbled over the bank. He sprinted to the edge and slid down to the water a ways upstream and quickly worked his way toward her, trading roots along the way. In no time, he held the same root that snared her arm, and he swung one of his around her waist.

Under the cold rushing water, she felt something grab her from behind and cried out, thrashing wildly to shake loose as the tree root, her saving grace, sliced deeper into the crook of the arm trapped over her head.

"Whoa there. Settle down. I gotcha."

"Goddamn! Weah he come from?" Jimmy yelled, pointing.

"Wha?" Davey Johnson gaped.

"Who da hell dat?" Bobby added.

Chloe coughed up dirty water.

"It's okay, girlie. Just you hold on. You're gonna be fine."

Wide-eyed and breathing hard, she peered into the boy's eyes, sky blue dusted with snow. She'd never seen eyes like these, and they distracted her.

"Look, we'll get outta here. You just gotta let me help, see?"

No more screams, and the sobbing eased, but Chloe still couldn't catch her breath. She was hyperventilating as PJ leaned into her, his cheek behind her ear. "It's okay, girlie." He unwrapped her right hand from its fistful of mud and led it to another root, which she grasped tightly. PJ hung behind her, while she worked to breathe, the terror subsiding.

He pushed up behind the elbow of her trapped arm and dislodged it from the loop, and she quickly took hold of it with her freed, numb hand. She held herself firmly now, and, feeling PJ's torso pressed against her back, she felt relief, some sense of control.

Davey Johnson, regaining what wits he possessed, started in again. "So, iffa taint runt boy!" He barked down the bank, "Seem you cot yaseff a coon! Whacha goan do wit it?"

"Look like he goan fuck in da mud, like a stuck pig!" Bobby cried. Davey guffawed, slapping Bobby on the back as the young comic beamed with pride.

"Don't pay 'em no mind. Here's what we're gonna do." PJ pointed out a place on the bank downstream where there was a more accessible slope with no overhanging lip at the top. "We just make our way down the bank some, climb right up."

No response.

"Easy as pie."

Chloe looked him in the eye again. What she saw was calm, and calming. She looked downstream and could envision the plan, but when she considered letting go of her root, a wave of fear swept over her, stiffening her body. The whimpering returned. She lowered her chin, trembling. "Non, non, non." She was in shock, and PJ knew nothing about shock. He just knew it would work. It was about doing, was all.

"We just hold on 'til we're done. We ain't in no hurry, all right?"

"Non, non. S'il vous plaît."

He pressed his body against hers and propped her up as best he could. He held on to two roots now, one on either side of the girl.

"Hey, boy, you an yer nigga fren enjoyn yoselfs?" Davey Johnson was in full stride. Raising his arms to the sky, he shouted, "Beootifah day foe a swim!"

"And a stuck pig fucken!"

"You sayed dat, you mongeroid." Davey groaned, butchering the slur.

Jimmy piled on, "Yeah, Bobby, doan be a dummy." He looked back to Davey for approval that wasn't granted.

PJ repeated what they needed to do.

"Non, non." Chloe moaned, quietly. "I cannot swim. I will die."

"You don't gotta swim. You just watch where I put my hand, then you do it." He didn't wait for another response. "Like this."

He reached out, stretching to the closest root hanging a foot or so downstream.

Chloe grimaced and watched. "C'est très difficile." A squeak made its way up her throat as she let go of the root and reached out, taking hold just above PJ's fist. She squeezed her eyes tight, fighting the fear.

"See? Now we're doin'. Just move the other hand to the one we just let go of, like this."

Chloe reacted immediately, emulating PJ's move. A searing pain shot from her shoulder down her arm and back up her neck. It hurt but didn't frighten her. It felt like success.

"Nothin' to it."

She cooed, suffered a coughing fit, then let out a little laugh. PJ could feel the girl relaxing, leaning back into him. "Let's go." He reached to the next one, and they repeated the movements maybe a dozen times. Chloe looked up, astonished to find they'd reached the place where they could climb out. PJ pushed on her bottom and legs as she scrambled up the muddy ledge. Her dress snagged on more roots, but soon they were both on their knees on the bank. Chloe breathing hard, but out of danger.

Panting, she spoke rhythmically, "Merci beaucoup. Merci beaucoup. Merci beaucoup." With her forehead on the ground, she coughed hard and tears dripped into the soggy dirt as she retched, vomiting dirty water.

He looked this way and that. "Think them jackasses skedaddled."

Chloe snapped to attention as panic gripped her yet again, her head swiveling to confirm what her rescuer had said. "Quel soulagement." Her tormentors were gone, and this panic subsided almost as quickly as it had come on. He fidgeted while she tried to steady her breath. Climbing to her feet, she smoothed her dress as best she could. Muddy and torn, nearly shredded, the soggy matted fabric clung to her little body. PJ could make out the silhouette of her thin legs quivering behind the sagging cloth.

She rubbed a tiny embroidered flower between her thumb and forefinger. "Ma belle robe blanche, en ruine." Her limbs were covered with wide reddish blue scrapes and cuts oozing blood. She twisted around to see her back, where much of her dress had torn away, to find skin bruised and swollen. Her arm was still numb, and nervous pain shot up from her shoulder into her neck. A puffy red diagonal line stretched across the crook of her elbow. It looked like the work of a bullwhip.

"That's some welt you got there." He pointed.

"Oui. Ah, yes. It is there." She paused. "But I am good." She flexed her arm, then raised her other hand to her mouth to clear her throat.

PJ kicked at the dirt. "You from 'round here? Is that French you been sayin'?" In the two weeks since he'd come to Abbeville, PJ'd learned that a lot of folk in Vermilion Parish spoke French Creole, mixing it with plain English. But this was the first Negro he'd met since arriving, and he didn't know much about any of it. His daddy used some Creole words, but he didn't talk like how they talked here. Maybe the black folk were more Frenchy.

She did her best to smooth her dress. "Yes. I am French. Well, I have been living a long time in France. I am new to this place."

"How 'bout that? Me, too. Got here just a couple weeks ago." He stuck out his hand. "Name's PJ Benoit."

"Enchanté, Monsieur PJ Benoit. I am called Chloe Boisvert." She took the boy's hand into her own. He shook it hard, his coarse manner startling her yet again. It seemed something had startled her most every day since she'd left Paris some eight weeks past.

"Chloe." PJ pondered the sound of it as he rubbed his head, picking at some mud caked in his hair. "Your eyes."

"My eyes?" she asked.

"They're like..."

"Yes?" She smiled and swung her shoulders a bit. She had heard about her eyes before, and often.

His own eyes darted as he searched for a description.

"Honey!" he exclaimed. "Your eyes look like they're filled with honey."

Chloe giggled, and her shoulders released the last of her tension. She composed her posture and once more raised her hand to clear her throat.

"Ahem. Pardonez-moi, s'il vous plaît. So sorry. Moment." Holding up a finger, she paused to cough, then to catch her breath. "Thank you for your kind words, and thank you again for saving me from the water. I was sure to ... noyer ... without your ... your assistance."

"*No yay?*"

"Oui. Pour noyer. To ... to die under the water."

"You mean drown?"

"I am happy to have you save me."

The boy blushed and scooped a dollop of mud with his toes. "It wadn't nothin'." Looking back into the underbrush, he said, "Them boys are jackasses."

Her shoulders slumped. "You know them, the boys?"

"The big one's named Johnson. I started school here last week, and he and his pals grabbed me the first day."

"Did they push you, also?" Chloe wondered.

"Nah. But that Davey Johnson thinks he's the boss. He's just a grade above me, but I figure he's thick. Got held back. Wouldn't doubt a couple times. Anyway, told me if there's anything I need, come to him."

"Well, that is . . . *friendness*, n'est pas?"

"Nah. He's just actin' like a big shot. You know, like he's in charge." PJ spat on the mud. "S'pose he's the lead jackass 'round here."

"What is this, this *jackass*?" she asked, politely.

"Ha!" He slapped his thigh and found blood there. Chloe's blood. He wiped it on his chest.

"He's mean and dumb. Tries to push you 'round, know what I mean? A jackass. Like a donkey. You know *donkey*?"

"Don-key? Ah oui, l'âne! Je comprends." She nodded. "Very . . . stubborn. The animal bites. Très difficile, oui?"

PJ got *difficile* and blurted out, "Ya think?" He poked her in the shoulder, making Chloe flinch in pain, which made his stomach fall. Shrugging, he joked, "Hell, he tried to *no-yay* you. I'd say that's bein' purty *deef . . . eee . . . seal.*"

"Oui. Yes." She laughed nervously. Looking into his eyes, she thrilled to the memory of Parisian skies. "Le miel et le ciel." She giggled. "C'est la poésie!"

"Huh?"

"Honey and sky." She giggled at herself, the poet. "Thank you so much, PJ Benoit. Maintenant, we are friends, yes?"

PJ just stared and mumbled. "Angel cookie."

"Pardon?"

He flushed and remembered something else. Cinnamon and sugar. Big Jack used to spoon it from the little glass bowl onto his hot buttered toast. That was the color of her skin. "Two parts cinnamon, one part sugar." He'd said it to himself, out loud. She gave him a quizzical look, and he started pawing at the mud with his toes again. "Yeah, we're friends all right." He looked up. "You know somethin'? You're the first friend I've made since I got here."

Chloe beamed, light flickering in her amber eyes. "Moi, aussi, PJ. You are my first friend, also."

He made out a few dark freckles on her cheek that formed a W. "So where to?"

She inspected her muddy, bloody, ragged self, then looked up and down the coulee. She informed the boy how she'd come to Abbeville to live with her aunt and sister behind the café, but now she realized she'd completely lost her bearings. "And you are new to here, also, yes?"

"Yeah. Hopped a train from Texas. But ya know, this town's pretty puny. How 'bout we just head back that way, and we'll ask where it is?" With a crooked, toothy grin, he took Chloe's hand into his own. She swung their hands and smiled.

"Oh, almost forgot!" He ran to collect his shirt and shoes from under the tree. He rolled up his soggy pant legs and smiled up at the rope. "Yeah." Running back to the girl, he stuck out his hand again. "Let's go, Honeybee."

They found the path that cut over to the railroad tracks and walked it in silence. A girl from France and a boy from Texas. Brand new friends, each lost in their own thoughts about what just happened.

The pair stepped onto the iron span railroad bridge. The clouds were parting, and they squinted into the sparkling sunlight that was reflecting off the Vermilion River. PJ spat to see if a fish would rise, and Chloe studied his profile. Long blond eyelashes, turned-up nose. A little ball of mud in his ear. A line across his bicep. Above the line, smooth lightly tanned skin up to a darkened red neck. Below the line, freckles on a deeply tanned forearm. Their eyes met, and he blushed but didn't turn away. That's when she noticed there were two blue rings in his eyes, the lighter one on the outside. They looked like the sea off Nice where she spent time with Yvonne back when Yvonne was still sweet. That lovely white-sand beach lined with shiny white deck chairs and all of those striped yellow towels. Sunlight twinkled in aquamarine just off the shore, and beyond the little pontoon dive barge, it sparkled in rich Persian blue. The colors in her new friend's eyes. His Mediterranean eyes. Then the hate in Davey Johnson's eyes. She shuddered and looked down at the flat brown river below.

She squeezed his hand, and turning to her new friend, she asked through a shy smile, "PJ Benoit, do you like pie?"

1
CRICKETS

FEBRUARY 1927

No one had even *heard* of rain like this. It had rained some, and more often poured, most every day for the past five months, and Alabama was soaked. But this week the sun owned the sky, and every magnolia tree in Montgomery County had burst into bloom.

Shaded by the tall pines that lined the river, the undergrowth behind PJ was thick with honeysuckle, and the pungent scent mingled with the sweet pine riding the evening breeze. The river was way up and running hard, but even so, Big Jack had taken his birthday boy up Blue Ridge way to give the catfish a go. It was early evening Saturday, February 26, and PJ rocked from cheek to cheek on his cold, damp bottom as the sun nestled into the pines on the far bank. With the tip of his sun-bleached cane pole, PJ scribbled his initials across that blue-green pine canvas.

    P J B

The weight of the long stiff pole pressed into his palms. "Like a seesaw," PJ whispered to himself, thinking how he loved fishing. The critter chorus was just warming up as the sun dropped from sight. "And crickets. I love crickets."

"What's that, PJ?"

"Daddy, doan choo love crickets?"

"Sure do." Big Jack leaned into the boy. "Crickets, you see, when the sun starts goin' down? They get all riled up, 'specially on a Saturday night. Sounds like they're pullin' together a big ol' hootenanny tonight, yeah."

"Crickets have parties?"

"Wouldn't you, out here on such a fine night? Somma the stars are already peepin'." Sunset on the Alabama River, the color of a ripe peach, never failed to make his daddy smile.

"But I thought they's jus' spreadin' rumors. Dat's what you said."

Big Jack mussed his hair. "Nah, I was talkin' 'bout the ol' church lady crickets back in town. See, every Wednesday night they sit in their ol' cricket rockers on their ol' cricket porches, then they spread all the gossip and nonsense they picked up durin' midweek service at the ol' cricket church. You know, they's all Baptists, them town crickets. That's why you can't take just one fishin'."

"Huh?"

"Cuz he'll drink all your beer!"

Silence.

"You're a smart kid. You'll figure out crickets in good time." Big Jack pulled in his line and reached for PJ's pole.

He tipped it away. "*Pleeease?* Can't we stay for one more bite, Daddy?"

"Can't do it. We're late already and no doubt your mama's startin' to steam like a kettle. Pull in that stringer." Big Jack unwrapped the cord from the bush at the river's edge and handed it to the boy. "Remember how they get perky when you pull 'em out. Wrap the cord 'round your hand first, so it don't slip. Always prepare, PJ."

PJ nodded. "Always prepare."

He looped the cord around his palm three times and steadied himself. Backing up slowly, he pulled the stringer up the bank. Each of four keeper channel cats twisted and turned as they left the water, tails splashing on the way out, and PJ Benoit struggled the whole flopping mess onto the bank.

"Good boy! Seven, maybe eight pounds. Gonna make a nice fry, PJ." Big Jack tossed the fish into the flatbed with the poles. "Gotta get. We'll clean 'em when we get home."

PJ's daddy earned his nickname by fighting bigger than he looked way back in grammar school. The man stood all of five foot six, so from *Big Jack* one could infer irony or strength, and everyone who came to know him understood it was the latter. He engaged the world with a cool confidence that put folks at ease, assuring them they were in good hands, and his youngest son felt it. Today was his fifth birthday. Jacques Louis Benoit, Junior. He didn't mind his nickname so much, not the way it sounded, anyway. *PJ*. But he'd already had his fill of the implication. He was Petit Jacques. *Little Jack*. Not that there was something to be done about it. Maybe some fussing, but fussing wasn't his way.

Big Jack swung the flatbed Ford onto Swanson Road and started for home. He struck a wooden match to fire the Chesterfield dangling from his lips, then surprised the boy with an astonishing offer. "How'd you like to fly with me, PJ?"

It was dusking to dark when the truck squeaked to a stop in front of the drab, shotgun-style house. Big Jack squinted through a curl of smoke at the light glowing behind the front window's thin curtains, then flicked the butt out onto the street. PJ was in a trance. His clock had stopped back when those magic words hit the air. "Fly with me," he whispered now, wriggling his bottom. The whole drive home, he'd imagined what it would be like to fly. The best he could figure was standing up in the back of the truck as it rambled along Highway 31, something he'd been scolded on more than once.

"Don't say anthin' to your mama about the flyin'," Big Jack said sternly, cocking his head the way he did whenever he insisted on being understood. "Yeah?"

"Yes, Daddy."

* * *

PJ's mama, Elaine Benoit, was an Alabama girl, and her father, William Brewster, was in commodities brokerage. Cotton, soybeans, peanuts. A moneyman for tenant farmers and sharecroppers who'd had trouble with the weather. The closest equivalent up north was the loan shark. When a soldier boy, one Private First Class Jack Benoit, impregnated his daughter Elaine, Brewster made arrangements with a convent in Maryland. But Elaine had a different idea and hopped a train to Virginia, where she tracked down Big Jack and married him. That was in 1916, two years before Big Jack shipped off with the American Expeditionary Forces to assist the French in the trenches at Château-Thierry, leaving Elaine behind to care for their toddler, Frank.

Upon his return from the Great War, Big Jack entered the army flight school, eventually flying test missions. It was early 1926 when Lieutenant Benoit was made the army's liaison to the House Military

Affairs Committee and its powerful chairman, Congressman J. Lister Hill. Hill hailed from the great state of Alabama and was intent on turning tiny Maxwell Field outside Montgomery into the largest US Army Air Corp training base. As part of Hill's plan, Big Jack was ordered to move his family from Washington, D.C., to Montgomery, and he'd been officially stationed at Maxwell since last July.

Elaine was less than thrilled, stuck on the outskirts of town in a "damn little shotgun shack" and regularly subjected to her father's thinly veiled disgust. She missed the Capital scene, with its dinner parties and the Army Officers' Wives Club. Cards, cocktails and gossip. Alabama all but ended her social life, so she started hosting cocktail parties for one.

* * *

"Fetch the red bowl, PJ."

Big Jack retrieved the filet board and tools from the shed and set up on the Ford's tailgate.

"Nice stringer, Daddy!" Frank bounded out the side door. Big Jack slammed the largest catfish down, impaling its head on the tenpenny nail sticking up through the board. "Can I do it?"

"Knock yourself out, T-boy."

PJ's big brother Frank obviously loved everything about hunting and fishing, including the cleaning. Always had a little pride on his face when he provided for dinner. PJ was disappointed he couldn't do it yet but knew not to ask about using the filet knife.

Big Jack punched his oldest's shoulder. "Sorry you missed out. Next time." That morning, as the Benoit men loaded gear, Elaine handed eleven-year-old Frank a list of chores, then got after his father. Big Jack wasn't game for an argument, so Frank missed out on the river, and he got the chores done in a hurry.

Big Jack shook out a cigarette and tapped it on the tailgate. He struck a match. PJ liked the sound of a struck match, the smell, too. Their daddy went inside while PJ stayed to watch his big brother clean the fish. PJ adored his big brother and often watched intently as he did this or that. For a five-year-old, PJ had a keen eye and noticed how Frank approached tasks differently than their daddy did. Like when they packed fishing gear, Big Jack would make a list then check it off as he tossed rods and whatever all in the truck bed. But Frank always took a little extra care, placing everything just so, making sure the lines didn't tangle. He would wrap the reels in cloth to keep them clean and poke loose hooks into a cork. If it looked like rain, it was Frank who made sure everyone packed for it, extra socks, and he would cinch a tarp over the gear.

PJ marveled over the job at hand. To clean a sunfish or a bass you just needed a sharp knife. But for catfish, it meant also hammer, nails, knife and pliers, and when Frank worked a mess it was like a well-oiled machine. PJ couldn't wait until he could clean his own fish.

Frank cooked the dinner. Big Jack and the boys devoured the entire fry and a pot of baked beans while Big Jack retold stories about famous aerial battles fought over the trenches during the Great War. Elaine had retired early with a headache, and when she woke near midnight, she found the dishes done, the iron skillet soaking in the sink.

The next morning, PJ jumped from bed and peeked out the boy's window curtain. Pre-dawn, but no clouds. "Sunshine today." Excitement overwhelmed his need to pee as he sprinted in his jammies through the house and out the front door to find his daddy stretching. PJ completed all eighteen minutes of Big Jack's calisthenics routine, the one Big Jack learned from Canadian flight officers back in France. PJ joined his daddy's routine after the move to Alabama, and he was proud that now he could complete it without any breaks.

Frank had breakfast waiting inside, and they ate quickly.

"Delicious, T-boy. Put the dishes in the sink, boys, and let's get out of here." Big Jack waved a piece of crispy bacon toward the door. "It's showtime."

"So there'll be generals there?"

"Sure will, T-boy. All kinds of brass gleamin' in the sun. You know how to behave."

"Yes, sir!" The brothers answered in unison as they double-timed to keep up with the lieutenant's strides.

February 1927, and Maxwell Field still wasn't much in the way of a military base. Ten years earlier it'd been the site of a substantial army training facility, with doughboys coming through during the last year of the Great War. Since then, army presence had dwindled to a handful of staff. But at Congressman Hill's insistence, Maxwell was hosting something special today. The Three Musketeers.

Based in Texas, the Three Musketeers was an aerobatics team composed of select flyers from the 1st Pursuit Squadron and led by airman and instructor Captain Claire Chennault. Chennault's team showcased the Army Air Corp's fighter pursuit abilities by barnstorming a trio of Boeing Model 15 biplanes across the country. Congressman Hill arranged for this show at Maxwell to mingle key politicians and army brass with executives from the aircraft manufacturers Boeing, Curtiss, and Wright.

During the decade of peace since Armistice Day, a heated debate had grown within the army regarding the value of pursuit aircraft. Most high-ranking officers felt that because the small fighters were slower than big bombers, they were useless as defensive equipment, a reasonable conclusion to draw based on the results of numerous training missions. By the time a bomber group could be identified from the ground and its location communicated to the nearest airbase, a pursuit squadron of fighters simply couldn't climb and catch the attackers before they reached their target. Bombers were clearly better than fighters for offensive tactics, so, on the surface of the argument, the idea that pursuit aircraft had no use whatsoever was the correct conclusion. However, the opposing view, shared by a small minority of army air officers, was that pursuit fighters could be very effective if deployed properly. The key was technology. Fighter groups could maintain staggered patrols, circling above the enemy's targets, then diving with speed and concentrated strafing into approaching bomber formations. Equipped with portable two-way radios, a recent technological advance, the fighter patrols would be supported by immediate, direct ground-to-air communications. This would enable air cover to intercept approaching bomber groups quickly and with precision. Holders of the minority view believed that forthcoming advances in aerodynamic engineering and power in compact engines would soon level the playing field between large and small planes.

The Air Corps' highest brass was composed mainly of aged cavalry officers, and their vision was limited by experience on the ground, not emboldened by the unlimited potential of three-dimensional engagement in the sky. What Chennault accepted as fact was something the old veterans refused to even consider. Over millennia, the nature of warfare had evolved with humanity's advancing technology, from rocks to spears to arrows to guns. Then the Industrial Revolution enabled fundamental change over a period of years, not centuries, and now, technology was driving change in mere months. Chennault knew that advancement in pursuit aircraft design would alter warfare more fundamentally than the machine gun did and believed the United States should lead the world in design and implementation. A staunch and vocal advocate for the minority view, he used the Three Musketeers as a promotional tool to buy time while younger senior officers came around. Today, Congressman Hill was shilling Maxwell Field. Claire Chennault was shilling pursuit aircraft.

Big Jack saluted. "Captain, these are my boys, Frank and PJ. Boys, meet Captain Chennault of the renowned Three Musketeers."

Chennault cut a dashing figure. Muscular, with a rugged face, square jaw, and dark, piercing eyes. Unusually tall for a pilot, he stuck a hand out to the boys and made an easy grin. "Beautiful day for flying!"

"Yes, sir!" The boys answered, again in unison, taking turns shaking the captain's hand.

"Jack, I'd like a word." Chennault clapped the boys' daddy on the back, and the two men ambled toward three olive-green biplanes with red stripes wrapping their wings and tailfins. "I need a favor." Standing almost half foot taller, Chennault threw an arm over the lieutenant's shoulders. "Billy took ill. He's in the town hospital with an awful stomach. We just received word his appendix burst this morning, so the docs are working on that mess as we speak. Hell, I hope he makes it . . ." Chennault trailed off, then continued. "My alternate has some kind of bug, too. Fever, poor guy's sweating like a Brahman bull in August. Fact is, I'm one musketeer short. You game?"

Straining to overhear, Frank caught enough and yelped with glee, earning himself a stern look from his daddy. PJ was watching two mechanics check the wing struts on the nearest PW-9, the army's designation for the Model 15. The top wing was much longer than the bottom wing, a configuration that enabled both versatility in aerobatics and stability in power dives.

"I'd be honored, Captain. Tell me what you need."

"Good man, Jack." Chennault grinned. "Of course, we'll have to tone it down some, seeing as you don't know the routines. Less crossing, more parallel work. Dives, climbs, pursuits. We'll skip the part where we tie the wings together. With the radios, we'll make it work fine. Let's have a chat with Harry to sort it."

Big Jack put the boys under a corporal's watch and walked off with Chennault. The three airmen reworked the program, taking Big Jack out of play during the close-quarter turning and mock dogfighting. They agreed he would fly large arcs and climb and dive on the perimeter of the other flyers' skirmishes and aerobatics.

Intermittently, the three would coordinate on more basic close-in maneuvers, with Harry and Big Jack tight on Chennault's wings.

The sky was robin's-egg blue, dotted with puffy white clouds drifting east. The boys sat cross-legged on the ground, all eyes up. The corporal stood at ease between the boys and the bleachers.

"Remember the cotton?" Frank poked PJ in the leg.

"Huh?"

"The cotton. On the side of the road last fall. Daddy stopped so we could pick some up." Frank pointed to the sky. "We made clouds outta it, like that."

The clouds today were the puffy kind, with a few of the stretchy kind in between. He remembered pulling the cotton into the long, stretchy kind of cloud. "Yeah, you tied it around my ears!" He said, pouting, but the light in his eyes gave him away.

"Look!" Frank pointed again. "The plane climbing out to the right, there. That's Daddy."

PJ's tummy tingled. He stuck two fingers in his mouth and tried to whistle.

"You sound like a pig fart."

"You *smell* like a pig fart!"

Frank whacked him in the head.

Big Jack rolled his PW-9 into a steep dive. As the biplane screamed toward the field, he released a trail of white smoke while the other two flyers eased their wings into identical, graceful loops, painting parallel corkscrews of smoke across the sky.

"Look at that!" Frank exclaimed.

But PJ's gaze was fixed on the dive. The pitch of the PW-9's engine rose as it screeched toward the reviewing stand. Big Jack pulled up and buzzed the bleachers at a hundred feet. He cut the smoke on the climb, leaving a long white fishhook to float over the administration building. PJ squealed, jumped to his feet, and chased after his daddy's plane. Frank hollered and was struggling to his feet when the corporal grabbed an ecstatic PJ by the shirttail. The soldier spun him around toward Frank, who PJ promptly body slammed.

"Did you see dat? Did you see dat?" Jumping up and down. "Oh boy!"

"Sit down, kid, before you get us in trouble." Frank pushed down on his shoulders. "Sit!"

PJ's chest pounded as the biplanes cartwheeled in the sky. "I'm goan fly! I'm goan fly all around!"

At last, the Three Musketeers landed in unison, wingtips not ten feet apart. They circled on the tarmac to polite applause.

"Why does da sound change when he goes up?" PJ wondered aloud.

Frank explained it wasn't the up and down, but the coming and going.

"Why?"

"I don't know. Ask Daddy."

Frustrated, PJ pressed, "Doan choo wanna know?"

"Shut up and get up." Frank glanced around. "We need to be ready to go when Daddy wants us."

PJ huffed and clambered to his feet. He studied the three PW-9s growling in a power chorus with a combined 1300 horsepower. He looked to the sky where the smoke trails were diffusing under the clouds. He looked at his fingers, remembering the texture of the stringy cotton between his fingers.

The presentation was a success even without the more dangerous, impressive tricks Chennault had designed. The PW-9 was the most powerful pursuit aircraft in the world, and Big Jack topped 170 miles per hour as he leveled over the brass in the stands. The wood-frame wings were perfectly balanced, and the fabric over the welded steel tube construction was taut, with no noticeable vibration in flight. His plane was tuned like a concert piano.

Chennault slapped Big Jack on the back. "What'd you think?"

"That machine is tight, Captain. Tight! I'd like to meet your crew chief and shake his hand."

Chennault beamed. "Jack, I know you can see it. You could feel it, right?" He glanced at the reviewing stand as a handful of highly decorated geezers climbed down, surrounded by attentive army-brass lackeys. Chennault shook his head. "We're going to win this battle, dammit. It might take a few years, but this . . ." He waved toward the equipment. "*This* is going to win the day. They'll see."

The boys waited in the hangar while their daddy and Chennault talked with Sergeant Hank Novak, the crew chief.

"The tightest equipment I've had the pleasure to fly, sergeant."

Hank grimaced and muttered something about a wing strut.

"That's right, Hank," Chennault chuckled. "You keep worrying. Our babies need to be perfect. Perfection in the sky!"

"These the new cadets, Captain?" Hank joked as the boys approached. "I swear they're getting younger all the time."

"Boys, come here!" Big Jack waived them closer. "This is Sergeant Novak. He's the one who keeps these beauties in tiptop shape."

Frank approached the bear of a man and stuck out his hand. "Pleased to meet you, sir."

PJ hurried to emulate his brother. "Please ta meet you, sir." Hank's paw wrapped around his little hand with plenty to spare. PJ saluted him, then Chennault, then his daddy.

"That's a lot of saluting, young man," Chennault chuckled.

"I'm goan be a flyer like my daddy," PJ said, matter-of-factly.

"I don't doubt that," replied the sergeant, then he asked Frank, "You gonna fly like your daddy, too?"

Frank shrugged and shuffled his feet. "I'm not sure, sir, uh, Sergeant. I think I might like to try college."

"Smart kid," Chennault interjected.

On the drive home, Big Jack hummed and tapped the steering wheel. Next to his daddy, with furrowed brow and arms crossed, PJ worked hard to remember the show in its entirety, trying to run all the tricks through his mind again and again. But Big Jack's incredible dive kept bursting through his concentration. The air show was the most thrilling thing he'd ever seen, and PJ couldn't wait to fly.

The thought made his tummy tingle again. He wriggled in the seat between his daddy and his big brother.

"You gotta pee, PJ?"

"No, sir." He shook his head and closed his eyes, returning to his daydream.

Frank rode with one arm stretched out the window like a wing. The air whistled through his fingers as he made a low, rumbling noise in his throat. PJ joined him, eyes still closed as they harmonized, two little PW-9s in the old flatbed's bench seat. Frank peeked at Big Jack and elbowed his brother to look. PJ saw a bigger grin on his daddy's face than he could remember.

"That looked like a lot of fun, Daddy. The flyin'," Frank offered.

Big Jack finished a drag off his Chesterfield and blew smoke out the window.

"You said it, T-boy. That . . ." Big Jack pointed his smoke out the window. "That!" he repeated, spinning the butt in circles, "was nothin' . . . but . . . fun." He took another long drag and exhaled slowly. "Nothin' but fun." He flicked the butt out the window and slapped the outside of the truck door three times, hard. "Deep in the heart of Texas!"

PJ flinched and looked up at his daddy in surprise. He turned to Frank and found his brother wide-eyed, looking confused.

Elaine Benoit was fairly gone drunk when they arrived home. She had dinner ready despite but was not at all receptive to Big Jack's news She quickly excused herself to their bedroom. While Frank washed the dishes, PJ dried as best he could. Through the kitchen wall they could hear their parents' argument.

"Mama's pitchin' a fit."

PJ nodded.

Their daddy raised his voice a little more each time he spoke. This didn't happen often, but nothing good ever came when it did, and the boys were getting anxious. Suddenly, there was a loud crash, and their mama wailed. The door slammed, and Big Jack stomped down the hall and straight through the kitchen, the screen door slamming hard.

Swinging wildly as she lashed out at her husband, Elaine had connected with the lamp on the bedside table and sent it crashing against the wall, the ceramic base shattering on the floor. Now the boys could hear her sobbing, and PJ was scared, and tears welled in his eyes.

"It ain't nothin'." Frank elbowed him. "Pay attention to the dryin'."

Their mama cried herself to sleep while the boys put the dishes up, and Big Jack still wasn't back when they put themselves to bed. Frank made sure PJ brushed his teeth and washed his face. In the morning, the boys made and finished breakfast with their daddy before their mama emerged from the bedroom. Big Jack stepped out, so the boys played cards at the kitchen table.

"Would you like some eggs, Mama? There's bacon." Frank moved over to the stove.

Elaine snatched the coffee pot, pulled the top, and stared inside at the lukewarm brew. "Seems we're moving to Texas."

She slammed the pot down on the cold burner, spun dramatically on her heels, and returned to the bedroom. The boys could make out a sarcastic sounding "yeehaw" from down the hallway, just before they heard the door slam. PJ sat at the table struggling to hold a mess of playing cards in his little paws. Frank wolfed down a piece of bacon, then rubbed his little brother's head.

"Bath day." He tweaked PJ's ear. "C'mon, I'll help you with the tub." They didn't see their mama again until the following morning.

* * *

The army air brass at Brooks Field in San Antonio was much more interested in enhancing the pursuit fighter agenda than the generals in Washington, and they paid no mind to Congressman Hill's plans for Maxwell. Chennault needed to strengthen his squad and had asked if Big Jack would like to come out and join him at Brooks. Strings were pulled around the congressman, and Big Jack was to receive orders no later than April. The transfer meant a meaningful base with regular flying. He would serve as an instructor at Brooks and travel as alternate for the Three Musketeers.

Elaine Benoit fell into despair. She so wanted her husband to be called back to Washington, where she could rejoin her clubs and the other army wives. Now they were headed to "Godforsaken San Antonio, Texas." She'd snorted, "Might as well be Timbuktu."

"Is there huntin' in Texas?" Frank asked his daddy, who was bent under the Ford's hood.

"Sure, T-boy. Deer, turkey, quail. Not so much fishin', I think. I hear the rivers ain't much more than creeks."

The enthusiasm his daddy and brother shared was rubbing off on PJ, but he still had some doubts.

"Dey got catfish, Daddy?" PJ was too young to hunt, but he knew how to catch catfish and sunfish with his cane pole. To his relief, Big Jack nodded.

Frank asked. "How 'bout Mama, Daddy? She don't seem all too happy."

"Your mama'll be just fine, T-boy." Big Jack wiped his oily hands on a rag and lowered the hood. PJ looked at Frank, and Frank raised his eyebrows. PJ struggled to raise his, too, a comical effort, and Frank mussed his hair. PJ growled and snapped his teeth.

2

LE MARDI GRAS

MARCH 1927

Little Chloe plopped down on the bench, straightened her posture, and stretched her tiny fingers over the piano keys. The morning sun angling through the window painted the parlor wall with a trapezoid of light, the first sunshine in weeks, which had seemed like months to the Chantale girls, and Chloe silently vowed to practice until the light moved all the way off the wall and settled on the floorboards. To her immediate right stood the Victor Automatic Orthophonic Victrola 10-50, the first phonograph to offer an automatic record changer. It could play up to twelve discs in succession, and its revolutionary acoustic horn delivered the best sound in electronic music. The official release date for the 10-50 was April 1, but through his connections, Theodore Chantale had obtained this pre-production unit in February. Housed in a sumptuously carved, dark-stained cherry cabinet, the Victrola was one of only a handful of post-prototype units manufactured, and the first to find its way to New Orleans. It set him back six hundred dollars, nearly twice the cost of a new Ford Model A sedan. Since its arrival, the machine hadn't stood quiet for a single day.

Chloe's mommy, Pascale, hummed along with the piano while she snapped green beans over the kitchen sink. She appreciated effort almost as much as kindness, and she was proud of her youngest on both counts.

Chloe's papa was home, which was uncommon for a Saturday morning. He stood outside smoking on the drive, issuing instructions to some men. Between songs, Chloe shuffled her sheet music while voices drifted in through the kitchen's screen door, both her papa's commanding baritone and the muffled, contrite responses. Tall an straight, Theo Chantale was an imposing figure, his sinewy frame hanging from broad, angular shoulders, a large pointed Adam's apple protruding from his long neck. Thick lips, a broad nose and deep-cut dark eyes under heavy eyebrows and a worn, tan golf cap. He usually employed his temper judiciously in his business dealings, but this morning his men were on the receiving end of some powerful wrath. Chloe didn't like when her papa got mean. It wasn't that she got scared, he'd never raised a hand to her. But it seemed that every time he brought his business home, he was yelling out in the drive.

She was rifling papers on the music rest, searching for "Atlanta Black Bottom," when the voices fell silent. The hinge on the kitchen door squeaked, and car doors slammed in the street.

"M'abeille musicale!" Her papa was leaning against the kitchen doorjamb, eyes shining over his yellow toothy grin.

Out front, the car's engine revved, then it's growl faded south on Bayou Road.

Her papa blew a kiss. "Mwah!"

Chloe snatched the kiss from the air and pressed it to her cheek. He went into the kitchen and took Pascale's hand, pulled her close and kissed her smiling lips.

"Yes!" Victorious, Chloe held up the sheet music, her own grin missing a baby tooth.

"When we meetin' your brother?"

"We'll be leaving soon. You need to clean up, my butterman." Pascale patted the big man's chest.

At six feet four inches tall, Theo Chantale towered over his pretty wife by a full foot and a half. She looked into his dark eyes, her own glistening like Colombian emeralds. Cinnamon freckles dusted her upturned nose, a dimple creased her right cheek.

"We're meeting my dear Paul and his Yvonne at one o'clock, at the Travelers. So I'm making us an early luncheon. Remember, the parade should arrive on Basin Street by two thirty thereabouts."

"The Zulus!" He squeezed his wife's bottom with both hands. She swatted him away, and he tiptoed to the parlor to sneak up behind his little Chloe, who was intently focused on her blues. The girl squealed when he seized her shoulders and whispered, "M'abeille, are you ready to capture the coveted ... *golden coconut?*"

Chloe jumped to her feet, beaming. "Yes, Papa!"

Pascale peeked from the kitchen, and the girl ran to her, burying her face in her mommy's apron. "Mmmm. Rosemary?"

"Very good!"

The girl opened her arms to her father. "I'm so excited!"

Laughing, Theo dropped to his knees. Chloe giggled and fell into him. It felt like his arms could wrap around her twice.

"Are you sure you're cunning enough? Quick enough?"

The odor of her papa's shirt, Spud menthol and sweat, replaced the rosemary her mommy's apron had left lingering in her nose. She didn't mind. Both scents smelled like love.

Francie burst from the hallway into the parlor. At ten years of age, she had nearly six years on Chloe. She slammed into the group, shouting. "Zulu! Zulu!" Bouncing up and down, she repeated the word a dozen times before Pascale could distract her.

"Francie, Francie! A biscuit, with jam?"

"Biscuit! Biscuit!" Francie shouted as she stomped around the kitchen.

Chloe felt her papa's hug go slack. He stood and quickly disappeared down the hall, as Francie held on to the kitchen countertop, hopping.

"Biscuit!"

The house rattled when the bedroom door slammed. Pascale took Chloe's head in her arm, pulling her tight.

"Will you help Francie with the biscuits, m'abeille?"

"Yes, Mommy."

* * *

After lunch, the girls cleared the dishes, and the Chantales were out the door, headed from Tremé to the French Quarter. Theo led the way striding in his ivory suit. He cut a dashing figure, from his crisp, new straw boater down to his shiny, two-toned spectator shoes. The girls each held one of their mommy's hands as they worked to keep pace.

Chloe couldn't remember anything from last year's Mardi Gras, and she was beyond thrilled, and excited by the crunchy sound of gravel under her shiny new Mary Janes, shoes that debuted at St. Augustine Catholic Church just that Sunday. As they made their way, a confluence of people amassed, quickly forming a dense crowd hustling south, and Pascale squeezed both girls' hands a little tighter.

The Zulu Krewe was the oldest Negro social aid and pleasure club in New Orleans. Originating as the Tramps some twenty years earlier, their parade quickly became a can't-miss for the Crescent City's black community. The white krewes tossed glass beads and gold-colored coins into their parade crowds. Since the Negroes didn't share in the economic prosperity their white neighbors enjoyed, the Tramps' founders thought it both practical and funny to toss gold-painted chestnuts to their adoring throngs. The children delighted in the offering, but everyone from young to old hoped to catch one of the rare golden coconuts the Zulu King himself tossed toward a lucky few. Many whites came to enjoy the spectacle as well, striving for the goodies with an urgency equal to their presumed superiority, oblivious to the irony attached to each painted nut.

"Pascale, ma chatte!"

"Paul!" Pascale dropped her daughters' hands and ran to her brother.

Chloe marveled at the sight of her uncle, a very handsome man, but so small when compared to her papa. Sporting wavy, slicked-back hair with sideburns that pointed to his chin and framed a jet-black pencil-thin mustache, Paul Benoit stood straight in a rich, burgundy velvet suit. Over his crisp, cream-colored shirt, a splendid burgundy silk tie speckled with brilliant yellow stars was tucked snugly under his canary-yellow vest. Then there was the hat he held against her mommy's back as they embraced, a top hat, also burgundy, with two long, thin yellow feathers sprouting from its cream-colored band. When he placed the hat atop his head and twirled his silver-tipped walking stick like a baton, Chloe couldn't help but to clap. She thought he looked like a slice of red velvet cake adorned with shaved lemon zest. Paul's eyebrows danced when he spoke, and this would become the first memory of her uncle that would stay with Chloe forever.

Theo turned to Paul's wife. "Yvonne, how are you?"

"Je me sens merveilleuse, Theo!" She lifted her gloved hand, which he obliged with a kiss. She tipped her head. "Enchanté."

Chloe was stunned by her aunt's beauty. As with many young girls, she believed her mommy to be the prettiest woman alive, but her aunt Yvonne looked like one of the angels Father Damon described on Sunday. Wrapped in eggshell white, her linen dress snug against her thin yet busty frame. Satin gloves reached above the elbow, and her cut-glass earrings dangled like chandeliers. A touch of rouge accentuated her high cheekbones. Yvonne's smallish, upturned nose reminded Chloe of her own, as did her aunt's mouth. For the

Zulu parade, anybody could wear anything, and many wore much of nothing. Yvonne Benoit looked ready for the ballroom, not the street. Stroking the ribbon tied into her own hair, Chloe marveled.

"Oh, Paul, mon frère!" Tearing up, Pascale kissed his cheeks.

Theo extended his free hand. "Welcome, Paul. Welcome to our home."

"I was not aware you owned this establishment, Theo." Yvonne pulled a draft of smoke through her ivory cigarette holder.

Paul mock-scolded his wife. "Do behave."

"How was the train from New York? Uneventful, I hope?" Pascale inquired. The Boisverts had just arrived in New Orleans after a short week in Manhattan, where Paul had been on business.

Yvonne answered for her husband, "If by uneventful you mean *boring*, then yes. Now the crossing from Le Havre, that was something." The couple had traversed the Atlantic aboard the S.S. *Ile de France*. "The new flagship of the French Line, the CGT, yes? In fact, the *Ile de France* has still not been christened. I believe the celebration will come in the summer, no?" She glanced at her husband. "However, Paul, *mon chat extraordinaire*, he acquired passage for us on the first crossing, the . . . how to say, *the sea trial?* Oui? We were two of just thirty . . . yes, thirty-six passengers in the most fantastique, beautifully furnished ship. Art deco!"

"Stem to stern," Paul interjected.

As the proprietor of one of the most popular nightclubs in Paris, Paul Boisvert maintained relationships with all kinds of people, from musicians and writers and bohemian artists to the most powerful European politicians and captains of industry, including the chairman of the CGT.

"Magnifique! Simply gorgeous, and the food was inspired. Truly divine." Yvonne pressed on with an elaborate description of the dishes they'd tried. "Moët to start, and the very best vinho do Porto to finish."

Chloe'd never witnessed such exuberance. She had no context for any part of her aunt's story, but the language she employed, the enthusiasm with which she spoke, the very essence of Yvonne Boisvert, entranced the girl.

"I'm afraid you're going to set my children to drooling," Pascale quipped as she rubbed Chloe's neck.

Francie shifted her weight from foot to foot.

"And I love your dress. It's stunning."

"Yours is quite pretty, too, darling Pascale. My husband here, however..."

Chloe stood mesmerized.

"My dear husband thought it best to dress, well..." She looked Paul up and down.

Paul rolled his eyes and squeezed Pascale's hand.

"I told him he looked ready for a costume ball, masquerading as coq au vin!"

Pascale laughed so hard she snorted. Covering her mouth, she blushed and apologized.

"A purple rooster." Theo mockingly scratched his chin. "Yeah, I can see that."

Paul took it all in stride. "You see, my lovely bride has never before experienced the splendid extravagance we know so well as Le Mardi Gras. *Le coq au vin?* Oui!" He tapped his chest with the ivory handle of his cane, rapped the tip on the floor, and spread his arms in a vaudevillian gesture. "Voici! Cocorico!"

Chloe laughed with the adults. She was proud to have understood the joke.

Theo pulled a golden timepiece from his waistcoat. "We best get on our way. The street's gonna crowd up fast. Let's move on to the Brewster place while there's still room to walk."

They exited the Travelers Hotel, and, in a flash, Chloe was holding a glass of cherry lemonade in the Brewsters' apartment on Basin Street.

Theo Chantale leaned over his youngest. "Keep with your sister, you hear?"

Chloe turned to Francie, who was hunched over a mostly empty glass, slurping through a bamboo straw from the small pink puddle at the bottom. The sisters wore matching satin crème dresses with purple velvet sashes, and Francie was already disheveled.

Chloe's sister was slow. Some might say stunted. Her efforts were strained, and managing her was an effort that strained the whole family. Unlike her mother and sister, both blessed with bright eyes that shone through lovely heart-shaped faces of silky smooth, cocoa skin, Francie's flat round face framed oriental eyes with swollen lids and held a mouth that rarely closed, which, all together, announced her condition to an intolerant and often cruel world. After Francie's birth, her mother was bombarded with advice that blended good intentions with disgust. Friends suggested sanatoriums "for this kind of thing." They told Pascale how she would only know burden and sorrow, and the girl would never know the difference anyway.

Pascale would have none of it. Two years in was the last time Theo suggested they put Francie in a home "for her own good." Pascale shouted him down and for years resented him for making the proposition. As time passed, she found Francie wasn't as challenged as people had predicted. Between six and ten years of age, the girl had improved a good bit. People didn't consider mongoloids capable of maturing, but Pascale's determination and dedication had allowed Francie to do just that, and the girl was starting to come through, albeit slowly. Even so, approaching just five years of age, Chloe had already taken on some responsibility for her big sister.

"Hey, y'all! Hey! Hey!" Marvin Brewster hollered over the crowd. "My sources say the Zulus are just a few blocks up and heading this way! So, please, freshen your drinks and take to the balconies!"

Voices rose in anticipation as folks migrated to the second and third floors for better viewing.

"Let's go, girls!" Theo boomed, startling both his daughters. He snatched their drinks and handed them to a servant. "Let's go mine some Zulu gold!"

Thrilled and giggling, the girls struggled to keep up as their papa pulled them out of the apartment and into the masses on the street.

Pascale and Paul called at them from the third floor balcony, but their voices were lost in the shouts, cheers, and laughter below. They tracked Theo's straw boater as it tacked through the pulsing assembly like a speedboat navigating a regatta. The big man led his daughters by the hand, pulling them through the drunken, rowdy rabble.

"Chloe!" Yvonne waved from the lower terrace as the girl's gold-and-purple hair ribbon submerged under the mass of humanity. Leaning over the railing, she looked up to the girl's mother, beaming. "Chloe est exquisite, Pascale!"

"We love our *daughters* very much, Yvonne," Pascale shouted down.

Paul placed a hand on her shoulder. "Yvonne has said to me how Chloe reminds her of her younger self."

Pascale flashed him a look.

"I must say, dear sister, for a relation by marriage, there is an uncanny resemblance between the two." He cupped her chin and gently brushed her cheek with his thumb. "I will return in short order with fresh libations."

Yvonne made her way upstairs and joined them on the upper balcony. "You are a saint, Pascale, with what you do for poor Frances." She sighed. "I do think that in *most* circumstances, the child would be with *her kind*." She requested a cigarette from the man standing next to her. "Merci." She inhaled deeply and exhaled dramatically. "No, I do not see how you manage it at all."

While Yvonne Boisvert leaned over the railing, pointing and laughing at some feathered revelers. Pascale was reminded why she was grateful for the ocean between her family and her brother's wife. The Zulus were turning onto Basin from Orleans Avenue. It was party time.

Paul reached around Pascale with a glass of champagne and whispered in her ear, "She is right, you know. You are a saint. But in so many ways, yes? And I thank you for it." He tipped his head toward his elegant wife.

Pascale's anger melted. She loved her brother and knew he loved her, and her family. "Je t'aime, mon frère."

Below, Theo towed the girls through the crowd. Chloe was breathing hard and clinging tight to her papa's suit coat. Francie stumbled and whined. In the throng on Basin Street, amid the crowding and jostling, the stumbling and pushing, the air was sticky and stale, smelling of sweat, booze, cigarettes and cheap perfume, as though a speakeasy had taken to the street. Chloe knew her papa would never put her in harm's way, but she felt anxious.

"Here! Here it is!"

Three men standing under a lamppost greeted Theo Chantale with deference. "We's got it all here, Missah Chantale. See, we's got the cinderblocks inside, jus' like you say."

Theo scooped up Francie and stood her on the wire milk crate.

"You boys stand back there, like that, so no drunks knock her off. Nobody pushes 'round here, understand?" He swung Chloe onto his shoulders. "Okay. Now you girls can see over everybody!"

Chloe saw Francie below with a huge grin on her face.

"Papa! Papa!" Francie hopped on the crate. "They come!"

Theo scolded the girl to hold still, and Chloe leaned over to stroke her sister's hair.

Drumbeats pulsed, pounding Chloe's chest as the parade eased around the corner onto Basin Street. Chloe leaned forward on her papa's shoulders to see up the street. Losing her balance, she squeezed her arms tight around his face. Chuckling, he unwrapped the little arms and placed each of her hands on a shoulder. The drum major danced wildly in front of the drum lines, which spread the entire breadth of the street. Four lines of men playing percussion on a variety of drums, clapping wood blocks and banging hollow lengths of bamboo. All the drummers were clad in black turtlenecks and black leggings under palm-grass skirts. The drum major pumped and twirled a baton painted gold with a fluffy burst of green-and-gold feathers fluttering off one end. He wore black, too, but instead of a grass skirt, his leggings were covered with chaps made from ostrich feathers bleached a brilliant white and tipped in indigo. He wore blackface with a bright-white circle over his left eye, and a massive ostrich feather headdress cascaded over his shoulders and down his back. The long, flowing feathers made their own dance atop the major's head.

"Look Chlo, look!" Francie jumped and jabbed with both hands, her fingers spread like she was pounding a piano in the air. The major's movements, an inspired blend of purpose and chaos, was mesmerizing. In his mouth, he held a whistle attached to a bear-claw necklace. Francie howled as she clawed at the street. The major whistled the beat, then blew eight hard notes. The Zulu Krewe halted. The brass lines raised their instruments and, on a count of four, kicked the party into high gear. The ecstatic throng raised their arms and rocked to Dixieland jazz.

Chloe bounced on her papa's shoulders as Theo lost himself in the music. The drum lines synchronized their steps, and the major was all in. When they finished the first number, the crowd erupted. The major blew a hard eight count, and the Zulus started up a second number, and entered a slow march.

The block was euphoric. Dozens of krewe dancers, all in grass skirts and spotted blackface, worked the crowd into a frenzy, tossing gold-painted chestnuts at the revelers. Theo called out "Charlie," waving at one of the Zulus who bore a spiral of small white dots on each cheek. The man came over and leaned into the crowd. Theo shouted into his ear. Charlie nodded and ran off.

As the largest and last float, the king's float, reached their lamppost, the Zulu King stood. Over his blackface, he wore a stark-white circle over his left eye and another that encompassed his mouth. He was covered from head to toe in royal satin and feathers, his costume featuring a headdress of brilliant white feathers tipped with indigo, like the drum major's chaps. The ostrich feathers draped all the way down his back, layered over his purple and green satin cape.

Charlie returned to them and twirled, throwing his hands out toward the Chantales. From atop the float, the Zulu King pointed at Theo and pitched a coconut his direction. Squealing, Chloe reached for it, but someone aside them grabbed at it, slapping it down. The hairy golden ball bounced back into the street and rolled away. A float tire squashed it, eliciting a collective *awww* from the crowd. The Zulu King looked over the side of his ride, shrugged at Theo, and exclaimed, "Spilt milk!"

Chloe was overcome by disappointment. The float passed and the music faded, to the delight of the thousands of revelers who were waiting on Canal Street. Francie threw her head back and moaned.

Some of the crowd shuffled into the street to follow the parade, and others dispersed to the speakeasies or to home. Charlie popped up out of nowhere, tossed something shiny at Theo, screamed like a banshee, backflipped into the street, then shimmied away to catch up with his fellow Zulus. The drumming faded as did the chaos.

Chloe sprinted up the stairs and across to the third floor terrace of the Brewsters' apartment, arriving out of breath. She tugged on Pascale's dress. "Mommy! Look! Look what we got!" She pointed back to Francie, who was trailing not far behind and holding a closed fist over her head.

"What do you have, dear girl? Let us see."

Francie slowly lowered her arm with a glistening gold chestnut pinched between her thumb and forefinger. She stared at it as she lowered the prize, as though she was witnessing a jewel descending from the heavens.

"Well done, Francie! How lovely!"

"Chlo caw't!" Francie punched her sister's arm. "She gay ta me!" She pushed through to the balcony railing, checking whether the parade was still in sight. With her straight, light-brown hair and pale skin, splotchy from the heat, at a glance Francie looked like a plump white girl. All of the Chantales were light-skinned, and Francie was much the lightest.

"You're a good sister, m'abeille." Pascale kissed her little one's forehead. "We have beignets, fruit pies, champagne, and coffee waiting for us at home. Shall we thank our hosts and make our way?"

"I am just dying to see the new Victrola," Paul replied.

Francie exhibited her prize to the Brewsters while the party thanked their hosts. The family headed up Orleans Avenue, the crowd thinning as they moved from the French Quarter into Tremé. Chloe peered around her mommy, and what she saw made her tummy tingle. Francie, leaning over cupped hands, cradling the shiny chestnut like a fragile egg. Paul entertained Theo and Pascale with a story born in New York just a few days earlier, something about some very high horn players backstage at the Lafayette Theater. Yvonne glanced over her shoulder at Chloe, who was smiling, skipping, and swinging her mother's hand.

Leaning into Paul, she whispered, "I want to take her home with me."

When the party entered the Chantales' lemon-cream, double-gallery house on Bayou Road, Paul boomed, "C'est magnifique!"

Theo grinned. "Beats that old shack we were in last you were here."

"So much improved, Theo. Very comfortable, yes." Paul headed straight to the Victrola's luxurious cabinet, caressing the brilliant millwork. "Gorgeous, truly! Let us hear from this work of art. Please, make it sing!"

Francie giggled and ran to the girls' bedroom, slamming the door behind her. Pascale noted the repulsion on Yvonne's face, while Chloe watched her papa stack a dozen records into the Victrola's changer. The machine clicked. Theo Chantale spun on his heels and spread his arms wide like a showman.

```
They play that strain
Works right on their brain
```

"C'est Louis!" Paul exclaimed.

```
Now it goes Black Bottom
A new rhythm's drivin' the folks insane
```

"Yes," Pascale said. "His Hot Five released this 'Irish Black Bottom' not two weeks ago."

"We saw Monsieur Louis just Friday, in New York." Yvonne's tone was aloof. "He hosted us in his dressing room after the show."

Chloe jumped to her feet. "Was Miss Lil there? Did you see Miss Lil?"

Yvonne looked at the girl, perplexed.

But Paul intuited the origin of the girl's interest. Lil Hardin Armstrong was many things to the great horn player, Louis Armstrong. Manager, writer, pianist, and wife. "No, Chloe. Miss Lil was not with Louis. I understand she is leading her band on a tour that should be in . . . *I think* Philadelphia about now, yes. We had the pleasure of hearing Louis leading his big band at the Savoy Ballroom in Harlem to the admiration of thousands. But I must say, it is quite impressive of you to know Lil was the accompanying pianist for the Hot Five on this record, this 'Irish Black Bottom'."

"She writes music, too." Chloe nodded, knowingly.

As the proprietor of the nightclub Le Pomme d'Or in Montparnasse and an investor in Josephine Baker's restaurant and club, Chez Josephine, no one was more in touch with the Parisian music scene than Paul Boisvert. His clubs hosted the best of the best, and he traveled at least once annually to the States to seek out musical talent he might have otherwise missed. New Orleans meant pleasure with his sister and her family, but it also meant business. He had meetings here in the Crescent City, and Chicago was next, then to Montreal, followed by the crossing to London. The club owner was quite familiar with the Armstrongs' skyrocketing careers, and in New York, he'd prodded Louis to make his first European tour, and to start in Paris at Le Pomme d'Or.

"I practice the piano part to it."

Paul lit up.

"It's pretty much the same as 'Atlanta Black Bottom,'" Chloe added.

"Well, I can't say I've ever compared *those two bottoms*." Theo raised a glass to his joke as Pascale rolled her eyes. She handed a champagne flute to Yvonne.

"Oh, darling Theo. Darling Pascale! You must be so proud of your child," Yvonne effused, raising her glass toward Chloe. "Yes . . ."

"Yes, we are very proud of our children," Pascale raised her voice to interrupt as Francie returned to the room. Pascale stood and hugged her, who struggled to free herself, letting out a horrific growl.

"Chlo play! Chlo play!" Francie pointed at her sister with the fist that still clenched the chestnut.

"After the records!" Theo snapped.

The room fell silent but for the Victrola's mechanical clicks as it set down another record. Into the pause, Pascale suggested that Theo restack the recordings, so Chloe could accompany the newest release. "We will hear Louis again, and this time with m'abeille playing with Miss Lil!"

Paul was astounded by Chloe's prowess. There were errors, plenty of them. But the fluidity with which she played, and her ear! One could add years of lessons and expect a lesser result. As the song concluded for the second time, Francie bounded to the piano bench and threw her arms around her sister. Squeezing hard, she commanded, "Again! Again!" The Victrola changed records, and Pascale offered Francie the distraction of readying the king cake in the kitchen. "King cake! King cake!"

Theo winced as Francie bolted to the kitchen. Yvonne raised her eyebrows and motioned to her husband for a cigarette.

```
I've come to you sweet man
Falling on my knees
```

Yvonne looked down her nose as Sippie Wallace sang the blues. Paul offered his hand to Chloe.

"May I have this dance, mademoiselle?" He took her up and swung her through the air, her little feet landing on the piano bench. "Shall we dance like the Zulus?"

Chloe gyrated wildly and laughed through her tooth-missing grin.

Francie ran back into the room. "Me! Me!"

Paul lifted Francie up onto the bench with her sister. He held one hand each as the girls wriggled and howled. Everyone was laughing and clapping, except Yvonne, who stood at the window with her smoke.

Chloe was too young to remember the only other time she'd met her Uncle Paul. It wasn't quite two years earlier, the summer of 1925. A photograph confirmed the Boisverts had been in attendance at her third birthday party, the 23rd of July. It was taken in the Chantale's tiny old house in the Ninth Ward, when she was a smiling toddler seated behind a large apple tart, cloistered by family that included everyone now present in the room.

"Look!" Paul pointed. The framed picture sat on the piano, a handsome Hamilton Mission Oak Craftsman. It sat among others photos, including a cracked and weathered likeness of Pascale as an early teen, dressed for church and standing in front of a large tree.

Her dress was dark with white polka dots, and Chloe had studied that photo often, loving the thought of her mommy as a young girl, knowing they would have been the best of friends if they had been the same age.

"Who is this?" she asked the room, pointing to another faded picture.

"That's your papa as a boy with his brother and sister. This is your Uncle Charlie, and that's your Aunt Armintha." Pascale smiled.

Chloe'd never met her papa's siblings. Looking closely for the first time, she noticed how much darker they were than him. She looked around the room. "Darker than everybody," she said aloud.

The Victrola dropped another Louis and the Hot Five number, "The King of the Zulus" appropriately enough, and Francie rocked next to her sister while Chloe followed the banjo with a flawed but hearty effort on the ivory keys.

* * *

Later, over cigars on the porch, Paul answered the question Theo had put to him earlier.

"Let me have a think. I am sure to bring you questions because it is an interesting proposition, ripe with potential."

"Don't take too much time."

Theo was pleased his brother-in-law seemed receptive to the idea. He'd invited Paul to participate in the European distribution of muskrat pelts from the processing plant in the south of Algiers, or from St. Louis, if that deal worked out. "I'll be headin' to the new fur exchange in St. Louis to talk to some brokers. I need to move quickly to solidify the advantage."

Paul grasped Theo's shoulder and changed the subject. "I want to thank you for taking such care with my sister, Theo. Pascale means the world to me, and she is very happy with you. Anyone can see."

"Baby! Baby!" The shout sliced through the window screen, and Theo winced.

"I suspect Francie found the baby in the king cake," Paul said cheerfully, pointing his cigar. "You are a good man."

As a rule, Theo Chantale did not blush. He regained his composure most immediately. "So Charlie's done you right, set you up for Chi-Town?" he asked.

"Yes, yes." Paul nodded and sipped his bourbon. "Your brother has established quite an itinerary for me in Chicago. I believe he has it covered."

Theo nodded, pleased Charlie had put his best foot forward. "Charlie knows everybody in town. Everybody who matters in music, anyway. But are you sure you want to get involved there, directly? Since Tarrio got shot and Capone took over, things aren't so . . . subtle, anymore."

"Yes, yes." Paul repeated his nodding and his sipping. "I am well aware of the . . . let us say, the *changing* landscape of Chicago. I am not concerned that making connections with the syndicate-controlled music venues there will threaten my independence in Paris."

Theo wasn't so sure. He'd no doubt his brother Charlie's position in the Chicago music business was closely associated with the Outfit. To date, Theo had kept his own relationship with Charlie purely familial. But this St. Louis business might change things. Chicago could make sense, depending on what happened in St. Louis in the coming weeks, and Charlie would be useful for making introductions to Capone's people.

His plan was getting more complex, and it made him a little uncomfortable. He was getting away from his motto. *Keep it simple and work it hard.*

Paul drained what bourbon was left in his glass. "Now, I think I would like to have a taste of that spiced rum you mentioned."

The men entered the parlor where Francie slammed into her papa. She punched her hand up at his face. Pinched between sticky, purple and green fingers, she held a tiny, white porcelain baby.

Paul noted the obvious. "Seems someone mined the king cake."

Francie beamed and licked the baby clean before turning to run down the hallway to the bedrooms. The men went to the kitchen and poured fresh glasses.

"Salut!"

"To family and to profit," Theo added with a smile. They threw back the rum and shook hands.

3

GREENVILLE

APRIL 1927

The Roaring Twenties were at full roar, with the rich getting richer off a stock market that just kept climbing. Serving the rich was no longer a job reserved for servants, and a rapidly expanding middle class of professionals and merchants started making money up, down, and across the American economy. Money flowed into thousands of urban homes for the first time, as did electricity and plumbing with clean water. Automobile sales skyrocketed. By the mid-twenties, it seemed as though every woman in Manhattan wore a fur coat, and every woman in Pittsburgh wanted one. Mink and sable at the top, and for the rest, it was muskrat. And the Delta south of New Orleans, the lowlands of Plaquemines and St. Bernard Parishes that jutted into the Gulf of Mexico, was prime muskrat country.

Nobody paid much attention to land titles for the swamps and bayous in the Delta, not since the Louisiana Purchase, way back in 1804. Ownership and deed transfers were recorded for the cultivatable land, but except for some subsistence trapping here and there, the swamplands that laced the farmland held no significant value. By the 1920s, ownership was pretty murky.

As of 1927, trapping in the Delta was brisk business. There'd never been such a demand for pelts, and due to a decade of good weather, Plaquemines and St. Bernard Parishes offered the world's most fertile environment for muskrat reproduction. Prices for pelts quadrupled the past two years, and profits swelled from New York City's Gimbel's Saks Fifth Avenue all the way back to Pointe à la

Hache in Plaquemines.

Most of the area's cultivatable lowlands were owned by smallholding rice farmers who doubled as oystermen, and, until recently, they'd paid no mind to the occasional pelt poacher. But with prices where they climbed to in the summer of 1926, some of them started to mind.

Leander Perez was a prosperous businessman and the district attorney, controlling both business and law which, in the Delta, were indistinguishable. Among his many holdings and titles, he headed the St. Bernard Trappers' Association, and a cousin of his was the largest landholder in St. Bernard's Parish. So Perez set his mind to collectivizing the trapping business all around his cousin's land. As pelt prices climbed, he grabbed even more profit by squeezing the trappers with higher association dues.

Manuel Molero, the Isleño kingpin of Delacroix Island in Plaquemines Parish, controlled one of the largest prohibition-era bootlegging operations in the country, running Puerto Rican rum and Scottish whisky up the Mississippi River to slake middle American thirst from Arkansas to Minnesota, and, until recently, he and Leander Perez had left each other alone. But when Perez stuck it to the trappers on dues, Molero saw opportunity in their frustration, and he brought the small landowners of Plaquemines Parish together into their own separate collective. He also picked off disgruntled trappers from Perez's association and welcomed new trappers who worked St. Bernard Parish marshes. Molero set prices in his collective so that everyone made good money, and so brought the Delta trapping business to industrial scale. But his personal focus was on the bootlegging business, and he entrusted his right-hand man, Theo Chantale, to run the fur trade. The plan worked well, much to Leander Perez's detriment.

Perez held a begrudging respect for Molero and envied his fast-growing operation. So in September 1926, he sent his representatives to Delacroix Island with a lowball offer to buy him out of the fur trade. Molero declined, knowing his refusal would trigger a fight. He charged Chantale with ensuring the landowners' and trappers' allegiance to his collective, and also with defending the business from encroachment by Perez.

For weeks, conflicts flared across the marshes as Perez sent his trappers west and south into Plaquemines. The fight also entered the courts, where violence and corruption both played their parts. Perez filed a lawsuit, which he surprisingly lost, but his appeal to the Louisiana Supreme Court proceeded swiftly and successfully. However, the legal reversal didn't hold water on the bayous. Violent conflicts increased in number and intensity until Perez grew tired of Molero's obstinacy. On November 15, he sent men, including mercenaries brought in from Texas, to Delacroix Island "to make Spanish soup" of the Isleño trappers there. Perez's thugs commandeered an oyster lugger named the *Delores* and mounted two machine guns on the hull. But when the boat approached the Delacroix Island dock, Perez's men were surprised to find some four hundred armed trappers who'd come that very afternoon to discuss matters with Chantale. The *Delores* was quickly overwhelmed with gunfire and turned tail.

Perez protested Molero's attack to everyone in power, including the United States Marshal, the New Orleans Superintendent of Police, all the way up to the Governor of Louisiana. But even though the high court had ruled the lawsuit in Perez's favor, this time the powers-that-be refused to come to his aid. They'd had enough of the Trappers' War, and Perez was left without recourse.

Theo Chantale continued to consolidate Molero's power in Plaquemines Parish and expanded operations well into St. Bernard Parish, Perez's own turf. The muskrats continued to breed, the trappers continued to trap, and the money continued to flow into Molero's organization, and into Theo Chantale's pocket. He had consolidated the trapping business throughout Plaquemines, from Pointe à la Hache to Port Eads, up around Black Bay and into St. Bernard Parish north and east of Lake Coquille. Everyone knew that Chantale not only represented Molero, but that his word *was* Molero. By February 1927, he ran trapping in the Delta.

Licking his wounds, Perez turned his attention to other business pursuits and quickly became one of the most influential men in Louisiana, a famous segregationist known to say, "Good Negroes are darkies. Bad Negroes are niggers." Between toasts at his 1927 New Year's Eve party, Perez was overheard complaining. "I can live with Molero. But the nigger Chantale's gotta go."

Despite months of incessant rain, come spring of 1927, Theo Chantale's business was booming, collecting three times the number of pelts as the prior season. It was money time, and Theo Chantale had ideas about how to make even more of it.

The pelts were processed in Algiers and shipped directly to the New York furriers. But this season's harvest was so productive, there was more supply than the eastern furriers could take in. With demand growing all across the country, and even faster in Europe, Theo was considering how to expand his distribution network quickly and without diluting prices in the Northeast. Brokers working at the newly opened International Fur Exchange in St. Louis were offering top dollar for pelts, including terms on shipping that mitigated the risk of loss and the cost of insurance for cross-Atlantic transactions. If Chantale's brother-in-law, Paul Boisvert, could work his connections in Paris and London, the pair would be able to come at the St. Louis exchange from both directions.

Chantale made arrangements for a mid-April trip to St. Louis, hoping to make a lucrative deal. 1927 was the year Theo Chantale woulc cross that wide line between *making* money and *having* money.

* * *

Now she wants a butter and egg man
A great big butter and egg man from way down South

"How's *my* great big butter and egg man?" Pascale cooed as they swayed to the record.

She touched his cheek, which spread Theo's toothy grin. He put his hands over hers and raised them to his lips.

"Your Butterman." He wrapped his strong bronze arms around his wife and squeezed her tight.

"Je t'aime." Pascale smiled and slipped into a coughing fit that lasted so long she couldn't catch her breath. Lightheaded, she buckled.

Theo scooped her into his arms and set her in the wingback chair coughing so hard she passed out. When she came to, her face was ghostly pale, her forehead trickling sweat. The house was silent but for the clicking of the Victrola, changing records. The speaker amplified the crackles and pops before Richard Jones and His Jazz Wizards started "Dusty Bottom Blues." Chloe, woken from her nap by her mommy's coughing, entered the parlor.

"Your mommy's gonna be fine, m'abeille. Say, you sit and play along some."

Reassured, Chloe accompanied the record on the upright, her papa beaming with pride as she matched the banjo solo, then the piano solo, note for note. Pascale coughed lightly.

"How you feelin'?" Theo dabbed her forehead with a damp cloth.

"I'm fine, baby. Just fine." But her voice was weak and scratchy. "I just have a tickle in my throat. Some water, please?" She coughed again while Theo was in the kitchen, a deep, honking growl of a cough. The water helped, and Theo wasn't concerned. Since he'd known her, Pascale'd never fallen ill for more than an overnight. She was so strong-willed, it was as if she just wouldn't tolerate it. He had failed to take note that this cough had lingered for days.

Chloe focused on the song, and Theo approached her at the bench.

"You play that boogie something serious! Should be bangin' out Beethoven or somethin' at the Tulane Theatre." He kissed his youngest on the head. "I gotta pack." The big man's boots clomped down the hall toward the bedrooms. Pascale sipped at her water. The record player finished the stack and shut down.

"Mommy?" Chloe said, as her mother worked some loose records into their sleeves. "I'm worried about Papa."

"M'abeille, whatever for?"

"It's the rain, Mommy." Her voice held an uncharacteristic whine.

"Your papa, he's traveling in this rain all the time. He's been down to the Delta and back countless times in downpours worse than this, m'abeille. Seems all your papa's ever doing is driving in the rain."

"But, Mommy!"

Chloe's nature was calm, extraordinarily so, and Pascale believed her youngest's serene spirit was a gift, one that enabled her to focus on Francie's needs. But this morning the girl was unusually agitated.

"Papa isn't driving to the Delta, Mommy. He's going north!" Her voice rose.

"He will be fine."

"How do you know that? How do you know that?" She was yelling now, approaching frantic. The girl was used to her papa's lengthy stays away from home, south of the city. But the other direction, the unknown, disturbed her. As far as she knew, no one in her family had ever traveled so far as St. Louis. Except for Uncle Paul. But that was different. He was *from* far away. She sobbed into her hands.

"The trainmen know their jobs, m'abeille." Pascale rubbed her back. "They drive those trains on the same tracks every day. Day, night. Sunshine, thunderstorms. Even snow! It's not like the roads, where the rain breaks them up, making big holes. The tracks are built high up. It's all going to be just fine."

Theo returned to the parlor and sat next to her on the piano bench. "I'll tell you what, m'abeille. Next time, how 'bout I bring you with me? Maybe go all the way up to Chicago. Would you like that?"

Chloe couldn't look at him. Tears streaming through her fingers, she was inconsolable.

Since last summer, the entire Mississippi River Basin had been pounded by record rainfalls, from the headwaters of Montana to the Gulf Shore of Alabama. Since New Year's, wide swaths of mid-America were experiencing three to six, even eight inches of rain in a single day's time. It was unheard of. Just after Mardi Gras, New Orleans had been deluged by a daylong downpour that totaled fifteen inches of rain, which sent two feet of water rushing into the Tremé District. It rose over the Chantales' porch, cresting inches below the front door.

By April, the mightiest river in the world was swollen, as were its feeders, and the rain refused to relent. At every turn south of Memphis, the Mississippi was running near the top of cracked and leaking levees. Folks were so nervous that armed guards patrolled both riverbanks because the landowners and politicians worried someone from the other side might choose to save their own property by dynamiting the levee on their side.

Chloe could feel the tension in New Orleans, and it heightened her reservations about her papa's trip.

The following morning, Theo kissed Pascale, Francie, and Chloe each on the forehead, then rubbed Chloe's earlobe.

"I see you've turned that frown upside down."

Chloe hadn't stopped smiling since last night's wonderful dream. In it, she was sitting next to her papa, sharing an ice cream on a train, the landscape speeding past her window. Her daddy held her skinny calves as she poked her head outside. The sun was bright in her eyes and warm on her face, while the whistling wind whipped her hair.

Theo pinched her cheek. "I should be home in a week's time."

He collected his suitcase, tipped his brown felt hat, and made his exit. The screen door groaned as the spring stretched. Chloe ran to catch it as it swung closed.

"Come, girls." Pascale clapped. "Let us play some records. Francie, you choose six, and Chloe, you pick six as well. I will mix them up, and we'll have a dance party."

Francie stomped and swayed, her head back, eyes closed, arms wide. Pascale took Chloe's hand and set her to twirling. The girl was giddy and a little dizzy, and all was right again in the Chantale household. The last record in the stack was a sad bluesy number by Sidney Bechet and Rosetta Crawford.

```
My path before me is mighty dark
To travel with a broken heart
```

* * *

The porter tugged Theo Chantale's sleeve. "Sir, if ya please."

Theo raised the brim of his hat and blinked, surprised he'd slept so hard.

"You axe me to wake you when weez comun up ta Greenville, sir. Weez bout theyah, yessah. Just unda ten minute now."

Theo stripped a fiver from his money clip and pressed it into the porter's palm. "Thank you, Cassius. It's Cassius, right?"

"Yessah, Missah Chantale. Anthin you needs. Membah, weezs only sixteen minute in Greenville takin watta. It startin up hard rain again, so I brought you dis umbrella so as you kin keeps yoseff some kinda dry durn yo meetin."

* * *

James Hall waited at the Greenville station, raindrops splashing in the full brim of his saturated bowler. He spied Theo stepping out of the black car.

"You Chantale?"

"You Hall?"

Hall motioned toward an overhang at the south wall that did something to block wind and rain. He leaned against the slick wet bricks, fighting nature to light a cigarette and sizing up this impeccably tailored Negro.

Theo wondered if Hall was slow, out in this weather with no umbrella. His brother, Charlie, had told him this guy was pretty high up in Capone's organization and oversaw much of the Outfit's bootlegging from Canada. Theo wasn't sure if he would just ship pelts to St. Louis legit, or, if he could find an angle, maybe he could expand Molero's bootlegging enterprise east of the Mississippi with Puerto Rican rum to Chicago, maybe even compete with Scotch whisky. Before another word was said between them, Hall craned his neck to look past the big man.

"This nigga bah'thrin you?"

Theo turned to find three men standing shoulder to shoulder. The one who spoke, the one in the middle, was a wispy fella about swallowed up by an oversized trench coat and a sunken, rain-soaked fedora. The man cupped a match to relight the butt pinched between his lips, but a huge drop off his hat brim extinguished the flame. His two companions wore military khaki under doughboy helmets. Both held carbine rifles and looked tired.

"He's with me." Hall stepped forward. "There ain't no problem here."

"Y'all know the river's 'bout to top the levee. We're collectin' volunteers to work sandbags."

Under the fedora was Joe Slinger, foreman at the Greenville Seed Company. In recent weeks, he'd been charged by the Greenville city council to oversee the collection of workers to reinforce the levee on the east bank of the Mississippi River. That meant corralling Negroes. Drunks, and other unemployed ne'er-do-wells, sharecroppers whose fields and loans were already underwater. More hands were needed, too many, in fact, so today, Slinger and his men started rounding up all the black men they could find. The governor had activated the National Guard to support the efforts on the levees and to coordinate relief with the American Red Cross. This dark, wet night, Slinger was accompanied by Bill Smith and Benjamin "Curly" Wilson, both guardsmen from down in Jackson.

Theo spoke. "We're meetin' here for just a minute. Got a seat on that there train, heading north."

"You think I was talking to you, boy? Shut . . . yo . . . mouth!"

Theo looked at James Hall, then at his watch. "Look, we ain't from around here, and I have a seat on that train." He took Hall by the coat sleeve and started walking toward the colored car. "Good evenin', gentlemen."

Police say, work, fight, or go to jail, I say I ain't totin' no sack
And I ain't buildin' no levee, the planks is on the ground and I ain't drivin' no nails

    Slinger whacked Curly Wilson on the arm. The corporal raised his rifle and pulled the trigger. Not ten feet away, the bullet penetrated the back of Theo Chantale's skull and exited the front, taking his right eye and some of his nose with it. The big man fell like a tree struck by lightning, cracking what was left of his face on the wet platform. Hall looked back at the trio. The guardsmen both sighted their rifles on the Yankee in the bowler. Slinger approached him.
    "I suggest you collect yer nigga," he flicked the soggy butt at Theo's body, "and get him, and yer nigga-loven ass, off this platform, ya heyah?" He motioned to the guardsmen, and they disappeared into the rain.
    Hall stood over the corpse as the scene attracted a small crowd. He cupped a hand over his brass lighter, fired a Lucky Strike, and blew out a dense, blue-gray plume that the rain smashed to bits. Hall walked away, toward an idling Nash sedan.

4

THE LEVEE

APRIL 1927

Congressman Hill wanted Lieutenant Benoit down in New Orleans. Elaine, meanwhile, was planning a visit with friends back in Washington. When Big Jack asked her about the boys, she was flippant. "Just leave 'em with my mother."

When he told the boys the plan, Frank proposed an alternative. "Daddy, me and PJ can stay here in the house. I can cook and get us to school, no problem. You'll only be gone a few days, right?"

"More like a week. Maybe then some."

Big Jack was proud of his oldest. Frank was always respectful and polite, and for an eleven-year-old, he did a fine job presenting how his idea would work out best for everyone.

"The Sills and the Coughlins are right down the street. If anything comes up, I'll ask 'em for help."

Big Jack told the boys he'd think about it, but for the time being they were to be agreeable with their mama, who wasn't going to leave for a couple more days. So Frank told PJ they'd let it simmer with their daddy.

"He'll come 'round."

They didn't know that Big Jack'd already made up his mind to bring them with him to New Orleans.

* * *

The entire Mississippi River Basin was saturated with water. From Cincinnati to Missoula, Minneapolis to Mobile, the streams, bayous, and rivers were angry and aggressive. Lakes in Missouri and Arkansas swelled, and swamps in Louisiana flooded. The runoff from the saturated ground drained down the massive Mississippi River, and, on April 21, the levees could take no more.

The first break was at Mound Landing near Greenville, Mississippi, where the churning river broke the top off the eastern levee, a dirt-and-stone barrier over a hundred feet tall. Within minutes, the unforgiving torrent carved a slough twenty feet deep and a hundred yards wide all the way through the quarter-mile thick structure, and water sprayed east toward Greenville with the force of Niagara Falls. Soon, new breaks occurred downriver and, in short order, sixteen million acres, twenty-five thousand square miles across the states of Mississippi and Louisiana, were under cold brown water.

Big Jack's mission was simple enough. Before the levee breached, the powers-that-be had demanded air reconnaissance, and, at the governor's request, a navy carrier put a plane off in New Orleans for the use of the Louisiana National Guard. But the guard was supplied by the army, and so army personnel was required to support the plane. A flight crew was coming up from Brooks in San Antonio, but Congressman Hill thought including a flyer from Montgomery would make good press for Maxwell, and so he insisted on Lieutenant Benoit. Regardless, nature didn't wait for the army to arrive.

* * *

The drive was an overnight adventure full of new sights and sounds for the boys. Big Jack steered the Ford flatbed southwest from Montgomery, and the trio spent the night in a highway motel just south of Mobile. When they rose early and eager the next morning, the Crescent City beckoned. As Big Jack eased the truck through a stretch of lightly flooded highway, he drummed the steering wheel in high spirits. "Almost there." By the time he turned onto a rutted dirt drive, PJ was ready to burst with excitement.

"It's a farm," Frank deadpanned.

"Ain't no airport down here, so the guard leased this man's property." At the end of the drive a sturdy red barn adjoined a close-cropped hayfield. "Not too far out in the boondocks." Big Jack parked the pickup next to the barn. "Maybe we'll get into town. Suck some crawdad heads."

The nose of a plane was sticking out the barn door, and a couple men in green overalls were doing something with the propeller.

"If y'all gotta go, do it over there. I gotta talk to the sergeant."

As the boys laughed and crisscrossed streams against the barn wall, they heard Big Jack from around the corner.

"Great day for flying!" He surveyed the PT-3 Courier biplane. A yellow canvas two-seat trainer with a 550-mile range, nearly double that of the PT-3 Trusty it had replaced. Its nine-cylinder circular plant sat behind a slick varnished wood propeller tipped in cherry red. From the front, the engine looked like a black metallic wagon wheel, the hubcap a brushed-metal cone. The tapered exhaust pipe curved down and to the port side of the aircraft. It looked like an elephant's trunk had been stuck to the rig.

"She sure is a beaut!"

The boys rejoined their daddy just as Sergeant Hank Novak climbed down from the biplane and wiped his greasy hands on a rag. He saluted Big Jack. "Mornin', Lieutenant."

PJ hadn't known Hank would be there, and he'd forgotten how big the sergeant was.

Big Jack teased, "What do you do in your spare time, Sergeant, wrestle bears?"

"No, sir. Just eat one every now and then." Hank flicked a thumb at the kids. "One of them your copilot, Lieutenant?"

"I am!" PJ shouted.

"You remember my boys, Sarge?"

"How could I forget? The college man and the fighter pilot."

PJ ran right up to Hank and stuck out his hand. "Glad ta see you, sir."

Hank chuckled, wrapping his giant paw around the boy's hand.

"The only *sir* here is your daddy, son." He leaned over and whispered loud enough for Big Jack to overhear, "But I won't take no offense."

Big Jack rubbed the propeller blade between his fingers. "How's she lookin'?"

"Good as gold, Lieutenant. I gotta say, I like this new Wright radial engine. It's a smooth piece of work. We did have a problem with the spark. Saltwater. But I was able to settle that easy enough. Don't see why the navy didn't get at it. Anyway, I replaced the plugs and the seals and made some adjustments to the distributor, and I'm bettin' we get a little more horsepower. A cruisin' speed over a hundred ain't out of the question."

"I'd like to take her up."

"Sure nuff, sir. It's fueled. The boys can help me out here 'til you get back."

PJ pointed up. "I'm going!"

Hank laughed, then stopped short when he realized the boy was serious. Frank stepped forward.

"Me too, Sergeant," Frank said.

The big man frowned at the lieutenant, who nodded. "You had it right, Sergeant. These are my copilots."

"But, sir . . ."

"But what? You just told me she's good as gold. Unless by that you meant she's gonna drop out of the sky like a brick of the stuff."

Hank pawed at the dirt floor.

Big Jack paused, weighing the mechanic's confidence, then he mussed Frank's hair. "Let's get at it, T-boy. C'mon PJ."

Squeezed into the instructor's seat with his brother, both boys were perched on yellow life preservers, and PJ's adrenaline reached an all-time high as Big Jack ignited the engine. Hank climbed up the ladder to the front trainer seat.

"This is all we have, Lieutenant!" he shouted, holding up two parachutes. Big Jack motioned for the boys to sit on them, too. Stacked atop the life preserver and the parachute, PJ could just see over the fuselage, and he squealed with delight. Big Jack wasn't concerned with parachutes. Even if he were alone and ran into trouble, his best bet would be to glide the rig into a pasture.

The roar of the engine inside that barn was the loudest noise PJ'd ever heard. When he pressed a hand against the inside of the taut canvas fuselage, intense vibrations convulsed through his palm and into his arm.

Frank hollered at his brother, a jiggly *aaaaaaaaaaah!* and PJ made it a chorus. Hank recommended Big Jack take off along the crest down the middle of the pasture where the water had drained the best. Big Jack nodded and circled his arm over his head. He eased the biplane into the sunshine and across the rutted barnyard to the mowed field. He turned to check on the boys. With a gray scarf bunched high, all that showed of PJ's face under oversized goggles were the tip of his upturned nose and two rows of tiny white baby teeth, a dark hole where the front top two used to be. Next to him, his brother howled with joy.

In the barn Big Jack had told them it would be too loud to talk much once they were airborne, and he smiled to find PJ chattering away in back anyway. As the PT-3 picked up speed, the small aft wheel bounced along the pasture, and the boys belly-laughed with their heads bobbling wildly. Big Jack pulled back the stick, and the plane left the ground. The head bobbling abruptly stopped, and the engine roared like a lion. At a thousand feet, Big Jack arced the plane northwest. They were going to see the flood.

He signaled downward, yelling, "That bright green down there! See it? That's oats! The dark green over there! That's beans!"

The outskirts of New Orleans fell away as the biplane rose over a patchwork of yellow, ochre, and green farmland stitched together with tree rows and dual-track roads. The scene reminded PJ of his nana's quilt. She'd gone to heaven when he was a baby, so he only knew her from the photograph Big Jack kept on his dresser and the quilt draped across the back of the big red chair in the front room. He figured the spread beneath them must be for Nana's benefit, her having ass-ended into heaven last year. The damp air splashed between his clumsy goggles and the loosening scarf, trickling down his neck like cold water. With the wind rushing across his face, he was surprised by how slowly everything below was moving.

Twenty minutes in and leveled at four thousand feet, they found the flood. Frank kept elbowing PJ and pointing over the side of the plane at something, but PJ couldn't see. The life preserver under him had shifted, and he had to pull himself up to see anything at all beyond his own side of the instructor's cockpit.

Big Jack stabbed a gloved hand toward the ground starboard and guided the biplane into a slow arc that direction. As they tipped, the flat brown water came into PJ's view. It looked like a paper bag splattered with tiny green dots of paint and little tin-gray rectangles, spread as far as the eye could see, all perfectly still but for a random, silvery shimmer here and there. Big Jack banked harder, bringing into view a long and thin winding figure further west.

He yelled into the back, "See the curve there? Looks like a big ol' copperhead swimmin'!"

PJ worked to steady the goggles that were trying to swallow his face. He wriggled against the harness, stretching for a better look at the squiggly dark line almost a mile down and some five miles out, squeezing his butt cheeks, trying to keep the life preserver from squirting out from underneath him.

There were two lines, twisting and turning together. They looked as though they'd been drawn in parallel with a fat pencil across the brown paper sack.

"Atchafalaya River! Levee breaks on both sides!"

While Big Jack dropped altitude, PJ couldn't get the life preserver to cooperate. He took a deep breath and closed his eyes, focusing on the harmony of the rumbling engine and the jiggling underneath him. The canvas hull sounded like a flag in a storm as it rippled in the turbulence. Frank jammed the yellow preserver back under his brother's bottom.

Both boys stared in awe as the levee passed slowly below them. Neither of them had ever seen a levee before, and these were massive. Some thirty feet across the peak and hundreds of feet wide at the submerged base.

"Where're the trees, Daddy?" PJ shouted, his little voice lost in the roar of engine. "Where're the houses?" Big Jack lifted an earflap. The boys both shouted the question as loud as they could.

"Underwater, T-boy, 'cept those. See?" Big Jack pointed at three treetops near a gray square of tin roof about two hundred yards from a similar second cluster. A few dozen oaks poked from the water in parallel lines for a quarter mile or so, no doubt bordering a submerged road. "Over there, that's Columbia!"

"Where, Daddy?"

"What? Speak up!"

PJ yelled again. "Where's the town?"

Then, it struck him like a thunderbolt, and his heart raced like it did whenever his mama chased him with a switch. He scanned the levee and screamed from the instructor seat, "Daddy, it's wrigglin'! Is it a snake, Daddy? *Daddy*?" His words rattling out fast, like machine gun fire.

"Settle down!" Frank punched his arm.

Big Jack laughed hard. He raised his goggles to his forehead and set his stormy blue eyes on his PJ. Despite his confusion, the relentless noise, and his smeared goggle lenses, looking into his daddy's eyes eased the little one's anxiety.

"Ain't no monster snake, PJ. It's a levee. A big long hill. The only spot of land 'round here tall enough to top the water."

"What's makin' it move, Daddy?"

"Them's people. The levee's plum covered in Negroes. Thain't got nowhere to go, so, there they are." Big Jack waved his arm in a circle, banked the plane hard, then leveled off toward New Orleans.

PJ could no longer see the catastrophe below. His view was once again a hazy gray sky dotted with puffy white clouds with dirty bottoms.

He breathed out the words. "Plums. Negroes."

5

ST. LOUIS NO. 3

JUNE 1927

Founded in the Tremé District of New Orleans in 1841, St. Augustine was the oldest black Catholic parish in the country. *Les gens de couleur libres*, as free blacks in Louisiana were known before Reconstruction, won the *War of the Pews*, purchasing three times the number of pews bought by whites, along with the two side aisles where the property of slave-holding parishioners could sit.

    Chloe and Francie were up front, waiting as the altar boy made preparations. Francie rocked, swinging her legs under the pew, while Chloe sat still with her head down, her tiny silk-gloved hands folded in her lap. She was thinking about the crypt, remembering the first time they'd gone there, only a few weeks past. A big, cold white box with sharp corners and a strangely tall step out front. She pictured the pretty white angel perched on the top of the box, her arms and wings spread wide, like Jesus draped in a white robe before he got all bloody.

    She tried to picture her papa's name carved into the gray marble plaque set in the wall. How the plaque looked like the New Year's party invitation her mommy and papa received from the Brewsters before Christmas. A dozen tears dripped into her lap before her Uncle Paul dabbed her cheeks with his handkerchief. He pressed the moist cloth into her gloved hands.

    "This is a day for sorrow, yes. We have lost so much."

He leaned across her to gently pat Francie's leg.

"Awh!" Francie's howl echoed off the high ceiling. She neither looked up nor altered the pace of her rocking.

Paul returned his attention to Chloe. "This is a time to be strong, and to take comfort knowing the angels will care for your mommy."

She pictured the angel on the crypt. "The Jesus girl, with the wings?"

She studied the wooden box set to the right of the alter. It was just like the other wooden box the men pushed into that big white box before. *Was Papa a skeleton in his wooden box? How long before Mommy would be a skeleton? If Papa was in heaven and not in his wooden box with his skeleton, how would Mommy find him?* She was sobbing, and Paul pulled her close, under his arm, where her nose dripped onto his gold-and-black paisley waistcoat. Francie continued to rock. Chloe looked through the skylight over the alter, at the Eye of God, as it was known, and wondered if God was looking back.

* * *

When the mourners processed from St. Augustine's to the St. Louis No. 3 cemetery back in May, an early morning rain had cleared the air. Despite her friends' objections, and their pleas that she ride in a car, Pascale walked the whole way, holding tight to her daughters' hands. Each time she felt a cough coming on, she squeezed hard, then pulled away to raise a handkerchief to her lips. Chloe's fingers were sore for two days.

The procession for Theo Chantale was huge, with some five hundred mourners paying tribute to the hard-working man who'd driven poverty from the Delta and industry to Algiers. With each of the widow's coughing fits, the band's dirges slowed, and the procession stalled to accommodate her.

Now, when Chloe arrived at the crypt this time, she learned why her papa's name and those numbers had been carved on the left-hand side of the plaque. That carving was now balanced by the new letters and numbers on the right.

Pascale Amélie Chantale
August 17, 1898 – June 22, 1927

Paul lifted her, and Chloe pulled off a glove to trace a finger through each of her mommy's carved letters, every number. Her chest felt tight, like she was being smooshed against a wall, the palm of someone's hand pressing hard on her heart. Tears streamed down her face. Francie sat on the tall step, swinging her feet, bent over a closed fist.

* * *

Just days after arriving home in Paris, Paul Boisvert learned of his sister's illness, and he sailed straight back to America. His wife, who couldn't have children of her own, made it clear what she wanted. "If the worst comes to pass, heaven forbid," she crossed herself, which was not her habit, "bring my precious Chloe to me."

Yvonne Boisvert then made it equally clear that there would be no room in their apartment on Rue de l'Odéon for the older girl, and she pressed her husband to promise he would "do the right thing" and put her in a home "where she can be with her kind."

Paul arrived at the Chantale house on Bayou Road with no time to spare. He set his train case in the parlor and entered Pascale's room to find her in a terribly weakened state. She could only manage a whisper, and he leaned in close. When she finished, he stood, his wide eyes betraying his concern. Pascale raised a pale, trembling hand.

"Promet moi, mon frère," were her last words.

"Oui, ma chatte. Je promets." Paul Boisvert kissed his sister's forehead as she died.

* * *

Paul hired a neighbor woman to stay with the girls while he set out to clear the paths to their futures, and when he returned at dusk four days later, he was greeted by song.

```
Oh Candy Lips
You're sweet as you can be
```

An old Eva Taylor record accompanied by Chloe on piano. Paul set his bag on the stoop and stretched, his back stiff from the three-hour drive. Closing his eyes, he let the music envelope him, and he pulled a cigar from his inside breast pocket. He clipped and fired the stogie as the Hot Five followed Ms. Taylor and, oddly, Chloe played tandem with Louis Armstrong on his cornet.

```
Gimmie, gimmie, gimmie, gimmie what I cry for
You know you've got the brand of kisses that I'd die for
```

Chloe didn't notice when he entered the parlor. He poured a bourbon and watched, leaning against the kitchen doorframe. The Victrola finished the stack, and the mechanism shut down. Chloe sat silently on her bench, staring up at the old photo of young Pascale in her polka-dot dress.

"I have brought you something."

Chloe let out a startled scream.

"I didn't mean to frighten you, m'abeille."

She stood and stomped her foot, yelling at him. "Do not call me that!" She ran down the hallway and slammed the bedroom door. Moments later, Francie appeared.

"Wha you do? Wha you do ta Chlo?" she demanded, face red, hands on hips.

"I brought chocolates." He opened a fancy tin with red cursive lettering. Francie jumped to him and grabbed at the box. "Ah, just one, Francie dear, yes?"

She snatched a milk chocolate pecan cluster, the whole of which went straight into her mouth.

"Very good." Paul nodded and closed the tin.

The girl's eyes and smile grew large as she savored the morsel. She crinkled her face while swallowing hard, then stuck out an open palm.

"Perhaps later."

Her hands returned to her hips. "Wha you do ta Chlo?" Her face was stern again.

He told Francie the truth.

"No good." Francie vigorously shook her head. "Only Mommy and Papa. Nah for you ta say."

Paul found Chloe crying into her pillow. He sat on the bed. "I am so very sorry, my dear girl. It was terribly presumptuous of me to call you by your dear parents' pet name for you. Can you please forgive me?"

But she was inconsolable, and having spent little time with children, Paul was at a loss. He waved a chocolate under her drippy nose. She twitched and opened her wet eyes, then quickly squeezed them tight again, pressing her face into the pillow. He left two of the treats on the nightstand between the girls' beds, laid his handkerchief on the bed sheet, and exited the room. Francie confronted him in the hallway.

"I left two for your sister on the table in there. So you can choose one more now, okay?"

Francie giggled and snatched a dark chocolate sphere. Popping it into her mouth, she smiled up at her uncle as she chewed. Inside was a preserved cherry, and when it burst with gooey sweetness, she pressed her hands to her cheeks and squealed with surprise and delight.

"Now you leave the others I left on the nightstand for your sister, yes?"

She frowned at him, pursing her lips.

"*Yes?*"

Francie nodded and disappeared behind the door to the girls' room. Paul let the help go home and carried his tall bourbon to the porch. He loved the sound of the screen door spring as it stretched. He noted the Appalachian landscape painted on the headrest of the black spindle-backed rocker on the porch, tossed a cushion from the bench swing onto its seat, and settled in, re-firing his smoke. Chloe peeked out the window, watching each draw he took stoke the tip of the cigar, forming a tiny, setting sun against the dusking sky.

Having had three hours to think it through during his drive back to New Orleans, Paul was confident he'd found the right path for the older girl. "No sanitarium. She stays with family," Pascale had whispered. "Promise me, my brother." He'd driven some 150 miles west of the city, to Abbeville, where he'd found Theo Chantale's sister, Armintha Williams.

* * *

Armintha Williams was married to a sharecropper named Terrance Williams. But the brutal rains had pounded their crops so badly, there was no way they could pay off their debts. On a Tuesday morning back in October, Armintha woke alone in their bed. She heard rumors Terrance had jumped a train to Chicago, but no one knew for certain, and no one but Armintha much cared.

Before she married, Armintha had cooked and cleaned for a white family in Baton Rouge. She was a wonderful cook who made tantalizing jambalayas, étouffées, and gumbos, and she was a fine fryer and baker as well. When Paul found her, she was living in a shed behind an acquaintance's home on the southern edge of

Abbeville. She'd been trying to find work to no avail and was living off charity and losing weight something awful. She'd heard mention of Pascale's brother from her own brother Theo way back when, but when the dapper gentleman introduced himself to her in that shed, she didn't understand who he was or what he was offering.

While Paul walked her through it a second time, Armintha became certain this was a swindle of some kind. The man was nothing but a cruel liar and charlatan. She cursed him, wildly swinging a rusty hoe as she drove him away. Paul thought it best to excuse himself, placed his calling card on a broken stool and tipped his hat as he backed out of the shed.

He drove into town, considering how he might try again. An idea sprouted as he rolled past St. Mary Congregational Church, inside of which he approached two women cleaning windowsills and glass panes. He learned the pastor's address.

The Reverend Doctor James Herod lived on Victor Street with his wife, Josephine. Twenty some years earlier, the preacher had started a school for Negro children in the church and later moved it into his second home. A fervent educator and successful businessman, the reverend was on the Board of Directors of the Abbeville Chamber of Commerce, an extraordinary position for a black man in 1927 Louisiana. His wife, Josephine, graciously welcomed this resplendent stranger who held his new country gentleman's hat against a lavender silk waistcoat and tie. She delivered Paul to the preacher's home office, where he was found reading. The reverend stood and stiffly made his way out from behind his desk. Approaching seventy years in age, the graying preacher had walked for half a century on a peg leg. Introductions were made, and Josephine called for the house girl to bring lemonade, then took a seat among the men.

The reverend wasn't one to boast or even self-profess, but he so appreciated this rare element of Parisian sophistication in his parlor, especially Paul Boisvert's affable nature and conversational skills, that he took some liberties from his usual decorum and told Paul, with a few omissions, the story of his life. After an hour or so of varied and interesting talk that pleased all the parties involved, the preacher turned to the purpose of Paul's visit.

"So how may I be of service, Mr. Boisvert?"

Paul protested the reverend's formality for the last time, then started his pitch. "I need your help so that I may assist a woman, a

Mrs. Armintha Williams. She lives here in Vermilion Parish, just outside the Abbeville city limits, if I have my bearings correct."

Paul filled the Herods in on the recent history. The murder of Armintha's brother, followed quickly by her sister-in-law's death from pneumonia. Francie's *condition* and the promise he had made to his sweet sister, Pascale, on her deathbed. He couldn't bring Francie to Paris, to live with him, an owner of nightclubs. Even if he had had the skills to raise Francie, or could hire someone to do so, it wouldn't be fair to the girl for his attention to be so otherwise directed. He conveniently avoided his marital status and the existence of Francie's sibling. From what Theo and Pascale had told him, Paul understood Armintha to be a wonderful cook, though she'd left behind that occupation upon marrying Mr. Williams and taking to farming some years ago. But given her husband's recent desertion, the dear woman's immediate situation was dire.

So the proposition was made. Francie was sole heir to her parents' estate, what was left of it after the ruinous flood. Paul would liquidate everything for Francie's benefit. If he found Mrs. Williams capable of managing financial distributions for Francie, he would deliver the money to her. If he found otherwise, yet still deemed the woman capable of caring for the girl, he would establish a trust from which he would distribute the money over time.

The Reverend and Mrs. Herod were entranced. Paul could tell a story, and he'd just presented a mystery that demanded an ending.

"Do tell, Mr. Boisvert," Josephine couldn't help herself, "how did you find Mrs. Williams? That is, in what state of distress or comfort?"

"Ma'am, Mrs. Williams chased me off with a rusty hoe after I failed, and quite miserably so, to communicate my intentions to her. But from the little I had heard from her brother, and from the little time I did spend with Mrs. Williams, I believe she is capable of caring for Francie. Regarding the money, well, *that* is a different matter altogether. I may be wholly mistaken based upon my limited observations, but I do believe she would struggle with the management of a tidy sum. A likely target for predation and fraud."

The reverend's expression was serious, and he nodded, slowly, pensively. He was now aware of the small, yet fundamental, generosity Mrs. Williams's current host proffered, but he admitted to knowing nothing of the woman herself beyond the cause of her predicament as described by his guest. She wasn't a member of St. Mary, nor, to his knowledge, was she active in Abbeville's seedier side of colored life. The reverend and Josephine looked into each other's eyes, already knowing they would help poor Francie Chantale and her aunt Armintha start a new life together.

Josephine Herod orchestrated meetings with the woman that included herself, the reverend and Paul, and together, over the course of three days, they laboriously moved the proposition forward. Paul could not have been more pleased. Josephine was successful in pulling to the surface what little strength remained in Armintha Williams and nurtured it with encouragement and love. The result was nothing short of miraculous. In just a few days, Armintha came to fully understand the proposition, then reframed it, and an agreement was made.

With the proceeds from the estate, the reverend would assist Armintha with the purchase, renovation, and repurposing of a building on South Louisiana Street. The result would be a restaurant and her new home, and she would take in Francie as her own. The remainder of the money would be put in a trust for Francie. This, Paul insisted, would legally protect the sum in case the moneymen came after Terrance Williams's estranged wife. Armintha didn't understand the trust, but earlier that week she'd been wasting away on a flea-ridden pallet in a broken-down shed, and she was truly grateful to this stranger from Paris. She put away her objections.

As New Orleans came into view over the Packard's dashboard, Paul put a match to his cigar. Any idea of bringing Francie home with him was untenable. He was a man who knew his limitations and was well aware of the limitations his wife carried with her. Technically, he hadn't lied to Pascale. Francie *would be* with family. But he knew that wasn't how his sister understood his agreement. Then he flat out lied to the Herods, and in the hours to come, he would lie to the girls. He pulled out his handkerchief and dabbed his eyes. He took a deep draw on the cigar, blew a slow, long plume of smoke out the window and pushed the guilt down as deep as it would go.

* * *

The next day, after a luncheon of sandwiches and fruit with the Chantale girls, Paul walked to the Travelers Hotel to have a drink in the lobby bar with adult company. Within minutes, he was holding court with a handful of delighted strangers, regaling his new friends with fascinating tales of Parisian nightlife. Several hours later, he returned to Bayou Road refreshed. Chloe was at the piano playing fast scales, while on the floor behind her, Francie played jacks.

"Bonne après-midi!"

Chloe's heart leaped. Francie bounced the ball and spun a jack.

"We are dining out tonight, girls! Anywhere your little hearts desire. What would you like to have this evening? Chicken? Shrimp? How about a sizzling steak with potatoes and carrots?"

Chloe shrugged. Her only thought was how good it was to have her uncle there. Francie bounced the ball and spun another jack.

* * *

"What is it like, Uncle Paul?"

"What is what like?"

"Paris."

Paul sipped his wine. "I will tell you this, Chloe. Paris is like no other place in the world. *La Ville des Lumières*. The City of Lights! The music, the food, the art, oh the laughter. People who live in Paris . . . they think like people are *capable of* thinking. Not like elsewhere, not like . . ." He swept his hand across the room as a scowl replaced his smile. He drained his wine glass and shook it toward the waiter. His smile returned, and he leaned over the table. "The evenings are lifted by the moon as she rises over the Seine. Then . . . before you know it . . . *poof!*"

"Poof?"

"Yes. Poof!"

Francie looked up at him. He thanked the waiter for the fresh glass.

"Magic."

"Magic." Francie mimicked.

Chloe tried to imagine magical Paris. But Paul's lyrical expression was too much, or not enough, for the little one to clearly see.

"And we will see to it you have the best of musical instruction and schooling. All of this is possible in Paris."

Chloe felt peace in the moment. She could feel that her uncle cared for her, and, for the first time since her mommy's passing, she didn't feel empty inside. Through the restaurant's paned window, a harvest moon shone brightly from just over the building across the street. Chloe pointed at the Tycho Crater. "Kitty whiskers."

* * *

The sale of the estate was completed within a week. The house and furniture, the entirety of the Chantales' possessions, all liquidated. The proceeds weren't as substantial as one might have anticipated just weeks earlier.

Back in April, on the day of the first levee breach at Mound Landing, Mississippi, the civic leaders in New Orleans concluded a week's worth of heated debate. The city was vulnerable with river water lapping at the very top of the levee that bordered it to the west and the south. The structure, more than four hundred feet in width, was fully saturated from the rains and was cracking all along the city's border. Conditions worsened by the hour, and leaks grew in size and number. Lying below sea level, the entirety of New Orleans would be devastated by a levee breach. So the city's power brokers decided to take an extraordinary precaution. Downriver at Caernarvon, they would dynamite the levee on the opposite bank to open a chasm and relieve the pressure. Put another way, New Orleans politicians and businessmen decided to flood the Delta and drown Plaquemines and St Bernard Parishes in order to save their city. Everyone in the Delta was forced to evacuate, and on April 30, the day after Pascale learned of her husband's death, the first explosion was triggered on the southern levee. Thirty-nine tons of dynamite later, both parishes were completely submerged, and the Delta trapping business ceased to exist.

When Manuel Molero learned of Theo Chantale's murder, his first thought was to exact vengeance on Leander Perez. He promised Pascale he would make things right for her and her daughters, but first and foremost, Molero had to turn his attention to city politics. The sacrifice of the Delta had been agreed over his strenuous objections, and those of his rival, Leander Perez. Molero and Perez negotiated for compensation for their people's lost homes, farms, and businesses, and they received promises that the communities in Plaquemines and St. Bernard would be made whole for property losses.

In time, the water receded, but the promised reparations were never made. Instead, the politicians seized the opportunity to condemn Delta property en masse and lease it to the Getty Oil Company. As a result, oilmen and their patron politicians became very, very rich, while the Delta's farmers, shrimpers, and trappers never received a dime for their losses, let alone royalties for the oil extracted from under their property. Manuel Molero was powerless to help even himself, let alone the Chantales. Pascale had been left with the house and the possessions inside it, along with a small bank balance. Theo Chantale had tied up most of his money in business transactions that were now impossible to complete.

And so when Paul liquidated the estate, it was transformed into a short stack of cash, but for the Victrola 10-50 and the records. Paul had mentioned the record player to Armintha, who asked him not sell it. Instead, he hired a truck to transport the machine and nine peach crates stuffed with shellac discs up to Abbeville.

* * *

The Reverend and Mrs. Herod came to New Orleans to visit friends and collect Francie. Paul Boisvert suffered no regret, no shame, until it was time to tell the girls that, while Chloe would sail to Paris, Francie would be traveling Highway 90 to Abbeville.

That night was filled with tears, screams and tantrums, all eventually overcome by exhaustion and whimpers. The girls fell asleep together in their bed at the Travelers Hotel, the little one wrapped around her big sister. Paul touched each girl's head as they slept. He brushed Chloe's hair from her eyes to find they were as puffy as her sister's. He stepped out onto the sidewalk and lit a cigarette with a trembling brass lighter. His eyes filled under the smoke he sent curling into the night sky.

The morning went as well as could be expected. The girls were still in shock, emotionally spent, and incapable of causing any real problems. Paul had the neighbor woman come down to take Chloe for breakfast and to walk the shops while he kept Francie at the hotel. Francie repeated the word "parade" at least a dozen times on the elevator ride down to the lobby, where Paul saw the Herods rise from a sofa. Following introductions, Mrs. Herod did all she could to soothe and manage Francie. It didn't go well, but it could have been worse. To avoid complications, Paul enacted the trust naming Dr. James Herod as trustee in favor of its beneficiary, Francie Chantale. He handed the preacher a copy of the documents and the satchel that held the cash necessary to complete the real estate purchase and renovation in Abbeville. It occurred to Paul as he let go of the bag that he didn't really trust anyone in this world, but the reverend was as close as they came. In saying their goodbyes, Francie rocked sideways, from foot to foot, while Mrs. Herod held onto her limp hand. Paul watched Francie flex a fist with her free hand, and as she opened and closed her fingers, he caught a glimpse of the gold-painted chestnut.

During the Atlantic crossing, Chloe's emotions rocked more than the ship. Paul was attentive and made every effort to cheer and distract her. Despite her grief, she found some joy at the piano as the shock and pain subsided. The head steward accommodated the girl with the graciousness forty dollars afforded, and many of the passengers appreciated the early afternoon novelty of hearing the blues played by such a little thing.

Red Hot Flo
From Ko Ko Mo

It would have been natural for Chloe to blame her uncle for the loss of Francie, but she was at ease with Paul. Maybe it was because since her papa died, while her mommy was sick, she had no buffer, no meaningful help with her sister. Francie suffered and struggled such that Chloe carried not only her own burden, but also the burden of her sister. What Chloe felt on the ship was relief, but she was too young to understand it.

"Hit me."

Paul flipped the five of clubs.

"Vingt-et-un!" Chloe cheered, as he slid two matchsticks from his pile to hers.

"Do you like this game best, or acey deucey?"

"I like how acey deucey is fast. But I like winning the sticks in this game. How did they decide on twenty-one, Uncle Paul? Why not a different number?"

The girl and her uncle played games on the small tables set between their favorite deck chairs on the shady side of the ship. Port in the morning, starboard late afternoon. The cool sea breeze mussed her hair as she sipped an iced drink, and Paul shuffled the cards. Despite the occasional salty mist, Chloe felt dry for the first time in months. She recited song lyrics she'd memorized, and Paul translated them into French. They sang the blues in two languages, pounding out rhythms on the stern taffrail while scanning the horizon for whales.

"But they don't rhyme anymore."

"That is how language works. French songs do not rhyme when they are sung in English, either."

Every evening she and her Uncle Paul sat down to a sumptuous meal served with white gloves under chandeliers, but Chloe didn't care much for the rich, creamy food. She preferred her mommy's spicier dishes. Blackened catfish, red beans and rice, crawfish étouffée. She missed the smell of her mommy's kitchen where shrimp fried and crawfish boiled. The ship's dining room smelled of beef and asparagus. They shared large tables with other travelers, some of whose overbearing colognes made her nose itch. The dining room was where she got sad.

After the evening meal, the pair would climb the stairs to walk the perimeter of the deck while Paul smoked a cigar. Invariably, Chloe's mood would cheer before they completed the first lap. "I like the sound of the ocean because no one is making it."

Before she retired each night, Paul reread the copies of *Topper* and *The World of Winnie-the-Pooh* that he'd found in the ship's library. One night, they decided on a change, so he started *The Sun Also Rises* in English. He hadn't previously read the book, and, thinking it too much for the young girl, he set it down, but Chloe begged him to finish.

"I like *Winnie the Pooh* very much, and *Topper* is funny. But I like to think about what Paris will look like when we get there."

They finished Hemingway's novel across two evenings. The dark, mature themes didn't faze the girl.

Across the final days of the crossing, they developed a nightly ritual. Winnie the Pooh read, forehead kissed, covers tucked. Her uncle was gentle, like her mommy. Paul would close the door behind him and join adult company in the main lounge while Piglet worried, Pooh pondered, and Chloe faded into slumber.

* * *

Paul couldn't have put his faith in more trustworthy souls than the Herods. As the reverend conducted business on Armintha's behalf, his wife, Josephine, made every effort to bring the poor woman more fully into Abbeville's reputable black community. With better nutrition and fresh clothes, Mint's confidence and dignity returned. Josephine arranged for Armintha and Francie to stay in the homes of welcoming Congregationalists until their new house was ready, which, in just six weeks time, it was.

The reverend directed the conversion of a dilapidated, rat-infested duplex into the restaurant and new home of Mrs. Armintha Williams.

The living area in the back was cozy, with two small bedrooms, a bathroom, and a sitting room featuring two wingback chairs and a rocker. The restaurant, which faced west on South Louisiana Street, held two wooden booths abutting the north wall and three along the south. Two eight-top community tables split the room down the middle, and a high shelf ran above the windows along each side. A half wall with saloon doors separated the seating area from the kitchen, and the Victrola cabinet stood in a corner of the dining room, the high shelves filled with the record collection. And so, the Music Box Café was born.

At first sight of the dining room, Francie ran to the Victrola and hollered excitedly. "Play! Play!" She turned to Armintha with bright eyes and a toothy smile. "Dance me, Menta!"

Mrs. Herod was there, and what she saw in Armintha's face as Francie tumbled across the room, slamming into her aunt and pulling her toward that record player, was resurrection, and it brought tears of joy to her eyes.

* * *

Paul and Chloe rode the train from the port at Le Havre and entered Paris at Gare Saint-Lazare. Chloe looked up at the high glass skylights in awe and twirled. Only once before had she seen so many people crowded together, and that was at the Zulu parade. But here everyone looked so clean and tidy, so purposeful, scurrying here and there mostly in pairs. It was all very loud and very busy, but not at all like the parade.

Porters wheeled their bags to Paul's car, which was idling on Rue d'Amsterdam. His man Dumont held the door. "Bonjour, Monsieur Boisvert. Bonjour, Mademoiselle Chantale." Dumont, a tall, somber-looking Ethiopian, was prematurely gray in his mid-thirties.

Chloe giggled, sliding back and forth across the cordovan-leather bench seat of the shiny new Duesenberg Model X Locke. A tapered glass vase holding a white rosebud was tucked into a brass loop set behind each of the back doors. As the car ambled forward, Chloe climbed to her knees and pressed her nose to the window. The sun was setting as Paul instructed Dumont to circle the Arc de Triomphe, then head south to Pont d'Iéna. As the driver angled the long automobile onto the bridge, Chloe gasped. Directly in front of them was the most wondrous sight.

"That is the Eiffel Tower."

"It's all in lights!"
"Yes. In the City of Lights."
"What is Citroën?"
"That is a type of automobile."
"Is that where they make them? In the Eiffel?"
Paul laughed. "No. That is where they advertise them, dear girl."

6

THE KING RANCH

NOVEMBER 1931

PJ climbed into the booth and scooched up against the wall. Frank hopped in next to him, and Big Jack plopped down across the table.

"Three Co-Colas, sweetie."

The dark-haired girl smiled and returned to the counter.

"Pretty li'l señorita!" He winked at Frank.

Frank watched the girl work while PJ inspected a framed photo nailed to the wall above the booth. He counted thirteen longhorn cattle staring at the camera from behind the dusty wooden slats of a plank pen. Two vaqueros in chaps leaned against the fence posts, one holding a branding iron, the other a stiff rope. "Fifteen. You're fifteen," he said mindlessly to Frank.

The sodas arrived, and Big Jack raised his bottle. "To dogs and ducks."

The boys raised their bottles, and everyone took a swig. Three years into the Depression and it showed at Juanita's Cantina in Alice, Texas. Other than the Benoits, Juanita, and her daughter, the place was empty, and it was straight-up Saturday noon.

"Don't forget the quail, Daddy," PJ added.

"Weather's perfect. The norther's gonna come in quick. Probably catch up to us at the ranch tonight, and before you know it, the sky'll be full of Yankee ducks and geese."

The boys were ecstatic.

"Oh, and I forgot. Somethin' that just come up before we left. I got a extra day of leave, so, dependin' on the weather, we might have a little time to take a side trip to the coast and do some fishin'."

PJ and Frank, laughing, knocked heads.

"It's not a deal yet. If we get sleet, I ain't gonna be up for getting out on the water, so we'll see how things do."

"Gee, Dad!" Frank exclaimed. "This is so neat!"

Frank had always been a quiet boy. Reserved. But this was too much for even him. Hunting on the King Ranch, the largest ranch in the country where they ran more than twenty thousand head of cattle over a million acres of southeast Texas. Major Chennault had invited Big Jack and the boys to join him and some old friends for their annual quail hunt, shooting over German Shorthaired Pointers. On the King Ranch, game was plentiful, as were steak, tamales, and rye whiskey. There was plenty of water near the coast, too, so the plan included time in a duck blind.

"You know, this town was named after Mr. King's daughter."

"Who's that, Daddy?" PJ inquired.

"Really, kid?" Frank said, and Big Jack laughed. "How 'bout you give it some thought?"

It took PJ a moment. "Alice!"

He was nervous. At nine years of age, it wasn't certain how all this hunting would play out for him. No one in his grade at school was allowed to hunt quail yet. Not 'til next year, or the next. But Frank'd had him out shooting each of the past eight weekends. They took the truck outside town, and Frank taught him how to aim at the cactus along ranch roads. Prickly pear made great target practice. PJ squeezed the trigger on the single-shot .410, and the boys ran to check the spread in the plant's flesh. Frank showed him how the pattern was wider and thinner the longer the shot. They would talk into the night about leading birds. "You shoot where it's goin', not where it is, 'cause it takes time for the pellets to get there."

They played catch at home, and Frank would run across the yard and have PJ throw him a baseball. At first, PJ kept throwing behind him. Then he started leading Frank with the ball.

"Wingshootin's like that. If you just let yourself see the path, then your arm follows. It just does, natural like. So you'll end up shootin' where the bird's goin', just like you started throwin' where I'm runnin' to."

The past three Sunday evenings, Frank taught PJ how to swing the .410 on dove. They positioned along a fence line between a patch of cut sorghum and a cow pasture with a small muddy tank in the corner. At dusk, the dove would fly in for water and sand. The first Sunday, Frank showed his little brother how it was done, bagging eight birds. But each time PJ shot, he was behind the speedy flyers, and his frustration grew. As the evening light faded, and they could no longer see their quarry, PJ kicked at the ground and cussed.

"Hey!" Frank's voice rose. "When you're carrying a gun, you keep your cool, you hear me?"

PJ pouted.

"You're swingin' smooth. Just a little behind, that's all. It'll come."

But it didn't come. PJ didn't down a single dove.

Big Jack had left the training entirely in Frank's hands. He told his eldest if he thought PJ was ready, then PJ would join the men on quail. Shooting over dogs, in a group of hunters with guides and beasts in the mix, hunting quail was dangerous sport. Shooting up from a duck blind was a much easier proposition. Chennault's party was at the King Ranch for quail. They had plenty of ducks back home in Louisiana. But the thoughtful host had arranged a separate duck hunt for the Benoit boys to make certain PJ had his chance.

The waitress brought three steaming plates of enchiladas with rice and beans, and Big Jack asked her name.

"Maria."

"Well, Maria, I'm Jack, and these are my boys, Frank and PJ. Frank, meet Maria!"

"Pleased to meet you, Maria," Frank said without enthusiasm but with a blush. The girl nodded and asked if they would like more Coca-Cola.

"Tres, por favor." Jack grinned and kicked the boy's leg under the table.

Frank frowned as the girl walked away. "Daddy, why are you always doin' that to me, with girls?"

"Practice makes perfect, T-boy. Right, PJ?"

"Yes, sir." PJ heard that phrase often, including during their morning calisthenics.

Later, PJ watched his father pay at the counter. After Maria closed the money drawer, Big Jack pressed some bills into her hand.

"Gracias, señorita. Buenas tardes!"

***

The ranch house was a long single story, painted white, with large, square-paned windows. It was skirted on three sides by a wide covered porch bestrewn with swinging benches and rocking chairs. Big Jack eased the Ford into an opening among the vehicles parked along one side. The Benoits were the last to arrive, and Big Jack and the boys would share a corner room furnished with two stacks of bunk beds. It was suggested they might do their washing up before dinner because morning would come early.

As they entered the great room, they were greeted by warm, toasty air laced with the scent of oak and a touch of mesquite. At the far end of the hall, a blazing fire hissed and crackled inside a massive limestone fireplace, and the heat rose to the rafters where the two ceiling fans circulated it throughout the hall. Facing the fire, a large, burnt-orange cowhide sofa stood flanked by sturdy oak side tables and puffy brown leather chairs. The room's centerpiece was the twenty-foot table lined with ladder-backed chairs with seat cushions that PJ thought looked like Indian blankets. At the far end of the room stood a tall, polished oak-and-brass bar backed by a huge mirror where men were laughing and talking loudly. PJ watched the nearest fan spread blue pipe smoke across the ceiling.

"Well, well. Here they are!" It was Chennault with pipe in hand. "Glad to see the Benoit men made it." He shook Big Jack's hand and turned to the boys. "Frank, I hear you're a fine shot, and you're making a hunter out of this little one here, too." He mussed PJ's hair.

"Yes, sir."

"I have some people I'd like you to meet. This is my age-old friend, Eddy Sweetwater, and his boy, Matthew. Eddy and I matriculated together at Louisiana State University."

"Edward Sweetwater." Sweetwater extended a hand in the general direction of the Benoits.

Frank reached out. "Mr. Sweetwater, nice to make your acquaintance."

Sweetwater was taken aback that the boy was first to close the gap, and the firmness in his grip made an impression. "My boy Matt here's a heckuva duck hunter back home. Just had his fourteenth birthday, and he's here for his first quail."

Unlike his rather pasty, spongy-looking father, Matt had a healthy glow about him. The older boys nodded to each other, and Frank pulled PJ forward by the elbow.

"This is my brother, PJ. It's his first time out, too."

Frank was already taller than Big Jack, and he towered over little PJ, who seemed to be taking after his daddy in height. If one guessed PJ's age by looks, seven years might come to mind, instead of his proper nine.

PJ met the elder Sweetwater's eyes. "I'll be ten years old in February, sir."

Big Jack swirled ice in a glass of rye as he watched the scene unfold.

Frank threw his arm around his brother's shoulders. "We've been on dove this season. Looking forward to working with the dogs."

Chennault smiled. "No better dogs in the world than right here at the King Ranch, I tell you. My favorite is Criquette. She's one hardworking, staunch bitch. A fine animal."

All the men raised their glasses toward the major, but the Benoit boys didn't have anything in hand.

PJ'd never eaten a tastier meal than that evening's braised venison. Chennault said the secret was apple juice. The meal included grilled bacon-wrapped dove and, made special for Chennault's party, jambalaya with andouille sausage the Sweetwaters brought down. Drink flowed liberally, and the boys were allowed as much Coca-Cola and Dr. Pepper as they wanted. Big Jack coached them. "Be polite in the asking and generous in the thanking. It's a party, and we're guests. Thank the hosts. Thank the help."

It was late when the boys climbed into their bunks, but still long before their daddy called it a night. PJ's mind raced, and he whispered to Frank. "This is so much fun 'cept for having to pee."

Both boys had downed so much Dr. Pepper that it made for a busted-up night's sleep. But with dawn's arrival, excitement overwhelmed exhaustion. The great room was toasty again from the fire, and the smell of coffee and sausage wafted throughout. A breakfast buffet lined the bar. Big bowls of scrambled eggs, ground chorizo, corn tortillas, butter, and fruit.

"Got everything? Hat? Shells? Gloves?" Big Jack was in a great mood. As they headed to the trucks, pungent mesquite smoke circled the house from out back where the barbecue pit was already hard at work on the evening meal.

After bumping a couple miles along a dual-track ranch road, they stepped out behind four pickup trucks stuffed with dog boxes and gear. Ten minutes of talk, and the hunting party split in two. One group started there, and the other rode downwind another a mile to walk the pasture back up to this spot, where two of the vehicles would be waiting. After dropping off the downwind party, ranch hands drove the other trucks a like distance upwind, where this group would end up.

The Benoits went out from the meeting spot with Chennault and the Sweetwaters. Six guns and a guide named Mikey, hunting over two dogs. Max was a trim, muscular German Shorthair, a beautiful specimen in dappled cream with solid black ears, a black saddle, and a small black tip on his tail. The other was Criquette, an Epagneul Breton bred in Montana to run big on Hungarian partridge and sharp-tailed grouse. "Maybe the only French Brittany in all of Texas," according to Chennault. At twenty-five pounds and just a third the size of Max the Shorthair, Criquette was tricolored, mostly white, with a black saddle slipped to one side, some black dapple, a liver muzzle, a liver-and-black nubby tail, shiny black feathered ears, and brilliant white feathered haunches. PJ thought she was the prettiest animal he'd ever seen.

Max ran big, two to three hundred yards out, while Criquette quartered much more tightly, leading the hunters on the walk. Frank and PJ were fascinated by her work. Max might cover twelve to fifteen miles in a day's hunting. He'd point numerous coveys but would also canter past some birds. Criquette, on the other hand, loped over less ground but missed nothing. Even in the driest weather, she always found birds. The Chennault group was still loading their guns when PJ looked up to find Criquette thirty yards out, rock solid, haunches up, head at ninety degrees from a body frozen mid-trot. She was pointing toward a large spread of prickly pear cactus.

The hunters approached slowly in a line six across, three on each side of Mikey the guide. PJ's single-shot .410 was empty, the bolt open. Frank carried a side-by-side 20 gauge, which was also empty and open. He would watch the first couple of rises next to PJ. The guide had the men stop some fifteen yards short of the dog. Then he issued the command. "Flush!"

Criquette immediately released at the cacti. The burst of wings startled PJ as some twenty quail launched into the air. As the birds leveled, five shots rang out, and three brown spots dropped from the sky. The spaniel was staunch at the prickly pear, straining her neck to catch sight of the falling birds.

"Open, please." Mikey requested the party open their guns for safety. He pointed at the arc of the closest downed bird. "Hunt dead."

Criquette released and quartered slowly and tightly, about five yards across, in the direction the guide had pointed. Seconds later, she buried her head under a sage bush, then trotted back to Mikey with a quail soft in her mouth. She set the bird in his hand, sat, and looked him in the eye. He threw his arm out again. "Hunt dead."

"Three in the bag, and we hardly left the truck!" Chennault beamed. "It's going to be a fine day of hunting, gentlemen."

Both Frank and PJ were astounded by what they'd just witnessed. Big Jack patted Frank on the back. "Whaddya think, T-boy?" Dumbstruck, the older boy just grinned and shook his head. "How 'bout we give Criquette another point, then you join in? Coach your brother, now."

Big Jack left the boys to join the others, where Edward Sweetwater was taking credit for two of the birds. "How about that double?" He crowed.

Chennault grimaced, knowing he'd knocked down two of the birds himself. "I think we'll see a lot of action today. Plenty for everyone. Right, Matt?" The boy smiled nervously, and the party regrouped to walk a line. Mikey set Criquette off again.

Max had long disappeared over the horizon, and they found him thirty minutes later, still as a statue of Stonewall Jackson. Max was staring into the sage under a twisted mesquite tree. As they approached, Criquette locked onto the pointer. The party walked past the Brittany to join Max, and they bagged four birds on the rise.

Criquette always stayed in sight. Methodically loping from side to side some thirty yards ahead, her feathered haunches looked like a little white sailboat tacking across a dusty brown sea. During the first four flushes, Frank kept his gun down and taught PJ what to look for and how to swing on the birds safely over the dogs.

After shooting over Max, there were eleven birds in the bag, and finally, Frank got the go ahead. He'd come to the ranch an excellent wingshooter on both duck and dove, and he proved his mettle now, bagging doubles on each of the next three rises. PJ was beside himself, happy for his brother, but anxious as a cat in a parade.

"Not my first rodeo, kid," Frank teased him with one of their daddy's favorite sayings.

A mile and a half and ninety minutes later, the group crested a hill to find the trucks parked on another double-track dirt road. There were a lot of birds in the bag. Max and Criquette had both performed brilliantly. Mikey watered the dogs and treated them to bits of jerky, then put them up to rest in the crates while the hunters lingered over coffee and snacks.

"Major Chennault, you weren't kidding about Criquette," Frank said, exuberantly.

"Max and Criquette do what their ancestors have done for hundreds of years," Mikey offered. "Some trainers think they gotta be hard on their dogs to get performance, but with the great ones, it's best just to stay outta their way."

"You do yourself a disservice, Mikey," Chennault said, slapping him on the back. "You and these dogs work like a well-oiled machine. Together, you deliver undeniable excellence. A living work of art."

Everyone was excited about the walk and how the quail coveys had burst into the sky. Max's stoicism. "He pointed for a half hour!" PJ raved. Criquette's diligence, her excellent retrieving skills and soft mouth on the birds. PJ poked his brother. "She's always smilin'."

During their walk, the sky had darkened some, and the wind had started picking up. The norther hit while they were having coffee and sodas after their second walk. The bitter wind pinched PJ's cheeks. He was sweaty from the walks and got chilled to the bone. With so much success in the bag, the men decided to return to the ranch house and warm up. They'd give it another go come afternoon.

"Two dozen birds is a heckuva day." As he climbed into the truck, Edward Sweetwater seemed to be suggesting his day of hunting was done. PJ's heart sank at the idea, and he looked at his daddy with searching eyes. He'd figured he was going to get to load and hunt that afternoon, and now he was beside himself with worry as they bounced toward the ranch house. He whispered a whine to his brother, "Are they talkin' 'bout stayin' inside?"

Frank hissed low, "Hush it!"

Big Jack chimed in. "Don't worry. You'll get a shot before the day's out."

PJ was relieved to hear it, but now he needed to pee something awful.

Edward ensured an end to the Sweetwaters' day in the field by draining two tall whiskeys before lunch. In fact, the norther came in so hard that all of Chennault's Louisiana guests decided against braving the cold that gusty afternoon and agreed it would be poker instead.

Chennault pulled Big Jack aside. "Don't feel you need to stay with us, Jack. If you want to take the boys out, Mikey'll be happy to oblige. I'll ask him to take you to a sweet spot, so Criquette can put up plenty of birds in short order." He tipped his head toward Frank and PJ, both looking forlorn at the end of the dining table. "They'll knock a few down. Y'all'll have a ball."

Big Jack thanked the major and told the boys they'd head back out again in an hour or so. PJ's face broke open with a huge grin. The boys raised their Dr. Peppers and clinked the bottles together. Even Frank was giggling.

* * *

As they stepped out of the truck, Mikey explained the strategy while the Benoits loaded up. "We'll make an oval, not too big. Start by walking the road back the way we came in, then turn into the field for a hundred yards or so. We'll walk back up this way, into the wind, and maybe past the truck some if we feel like it. We should see some birds here. They'll be tucked in tight under this weather, but our girl is up to it."

"Take a breath, PJ." Big Jack rubbed his youngest's head. "You got this, T-boy?" he asked Frank, knowing the answer.

Criquette got a nose full of nothing as they made their way downwind, the norther gusting from behind her well over thirty miles per hour. Soon they turned into the pasture and rounded back toward the truck. PJ's eyes watered something fierce as he bent into the wind, and the cold damp found its way down his neck. Quartering along the road, Criquette froze some twelve yards ahead, and PJ readied to shoulder the .410. Mikey was about to command the flush when a small covey burst from a cluster of sage just beyond the dog. Eight birds rose and curled with the wind to cross on their left. Frank and PJ swung and shot. Two birds down. Frank told PJ to open his bolt to kick out the shell. "Leave it open."

Criquette worked her retrieving magic, and two birds were in hand.

"Congratulations, Mr. PJ." Mikey handed him the trophy. "You are now officially a quail hunter."

The boy inspected the bird through eyes tearing in the biting wind. It was a beautiful male with brown feathers speckled with white and black. A tiny drop of blood sat at the corner of its beak under a closed eye.

"That's dinner, PJ." Big Jack thumped him on the back. "Baked quail on rice. Nothin' better."

PJ beamed with pride. He was a hunter. Now he could help feed his family, like his brother did.

"So?" Chennault hollered as a blast of frigid air pushed the Benoits into the great room.

Frank looked up at his father and said, "Eight in the bag, sir."

Big Jack accepted the shot of rye from Chennault's outstretched hand, threw it back, and shook out a shiver. "The boys got all of 'em. Frank knocked down six, and PJ two." He turned to his sons. "Why don't y'all peel down by the fire there and warm your bones." Big Jack turned back to Chennault. "Helluva day, Major. Thanks loads."

Frank approached Matt Sweetwater, who was sulking in a chair by the fire. "I think we're gonna go for geese tomorrow. I suppose you'll be out for quail again, but you're sure welcome to join us, if that'd work for your father." The boy, who hadn't any success during the morning hunt, brightened some. As his father had said, he was a pretty good shot in a duck blind, but he couldn't seem to get the hang of it over the dogs. The moment passed without Edward Sweetwater's notice, and Matt sunk back into his chair to stare at the fire.

As they hung their coats, PJ leaned into Frank. "I think he's scared to ask his daddy."

"I'll ask Daddy to talk with Mr. Sweetwater to see if he can come." Frank looked across the room at the elder Sweetwater, propped at the bar, talking to the other men. "If Matt brings back a couple o' honkers, his daddy'll be proud of him."

At dinner that evening, the whole party cheered as a large plate piled with fresh-baked quail was placed at the center of the table. The barbecue would wait.

"To this wonderful King Ranch, to our guides Mikey and Charlie, and to the best damn dogs on the planet, Max, Criquette, Hans, and . . . who's the other one?"

"Willie!"

"Yes. To William the Quail Conqueror! Salut!"

PJ loved the major's toasts. They felt like friendly punches to the arm.

"Which one is mine?" PJ asked.

"They're all *ours*, PJ," Chennault replied, waving his hand across the table. "That's how it works. We hunt together, we eat together. We're a team."

PJ felt a twinge of disappointment. He wanted to eat *his* bird. Then he gave it a short thought and mumbled to himself. "S'pose it's like corn or somethin'. Ain't gonna say, 'Where's that ear of corn I picked,' yeah?" He pulled a leg off the bird on his plate and ate it like a tiny chicken's drumstick. It was better than candy. For the second day in a row, PJ ate a tastier meal than any he'd ever had before.

Plans were laid for the next morning. The whole party, save the Benoits and Matt Sweetwater, would start out for quail late morning. "No sense getting up early just to freeze," as Edward Sweetwater put it. The fowl hunt would start predawn, and they would set up between a field of cut corn and a couple large ponds off San Fernando Creek. That night, Charlie had a couple hands drive out to the field to set up some goose and duck decoys in the dark. Morning would come early, so after dinner, the Benoit boys went straight to bed. Big Jack stayed in the great room to socialize for a couple more hours but called it an early night compared to the Louisiana gang. After miles of walking in the cold, a big hot meal, and a long soak in a steamy bath, PJ passed out when his head hit the pillow. Through the entire night, exhaustion won out over his little bladder.

Breakfast consisted of quail meat tacos with jalapeño hot sauce and flour tortillas, and the roasted potatoes leftover from dinner. Charlie drove Big Jack and the three boys in a dusty old Packard sedan with two spare tires tied to a metal roof rack. Big Jack tried to drink coffee from his thermos, but the ride was too rough. The boys wobbled in the backseat like carnival game bowling pins that refused to tumble over. They set up on a tree line bordering the cut corn. Two dozen goose decoys were spread out some thirty yards in front of them, and a dozen duck decoys bobbled in the pond to their right. Big Jack and the boys plopped onto wooden stools, and Charlie helped them pull scratchy wool army blankets over their shoulders. The wind was biting cold, but it wasn't blowing as hard as the day before. PJ's cheeks were bright pink as he shivered on the stool.

Thirty minutes later, they heard faint honking up high and in the distance. With a predawn glow starting on the eastern horizon, the overcast sky started to lighten, but visibility was poor with a low ceiling. A few times, honking drew nearer, pulling up PJ's adrenaline, only to blow away with the wind. The hour that passed as the sky continued to lighten felt like an eternity. "This gun's heavy," he whined to himself. "My feet are so cold." At least he didn't have to pee.

There was little hope of downing a Canada goose with his .410, so he held one of the ranch's long-barreled, 12-gauge, pump-action shotguns. Charlie'd given him a tutorial on how to work the pump. "Just click that button to turn off the safety, aim, and shoot. Then keep the barrel up and pull this back. It'll kick out the spent shell and load another. Aim and shoot again."

More honking from high above, but this time it quickly closed distance as Charlie blew his goose call. He honked loudly, then made lower noises that sounded to PJ like clucking chickens. The honking from the gray mist above grew louder and louder, until finally PJ heard it low and directly behind him, beyond the tree-lined fencerow. It was like the geese were sneaking up on them.

Charlie clucked some more, and the hunters were surprised by the large flock of geese that zoomed directly over the field, then banked up and to the group's right. Charlie kept at the clucking, enticing the geese to circle back to the decoys. As they approached, he spoke low from behind the boys' stools. "When they cup their wings and drop their feet, that's when you stand and shoot." Moments later, the geese did exactly that, and Charlie shouted, "Go get 'em!"

Big Jack and the three boys stood, the heavy blankets dropping from their shoulders. Matt was the first to shoot. He felled a honker just to the left of center. PJ picked out a goose, then his sightline was interrupted by closer birds, and he lost focus, dropping the barrel of his shotgun.

There must have been two-hundred birds in the air, all reacting to Matt's shot by pulling up their legs and flapping their wings wildly to reverse direction and regain altitude. It was chaos in the air as the birds started climbing this way and that, and a half dozen shots rang out in short order. PJ raised the barrel and put the bead on a bird that seemed to be hanging still in the air, right in the middle of the flock. He squeezed the trigger and *BOOM!* The recoil from the shotgun smashed into his shoulder, and he struggled to keep his footing, watching in awe as the limp bird tumbled from the sky to the field. Matt and Frank, using similar Ithaca 10-gauge double barrel shotguns, both bagged doubles. Big Jack downed one bird. All in, they had six fat Canada geese on the ground. As the rest of the flock rose into the gray sky, the hunters strode out to collect their quarry. PJ was staggered by the size of his bird.

"The leg's bigger'n a whole quail!"

Charlie lined the birds up behind their stools.

"Look at all that gumbo!" Big Jack laughed. "Matt, T-boy, fantastic shooting!"

Both boys beamed.

"My PJ!" He hugged his little one, who was grinning from ear to ear, looking up, deep into his daddy's blue eyes.

"So, how was it?" Charlie asked. PJ'd forgotten all about his shoulder until then, and now he poked himself to find it was bruised pretty good. "Gotta keep that stock tight in the crook of your arm, there," Charlie said. "Tuck it in there good and you'll be fine." He showed the boy how. PJ liked that he could feel it, the bruise. Like he'd earned his bird.

"Nice shooting everybody!" Big Jack summed it up. "Let's reload and do it again."

Under Charlie's supervision, PJ pumped a shell into the gun chamber and clicked the safety switch on. He settled back onto the wood stool, and Charlie draped the wool blanket over his shoulders. It was scratchy on his neck. Felt like hunting.

* * *

In the end, the quail party had decided to sit the frigid morning out, and when Big Jack burst through the door to the great room, he held his hat like a microphone, announcing, "May I introduce to you, the one, the only, the king of Canadian geese, Mr. Matthew Sweetwater!"

Three big grins filed through the door into the great room. The men rose from their card game and joined the frosty geese hunters near the fire, where Matt launched into the morning's story. Sixteen birds in the bag, and Matt had four doubles. When Big Jack threw his arm around the boy, he glowed.

"If you want to eat good, this is the man to have in the field with ya! We would've been back sooner, but the boys insisted on doin' some field dressing. Down swirling everywhere in that wind. Looked like a damn snowstorm!"

Matt approached his father looking a bit sheepish. "I was thinking maybe Frank could come visit us in Louisiana sometime. Maybe in the summer? Do some fishing?"

All eyes turned to Edward Sweetwater, who, at eleven in the morning, was well down the path to drunk. He nodded, and the room cheered.

Chennault crouched in front of PJ. "How'd you do, son?"

"Just one, sir."

Chennault rubbed the boy's head. "You should be proud, knocking down quail and geese at your age. You're going to be a helluva shot soon enough, PJ Benoit. Mark my words."

The following day they woke to rain, and by nine that morning, sleet was blowing sideways, so everyone spent the day inside. The men played nickel-limit poker, and the boys played for matchsticks. It was a day for reminiscing among the Louisiana troupe, talking ducks and gators. Big Jack and Chennault talked airplanes, telling fantastic stories about the Three Musketeers. Stalled engines, clipped wings, exploding pigeons and crash landings. The weather wasn't expected to break for at least another day, which would be the last day of the trip, but everyone was having a superb time despite. That night's barbecued ribs were to die for, and the boys couldn't get enough of the German potato salad. The norther settled down just in time for the drive back to San Antonio. Big Jack left the radio off to enjoy the boys' enthusiastic chatter. When they hit Alice, he pulled up to Juanita's Cantina. Frank hopped out of truck cab and grabbed four cleaned geese from a sack in the bed as PJ watched from his knees on the seat. Frank walked the meat into the cantina where Juanita held her heart, Maria smiled sweet, and Frank wished them well.

7

MARIA AND MARIE

SEPTEMBER 1932

"Bonjour. Buenos días. Buongiorno. Dobraye ootro. Goeiemorgen. Guten Morgen."

Her pronunciation was remarkably good today. Every morning, Mademoiselle Venet would shuffle the order of her classroom greeting, and every morning on the way to school, Chloe would try to guess which greeting would be first. "Buenos días."

"So, Spanish today?" Miss Sophie said.

Chloe nodded.

"Well then, buena suerte, sweet girl." Standing outside the tall, spiked gate of patinated bronze, Miss Sophie let go of Chloe's hand and bent to kiss her forehead. Then she winked, as she did every morning. "Run along."

Miss Sophie Landren hailed from London's East End. The daughter of a Welsh cobbler and a French seamstress, her father died when she was a child, killed in Tripoli during the Great War. Sophie and her mother spoke French at home, and, to make ends meet, Sophie assisted her with the costumes for the small London playhouses. That was where Paul Boisvert took note of their work. He offered to bring the widow and her daughter to Paris to work costumes for the shows at La Pomme d'Or, but the widow declined, choosing to stay in London to care for her struggling mother-in-law. But she encouraged her daughter to go, hoping work at La Pomme d'Or would provide Sophie with the security and opportunity that the widow, and the East End, could not. For two years, the girl lived with Paul Benoit's head seamstress. But as the Depression took hold of France, then squeezed it tight, Paul had to cut back on costuming at the club, and Miss Sophie transitioned to nanny, cook, and laundress for the Boisvert household.

"Au revoir, Miss Sophie." Chloe blew her nanny a kiss, skipped through the gate, then struggled open one of the heavy wooden doors and disappeared into the building. Three classes of children were gathered for the morning greeting and the reading of the activities plan.

The teacher clapped her hands. "Russian first."

Chloe tapped her foot and huffed.

"Dobraye ootro, Mademoiselle Venet!" replied thirty-six voices in a chorus.

Chloe loved her school, the one Maria Montessori had established five years ago, the summer of Chloe's arrival. The few children she knew from outside the school whined about strict nuns or harsh Germanic administrators. *Her school*, on the other hand, was interesting and exciting, and the teachers were kind.

The common room was brightened by a large skylight and tall, narrow windows where lush plants thrived in the sills. Some of these plants Chloe recognized from le Jardin du Luxembourg, with other species having come from the Greek isle of Mykonos. In the common room, twin terrariums were dense with flora from the Belgian Congo. One glass box was the humid home to tiny yellow frogs with bright red eyes, multicolored geckos, and large leggy insects. The other box held a snake nearly three feet in length.

Dr. Maria, the name she preferred her students to use, appreciated experimentation in the classroom, and her model had been enthusiastically received by the city's more liberal thinking well-to-do parents who rejected the tradition of boarding school.

What Chloe liked best, besides the colorful tree frogs, was how language flowed through the room. The children were taught in French and Italian, but German, Russian, English, and Spanish all made their way into conversation.

During the late 1920s, the Italian dictator Benito Mussolini had pressured Montessori to support and encourage what he called *Corporatism* in her curricula, and she grew weary of the meddling Fascist bureaucrats and angry over their ever-increasing pressure and threats. Instead of capitulating, she shuttered all of her Italian schools to refocus her efforts in Germany and Holland, where enthusiasm for her methods swelled. Chloe's school was the only Montessori program in all of France. Dr. Maria now called Spain home, but she enjoyed Paris so much that Chloe saw her a few times each year at the school on Rue de Vaugirard.

They also saw each other at salons and parties. Yvonne's weekly routine included attendance at an intimate Thursday evening party, a large Friday evening party, Saturday dinner out, and a Sunday salon, and she insisted that Chloe accompany her most every Thursday and Sunday. Yvonne loved to show off her adopted daughter, her *"petite moi,"* often boasting about the girl before moving on to more directly flattering topics, leaving nine-year-old Chloe to fend for herself in the company of adults. Sometimes at the salons, Chloe would find Dr. Maria encircled by inquisitive admirers, like a flower bud surrounded by petals. "If only she didn't always wear those long black robes," she said to Miss Sophie more than once. Dr. Maria's manner of dress was solemn, and it belied the light and love in her heart that radiated through her kind, dark eyes.

* * *

In the early 1930s, the artist Marie Laurencin's salon evolved into a rather large, invitation-only event supported by an ever-changing combination of benefactors. The salon was held the third Sunday afternoon of every third month. This was Chloe's second visit to Laurencin's home, and the painter was wholly taken with the girl.

"Yvonne, how wonderful to see you, and you brought us your Créole princess!"

Yvonne bristled and kisses were exchanged.

"You've heard what Josephine Baker is doing, yes?" Laurencin continued. "It is a formidable undertaking, and quite a tribute to this little one."

Yvonne Boisvert fed off praise for Chloe. But when attention paid to the girl threatened to exceed the fawning over her own beauty, the woman hardened, and she might ignore Chloe for the remainder of the event.

"I know you." It was Dr. Maria.

Chloe beamed and curtseyed.

"Dr. Montessori, is Chloe one of your students?" Laurencin asked.

"Most certainly, and she is a pleasure." Dr. Maria smiled. "Chloe, I understand you named our friend from Ghana, who lives in the terrarium. Tell us about her, Chloe."

"Queen Nana Yaa is a ball python. She is brown, dark with light spots. She measures longer than a meter. I was awarded the privilege of naming her when I won an essay contest. I wrote about Queen Mother Nana Yaa Ansantewaa, the leader of Ghana who fought the British for independence at the turn of the century. So this is the name I gave to her."

Laurencin was impressed, and Dr. Maria glowed with pride. Yvonne waved to someone on the other side of the room and excused herself from the discussion while Chloe illuminated her audience with facts about the jungles of West Africa.

"That sounds lovely, and dangerous!" Laurencin exclaimed. "Is that how you will be, Chloe, when you are grown? Lovely and dangerous?"

Chloe blushed, swaying her shoulders from side to side.

"I would like to paint you. I will put you together with my Afghans. Would you like that? Do you like dogs?"

"I do not know any dogs well, Mademoiselle Laurencin. But I do like Chiquita very much."

"And who is Chiquita?" Dr. Maria inquired.

"Auntie Josephine's cheetah."

Laurencin and Montessori burst out laughing.

"I do not foresee Josephine Baker's cheetah sitting in my studio, Chloe. But yes, I do intend to speak with Yvonne about having you sit for me, with or without the hounds."

"Magnificent!" Yvonne burst back into the conversation, a glass of champagne in each hand. "Dear girl, you could wear that glorious, blue lace dress we had made for you in Bruges. Doesn't she have the sweetest face?" Yvonne stroked her own cheek with a glass, dribbling a little champagne on her shoulder.

"What are we talking about here, ladies? Solving the world's problems, or gossiping like washwomen over the tub?"

"Talking about the wolf," Marie joked.

"Auntie Josephine!" Chloe threw her arms around the elegant woman donning an exquisite, maroon-and-black sequined dress and matching gloves.

During the eight years since her arrival in Paris as a teenager, Josephine Baker had become the most sensational and beloved entertainer in all of Europe, and she based her act at La Pomme d'Or, Paul's club in Montmartre. But due to the worsening economic depression, fewer and fewer Parisians had money for clubs and parties, and both Chez Josephine and La Pomme d'Or were struggling. Paul Boisvert was part owner of Chez Josephine, Baker's club, he having saved the establishment just last year. Josephine adored the Boisvert's adopted daughter, and the two often adventured together.

Josephine cupped Chloe's face. "I'm so happy to see you, child!" She kissed her cheeks and raised her off the ground with a tight embrace.

"How is Chiquita?"

"My fickle feline is at home on her settee, no doubt sleeping off her Sunday bunny."

"Oh, dear," Yvonne scoffed, handing an empty flute to a waiter and waving at a nearby gentleman for a cigarette.

The cheetah often joined Josephine onstage, at times getting loose and wreaking havoc in the orchestra pit. "Chiquita misses you, Chloe. You must come spend time with us again, and soon. Yvonne, perhaps, say, week after next, your dear daughter may come spend a few nights in the house with my kitty and me?"

"Why, of course, Josephine. I'm certain Chloe would enjoy that very much." Yvonne blew a smoke plume overhead.

"Chloe was telling us about Africa. What she has learned from our books and terrariums," Dr. Maria said, still glowing over her student's impromptu oral report.

"Yes, it has yet to be determined which path Chloe will follow, pianist or lion tamer." Yvonne waved at another server.

"Will we see Paul this afternoon, Yvonne?" Josephine asked.

"We won't," Yvonne responded, coldly. Her jealousy of the close working relationship her husband shared with Miss Baker, and her general suspicion of the many beautiful women with whom Paul worked, was thinly veiled. In a few cases, her suspicion was justified, but there was nothing but business and laughter between Paul Boisvert and Josephine Baker. The singer loved Chloe, and though the girl called her *Auntie*, Josephine really thought of herself as more of an older sister.

The hostess redirected the conversation. "Yvonne, let us set an appointment for Chloe to sit for me. Near the end of this month, yes?" It was agreed, and Laurencin then redirected them back to Baker's new project.

Josephine was exuberant in the telling. She was reviving Jacques Allenbach's nineteenth-century opera *La Créole*, a love story about an adventurous French musketeer and a beautiful Créole girl from Guadeloupe named Dora.

"I will sing Dora." She stroked Chloe's hair. "When I read the opera, it was this Créole girl that I saw in my mind's eye." She spread her gloved arms and sang.

```
Un ramier tomba, en volant
Amoureux d'une tourterelle
Elle était noire, il était blanc
Ils n's'en aimer'nt que de plus belle
```

Chloe was in heaven, having inspired her Auntie Josephine to sing an opera! Laurencin excused herself to attend to other guests, and Dr. Maria turned the talk to politics.

It was approaching three years since the Great Crash of 1929, and across Europe the Depression continued to deepen. So many people were frightened and understandably longed for security and stability, and, as a result, reactionary Fascist movements had quickly grown in strength. As the number of financially secure intellectuals rapidly dwindled, so too did the number and lavishness of the salons, and so did progressive talk. The economic crisis had spread far and wide, and desperation was taking hold. Across the Rhine, terrible unemployment and hyperinflation accentuated Germany's economic stagnation. "I hear that in Berlin, it takes a pail full of German marks to buy a single loaf of bread!" Fervent Communists advocating global revolution were pressing Soviet Socialism into Western Europe. Reactionaries were collecting into larger, more powerful and violent Fascist organizations, and the Anarchists added to the general unrest. Return to European monarchy was out of the question, and American democracy seemed too fragile to prevail over this global financial collapse. In Parisian cafés, intellectuals ran themselves ragged with political debate, retreating when they could to the comfort of art, music, literature and love as the four cornerstones of a life worth living. Marie Laurencin's salon was one of just a few such large-scale affairs to survive.

Laurencin returned with some papers in hand. "Dr. Montessori, it seems your Italian nemesis, *Il Duce* has done some writing. These are excerpts from Mussolini's recent entry to the Italian encyclopedia. She paused for effect.

He calls it *What is Fascism?*"

The Fascist State organizes the nation, but leaves a
sufficient margin of liberty to the individual; the
latter is deprived of all useless and possibly
harmful freedom, but retains what is essential; the
deciding power in this question cannot be the
individual, but the State alone.

"'Deprived of all useless and harmful freedom?' So a few arrogant men will decide what will, and will not be, considered freedom?" Montessori shook her head in disgust. Laurencin read on:

Fascism denies, in democracy, the absurd
conventional untruth of political equality dressed
out in the garb of collective irresponsibility, and
the myth of happiness and indefinite progress.

"This despot tried to consolidate power in Italy with Socialism, with Collectivism, and he failed miserably," Montessori went on. "Now he's giving it another go with Fascism. He doesn't believe in anything. He merely desires control. He is a herding dog, leading mindless sheep to the slaughter, if we let him. The *myth* of happiness and indefinite progress? He's a reactionary bore, an amoral swine with dangerous teeth."

Laurencin laughed nervously at the educator's pun. "Is that from the speech you gave last month at the International Peace Conference in Geneva?"

"Heavens no." Dr. Maria's dark eyes hardened. "But humanity cannot survive peacefully if peace is merely a *reaction* to aggression. The only way to enable humanity to act humanely is through education. Il Duce would no longer allow my schools to teach without the taint of his politics, without serving his primary interest, propaganda. So I am finished with Italy, although I apparently cannot stop the Fascists from using my name, because all of the judges in the courts there are complicit with the dictator. In Geneva, I spoke about how we must change *ourselves* before we are called upon to react to aggression. We must change ourselves first."

The discussion was well beyond the limits of Chloe's understanding and interest, and her adoptive mother was nowhere to be found. So she excused herself with a curtsy, grabbed a handful of gingersnaps from the buffet, and skipped into the garden, where butterflies skittered from sunbeam to shade under a rustling canopy of hazelnut leaves. She sat down and had a talk with herself. "I wonder if butterflies enjoy music. Do they talk about politics?" The more she thought on it, the more resolved she was in her conclusion. "Butterflies are happy when the sun shines and the flowers are open. They are sad when it is cold and rainy. Butterflies never get bored."

 A gust of wind snapped a dry tree branch, which snapped the girl from her daydream. Pale gray clouds were intruding on the bright blue sky, and the chilling breeze swirled through the courtyard. "Yes, it will rain soon." She watched the butterflies dance among the flowers, a menagerie of white, pink, and yellow. "I hope they will stay dry and happy."

* * *

Late afternoon, and the kitchen counter was dusted with flour. So was the floor. As hard as she tried, Chloe just couldn't keep her space clean when she baked, but Miss Sophie appreciated her charge's enthusiasm. Chloe gladly assisted Miss Sophie with the meals, but best of all she loved to bake, losing herself in the aromas, and singing songs with her nanny. Miss Sophie, too, wondered aloud about Chloe's future. "Piano or pâtisserie?"

 At dinner that night, Uncle Paul seemed sad, as he seemed most of the time these days, but at least he was home. Chloe and Miss Sophie had baked his favorite dessert as a surprise, and when Miss Sophie cut into the beautiful cinnamon apple pie with gruyère cheese baked into its flaky lattice crust, Chloe at last saw a sparkle in her uncle's eyes.

 He straightened. "Magnificent! Really, Miss Sophie, you have outdone yourself."

 "Thank you, Monsieur Boisvert. But it was a team effort, and Mademoiselle Chloe was the primary artist this time."

 Paul laughed, Chloe blushed, and Yvonne lit a cigarette. When he'd finished his pie, Paul fired a cigar. Seemingly refreshed and renewed, Paul now spoke excitedly. "Next week, we'll have a very interesting visitor in the club."

 Yvonne puffed away, looking bored.

 "Ernest Hemingway is coming to Paris." Paul raised his eyebrows. "We haven't enjoyed his company in the city for some years now. Six years, isn't that right, Yvonne? I am not sure how long he will stay, but it should be a load of fun while he is here. Josephine is creating a new composition, just for him. Isn't that brilliant? Chloe, do you remember when we read *The Sun Also Rises* during our crossing?"

She nodded. "I read *A Farewell to Arms* during free time at school."

Yvonne tucked a fresh cigarette into her slick black Bakelite holder and leaned over a silver-plated art deco table lighter. "Why does that dour old Montessori woman wear such wretched clothing?" she drawled. "All the style of a Victorian spinster."

"So, tell us about *A Farewell to Arms*. What did you think of it?"

The table was quiet as Chloe pondered the question.

"She died."

"Who died?" Yvonne hadn't been listening.

"Yes, she did. And?" Paul probed.

Chloe leaned forward with a pained look on her face. "Many people died, Uncle Paul. I think many horses were killed, too." The girl paused and spun her dessert fork between the palms of her hands. "He went to Switzerland." She stabbed a slice of cinnamon baked apple. "I suppose the horses in Switzerland were happy. There was no war in Switzerland."

Paul smiled and shook his head incredulously at his adopted daughter's intuitiveness. He tapped cigar ash onto his empty dessert plate. "The way you think, girl. Truly astounding."

"The way she thinks about what?" Yvonne snapped, teetering on inebriation.

"The way her mind works. She thinks like a song. A song that has so much more to it than most people can hear."

Yvonne stubbed her cigarette into her untouched pie. "To hear you talk, Paul Boisvert, one would hardly think you keep a bar." She rose. "Excuse me. I must say goodnight, what with this awful headache."

Chloe kept her eyes on her apple slice. She couldn't remember the last time her adoptive mother had given her a goodnight kiss.

As Yvonne climbed the stairs, Paul pointed his cigar at the girl. "A beautiful mind is a gift not everyone appreciates. Now, please be a sweet girl and help Miss Sophie clear the table. It's late, and she'll need to get home once the dishes are finished."

Chloe saw the sadness return to her uncle's eyes. He'd become so quiet as of late. She'd heard him say people didn't come to the club like they used to. But whenever she was at the club, the people were still loud and laughing. She was happy her Uncle Paul had been talkative tonight.

Miss Sophie handed her another plate to dry, and Chloe remembered the last time Uncle Paul had brought her to La Pomme d'Or. It was Bastille Day, and the place was jumping. Just after midnight, Auntie Josephine was in the middle of some crazy number when Chiquita slipped her collar and got after one of the male dancers who was shirtless, barefoot, and wearing a grass skirt. Chloe laughed so hard as the dancer's feathered headdress whipped this way and that while he screamed and ran in circles, all the while the cheetah pawing and nipping at the grass pom-poms on his ankles. Chloe laughed out loud at the memory.

"A franc for your thoughts?" Miss Sophie handed her another wet plate.

"Chiquita's a naughty girl."

* * *

Chloe still sat at the piano and enjoyed playing, more so when Yvonne was out of the house and she could play blues and jazz instead of the classical pieces in which she'd been trained. Paul stopped her lessons for lack of funds, but she didn't mind. Her interest started to wane when she began baking after school with Miss Sophie. She loved the smells, the warmth of the oven, and the textures of their creations, delicious morsels that her uncle enjoyed very much, and his joy made her happy. But most of all, she loved spending time with Miss Sophie. When summer came, Chloe couldn't walk past a patisserie without smiling, whether she was out strolling on her own or holding Miss Sophie's hand.

* * *

The French economy continued to decline. Factories shuttered, businesses closed, and more and more people found themselves unoccupied, many on the street. Paul Boisvert did what he could for his employees, keeping them on partial wages. He was in fair shape financially, but Yvonne's refusal to change her spending habits caused a serious drain. The air in the apartment was always tense, and it seemed to Chloe that her parents hardly spoke to each other anymore, and Paul had taken to working most every day and night at the club, having cut loose the thief that had been his manager.

Midsummer, Miss Sophie moved into the apartment and took on all the household duties in exchange for room and board and a little pocket money. It was Miss Sophie's best option, and the only way Paul could afford to keep her. Yvonne did nothing around the apartment yet resented Miss Sophie's presence anywhere outside of the kitchen.

The summer of 1932 was the first summer Chloe didn't accompany her adoptive mother on a vacation to the south of France, or to Italy or Spain. With Yvonne gone, life in the apartment was much more relaxed. Though her uncle's stress was still palpable, by summer's end, he was back home for dinner at least a couple of evenings most weeks, insisting each time that Miss Sophie join him and Chloe at the table.

One evening, Paul was so enjoying the girls' company that he phoned the club to say he would stay home. The trio played card games and charades late into the night, and it warmed Chloe's heart to hear her uncle laughing. She remembered him teaching her vingt-et-un on the ship. Waiting her turn to bet, her gaze wandered to the photos atop the buffet. There was a toddler, surrounded by family, sitting behind a tart. Her amber eyes clouded.

"Your Auntie Josephine was asking about you." Paul struck a match to add fire to his cigar.

Chloe sniffled. "Really?"

"We agreed another sleepover was in order. It has been much too long."

* * *

Chloe stroked Chiquita's soft fur while the big cat napped, rhythmic purrs reverberating through her hand. "You love to have your ears rubbed, don't you, kitty?" As she massaged an ear, the cheetah flicked the other one. There was a tiny red spot on her cheek.

"Bunny brunch," Josephine whispered, having tiptoed up to her two favorite girls, lounging together on Chiquita's settee.

Instinctively cheetahs won't prey on adult humans because they're too delicate and know not to risk injury, but they will go after a child. So Josephine always made sure Chiquita ate a hearty breakfast the morning of Chloe's visits. She whispered again, "Everybody has to eat something, or someone!" She giggled and tweaked Chloe's earlobe.

Her auntie's radiant smile filled Chloe with joy, but sometimes she felt guilty for wishing Josephine was her mommy. Other times she felt guilty for wishing the same about Miss Sophie. She couldn't remember Pascale. Even in her faint memories of the Brewster's balcony that Mardi Gras, her mommy was missing. She only had the image in the photographs her Uncle Paul brought across the ocean. She knew she should feel grateful for her Parisian parents, but she also understood Yvonne didn't even truly like her. It had been a long time since they'd done anything together, and Chloe couldn't remember her adoptive mother ever treating her with a real kindness. Every thought of Yvonne was enveloped by a haze of smoke and that unique blend of Nat Sherman tobacco, Joy perfume, and Château Haut-Brion wine.

8
ASHES

FEBRUARY 1934

PJ pleaded to wash his face. "I ain't goin' nowhere, so it ain't like nobody's gonna see me without it." Cutting carrots for a stew, Elaine Benoit hummed a hymn over the sink, the black cross on her forehead still pristine from the morning's Ash Wednesday service. When PJ returned that afternoon from school, his mark was barely discernible within the smudge across his forehead, so Elaine burned some paper and reapplied the cross herself. Now, the boy sported a thick black X over a field of gray.

"Be thankful Jesus cares about you at all."

PJ was bored silly at school. Like other boys his age, he preferred to be outdoors, running, jumping, fishing, and climbing. But he had to graduate high school in order to fly for the army, so he was willing to do what was necessary to pass.

Elaine poured herself a drink. "You have to sit there for eight more years. Seems you could pay a little attention while you do it." PJ hated the smell of gin. As much as he disliked school, home wasn't much better. Frank didn't return after his second summer working at Edward Sweetwater's lumber business. He'd married Sweetwater's daughter Odette and stayed in Louisiana. PJ hadn't seen his brother in eight months. He pushed out the screen door, letting it slam behind him just to aggravate her. Pumpkin bounded from around the house and joined him under the swing tree. Not yet a year old, the Golden Labrador puppy laid in the shade while PJ wound up the swing until he could just touch the dirt with one toe, then leaned back to watch the blue patches in the tree's dusty canopy spiral above him. When it came to a stop, he thought again about his daddy and mumbled, "Not my first rodeo, kid."

* * *

Months ago, on a brisk November afternoon at Randolph Field, Captain Jack Benoit was stress testing the Boeing XP-936, the prototype for what would become the P-26 Peashooter. The first all-metal aircraft designed for the US military, the XP-936 sported a powerful 600 horsepower engine capable of reaching 230 miles per hour. Early testing found that the snub-nosed plane had a tendency to flip forward upon landing, so they'd added a tall headrest behind the open cockpit. Now, Big Jack would put the updated prototype through its paces.

The Texas sky was powder blue, the east-by-southeast wind gusting to fifteen knots. Big Jack took the prototype up to ten-thousand feet and engaged a series of maneuvers to stress the wing flaps. The aircraft performed well, the flaps responded, although he did feel some vibration in the tail during a roll. He radioed the spotter aircraft upon completion and descended to the runway. When he touched down, the plane tumbled over its nose. The prop shredded on the concrete, filling the air with the sound of an industrial metal grinder. As the machine skidded belly up, the headrest snapped.

That morning after calisthenics with his daddy, PJ fried up some bacon, scrambled a couple eggs, and wrapped it all in corn tortillas. He filled an army canteen and headed out with his cane pole, a filet knife, some butcher paper, and a bean can half full of black dirt and red worms. He was going for largemouth bass in Cibolo Creek. It was noonish when he returned to the house with eight wrapped filets to find an army car parked out front of the house. Sergeant Hank Novak was sitting on the front porch and rose when he saw PJ coming up the street.

"How's it goin', Sergeant Hank?"

"Been fishing, PJ?"

"Yeah. My daddy home?"

The screen door squeaked open, and the base commander, General Leland Samuels, stepped out of the house. "PJ." The general saluted.

"General." PJ saluted.

The general turned to the boy's mother. "Elaine, if there's anything we can do . . ."

Hank squeezed PJ's shoulder. "You come by if you want to, okay?"

Elaine leaned against the doorjamb, swirling a yellow liquid in a canning jar as the car pulled away.

"What is it, Mama?"

"A widow's world." She turned and disappeared into the house, letting the door slam behind her. The next morning PJ walked to the base. Hank was off, but the on-duty crew tracked him down. Terribly hungover, he waved the boy over to the Jeep. "Hop in." They headed southwest, toward the city. "There's a soda shop in Alamo Heights with really good ice cream. My treat."

It was closed, being a Sunday. "Sorry, PJ. I wasn't thinking." They found a bench in the park across the street, but Hank didn't know what to say. "How's your ma taking it?"

"In a bottle." PJ kicked at the grass under the bench. "But that ain't no differ'nt than before, so . . ." He trailed off and looked Hank in the eye. "How'd it happen, Sergeant Hank?"

The big man hemmed and hawed, but PJ didn't let him off the hook, so Hank described the test flight some. The turns, the dives. How it all went smooth as silk. "But the damn thing's nose-heavy. It flipped when he touched down."

PJ toed at the dirt. "Did my daddy burn up, Sergeant Hank?"

"No, no. Nothing like that."

A tear dangled from the end of the boy's nose. He sniffled and it dislodged, landing in the grass between his feet. Hank rifled his pockets for a handkerchief but came up empty. The bachelor sergeant was way out of his depth.

"Your daddy was a helluva pilot and a fine trainer. He was good man, PJ."

"Can you tell Frank?"

"What's that?"

He sniffled. "Frank needs to know. Can you send him a letter?" PJ swallowed hard. "I don't know what to write."

"But your ma . . ."

Another tear dripped off his nose.

"Sure, kid. I'll write Frank straight away."

PJ stared out the window on the ride home. The house was quiet. He pushed open his parents' bedroom door. It smelled bad in there. "Mama?" PJ shook her by the shoulder. She was snoring, lying in a wet yellow stain.

* * *

The funeral was all uniforms and straight lines. PJ grumbled, "This ain't like Daddy." He closed his eyes, imagining Big Jack arcing, looping through the clouds. Everything smooth and easy, like how he cast spinbait. Flipping pancakes when they went camping, all casual like his easy smile. But today, everything was neat and white with corners, and it made him uncomfortable. Angry even. He eyeballed his mama. *At least she's sober.*

The line of soldiers shot the air three times before they tucked their carbines down. The general handed his mama the flag, which two corporals had folded into a triangle. PJ ran off, and Elaine muttered to the general, "That child's a goddamn embarrassment."

Hank found him behind the hangar, sitting Indian-style in the grass. "What's on your mind, kid?"

The boy was rocking, his brow furrowed. "I'm gonna fly." He spat out the words. "And I ain't gonna die doin' it."

"I don't doubt that, PJ. No, I don't." Hank sat down next to the boy. "But you got a while yet. You got some schooling to do."

PJ nodded vigorously and lied, "Seven years." He looked at the sergeant with resolve. "I'm flyin' that damn plane. It ain't gonna kill *me.*"

9

LOUIS'S STAR

FEBRUARY 1934

Chloe swung her crossed legs as she sipped her tea. It was an unseasonably warm and gorgeous afternoon for reading at her favorite sidewalk table outside the café Le Select. Simone, the café cat, had already dropped off her perch near the staircase to visit Chloe twice, butting her head against the girl's ankles, then returning to her spot before it cooled. Chloe made little progress with her book. She'd been having a hard time focusing on anything since the incident, just before Christmas. That's what everyone called it. *The incident.* The shock had passed, but she was always tired now and was failing at her studies. It was as though a weight pressed down on her, like the air itself was heavy. Baking with Miss Sophie provided her only relief, but even then she would lose interest before long.

Miss Sophie looked sad, too, but they never talked about the incident. The house was so quiet. The pair baked for themselves, and not often, because money was too short to fund sweets for teachers and schoolmates the way they had done before. The stray cat they'd taken in the day of the first snow had disappeared sometime last week, still without a name.

A deep horn blared from the corner at Rue Varin, and her heart leaped to see the shiny new lavender Delage Cabriolet ease around the corner, the front fender shaped like the hip of a curvaceous woman lying next to the bonnet. Chloe set a worn fifty-centime piece on the table, sprinted to the curb and stepped up on the running board to lean through the passenger door window.

"Going my way?" Josephine held an absurdly long, carved-ivory cigarette holder between her teeth, and squeezed the girl's gloved hand as Chloe climbed into the passenger seat. "Colette will be reading for us today! Isn't that divine?"

Auntie Josephine threw the car into gear and pressed the gas pedal to the floor. The tires screeched through a U-turn then, in what seemed like a blink of the eye, screeched again to a halt in the Latin Quarter where Gabrielle Laurent, heiress to her industrialist father's fortune, was hosting her bohemian salon.

The sprawling apartment was quite lively, stuffed tight with Parisian wealth, intelligentsia and hangers-on. The sumptuous buffet included a wide variety of rich cheeses, tasty meats, breads, and pickles. Gorgeous dessert towers held climbing spirals of hundreds of tiny cakes, and antique porcelain bowls piled high with luscious, colorful berries. The contrast between this presentation and the hunger in the streets could not have been more pronounced.

After a delightful luncheon, but feeling alone as once again the only child at the party, Chloe invited herself on a tour of the crowded apartment.

Each step of the marble spiral staircase held at least one, if not two people. A human corkscrew going nowhere. Chloe rudely sliced her way through the stationary mass, offending numerous partygoers. The salon's main attraction was on the third floor of the four-story apartment, and having battled halfway up, she squeezed through the smoke-veiled bodies on the second floor landing and into a cozy, surprisingly open sitting room where a pair of old women sat fanning themselves. A young woman in the corner was playing something baroque on a cello. Chloe moved to the window, pushed it open and stared down at a beggar in the street below as more anger welled up inside of her. Some deep breaths later, she returned to the staircase and pushed toward the third floor where she skirted along the edge of the packed room until she reached a window seat. She stepped up to have a better view.

Across the room, a woman with small red rosebuds woven into her hair read from a manuscript.

```
You don't think before you do something foolish.
You do your thinking afterwards.
```

The words stabbed her in the heart. She wondered where her Uncle Paul was, and whether he could think at all. She closed her eyes and tried to picture him in heaven with her mommy and papa but was too distracted by her anger, which was nearing rage. She mumbled, "Damn heroin." She wondered where Yvonne was, and hated her. Living down in South America somewhere for, what, two years now? "Damn bitch."

"Here you are." A smiling lady said in a sing-song voice, holding out her hand. "You must be Chloe Boisvert. Josephine was telling me about you. I am Gabrielle Laurent, but you may call me Gabbie. This is my home. Are you enjoying the reading?"

The interruption tugged Chloe off her path to rage. She shrugged. "She sounds like an actress in a movie."

The hostess muffled a laugh. "She does, doesn't she? Would you like to meet her?"

Chloe wasn't interested, but politely said yes. They stood quietly for a moment, while Chloe studied her hostess out of the corner of her eye. She was a handsome woman, very tall and straight, with warm, kind eyes.

Gabbie leaned over to her. "I think you have the best seat in the house. Plenty of room."

Chloe flushed with embarrassment. She'd forgotten where she so rudely placed herself.

"Oh, mademoiselle, I am so sorry." She began to climb down.

"Dear girl! Please, stay and think nothing of it. You're putting that window seat to the best use it's ever had. And isn't that the way of things? Shouldn't we put them to their best use, convention be damned?"

Gabbie's smile was so warm, so genuine, Chloe lost her anger and found guilt. The hostess craned to see something across the room. "Please excuse me, Mademoiselle Chloe. I must attend to another guest. If you will stay here, I will collect you after the reading, and we will introduce you to our dear Colette. Yes?"

The reading went on for some time, and Chloe watched while more and more onlookers grew fidgety as the room grew hot and stuffy. She cracked the window behind her. No one was smoking, which was nice, and she supposed Mademoiselle Laurent had a special rule for this room.

As promised, Gabbie returned and delivered Chloe to Colette. So many people were vying for the writer's attention that Chloe felt like she was in the way and made her excuses as politely as she could. She smelled Joy Parfum, which invited thoughts of Yvonne Boisvert. Her anger surged again, and she had to get out of there and find some air.

The cobblestone courtyard lay open to the backstreet, and a breeze wriggled the slightest of the bare tree branches. She searched for budding life in the flowerpots, but finding none, she remembered it was just an extraordinary weather day in February. Josephine was across the way, amidst a cluster of her admirers.

Chloe wanted to leave, but she didn't want to go home. As she made her way across the courtyard, there was a commotion in her auntie's party.

"Monsieur Pops!" Chloe gasped.

"Well, looky, looky! Who we have here but our little mademoiselle, Chloe Boisvert?" Armstrong grinned and they embraced. "I think you've grown a good half foot since I last saw you, young lady. Have you been practicin' the keys like a good girl?"

Chloe's newfound joy quickly shifted to embarrassment. She didn't want to admit she hadn't played the piano in months.

Josephine interjected, "Say Pops, I understand Lil is coming to town."

Armstrong's eyes widened. "Yes, yes she is."

"Well, we must get together. You will bring her to Le Vésinet. We'll have a quiet dinner without distractions."

Armstrong leaned in to whisper, "Think I might prefer distractions!" Armstrong had been avoiding divorcing his wife for going on a couple years. He asked how Josephine's operatic production, *La Créole,* was coming.

"We will open late this year."

"So, what's my part? How 'bouts the Zulu King?" Louis joked. "Yo' boys kin carry me 'round the opera house while I pelt the crowd with coconuts."

Chloe startled. In her mind's eye, a golden coconut burst under a tire on Basin Street.

Soon the discussion turned to politics, as it often did these days.

"Them Nazis are talkin' crazy. Gettin' everybody's blood up." Armstrong sighed. "Damn Brownshirts causin' all kinds of trouble. They be roundin' up Jews, gypsies."

"Homosexuals," Gabbie interjected.

Armstrong nodded. "Anyone who ain't white and full o' *you know what.*"

"They think they can pull themselves up by pushing others down," Gabbie added. "Oh, here! Come here please." She waved over a petite woman wearing a short blue dress. "Josephine Baker, Louis Armstrong, Chloe Boisvert. Please meet Adrienne Bernard, my sweet Addie."

Introductions were made, then Gabbie returned to the subject of growing persecution in Germany. "Monsieur Armstrong, is it true what I have heard about you, that you were raised by Jews back in the States?"

"You've got it almost right, yessiree."

Louis Armstrong was born and raised in the Battlefield neighborhood of Storyville, New Orleans's prostitution district. He'd found trouble in the streets at an early age while his mama lived on and off with a series of pimps.

```
If you don't want me
Please don't dog me 'round
```

If not for the kindness and generosity of the Karnofskys, a Jewish family who'd escaped the pogroms in Lithuania and migrated to New Orleans, it was likely young Armstrong would have found himself in prison or an early grave. The Karnofskys gave him work and food, and a place to sleep when he needed one. Enough support and stability to instill in the young man a strong work ethic, hope, and an appreciation for their generosity of spirit that stuck with him for the remainder of his life.

He unbuttoned his collar and pulled out a braided gold chain and medallion, a Star of David. "See this? I never take this off. Never. I wear it to honor the Karnofskys. Without them, I wouldn't be here today, no way, nosiree." He tucked the pendant back into his shirt and straightened his tie. "Them German folk gotta stop their damn Nazis, or it's only gonna get worse."

Chloe spoke up. "The Nazis closed Dr. Maria's schools in Germany."

Addie touched the girl's shoulder. "Do you attend the Montessori school here, Mademoiselle Chloe?"

"Yes."

Gabbie shook her head. "Fascists. Nazis. I don't know how they can be stopped, but it must be so. People are looking for strength, but men like that, they never stop on their own. Never. It always comes to conflict because they think only in terms of control, of violence, of domination. We have this beautiful world to live in, and they just want to use it up, grind it into nothing, and use up the people who live in it, and grind those up who are not like them. They have no respect for nature, or the *true* nature of things. And those of us who disagree, who speak out, they want to snuff us out like candles that shines light on their grotesqueness."

Addie spoke up. "I've always found it odd how these men focus on the color of their skin. It seems there could not be a weaker argument for claiming superiority, as though they have nothing else to rely upon. I envision each of them like a petulant child, pointing at boxes under a Christmas tree. 'This one is wrapped in brown, one is yellow, another red. Oh, here is one with a white wrapper. This must be the best!' But the box, it is empty. Nothing inside. All of the boxes are empty unless we put something inside. That is how I think of these self-proclaimed racial supremacists. They have nothing real to contribute, nothing inside to generate contribution, so they just make up a story that places them at the top. Then they enforce the story with violence. They stomp on all the other boxes under the tree. It would all be silly, *truly silly*, if their behavior didn't have such horrible consequences."

Everyone was quiet until Gabbie broke the silence. "My lovely ray of sunshine, my dear, dear, Addie!" They hugged and the whole group laughed. "My friends and guests, it is a glorious Sunday afternoon, and there are no Nazis or Fascists *here* to steal our joy. So let us celebrate the freedom we have to be ourselves, each of us."

She waived at a server, and they all snatched a flute from the tray. Gabbie made a toast with her mimosa held high. "To our joy."

Addie invited Chloe to check on the sweets table with her. Gabbie excused herself to mingle with the other guests, and Josephine and Louis found a quiet corner, where he asked her about Chloe.

"Louis, you know how I live. It's no place for a girl like Chloe."

"And Louisiana *is?*" He saw pain and guilt flash in Josephine's eyes.

"She'll be with family. Her sister. Her *real* aunt." But her eyes betrayed her sadness. "Look, Pops, I've corresponded with this Reverend Herod. He's well educated and highly respected. Hell, he's on the damn Chamber of Commerce! I don't know exactly what that is, but I understand it's full of rich white men and this one educated preacher man. Proper schooling and a stable family. That's gotta be better for the girl than traipsing around Europe with a crazy cabaret singer." She looked at him, pleadingly. "My tour begins in three weeks, and I'll be months on the road. That's no life for a child." She shook her head and lit a shaky cigarette.

Louis touched her arm and nodded. "You right, dearie. You right."

She took his hand, and they watched Chloe from across the courtyard. She was on a bench talking with Addie, swinging her legs and pointing her toes. Josephine welled up.

"Fuck, Pops!" She took a long drag and put her head on his shoulder. "Just . . . fuck."

"You said it, baby."

* * *

"How was it at Mademoiselle Laurent's?" Miss Sophie asked, slicing potatoes over the sink and sounding in a good mood.

Chloe said her tummy hurt.

"Too many sweets, no doubt. Well, I have some very good news to share with you." Miss Sophie told her about her new job, how Marie Laurencin had gotten her an appointment with Colonel W. de Basil, the Russian benefactor of the ballerinas who modeled for Laurencin's paintings. She was now to work for him as a seamstress and baker.

"So, will you still walk with me to school? And what time will you come home after your work?"

Miss Sophie was caught off guard. Josephine was supposed to have informed Chloe today. "So, you don't know . . . about the apartment?"

"What about the apartment?"

Sophie gasped. She asked Chloe to sit with her. Then, she told her that the bankers were foreclosing on the apartment and explained what that meant.

"Do you mean we can't live here anymore?"

Miss Sophie nodded.

Chloe looked around the dining room. "So where will we live?"

Miss Sophie explained how she would have quarters in the colonel's house. "I will share a room with the cook and laundress."

Chloe didn't understand.

"Didn't Miss Josephine explain to you? Where you'll be going?"

Chloe shook her head as panic rose and tears moistened her eyes.

"You're going to live with your aunt and sister in America."

* * *

The next morning, when Miss Sophie went to wake Chloe for school, she found the girl curled tight in her bed and could not roust her. Her eyelids were dark and puffy. Miss Sophie straightened and tucked the bedclothes.

The next day, while Chloe was at school, Josephine came to talk through the plan with Miss Sophie.

"So, the bank takes everything?" Miss Sophie frowned. "I thought since Monsieur Boisvert passed, Chloe would have an inheritance."

But the coroner determined that Paul Boisvert's death was a suicide, and that changed everything.

"No insurance payout, and the bank can act like he's still alive and bankrupt. Everything goes to pay the damn loan."

"Chloe gets nothing?" Miss Sophie pondered the thought. "Chloe has . . . *nothing?*"

"He overdosed, but no doubt the damn bankers paid off the damn coroner."

Just then, Chloe entered the apartment, though school wasn't scheduled to let out for another two hours. She looked in a stupor.

"Are you okay?" Miss Sophie said.

Sighting Josephine, Chloe screamed with joy and ran to hug her as tightly as she had ever hugged anyone, tears rolling down her cheeks. "Auntie Josephine, are you here to take me home with you?" The question pierced the woman's heart. Even before Josephine finished her explanation, Chloe broke down. "No!" she screamed and ran upstairs.

They heard a door slam. Miss Sophie asked, "Is it the only way?"

Josephine looked away. "It is the best way."

Lil Hardin Armstrong, Louis's wife, was in Paris. She'd crossed the Atlantic to obtain his signature on divorce papers. The couple's relationship was still amicable, but they'd been living separate lives for years, and Lil was ready to move on. So Louis and Josephine made arrangements for Lil to escort Chloe back to the States. Lil would deliver the girl to her Uncle Charlie, in Chicago, who would see to it she reached Abbeville, Louisiana, where her sister was living with her aunt, Armintha.

Josephine gave Lil two envelopes. One held cash to cover Chloe's travel expenses, and the other held two thousand US dollars for the girl's aunt.

"So, what about Yvonne?" Miss Sophie asked, cautiously.

Josephine cursed the name. "Paul heard nothing from that wretched bitch for going on two years. I doubt she even knows he's dead, and, frankly, I prefer to think of her in the same condition, rotting under Argentine mud." She rose to take her leave.

"Don't you want to say goodbye?" Miss Sophie raised her eyes toward the stairs.

Josephine lit a cigarette with a shaking hand, not bothering with her holder. She inhaled deeply, and slowly exhaled a large plume of smoke over the table. "I will see her off."

It was then that Miss Sophie witnessed something rare. Josephine Baker slumped back into the chair and sobbed violently into her hands.

10

ON TOUR

MARCH 1934

A damp gust blew her coat open as she stepped off the train at Gare du Havre. Chloe had spent all day in the stuffy, third-class car with her two chaperones and twenty-one strangers. She shivered and struggled the coat's large black buttons into their holes, then scanned the station from end to end while Lil Hardin Armstrong and Sarah Brown spoke with a porter about transportation to the ship. The newsstand at the far corner looked familiar, and Chloe watched a man buy a magazine while a woman hurried by towing a fussy little boy by the elbow. Nearly seven years ago, Uncle Paul had taken her off this very platform, right about here, and set her on the train that would take her to a new life in Paris. She wondered if this was the same train taking her from that life. She spent the past week in a daze, clear only in the knowledge that she would never again see her sweet Uncle Paul. Standing just out of earshot from the loud animated ladies, dread took hold. Uncle Paul was gone. Miss Sophie was gone. Mademoiselle Venet, Doctor Montessori, Paris. All gone. She would return to Louisiana to start a new life again, this time with an aunt she'd never met and a sister she couldn't remember.

This Atlantic passage wouldn't be as luxurious as her first voyage. No filet mignon. No orchestra. One of the passengers, a handsome young man named Ricardo who played the guitar would accompany Lil as she entertained the other travelers on the piano.

CHLOE'S MISTIGRI

```
She can start a fire in the coldest man
She's a hip slick sister known throughout the land
```

Chloe didn't play at all, and no one on the ship paid her much mind, a circumstance new to her. At school, at Le Pomme d'Or, at the salons, she'd always gained attention with little to no effort. On this ship, she felt invisible. Sarah Brown was pleasant enough, and Lil was cordial. But their attention was on the other passengers, and the other passengers' attention was on them.

Two days in, they were thrashed by a punishing nor'easter. The air grew frigid, and the ship was pelted with hail and sleet. Their bit of ocean roughed up horribly, with swells cresting near thirty feet. General orders were issued for the passengers to stay put in their rooms, and many took ill. Chloe was queasy in the stomach and dizzy in the head, but she didn't get sick. Sarah Brown wasn't as fortunate. They couldn't open the porthole, and even propping the door failed to dissipate the stench of vomit in the tiny compartment. The ship heaved so violently that Chloe couldn't focus on a book, so she curled up on her bunk, clutching her knees, trying to recall her first trip across this ocean. She remembered naming the clouds that were floating in the clear blue sky, playing vingt-et-un and singing the blues in French with her Uncle Paul.

In a day's time, they passed through the storm to calmer water and overcast skies. It didn't rain again until New York peeked at them over the horizon. Chloe was on deck with Sarah, stupefied by the scene. To stern, the piers and warehouses of Red Hook loomed dark under the dirty gray clouds billowing from countless smokestacks. In the distance, the Manhattan skyline beckoned, its massive cluster of towers growing taller as the ship steamed in. New York looked nothing like Paris, which spread beautifully, elegantly, in its daffodil hue below Montmartre. This city was not beautiful. It was metallic, mechanical, powerful, menacing. It was awesome.

They crossed the deck and joined a bustle where hundreds of passengers strained to see Miss Liberty. Cheers rose from a group of Hasidic Jews all in black, rainwater dripping from the brims of the men's shtreimel hats as they raised up small children to give them their first glimpse of freedom.

A tugboat pressed the ship against the dock at Ellis Island, and, as if on cue, the rain stopped. From the west, slivers of light trickled through the spreading clouds, illuminating the green-crowned goddess on Bedloe's Island.

"Shall we collect our bags?" Chloe said, anxiously.

"This ain't us. This here stop's for them immigrants. We get off in Manhattan, over there. But yeah, we'll grab our bags after these people move along and make some room. Travelin' light makes it easy."

When the ship finally steered into Chelsea Pier, Chloe felt excitement for the first time in months. Still frightened and not knowing what was to come, but she was ready for something new. She wanted the new.

The ladies trailed the redcap who was carting their bags up Eleventh Avenue, and Chloe wondered why they passed by two taxi stands. They stopped at the third while the porter waved for Harlem cabs. It took some time before a man stepped out of a black-and-yellow checkered sedan to open the trunk hatch. As he and the redcap maneuvered the bags, it occurred to Chloe they were all Negroes. All five of them. And everyone nearby was black. She looked back at the last taxi stand they'd passed. Everyone there was white.

"C'mon!" Sarah yanked the dazed girl's coat sleeve.

The driver closed the door behind Lil, and Chloe spun around, climbing to her knees to see out the back window. The redcap pulled some bills from his pocket, counted and folded them, then quickly secured the straps on his dolly and trotted back down Eleventh. That's when she noticed the sign over his head. *Colored Cars.*

Uptown, the sun was bright, and the shower had cleared the smog and cleansed the streets. She followed Lil out of the cab and skipped up the sidewalk a bit. The clean air smelled like Paris after a spring rain, but before the blooms. Lenox Avenue was teeming with life, some of it shaking umbrellas, and all of it black. A tall, thin man with gleaming white teeth and arms spread wide burst from the Lenox Hotel. Lil shrieked with joy as he pulled her into a bear hug.

"Miss Lil! You back!" Mr. Willard, the day manager, welcomed the living legend home. Two bellboys and another young man competed to collect their bags.

"Tiz good to be here, Willy. Yes tiz. You 'memba Sarah Brown."

Mr. Willard pinched the brim of his hat. "Miss Sarah, welcome back."

"And this here's Miss Chloe. She be Paul Boisvert's kid."

Chloe startled.

"Well, I'll be. Welcome to the Lenox Hotel." Willy took up her gloved hand and bowed. "At your service, Miss Chloe."

The way the women started talking on the ship was even more pronounced here. She wondered why their language kept changing.

"Miss Lil could use a drink! Whaddya say, Willie?" Lil slid her arm around the man's waist and tugged him toward the door.

"You know hotel policy, Miss Lil. I cain't drink witch you." Willie looked around, pretending to check if the coast was clear. "So it'll have to be just the one."

The news of Lil Hardin Armstrong's arrival spread through Harlem like wildfire, and in an hour's time, the Lenox Hotel bar was packed with dozens of people, laughing, drinking, smoking, and stomping with the piano player. Chloe felt at ease for the first time since leaving home. Someone shouted a toast.

"To the Yell-ooooow!"

The crowd echoed. "Yell-ooooow!"

On clear mornings, the dawn lit up the hotel's limestone façade, extracting a rich yellow hue from its typically dusty complexion. Dawn was when many of the musician guests returned to the hotel from their night's work, and play, and a few years back, on one such morning, Count Basie took to calling the place "the Yellow." Management responded by painting the lobby lounge a sunflower yellow that burst from the walls in luminous halos issued by yellow, stained-glass side lamps.

Perched on a stool around the curve of the bar where Max, the gray-haired bartender, had placed a bowl of boiled peanuts, Chloe watched the crowd quickly swell to bursting. Cheers rose every time the door swung open and more folks tumbled in. The joint was jumping when, through the din, Chloe made out a faint cuckoo sound. Above the bar, a silly, wooden bird poked from a carved Bavarian clock, crying out for the crowd's attention in vain.

"What'll you have, sweets?" Max wiped the bar. "How's about a nice Shirley Temple? Something new, named for that little curly haired actress."

Chloe stiffened.

"It's on the house."

Sarah was cozying up to a young man with conked hair and a coal-black zoot suit with wide ivory stripes.

Chloe giggled when the highball glass Max slid down the bar stopped dead in front of her.

"There you go. See if that don't light cho fire."

The liquid inside was rose red on the bar, and two maraschino cherries speared on a green toothpick bridged the rim of the glass. She lifted the glass to a sidelight, and it glowed a luscious orange-red like a Montmartre sunset in the fall. The sweetness of it was lovely, and her toothy grin lit up the old man, who was drying a martini glass.

"Merci, monsieur. The drink is very pleasurable."

He leaned on the bar and waved a finger toward the raucous crowd. "When you get tired o' all this, I'll take you to Mrs. Scott. Mrs. Scott'll make sure you get settled in yo' room, all right honey?" He tapped the little hand she had resting on the bar.

* * *

The next morning, she woke early from excitement to find the other twin bed undisturbed. She washed, brushed her teeth, dressed, and headed downstairs. The lobby was quiet, the restaurant still.

Lil Hardin Armstrong's All Girl Orchestra was to perform two nights this weekend at the Apollo Theater, kicking off the new tour, and rehearsals started this afternoon. But for one horn, the entire outfit had been with Lil during a tour that ended in New York just before her trip to France. The set list was largely the same, too, so the band was already pretty tight. They would be twenty-five days from New York to Chicago, starting with mixed shows at the Apollo followed by two colored gigs at the Pearl in Philadelphia. A colored show and a white show in each Baltimore and Washington, D.C., then hootenannies in Cumberland and Morgantown before white one-nighters in Pittsburgh and Cleveland. The final leg would include split shows in Detroit, a colored show in Flint, then the finish with split shows at the Chicago Theatre. In Chicago, Chloe would be delivered to her uncle, Charlie Chantale.

The evening of the opening at the Apollo, Chloe shuffled cards in Lil's dressing room, where Sarah was fretting. "Sales ain't so hot, Lil."

The bandleader snorted. "There's a depression all right. A depression in my pocketbook." Laughing, Lil fired a reefer. Sarah took a long drag and waved the joy-maker at the girl. Chloe shook her head.

"Girl, what's yo' problem?"

"Oh, leave that one be, now." Lil smiled.

"She jus' too damn serious all the time." Sarah took a long drag.

"She fine." Lil pinched the joint. "Jus' a couple o' weeks an you gonna be with family. Ain't that excitin'?"

Chloe shrugged.

Lil popped up and shimmied. "Well, then, how 'bouts I cheer you wit' some music?" She was snapping her fingers.

```
Is everybody ready?
Is everybody ready for?
Is everybody ready for the All Girl Orchestra?
At the Apollo?
New York City!
At the A-pol-lo!
```

Lil took up Chloe's hands and shook them all around. "We's gonna kill 'em."

That night the Apollo was just over of half-full, but the band jumped and wailed.

```
Like the beat, beat, beat of the tom-tom
When the jungle shadows fall
```

Chloe stood in the wings, lost in the music. She saw how Lil directed her orchestra like Louis did his band at La Pomme d'Or, except Lil wasn't quite as showy. And she wasn't at all like Auntie Josephine. When Auntie Josephine was onstage, it was all about Auntie Josephine. Chloe liked the way Lil let the other ladies shine during their solos.

The shows in New York and Philadelphia failed to sell out, but the venues in Baltimore and DC were packed. Traveling was hard, the bus cramped and always smelling like something that shouldn't be there. It got cold after the heater busted on the way up to Pittsburgh. They were approaching Detroit, and Chloe eavesdropped on her chaperones.

"He a jackass." Sarah passed Lil her last pint of Cumberland moonshine.

"A drunken fool and thievin' sonuvabitch, too. Ain't no money, girlfriend. But he gone now. The white show in Detroit's sold out, an' the black one's close. Word's been spreadin' west."

"But we runnin' outta shows!"

Lil nodded and said something about extending the tour. "We be green when we get the cashbox in Pittsburgh. The girls'll get paid."

Chloe had heard them grousing about their front man before but was surprised to learn he was a thief. Lil confronted him after he got caught him skimming off the Morgantown hootenanny, and he ran off with most everything. "Can't sue whitey."

Lil was kind to Chloe. She was kind to everyone. And though Sarah was quick to complain, she was okay, too. She spent a lot of time hungover, and she sure enjoyed her men. Lil would say, "Sarah like her a sharp suit."

At the hotel in Pittsburgh, Chloe sat on the edge of her bed and swung her feet. Her dull patent-leather Mary Janes were squeezing her toes.

"Do you think he'll look like my daddy?"

Sarah was finishing up her lipstick. "What you talkin' 'bout, girl?"

"My uncle. Do you think he'll look like my daddy?"

"Well, I'd think so, they bein' brothers."

When Chloe thought about meeting her uncle Charlie, which was often, she pictured him young and gray, like in the photo of him with her papa and their sister, Armintha. Except, he was always on a train platform, with the same expressionless face under a low-slung hat.

Cleveland, Detroit and Flint all sold out. The band was tight, the crowds were loud, and when the bus rolled out of Flint at three o'clock in the morning, Lil announced they'd added a second white show in Chicago. As the bus rumbled west, Chloe dozed on and off. She leaned her head against the window, letting it bounce on the cold damp glass.

Dawn stretched between Gary and Calumet City as they rolled past a seemingly endless hobo camp made from splintered pallets, tree branches, corrugated tin and cardboard. Yellow sparks rose from burn barrels that glowed fiery orange through rusted holes, illuminating lumps spread across the dirt, men curled under blankets, under newspapers.

**

The bus hissed to a jerking stop on South State Street. The driver slammed the door open and a couple dozen very tired women, stretching and groaning through teeth caked with the night's funk, tumbled onto the street. It was eight o'clock on Friday morning, and most everyone was in a bad mood. Day twenty-four of a twenty-seven day tour is hard enough, but most of the girls had no idea what was in store for them after the this stand at the Chicago Theatre. Barnstorming south? A return east? Or would they just be cut loose to scrape up gigs here Chi-Town, up in Racine, in Milwaukee?

Lil had ideas she wasn't sharing. She was hoping to cut at least two new orchestral songs, if not four, while in Chicago. The All Girl Orchestra had trotted out a couple new numbers in Pittsburgh and Detroit to great reception. It wasn't Lil's nature to leave folks hanging, but the arrangements weren't certain, so she held off on telling the band. Times were tough, and she tried to strike a balance between giving hope and getting hopes up.

At the corner of Pershing Road, Chloe gazed north up State Street. Gray buildings, cracked gray sidewalks shaded by the blackened elevated trains that rumbled overhead, drowning out all other sound when they passed. Everything looked dirty.

"Sweet home Chicago!" Sarah was smiling big. She had a beau in town named Raymond, and, despite her proclivity for local rendezvous, she hadn't shut up about him since Detroit. A couple hobos huddled near the corner, one jangling pennies in a cup, another bumming for a smoke. Chloe still wasn't used to the blackness. The blackness of every hotel, every neighborhood. The back entrances at the venues, the colored toilets. Except for the white audiences, everything they'd done from New York to Chicago, they'd done with Negroes. At Dr. Maria's school, there were children and teachers from all over Europe, Africa, and Asia. The salons were mostly white people, but black musicians, writers, and artists were prevalent, and she'd met plenty of brown people from Morocco, Persia, and South America. Since her arrival in the States, Chloe's interactions were exclusively with black musicians, black stagehands, and black waitresses, many of whom she couldn't understand. She hadn't said it out loud, but she thought it. "They all talk like they are drunk and chewing bread."

During the tour, both Lil and Sarah slipped more and more into the rhythm of the street, and Chloe sometimes had a hard time understanding them, too, especially when they were drinking or smoking marijuana. Dr. Maria's school was a wonderful place to explore, with the freedom to learn what you wanted to learn. But with language, there were rules. *Bonne énonciation, s'il vous plaît. La capacité de communiquer est notre compétence la plus importante!*

English was Chloe's third schooled language after French and Italian, and she and Miss Sophie usually spoke French together. All the women on the tour seemed to understand each other just fine, but it wasn't the English that Chloe had been taught, and she found it exhausting trying to listen, focusing in attempt to comprehend.

The All Girl Orchestra couldn't have their rooms at the Washington Hotel until five o'clock that afternoon, so they were in an awful rush to prepare before the show. The bathrooms were overrun, and by the time Chloe gained access, there was only cold water left. Hurrying to dress, she dropped a shoe behind her bed. Retrieving it, she crawled through dust past an empty gin bottle, some gum wrappers, and two used condoms.

"I sent your uncle a note. He s'pose to come tonight."

Chloe jumped to her feet. "When, Ms. Sarah? After the show?"

"How would I know, girl? He s'pose to be there. That all I know 'bout it."

Chloe squeezed her eyes tight and tried to imagine what he would look like, in real color. Would he be kind? What if she couldn't understand *him*, either?

The Chicago Theatre was magnificent. She marveled at the frescoes that covered the high, domed ceiling. Angels and cherubs, plump, lovely, and white. Management was white, and most of the stagehands were white. Lil's dressing room was by far the most comfortable of all the venues on the tour. Sarah asked the girl one last time, just before the show started. "You sure you wanna wait back here? Cain't know when he's comin'."

"Yes, ma'am."

"Soocha self!" Sarah took a swig of gin, tucked the bottle behind the lighted table mirror, and left to watch from the wings.

Chloe was intrigued by how show nights evolved. The hustle and bustle, the shouts and fussing and laughs, followed by the chorus of clicking heels as the band members rushed up the hallway. Always some straggler who was fixing a reed or pinning a popped button, crying out, "Wait up!"

She listened through the open dressing room door to the last of the footsteps clomping across the stage as the crowd's welcome grew louder. Tonight was a white show. There'd be tomorrow's colored matinee, then, the tour's finale, the second white show Saturday night. All three performances were sold out. She tipped her head this way and that in front of Lil's lighted mirror to check the ribbon that tied back her hair.

```
Savoy, the home of sweet romance
Savoy, it wins you at a glance
```

The crowd exploded with applause, and Chloe could tell it would be a fine show. She was happy for Lil and glad everyone would get paid and be in a good mood. She twisted a curl in the mirror, and the noise faded behind her as the dressing room door closed.

"Well, well. Whadda we have here?"

Chloe gasped. "Pardon? May . . . may I help you?"

"Ha!" The man spit tobacco juice and rubbed his stubbly chin. He popped the cap off his head to run a hand over his salt-and-pepper crew cut, staring, licking his lips. "Yeah, I'm pretty sure you can help me." In three pounding steps, he was across the room. She tried to run past him, but there was no room, no way. He grabbed her by the arm and threw her against the dressing table. "Yeah, you'll do fine."

The big man straddled her legs as he unclipped the straps to his overalls and pushed the denim to his knees. Her scream drew a hard right cross that slammed into her jaw. The back of her head hit the mirror and skated across it, bursting three light bulbs. Sarah's pint bottle of gin shattered on the floorboards. The brute flipped her over and gripped her neck, smashing her face against the vanity table. He raised her cotton dress. She felt his cold rough hands on her buttocks and thighs.

"Yeah, just fine."

Something warm was rubbing on her bottom, then between her legs. The band got louder.

```
Why do you try to make me feel so blue?
```

There was a loud crack.

```
I've done nothing to you
```

His face crashed into hers, and his chin stubble scratched across her cheek. The big man was crushing her, pressing the air from her lungs. She gagged on his breath, a sour blend of tobacco, onion, alcohol, and rotting teeth. He slid off to the side and hit the floor with a thud. The music died down again.

"You alright?"

It was a different voice. A man's voice, but with a high pitch, almost like a child. Terrified, she couldn't move. The young man hung a wooden cane on the mirror, straightened the girl's undergarments and smoothed the dress over her bottom and legs. He eased her up by the shoulders and helped her onto the stool. She was trembling and in shock. The young man knelt in front of her and collected her hands in his own.

"You okay now. Everythin' gonna be jus' fine, understand?"

She shuddered, and her eyes widened. She tried to pull away, but he still had her hands cupped in his own. The big man on the floor groaned and raised his hands to his head. He was pushing himself up when the young man snatched the cane off the mirror and swung it like an axe onto the man's head with such ferocity that Chloe squealed with fright. He brought the cane down on the brute's skull three more times, each blow making that same loud crack she first heard. The man wasn't moving anymore.

"Wooh! Lucky this here cane was in that there umbrella stand."

"Lucky . . ." She was still in shock.

The young man nudged the lump with his foot. Nothing. He kicked him in the ribs. Still nothing. "Don't think he gonna be a bother no more."

Chloe stared at this man, this boy, really, with the cane slung over his shoulder, hovering over the big man on the floor. He tipped his Stetson fedora her way, tucked the cane under his arm, and presented his hand to her.

"James Hamilton Jones. You kin call me Hamilton."

Chloe accepted the hand in silent, shocked astonishment. He was wiry and very tall, nearly two meters she supposed, with a thin, handsome face and a long nose under a head of wavy jet-black hair slicked close to his scalp. He wore a crisp suit, blue pinstripe, with a red carnation tucked into the lapel buttonhole.

"I work for your uncle Charlie. Well, that is unless I'm mistaken as to your identity. You Miss Chloe, ain'tcha?"

She just stared.

"Alright then, Miss Chloe. We best be movin' along. I figure these theater people ain't gonna be none too happy 'bout Mistah Smashhead, here. In fact . . . s'pose we best do somethin' with him."

He kicked the heap again. "So as to avoid gettin' you mixed up in this, understand?"

There was music in his voice. The rhythm of it soothed her some.

"Is . . . is he dead?"

"Not sure." Hamilton leaned over the body with his hands on his hips. "He's done gone pissed his pants. They do that, they usually dead. At least he ain't shit himself. Look, you sit here while I take a peek down the hall. Gotta manage the situation, understand?"

Her eyes widened with panic. He took a knee and collected her hands in his.

"Now don'tcha be frettin'. I jus' need to figure if I can do somethin' with this heap, that's all. If not, we just up and go. Got it?" He squeezed and gently shook her fingers until her eyes started to calm.

"Gonna do this now."

The boy eased the dressing room door open. He stepped out, pulling the door closed behind him. Chloe's panic made a rush. She pulled her legs up to her chest and rocked on the stool, eyeing the body on the floor, the door, the body, the door. A pool of blood was spreading from under the man's crew-cut head, a puddle of urine from under his pale hairy ass. She trembled as anger wrestled with her panic. A tear trickled down her cheek.

"I hope you *are* dead."

She shrieked when the door burst open. Hamilton slipped in and held a finger to his lips.

"There's a prop room right across the hall. Ain't no one 'round, so I'll just pull him over there, nice an' easy. But I need you to help, young lady. You gotta open and close doors, understand?"

Astonished, her mouth agape, she shook her head *no* and started to rock again.

"Yeah, you heard me right. I need you to work the doors 'cause I can't pull whitey's fat ass over there and work the doors at the same time."

Still rocking, tears dripping off her cheeks, she stopped shaking her head.

"Good girl. So when I get 'im across the room here, I'll peek out. When the coast's clear, you run across the hall and open the other door real quick, while I'm draggin' him out. Got it?"

She nodded.

"Then you close that door behind me and come back in here, right?"

She nodded again. She felt like she was going to pee herself.

"Alright. Let's do this."

The plan went off without a hitch, like a play they'd rehearsed for weeks. Hamilton covered the body with costumes in the back of the prop room, and then, back in the dressing room, they both breathed sighs of relief as Hamilton wiped his brow with his kerchief. Chloe was coming out of shock, crying hard. Hamilton handed her his kerchief and pulled a black feather boa off the coat rack to wipe up the blood and piss as best he could.

"We gotta go." He cracked the door open and took a peek down the hall. He waved for her to walk through.

Chloe shook her head and held tight to the stool.

"Come on, we gotta go, now!"

"But what of Miss Sarah? What of Miss Lil?"

"Under the circumstances, we best get movin'. I'll come back and talk to the ladies, now c'mon."

She held tight to the stool. He snatched her up and stood her on her feet. "This way."

He pulled her by the hand down the hallway and on through multiple corridors. The band finished a number and applause was rocking the building as the pair slid out the back. In the alley, an awful garbage stench filled her nose, but the cool air helped clear her spinning head. With Hamilton holding her hand tight, they hurried around the side of the theater. He pulled his hat down, tucked his chin and led her across State Street.

"What about the man?"

"What about him?"

They stopped on the corner a block south. He squatted to look her in the eyes. He told her that with Lil's three gigs scheduled, he figured no one would be going into the prop room for at least a while. "No one'll be the wiser 'til he starts smellin'." Her eyes clouded behind pools of tears.

"Hey." She was still clutching the kerchief, and Hamilton raised her hand to her cheek. "He was a very bad man, understand? And he ain't gonna try that with no one never again. So you jus' put it outta your mind. It don't mean nothin'. *He* don't mean nothin'."

The tears came harder. She couldn't control herself.

"So what happen' back there, that jus' between us two. Jus' you and me, got it?" He moved in close and took up the hanky. He dabbed her eyes and wiped her nose. "You don't tell no one, never, right?"

She nodded, sniffling.

"And you start *not tellin'* by not tellin' Vera."

He led her across Randolph Street and opened the passenger door of a dark 1930 Ford Model A Cabriolet. He lifted Chloe in over a beautiful dark young woman wearing a bright-red dress, bright-red lipstick, and a strand of small pearls. Chloe straddled the hand brake.

Hamilton leaned in and kissed the young woman's cheek. "Miss Chloe, this Miss Vera. Vera, this Chloe."

The girls looked at each other.

"Enchanté." Chloe raised her hand.

Vera just looked at it, pulling hard on a filtered Chesterfield. She aimed a large blue plume at Hamilton's face. "I need a drink."

"Not jus' yet, baby. I be right back." He closed the door and trotted back to the theater, where he found Sarah Brown in the wings.

"Charlie Chantale sent me to collect the girl. I got her with me. Somethin' came up. Everything's jake, but I gotta go."

Sarah pressed him for an explanation.

"You don't need to know, woman. You best not, got it?" Hamilton's tone was serious. "The girl's fine. We'll come 'round the Washington for her things. Don't say nothin' to nobody 'bout nothin', understand?"

Sarah didn't understand, but she was done asking questions. It was apparent something was going on, and this boy meant business. Hamilton peeled a twenty from a gold-plated money clip and pressed it against her palm.

* * *

Hamilton settled the girls in his room. "I gotta go see Charlie. Won't be long."

The evening wasn't heading in the direction Vera had envisioned. She let out a loud sigh and pouted. "I'm starvin'. Get us sump'n ta eat."

Hamilton lifted Chloe's chin toward the table lamp and sized up the purple lump on her jaw.

"I'll getchoo some ice."

CHLOE'S MISTIGRI

Vera struck a match as Hamilton closed the door behind him. Bobbing a crossed leg, she fired her smoke and shook out the flame. "So, you from France, huh?"

"Oui. Yes. From Paris, in France." Chloe tried to guess her age. *Sixteen?*

Vera heaved a sigh and took another long drag. She looked Chloe up and down. "You a pretty li'l thing, ain'tcha? You an yo paper bag and all that."

Chloe dropped her eyes.

"Yeah, pretty li'l paper baggy, that you."

Chloe was confused.

"So what, you don't know that, huh, Frenchy?"

Chloe shook her head.

"Them uppity house niggers." Vera took another draw and pointed her cigarette at the window. "Society folk 'round the university and all. If you's lighta than a paper bag, you kin be one a them." She pointed the glowing stick at the girl. "But you gotta talk right, too, see?" She paused to take another drag. "Yeah, you got it all, Frenchy, yes you do. Got *it*. They eat choo up with a silver spoon."

Chloe pictured Auntie Josephine. She wasn't lighter than a paper bag. She was quite dark and fit in just fine with university people at the salons.

Hamilton returned in short order with two sacks. From one, he pulled a bottle of milk, then dumped three sandwiches wrapped in butcher paper on the bed. He handed Chloe the bottle. "Didn't have no ice to sell, so hold that on your face." The other sack held a pint of rye whiskey. He pulled the cork with his teeth and poured shots into two stained highballs. He handed a glass to Vera, and they threw back the shots while Chloe picked the crumpled bag off the floor. She held it across her forearm under the table lamp.

* * *

Charlie Chantale didn't look pleased when he heard of the extracurricular activity that took place at the Chicago Theatre, but he commended Hamilton for his quick thinking.

"It ain't gonna do to have that body found there. Whitey'll pin it on some black man. Prob'ly somebody 'round Lil. We gotta get his fat carcass outta there."

Hamilton wanted the job, but the boss put someone more seasoned on it. He instructed Hamilton to collect the girl and her things and bring her to Saucy's place. Charlie Chantale had been estranged from his wife for some time, and he kept his mistress Saucy in a comfortable, two-bedroom flat on Twenty-Ninth Street. Saucy would keep the girl for a couple of days until Hamilton was freed up from another project that required his attention. "You gonna take the kid to my sister in Louisiana. Until then, gotta put some distance between her and Lil, got it?"

Chloe didn't get to say goodbye to Lil or Sarah, and she never even met her uncle. She was watching people on the street below Saucy's second-floor window when the Ford Cabriolet screeched to a halt out front. Hamilton and another young man stepped out. All Saucy said was, "Good luck, kid."

The new boy tossed her bags into the rumble seat, and Hamilton lifted her and set her in next to them. Flushing, she wondered if this was what it was like to have a big brother. During the short ride to Central Station, she thought back on Paris and longed for her Miss Sophie. She missed Josephine and giggled at the memory of Chiquita twitching her ear. Hamilton caught a glimpse of the girl's smile in the rearview mirror and smiled back. Every time he whizzed around a corner, she tumbled around in the leather seat, belly laughing. The plan was to take the train to Lafayette, then hire a car to Abbeville. To her delight, Hamilton would accompany her the whole way. She'd be settled into her new home in two days time.

The train trip was pleasant. Chloe reread the few books she'd brought from home, and Hamilton read back issues of the *Chicago Defender*. A chill ran down her spine when she noticed an ad on the back page for the All Girls Orchestra black show at the Chicago Theatre.

Hamilton pulled out a deck of cards. He taught her poker games, stud and draw, and she taught him acey deucey and vingt-et-un. She showed him the deck of cards she'd saved from the apartment on Rue de l'Odéon.

"You see, where you have a K for king, we have an R, le roi. Where you have a J, have a V. Le valet."

Hamilton studied her jack of clubs.

"This card, le valet de trèfles, we know as *le mistigri*," Chloe said.

"Misty gree?"

"Oui. Very good!"

"So in France, the cards, they got separate names, like people do."

CHLOE'S MISTIGRI

"Oui, le valet de trèfles est le mistigri."

South of Memphis, Hamilton joined a couple of men in the backbench of the colored car for a game of draw poker. Otherwise, the two were together the entire trip. Hamilton was riveted by Chloe's stories of Paris, her descriptions of La Pomme d'Or and Josephine Baker's act.

"What's a cheetah?"

She explained.

"So like a leopard?"

"Oui, but tall and, how to say, maigre. Slim, yes? Like you." She giggled.

"How 'bout Louis Armstrong? He's over there in Paris."

"Monsieur Pops, oui."

Hamilton seemed astounded by her stories and impressed by her maturity and eloquence. At eleven years of age, Chloe Boisvert was already more interesting than Vera Jackson or any of the others would ever be. By the time they reached Lafayette, Chloe's anxiety had completely dissipated. She was comfortable with Hamilton, except for those times when he caught her looking at him. Then she blushed. As they stepped onto the Lafayette rail station platform, she asked his age.

"I'm twenty-one."

She nodded.

"Actually, I'll turn eighteen this summer. Don't tell nobody." He winked.

Chloe wore her biggest grin.

Hamilton struck up a conversation with a man who was pulling planks from the bed of his truck and offered him five dollars for a round trip to Abbeville. On the drive, he asked about musicians in the area.

Chloe listened intently. She thought Hamilton would fit right in at the Paris salons, except that he finished too many of his sentences by saying, "Understand?" or "Got it?" And maybe he cursed too much. She was getting nervous. It was only minutes before she would meet her aunt and her sister.

Hamilton asked the man about Nellie Lutcher.

"Cain't say I know o' her. But you know, missah, they's call it the *Big Easy* down theyah foe good reason. Maybe it *be easy* to find her."

The flatbed bumped across the Vermilion River bridge and turned south onto Louisiana Street. "That's it." Hamilton pointed. "Pull over."

The truck squeaked to a stop, and the driver cut the engine. Chloe read the sign out loud. "The Music Box Café."

"Miss Chloe, I do believe you home." Hamilton told the driver he'd be a few minutes. As they approached the restaurant, Chloe's heart raced, and she eyed the weeds sprouting between the cracked stepping-stones. The yard was dotted with bright yellow dandelions and a few puffy white ones. The pair climbed the creaky porch steps and faced a rusty Coca-Cola thermometer nailed next to the doorframe. Hamilton set down Chloe's bags and opened the screen door. "Well, c'mon."

The place was empty, and quiet save for the Regulator clock ticking on the wall. Seven minutes past three. Hamilton checked his wristwatch.

"Hello?"

Nothing.

"*Hell-oh!*"

This time the call was answered by heavy footsteps coming from behind the kitchen. A teenager in a worn blue dress burst through the chest-high saloon doors and into the dining room. She placed her hands on her hips. "We close."

Chloe was startled by the girl's face. Those eyes. That mouth. She stepped forward. "Et-tu, Francie?"

The girl in blue dress pressed her hands to her cheeks. "Chlo!" Francie ran to her little sister and squeezed her tight.

11

IT AIN'T THE ALAMO

MARCH 1934

PJ twisted in the swing, scraping the dusty ground with his toes. The moon was shining bright, and he wondered if there was good fishing up there. He liked it best when the moon was big, when he could see the kitty nose and whiskers near the bottom.

"S'pose now's as good a time as any."

Pumpkin, sleeping in the grass, woke when he hopped down. The puppy followed him into the shed where he shook the potato sack free of the last three spuds. She sat on the porch, trying to catch glimpses of him as he crossed back and forth in the kitchen.

Stepping over the squeaky board, he pulled the red-and-white checked tablecloth from the buffet drawer and brought it to his room. He stacked some clothes on it and tied up the corners. Back in the kitchen, he wrapped four apples in a dishtowel and snatched the ham steak from the icebox. He stuffed everything into the potato sack, along with his full canteen, and slung the whole mess over his shoulder. Looking back into the darkened hallway, he got a little sad, then turned and walked out, letting the screen door slam behind him.

"I'm gonna miss you." He knelt and rubbed the Lab's ears. "Stay." But she wouldn't stay. She followed. "Git! Go on home!" The pup wouldn't do it, and she crept behind, at a distance. So he walked her back to the yard and clipped her to the doghouse. PJ dug into his bundle and pulled out the butcher paper. He tore off a piece of ham and held it to her nose, which wriggled, but she didn't bite. She just stared at him.

"I can't take you with me."

Her eyes asked, "Why not?"

"Goddam. Okay. We'll figure it out."

He'd walked with Pumpkin to the train station last weekend to see how long it would take. It was past midnight, and he figured they'd get there around one o'clock. When they arrived, a bright light was shining through a single window of the station house. He tied Pumpkin's leash and rubbed her head, then they snuck around the back, following the tracks a hundred yards or so to the east. And there they sat, waiting for their ride.

The full moon was heading west and everything, the tracks, the gravel, the telegraph line, seemed to glow. He pulled an apple from the dishtowel and polished it on his yellowing T-shirt. Then he felt it. The vibration in the rail. He tucked the apple back in the towel, the towel back in the sack. Then came the whistles.

"Let's go, girl."

The pup followed as he skated gravel down the embankment to a line of scrub brush. His stomach and groin were tingling when the freight train's headlamp cast a halo of light over the tracks above him. Another long whistle blast. "You ready?" Behind the engine were some twenty cattle cars, but as the line came around the soft bend from the station, he saw open boxcars near the tail. He checked to see if the coast was clear, then scrambled and slipped his way back up the gravel to the tracks, Pumpkin right there with him.

The shuffling, grunting, and snorting in the cattle cars was intimidating, and he was surprised the train was traveling as fast as it was. As the first open boxcar arrived, he and Pumpkin trotted alongside and panic jumped the boy. It was so high. How was he going to get her up there? They needed to do this quickly, or he would lose his breath, and the opportunity would pass. Slowing to the next car, he tossed the potato sack into its dark bay and stumbled, the boxcar pulling away. He sprinted to catch up, and Pumpkin was right there with him. He realized now he could never get her in there. The bay door was too high, too high even to get a handhold and pull himself up. That's when a thin, pale hand poked out of the darkness. Instinctively, PJ grabbed it.

Dangling by one arm, he heard the man grunt. His ribcage scraped against the ragged edge of the floorboard as he was pulled into the bay. On all fours and out of breath, he heard panting that wasn't his own. A dark figure of a man on his knees was wheezing, coughing. PJ crawled to look out the bay door. The train was speeding up, and the pup was in a full canter to stay abreast of the boxcar. Tears welled in the boy's eyes. He yelled, "Go home!"

"What's yer name, boy?"

He spun around, startled. As the train rounded northward, a rectangle of moonlight spread into the boxcar, creeping toward the hobo, who was still on his knees. He was sickly pale, unshaven, and dirty with sunken eyes, hollow cheeks, and a thin, stretched neck. He started coughing again. After the fit, he hacked and spit up phlegm, then wiped his mouth on the sleeve of a worn leather jacket.

"Well?" He hacked and spit again.

PJ was looking back into the darkness. He wiped a tear from his eye. "My name's PJ Benoit."

The man eyed the potato sack. "You got food?"

PJ nodded.

"Well, how 'bout somethin', in trade for the help I just give ya?"

PJ reached into the sack and pulled an apple from the towel. He tossed it to the man, who fumbled it, the apple bouncing off his lap and rolling to the back of the car.

"Get that, boy."

He retrieved the apple and handed it to the man, who pulled out a small jackknife and cut off a slice.

"A li'l green, but'll do."

PJ tried to focus on what he needed to do, but he was awfully worried about Pumpkin. When the train reached speed, the clacking from the tracks was fast and loud. He thought things through the best he could and figured the next thing was to find out if this train would go all the way to Louisiana or, if not, how to get on one that would. He wanted to ask the hobo and remembered something his daddy used to say. *Everybody's more agreeable with a full belly.*

Turning his back so the man couldn't see what he was doing, PJ pulled the towel from his sack and, with his lock blade, cut off a piece of ham. The man had eaten half the apple and was wrapping up the rest in a stained cloth.

"Would you like some ham, sir? I ain't got much, but you can have what I got."

"Ham? Yes, boy. I'd like some ham."

PJ walked it over to him.

"Name's Brito. Walt Brito." The man didn't save the ham. He wolfed it down, triggering another coughing fit.

PJ made his inquiry. "Where does this train go to?"

No answer.

"Does it leave Texas?"

Brito didn't look up. "Where you headed, boy?"

PJ didn't know why, but the question made him uneasy. "Louisiana. I gotta get to New Orleans."

"Ain't that somethin'? I'm from New Orleans." But still no answer to the question.

"I gave you my ham. How 'bout somethin' in trade?"

Brito chuckled and started coughing again. After his fit settled, he nodded. "This here train is headin' to New Orleans."

A week ago, when he and Pumpkin walked down to the rail station, he poked around some and learned that trains heading to New Orleans went through Lafayette, and Lafayette was close to Perry.

"But them cattle cars, they'll get switched in Houston. Them cows are bound for Galveston."

The boy was puzzled. "So we just stay here, in this car, and they'll pull it all the way to New Orleans?"

"That ain't how it works, boy. See, in the switchin' yard, they got bosses that'll beat ya shitty if they find ya in a car, and they're bad in Houston. So ya gotta jump before the yard, then make yer way 'round the other side. Catch it on the way out."

This wasn't going to be as easy as PJ had thought it was going to be.

"So which way are you goin'? Outta Houston, I mean?"

Brito smiled wide, a dark rectangle where his three of his front teeth used to be.

"Well, I'm going to New Orleans, just like you, boy." The man's grin wasn't right. He looked a little crazy. PJ couldn't tell if it was because his eyes were so big and hollow, or if maybe he *was* crazy.

"Houston's a couple hours. Might as well get some shut-eye, boy." The hobo rolled to his side, belched, and suffered another long cough before going quiet.

PJ fought sleep for fear of messing up the switch. He thought more on Pumpkin, wondering if she'd turned back for home, or if she was still following the tracks. But exhaustion made its play and won the hand.

The crackling fire was toasty on his shoulders. He was sitting Indian-style, and Criquette was nestled between his legs. It tickled when the spaniel stretched to lick his chin. Her eyes closed by half while he rubbed her soft, feathered ears, then Pumpkin burst into the room, sniffed at the Brittany, then buried her nose deep in the boy's crotch.

PJ opened his eyes to find Brito hunched over him. The gaunt man was breathing hard with a hand down PJ's pants, the other stuffed down his own. The stench of rotting teeth in his nose, PJ pushed at the man's chest. He wasn't big, but the boy had no leverage and couldn't budge him. He jammed a finger into one crazy eye, and the man howled, reeling back. He couldn't catch himself and tipped onto his side. The boy scrambled free, but the boxcar was rocking, and he fell on his backside. It hurt where he landed on his lock blade.

As Brito struggled to his feet, PJ's steel glinted in the moonlight. The hobo fumbled for something in his back pocket. PJ took a deep breath, and everything slowed down. His mind was clear, and he rushed the man.

Before Brito could react, PJ lowered his shoulder and drove as hard as he could into the man's legs. Brito lost his balance and fell toward the open slide door. Up on one knee, he was overtaken by another coughing fit. PJ got as low as he could and rammed the man in the side. Brito tumbled out the opening, floppin on the dirt below with a thud. PJ watched as the coughing body rolled down the slope and disappeared in the dark. He stood there, holding the knife. He didn't know if he'd stabbed the man. "Fuck 'im if I did."

His hands were trembling, and he wiped the knife blade with his thumb. It was clean. He snapped it shut and plopped down, dangling his legs out the bay door. The moon had sunk below the horizon and to his right there was only darkness. To his left, dawn's glow. He worried some about Pumpkin, then his mama jumped his head. "Won't crawl outta bed for hours. Fuck her, too." He forced himself to think about something else. Frank. He would think about his brother. Sitting with Frank in a deer blind. Predawn, just like now, but quiet. Peaceful. "Gonna see Frank soon. Gonna meet Odette, too." The train was slowing. He leaned out to see what was coming, but it was turning on a long arc, and all he could see ahead was hedgerow. The whistle blew.

* * *

Twisted rusty barbed wire, busted-up boards and wastepaper were strewn alongside the tracks. The more whistles, the dirtier the scene. Then came a line of ramshackle shelters cobbled together with refuse wood, torn tarpaper, tree branches and rusty corrugated steel lying just beyond the clumps of scrub brush. The boy tucked everything back in the potato sack and positioned himself to jump. The whistle was blowing while his boxcar crossed a rutted dirt road. He had no idea how far the switchyard was, but the train was slowing even more as it rolled past a larger hobo camp where people were sleeping on the ground or circled around campfires. As good a time as any, he figured. He tossed the sack out and followed it to the ground, tumbling headfirst and rolling to a stop. He was glad it was dirt and not gravel. He gathered the sack and watched as the last of the boxcars rolled by. The camp was some fifty yards back.

Two men hovered over a coffee pot on a flat rock at the edge of a low fire. They eyed the boy warily.

"Do y'all know how to pick a train to New Orleans?"

"Going to New Orleans, are ya?" It was the one with a tobacco pipe hanging from a crooked mouth.

PJ felt more at ease here than he'd felt from the get-go in that boxcar with Brito. "Perry, Louisiana, sir. I've heard the train to New Orleans goes by there, by Lafayette, sir."

The man's eyes lit up. It'd been a long time since anyone had called him sir.

"You on your own, boy?"

PJ hesitated. The men looked at each other.

"I'm just saying, because it can get dangerous 'round here. On the road and all." He pointed his pipe at the boy. "Not everyone's so friendly, if you get my drift."

PJ took a deep breath and decided he was done being afraid. *Fear ain't gonna get you where you're wantin' to go.* Another of his daddy's sayings. He figured he could outrun these tired old men if it came down to it, and if that didn't work, he had his lock blade.

"I'm gonna stay with my brother. And his wife. I heard there's a switchyard in Houston, and I gotta find a train to New Orleans. I was on one but . . ."

The man with the pipe nodded. "Someone told you they'd be switching cars in the yard."

"Yes, sir."

"Well, he told you right. If you didn't jump when you did, you mighta got the hell beat out of you by the yard bulls up yonder. Have a seat." He pointed his pipe around the circle. "We'll get you straightened out. All we got is beans and bad coffee, but you're welcome to both."

"No, thank you, sir."

A third man with a blanket over his shoulders joined them at the fire. Introductions were made. PJ, two Johns and a Johnny. Pipe John knew all about the Houston switchyard. He drew a map in the dirt with a stick and explained which spurs went which direction. Dallas, Corpus Christi, New Orleans.

The Johnny spoke. "I'm heading east, kid. We can go together. Ain't no jobs in this damn town. Maybe get some boat work over Louisiana way."

Pipe John blew a series of smoke rings. "Sure you ain't hungry, PJ? Go ahead." Bobbing his chin at the boy, he held out a tin cup of hot beans.

"Thank you, sir." PJ sat cross-legged by the fire and wolfed down the beans. He hadn't realized how hungry he was. He looked up at the Johnny and wriggled on his bottom to feel the lock blade in his back pocket. "Ain't no way I'm goin' with nobody," he mumbled into his cup.

Something about having the boy there opened up the menfolk. They started telling stories, most of which landed dead center between sadness and misery. They'd all left wives behind, and children, and they all needed work to send money home.

But Pipe John's stories, about traveling the world as a merchant marine, they were fun, and they all ended with a surprise. Here would come the twist, with the other men on the edge of their seats, waiting for more, but there wasn't more. Pipe John would just lean back and chew on that pipe. Then it'd start dawning on the others, one by one. Someone would laugh, slap a knee, say something like, "There ain't no girl like that!" Except for PJ, they all knew Pipe John was bullshitting, they just didn't know by how much, and that was where the fun was. Pipe John chose to pass the time making cheer, and to do so, he took liberties with the truth. Since PJ wasn't wise to the ways of the world, he had a hard time picturing tattooed Oriental girls holding clams between their thighs.

* * *

The Johnny was tapping his shoulder. "Time to go, kid. We got some walkin' to do."

PJ scrambled to his feet. It was midmorning, and two other men were standing behind the Johnny, each with a sack slung over a shoulder.

"We're all goin'."

As the four of them walked eastward toward the rail yard, the Johnny explained how things would go.

"Look, kid. This yard's got some of the hardest bulls on the line. They mean business, see? They catch you, they beat you. They ain't gonna give a good goddamn yer just a kid, and they won't lose no sleep from splittin' your head wide open."

PJ could tell he wasn't fooling.

"We'll split up. You come with me, and those two'll pick a different car. If someone finds trouble, then the others might make it out clean, see?"

PJ wasn't thinking the way he did last night. The image of the yard bulls shook him, and he was glad to have help figuring this out.

The men took every precaution to move undetected, and it was quite a while, running, stopping, looking out, running, before they made it fine. The Johnny peered into a boxcar with the door slightly ajar.

"This'll do." He boosted the boy, then asked for a hand. A large wooden crate sat on pallets in the middle of the car, and the pair positioned themselves behind it. "It ain't the *Alamo*, but it'll do."

"Huh?"

"The bulls'll shine a light in here but won't bother climbing up." The Johnny tipped his hat down, over his eyes. "If I start snoring, you poke me, ya hear kid? I can't be givin' away our position, see? So you stay awake, got it?"

PJ had every intention of staying awake, all the way to Lafayette.

* * *

After dropping some cars in Beaumont, the train rambled east without further interruption. PJ shared his apples and what was left of the hamsteak with the Johnny, then broke the promise he'd made to himself by falling asleep.

"This is it, kid." The Johnny shook PJ's foot. "Wake up. You gotta jump soon."

"Where are we?"

"Rolled through Lake Charles a while back. I'd say we're less than half an hour outta Lafayette."

PJ hopped to his feet, adrenaline pumping. He needed to pee something awful and made an arc out the bay door into the black night, the nearly-full moon obscured by thick cloud cover. He could just make out some crops through the tree line along the tracks.

"Sugar cane." The Johnny put a match to a freshly rolled smoke. The train whistled. "We're slowing down. Get yourself ready. You gotta jump before we pick up speed again."

PJ checked the knot on his sack.

"Remember, Highway 167 south. Take it to the end. Just ask people about your brother. Give 'em the address. They'll help a kid." The Johnny poked his head out the bay door. "Looks like some grass comin'. We ain't gonna slow down more than this, so remember, when you hit the ground, just roll with it."

The train eased southward.

"This is it." The Johnny patted his back.

PJ looked the man in the eyes and stuck out his hand. "Thank you, sir."

The Johnny grinned, and PJ was surprised to see a hole where a front tooth should've been. "Good luck."

The boy tossed the sack and followed it down.

* * *

It was nearing morning light when he heard voices on the road up ahead. Two Negro men bent under the hood of a broken-down flatbed.

"Excuse me."

"Yessah?" A big man in overalls wiped his brow with a blue bandana.

"Can y'all tell me somethin'?" PJ said, pointing to the bridge just up the road. "Is this Abbeville?"

"It is. Right theyah, 'cross ta way." The men studied the little white boy with the potato sack slung over his shoulder.

"Sorry to bother you," PJ added.

The men looked at each other and the big one smiled. "No botha, nosah. Wha choo need, young man? Kin I hep ya?"

"I need to get to Perry. Can y'all tell me how to get to Perry?"

"Sure ting. You jus cross ta bridge into town, theyah. Den a cuppa blocks yous turn south, deyah, on State Street. Yous walk cleyah outta town bout oh mile, no, two mile, and yous get to Highway 82. Yous turn back ta dah riva, so dat right. Take you in ta Perry, yessah."

He'd walked twenty miles through the night and was nearly to Frank's. Adrenaline overwhelmed exhaustion. "Thank you very much, sir."

It felt like forever when some forty minutes later he was standing in the bright morning sunshine on Main Street in Perry, Louisiana, facing a green cottage with tan shutters. He climbed the porch steps and traced his fingers across the raised numbers tacked to the doorframe. Two. Zero. Three. He rapped the door with his knuckles a little too hard, especially for this early hour. A pretty young woman with sandy bobbed hair and big brown eyes, her dress wrapped with a white apron with red checks on the pockets, leaned open the screen door. She was cradling the tiniest baby in her arms.

"May I help you?"

"You must be Odette." The boy dropped his sack and put out his hand. "I'm PJ."

12

INTRODUCTIONS

APRIL 1934

Chloe sat in a spindle-backed chair with a cane seat that crunched when she wriggled. She swung her legs, crossed at the ankles, and surveyed the room, which was a little dark on this overcast day. She recognized the French toile print on the faded wallpaper that lay behind two framed oval photographs, a middle-aged woman and a middle-aged man, both with glassy eyes set in stern faces. The floor was covered with a large braided oval wool rug, and the lamp table next to her chair was oval shaped, too. She couldn't recollect ever seeing so many ovals in one room.

"Hol' still," her aunt scolded. "The revrun's a busy man. He'll see us when he ready."

The house girl returned and led them to Dr. Herod's office.

"Please, come in. It is so good to see you, Sister Williams. It seems we only ever have the chance to speak in the receiving line after Sunday service."

"You wehcome down ta café, Revrun, foe ta best jambalaya . . ."

"Yes, yes, I would like that very much, Sister Williams. Yes, I would. But remember, *God resisteth the proud, but giveth grace unto the humble.*"

She bowed her head. "I's sorry, Revrun."

A gray-haired black man with full dark eyebrows, heavy lips and a serious look, the preacher wore an aged but well-kept tan suit. He stood straight and held his chin like her Uncle Paul's driver, Dumont, back in Paris before the money trouble. There was a short dark scar on the preacher's cheek. "Digne," she whispered.

Dr. Herod made his way around his desk with the help of a cane. He'd aged significantly since his involvement with this family began nearly seven years ago. He stuffed his pipe and struck a match. Plumes of blue-gray smoke curled slowly overhead as he began the conversation with a description of the meeting in his office with Paul Boisvert so long ago. It had been some ten minutes when he paused and tapped the ashes from his pipe.

"Chloe, dear child, are you crying?" An obtuse question from a learned man. She was crying, and predictably so. The reverend had recounted the death of her parents, her estrangement from her sister, and the death of her uncle, and his tone was such that he could have been reading from a newspaper. Chloe's time with Hamilton had so eased her burdens, and her reunion with Francie had so lifted her spirits. Now, here she sat in front of this serious man trying to fight off depressed apprehension. The reverend extracted a paper from a stack on his desk.

"Well, well. Yes. Here it is," he said. "Miss Josephine Baker. This is the correspondence I received from her, an explanation, to be precise. I am somewhat familiar with Miss Baker's exploits, but as a man of the cloth, I must say I am relieved this child of God will no longer be subjected to the rampant depravity and sin that dominates the industry in which Miss Baker thrives. Praise the Lord that she has been delivered unto us, Sister Williams, so that we may assist in the cultivation and emancipation of her soul."

"I got some bad news, Revrun." Armintha fidgeted, and Chloe wiped tears. "The envelope Hamilton Jones brung t'me did't have two thousand dollars in it. They be jus one bill. *A fifty-dollah bill.* No more." She began to cry into a piece of dishtowel.

"Sister Williams, I can't say I am at all surprised to hear this, no, ma'am. What with the likes of those music people who delivered this child to us, it's a wonder any money arrived at all, that is, if there ever was such a sum to deliver."

Chloe jumped to her feet and screamed through her tears, "Auntie Josephine would not lie. She is my auntie! She loves me!"

Dr. James Herod puffed his pipe and raised his eyebrows. Armintha Williams raised her voice and her hand. Chloe Boisvert ran out of the reverend's office, out of his house, and down St. Victor Street.

***

On his first day at Abbeville Public School, PJ's new teacher held him after class to set him straight on how things were. Though he hadn't caused any trouble, the teacher delivered her proactive scolding. When he stepped out of the schoolhouse and into the afternoon light, three boys were leaning on the stair rail. The largest hopped up and crossed his arms in front of the new kid.

"Whacha think you doin, boy?"

"Yeah, whacha doin'?" parroted one of the sidekicks.

PJ eyed all three. Even from two steps higher, he still had to look up at the big one.

"Goin' home." He tried to pass, but Davey Johnson blocked his way.

"You ain from rown heah."

"That's right."

"Weah you from, boy?"

"Yeah, weyah you from?" It was the other sidekick.

"Texas."

"He! Texas!" Davey exclaimed. "Sheeit. You cain be from Texas." He turned to the other two. "Doan tha say evtins biggern Texas?"

Davey's stooges, Jimmy Sweeney and Bobby Talent, guffawed and nodded vigorously. Davey turned to PJ and poked him in the chest. "An yous jus soam squirt. Yous a runt!"

"Ehva litta got a runt," Bobby added, and the trio laughed.

A dozen or so kids had collected around the steps, having heard something about a fight coming after school. Davey Johnson made an announcement.

"Look like we got us a Texas runt heah now, yeah. Ain we lucky?"

A handful of boys in the front forced hard laughter. A few others laughed nervously, and the rest of the crowd remained silent. All of it confirming Davey Johnson's status at the school.

PJ's blood was coming up. Head cocked, he was readying for the fight when a car horn blared from the street. All the kids walked to school each day, so they all looked surprised to see a young woman behind the wheel of a dusty old Model T with a torn top, waving out the window, oblivious to the tension on the schoolhouse steps.

"Look like ya mama's heah," Davey scoffed. "Go run ta mama, runt boy. I deal wit you laitah."

PJ squared his shoulders and looked the bully straight in the eye. He looked at Jimmy Sweeney, then to Bobby Talent. He scanned the semicircle of onlookers. Some were gawking, but just as many were looking down at their shuffling feet. And there was Odette, still beaming and waving big out the car window. He cocked his head again, trying to read what confidence, if any, actually resided behind Davey Johnson's muddy-brown eyes. Then he turned and walked away.

"Shicken!" shouted Jimmy, emboldened by the retreat.

"Bauk bauk bauk!" Bobby added, grabbing his shirt at the chest and flapping his arms.

"Dat right. Go ta ya mama, runt boy!" Davey Johnson folded his arms on across his chest. "Maybe she offya a teat en fatten you up some."

Pursued by laughter, PJ strode to the Ford, where he paused. The onlookers were dispersing, starting for home, except for a small red-haired boy Davey Johnson had in a headlock. "Welcome to Louisiana, boy!" He shouted. "Anthin you neet, jus come see me, yeah."

Odette couldn't make out the boy's words. With a radiant smile she asked, "Your first day went good, PJ?"

PJ answered with a sigh.

13

THE MUSIC BOX CAFÉ

APRIL 1934

People stopped and stared at the two kids walking hand in hand up State Street, and it wasn't because of their muddy torn clothes and smudged faces.

"Wha ta hell you doin, boy?"

They heard numerous variations of the inquiry, and not a single one addressed to the girl. The Music Box Café was situated on South Louisiana Street below Railroad Avenue, and PJ held the screen door open for his new friend.

"Merci." Chloe stepped past him.

The dining room smelled of fried shrimp but was empty and quiet, dark with the shades pulled against the afternoon sun. PJ let the screen door slam behind him, and a voice came through the kitchen.

"Menta, who dat?"

"Francie, *go see* who dat."

Francie Chantale bounded through the swinging half doors into the dining room where she stopped abruptly, mouth open. She raised a finger and pointed.

"Who dat?"

"This is my friend, PJ Benoit. PJ, I am pleased to introduce you to my sister, Francie."

"Glad to meetcha," he said with an easy smile.

Francie just stood there, frozen, eyes locked on his outstretched hand.

"What is the trouble?" Chloe asked. "Francie? Est-ce que ça va?"

"He white." She walked back to the kitchen, leaving Chloe confused and embarrassed.

"Don't worry nothin' 'bout that," PJ offered.

Armintha entered from the kitchen. "Sha bon Dieu! Wha done happen ta you, chile?" Her eyes widened on the boy.

"Had a run-in with some jackass bullies down on the creek," PJ offered. An expression of horror spread across the woman's face, and PJ figured it was his language. "Oh, sorry, ma'am."

Armintha collected herself as best she could and set them in a booth, hollering for Francie to bring sweet tea. While Chloe told the story, her aunt stood listening, hands on her hips, mouth agape, trying not to get caught staring at the wiry little white boy. She couldn't help but keep whispering, "I nehvah." When Chloe finished, her aunt cradled her head and kissed her filthy, matted hair.

"Tank you ehvah so, Missah Benoit, for save en dis swee girl."

"It wadn't nothin'. A little swim, y'all."

Chloe leaned across the booth and kissed his cheek. Her aunt's jaw dropped as PJ turned red as a radish. Armintha stuttered, almost yelling, "You, you, you go wash, chile. Weah soak ta dress an seef we kin save soam it."

"Yes, Menta." Chloe skipped off. *Menta* is what Francie had been calling her aunt since the girl arrived in Abbeville all those years ago.

Francie set down two glasses of tea, and as her sister climbed out of the booth, she threw her arms around her, squeezing hard, rocking her from side to side. A foot taller, the older girl leaned her head on the little one as they walked hand in hand toward the kitchen.

"I getchoo a clean towl, Missah Benoit."

"Yes, ma'am, thank you."

Menta walked off, shaking her head. "Bon Dieu."

*　*　*

PJ was working on a fat slice of berry rhubarb pie, crumbs stuck to his somewhat clean face, when Chloe reappeared in a green linen dress with fresh white socks and soggy but hastily polished Mary Janes. Her curly locks lay wet on her shoulders, and to PJ she looked older. The room was dusky with the shades down, but the girl's eyes shone full of life. She kept smiling at him, rocking her shoulders, and his heart fluttered.

"I been tell'n Missah PJ heah bout ta Music Box." High shelves lined with music records ran along each side of the café, and a Victrola sat in the corner. "Toll im how dah records come from yous papa and mama, come tah me wit Francie heah. Would you like to heah soam songs, Missah PJ?"

"You bet."

Melancholy crept over Chloe as it did each time Menta played a stack of records, which was often. The first time, Francie had burst out, "Play, Chlo! Play!" and then talked a mile a minute, telling the whole café how in New Orleans her little sister played piano along with the records.

The first record in this stack dropped. It was Lil Hardin Armstrong's *You're Next,* which opens with a classical piano riff, bridging to the groove that sets up Louis Armstrong's cornet and the smooth Dixieland ballad that follows. During the classical introduction, Chloe worked her fingers along the edge of the booth table as though it were a piano. Her smile lit up the place, and Francie clapped along, cheering, "Go, Chlo! Go!"

The Victrola clicked and dropped the next record, and PJ surprised the ladies by saying he knew it.

"You doan say?" Menta exclaimed.

"How bot dat, Menta?" Francie plopped down next to Chloe and started rolling a small gold ball from palm to palm across the tabletop.

"My daddy liked listenin' to records. He had a colored mechanic, a boy named Sergeant Brown who knew lots 'bout music. Sometimes Sergeant Brown'd bring Daddy a race record from the east side."

"Tah ease side?"

"Yeah, in San Antonio."

"Ain't dat sumpen?" Menta was astounded. "Tis heah a fine dancin song, yessah. Didjor daddy dance wit yah mama to dis song, Missah PJ?"

"No, ma'am. Mama wadn't much for dancin'." PJ's mood visibly darkened. "Not for a long time anyway, since back in Alabama, I s'pose. Mama didn't care much for the race records. One time, my daddy took me with him to somethin' . . . somethin' called . . . a *chittle circus?*"

"Chitlin circuit?"

"Yeah. A travlin' band, right? I think the man's name was Walt. Walt the Creole?"

Menta raised her eyebrows so high she looked like an exclamation point come to life. "Waltah Bahnes an ta Royal Creolians?"

The boy shrugged. "S'pose. It was kinda late at night. We didn't stay long." He scrunched his face and thought hard. "Daddy'd go see a man named Don Albert all the time with Sergeant Brown. Maybe he did some dancin' then. I wadn't there."

Menta burst out laughing. When PJ cocked his head, she covered her mouth, startled by this white boy telling them his daddy went to hootenannies with a bunch of wild, sweaty, and no doubt very drunk black folk. And he brought the boy!

"Didjou dance in Paris?" PJ asked, watching Francie roll the ball.

"Oui, yes. We had lessons at school. Miss Sophie and I would dance at the apartment, also," Chloe recalled wistfully, but there was light in her eyes, and her lips curled into a smile. "It was not like the dancing at La Pomme d'Or, with the jazz music. At the school we danced the waltz."

Menta slapped the table. "Now you waih heah. I be jus a minute," as if they had somewhere else to go. She returned in no time with three plates of peach pie. Francie stopped rolling her ball to reach out with both hands.

"Tankoo, Menta."

"Some day, huh?" PJ sprayed crumbs from his pie-filled mouth. Instead of using the napkin Menta placed in front of him, he wiped with a forearm and laughed. "I tell you what, I'd pull y'all outta a creek fer somma this here pie anytime!"

Menta beamed.

"May I ask you a question, PJ?" Chloe inquired.

"Shoot."

"You said to me that you are new to this place. You came to this place from Texas. Where was it you lived in Texas? I do not know this *Santonio*."

PJ asked for a glass of water and started talking. He told them about moving from Alabama to Texas so his daddy could fly with the Three Musketeers. How there weren't pine trees in San Antonio, and how the rivers in Texas seemed more like creeks running down the middle of a wide patch of stone. "No catfish, y'all." He spoke of wingshooting with his brother, Frank, "Until he moved to Louisiana to work for Mr. Sweetwater." He told them about his daddy's plane crash, how his mama was sick, and how he'd caught a train to Lafayette just two weeks ago.

"But who will take care of your mother?" Chloe asked in a worried voice. A few faint memories of her own real mommy had come to her through the Victrola during the past few days, and they were hurting her.

PJ didn't respond, and Chloe continued, "My mommy was ill. Then she died."

PJ nodded. He didn't want to talk about his mama, but they were all looking at him.

"She ain't that kinda sick."

"Pardon?"

He cocked his head and grimaced. "She's a damn drunk." He picked the last bit of crust from his plate. "And a cokehead."

"Pardon?"

Menta touched Chloe's arm and shook her head.

"My mama's a drunk, and she's on the cocaine. Don't do much of anything but sleep and get high."

"Oui."

PJ straightened up. "Nuff 'bout that." He pushed his empty plate to the middle of the table. "I figure Odette's wonderin' 'bout me. Think I gotta be goin', y'all."

"Missah Benoit . . ." Menta started.

"Dammit!" PJ interrupted her, spitting out her name. "Menta, my name ain't Missah! It's PJ, got it?"

"Yes, Missah PJ. I undastan. If they be anthin I . . ." She waved her hand toward the girls. "Anthin *we* kin do foe *you*, doan choo heztate to axe."

PJ headed to the door. "Nice to meet y'all."

Chloe ran after him and took up his hand. "PJ?" She pulled it to her chin and looked into his eyes. "May we be friends?"

"We already worked that out at the creek, remember?" He was still frustrated, and it showed. Menta came quickly and handed the boy a tin. "Dis fo yo brothah an his bride."

"Thanks."

"They's lucky tah haff you, Missah PJ."

The boy shook his head, but he was smiling again. He looked Chloe up and down, spun on his heels, and headed home.

* * *

Odette gasped. "Sha, bon Dieu!"

Frank came to the door. "Damn, PJ! Where the hell you been?"

PJ handed Odette the tin. "This is from Menta, the lady at the Music Box Café."

Odette opened it to find a pie. Puzzled, she looked at Frank.

"The Negro restaurant in Abbeville?" he asked.

"I met a girl who lives there. Name's Chloe. Pulled her outta Galleque Creek."

"Coulee."

"Huh?"

"It's Coulee Galleque," Frank corrected him.

PJ rolled his eyes.

Frank and Odette stood speechless, looking at this filthy ragamuffin.

"Her eyes shine like a honeycomb in the sun." He tried to pass into the house.

"Stop right there." Odette put two fingers to the boy's chest. "Nobody comen in this house coam a coashon. See that water pump over there? I get you a towel, some soap an some good cloes. You had betta wash good, then you tell us wha happen."

Odette brought out a clean T-shirt, some underwear, and his second pair of dungarees while PJ doused himself with buckets of cool, clean water from the old well. When he finally made it into the house, he found Odette had cut thin slices of the pie, and the three of them stepped out to the porch so the boy could recount his adventure.

"PJ, you make me proud." Odette squeezed him tight, tousled his hair, then licked her fingers to smooth it back down.

Frank held the door for his bride, who took the dirty plates inside. He warned, "You might keep some distance from that Johnson boy. His daddy's Bubba Johnson, the sheriff here in Vermilion Parish. You get sideways with the Johnsons, and things'll come down fast and hard."

PJ frowned. Frank and Odette had been nothing but good to him since he'd shown up on this porch two weeks ago. Frank had always been stern with him. Stern but fair.

Frank shook the boy's shoulder a little and smiled. "We're both proud of you, PJ. You did good today. But don't be makin' trouble that don't need to be made, ya hear?" He turned and went inside.

PJ hollered after him. "Not sure I'm whistlin' Dixie next time I find 'em drownin' somebody, Frank."

Frank hollered back. "Jesus, Mary and Joseph, PJ! What I'm sayin' is leave trouble be when you can leave trouble be."

The boy's arrival in Perry had been a complete surprise to Frank and Odette. He'd written a letter but never mailed it, thinking Frank would put a stop to his plans. He did leave a note for his mama.

Mama,

I am going to live with Frank and Odette.

Goodbye,

PJ

Now Frank had to look past his own grudges and reconnect with Elaine. He'd heard about his daddy's death from Sergeant Hank, whose letter arrived days after the funeral service. His mama never even called. He'd tried reaching her by phone but only ever got PJ, and the last time Frank tried calling, the line had been disconnected. He knew his mama drank hard but didn't know how far it had gone. PJ hadn't said much since arriving, but from what little he had said, it seemed he'd been pretty much making his own way.

Odette suggested there'd be no harm in keeping the boy for a while until the situation could be sorted out. There were six weeks of the school year left, so she had enrolled him at Abbeville Public School, and Frank had informed his little brother he'd be returned to San Antonio sometime during summer. PJ just kept his mouth shut. He had no intention of returning to Texas and figured if he could make himself useful to Frank and Odette, he'd earn his keep here. This played in his mind as he pondered Frank's warning about Davey Johnson.

* * *

Frank first met Odette while visiting the Sweetwaters in Lafayette during the summer after the King Ranch hunting trip, the summer of 1932. Frank and Matt got on so well that Edward Sweetwater invited Frank to stay the rest of the summer and work in the family's peckerwood business, which could use the help. Frank was happy for the job and secretly thrilled to remain in close proximity to Matt's twin sister.

During the 1920s, single-family homes exploded in popularity across the country, and to meet demand for lumber, large timber companies grew even larger extracting tons of ancient cypress trees from the old plantation lands of Louisiana. By the early 1930s, most of the easily accessible old growth had been cleared, and the big outfits moved on. Edward Sweetwater's company took to picking at the remains, focusing on quality trees in locations that made it more difficult to extract. He set up small, temporary mills to cut planks on the spot, which he shipped directly to the builders, cutting out the middleman to make an extra buck. The business got its name, *peckerwood,* from the woodpeckers that sustained themselves by flitting from tree to tree, getting a little to eat here and there. The big operators used the term derogatorily, which irked Edward Sweetwater to no end.

During Frank's first visit, Sweetwater told him how he saw it. "Pretty much every month now, one of the big boys closes another mill. They're all leveraged to the hilt and going bust on soft woods. I make a profit, dammit, so who should be laughing?" Frank worked hard and proved resourceful, bringing some good ideas, so Sweetwater invited him back for the following summer, and, at seventeen, Frank was made assistant foreman at one of the sawmills.

That second summer, Odette joined Matt and Frank every other weekend when the boys had two days off to camp on the Ouachita River. She would sit in the shade and needlepoint, while the boys bait-casted for bass and worked catfish with bloodbait on treble-hooks. The boys got along famously, and Frank and Odette's flirtation grew. To Ameline Thebodeaux Sweetwater, the girl's mother, the attraction was obvious. Edward Sweetwater, on the other hand, took no notice, which was for the best. If he had, he would have put a stop to it. He acknowledged Frank for what he was, a hard worker and a quick study, but Sweetwater was intent on his daughter marrying a college man. He was a graduate of Louisiana State University and expected Odette to land a professional, an engineer or a banker. Even better if there was family money. Ameline, though, thought the kids made a good match. Frank was a serious boy, mature for his years. But he was also kind, attentive, and endearingly sentimental. She saw that the kids were in love, and she wanted her daughter to have the kind of relationship she herself never had. And so it was, that second summer, the summer of 1933, that Edward Sweetwater's plans for his daughter were circumvented by nature. Frank and Odette married in September with the girl three months pregnant.

The baby was born in March, a few weeks earlier than expected, so when PJ appeared on their doorstep, Odette and Frank were all of three weeks into parenthood. In their little Sears Model 147 kit home, PJ slept on the floor in baby Molly's room. He knew that to have any chance of staying, he would have to find a less intrusive solution.

* * *

Monday morning, PJ completed his calisthenics, wolfed down Odette's oatmeal, and walked the two-plus miles to school where he found Davey Johnson leaning against the stair railing, supervising Bobby Talent and Jimmy Sweeney as they tormented a pair of girls trying to hurry past.

"Iffa tain't Li'l Tex, ta nigga-loven runt."

PJ locked eyes with Davey as he climbed the steps. Jimmy took a quick step at him, then stopped short when Davey didn't move. "Nigga-loven Tex runt!"

The remainder of the day passed without incident. The afternoon bell rang, and PJ crossed to Louisiana Street and down to the Music Box Café, where he found Chloe reading in a booth.

"Hey, Honeybee."

"PJ!" She ran to the door and hugged him. "How are you?"

"Hungry," he said through a crooked grin.

"Then you shall have pie." Chloe went to the kitchen, and PJ strolled over to the Victrola. The cabinet was as luxuriant as it was when it arrived seven years ago. Menta kept it polished and never let anyone but Francie touch it. Francie was very careful with the machine and the records.

"Peaches. C'est bonne, oui?"

"Yes." PJ was so happy to see her. "Thank you."

The children talked as the Victrola played through a stack of aged Hot Five records. Chloe shared stories about baking with Miss Sophie, and how she missed the scents that wafted from the patisseries she passed on her way to Dr. Maria's school.

"You should show your aunt how to bake those things."

"Oui?"

"Sure. You could sell loads of 'em."

Chloe wondered if Miss Sophie was well, if she was happy.

"So where do you go to school?"

"I do not . . . assisté l'école. No school."

"Why's that?"

"My aunt, she needs me, here, at the café. I have met Dr. Herod. The man who has, l'école noire . . . *the black school*, in Abbeville. Dr. Herod says my education is already, hmmm, further than I may achieve at his school."

"So, you're gonna work here?"

"Dr. Herod has offered to tutor for me. But I do not know . . ."

"Tutor? What's that?"

"To teach only one student in a manner unique. You see, Auntie Josephine . . . well, she is not my aunt . . ." Chloe struggled to find the words. "Money was sent with me. I did not know of it, during the travel. But then my Aunt Armintha . . . *Menta* . . . says to me someone stolen the money. I do not know if there is money to pay to Dr. Herod." Her shoulders slumped. "But, yes, I will work here, in the café. I am with my sister, Francie, and this is good."

"She seems nice. Is she a mongoloid?"

Chloe shuddered. "My sister, she has . . . des difficulties. Mais oui, we are fine." Her tone was angry. "Now that I am here with Francie, it will be good for us. Bon pour les soeurs, oui. Chloe Boisvert and Francie Chantale. The sisters."

They sat in silence while PJ finished his pie.

* * *

In late June, Frank took time off work to return PJ to San Antonio. He chewed jerky and watched his little brother sleep in a second-class seat, picturing the boy hopping those freight trains. That took brass, but he wasn't about to acknowledge it. Not knowing what he'd find at his mama's house, Frank checked them into a hotel, gave PJ a dollar for a sandwich and a soda and told him to not to wander off. PJ wanted to see Pumpkin, but Frank said "later."

No one was at the Benoit house when the cabbie dropped Frank there, so he sat shaded on the porch for a couple hours before an oil-burning Dodge coupe creaked to a stop in the street. Elaine stumbled out of the passenger's side. Frank made a thin man with a thin mustache and dark fedora behind the wheel. Elaine staggered up the walk.

"Who was that?"

"Just a man."

"Not much of one, if he can't even open the door for a lady." Frank pulled the screen door open.

Elaine clucked. "Much of a man." She reeked of cigar smoke and booze sweat. Ashen bags protruded from under her jaundiced eyes.

Frank tried getting straight to the point, but soon found there was no point to get to. His mama was a shell of a woman. No care, no remorse. He guessed the army pension wasn't enough to cover the mortgage and her habits. Probably why the phone was out. She ignored the question when he asked about PJ. Instead, she started griping about all the Okies coming into Texas.

"That's what they call it, you know. *Dust Bowl.* Fits perfect. Bunch of dirty, good-for-nothin' mongrels."

The irony didn't register with him, but it worked to convert what pity he arrived with to disgust. Less than twenty minutes later, Elaine was pouring her third drink, and Frank was done. He excused himself and walked out the door. He took a deep breath on the porch while a dirty yellow dog, not much more than skin and ribs, eyed him from across the road.

"Pumpkin?"

The sad-looking beast's ears perked some.

Frank unclipped a rope from the doghouse and approached the mangy Labrador, who backed away. He pulled the last bit of jerky from his shirt pocket, and flicked it to the dog, who snatched it out of the air and tossed it back like an oyster.

"C'mon." Frank waved at the dog and started the two miles back to the hotel on foot, Pumpkin following a ways behind. The day had become a scorcher, and he was soaked in sweat by the time he found PJ sitting alone, spinning an empty Dr. Pepper bottle on the hotel lobby bar. When Frank asked for a bowl of water, PJ lit up and ran out the door.

"Pumpkin!"

The dog startled and jumped back, then recognized the boy and crawled forward, her head low. PJ dropped to his knees and took her ears in his hands. They were gritty with mange and jumping with fleas. She sniffed at the jerky in his shirt pocket and nipped his finger as she tore it from his grasp.

"She's coming home with us." Frank set the bowl down.

"*Us?*"

"Yeah."

"What about Mama?"

Frank shook his head. He tied Pumpkin out back in the shade and gave the restaurant manager a dollar for some kitchen scraps and an assurance that no one would bother the dog. That evening, he and PJ ate tough steak and boiled potatoes at the hotel restaurant. Frank sipped a beer and thought everything through. Afterward, PJ sprayed Pumpkin with Flit, soaking her good, then soaped her up. Her belly was a flea-bitten mess, but the mange wasn't bad. He pulled off his sweaty T-shirt to let her sleep with it.

The next morning, the brothers boarded the train. Pumpkin, skinny and weak but clean, was tied off in the baggage car. The brothers played acey deucey, laughing for hours as the train rocked through East Texas. PJ showed Frank how to play vingt-et-un. "That's twenty-one in French. Chloe taught me." PJ kept walking back to baggage to check on Pumpkin, and she lit up more with each visit. As they crossed into Louisiana, Frank told him the story of their Creole ancestry, just as Big Jack told it to him years ago in a duck blind on the Alabama River.

The Benoits were of French descent, Acadians who crossed the Atlantic early in the eighteenth century to settle in what was now Nova Scotia. For three generations they did well with a fishing business until, in the mid-1700s, the British forced the Acadians out during the Great Expulsion. The Benoit clan migrated south to the Carolinas, where, for need of cheap labor, the British were more tolerant of other immigrants. Soon thereafter, the Benoit clan pulled up to start afresh in French Louisiana, where for another century they flourished on the water's bounty, crabbing and shrimping, then further inland with crawfish and catfish. PJ couldn't stop laughing when Frank told him about the origin of crawfish.

Odette met the train at the Lafayette rail station. They bought a watermelon and meat sandwiches at the market and had a picnic near the courthouse, where she suggested they tidy up the attic so PJ could have his own room.

The next day after school, PJ walked down Louisiana Street again. When she caught sight of him entering the café, Chloe sprinted from the kitchen and threw her arms around him.

"Mon Dieu, mais . . . you returned to Texas?"

"Didn't work out."

"You will live here, in Abbeville, yes?"

"Down in Perry, yeah."

"Mon Dieu!" She wiped a tear from her cheek and kissed both of his, pulling away from him with a big smile.

He wolfed down a cup of gumbo while Chloe sat and watched, grinning from ear to ear. Menta set a plate in front of him.

"Crawfish étouffée."

PJ started the story Frank told him on the train.

"So when the Acadians got kicked out of Canada, the lobsters missed 'em so bad, they set off to find 'em, see? Them lobsters walked and walked and walked, searchin' everywhere. The journey was so long and so hard, hikin' over mountains, sailin' the seas, that they lost a lotta weight. By the time they found us in Louisiana, they'd lost so much weight they were tiny! So everyone had a big ol' party, and the tiny lobsters got a new name."

"Crawfish!" Francie shouted.

Chloe was stunned. When PJ started laughing again, she understood she'd been fooled.

"I did not know your ancestors were Acadian."

"Yeah." He wiped his plate with bread crust. "This étouffée's somethin'. Thank you, ma'am."

"I, too, mmm, . . . je suis descend à les Acadians."

"Huh?"

"Mommy's people, they were French. The Boisvert family émigré . . . emigrate, yes . . . from France to Acadia early in the, the . . . le dix-septième siècle. Seventeenth, yes? A hundred years passed, and they were . . . how to say . . . exclue . . . expelled, yes? The same as with your family. But they returned to Canada from the Carolina after the British . . . assouplissement des restrictions. Some families then departed again . . . le dix-neuf siècle . . . the nineteen century, to try Saint-Domingue, l'île d'Hispaniola. Yes, in eighteen four the Haïtienne esclaves . . . the slaves, *yes?* . . . ont gagné leur liberté . . . gained liberty from the French. Ce fut la première rébellion vicotrieuse pour des esclaves en deux millenium. My Acadian family married les esclaves libérté, les gens de couleur libres, *yes?*"

PJ got the gist of it.

"La famille de ma mere . . . my mommy's family came to New Orleans from Haiti."

"So that's why your skin's so light. You ain't all black."

"Plus de sel que de poivre."

"Huh?"

"More salt than pepper, that is what my uncle Paul said to me." She continued. "My mommy's family . . . how to say . . . combiné de nombreuses ascendances . . . put together many . . . ancestries? Yes, from many places. France. Mikmaq. Espana. My papa, ses ancêtres etaient africains . . . from different . . . *tribes?* I know of Gyaaman, but do not know the other tribes. Slaves that had been brought to Louisiana. Mais . . . but the condition of the slavery . . . the masters put more salt to the recipe, yes? My uncle Paul told me this story. He moved from New Orleans to Paris before I was born in New Orleans, before my mommy married my papa. Uncle Paul showed a book to me, a book written by my mommy, a book that tells this story. But Miss Sophie and I could not find the book before *les banquiers*, they locked the apartment at Rue de l'Odéon."

He understood only some of what she said, but he loved to hear her talk. Her words felt soft and smooth. They floated in the air and caressed his ears. He soaked up the last drop of étouffée with the last bit of bread. "Sounds like we're related."

The sad look on her face melted away, and she covered her mouth, giggling. "It could be that some people from our families married in Acadia, in Carolina, maybe in Louisiana, yes?" She smiled. "But I do not think that makes us family, PJ."

He belched, nodded, licked his fingers, and looked up to find her staring. "*What?*"

14

FUTURES

MARCH 1939

The girl had hardly touched her plate.
"Lucille, you wunt some rice, Sha?" Odette held out the bowl.
"No, tank you, ma'am. It very tasty, but I couldn fit anotha bite."
Frank noted the disappointment on his wife's face. "I'm stuffed! The duck in that gumbo was real tender, Bebe. Great supper."
"I like it when the corns pop open when I bite 'em." Molly, the oldest, was nearing her fifth birthday.
PJ had started up with Lucille, one of the six Mouton daughters, last summer as they were both coming into their senior year at Abbeville Public School. Her daddy had been with the Louisiana and Arkansas Railway before he was let go back in '33. Two years later, he got a job as a WPA construction supervisor, working out west, so it was just the women at home, and Lucille and her sisters raised eggs and worked a few acres, canning okra for market. The money coming in from California was their saving grace.
Everyone knew PJ would join the army after graduation, and Frank tracked down Claire Chennault, who he learned was over in China, to request a recommendation for the boy's acceptance into the air corp. Lucille's mother figured life as an officer's wife would suit her oldest girl just fine. Odette thought Lucille shy and a little dim, but she was a sweet girl, and it could be a good match. What none of them knew was that PJ had interest in another, someone with whom he'd been seeing secretly for some time now. He appreciated the deception that dating Lucille enabled, and his real girl knew the truth

about his feelings. Still, some days he worried, and a lot more lately because he knew Lucille wasn't nearly as shy or as dim as Odette believed. In fact, Lucille had a crush on an older boy from up in Lafayette, a guy who'd resurrected an ancient Indian motorcycle that burned oil something awful. A few kids from school, including PJ, knew she'd sneak off for rides in that bike's rickety sidecar. PJ figured it wouldn't be long before Lucille got pregnant, and he was likely to get pinned for it.

When he'd returned from walking her home, Odette sighed, "She's so, so sweet."

"I ain't marryin' her!"

"Nobody a-dee-rein bout nobody gettin' married." Odette got her back up.

"You don't hafta say anything, Odette. Here's how it is. I don't need no wife to fly airplanes, and I ain't interested in bringin' Lucille Mouton along when I leave."

"Mais PJ, nobody a-dee-rien . . ."

He interrupted, even more tersely. "Look. I know you like her. I know Frank likes her. But I ain't interested, and I don't see the point of datin' her when it's all gonna be done in a couple months anyway. So don't invite her over here no more, okay? I'm not askin' her out again, and I'm gonna tell her that on Monday after school."

Frank agreed it was for the best. "He needs to focus on his career, Bebe, and maybe have a little fun." But when he and PJ were alone, he chided his little brother. "Don't you use that tone of voice in this house. It's disrespectful of Odette, and it's disrespectful of me."

PJ stomped out. "C'mon, Pumpkin."

***

"Come, sit here, child." Dr. Herod tapped the arm of the loveseat set in the corner next to his reading chair. "We have something important to discuss today."

Chloe folded her hands in her lap, curious and hopeful.

"I've known you for what, five years now? How quickly time goes by. I can remember the day we first met. Can you?"

"Not really, Dr. Herod, no."

"Ha! And here I presumed I made some kind of impression."

"No, no, it's just that . . ."

The reverend held up his hand. "Never you mind. My pride is uninjured, Miss Boisvert." He started again. "I remember very clearly the day we first met. You had your hair pulled back with a white bow. White gloves, legs crossed at the ankles. Sitting where you are right now, a little lady straight in from Paris, France. Une petite jeune fille, oui? My, my, Abbeville had never seen the likes of you. Here was a proper, thoroughly educated, eleven-year-old black child. Praise the Lord. I can't say Abbeville had ever seen a proper, educated child of *any color*, and here you were in my office. Mrs. Herod and I talked long into that night, I do recall. 'Whatever shall we do with this one?' was what I said. You had already surpassed the learning our school could provide, and certainly it would not do for you to waste away, serving red beans and rice in the Music Box Café for the rest of your life. I must admit, it was Mrs. Herod's idea. She deserves *all* the credit. She said to me, 'James, you take that sweet girl under your wing and school her yourself.'"

He paused, as if he were preaching to the congregation and was awaiting their response. Chloe squirmed a little in her seat. "Yes, Dr. Herod. I appreciate all you and the Mrs. Reverend have done for me over the years. I am deeply grateful."

The reverend beamed. "Listen to those words! Yes, praise God Almighty! Your diction is to be admired, Miss Chloe."

The girl flushed, wishing he'd get to the point, and she hoped that point would be what she was waiting for. But the reverend had a lot of words left in him.

"And what you've done for your sister, Francie. My, oh my. Just last week after service she told me the funniest story. Oh, what was it now? Something about a frog, yes. But her speech, the clarity! You've done wonders for that young woman, dear child. She sounds nearly like a normal person."

Chloe flinched.

"Miss Chloe, we have something to discuss."

She took a deep breath and exhaled slowly as the reverend cleared his throat.

"As you know, I took it upon myself to engage correspondence on your behalf with the leaders of the finest Negro colleges in this country. I believe with all my faith that you will make a fine student, and I communicated as much to my academic friends and colleagues."

Chloe scooched to the edge of her seat, her shoulders back and her eyes wide. The reverend took a sip of water.

"It is with great pleasure that I inform you, Miss Chloe, that my dear friend, the Reverend Mordecai Johnson, President of Howard

University, has confirmed his interest in your matriculation at his prestigious school."

"Mon Dieu!" she screamed, jumping to her feet. She blushed deeply and worked to regain her composure. "I am terribly sorry, Dr. Herod."

"It's nothing, child," he chuckled. "Let us interpret your exclamation as heartfelt thanks to the Lord. And better yet, let us pray."

The reverend leaned over and took her hand. "Our Heavenly Father and Christ, our Lord and Savior, please hear our words and accept our thanks and praises for all of the blessings you bestow upon us, and for . . ."

Chloe's mind wandered to Howard University. She didn't know what it looked like, had never even seen a photograph, and so pictured in her mind's eye the weathered gray façade of the Sorbonne in Paris. She tried to picture other students, like herself, and wondered how they would dress. Would they look like students in Paris, or students in Abbeville? Maybe they would look like adults. What would she wear? She couldn't possibly wear her old ragged dresses, not at Howard University. But she had no money, so what would she do?

The Dr. Reverend cleared his throat, and Chloe opened her eyes to find him looking at her.

"*Amen?*"

"Amen." She repeated.

Dr. Herod let go of her hand.

"You were squeezing pretty hard there, child. I thought I might lose a finger or two," he joked, and she fidgeted. "But I'm not certain your intensity was a fervent reaction to my prayer."

Chloe flushed again. She was sweating.

"No, Dr. Reverend. My mind wandered. I'm terribly sorry."

"To where did your mind wander, child?"

Chloe explained she didn't fully understand how it would work. She thought that Dr. Herod might be presuming a scholarship, knowing she could not possibly afford to pay for college. But even then, how would she live without any money? She pinched at her dress.

"Oh, Miss Chloe. There is sufficient time to prepare. You see, the Reverend Johnson, he was quite taken with your qualifications, but he expressed concern about your age."

"Pardon me?"

"Yes. He believes it best to give you another year of maturation before commencing your studies."

Her heart fell to her feet. Her disappointment was obvious, though the reverend chose to ignore it. "I must say, dear child, I agree wholeheartedly with Reverend Johnson's assessment. That is, you have been preparing yourself well for study at a fine institution of learning such as Howard University, but another year's growth will ensure it is a successful undertaking. That is why I recommended to Reverend Johnson that he defer your enrollment until next year."

The word echoed in her brain. *Recommended*. Heat rose inside her as she glowered at the reverend. She turned aside her head and bit her tongue. She would not let herself cry.

"Thank you for writing the letters, Dr. Herod."

She stood and asked to be excused.

* * *

A tear rolled off her cheek and dripped onto his chest.

"God I love you."

This is what she would say in the moments after she finished. She could feel her heart beating in her ears.

"I love *you*, Honeybee." He kissed her hair, black with a glow of rich auburn from the sliver of sunlight that pierced a crack in the barn wall. The air in the hayloft was heavy, like there was too much of it stuffed inside, but her tummy tingled. It always did when he called her *Honeybee*. Always, even when she was sad.

She cupped his cheek with her hand. "Do you remember last fall, when the monarchs came?"

PJ grinned crooked as Chloe bounced to her feet.

"They were *everywhere*. We looked out the bay door here, and hundreds, no, *thousands*, were fluttering that way, over the field, flying south." She sat at the edge of the loft, swinging her legs out the open bay. He loved it when she sat nude in the sun. "You were so silly, trying to shoo them out of here, as though they could not find their way without you." She giggled as he pranced around, miming a battle with a swarm of butterflies. "Imagine. Just imagine if our ancestors . . . if they did not come to Louisiana, PJ. What if they kept going south? What if they went all the way to Mexico like the monarch butterflies do, flying all that way from Canada? What if the Acadians had migrated to . . . to say, Michoacán, where the butterflies go? *Imagine*. Today, right now in this very moment, we could be meeting for the very first time. Here I sit, on a park bench in Zitácuaro reading my book, and you come walking along the path. You stop and ask if you may sit by me, and I look at you with caution, with suspicion. You ask me what I am reading. I tell you, but you are not listening. You tell me I have honey in my eyes." She wrapped her arms around his bare legs. "Yes. We would fall in love right now, this very minute. We would marry and have a future together."

PJ grimaced. He knew the tears were coming, and they came. He sat behind her, wrapping her in his arms, kissing her neck. Chloe leaned back into his embrace.

"Look." He pointed at the morning moon. "Moustaches de chaton."

She sniffled and tucked her head under his chin. The kitty whiskers always cheered her, even if just some. Suddenly, she pushed him off and shrieked. Bent over her clenched fists, she formed a ball of rage.

"Damn him! Damn him to hell!" She was up and pacing.

"Good grief!"

She seethed and paced. "The *honorable* reverend."

PJ waited for it.

"Maturation . . . maturation . . . maturation! That pious peg-legged sonuvabitch just wants to keep me here so he has someone with half a brain to talk to in this . . . this shithole of a town! *Maturation*."

PJ finger-whistled out the loft bay. Pumpkin trotted around the side of the barn and sat below them, looking up, panting through a smile.

* * *

For the longest time after Chloe first brought him to the café, PJ was a fixture there. The only white to stay there to eat. He showed up often after school, Francie always greeting him with a big hug. Pumpkin would lie out on the porch and greet every arrival with a wag, so all who came by, or walked by, knew when the white boy was at the Music Box.

After a while, the black folk hardly took notice but remained careful not to speak of any whites while he was there. PJ figured as much but didn't care one way or the other. He loved spending time at the café. He'd help scrub pots and pans just to be useful while scratchy old records played before dinner. When times got hard, there weren't many folks in for dinner, many days there were none.

The young friends would meet to walk and talk along the coulee. Sometimes they'd fish the Vermilion River, south of the railroad bridge. In town, they were known as *that Benoit boy and his nigga girl*, and as a result, most whites wouldn't have anything to do with PJ, and Frank and Odette would get an earful on Sundays at St. Mary Magdalen Church. All of Abbeville knew the black preacher tutored the French girl, and the whites referred to her as his *bouzin predicate*, the reverend's whore. Frank's father-in-law, Edward Sweetwater chaired the Lafayette Parish Chamber of Commerce, which often coordinated with the Vermilion Parish Chamber, and he was not at all pleased to be associated with this disgrace through the stupidity of his son-in-law's little brother. Eventually, Frank let PJ have it. "No more of this nonsense, you understand? You quit going by that black restaurant. You stop seeing that girl. You hear me? This is done."

It'd been two years since PJ last visited the café, and he and Chloe never walked through town together anymore. Instead, they passed notes, tucked behind a loose board in an abandoned shack in a part of town where whites never ventured. They traded coded maps, leaving times and dates for secret meetings. They saw each other at least once a week, most often in the woods south of the railroad bridge, or under the Big Tree off the coulee. It seemed a miracle they hadn't been caught.

Lately, they'd taken to meeting twice a week in an outbuilding on the Hebert farm east of town. The Heberts never missed services at the evangelical church set on the highway north of Lafayette, up near Opelousas, so their place was empty every Wednesday evening and every Sunday from morning until mid-afternoon. Despite Odette and Frank's efforts, PJ never joined them for mass at St. Mary Magdalen's anymore, and to Menta's chagrin, Chloe had been skipping the reverend's services ever since he informed her of her maturation issue.

The kids were in love, and they wanted to make love, but Chloe wouldn't allow intercourse.

"I will not bring life to your baby when I cannot live with you."

PJ suggested they use rubbers.

"So you propose we have intercourse but do not touch each other? That is mere fornication, and I will not have it."

Subject to Chloe's rule, they developed a loving, attentive rhythm, and a soft song of sex that would build to a crescendo, then build again, each time they sang it together. "It's no wonder your eyes shine like honey," he would tease. "You taste like you're plum full of the stuff." They were one, and unaware of just how fortunate they were in their intimacy. How rare it was. But they also knew it would have to end.

As was his nature, PJ focused on the moment, the joyous moment. But it was different now. Each time they finished, he pushed down the pain of knowing they would soon part ways.

On the days they didn't see each other, he was good at filling his mind with distractions. Chloe managed pretty well, too. She daydreamed of college, of learning new things, of talking with new and educated people from a multitude of different places, like in Paris. When her anger about the delay disturbed her, she turned her thoughts to the hayloft, and the lovely memories would calm her.

She started meeting Dr. Herod in his office again, but sporadically and only because the reverend had made requests through Menta across multiple Sundays, and she wanted to ease Menta's disappointment. He seemed delighted in their meetings, despite commencing each one by chastising her for missing services. Chloe remained certain she would be leaving for Howard in August if not for the old preacher's selfishness. She often found their meetings interesting, but almost as often she found herself suppressing rage.

* * *

As they dressed, PJ asked about college.

She responded curtly. "I told you last week. There's nothing left to say."

"Yeah, but you were gonna ask him about music."

Chloe huffed. "They are certain to have a piano somewhere at Howard University, and I am confident they will let me use it. That is, if I ever get there. You will have been gone for an entire year before I have any chance, so what do you care?"

PJ pressed on, trying to change the mood. "You know somethin'? After all this time, I've never heard you play. Never been to that church of yours."

Chloe burst out with a cynical laugh. "Oh yes! I can just see it. An usher escorting PJ Benoit, the little white nigger lover extraordinaire, to the front pew at St. Mary's Congregational Church. You would probably hoot and holler like an imbecile at a boxing match when I finished *Amazing Grace*. Maybe you could join the choir, yes? Singing horribly off-key, as you always do." She slipped her cotton dress over her head and walked to the bank of the coulee.

He wrapped his arms around her and squeezed. "That's not all that makes me hoot and holler. I love your amazing graceful . . ."

She put her lips on his before he could finish. They kissed for a long time.

"I am going to miss you terribly, PJ Benoit. That is all I know for certain."

They walked through the woods with Pumpkin at their heels until they reached the fork in the paths. They said their goodbyes and parted ways, and as PJ headed south on the road to Perry, a patrol car rolled up in front of him. It was Sheriff Bubba Johnson's newest deputies. Jimmy Sweeney behind the wheel and Davey Johnson riding shotgun.

"Iffa tain't PJ Benoit, ta Texas runt." After six years, *Texas runt* was still the best Davey Johnson could manage besides *nigga lovah*.

"What you want?" He didn't slow down or look up from the can he was kicking.

"No need ta get wown up. We lookin foe a nigga done stole somma Tippy Stonewall's shickens lass nigh. Figga you migh know sumpen."

Sweeney just missed PJ's feet with a stream of tobacco juice.

"Can't say I know 'bout Tippy Stonewall or her damn chickens, Deputy Davey." He kept walking.

"Hey!" Johnson called as Sweeney backed the car alongside the boy's path.

PJ cocked his head.

"I heah Lucille Mouton jilt you, yeah. Think maybe I hook mah train ta tha caboose."

PJ reached up with a hand and pulled down. "Woo-woo, Deputy Davey." He leaned into Sweeney's window. "Must be nice and cool inside that head of yours, what with the breeze blowin' in one ear and out the other."

"Fuck you, Benoit!" Johnson shouted and slammed his fist on the dash. Sweeney peeled out, spraying gravel on the boy and his dog, covering them in a cloud of dust.

"No shortage of stupid in this damn town, is there P-dog?"

* * *

It was early May when he showed up at the Music Box Café.

"Jus tree week you goan leaf us, Missah PJ." Menta stroked the boy's hair. "You goan fly up en dah sky, en dem airplane." She shuddered. "You could'n geh me in dem ting, no sir!"

"Yeah, maybe I'll fly over Abbeville sometime. Do some loops over the Music Box."

Francie lit up. "Please do!"

PJ smiled at Chloe. Chloe didn't return it.

"What I'll miss most is your pie, Menta."

Chloe glared at him. Menta smiled and wiped tables. She felt love for the white boy but knew it'd be best for everyone when there were some miles between those two kids. Chloe moved over to his booth.

"And why are you here, PJ Benoit? We agreed you would not come to the café."

PJ stuffed his mouth with preserved blackberry cobbler and chewed it slowly behind a big, crumb-flecked grin, his clear blue eyes locked on his lover. "My last piece in Abbeville. Gonna savor it." He chuckled to himself, and she leaned over the table.

"If you insist on being awful, that will be the *last piece* you have in Abbeville."

He laughed and coughed a bit of blackberry as she spun away.

Francie thumbed a deck of cards. "Twenty-one?" She dealt for just the two of them and turned up the jack of hearts.

"He! Mistigri!" Menta was standing over his shoulder.

"Mister Gree?"

"No, *miss-tee-gree*. Ta man wit one eye." She poked the card.

"No, le valet de trèfles, c'est mistigri!" Chloe insisted the jack of clubs was the true mistigri.

"Y'ain't en France no moe." Menta teased. "Y'in Louisiana."

PJ flipped up his down card. "Blackjack." Francie peeked at her down card, grumbled, and left the booth. PJ called after her. "You owe me a matchstick!" He worked on his pie. "Last piece. Yeah, that'd be a shame."

Chloe crossed her arms and squinted at him.

* * *

"You betta be sure bout this." Odette furiously worked her knitting needles, her face twisted as close to a scowl as the sweet thing could manage.

Frank sighed. "The boy's old enough to do what he wants to do."

"He not ole enough to join up, Frank Benoit!" Odette was tearing up. "We shoulda nevah let you lie bout that year in school when you came here."

"Men do it all the time," PJ said, frustrated.

"You hardly seventeen."

"And what were you doin' when you were seventeen, Odette?"

"Don't get smart!" Frank snapped.

PJ and his sister-in-law both angled their chairs away from the other. Frank shook his head and laughed.

"Bebe, remember when this boy showed up here what, six years ago? Jumped trains to ride four hundred miles, comin' all the way from San Antone."

"Mais . . ."

"But what?"

"Your daddy, Beb."

"You think PJ's gonna crash? Jiminy Cricket, Bebe, I've had two hands die on saws just this season. All kinds of work is dangerous. That's how it is."

PJ grinned at his brother, who'd taken up saying *Jiminy Cricket* since he took Odette and the children to see the new Walt Disney movie.

"Not sure you're helpin', Frank. Look, Odette, I've been wantin' to fly ever since I can remember. It's what I was born to do, and now I'm gonna do it. That simple."

She dabbed her eyes and blew her nose in her napkin. "Eh, and what if they doan wont you?"

Frank laughed hard at that one. "Lord, Bebe, look at the boy! He's short and built like a professional wrestler. He's made for an airplane cockpit. Or maybe a circus."

Odette sniffled. "Sha, you gonna look handsome in that unafom."

"I'll have a photograph made and send it to you."

She smiled, wiped a tear, and nodded. "You'll come see us?"

"Sure will."

* * *

Chloe and PJ snuggled on the old blanket they kept stashed behind the hay bales in the Heberts' barn. The midsummer breeze made its way through the loft, cool on their sweaty skin.

"I don't know what I'm going to do without you." She was crying again.

"It won't be long until you're at college, living a whole new life."

"You act like you don't love me!"

"Good grief. You're black. I'm white. What the hell, Honeybee, it ain't legal!" He took two deep breaths. Calming, he continued. "I wanna fly. You wanna go to college. We're gonna have the lives we want, 'cept not together."

She squeezed him tightly. "I know. I know."

He kissed her forehead, her nose, her cheeks. He kissed her ear and sucked the lobe. Chloe was grinding her hips as he worked on the ear. He kissed her neck and started working his way down, kissing and licking her belly. As he approached for another go, she grabbed him by the head, pulling on him to look into her eyes. She cupped his chin and guided him up until they were face to face. She spread her legs and pulled up her knees. Taking him in her hand, she placed him inside her.

They finished together quickly, and she started to sob. With a finger, he traced the small W of dark freckles on her cheek. "My Honeybee."

They walked silently back to town, holding hands. On the way, they crossed with a beat-up flatbed trailing a cloud of dust. Behind the cracked windshield, the surprise on the faces of Joseph and Suzanne Hebert quickly morphed into disgust. PJ looked back at the nine children bouncing on the flatbed to find not one was smiling.

On the café's stoop, Chloe was shaking.

"What's wrong?"

She pulled away.

"What is it?"

Staring at her feet, she whispered. "What if I get pregnant?"

Jack laughed. "You ain't pregnant."

Chloe slapped his face and ran inside.

* * *

Pumpkin lay on the backseat, panting, and Odette sat in front between her husband and his little brother. They started the drive to Lafayette, where PJ would catch the train to San Antonio.

"Plenty of time." Frank eased over the Perry Bridge.

"Good. I've got a stop to make."

Odette looked at the boy and smiled a sad smile.

"Goddammit, PJ."

"Frank! Fay pah sa. No cussin'." Odette chastised him. Her nerves were showing. "Let 'em say goodbye."

Frank cussed some more under his breath as the Ford squeaked to a stop out front of the Music Box Café. He tapped his pocket watch. "You got three minutes, young man."

PJ hopped out and strode to the porch. Francie burst through the screen door. "PJ, doan go!" She squeezed him tightly. "I will miss you very much."

"Francie, I need to see Chloe. Can you go get her for me?"

An eternity passed before the screen door squeaked open. The girl's eyes were red and swollen. "What do you want, PJ Benoit?"

"I want to say goodbye."

"Fuck you." She hissed, squinting at him through bloodshot eyes.

"Look . . ."

"No!" she shouted and looked over his shoulder at the car idling on the street. She pointed a finger in his face and whispered. "You look, PJ Benoit. I could have been pregnant, and you stood right there, laughing."

"But . . ."

"No!" She cut him off again. "You would go off and have your life, and I would be here, stuck forever in this shithole, raising your bastard alone."

She was furious, and he had no idea what to say. She straightened up and crossed her arms.

"But I have been fortunate. My monthly time has come this morning, so I do not have your child in me." She stomped her foot. "So, like you, I will leave this place, but next year. I will attend university, and I will not let a man have me that way again, not until I have achieved all I wish to accomplish. So you go, PJ Benoit. You go fly your airplanes, and you go make some white girl pregnant with your child, so you have to marry her and raise your own child."

He was dumbfounded.

"So, you will just stand there, with your mouth open, drooling like a fool?" She scoffed at him. "You left your mother. You left your Pumpkin. You have always intended to leave me, and that is what you do. You *leave*. I am done with you, PJ Benoit." She spun on her heels and left him on the stoop.

Frank tapped the horn, snapping PJ out of it. But for Pumpkin's panting, they rode in silence all the way to the Lafayette station.

Frank broke the silence on the station platform. "Funny. You came here on a train from San Antonio, and now you're taking a train right back there." He mussed his little brother's hair. "You're gonna make a helluva pilot, PJ." He paused. "You know, you should go see her when you're settled in."

Nothing.

Frank changed the subject. "Here's the *Alamo*."

"The Alamo?" PJ asked.

"The passenger train from New Orleans to San Antonio. It's called the *Alamo*."

"So that's what the Johnny meant." PJ grinned, thinking back to the boxcar he'd shared with the kind hobo. He shook his brother's hand, kissed his sister-in-law's cheek, rubbed his dog's ears, took up the cardboard box he tied with twine, and stepped onto the train heading west.

15

HOWARD AWAITS

APRIL 1940

It was the Saturday after Good Friday, and St. Mary's Congregational Church was buzzing in preparation for Easter services. Chloe was at the upright piano in the sanctuary, paging through the sheet music, the notes in her head, when she felt something under her bottom. A tiny shard of palm from Palm Sunday, when each member of the congregation received a palm leaf tied into the shape of a cross. She trimmed the scrap with her fingernails, tied a tiny cross and tucked it into her hatband to make a gift of it to Francie. She placed her hands on the keys and gave herself to the music.

"That was magnificent, dear child. Just glorious, praise the Lord!"

"Thank you, Dr. Herod."

"Yes, I do believe some, perhaps many, in the congregation tomorrow will be taken aback by this unconventional selection of mine, especially for Easter services. Of course, this will be the sole detour from our traditional hymns and readings. Yes, yes, *He . . . has . . . risen!* Blessed be the Lord." The reverend was radiant, a little unsteady on his cane. "Chopin. All things beautiful, all things bold. His name be praised."

The reverend waited.

"Amen."

"Yes, dear child. We shall celebrate His rising! Our Lord and Savior, with hymn and prayer, and we shall celebrate His promise of everlasting life with your lovely recital of this timeless, classical piece."

Dr. Herod asked her to play it through again, and she obliged, performing flawlessly. The reverend opened his eyes, beaming.

"Miss Chloe, I have news for you. But first I must attend to the ladies helping in the back. They require my direction." Absent reading glasses, he held his pocket watch at arm's length. "Would you visit me at my home office at, say, half past one?"

She thought it must be about college.

Again, the reverend waited.

"Yes, Dr. Herod, of course."

She ran the whole way to the Music Box.

```
Hello, little school girl
Good morning, little school girl
```

Menta welled up at the news.

"Of course I am speculating. But what else could it be? I have not been in his study for months."

Menta smiled and patted Chloe's hand before hobbling back to the kitchen. The woman's ankles were swollen all the time now. Her wrists were stiff and thick, too, but the girls never heard her complain.

"What ah you spec-ooh-lating?" Francie sat down beside her sister.

She didn't know what to say. Francie knew of her college plans, but Chloe was reluctant to talk with her about them. Her idea of leaving for university was always tinged with the guilt of leaving her sister.

"I'm playing at St. Mary's tomorrow."

"I know that." Francie picked up a broom and started sweeping.

"The floor is fine, Francie."

"I keep busy," Francie answered, proudly. "Everything can be . . . improved."

Chloe sat back and considered how much her sister had changed since they'd become reacquainted. Francie was still young for her age, young at heart, and perhaps always would be. But she was so much better at taking care of herself now, and so much more articulate. Still, she worried how Francie would fare after she left.

Times were still hard, and few Negroes could afford to spend money at the café. The whites had quit buying pies years earlier, before the government work programs started putting money back in their pockets. Menta had the garden plat on the edge of town that Uncle Paul had leased for them, prepaid for a decade way back in 1927. Fortunately, the owners moved out west long ago, so no one was asking for rent. Less fortunately, rabbits and thieves ravaged most of the produce before it was fully grown. Best as she could, Chloe rationalized her departure. It was one less mouth to feed, and she would find a job near the college and send what money she could back home.

***

"Come, sit child." Dr. Herod tapped the arm of the loveseat next to his reading chair. "We have something important, and might I say, something wonderful to discuss." The reverend cleared his throat. "It is with great pleasure that I inform you, Miss Chloe Boisvert, that you have been accepted to matriculate this coming school term, commencing September 1940, at Howard University in our nation's capital city, Washington, D.C."

Her heart soared, and she envisioned a lightning bug, freed from a child's cupped hands.

"But!" Dr. Herod punctured the air with the word, and her heart fell. He scooted forward in his chair. "But, that's not the *best* part." She was confused, and he paused again for dramatic tension. "You will receive a full scholarship for tuition, *and* you will have employment at the university, which will cover the costs of your room and board and leave you with a little something extra to cover your incidentals."

Chloe threw her arms around him, startling the old preacher as she tumbled into his lap. She cried out, "Oh, how wonderful! Oh, thank you! Thank you! Thank you!" She kissed his cheeks.

The reverend flustered and patted her back. "There, there, now, child, please, return to your seat."

She was all giggles and tears, a sniffling mess. He handed her his kerchief.

"It was your doing, child. You worked so hard during our private lessons and read so, so many books, it was all I could do to supply them! English, French, Spanish. Young lady, I merely communicated the facts to my dear colleague and friend, the Reverend Mordecai Johnson, and fate was sealed."

Dr. Herod paused to fill his pipe. She tried and failed to suppress the giggles behind her beautiful wide smile. Dr. Herod struck a match and puffed toasty blue smoke into the air.

"I am so grateful to you, Dr. Herod, for guiding me through my studies."

"Well, young lady, while Mrs. Herod and I are rightly proud of the achievements of the students in our school, your preparation in Paris would have been wasted in that comparatively remedial environment." He paused. "And I must add, I not only took great joy in our academic relationship, but your coming here blessed me with the opportunity to learn French, for my own edification and pleasure. I'm sure you do not know, how could you? But I recently finished Victor Hugo's masterpiece *Les Misérables*, at over nineteen hundred pages. This was made possible because Our Heavenly Father, in His infinite wisdom, sent you here to me, ahem, to *us*."

Chloe couldn't feel the ground as she skipped across St. Victor Street, but before she reached Louisiana Street, the seething resentment she'd worked so hard to repress for nearly a year's time overwhelmed her, stopping her in her tracks. With clenched fists, she bent to her knees and screamed, letting loose a terrible, guttural yowl. Breathing hard, almost panting, she was overwhelmed by rage. Rage at the prison, Jim Crow's prison, that she would finally escape. She fell to her knees and wept.

* * *

"Hey, Lieutenant, you wanna join us for a cold one?" Master Sergeant Hank Novak was raring to go.

PJ pulled the big sergeant aside. "I'm comin', but no slipups, all right? I don't need people hearin' nothin' 'bout *Petite Jacques*. The name's Jack."

He didn't know Hank's longtime buddies from the hangar had already heard all about Big Jack Benoit and his sons long before Second Lieutenant Jack Benoit Jr. showed up at Randolph Air Base, or that Hank had sworn them all to secrecy with a clenched fist. Even so, it was only a matter of days before all the officers were addressing him by his childhood nickname.

Like his father before him, the young flyer broke rank to socialize with Hank's pack. The only difference was PJ didn't smoke or care much for alcohol, which made the enlisted men a little uneasy at first. "I don't like a scratchy throat or coughin' in the mornin', and I like to keep my wits 'bout me. Not sure what's so damn wrong with that."

The men frequented a barbecue joint call *The Rack* for brisket, jalapeño venison sausage, and beef ribs that fell off the bone. They washed it down with Shiner Bock longnecks and ice-cold Dr. Pepper over conversation on three topics: baseball, girls and planes. A lot had changed in each of those categories during the twenty-three years Hank had spent in the service.

"During the Great War, we trained flyers in Jennys, pulled by all of ninety horses. Might as well have been riding bicycles up there." He laughed. "We got some Packard Le Pères after the war. Four hundred-fifty horsepower liquid-cooled performance, but fussy little bastards with bad valves." He told tales of air battles over France where biplanes dueled the Kaiser's triplanes, harassed his zeppelins, and hand-tossed twenty-pound bombs into the German trenches below. "On our best days we got 120 miles per hours out of those crates. Now, the lieutenant here is diving near four hundred! And look at what them Nazis did in Spain. They dive-bombed the fuck out of them Republicans, torn 'em to pieces. Pardon my French, Lieutenant."

"No problem, Sarge." PJ sipped a sweating bottle of Triple X root beer. "But I don't think that's French." He whistled to the bartender and waved a circle in the air. "My round, men."

When the Shiners arrived, PJ took one up. "To you guys who keep us up there. The best damn ground crew in the Army Air Corps."

* * *

August was hot as Hades. Plane tires burst on touchdown during afternoon runs, so all training and test flights were scheduled to conclude by 1100 hours. PJ was having a blast. With hostilities in Europe at full tilt, it was just a matter of time before the States would be pulled into the war. Since June, army pilot training had increased a hundredfold, and PJ was pulling time and a half as an instructor. To help meet the need for training hours, PJ and his colleagues were relieved from exercise and drills, but PJ still completed his predawn calisthenics routine every morning, and it drove his voracious appetite. From top to bottom he was muscle-wrapped bone, chiseled features on a compact V-shaped frame. Claire Chennault hadn't known the boy was underage when he sent a letter of recommendation to Washington, and another letter directly to Randolph's commanding officer, General Whitney Briscoe, who made certain PJ was routed to the new airfield that replaced Brooks outside San Antonio. So Briscoe was unaware one of his top trainers was just eighteen years old.

* * *

CHLOE'S MISTIGRI

One fine fall evening, PJ returned to the officers' quarters with a belly full of barbecue to find a letter addressed in Odette's handwriting lying on his bed. On the back of the envelope he found little flowers drawn with a colored pencil.

October 25, 1940

Dear PJ,

Everyone is getting back to how things were before the flood. The people are back home who are coming home, I suppose. Much of the damage has been cleaned up, and we are hopeful to have normal by Christmas.

The children are growing fast. I think you would not recognize Junior. He has sprouted at least a half foot since you left us last summer. Molly wrote the most wonderful poem at school, and I have enclosed a copy she made for you.

Frank says, "Hello, PJ." He doesn't want me to write anything about it, but the business is hurting. You know it was not doing good, then the storm broke down two of the big saws. I am worried, but Frank always says worry is wasted on nothing. I pray for him and hope for the best. Your brother is a good man, and I am fortunate to have him. I know with God's help he will find a way through the trouble.

I have news about your friend, Chloe Boisvert. She was ready to go to Howard University this term, but her aunt fell ill. The poor woman is incapacitated. It is her feet. Chloe is staying in Abbeville to run the café and take care of Menta and Francie. I bought a pie from them last week, and Chloe was cheerful and said she would try for college next year. I do not see how that can happen unless Menta recovers. Only God knows. They are fortunate to have Chloe. Imagine if she had not returned home from France.

PJ didn't want to imagine that. He loved the girl, and it hurt to read of her misfortune. He'd been on dates in San Antonio, with uninteresting girls whose conversation bored him straight through. He could see now how remarkable Chloe's stories and ideas were. How much he enjoyed listening to her imagining her future. Chloe was so smart, and yet he never felt dumb with her. He'd been ignorant of so much she'd introduced to him, from her early life and from the books in Reverend Herod's office. He still didn't understand much of what she'd said, but he could see now how she'd brought him into a world of ideas. It was so easy being with her. The San Antonio girls were interested in dancing and marriage, and not necessarily in that order, and they never ceased with the compliments. He didn't want to spend his life driving home to the wife after training pilots all day. Because of Chloe he knew there was a much bigger world out there, and he wanted a piece of it.

16

THE RECRUITMENT

JUNE 1941

The strip of sweat running down the back of Sergeant Hank's khaki shirt spread quickly to form a large, dark triangle from collar to belt as he squinted up into the afternoon sun. Summer came early to Texas, and at 1700 hours on this early June day, the concrete tarmac was pushing 125 degrees. The master sergeant felt like he was standing on a skillet.

Through his binoculars, he watched the P-40B fighter aircraft dive from 8,000 feet, the hum of its 1,150 horsepower engine transforming into a high-pitched scream as it approached the floor. The Tomahawk pulled up and out starboard as it blew past the onlookers less than 200 feet off the deck. Wiping his brow with a red bandana, Hank mumbled, "That kid's gonna give me a goddamn heart attack."

The fighter circled, approached for landing, and came in without issue. It taxied past the sergeant toward the hangar bay door, and ground crew placed a stepladder under the wing. PJ powered down the plane, and Hank inspected the left tire, hands on his hips.

"Jesus, Mary, and Joseph, look at this! Rubber's just no good. Look at that shred, and they're already shipping these birds to Africa." He shook his head. "Gotta be somethin' better than this garbage. In the desert, they're gonna have to change the damn tires after every damn sortie."

The men took shade in the hangar.

"You're a sweaty mess, Sarge," PJ laughed, his own uniform soaked through. He pulled two Dr. Peppers from the cooler. "Buy ya a beer tonight?"

Hank looked at him sideways. "You gonna try to take me to that colored joint again?"

"The only place in town with real music."

"I ain't goin'."

"You're just sayin that cuz you can't dance to save your life."

Hank was red from the heat and getting redder.

"All right, all right." PJ threw up his hands. "We'll go to that fleabag you call a saloon where they play that hillbilly station all night."

Hank chugged the soda and perked right up. "Now you're talkin, Lieutenant."

It was approaching a year since PJ had come to Randolph Field and two months since the last time he'd had the nightmare. Shooting marbles on the dirt patch near the tire swing when the army car squealed to a stop. Two skeletons step out. One's wearing a flyer's helmet and goggles. The other has a big, clanking chain around his neck, with a silver crucifix swinging as the two sets of bleached bones double-time up to the front porch.

"You know somethin', Hank?" PJ said, twisting on his barstool and sipping a ginger ale. "No one ever told me how he died."

The master sergeant kept turning his beer mug on the bar. "He crashed, Lieutenant. You know that."

"Yeah, but how . . . how'd he die? The plane rolled, right?"

Hank drained his mug and waved the bartender over. "Big Jack . . . your daddy was testing one of the new Peashooters. Those little bastards were the engineering equivalent of a carnival freak show. Unstable, resonance into the fuselage, nose-heavy. A complete mess. So Big Jack bounces in, and the damn thing comes right over its nose." He slapped the bar. "The propeller shreds as it flips, and there it is, damn thing top down, tipped on a wing." He picked up his fresh mug and swigged. "Had an open cockpit with a reinforced headrest, on account of being nose-heavy. But that weld . . . well, damn thing snapped clean off. Drove a stress fracture, a big ol' crack, right back through the fuselage all the way to the tail. Never seen anything like it, before or since." Hank bowed his head. "Broke your daddy's neck, Lieutenant."

"But these P-40s," Hank continued, "they're something else. Goddamn beasts. The B Model modifications cleared up a lot of the problems. You remember the seals on the A Model were shit."

PJ nodded. It felt good in the Tomahawk. Sturdy, rugged even, pulled by a powerful, air-cooled engine that tuned well. The new model could climb 3,000 feet a minute, faster than anything else in the sky. A cruise speed of 350 miles per hour and full-throttle dives topping out at an indicated speed of 420 miles per hour which, dropping from 20,000 feet, was actually well over 500 miles per hour. At those speeds the pilot had to counter extreme torque using the left flap pedal to prevent yaw, which resulted in PJ's developing a left calf muscle a full two inches larger in diameter than his right.

He pointed his empty ginger ale bottle at the bartender. "They're saying the British Spitfire and some Jap models could out-turn it. One of the engineers said it's somethin' like the German Messerschmitt 109, but with more power. It's a hit-and-run machine."

"Makes sense." Hank agreed. "Get in, get out. But Goodrich, Goodyear, one of 'em, they gotta figure out somethin' that won't shred on a desert runway."

They toasted the P-40B and clinked mugs.

Moon in all your splendor know only my heart
Call back my rose, rose of San Antone

"I liked this song better before they added the words." Hank finished his beer. "Your daddy was a good man, Lieutenant." He grimaced and belched. "But he was . . . he pushed it hard."

"He was a test pilot, Sarge. That was his job."

Hank shook his head. "I don't mean any disrespect, Lieutenant. I admired your daddy. I still do, dammit. No one worked harder 'round here than Big Jack. But sometimes, well, I just think he took some risks that maybe he didn't need to take. It's a dangerous job, sure, and you're damn good at it yourself, Lieutenant."

PJ smiled.

"But like that pullout today. You ain't testin' nothin' at two hundred feet that can't get done at five hundred, understand? It ain't war, not yet anyway. Yeah, you gotta stress the machine. But don't add risk when it don't add nothing, that's all I'm sayin'."

"You sound like Odette, Sarge." PJ paid the bill. "Let's get outta here. Tomorrow's another early mornin'."

PJ drove the Jeep back to base. He'd had his ginger ale and nursed a Shiner Bock.

The next morning, he took a squadron of navy flyers up on a predawn sortie. They were cocky to a man, navy always were. The other army trainers griped about the navy flyers' attitudes, and how they were always saying they were looking forward to "getting the hell outta there" as soon as possible. But PJ didn't mind. Whether it was natural disposition or stemmed from his disciplined habits, so long as the people he worked with showed respect through effort, he didn't care what they had to say. Landing on a carrier that's rolling on twenty-foot seas is tough business, and so long as their confidence didn't make for recklessness, their cocky attitudes were just fine with him.

PJ flew above and off formation, admiring the tight V of the squadron, the rising sun reflecting brilliantly off each silver fuselage. He gave the order, and the squad leader rolled and dove, followed first by each of the four planes off his right wing, then the three on the left, the formation looking like a strand of pearls pulled toward earth. It was a sight to behold.

PJ touched down first, just past a thick yellow line on the runway, then throttled back up. The navy flyers followed suit with touch-and-goes between the carrier runway patterns painted on the tarmac. Each pilot hooked a cross wire on his last touch.

* * *

Both the army and the navy had dramatically increased the number of pilots in training. The politicians didn't talk about it, and the civilian population wasn't ready to hear about it, but war was coming, and the services understood. Really, the United States was already fighting the German Nazis and the Italian Fascists through lend-lease, supplying the British and Free French with war materiel in England and North Africa. Likewise in Asia. America was leading the neutral country embargo of resources to Japan, impairing the Empire's ability to complete its four-year-old invasion of China. Roosevelt was secretly considering a complete halt of oil exports to Japan. With the Empire relying on the States for 90% of its oil supply, a full US boycott would all but require the Japanese to either sue for a settlement with China or gamble everything by invading Siberia, British Malaya, or the Dutch East Indies to obtain oil. It was highly unlikely the Japanese would be willing to lose face in China, and given the Tripartite Pact among the Nazis, the Fascists, and the Empire, war with one nation would mean war with all three. Roosevelt's secrecy notwithstanding, the high brass in the armed services knew it was just a matter of time before Americans would be fighting all around the globe.

* * *

PJ took a pull from his Dr. Pepper and watched Hank fiddle with a fuel pump. A new mechanic named John McClintock who arrived at Randolph just that week came by with a message.

"Lieutenant Benoit? Yeah, the commander wants to see you. Sent a major over here. If I may say, sir, the major seemed pretty hot."

PJ shrugged and snagged a corporal to drive him to headquarters. The Jeep's brakes squeaked something awful when they stopped in front of two MPs.

"Really, Corporal?"

"Sorry, sir. I'll see it's taken care of right away."

Inside, PJ saluted the colonel. "Sir."

"At ease, Lieutenant. Have a seat." Colonel Landon struck a wooden match with his fingernail and started his pipe. "So, Washington has a plan to help the Chinese."

"Sir?"

"No doubt you're aware the Japanese own the air over China. Their bombers are making hell on the mainland, no resistance. Terror from the sky."

"Yes, sir."

"Well, there are some recruiters here, and even though I have thousands of pilots to train, my orders say I'm not to get in their way." The colonel blew three perfect smoke rings. "You've heard about this?"

"No, sir."

"They arrived yesterday. They'll be at the Gunter Hotel for a couple of days, tempting my pilots and crew." He leaned back, puffing his pipe.

"Thank you for informing me, sir."

Landon blew a puffy ring over PJ's head. "Well, General Briscoe thought you, particularly, would want to know. That's why I called you here."

"Particularly, sir?"

"Because of Chennault."

PJ's adrenaline surged. "Claire Chennault, sir?"

"That's right. No doubt you know he's been training the Chinese Nationalist Air Force for a few years now. Seems they're itching to bring the fight to the Japanese homeland. Looking for multi-engine drivers and escort flyers. They want to hit the Japs where they live. Burn Tokyo. Put some competition in the air. Something along those lines."

PJ pondered. "Anything else, sir?"

"That's all, Lieutenant."

"Thank you, sir." As he was leaving, he turned back. "May I ask, sir, what do you think about all this?"

Colonel Landon lit another match and put it to his pipe. "No, Lieutenant, you may not."

* * *

That evening, PJ drove a borrowed car to the Gunter Hotel in downtown San Antonio. The basement was locally renowned as the Caveteria, a massive cafeteria-style restaurant known for its generous Mexican dinners of tamales, frijoles, and chili. It was *the* place to be after a night at the theater, or as its own destination for a family night downtown. PJ spotted some uniforms way in the back corner. A man in civilian clothes held the interest of a half dozen enlisted men. As PJ reached the table, their conversation was just finishing up, and the soldiers eagerly shook hands with the civilian, who was wearing a summer suit and a black and white polka-dotted tie loosened at the neck.

"Evening, Lieutenant." It was John McClintock with a big grin on his face. PJ returned a salute as the enlisted men tumbled away.

The visitor introduced himself. "Skip Adair, CAMCO."

"Lieutenant PJ Benoit. Say again?"

Adair waved PJ to a chair, lighting an unfiltered Camel. "CAMCO. The Chinese Aircraft Manufacturing Company. I work for a man named William Bond. We're looking for help."

A young Latina waitress in a white peasant dress approached, and Adair shook his glass. "I'll have another bourbon, sweetie. Ice. You?" He gestured to PJ with an open hand.

PJ met the girl's gaze. Her dark eyes reminded him of the waitress in that little town on the way to the King Ranch. *Juanita? Alice?*

"Just a glass of water, please, with a slice a lime."

She curtseyed. "Sí, señor."

The shape of her smile and her lowered eyes betrayed her interest, and as she walked away Adair said, "You got a way with the ladies, huh, Lieutenant?"

PJ smirked. "Not so much, Mr. Adair."

"Hell, call me Skip," Adair laughed. "So, Lieutenant. What do you know about this endeavor?"

PJ related what he had heard from Colonel Landon. "Major Chennault and my daddy flew together. I met him when I was just a kid."

Adair grinned. "That long ago, huh? Then I suppose you know he's a colonel now with the Chinese, basically runs their air force."

"No, Daddy . . . my father . . . he died a few years back. I can't say the major, that is, the colonel and me . . . well, we haven't kept in touch."

"No, I wouldn't suppose so." Adair smiled as the waitress returned with their drinks.

"So, what's it all about?" PJ asked.

Adair explained. Chennault had been training the Chinese Air Force in antiquated Russian equipment for the past three years. "Not a chance against the newer Jap equipment," he added. "So Chennault proposed to Generalissimo Chiang Kai-shek, the man who runs China, that they make a run at the US for materiel support. The Generalissimo's wife, Madame Chiang, well, she's a Wellesley girl."

"*Wellesley?*"

"A fancy college up in the northeast states. Very cosmopolitan woman, Madame Chiang, and very well connected here in the States. She came over a while back and made a hell of an impression in Washington. It's taken some time, but Roosevelt's all in. Of course, this is all on the q.t., politics, you know. Roosevelt agreed that in addition to supplying equipment, we could recruit American pilots. So," he stubbed his cigarette butt, "here we are."

"So we're going to war with Japan?"

"Not exactly," Adair continued. "We have permission to recruit. When we get a *yes*, the serviceman immediately resigns his service. We hire him to work for CAMCO, and he has no more ties to the United States military. He gets papers and a passport that lists some occupation that has nothing to do with the military, not even with flying. We're scheduling the first supply trips for later this month, early July at the latest. The crews closely follow."

Adair added some details, and the whole idea was astounding. The United States was officially neutral regarding the Second Sino-Japanese War, but the president had secretly agreed to send American planes with American crew, not only to defend the Chinese from Japanese air attacks, but to bomb the Japanese mainland.

PJ was stunned. He leaned in. "So, if I'm interested?"

"Squadron leaders will be paid $700 a month, flight leaders $650, and pilots $600. And Madame Chiang's promised another $500 for each confirmed Jap kill."

"Holy cow!"

"So, Lieutenant, what's your story?" Adair lit another Camel and swung his legs up onto a chair. "Because to tell you the truth, you look like you should be in high school."

PJ described his nearly two years in the air corp. No one had logged more hours in P-40s than the test pilots at Randolph, of which he was one. He let the crack about high school go.

"Sounds right. Your colleagues, R.T. Smith and Paul Greene, they signed on earlier today. Smith is coming in as a squad leader. Makes sense you'd come in as a flight leader. How's that sound?"

"Why not?"

The men stood and shook hands.

"Sure you don't want a drink?"

PJ declined.

"Right. You go to the commander's office at Randolph, and then we'll be in touch."

As PJ turned to walk out, he bumped right into the dark-eyed waitress.

"Sorry, miss." He strode out with his head buzzing, passing another handful of enlisted men who were making a beeline to the table in the back.

* * *

"I hear you had a big date last night, Lieutenant."

It took a moment for PJ to catch Hank's drift. "Well, you might want to go on a date yourself, Sarge," PJ winked.

Hank shook his head. "Old dog, new tricks."

Everything was settled by the end of the week, and a few days later, PJ had booked a second-class seat on the *Alamo* and was standing on the train platform next to his duffle. He wasn't much for possessions. He owned a fly rod, a cane pole, two shotguns, and a short stack of records with nothing to play them on. All of that plus his winter coat, he was storing in a friend's attic. When the whistle blew, he thought back to his first train out of San Antonio, Pumpkin running aside, fading into the night. A whistle woke him some hours later. The train was slowing into Houston, and he looked out at a familiar sight. A hobo camp. Not so big, this one. PJ pulled out his old knife, locked the blade in place and turned it in the sunlight. He wiped a smudge with his thumb. "What was that piece of shit's name?"

17

GOODBYE

JUNE 1941

He stepped off the train and into the humid blood-orange sunset, his crisp, cotton shirt open at the collar, a razor-sharp crease running the length of each leg of his army-issue khakis. Lafayette had grown enough to support a taxicab, and there it was, the driver asleep behind the wheel. PJ slapped the door. "Take me down to Perry?"

"Sure thing, son. You wanna sit in back or in front?"

As the car rumbled down Highway 167, he dangled his arm out the window and watched the fireflies dance over the ditch weed. Mars and Venus shone through the dusk near a bright quarter moon. A small covey of quail were eating sand up a side road, and he counted seventeen whitetail deer before the cab reached the Vermilion River bridge. He instructed the cabbie to stop outside the Music Box, where the *Closed* sign hung crooked behind the screen door. A rectangle of low light glowed behind the drawn window shade.

"You gettin' out here, son?"

"No. Take me back to the hotel."

"What hotel?"

PJ leaned his head back and closed his eyes. "The Lafayette Hotel."

* * *

It was Sunday. He woke predawn, completed three sets of calisthenics, had a quick shave and shower, and was out the door walking south before anyone else had stirred. The morning air was cool, the grass heavy with dew. He'd walked five miles in the dark when a farmer in a flatbed slowed and offered a ride. PJ gave him a lazy salute and climbed in the cab. He hopped out at the bridge. "Much obliged."

"Good luck with your girl!"

PJ mumbled, "If he knew."

He pulled the screen door, and the stretchy sound of the spring made him smile. The smell of last night's fried chicken lingered in the dining room.

"PJ!" Francie bounded in and body-slammed him. The intensity of her embrace warmed his heart. It occurred to him that he'd spent the past year with no intimacy. He closed his eyes and squeezed her tight. She was twenty-four years old, but he still didn't think of her as a grown woman.

"Why haven't you been heah foe so long, PJ? You want pie?"

"Is Chloe home?"

"Of course. I go get her. You stay here, okay?" She disappeared through the kitchen.

He walked toward the record player and picked a book up off a booth table. *Native Son*. He lifted the stack of records on the turntable, set the arm, and started the machine. As the first record dropped, Chloe stepped through the swinging door.

But if Dinah
Ever wandered to China

"To what do I owe the pleasure?"

I would hop an ocean liner
Just to be with Dinah Lee

His heart ached something fierce. "Just thought I'd come by to see y'all."

"Y'all?"

"Sure."

"Please, have a seat." Chloe wiped a table that was already clean. He sat his sweaty self down. "I'll make you some breakfast."

Luis Russell's "Louisiana Swing" played while Chloe watched PJ eat his fill of eggs, ham steak, and biscuits.

"Good coffee," he offered. "Everything's great."

Chloe lifted her chin and sighed. "I must say I am taken aback by your arrival here. It's been quite some time since we . . . last communicated."

He hadn't written. But he'd thought that was how she wanted it. He wiped his mouth with the faded, checkered napkin. "I wanted to see you. I'm goin' away."

Chloe huffed. "You are *going away?* Ha! PJ Benoit, you are already away."

He tossed the napkin on the table. "You done?"

Francie came over and cleared. "Do you wan moe coffee?"

"No, thanks, Francie. Everything's real good. I'm all set."

She beamed and left for the kitchen.

"So where *are* you going, may I ask?"

"China."

"*China?*" Her eyes grew the size of saucers.

The best he could do was smirk. "Gonna fly for the Chinese. Fight the Japs."

She was speechless. She'd had him back for all of thirty minutes, hadn't even forgiven him yet, or whatever it was she would do, and he was off to China.

He waited.

"So we are at war with the Japanese? There has been nothing on the radio."

"No. I'm done with the army. Gonna work for the Chinese. You remember me tellin' you 'bout Captain Chennault, the one who did airplane tricks with my daddy?"

"I do remember."

"He's runnin' things there, the Chinese Air Force. I'm gonna fly for him. For the Chinese."

Chloe closed her eyes. "So, you will be a mercenary."

"What's that?"

"It means someone who is paid to fight someone else's war."

"Yeah, sounds 'bout right."

Chloe nodded, her brow furrowed. "I understand the Japanese have done atrocious things in China, to the people there."

"Yeah, I hear that, too."

```
Chloe! Chloe!
Someone's calling, no reply
```

She went to the corner, raised the arm on the record player, placed it in the holder, and switched the machine off. She stood there with her back to him. "When do you go to China, PJ Benoit?"

"I'll be on a train to San Francisco in a week or so."

She spun, eyes shining, lips spread over a wide smile. She didn't know why, but she felt relief, peace, really, for the first time since he'd left her. It would be some time before she understood why she felt this way, only after she'd given it a long thought under the Big Tree. They were kept apart by singular stupid cruelty. Soon, he'd be fighting against stupid cruelty, even killing the perpetrators. They weren't white. They were yellow. Or were they brown? It didn't matter. These weren't her thoughts, yet, but looking into the eyes of the man she loved, her sorrow eased.

"May I write to you?"

PJ's chest hurt. "Yeah, we can get letters."

"And I presume you may write them as well, that is if you have not forgotten how to write."

"Sure, I'll write you . . . Honeybee."

The word pierced her heart. "Come here, PJ Benoit. My sweet mercenary." She placed a hand behind his neck and pulled him to her. She kissed him deeply, passionately. Looking into his eyes, she stroked his hair, cupped his chin. She quickly kissed both of his cheeks, a tear trickling from her eye. "I love you dearly, PJ. Please keep yourself safe. Use your discipline to keep yourself safe."

He took up her hands and kissed her fingers.

She walked him out, holding his hand. Her eyes shone like peppered amber. She pulled him close.

"Come back here, to the café tonight. I want us to love again like we used to love. Let us share ourselves again."

PJ's heart raced, and he grew hard. Chloe caught herself. They were outside on the porch. She pushed him away and stepped back, whispering. "You will tap on my window, yes?"

A flatbed burning oil came chugging around the corner, and PJ whistled. A rail-thin old black man sat behind the wheel with two little ones at his side.

"Can I get a lift? I'll pay you a rate."

The man recognized him from times past at the café. He backhanded the nearest of the two boys. "Go on, git in back." They scampered through the hole that had been the truck's rear window. You headin ta Benoit place?"

"Yes, sir."

"Since you lef, Armintha make some new kinda pies."

"That right?"

"Yessah. You migh wanna try some dat, if you doan mine me sayin, sah."

PJ laughed, thinking he would soon get some honey pie. The flatbed squeaked to a stop in front of Frank and Odette's bungalow. Pumpkin barked from the porch. PJ pulled out a two-dollar note.

"No, cain sep dat, nossah. Sho my pleshah bringin you outch heah, yessah."

PJ tossed the bill on the seat. "You take care."

"Blessya, sah. Blessya."

Pumpkin whined as PJ rubbed her muzzle. "You're getting some gray, girlie girl."

* * *

"Mais, look at you! Sha, you all growed up!" Odette, still dressed from church, cried and laughed as she led PJ to the table. "Frank's not home. How long you here foe?"

He told here he would catch the train to California noon Friday.

"Naw, you gonna miss em! Sha, PJ. One more day."

Odette brought out biscuits and jam left from breakfast. She poured apple juice, sat herself down, and patted her brother-in-law's hand. PJ didn't mention this was his second meal of the morning.

* * *

That night at the café, as the katydids serenaded them through the window screens, the pair made love the old way, on a blanket under a booth. Chloe tasted sweet, even more so than he remembered, and he insisted on two servings before it was his turn.

She laid her head on his chest.

"What's that smell?"

"Smell?"

"The scent? You're wearin' a perfume."

Chloe giggled and shushed him. "You must whisper so as not to wake Francie."

Loud snoring was coming from the house through the kitchen. "We needn't worry about wakin' ol' Menta, that's for sure," he said, making her laugh. She shushed him again.

"So?"

"Yes. It is perfume. Do you like it?"

"Very much."

"That makes me happy. It is mine."

"Huh?"

"I made it."

"You made it?"

"Yes. In a jar, I put lavender."

PJ pressed his nose into her neck and inhaled deeply. "But there's something . . . I smell the lavender, but there's something else."

She giggled again and squeezed him. "You are a very perceptive boy, PJ Benoit." She kissed him on the cheek. "You see, anybody can have lavender water. You pick the flower. You put it into the water. Voilà! But I have also a special ingredient, just for me."

PJ kissed her long and hard.

"And what is your special ingredient, Honeybee?"

"The Smiths have plum trees, yes? And those plum trees leak sap, so, I cut some sap off a tree trunk. It is soft amber. I place it in the jar with the lavender." She was radiant. "*My* scent, this is special. Lavender and amber. *Only for me.*"

PJ smirked. "Don't you mean 'only for *me?*'"

Chloe's expression saddened, and she looked away. "No, PJ. You had gone. My scent was for me." She snuggled in tight. "But yes, now, in this time we have together, it is for you."

With a fingertip, he traced the W of freckles on her cheek.

"Poor Cassiopeia," she said.

He didn't understand. She told him the story about the vain queen. "Banished, hanging helpless, upside down forever."

* * *

PJ was waiting in the shade, leaning against the Lafayette station office, when a Vermilion Parish patrol car pulled up in back. Davey Johnson climbed out.

"Goin' somewhere, Deputy Davey?"

"Iffa taint li'l ol PJ Benoit. Headin back to Texas, yeah."

"What can I do for you?"

"Nutin. I'm pickin up mah pa. He comin from N'Orleans. Been down theyah foe da police meetin wit ta govner."

PJ didn't bite.

Johnson pulled his knife, cut a big chunk of chew, and stuffed it in a cheek. "I heah tha coon a yoes goan ta some nigga college en Georgia."

PJ crossed his arms and waited for it.

"Wha dey learn en nigga college? Howta peel bananas, yeah?" He guffawed at his own joke and coughed up some chew juice. Spat a big brown mess onto the platform.

"That's a beaut, Davey. Bet ya could do that out either end, same result."

A whistle blew south of the station.

"Think I'll take a piss." PJ took up his duffle and walked off.

Hours later, while rolling west through Caddo Parish, about to cross into Texas, PJ stared at a cotton patch that seemed to stretch forever, a bunch of black folk hunched over in it. Back at the Benoit home, Odette hovered over Frank, who was hunched over the note PJ had left for him.

"Can you give me some room, please?"

"Ou, Frank, read it." She tapped a foot as he started reading. "So I can hear, Beb!"

Frank,

Sorry I missed you. I am off to California and a ship to Asia. Will help the Chinese fight the Japs but it is a secret so if anyone asks I am just working in China. The contract says that if anything happens to me my kin gets six months pay and insurance so I wrote your name. It will be 13,700 so I want you to do something for me and make sure Chloe gets to college. Get her money and get Nenta and Francie money so it will work out. There will be plenty left over for you and Odette.

Thanks for raising me and thank Odette too. Y'all did good. That's what I think. I will try to write to you.

PJ (but I am going to be Jack in China)

Odette put her face in her hands and cried.

18

THE JAGERSFONTEIN

JULY 1941

"Goddamn."

    The alarm bell smashed through his slumber like a splitting axe. PJ fumbled his hand across the nightstand, managing only to knock the clock to the floor, prolonging its assault on his throbbing head. Disoriented, he reached toward the shrill noise and, with his legs tangled in the top sheet, tumbled off the side of the bed, silencing the menace with his rib cage. Hanging there from his feet, the blood rushing to his head, he moaned and rubbed his eyes. His ears were ringing, his stomach felt like a volcano ready to blow, and he was desperate to pee. Finding his way to the toilet, which was spinning, he sat, and as he gained relief, he tried to remember how he'd made it back to the hotel.

    There was Chinatown. Steamed dumplings. A big dish of beef chow mein. Olympia beer, then another. The group split up. Some of the guys went down to the wharf. He caught a cab to the Top of the Mark with Billy, Sam, and Whatshisname. *The best view in all of San Francisco.* A bunch of stuffed shirts patting them on the back. Two bourbons. Three. *Four?* "Goddamn my head."

    He didn't remember the part about Whatshisname blabbing their mission, but he did remember a dark-haired, mustachioed man in formal attire informing the boys they wouldn't be paying for drinks that night. From then on, it was champagne, the best bourbons, and well-aged brandy. PJ had never imbibed so much alcohol.

"Dumb mug." He cursed the bleary-eyed man-child in the mirror and returned to the toilet where he violently filled the bowl. He stumbled back to the bed, where, squeezing a pillow between his knees, he rocked, trying to regain some sense of control. "Knucklehead."

The ship would launch at 3 p.m., and he woke with less than an hour to gather his things and get to the harbor where the Dutch merchant vessel awaited.

"If it ain't Mr. Dumpling!" It was Billy March, the first volunteer PJ met upon arriving in San Francisco on the Fourth of July. They'd spent a good bit of time together over the last few days. "You musta ate two dozen of those squishy things."

PJ squinted at him and wondered how he could be so damn perky. Billy was a hard-drinking man, and for him last night's festivities were ordinary fare.

"The dumplings tasted better going down."

Billy laughed hard. "You just need more practice, and I have a feeling you're gonna get some on this pleasure cruise."

The mate gave PJ directions to his quarters. There were four bunks in the room, three had duffles on them. A single chair sat in front of what looked like a lady's vanity, and that was the extent of the furnishings. He tossed his bag on the open bunk.

"Hey there!" A handsome face appeared in the doorway. "Toby Gyer." The man offered his hand.

"Peeeej . . . ah . . . Jack Benoit. Glad to meet you."

"You army?"

"Yeah. Randolph. Instructor and test. You?"

"Navy. Pensacola."

PJ eyed his new bunkmate. "Damn if you don't look just like . . ."

"Yes, I do."

Ensign Toby Gyer was a dead ringer for a young Cary Grant.

"Get it all the time. Would wear me out but for the girls. Not so awful in that department, if you know what I mean."

"S'pose not."

Two other men entered the room. One was Whatshisname. "Looks like the gang's all here!"

The other guy stuck his hand out generally in their direction. "I'm Rod Pierce. This is Gil Weathers. Navy, out of Norfolk."

Toby introduced himself through his thick Bronx accent. PJ introduced himself again as Jack. Toby punched his shoulder.

"Looks like we got you outnumbered, pal." He turned to Rod and Gil. "Jack's army."

Gil laughed and fired a Camel filter with his pocket lighter. "Yeah? Well, what crates have you army boys been flying?" As was the case with most navy pilots, Gil Weathers didn't think highly of the Army Air Corp.

"I was a trainer at Randolph. Mostly single engine, BT-13s, PT-13s. But I got some hours with multi-engines. Some experimental equipment."

Gil continued, "Well, at Norfolk a few weeks back, a Curtiss P-40 came in. Me and Rod here, we both got a couple hours in it," Weathers gloated. "It's a beaut!"

"Yes, it is," PJ deadpanned.

"You been in one?" Toby suspected he had.

"P-40B test crew."

"Really? How many hours?"

"Forty-seven."

Their jaws dropped. "You lucky S.O.B.!" Weathers shouted.

"So, how is it?" Toby was itching to know. They all were. Word was at least some of them would be driving P-40B Tomahawks over China.

"Handles great. Climbs good but a little soggy when its full of ammo. Dives like a hawk. It's a workhorse."

"Any problems?"

"We had a couple fires. Leaky gaskets in the A model. But the engineers worked it all out. Self-sealing fuel tanks, armored cockpits. She's a beast."

"I hear them Jap Zeros are fast and tight. They can turn like a bat," Toby said, accentuating with a little spin.

Rod laughed. "You better watch it. That's a good way to get a bad nickname. Start calling you Bat Boy."

"Ain't this something?" Gil blurted. "Damn, in a couple weeks we'll be killing Japs! This is gonna be fun."

It was obvious PJ was hung over bad. Toby suggested they get coffee, and they headed off in a pack to find the mess.

"So, Jack, you been at sea before?" Rod asked.

"Nope."

Weathers poked him. "You already look green."

PJ gave him a look. Something about *Whatshisname* Gil Weathers didn't sit well with him, but he couldn't put a finger on it.

"Don't worry." Toby put a hand on his shoulder. "You'll probably puke a couple times when we hit swells, but you'll get your sea legs fast enough."

PJ was filled with regret. It wasn't like him to get drunk, and this was the most hungover he'd been in his life. What bothered him most was the regret. He didn't appreciate regret and hated setting himself up for it.

The boys found the mess, and a whistle blew. A tug bumped the *Jagersfontein* into the harbor.

As the ship slipped out of San Francisco in unceremonious fashion at 1540 hours on July 8, 1941, very few people knew the *Jagersfontein* was filled with mercenaries sailing west to fight for the Chinese in the Second Sino-Japanese War. Thus far, the project had remained under wraps, with all participants sworn to secrecy. But while PJ found himself overindulging at the Top of the Mark, roughly a hundred of his soon-to-be colleagues were partaking in similar excesses all across the Bay City. What PJ couldn't remember clearly, the thing that was bothering him about Gil Weathers, was that last night the navy flyer had bragged incessantly about their mission. But Weathers wasn't the only one. *Adventurous* and *boisterous* sometimes come in a package, and as the ship steamed westward, San Francisco locals were already buzzing about the brave pilots and crew of the American Volunteer Group headed across the Pacific to fight the Japs.

That night, the mess served a tasty Salisbury steak with carrots and potatoes. Soon thereafter, the party that had taken place in pockets all over San Francisco the night before was consolidated into two general undertakings. Officers partied on the deck while the crew commandeered the mess. The ship was plentifully stocked with beer, whiskey, flavored liqueurs, cigarettes and cigars. One of the pilots rigged a speaker from the bridge radio over the on-deck pool. Soon the sounds of Benny Goodman and Artie Shaw backed the laughter and shouts of forty inebriated young men. The dinner helped to ease PJ's headache, but he wasn't up for another night of drunken revelry, and, from the look of it, he thought he might also be the only man on the ship who didn't smoke. Meandering back to his berth, he shook his head.

Don't drink. Don't smoke. Calisthenics every morning. He wondered if he had the ghost of some fussy old spinster trapped inside him. He was resting on his bunk when the door slammed against the vanity, and his three inebriated roommates tumbled in.

"Ar-meeee Ja-aaack!" someone yelled.

"Army Jack?" It was Rod. "You asleep?"

"How was it, boys?"

"The bee's knees!" Toby snickered and slowly stretched his arms wide. "Just the beginning of one looooong party!"

PJ felt surprisingly good. It was 0200 hours, and he'd woken from a solid six-hour sleep. With the food and some aspirin powder in his belly, his hangover had passed.

The room quickly filled with smoke, and the navy boys were sweating whiskey through the chlorine on their skin. In short order, all three of them were passed out in their bunks. PJ tried to return to his dreams, but the snoring, vaporized alcohol and flatulence overwhelmed him. He went topside for some air. The deck was devoid of human activity, and PJ leaned over the port taffrail. Under the cloudless sky, the view of the Pacific Ocean was breathtaking. A crisp nearly-full moon, pocked and scarred, irradiated the pale-green water to a horizon that glowed with a fuzzy white line. He'd spent time in the air over the Gulf of Mexico, but this was his first ocean voyage. First time on a ship.

The *Jagersfontein* was steady and cut a sleek wake on the calm water. The pulse from the steam engine entered his body through the soles of his boots and resonated into his forearms through the taffrail's top lifeline. The moon was as big as he'd ever seen it. Near the bottom, the Tycho Crater looked like it had been scored on white paper with a charcoal pencil.

"Les moustaches de chaton," he told himself. Out here it looked to him more like the remains of a dandelion puff after a strong wind. He worked some calisthenics in the cool, fresh air, completing four sets, a full hour's worth. It felt good to sweat out the last of the alcohol and work his muscles. He sat, dangling his legs over the side.

"I don't know how they do it, gettin' drunk every night. I'd feel like shit."

He wondered what was in store for them. What it was really going to be like. Weathers figured in a couple of weeks, they'd be killing Japs, knocking them out of the sky like they were swatting flies. PJ wondered how many of his new colleagues would be the ones dropping from the sky. Would he be one of them?

***

Toby Gyer couldn't have been more correct in his prediction about the voyage. It was one long party, so much so the mess stopped expecting anyone to show up for breakfast. Instead, they started cooking at their leisure and left out a buffet from 0900 through 1030 hours. There was next to no discipline onboard. Every day, the partying commenced by midafternoon and continued well into the following morning. PJ established a routine similar to his first night's activities. Starting between 0200 and 0300, he'd pace topside, complete multiple rounds of calisthenics, then read by moonlight. He'd think about flying, then, inevitably, think about Chloe. But after a few days, Toby pulled him aside.

"You got a problem with us?"

PJ had heard it all before. "I just don't like gettin' drunk, Toby. And even the best drunks wear you down after a few hours, you understand me?"

"I get it, Jack, I do. But the guys are talking." Toby squinted. "You might want to think about making some friends. We're gonna have some shit over there, you know? It doesn't pay to be the cold fish."

"I know. We're in this together . . ." PJ trailed off. He knew he was out of sorts and spending most of his time alone, and his routine wasn't exactly a load of fun. "I appreciate you sayin' something, I do. What say we find a game?"

Gambling on the ship had spread like kudzu on the banks of the Alabama River. Every afternoon and every night, dice and card games formed all over the ship. Generally, the pilots played on deck and the crewmen played in the mess or in the converted stateroom where most of them bunked. Most guys rolled craps. Some played spades or euchre, and there were a handful of straight poker games. Toby introduced PJ to a poolside craps game.

"I'll watch for a bit." He'd never played dice. Craps wasn't big at Randolph, which was more a straight poker base. After an hour or so of observing, he mumbled, "Lucky or broke."

"What's that?" Toby asked.

"From what I can see, in craps there are two kinds of players. Lucky and broke."

Toby blew on his dice and rolled. "Ah! Crapped out."

"I got an idea." PJ pulled Toby away. "Let's find a poker game."

"Poker?" Toby groaned. "Boring."

"Not when you win." PJ grinned. "You know a good game?"

"Yeah, follow me." Toby banged on a cabin door. "Guys, if you haven't already met, this is Jack Benoit. He's gonna sit in with me tonight if it's all right with everyone."

"Ebbe Windler."

"John Boyle."

"Buster Hobbs."

"Sal Capone."

PJ's eyes widened.

"Yeah, yeah. Sit down, or I'll show you what for." It was Sal's standard introduction, and his tone wasn't pleasant.

"I'm guessing you're down, Sal." Toby flicked his friend's ear.

"A hundred shinolas!" He pointed to an open chair. "Sit your butt there so I can start winning some of it back."

Sal looked nothing like the famous mobster, Al Capone. Duty had required his Italian American father to linger after the Great War in Belgium, where he met his bride, a displaced Swedish beauty. Their first son Salvatore was born as their ship docked in Brooklyn. Ever since Sal reached his teens, strangers struggled to reconcile the boy's James Cagney street-tough patter with his Nordic features and the bright shock of snowy-blond hair on his head.

Ebbe was the serious gambler of the bunch. He'd brought with him a beautifully carved walnut chest of clay poker chips crafted in Cuba. On the table lay a small notebook holding some numbers.

"What's that?" PJ asked.

"Buster's already busted," Toby laughed.

"I'm coming back," Buster slurred.

This was Ebbe's game. "We got a couple of weeks, and I figured everyone'll be goin up and down, see? So why bother with cash. We'll settle up when we make port."

PJ sat in. He drew three queens and, after numerous raises, took the pot.

"Dammit, Toby!" Sal was feeling mean. "Why'd you bring *him* here?"

"Sorry, boys." PJ pulled the chips to his pile. "Beginner's luck, I s'pose."

The whiskey flowed, and the smoke rose, but PJ felt great. They all seemed like good eggs. Even as each one slowly got stoned, PJ could tell they were loyal, salt-of-the-earth guys. They'd be there for each other, and for him. John Boyle was the only other army flyer, and PJ liked the navy boys fine. They had a swagger, for sure, each and every one of them. But he figured they'd earned it, bouncing off aircraft carriers on bad water. That first night, PJ cleaned up.

"Dammit, Jack." Toby smacked him the following morning. "How much did you win last night?"

"About three hundred."

"Oh, my head." Toby didn't look so much like Cary Grant with puffy bloodshot eyes.

"You need some coffee, my friend. I'll bring some back," PJ offered.

"And toast. No butter."

As PJ headed toward the mess, he reflected on the game. They'd been so drunk. He could scalp them every night! But he thought better of it. He'd enjoyed the game. Enjoyed the company more. If he kept his wits, he could clean up most every night, and, to keep the peace, he could throw some hands here and there. There'd still be some luck to it, but he could pretty much pick when and where to spread the money around over the next couple of weeks. The gang would be better for it, and that's exactly what happened.

Topside one afternoon, PJ was dealing twenty-one to Sal and Toby for matchsticks, just passing time, and a few of the crewmen gathered to watch them play. They'd never seen the game, and he told them how it originated in France, that someone he knew from Paris had showed him the game. John McClintock, the mechanic from Randolph, asked if he'd like to join a crew game that night. Said he was getting tired of draw and stud and thought this looked like fun.

Although they weren't maintaining military hierarchy, the men still socialized pretty much as they used to back in the service. The pilots and the handful of administrators who'd been officers socialized together, and the crew of former enlisted men stayed with their own. When PJ showed up for McClintock's game that night, it was extraordinary.

He was the last to arrive, and the men were an hour into a game. When PJ entered the room, McClintock stood out of habit. He sported a black crew cut that was so thick and flat it looked like blacktop road. His prickly, dark eyebrows lay heavy and low over muddy-brown eyes. He was a little pudgy, and PJ figured McClintock had packed on at least ten pounds since he last saw him at Randolph. A chain smoker, there was a huff in his breath and a flush in his cheeks.

He tapped a pack of Camel filters and offered one to PJ, who waved it off.

"This is the blackjack dealer I was telling y'all about."

"And this is one of best damn P-40 crewmen in the country." PJ nodded back.

"Don't be too sure." Carl Jones had worked on P-40s at Norfolk.

PJ introduced himself. "Jack Benoit."

"Joe Simmons."

"Bob Stanford."

Each crewman rose from his seat, not formally, but enough to reach PJ's outstretched hand, except for Carl Jones.

PJ murmured to himself, "Looks like Deputy Davey."

"What's so funny?" Jones asked.

"You remind me of someone."

"Yeah, that handsome, huh?"

The other men groaned.

"So, how's this game work?"

McClintock grinned. "We all play against the dealer."

"Well, I hope you brought plenty of greenback, Mr. Ben-waaah." Jones smirked.

PJ figured it would be a cash game, so he'd visited the purser to cash some twenties for singles and fives. As with the officers' games, this one was just something to do while drinking. PJ explained the rules and dealt a few practice hands. Unlike draw and stud, blackjack, as it was becoming known in the States, focuses all the attention on an individual player, in the order dealt, giving everybody playing against the dealer a sense of camaraderie, of being on a team. It also frees the hands of those who aren't immediately in play. As a result, the crewmen grew inebriated faster than usual.

The odds inherent in the game favor the dealer. A player can beat the house, but the longer the game, the more likely the house will win. As Chloe had told him, "It is math, no more." This night, it was math and bad judgment. As with most things in life, inexperience and inebriation significantly lower one's odds of achieving desired result, and the crewmen exhibited both characteristics.

The room grew raucous, every man cheering the player of the moment. PJ sipped a beer between decks while a different player shuffled the cards. But dealing kept him busy, so the fact that he was way behind the others in consumption went unnoticed.

The betting got wild and, of course, the crewmen lost. Every single one of them. Most lost their entire stash, but through the excitement of new experience, they didn't seem to mind much. Everyone was in high spirits. Everyone except Carl Jones, and PJ figured this was a man who was rarely in high spirits. The kind of guy who preferred laughing at the misfortune of others. An hour and a half later, everyone was tapped out save for McClintock, who still had fifty bucks. PJ had everything else. The rest of the men pounded beers and cheered on McClintock to make a comeback.

But Jones was sore. Real sore. Slurring badly, he put a fist to the table and shouted, "You're a cheat!"

The room fell silent. PJ cocked his head.

"Hey now," McClintock said. "No reason to get sore, Carl."

"He's the lucky one tonight," Simmons added, belching. "We'll skin him tomorrow." He popped PJ in the shoulder and reached for another beer.

But PJ kept his eyes on Jones, who wasn't having any of it.

"This sonuvabitch cheats." Jones yelled at McClintock. "*You* brought this cheatin' bastard in here, and he ain't taking *my* money outta here."

PJ set the deck of cards on the table. He picked up his winnings, straightened and folded the bills, and stuffed them into his pants pocket. "Seems the game's over," he said, looking Jones in the eye. "Sergeant McClintock, thanks for the invite. Boys, better luck next time."

Carl Jones sprang from his seat and, lurching forward, he knocked over the steel table, playing cards and dollar bills flying everywhere. He took a wild roundhouse swing at PJ, who saw the punch coming like a slow-moving train. Despite Jones' overwhelming size advantage, PJ easily deflected the blow with a forearm and drove his other fist hard into his attacker's nose. The crack was audible, and the force knocked Jones back. He staggered and cupped his nose, blood gushing from between his fingers. PJ put a left hook to his right eye, and the big man crumpled. The other crewmen stood over the unconscious man, silent, mouths agape.

"Jesus Christ!" It was McClintock.

"Sorry for the mess, boys." Standing over the heap of Carl Jones, PJ made a proposal. "Maybe next time we pass the deal. That way, we avoid . . . questions."

McClintock caught up with him down the hall.

"How'd you do that, Lieutenant? I mean, Captain."

PJ kept walking.

"You pack a wallop."

"I had a good time tonight, John. I hope the rest of the guys are all right with the results."

"Don't worry 'bout that. No doubt they're already on a search and destroy for more booze. None of us like that loudmouth, Jones, anyway. In the morning we'll have a good laugh about it."

"Want to go topside and get some air?"

"I figured that's for officers."

PJ stopped. "We're employees of a Chinese company called CAMCO. How 'bout we leave all that *officer and enlisted man* stuff back at base, John?"

McClintock laughed, and PJ stuck out his hand again. "Call me Jack," he said.

The men climbed topside, where, sure enough, the pilots were partying like there was no tomorrow. PJ led the way to the port quarter where they sat and dangled their legs over the side. McClintock smoked while they talked into the night about where they grew up, their families, the girls they knew. PJ was less than forthright than McClintock about two of the three subjects.

John McClintock was born and raised in Brooklyn, one of seven children. He told stories about the tenements, stickball in the street, nuns with thick rulers. They laughed about coming from such different places. Seemed they had only two things in common. They loved airplanes, and they'd jumped trains as kids.

Waking pre-dawn, PJ was greeted topside by a beautiful, cloudless sky just as the eastern horizon started to glow behind the ship. He was in his second round of calisthenics when activity stirred on the bridge. A ship's crewman slid down a stair railing and double-timed away. Others atop the superstructure scanned the water with binoculars. PJ hollered up to them, and an ensign called down that the ship was going on alert. The alarm blared and drown out the rest of what he was saying.

The bridge had been listening to Radio Tokyo, a Japanese radio station that broadcast jazz standard music and featured Orphan Ann, a sweet-voiced announcer who read news reports and propaganda sheets in English between songs. At approximately 0600 hours, Orphan Ann read a report about the AVG, describing their organization and mission in astonishing detail. She labeled the American volunteers criminals and spies. More disturbingly, she accurately revealed that a ship carrying members of the AVG to Burma was approaching the Hawaiian Islands. She spoke directly to the volunteers, informing them that their mission was futile and doomed, and suggesting they just go home. PJ joined the sailor atop the starboard superstructure to scan the waters for submarines. It was then that it came back to him. Gil Weathers, mouthing off at the Top of the Mark.

19

THE LAGOON

JULY 1941

By midmorning, Orphan Ann's message had spread to everyone onboard. The men hadn't been this subdued since the ship left port. But it wasn't long before anxiety transformed to skepticism, and skepticism was replaced by bravado. By midafternoon, the party had resumed, and by evening, the festivities had reached new heights. *Fuck the Japs* was that night's party theme, the words emblazoned on a bed sheet tied over the swimming pool. There were toasts to the Japanese Zeros that would drop out of the sky, their fiery spirals of death acted out by flyers who made twisting, acrobatic dives and bellyflops into the pool from precariously stacked deck chairs.

At the mess during dinner hour, McClintock waved Jack into line. "Captain Jack! Thought you should know Carl Jones was ordered to the infirmary this morning to get his nose straightened. Got a metal bridge taped under two big shiners. Looks like a raccoon that took a line drive in the schnoz."

"Happens, I s'pose."

"Happens. Ha! But don't you worry, he didn't say nothin' about the fight. Told the doc he got soused, tripped, and smashed his face on a table."

Back on base, it would have been extraordinary for an officer and a crewman man to fight. The enlisted man would get the stockade and lose at least one stripe, and the officer would earn a black mark that might just prevent him from ever getting promoted. Just then Carl

Jones entered the mess, and Jack caught his dark, puffy eyes. Jones nodded. Jack nodded.

Word of the fight spread across the ship as the Orphan Ann scare dissipated, and the administrative officers concerned themselves with how to go about disciplining those involved. But no one ever approached Jack. The lack of response seemed to bond the two groups in a new way. They figured the brass wouldn't be settling matters, it would be the men. The story also worked to raise Jack's stature among both groups. Carl Jones was a mountain of a man, and Jack Benoit, all five-foot-five, hundred-thirty pounds of him, had laid the giant out with two punches. A few of the pilots congratulated him for *putting the crew in their place*.

That night, he struggled to sleep and went topside for air. He was stretching when he heard an unfamiliar sound beyond the rhythm of the engines. It didn't sound mechanical, more like the sputter of a showerhead that had been long out of use. He walked toward the noise, and an odd movement in the ship's wake caught his eye.

"Goddamn submarine!"

He watched a large, curved shape rise from the water a hundred yards off the stern as a spray of water blew some thirty feet into the air over the shiny bump. He could see clearly in the bright moonlight. "A whale?"

The shape disappeared below the wake. Time passed. More time passed. "Well, at least it wasn't a sub." Then, a breach to his right. The whale had caught up to the ship and was swimming in parallel, no more than fifty feet off the port side. Jack took hold of the top lifeline and leaned over the water.

The two travelers eyed each other as the whale curved through her breach. He'd never seen anything so fantastic. The moonlight shimmering off her skin. That big, bright eye. The massive beast was so calm, so self-assured.

Anticipating the whale to stay on course and at speed, he ran forward across the beam to port bow, where he scanned the water for movement. She rose again, but to Jack's surprise and disappointment, she did so back at port quarter. She was cruising directly off where Jack had been standing, but this time only some twenty feet out. He cried out, "Wait!"

Just as he reached his original position, the whale submerged again. He decided to wait it out there, hoping she would try again. His senses heightened, he picked up the rhythm of the engines through his boots. In quick succession, three fish leaped into the air, each re-entry creating concentric circles of ripples that grew, glistening like silver necklaces on the glassy Pacific. Then it happened. The whale surfaced again, and he was eye to eye, just twenty feet down and twenty feet out, with the majestic blue whale, eighty feet from tip to tail. She rolled to get a better look at the *Jagersfontein* and its sole, topside passenger. She studied him for half a minute, cruising along the top water.

"God, you're beautiful."

The whale spun back below the surface, trailing her right flipper. Jack waited for the next rise, and minutes later, heard the showerhead noise again. She'd risen some hundred yards off the port bow. He heard two more blows, each more distant, before he lost sight of her altogether.

* * *

The ship anchored in Honolulu later that morning. A copy of Orphan Ann's broadcast had made its way to Washington and onto President Roosevelt's desk, resulting in a direct order from the Commander-in-Chief to assign an escort to the *Jagersfontein* for the remainder of her voyage. Two US cruisers, the *Northampton* and the *Salt Lake City*, would guide her to Singapore, where authority would be transferred to the British, who would escort her from Singapore to Rangoon, Burma.

From Hawaii to Singapore, the volunteers kept to their routine. Eat, gamble, ping pong, drink, shuffleboard, swim, eat, drink, tussle, sleep. Despit the fussy spinster inside, Jack bonded with the carousers, pilots and crew alike. In San Francisco, he'd abandoned the nickname he carried for nineteen years, and everyone on board knew him as Jack, but recently, a few of the pilots had taken to calling him Blackjack, for how he clubbed Jones. Most of the crew called him Captain Jack, which he preferred. Alone on the deck, he'd often wondered how this outfit would maintain discipline in combat conditions. There'd have to be some hierarchy of authority when they got in the shit. For him, "Captain Jack" seemed to hold the right balance between authority and friendship.

They arrived without incident in Singapore, where they would have a short week of delay, and therefore R&R, after which they'd be transferred onto British cruisers bound for Rangoon. Everyone was ready for shore leave, meaning everyone was ready for women. The crew would spend nights onboard the *Jagersfontein* while the pilots took rooms in the Raffles Hotel, luxurious accommodations that were otherwise sparsely occupied due to the looming hostilities. Jack interpreted the arrangements as confirmation that AVG management would enforce a more traditional military hierarchy in the outfit once they arrived at their destination. But there was borderline mutiny when the crewmen were told there would be no women allowed onboard. AVG administration quelled the uprising by proclaiming there would be no curfew, but each man was required to check in with the ship twice daily.

* * *

Jack plopped onto his bed at the Raffles. To his surprise, there was a Philco radio atop the chest of drawers, tuned into Radio Tokyo.

```
The boy left his love upon a distant shore
And sailed from the one his arms were longing for
```

There was no escaping the scent of tobacco which permeated the entire building, including his room, and the tropical humidity made the place stuffy. But the bed was so much more comfortable than his bunk on the ship, his single room was alcohol-sweat and flatulence free, and he had a private bath. A heavenly respite from the ship.

He stripped to his skivvies and lay back on the bed. Just as he started to doze, there was a banging on his door. Toby let himself in.

"Swanky place you got here. You ready to hit the town?"

"What do you have in mind?"

Toby had struck up a conversation with some British expats downstairs in the Long Bar. They cheerily recommended restaurants and a club called The Lagoon.

"Should be swinging tonight." Toby broke into a Lindy Hop.

The idea of live music fired Jack up. "A nice steak somewhere. Some jazz. Tell you what, Toby, I'm buyin'."

"You might want to reconsider that offer. Gil and Rod are in, too."

"I fleeced y'all good a few times on the way over. Least I can do."

"You're on! I got the name of this swanky restaurant. We'll meet in the lobby at 1900. Be there, soldier." Toby saluted and Lindy Hopped out the door.

Jack lay back and thought about his favorite songs, and his favorites from the past two weeks of Radio Tokyo. He knew what he would request at the club.

The boys had a great time at dinner, and no expense was spared. Gil and Rod were pretty far gone before they all declined dessert. Toby belched. "That was a fine piece of meat."

"Best steak I ever ate," Jack confessed.

"Ha! What'd I just hear this Texan say? What's that chill in here, is that hell freezin' over?"

"It's buffalo, sir." The waiter placed the check on the table. "From Thailand."

"That's for me." Jack pulled out his wad. "You take American?"

"Certainly, we can accommodate US dollars, sir."

"Accommodate that." He slapped down the twenties. Gil and Rod looked at each other, surprised grins on their faces.

"It's your money, boys. Well, used to be, anyway." Jack laughed. "Rod, you paid for the whole meal when you tried bluffing my three queens that very first hand of draw poker back on the ship."

"The waiter placed the bills on his silver plate. Very generous, sir. If there is anything else I might bring you, please."

"I'm pretty sure the dessert these fellas are cravin' ain't on your menu, bud. We're good to go."

An evening breeze took the top off the heat, the best one could hope for during a Singapore July, short of a downpour. The boys waved off the cabbies and rickshaws and walked the half-mile to The Lagoon, where they were greeted at the door with some irritation. No reservations. No jackets. The maître d' asked for a moment, and Gil commenced fussing and cussing.

A British Army colonel appeared, tall and handsome despite the birdy nose. "I'll venture a guess you gentlemen are with the American Volunteer Group. Major Archibald Mountbatten, 1st Burma Division, at your service." He stretched out his hand. "Please, do me the honor and join us."

"Sounds keen, Archie." Toby slapped the stiff Englishman on the back. "Damn *hospital* of you."

The major took it in stride and arranged for his table to be expanded. "The crowd is well into it this evening. Should be some laughs. We're up front, just off the stage."

Jack noted the stage was set for a band, but a recording of Louis Armstrong's orchestra filled the air. "S'pose they're on break?"

"Quite."

Introductions were made, drinks were ordered for the table, and the major made an announcement. "Gentlemen, tonight your money's no good. This evening is on His Majesty." The major stood and raised his glass. "To the 1st, to the AVG, and to victory in the Pacific!"

Jack sat between Major Mountbatten and Abhaijeet Dahrala, a Sikh sergeant major in the British Indian Colonial Army. "What's with the hat?" Gil yelled across the table. The sergeant major's look spoke more clearly than words could have.

Jack sipped a ginger beer with ice and asked the sergeant major about his outfit, learning he commanded a battalion in the 9th Division of III Corp in central British Malay. The sergeant major came off aloof, and Jack was astounded to be sitting next to a turban wearing Negro who led a whole battalion. He pressed for details, visibly irritating the sergeant major, whose responses grew increasingly curt, so Jack let it go and took in the room.

The joint was packed and loud with revelous voices, the walls lined with sturdy palms, evenly spaced, the ceiling lined with hard-working paddle fans sucking plumes of blue-gray smoke into the haze that obscured the frescos painted on the high ceiling. Straight lines, right angles. The crowd seemed composed of British officers, expats and their wives, and a smattering of Dutch businessmen, and it also seemed everyone save his Sikh neighbor was having a grand time. There was one small group of AVG pilots seated near the back.

"And now, for your continued pleasure, in an extended stay *required* by Singapore's more discerning connoisseurs of popular music, please welcome back to the stage, the Milton Stone Orchestra."

Jack leaned toward the sergeant major. "Just one more question. In the States, our names don't mean anything, but I've heard your names mean something."

The sergeant major raised his chin and narrowed his eyes on the baby-faced American. "Dahrala is an ancient Jet name. Abhaijeet, the name given to me by my parents, means 'victory over fear.'"

"Seems your mama got that one right."

The sergeant major's eyes widened. He roared with laughter and slapped the table. "Let us drink!"

Jack raised his ginger beer, and Abhaijeet raised his cognac and toasted, "To victory."

"And to hell with fear," Jack added.

The sergeant major smiled and threw back his drink, Jack took a swig, and Major Mountbatten interjected, "Captain, if you can make

Sergeant Major Dahrala laugh like that, we'd do well to get you out of combat and into diplomacy."

Toby poked Jack in the arm. The Cary Grant lookalike was well on his way to sloppy drunk. "We're gonna find us some pussy. You in, Blackjack? BJ want a BJ?"

He kept poking Jack in the shoulder while the band wrapped the number, and the crowd broke into applause. Jack was watching a woman in a glittering emerald-green gown accept the bandleader's hand at the side of the stage. Her silken auburn tresses were draped to one side, leaving the other creamy shoulder exposed. Her face had the heart-shaped look of Gene Tierney, and her lips were painted sharply in scarlet. Sparkling crystals dangled from her earlobes. When she reached the microphone and faced the crowd, he saw she was missing an arm.

"Another lovely night at The Lagoon." More cheers. "And a lovelier crowd."

"Holy cow."

The drummer started with a heavy beat, and Toby poked harder. "C'mon!"

"I'm gonna stick around here, pal. Y'all go ahead. I'll catch up."

Toby knocked over the sergeant major's drink while ogling the singer, a long leg bent through a slit that ran up to mid-thigh. Jack caught the brandy snifter before it hit the table. He set it upright and went back to ogling the singer.

"Some gams!" Toby drained his gin and tonic, spilling plenty down his chin and dribbling onto his khaki shirt. His friend was in a trance, like some cartoon wolf with his tongue hanging out. "Goddamn, Jack. She's got one arm. Don't you do anything normal?"

Never treats me sweet and gentle the way he should
I got it bad and that ain't good

Major Mountbatten asked Jack with a smirk. "Lovely voice, what?"

He just kept staring.

"I believe the American captain would like to make her laugh, too," Dahrala added, wryly.

"Dear God, another first," exclaimed the major. "The sergeant major made a joke! Seems a good thing you're heading to Burma, Captain Benoit. I fear if you accompanied the sergeant major upcountry, he would lose focus and III Corp would come completely undone."

Dahrala stiffened. Jack cocked his head at the two soldiers, then turned back to the singer. She was scanning the front tables, and their eyes locked. Rocking her hips during the horn solo, she raised a cigarette to her lips and blew a pink-hued plume through the red stage light. She released his gaze and rejoined the number.

```
And the things I tell my pillow, nobody should
I got it bad, I got it bad and that ain't good
```

"Who is she?" Jack blurted.
"That's Norah Davies."
"What's her story?"
The major cleared his throat. "She arrived in Singapore, what? Just over a month ago, I'd say. Was quite popular back home. Sang in some of the best clubs in London. I had occasion to see her perform on Little Newport Street. The name of the place eludes me. Of course, during the Blitz, everyone had a rough go. Singapore's as good a place as any to sing these days, I'd say."

Jack raised his eyebrows and waited for more.
"Do you mean the arm?"
He nodded.
"Right." The major lit another cigarette, drawing his smoke through a slim, ivory holder.

The Germans bombed London from September 1940 into May 1941. The Blitz, as it was known. During a night raid in March, a bomb entered the Café de Paris through a ventilation shaft just as Ken Snakehips Johnson was kicking off his band's second set. Johnson had asked Norah Davies, who was in the audience that night, to join him onstage. It wasn't common, but not unprecedented, for an integrated band to play in London, and Norah graciously accepted the microphone from the popular black bandleader.

```
Oh Johnny, Oh Johnny
How you can love
```

The Nazi's fifty-kilo bomb detonated on the dance floor, killing dozens and injuring many more. Snakehips Johnson died instantly, his body blown into the singer, knocking her under the piano. The building crumbled, with ceiling tiles, bricks, and rafters crashing down on the patrons and band. When Norah regained consciousness, her ears were ringing so badly she couldn't hear the other survivors' cries for help, or the commotion of the rescuers. She was twisted on her back under the partially collapsed piano, which miraculously stood on one leg under the debris. Her arm was pinned over her head. Twelve hours after the explosion, she was carried up to the street. Some days later she regained her hearing, but it was weeks before the agonizing headaches relented.

"The arm was a loss, but no doubt she would have been killed if she hadn't taken the stage moments earlier." The major stubbed out his butt. "Four months ago, she was under a pile of rubble in the West End. Now, look at the girl, sparkling like a resplendent jewel and singing like an angel. Brilliant."

"She's got moxie." Jack downed the last of his ginger beer, and the waiter appeared in an instant. "Just some water with lemon, thanks."

The band was swinging through a series of solos, and Norah was nowhere to be found. Jack jumped up, his head on a swivel. The Brit and the Indian laughed.

"Couldn't guess you just made port, Captain Benoit." Dahrala raised his glass.

"She'll be back. During this number, the band tends to trade some ten minutes of solos. Would you like to meet her?" the major offered.

Jack looked like a kid whose pop just offered to buy him a treat in the candy store.

"Right then. We'll make it so."

The sergeant major waved the server to the table for a quick word. He bowed and moved off.

"We'll see Mrs. Davies after the show."

Jack grimaced, disappointment painting his face.

Mountbatten added, "The *widow* Davies."

* * *

"May I introduce Captain Benoit?" The major presented his silver cigarette case to the singer, who was sitting on a stool. She pulled a smoke. He lit it then he pulled a second, tapped it, and set it in his holder to light. Norah eyed the flyer from head to toe, and back up.

"Name's Jack." He offered his hand.

"Yes. *Captain Jack Benoit*. Rolls right off the tongue." She exhaled blue smoke. "Has the ring of a hero in it."

Jack was oddly discomfited by her tone. She personified insouciance.

"I'll leave you to it." The major bowed slightly. "Early morning and all. Good night, Mrs. Davies. Goodnight, Captain."

Jack saluted. The major returned it, clicking his heels.

"He's a dear. So much as an officer can be, I suppose."

"He seems a good egg."

"We'll see what kind soon enough. The Japs are going to show up and try to crack some eggs."

"Then why are you here?"

Norah set her cigarette in a brass stand and put on a bedroom voice. "Because I'm not *there*, darling."

Jack yawned.

"Am I boring you, Captain?" She turned on the stool and dipped a shoulder. "Help a girl out?" Jack pulled the dress zipper down to her buttocks. "Good boy. Stick around?"

She disappeared behind the changing screen, and Jack plopped down at the dressing table. He listened to the rustling of her gown, her soft humming. She reappeared in a silk robe and slippers. Jack raised an eyebrow. "Oh, this little thing?" She smoothed the fabric, green with painted cranes. "It's enough to get me home." She placed a small beaded handbag inside a larger satchel and walked to the door. "Are you coming, dear?"

They climbed into a car waiting in the alley behind the club, and it carried them the few blocks to the Raffles Hotel, where they entered a side door to find a small elevator.

"A private lift for residents of the penthouse suites."

Norah's suite was neither opulent nor large, but it was quite nice. Off the parlor, one door led to the bedroom and one door led to a spacious private bath.

"Nice place." Jack was interested, but exhaustion was tempering his arousal.

"Take a load off, soldier." She held up a crystal tumbler. "Drink?"

Jack declined. "That'd put me to sleep."

Norah smiled wryly. "Well, we mustn't have *that*." She motioned to the bath. "Would you like to freshen up?"

He was taken aback. "Huh?"

"Please. You said yourself it's been a long day. I presume you share a bath back at the . . . where are you staying? Oh, never mind. You'll find a kit on the shelf. Razor. Soap. Tooth powder. Take your time. Refresh yourself." She poured a gin and tonic and sliced a twist of lime. "I'm a night owl. Really, no hurry."

He walked to the bath without thinking. Music played through the door while he lathered his face. He recognized a different voice coming from the sitting room. It was Orphan Ann, blathering on Radio Tokyo. As he toweled dry, he noticed a blue silk robe Norah must have delivered while he was in the shower.

"You were right," he said, entering the sitting room. "That felt great. Thanks."

Norah rose and walked to him. She ran the back of her hand across one cheek and her fingertips across the other. "Mmm. I do love a sparkling-clean man. I won't be but a minute." She waved him toward a small bar table near the window. "I had them bring up some tea and biscuits. Or, if you prefer, the juice is wonderful. It's papaya." She headed toward the bath.

"One fine caboose." Beyond the radio, Jack heard water filling the tub. "Gonna be more than a minute." He downed a glass of juice and poured another. After a few biscuits he felt rejuvenated and closed his eyes to picture the singer's auburn hair shining through the smoky cones of colored stage light.

Norah returned barefoot wearing ruby red lipstick and two fluffy white towels, one wrapping her torso and one wrapping her head. "I hope you don't mind wet hair?" she asked, rhetorically. "I so much prefer to spend the night freshly clean." She poured herself a cup of tea, adding milk and lemon. "Smoking's for the day, don't you agree?"

"I don't smoke, day or night. But I'm used to bein' in it."

Norah eased the bedroom door open. "My understanding is I'm . . . a bit out of the ordinary with my insistence on cleanliness . . . *in here*." She tipped her head toward the bed.

Jack walked in past her.

"I really don't understand why anyone *wouldn't* insist." She closed the door behind them and continued, "You see, I don't want the nasty residuals of the day on my skin and in my nose. I want *you* on my skin, I want *you* in my nose." She touched his neck. "I don't wish to taste dirt and sweat. I want to taste *you*." She ran her hand down his chest, his abdomen, and stopped at his crotch. "Just you."

She unwrapped the towel from her hair and let the other one drop to the floor. She twisted her wet tresses across her shoulder. "Now wouldn't you prefer to taste me, *just* me, and not the remnants of a hot summer day in the tropics?"

Jack was straining against the low-hanging cord that held his robe closed and grinning like an idiot. Norah dropped to her knees and slid her hand into his robe. "Let's start with you, shall we?"

She looked up at him with deep green eyes, like emeralds at night. He stroked her wet hair. Something classical was playing on the radio outside the door. He felt so good his thoughts wandered and found Chloe. His mind raced around her, and his heart sank. That wasn't all that sank.

"Is something wrong, dear?"

"No, no. Not at all. This feels swell."

She pulled herself up to him. "Swell? How . . . *American*." She crawled onto bed, draping her torso with the top sheet.

Norah was lovely, a classic beauty from her silky, sunset auburn hair to her long, creamy legs stemming from a tight pear-shaped bottom. When he pulled the sheet back, he found a torso splattered with pink scars in a variety of sizes and shapes. "A little something I acquired last spring from the renowned and incomparable German surrealist, Hermann Göring. He works in shrapnel." The stark reality focused his attention on her, only her.

She kept condoms in the nightstand. "I'd help but . . ."

He hadn't any more performance issues the remainder of the night, and Norah appreciated his attention to detail. They had chemistry, especially for having just met. When Jack awoke to a midmorning knock at the front door, his lover was sound asleep, her head on his chest, her arm across his abdomen. He slid out, collected the robe, and answered the door. A boy rolled in a breakfast cart. Jack tipped with American and closed the door. He turned to find Norah leaning on the bedroom doorframe, nude.

"It's too soon for breakfast. I want some more of that." She pointed. "Let's have dessert first, shall we?"

Jack bounded across the room, and she put her hand to his chest. "You know the rules, Captain." Tipping her head toward the bath.

"You're a funny girl, Norah Davies."

"Yes, Jack. I am rather set in my ways." They repeated the bathing routine and enjoyed a lengthy session in the bedroom.

She purred and rubbed his chest in slow, tender circles. "I don't know that I've ever screamed like that." She laughed. "What *will* the neighbors say?"

* * *

"It might be nice to see you again, Jack."

He tied his shoes, then rose and kissed her long and hard. "How about tonight?"

"Come see me at the club?"

"Sure thing."

As he pulled away, she snatched his arm. "Kiss me again, please."

She fiddled with her robe belt while they waited for the elevator. "So, where do they have you staying?" The door opened. He stepped in and, with a crooked grin and eyes locked on hers, told the operator, "Floor two, please."

* * *

Toby agreed to accompany him to The Lagoon that night, but it took some doing. "You sure got the hots for that dame."

Many of the boys were set on hard drinking and soft whores, with a focus on quantity. Jack's sober interest in jazz and steady companionship didn't fit the mold, so by the third night, he was the only AVG who saw closing time at The Lagoon. The next morning, he woke to the breakfast knock in an otherwise empty bed.

Famished, he dug in while Norah was still in the bath.

"I see you started without me." Her tone was cool, a bit of scold in it.

"Yeah, that was rude of me," Jack admitted while scooping half a kiwi into his mouth. "But I was really hungry, and that wasn't all my fault." He spanked her bottom as she walked past. Norah closed the bedroom door behind her, and it was an hour before she reappeared, perfectly coiffed. The radio was playing softly, and Jack was on the settee snoring softly. She picked up her silk clutch, checked her hair in the mirror, and left him there.

"How's Red?" Toby moaned, sprawled across Jack's bed and still wearing last night's clothes.

Jack ignored the question. "Y'all visit the *Salon* again last night?" That's what the men had taken to calling the brothels on Smith Street.

Toby sighed loudly. "Ordered Siamese twins. Boy, oh boy, was it bonkers."

"*Siamese twins?* That's bilge water, Ensign Gyer."

Toby swung his legs off the bed, pushed himself upright, and cradled his throbbing head. "Feel like I'm gonna upchuck." He staggered toward the bath while wagging a finger at Jack. "My baby dolls are from Siam, and they're twins. Makes them Siamese twins, smart guy."

The next morning, the pilots were called to a meeting in a sitting room off the Raffles main ballroom.

"What the hell is this about?" Gil Weathers groused, and he wasn't the only one complaining. The room was lousy with carping and smelled of sweat, whiskey, and tobacco. "I need some food, dammit."

"Ten-hut!"

Everyone piped down and looked up. Jack didn't recognize the voice or the face of the man who stepped up onto a chair. Short-sleeve khaki shirt, tie, shorts, and long socks, complete with pith helmet and a pistol strapped across his chest. He looked like a colonial officer. The man removed the helmet and tucked it under an arm, exposing a balding pate over his jowly cheeks.

"At ease, men. My name is Harvey Greenlaw. I'm Colonel Chennault's chief of staff and will command AVG ground operations."

Jack had expected to hear an English officer's accent, but this guy sounded more like a salesman from Pittsburgh.

"It has come to my attention that some members of this group have engaged in behavior lacking the decorum appropriate to the endeavor upon which we've embarked, and the housing which has been graciously afforded to you during this layover in Singapore."

Gil Weathers poked Jack in the ribs. "If I got that right, he said we've been drinking and fighting."

Toby laughed, and Jack whispered in his ear, "That's gotta be the first clever thing that meatball's ever said."

"For a military organization to properly function, discipline must be maintained on and off duty, the extent to which members of that organization . . ."

The chastising continued for an eternity, and by the time he concluded, what began as wisps of evaporating alcohol and bad breath had accumulated to a formidable stench seasoned with flatulence, wrapped in a thick layer of smoke.

Someone at the back of the room hollered. "Can someone turn on the fan? There's no damn air in here."

Greenlaw snapped, "This is precisely an example of what I have been saying. It seems whatever discipline exercised by the members of this outfit before you resigned your service has been overwhelmed by a lack of regimen during your crossing. This will be remedied soon. Shore leave is canceled. You are to pack your belongings and return to the ship immediately. Our departure has been expedited, and this unit will not transfer to British vessels. The *Jagersfontein* will raise anchor in short order. Report to the ship by no later than 1600 hours. That is all. Dismissed."

"What a jerk," Toby growled, firing a smoke.

The men shuffled out, and there was a commotion of low whistles and muffled catcalls as they passed Harvey Greenlaw in the main ballroom.

"Did you see that?" Sal Capone described a gorgeous dark-haired woman who joined Greenlaw after his speech.

"Turns out she's *Mrs.* Greenlaw. What a doll!"

Toby had his head on a swivel, straining to see. "Don't even think about it, pal." Jack patted his back. "Besides, you have what, five hours before we hit the plank?"

Toby stopped in his tracks. "Jack . . ."

"Yeah, I'll pack your stuff. You go pack your twins."

Toby quickly patted down his pockets. He found a tenner and six singles. Grinning from ear to ear, he waved the money under Jack's nose and took off like a shot.

* * *

"So that's it?" she spat out the words like a curse.

"I gotta go to work," he snapped. "And I work in China."

They were both angry, which only betrayed the feelings they'd so quickly developed. He enjoyed time with Norah, very much. The sex. The conversation. Just lying together, listening to the radio. The thought of Chloe occasionally interfered, but he was comfortable with Norah.

"Look . . ."

"No!" She interrupted. "Just go already."

He reached out, and she pulled away, plopping down on the settee. With a smooth, single-handed dexterity, she lifted the lid from a porcelain container and gave it a shake, making a cigarette jump high enough so she could trap it with her index finger. She raised the container and pinched the smoke out with her lips. He struck the table lighter for her.

"I want to say something."

She looked up at him through the smoke. Her innocent eyes belied her bravado. "You don't need to *say something*. You need to leave." Her eyes were wet and looking a little crazy.

"Look," he said, sitting down beside her. "You love singin' at The Lagoon. That's plain to see. But it's only a matter of time before the Japs come. You said it yourself. Could be months, could be weeks. Hell, I don't know, but they're comin', and it's gonna be bad when they do."

"And where do you suggest I go, Jack? London? Go home and give the frigging Nazis my other arm?"

"I don't know. Australia. New Zealand. Go 'round to Capetown. Somewhere south, away from here. The Japs are gonna attack you Brits. They're in it with Hitler, and they're going to hafta do somethin', and they ain't gonna start Down Under. It'll be Hong Kong, Singapore first. It'll be a while before they get down south, if they ever do."

She put on a brave face. "The authorities say there's nothing to worry about. Singapore's a fortress."

"Yeah? And when have these authorities been right about anything, Norah? The Maginot Line? The damn Krauts went right around it! The Japs, the Germans, the Italians. They're all bananas, and a bunch of cocky Brits in pith helmets and knee socks ain't gonna stop 'em with cannons on the beach. They're gonna bomb the hell out of this place, same as London."

He leaned in to kiss her. She stiffened. "Look, you deserve . . ."

She searched his face.

"Go down to Sydney."

Norah's expression softened and a tear trickled down her cheek. He wiped it with his thumb.

"No doubt they like music down there, the Aussies. There were a bunch of them at The Lagoon, right? They'll eat you up, just like I did." She laughed and bit her lip, tears welling in her eyes. "Well, maybe not *just* like I did. But there's gotta be at least one mug down there who don't mind soap so much."

Norah snorted and burst into laughter, loosening a whole stream of tears. Jack wrapped her in his arms.

20

THE OLD MAN'S SCHOOL

AUGUST 1941

Toungoo, Burma, sat just off the railway and roadway that ran along the Sittang River, halfway up the five-hundred mile route from Rangoon Harbor to Mandalay where the rail terminated in the north. There, all the material sent by rail to support China was loaded onto trucks to finish the journey to its military hub, Kunming, another seven hundred arduous miles across muddy switchbacks through mountainous jungle terrain. This was the *Burma Road*, China's lifeline since its coastal harbors had fallen under Japanese control.

At Toungoo, the east side of the roadway was lined with food stalls offering fruit, curries and cured meats. The west side, which fronted the hamlet's residential area, was lined with a tented bazaar where shopkeepers hawked everything from clothing and boots to rubies and jade to vehicle parts and vulcanized truck tires, along with an ever-changing supply of black-market booze and tobacco. Behind it lay a six-block grid of some forty houses, home to the British colonials who ran things and the Indian colonials who supported them. Claire Chennault had a place on Steel Road, as did Harvey and Olga Greenlaw.

When he first came across Chennault, Jack saluted. "Colonel."

"Well, look who's here." Chennault returned the salute and took up the young man's hand. "Damn if it hasn't been, what, some ten years now?"

"I believe so, sir."

Chennault was beaming. "Captain Benoit, it's good to have you here. If you're half the pilot your father was . . ."

"Yes, sir. I'm confident I won't disappoint you, sir."

Chennault finally let go of his hand. "So tell me, how's your family? How's Elaine? I hope well. And Frank and Odette, his Sweetwater girl. Are they still in Louisiana?"

"Very well, sir. Frank and Odette have a couple little ones. The boy looks just like his daddy."

Chennault looked happy to hear it. "We're going to do some big things here, Captain Benoit. Yes, we are."

From July through October, monsoon season, Toungoo was a steaming muddy mess, and even between the brutal, days-long downpours, it was impossible to stay dry in the oppressive humidity and heat. The Burma Road bustled day and night with trains and with loaded supply trucks headed north and empty vehicles returning to Rangoon Harbor, all carving deep ruts in the monsoon mud. Thousands of Chinese coolies lined the road day and night to free stuck vehicles and fill ruts.

The insects were nearly unbearable. Flying, crawling, biting, burrowing, and the only respite from their relentless attacks was sleeping under mosquito netting, where the incessant buzzing took some getting used to.

But what surprised Jack the most were the dogs. Smallish, feral mutts with pointy ears and noses, mangy brown fur soaked from the rain or matted with dried mud. They were everywhere. Packs and loners, many dragging a leg. The steady rumble of trucks was regularly punctuated by yelps as yet another dog was crushed or maimed while trying to reach a scrap of something discarded on the road. Each truck lumbering through the mud disturbed the mass of flies feeding on each carcass, sending them airborne to create a human-sized black cyclone. Urbanized vultures stationed themselves at regular intervals along the road, engaging in regular conflict with the dogs. The coolies assigned to rut duty also collected carcasses for burning.

The town sported one restaurant, the Savoy, housed in the rail station, and a single nightclub, the Silver Grill, which doubled as the brothel. A few houses in town rented out rooms where the men could stay when on leave from Kyedaw, the British airfield that lay some eight miles northwest, the AVG's new home.

Jack preferred base to town, even during leave. The airfield was far enough west of the Burma Road that the train and truck noise was more of a low, steady rumble, like distant rolling thunder.

Kyedaw Field consisted of a command center, a hangar, and a four-thousand-foot asphalt runway. The AVG joined the British contingent stationed there, Royal Air Force 67 Squadron, which was composed of thirty-two Brewster Buffalo fighter-bombers supported by some seventy ground crewmen and staff, and twice that number of Indian, Burmese, and Chinese laborers and servants.

Coolies built new barracks with split bamboo walls and palm-thatched roofs to house AVG personnel. The buildings featured half walls to allow for maximum airflow, and each cot was coupled with a footlocker and draped with mosquito netting. Two new mess halls were built, one for AVG pilots and one for crew. Coolies were constantly repairing damage to the buildings and grounds caused by the monsoon rains and runoff. Indian workers dug and covered latrines and emptied the men's chamber pots. Burmese men prepared and cooked the food, and Burmese boys served the meals and cleaned the cookware and dishes.

Though it was as hot as San Antonio and more humid than Abbeville, it was the bugs that got to Jack. Beetles. Spiders. Lice. Flies. Fleas. Mosquitoes. Centipedes. He considered taking up smoking just to keep the flying ones out of his face. The Brits swore that drinking gin was the best mosquito repellent.

Flit was sprayed on everything, including their bedding. As a result, the whole camp smelled like a Vaseline cocktail with a splash of kerosene. Smudge pots burned punkwood near all the buildings, and burn barrels smoked the air near the latrines. Nothing felt better than a shower, and it was the only way Jack could clear his nose. The men showered with rainwater collected in shaded cisterns, so it was usually below body temperature. Regardless, as soon as he stepped out of the water, refreshed and clean, he was swarmed by insects and grabbed the nearest can of Flit to apply a fresh layer. The other pilots took to teasing him because he showered so often, at least three times a day, but an additional benefit was he would think of Norah at least three times a day.

Despite the heat and the insects, he enjoyed the routine and kept up his predawn calisthenics. He worked out some evenings, too. Burning so much energy, he ate for a man half again his size, starting every morning with a big pile of eggs and ham.

He enjoyed the morning lessons conducted by Colonel Chennault, whom everyone referred to as the *Old Man*. In addition to classroom training, all the flyers were checked out on the P-40Bs through ground and flight maneuvers. Chennault involved Jack as a trainer because he already had so many hours in the equipment. The pilots finished their workdays by early afternoon, and boredom was an issue. They took naps, played cards and softball, and for many their grousing increased over time between weekly leaves when they were able to take advantage of the amenities offered in the rooms above the Silver Grill.

Whereas the pilots had plenty of free time, the ground crew never lacked for work. Some afternoons Jack hung around the hangar with the mechanics, helping out where he could. There was a shortage of parts for the Tomahawks, and he was impressed by the crew's improvisations. The plan had been for a contingent of a hundred planes with pilot and crew support for fighter defense and escort, but neither machinery nor personnel came close to those numbers, and the plan for bombers never came to fruition.

In the classroom, the Old Man hammered home his primary tactic for fighter defense. Pounce from above. Dive through the bomber formations in flights of three planes, consolidating fire on select targets. It was hit and run, pure and simple. Extra armor plating welded into the cockpit added weight that, combined with ammunition and full fuel tanks, slowed the Tomahawk's initial climb. But after burning fuel at altitude and cutting loose the fifty-caliber guns during an initial dive, the fighters could climb again much faster to reengage the enemy for a second run, lighter and faster than the first.

The crew had done a fine job with the plating, so the weight was balanced from side to side and front to back, maintaining proper aerodynamics. The electronic gunsights that had been ordered never arrived, so the crew fashioned their own design using a simple, mirrored mechanism. Tires were a problem, shredding on the steamy asphalt runway during landings, so all flight training was completed during the early morning hours.

The food at the Savoy was better than what the Brits were served in their mess, but AVG rations at Kyedaw were pretty good, a reason Jack didn't mind spending leave on base. Still, he went into town occasionally to walk the bazaar and play cards at the Silver Grill. Without exception, the men who climbed the stairs to enjoy female companionship preferred the lighter fare. There weren't any white girls, and so the few girls with mixed British–Indian blood were always busy, and commanded a premium. Down the list were the Indian girls, followed by the Burmese. The longest drinkers, the last to climb the stairs, would announce to the room, "Going dark!"

In September, Jack took up company with a lazy-eyed raven-haired Burmese girl named Sanda. Two years his junior, she wore her hair in a bob, the result of a recent botched attempt to eradicate a nasty lice infection. Neither the eye nor the bob worked in her favor above the Silver Grill. Jack liked that she wasn't in high demand and paid her on the side at a substantial multiple of the going rate. He enjoyed running his fingers along her silky skin, and she enjoyed rubbing his *soft spots*, the side of his abdomen, the inside of his bicep. They would lie in bed for hours, talking. With nothing in common, Sanda told him what she knew about the local fauna and flora. She adored flowers of all kinds and knew a great deal about them. Jack asked her what her name meant.

"My name is Ma Sanda Khaing. For you this means *young moon behind branch of the tree*. I came to be during a full moon. My mother told me it was light as day, so the Nats stayed away. She was looking out the window at the moon when I was born."

Jack twirled a curl of her bob around his finger. "Nats?"

"Yes. Spirits who live in the trees. They can make much mischief." She sighed. "My mother told me she thought to name me *hidden tiger*. She could see the tiger's whiskers on the moon, behind the branch. But my father said I would be moon, not tiger."

"So where was that? Where are you from?"

"I was raised to the south, in Phyu." She rubbed slow circles with her fingertip on the inside of his bicep.

"And your parents? They're in *Foo?*"

"My parents left five years ago."

"Where to?"

"My father left in an accident, while working in the jungle. My mother left with malaria." She circled his nipple. "And you, Jack? Tell me about America."

He told his story about moving around. Alabama, Texas, Louisiana, back to Texas.

"These places, they are close, or they are far?"

She was surprised to learn his family moved eight hundred miles across his country.

"Do you have grandparents in *Foo?* I mean, how'd you end up . . . how'd you come to Toungoo?"

"It is not a hard life over the Silver Grill, compared to the lives of many people."

He sliced one of the mangoes he'd brought and offered her a piece. They ate in silence on the bed. "Why don't you do somethin' else? Get a job in a shop or somethin'?"

"You see Toungoo."

"Yeah, but why not move? Go somewhere, like Rangoon."

Sanda stood and started to dress. "I must go back to work now."

"I'd like to keep you, *exclusive-like.*"

She didn't answer.

He tried again. "Just the two of us."

Sanda touched his hand. "I am flattered, Jack. But you will leave. Maybe not so soon, but yes. I must consider my future. Staying with Madam is the best way."

He lay back and stared at the cracked ceiling. Two large centipedes were approaching the corner on the far wall. He bet on the one on the left. "Sure. Let's just keep things how they are."

But Jack talked with Silver Grill management the next time he was in town. He offered a lucrative deal to keep Sanda exclusive, which was accepted, but soon thereafter he learned she worked plenty when he wasn't around. So, he, too, resigned to the possible.

* * *

The Tomahawks were shaping up. There weren't as many as had been planned, but what they did have, the crew had humming. It was late September, and the monsoons were relentless. Sixty-two pilots were training in fifty-four planes, each painted in green and khaki camouflage with the underside a sky-colored gray blue. Each wing sported the Chinese Nationalist emblem, a white twelve-point sunburst, each tail was wrapped with a stripe. White, blue or red, to represent one of three squadrons.

Each squadron coined a name and designed nose art. The first squadron chose the *Panda Bears*, the second the *Adam and Eves*, and the third, where Captain Jack Benoit was a flight leader, adopted *Hell's Angels* from Howard Hughes' famous movie about fighter pilots in the Great War. Their nose art was a red outline of a nude female with flowing hair and white wings, set in any one of a number of poses. Jack picked the reclining angel, her arms up, fingers locked behind her head. The squadron emblems were painted on the fuselage over the wing, just in front of the canopy and under the pilot's name. Each plane was numbered in white near the tail. Jack drove No. 91.

His wings handled like a dream, and the power was exhilarating. Over 10,000 feet, the flyers enjoyed respite from the heat. But this often came at the expense of nausea, which was triggered not just by repetitive climbing and diving, but also by the drastic changes in temperature.

"It wouldn't be so bad if I wasn't soaked in sweat before I left the runway," Sal complained through a mouthful of peanut butter sandwich. "It feels great at 8,000 feet, but at 23,000, it's like there's ice in my skivvies."

"That might come in handy after your maneuvers over the Silver Grill," Jack laughed.

"When do you think we'll see some action?" Toby handed his lunch tray to a boy and lit an unfiltered Camel.

Sal snagged a smoke from Toby's pack. "I've got September 25 in the pool, so it better be next week, or I'm out the dough."

Jack pondered out loud. "I don't get us pilots that got here in July ain't already tanglin' with the Jap bombers over Kunming. I s'pose the colonel's waitin' until the new guys get more hours in, so we'll have better numbers." They all shrugged.

* * *

Mail call, and Jack got a letter.

1 September 1941

Dearest PV,

Today I received your letter dated 23 July, and my heart leaped when I saw the envelope that brought a part of you to me from so far away. You were so thoughtful to write to me on my birthday and send me your wish for my happiness at Howard University. Sadly, I cannot say it will come true.

Menta's health has not improved, and I cannot leave her, so Howard University will do without me. I understand my duties to my family, but it is you only who may understand what this is doing to me. Often I think it would be better if I had never known Paris, had never known the freedom to be Chloe Boisvert. It is difficult to fight my bitterness. But it is done, and I must resign myself to what may be, not what I believe should be.

When I read about your insects, my first thought was to wish you butterflies.

Your Odette comes by the café every week to buy a pie. She is very kind to Francie and Menta, and to me. She stayed for talk and tea for quite a long time a few days ago, brightening the Music Box with her cheer. She brought articles about the war from the Abbeville Meridional, the New Orleans Times-Picayune, and the Daily Advertiser from Lafayette, but there is very little to read about China. I believe she misses you and worries and so comes to see me to think about you. Oh, yes, she brought Pumpkin with her. I enjoyed rubbing her ears, and she closed her eyes like she does.

Francie has asked me to write something from her. "PJ, I would like you to come home and play vingt-et-un with me. I have learned a new pie, and you would enjoy it very much."

In your letter you spoke of training and not of danger. I cannot help you, but I do wish we could share our thoughts like we did in the past. I hope you have a friend you can talk to about the things that are important to you. I miss that terribly with you gone from me. I no longer meet with Dr. Herod, and except for you, he was the only person with whom I could discuss the things that are important to me, if only some. Now I cannot help but feel anger toward the reverend. I am certain that if he had not held me here, like a prisoner for his own intellectual pleasure, I would have been at Howard University for two years now, having sent money to Menta during that time. She and Francie, and certainly I, would be better off for it. I cannot pretend to understand this white man's prison in which I must live. Dr. Herod professes to believe in a different kind of world, one of equality and opportunity, yet he is as much the architect of my prison as Jim Crow.

I have read what I have written thus far, and it is so bitter. I am sorry to burden you with these thoughts, but I am sending it out to you because you are the only one to whom I may say these things, and they are burning me inside. Please forgive me *for burdening you so, especially while you are in such personal danger.*

I love you, PJ. I think of you every day. The butterflies will be coming soon. I will watch them follow the bayou south for the both of us.

Please do all you can to stay safe.
With warmest regards,

Chloe

* * *

The Old Man pointed a wooden rod at a silhouette on the chalkboard.

"The Mitsubishi Ki-21, what we call the Sally. The heavy bomber used by the Imperial Army in the China Theater. A Sally can carry a 2,200-pound bomb payload and has a total range of 1,500 miles. From the underside, the Sally looks like a soaring hawk. See here, where the wings are attached near the middle of the fuselage. This is a good way to identify the aircraft from under or above. Making a leisurely comparison, it would be difficult to confuse the Sally with the older model Ki-30 Ann bomber. See here, the Ann's side view. A much shorter aircraft with this long, glass canopy on top. A much slower airplane, with a cruising speed of just 260 miles per hour. Only two crewmen in the Ann, too, the pilot and a single gunner/bombardier. So, just one gun in defense, rising from the back of the canopy. The best approach to the Ann is from behind and under, where it cannot be defended. If you're fortunate enough to find a squadron of Anns without fighter support, it should be a turkey shoot. But that's why you'll likely find fighter support with Anns. Now, the Sallys are a different story. Approaching a flight of Sallys is like walking into a shooting gallery."

Chennault went on to explain the configuration of the Ki-21 and its five machine gun defenses. "They'll light the sky around you with tracer rounds. It'll look like you're flying through a yellow spider web. But given the swing range on the various guns, some approaches will yield more success, more safely, than others." He pounded the chalkboard. "These, the Sallys, they're what have been tearing up

Kunming, and we're going to bring them down. On our first go, we'll likely find bombers without fighter support, because they've had no need for escorts thus far."

Jack had never cared much for school, but ever since Frank first showed him how to lead a duck with a shotgun, he'd been fascinated by three-dimensional shooting. Back in the classroom at Randolph, he'd loved learning about new model airplanes. Now, every day here at Kyedaw, he sat at the front of the lectures and listened intently, even as Chennault repeated himself for new arrivals. Next to him sat Lieutenant Shu Hao.

At twenty-nine-years-old, Shu Hao was half again Jack's age. The youngest son of a successful merchant trader, Shu Hao had completed university in England at Oxford, followed by partial credit against a master's degree in economics at Cambridge. In addition to Mandarin and multiple Cantonese dialects, he was proficient in English and possessed passing French.

Chennault called for a break, and Shu Hao leaned toward Jack. "The colonel is correct. The Japanese are very confident from years of bombing without interference. With appropriate preparation, in our first engagement, the only limit to our potential will be the number of planes in the air. If we have numbers and they have numbers, we'll down a meaningful total of their bombers. If that meaningful total is also a meaningful percentage, the Japanese command will halt their bombing campaign to reconsider strategy. We can give Kunming weeks of respite with one successful encounter."

Shu Hao was unusually excited and continued. "Hopefully, soon thereafter, we'll have our bombers, and we'll take the battle to Japan. Hit them at home. Put them on the back foot." He shook his head. "The Japanese do not respect the Chinese. Confucius said, 'Without feelings of respect, what is there to distinguish men from beasts?' This is the underpinning of Japanese cruelty. Nanking, and the countless other atrocities they have committed. Their delusional sense of superiority overwhelms any capacity for respect. Hence, they act like beasts. They must be stopped."

Jack found Chennault's lectures the most interesting when he discussed Japanese tactics. The Old Man had four years of study under his belt, having watched bomber formations and escorts with binoculars as bombed rained down on China. From operations and training manuals captured from downed enemy aircraft, Chennault probably knew more about Japanese fighter tactics than any single

Japanese pilot. To Jack, this sounded like the key. Everyone was always talking about Jap discipline, their strict adherence to orders. If it was in the manual, he figured that's what they'd do. They wouldn't finish a chase. They would entice dogfights. The Old Man said, "Hit and run." Jack figured that's just what he'd do.

Chennault spent most of his time at Kyedaw, readying the AVG pilots, but he was also responsible for the Chinese Air Force training at Yunnan-yi, just outside Kunming. The Old Man reported directly to Generalissimo Chiang Kai-shek, who took a strong personal interest in the air force and often made very specific orders regarding both strategy and tactics. He instructed Chennault to take four of the top Chinese performers and train them on P-40Bs with the AVG. And so it was that Shu Hao and three others had come from the Chinese Air Force training school at Yunnan-yi to join the fun in Burma.

Chennault made a personal request of Jack. "Make them feel at home. Unlike some of these boys from the States, the Chinese are very hungry to learn. This is their homeland, and they desperately want to fight for it. I see how you focus during the lectures, Jack, as do the Chinese men. Y'all can help each other. The best of our best will pull the entire unit's performance up, and pull the Chinese Air Force up, too. I expect you and Shu Hao to be in that top group, Jack. I know you won't let me down."

Sometimes when he and Shu Hao shared tea, Chloe would come to mind. They both used so many different words to communicate with precision, and they held such confidence in what they were saying.

"The Sallys are so well armed. They will make for difficult work," Shu Hao continued. "We'll need to keep in mind all of Colonel Chennault's tactics. Approach angles. Coming out of the sun. Concentrating fire. Escape paths."

"I think the hardest bit will be disengaging from the fighters," Jack cocked his head. "I get the Colonel's right. But runnin' ain't my nature."

"Yes, I've been thinking about this, Jack, and I no longer think of disengagement as retreat. Instead, I think of it like court dancing."

"What the hell is court dancin'?"

Shu Hao explained how European court dancing involves long, scripted movements and interactions. "For example, one may wish to twirl one's partner, but there are other maneuvers that must happen first, as part of the dance. One walks away, spins, jumps, claps. The twirling must wait. Diving out of an attack is just a part of our dance with the invaders. It's not running. It's a movement that is necessary to complete the dance successfully."

Jack liked the way Shu Hao explained things. It reminded him of Chloe, too.

"As the colonel has explained, the best way to distinguish the Nate from the Hayabusa is the landing gear. The Nate's landing gear is fixed. If you don't see wheels, it's a Hayabusa, and the Hayabusa can turn even tighter than the Japanese Navy's Zero."

"So what's it matter?"

"What do you mean?"

"Well, if we ain't gonna turn with 'em, get into dogfights, then it just don't matter . . . the gear."

Shu Hao laughed. "Yes, I see. But if we do find ourselves on a fighter's tail, we can know the Hayabusa will likely roll out more tightly."

Jack poured more tea. "You're right. Hell, you're always right, Shu." He studied his friend's face as they drank. Shu Hao was very handsome, with light skin and sharp cheekbones, jet-black hair, and dark eyes. Then it hit him, and he couldn't suppress his laughter.

"Would you care to share your joke with me?"

"You look like Lee Chan."

"Lee Chan. Who is Lee Chan?"

"He's a character in the movies. Charlie Chan movies."

Shu Hao grinned. "So, you think I look like a movie star."

"I didn't say movie *star*. Don't give yourself that much credit. Now *here's* our movie star."

Toby groaned as he sat down at the table.

"How was your night at the Silver Grill?" Jack turned to Shu Hao and teased, "No doubt he scored. All Cary Grant here needs to score at the Silver Grill is his devilishly attractive smile, that and fifty rupees."

* * *

In the morning, the flyers prepared for mock battles.

"Head-ons." Jack slapped Shu Hao's back. "Should be fun."

The two were paired for the maneuvers. A half dozen approaches dead on, a couple each high to low, low to high. "We roll to the right, Shu." Jack popped his friend with a finger gun. "Always to the right."

Standing on the wing of Sal's Tomahawk, the sun reflecting off his Ray-Ban aviators, Shu Hao did look like a movie star. He hollered over to No. 91. "Success depends upon preparation. Without preparation, there is sure to be failure!"

Jack mumbled, "Mr. Confucius."

They climbed together, and at fifteen thousand feet, Jack peeled off to put some distance between them. They kept in constant communication over the radio, transmitting altitude, direction, and air speed. This drill was designed to improve depth perception while flying head on toward the enemy. Without clouds for background reference, it was very difficult to gauge closing distance. But with each approach, the flyers became more comfortable holding their lines a little longer. By the end of the drill, Jack and Shu Hao were rolling out within two hundred feet of a head-on crash.

Back on the tarmac, the men embraced, laughing. "That was phenomenal!" Shu Hao said with a big grin. "Truly exhilarating."

"I think I got it. Felt good, know what I mean? Felt right."

Shu Hao agreed and pulled off his bomber jacket. They'd been on the ground for just a few minutes, and their foreheads were beaded with sweat.

"Did you hear about Bright and Armstrong?" It was Toby.

Gil Bright and John Armstrong were Panda Bears paired off for the same exercise. But during a run, instead of rolling out, Armstrong had bored through, like he was on a bicycle in a child's game of chicken. His Tomahawk sheared off Bright's wing, and Bright ejected as his one-winged plane spun wildly toward the ground. Armstrong didn't fare as well. Fragments of his plane were strewn along a mile of jungle. Some of his mangled body was still strapped in the seat.

"Is Bright all right?"

Toby nodded.

"He's a good egg, Bright." Jack offered. "Hey, wasn't it Armstrong who nearly collided with Charlie Mott last week?"

"Yes. Charlie was extremely angry. It almost came to blows in briefing."

Toby shook his head. "Thinnin' the herd."

"Excuse me?" Shu Hao was puzzled.

"Thinnin' the herd. Means stupid animals get themselves killed."

"It's never good when a comrade dies," Shu Hao said. "But, yes, Armstrong was a reckless man. When we're in battle, we must be able to rely upon each other. There will be no room for recklessness. The Japanese won't forgive it."

Chennault was sick again. Whether his constitution was at odds with the tropics or he just had bad luck, the Old Man had been run down by something or other almost continuously since the AVG arrived in July. Week to week, his complexion shifted from pale to flushed, ashen to jaundiced. Those steely eyes were now clouded. Jack knew Chennault as a man of resolve, and it was clear he was fighting through ill health to make this work, to pound his knowledge into the AVG pilots, many of whom carried thick heads. Chennault asked Jack to lead some classes. Jack found the lack of attention paid by some of his pupils extremely frustrating. Lack of attention that would not have been tolerated at Randolph.

A few times in recent weeks, a lone, unidentified aircraft had been spotted cruising over the airbase, but chase planes were never able to catch up, and the Old Man was nervous. The Japanese had quickly made themselves at home in Thailand, pushing aside the hometown Fascists. They were clearing runways and building airbases up and down the Burmese border. Sitting just sixty miles from the border with Thailand, Kyedaw was exposed and isolated.

It had been nearly a month since the Japanese last bombed Kunming, and Chennault knew the Japanese always stuck with their tactics until a change of strategy was being considered. He feared the Empire had shifted its strategy and was preparing for an eradication campaign against the British and AVG forces at Kyedaw in advance of a pre-invasion bombing campaign at Rangoon.

Chennault requested permission from the Generalissimo to redeploy the AVG south to Mingaladon Airfield outside Rangoon, where the British had numbers. As an alternative, he suggested moving the entire unit north to Kunming. Chiang Kai-shek did not speak English, and the Old Man did not speak Chinese, so they communicated through the Generalissimo's wife, Madame Chiang. The Generalissimo had left Chennault hanging for weeks with no response to his request. Fortunately, the Japanese still hadn't attacked.

"Hey, are you coming?" Sal woke Jack from a rare, late-afternoon nap.

"Comin' where?"

"The guys are auctioning off Armstrong's stuff."

***

On a clear and cool mid-November morning, Jack joined a large group of men who were milling around Charlie Bond's No. 5. Bond had seen a photo in the magazine *Illustrated Weekly of India* of a British-flown Tomahawk in North Africa whose nose was painted with a shark's head. He'd done the same with No. 5 using leftover white, red and blue paint. The shark's mouth was open, flashing menacing white teeth set against a blue and red background set below a red and white eye. It was agreed the war paint looked fierce, and within a couple of days, every AVG Tomahawk sported the same nose paint.

When No. 91 was done, Jack found the ground crew had added another detail. On each side of the fuselage, just behind the canopy, a playing card. The jack of clubs.

"It fits." Toby nodded.

"What the . . . ?" Sal yelled.

Jack and Toby hurried over to find Sal, hands on his hips, staring up at his Tomahawk. Behind his canopy was another playing card, the three of hearts.

"Makes perfect sense." It was John McClintock, their flight's lead crewman.

"Yeah, how's that, Chief?" Sal was confused and perturbed.

"Your reputation for double-dipping at the Silver Grill, sir. Three hearts."

21

ORION

NOVEMBER 1941

Chloe sat down under the Big Tree and read the letter yet again.

September 26, 1941

Dear Chloe,

    The monsoons stopped earlier than usual they say. It is a good thing after so much rain and mud. There are butterflies but not like the monarchs. Here they are mostly small and yellow or green. They make colorful little tornados.

    We haven't fought yet. I think it will be soon. Don't worry. We have practiced so much I am sure we will do good. When I see a flyer making mistakes I remember what you said. I will be safe.

    I know you don't like Dr. Herad but he has a piano in the church and you should play because it makes you happy. I don't know about college. Maybe you can go when you are older.

    Say hello to Francie and Menta. Pet Pumpkin for me, okay?

Jack (I go by Jack now)

***

Everyone was thankful the monsoon season concluded early this year.

The dusk air was dry and cool when the men leaned their bicycles against the white picket fence that bordered the lavish garden of the biggest house on Steel Road. Freshly painted green with shiny white shutters, a screened veranda wrapped around three sides of the ground floor, and a smooth cylindrical turret rose three stories on the corner of the ornate Victorian home. The shape of the place looked familiar to him. He was trailing Toby and Sal as they rushed toward the door when he some movement in a second-story window caught his eye. It was the silhouette of a slender woman backlit by low light. She raised a drink to her lips, then greeted him with a tip of the glass.

A trim Indian servant met them at the door. Jack entered last.

"What's your name?"

The man bowed. "Akarsh. At your service."

"What's it mean?"

"Sir?"

"Your name. It means somethin', right?"

"Yes, sir. In English, Akarsh translates to *something divine*."

"Like from God?"

"Yes, sir."

Jack could see he was embarrassing the man and thought better of pressing it.

"Akarsh." He shook the young man's hand. "My name's Jack, and it don't mean a goddamn thing."

John Fulton was Burma's country manager for the MacGregor Company, the largest teakwood supplier in all of Britain. Fulton oversaw the extraction of trees by jungle wallahs and their elephants and ensured the material made it downcountry and onto the ships that steamed from Rangoon Harbor back to England. A portly, monocled bachelor, Fulton was celebrating the anniversary of his arrival in the country, twenty years ago to the day.

As Jack entered, the host was introducing Toby and Sal to the room. He recognized some of the names, including General and Mrs. Bruce Scott. The general commanded the 1st Division of the Burmese Colonial Army. There was Major John James Clarke who led 67 Squadron, the Brewster Buffalos stationed at Kyedaw. With Clarke were two Brits he hadn't met, Captain Charles Thompson and Captain Phillip Edwards. Harvey and Olga Greenlaw were there. It wouldn't be a party without the Greenlaws. Sal, already halfway through his first drink, was making a beeline toward the wife, who was perched on an elegant chaise lounge, sipping a dull-green liquid from a martini glass. A Tiffany-style floor lamp, covered with yellow and green stained glass shaped like palm leaves, lit Olga as if in Technicolor, and a wavy line of smoke snaked from between her fingers up and into the lampshade. Across the room, the AVG chief of staff and the general were puffing pipes and looking serious.

"*Eddy* will do, mate." Of the two new Brits, Captain Edwards seemed the least uptight. "How about a drink?" He snapped his fingers at an Indian boy wearing a long coat the color of pea soup, just a little darker shade of green than Olga's drink. "What's your poison?"

Jack addressed the boy directly. "I'll start with some tea. Green tea."

"Good man! Excellent for the digestion," Eddy laughed. "Excuse me, but I'm going for fruit and cheese. Care for some?"

Jack declined.

The boy was still there. "How would you like your tea, sir?"

Jack thought him to be about twelve years of age. "You got honey?"

The boy nodded, then bowed and retreated.

Eddy returned. "Are you sure you wouldn't care to start with something a little more substantial?" But the question didn't register. Instead, Jack focused on the petite, blond woman drawing near, both of her wet eyes reflecting the orange glow of the cigarette she held high, her elbow propped by a crossed arm. The cigarette was tucked into a sleek, art deco holder that caught the light from Olga's lamp. She swirled the ice in her crystal highball glass, blending the brightly colored liquids inside. In rumpled olive slacks and a sleeveless white linen shirt that left her toned arms bare, the woman looked to Jack like a young tomboy. His eyes fell to the line of iridescent buttons that closed her blouse in the front.

"I'm not sure that's the right place to look," she said.

Jack raised his eyes. "Huh?"

"That's not the place to look for something *a little more substantial*." She shifted her weight, what little there was, and took a long drink.

Eddy laughed and gave the woman a squeeze around the waist. He raised his glass to someone across the room and excused himself. Jack checked the buttons again, then got the joke. He blushed.

"No . . . I mean, I like to pace myself. That is, I don't usually drink much. People say green tea is good for you."

"People say a lot of things." She peered at him over the lip of the sweating highball. "But I can't say I've had the pleasure of meeting an American who paced himself with anything, really." She passed the smoke into her left hand to accompany her drink and extended her right. "I'm Emma. Emma Simpson."

"Jack Benoit. I'm with the AVG."

Emma nodded, took a drag, then drained what was left in her glass. Immediately, a boy was there to collect it.

"Can I get you something? What was that?"

"A little too sweet and sticky for me, really." She pulled hard on her cigarette and glanced around for a smoke stand. "Johnny's a dear, really," she said of their host. "But he's always forcing these fruit-filled concoctions on everyone who doesn't insist on gin and tonic. I prefer your American bourbon, damn the mosquitos."

"Huh?"

"Gin, dear. It quite conveniently repels mosquitoes. But really, I can hardly stand the stuff. Hence the bourbon." She spoke to the boy. "Two Jim Beams."

The way she talked intrigued but discomfited him, like it was a game, and he didn't know the rules. They walked to the bar where another handsome, light-skinned Indian met Emma's request for bourbon by pouring two Jack Daniel's, neat.

She handed one to Jack. "Close enough." She said it as a toast.

"Huh?" He was confused again.

Emma took a swig. "Jack Daniels is a Tennessee sour mash, not a Kentucky rye. Join me out back, will you, Jack Benoit?" She turned to the barman with a little bow. "Thank you, Soheil."

No one noticed as they left the main rooms. Sal and Toby were taking turns making Olga Greenlaw laugh, while the general regaled the other guests with a story from his early days of soldiering in the Boer War. A hallway led past the kitchen and a line of pantries to the back of the house where the veranda widened into a large, screened-in room. Its white-painted wicker furniture and pale-blue cushions constrasted with the lush green jungle flora just yards away. The patio was lit with Chinese lanterns in yellow, red, and green spiraling out from the ceiling fan that was slowly spinning at the center of the room.

Emma plopped down on a loveseat, sitting over a bent leg. She patted the cushion next to her. "So, tell me something about yourself, Jack Benoit." She kept using his full name, how Chloe would do when she was mad at him.

"Benoit," she continued. "French? And your accent . . . you're from New Orleans."

"Tennessee whiskey. Kentucky bourbon. N'Orleans accents. Seems you're an expert on the States."

She scooted closer. "Was I right, about you?" Her eyes fired with anticipation, like a child's, and she returned to thinking out loud. "You're Acadian. What are they called now?" She threw her head back and squeezed her eyes tight under a furrowed brow. "Mmmm, Creole, right? But there's another word that escapes me."

"Cajun."

"That's it." She pointed at him. "But of course you would know. Well, perhaps I should have just asked!" She laughed and patted his thigh.

Jack sipped his whiskey. He preferred ice with his liquor, when he drank it.

"My daddy was Creole, so I s'pose that makes me Creole. Half, at least. I lived in Louisiana for a while, but not N'Orleans. A little town out in the country. Never much thought about my accent. I s'pose from over here, they're close enough to sound the same, Perry and N'Orleans, that is." He paused to think and watched Emma slide a hand into her pocket. "I s'pose it's like that in England, too. People sound different, even though they grew up pretty close to each other. But then, to me, y'all sound the same. Like you and all them Brits in there. I don't hear a difference, really, the way y'all talk. But I s'pose there is."

Emma nodded as she retrieved her silver cigarette case. She offered one to Jack.

"No, thanks. I don't partake."

She extracted a smoke, snapped the case shut, tapped the tobacco down, and placed it in the holder. "So, useless to ask for a light?"

Jack produced a lighter and fired the cigarette. She took a long drag and leaned back, watching Jack pocket his Zippo.

"To light up all the girls?"

"I bought a couple oil lamps. Helps keep the stench down some when I'm sleepin'. The number-one boy back at the barracks, he brings scented oils for me."

Emma had known American men in India and met some recently in Burma. She'd spent only a few minutes with this one who didn't smoke, drank almost reluctantly, and, *oil lamps?* "The number-one boy," she thought aloud, under her breath.

"What's that?" Jack said.

"Oh, nothing. Just a thought. It's flitted away." It was quiet for a bit. Emma plucked the butt from the holder and snuffed it in a marble ashtray. She sat up straight. "So, tell me something about yourself. How does Mr. Jack Benoit come to Burma? How does the boy from Louisiana find himself a mercenary, halfway around the world?"

He studied her face, a subtle portrait in yellow, red, and green. Her hair was sandy, like Odette's. A strawberry tint? He couldn't tell in this light. He was surprised by the wisp of gray at one temple, and some wrinkles starting in at the edges of her eyes. He figured her to be much older than he first thought, maybe in her thirties.

Jack met her eyes. They were hazel, with tiny black specks. A spray of freckles spread across her cheeks from the bridge of her smallish, upturned nose.

"Find what you're looking for?"

Jack smirked and flushed again. He took a breath and found his crooked smile. "Your freckles."

Emma raised an eyebrow.

He gently poked her cheek. "They look familiar."

"*Familiar?*" Emma said, with genuine surprise. She noted a faraway look in his eyes. He'd floated off somewhere with Chloe, naked and spooning in the shade. "How so?"

Jack snapped out of it and laughed self-consciously. "Huh?"

"How are my freckles familiar?"

"Well, I knew someone back in the States . . ." He stopped.

"Did you study her closely, too, Jack Benoit?"

He laughed. "You might say so, yes."

Emma jiggled her glass and took a swig. "It's Orion."

"Huh?"

"Orion. It's a constellation of stars in the sky." She connected the more prominent dots on her cheek. "This line of three running between the two other dark ones? That's his belt."

"Orion you say." He envisioned Cassiopeia.

"A hunter, like you. In China, he's known as Shen." She gave him a wry smile. "Perhaps our meeting was destined, Jack Benoit. Destined by the stars."

Her words made him tingle some. He didn't know if she was willing or making fun of him. He thought maybe both.

"So, are you ready for your war?"

"Can't say it's *my* war."

"Still."

Jack finished his drink and noticed Emma's glass was empty, too. "Another?"

"But of course."

Jack took her glass but didn't stand. "So how'd you come to Burma? I mean, why are you here? You a nurse with the Colonial Army?"

"*Why*, indeed. The eternal question."

A dog growled in the bushes just off the veranda. Another started in, then a third started barking. Soon it was a canine chorus.

"Damn mongrels." Emma's mood soured. "All they do is eat, drink, fuck, fight, and howl at the moon. Big surprise they're man's best friend." She stood, a little wobbly. "Let's go see about those drinks, shall we?"

The British captains were leaning on the piano, watching Major Clarke pound out a lively tune. The party had expanded significantly, and the front room was packed with bodies, heat, smoke, and laughter. At the center of the scrum, Sal was dancing with Olga Greenlaw, if you could call it that. The tall beauty was all but holding the drunken beast upright.

Emma ordered doubles from Soheil.

"Some ice in mine," Jack added.

They were served. Emma motioned with her head, and Jack followed her up a spiral staircase. Despite the baggy slacks on her tiny frame, he very much liked what he saw and hoped he would soon see more. At the top of the stairs, they crossed the upper floor, passing a toilet and a couple of closed doors Jack assumed led to bedrooms.

"The tower!" he exclaimed as they entered a round room encircled by a beautifully carved bench that ran the length the windows. Emma sat and stretched out, catlike. Jack spun on his heels to take it in, enjoying the pleasant breeze that crossed the room.

"So, you were saying how you came to Burma."

"Was I?" Emma pulled her knees to her chest and looked out the window. She sighed and took her time. "I was in India for a while. A long while." She paused. "How might I put it for you? Let's say, life took a *nosedive*." She shifted, sliding a leg underneath her like she had on the veranda. She patted the bench here, too.

Jack swirled his glass. He liked the sound of ice in a glass. He took a swig and sat down, close to her.

"I was married to an officer in Her Majesty's Royal Air Force." She straightened, stuck out her lip, and saluted. "We were in India for, how long was it now? Ah yes, an *eternity*. I was an RAF wife, doing what RAF wives do, for a frigging eternity."

She took a long drink, set the glass on the bench seat, and fiddled with her cigarette case.

"What do they do?"

"They who?"

"RAF wives in India."

"That, Jack Benoit, is an astute question."

He flamed her smoke.

"We plan. No shortage of planning. Dinner plans. Tea plans. Bridge plans. Party plans. Holiday plans." She smoked and drank, visibly agitated. "Then . . ." she paused for dramatic effect, pointing at him, swaying a bit. "We *execute* those plans."

"All right. I was just wonderin' how you came to be here."

"I came *here* to have a drink with Johnny! Flew up from Rangoon with the Tommy and Eddy." Emma shook her shoulders with her eyes closed and took a deep breath. She jumped up and pointed at the floor. "No doubt they're missing us terribly down there." Wobbling on her feet, she smoothed her slacks. "Shall we?"

The party was in high gear. There must have been fourty, maybe fifty guests in all. The radio blasted a rollicking swing tune from Radio Tokyo, courtesy of Orphan Ann herself. Like a mouse in a maze, Emma sliced and bounced her way through the crowd until she ran into a wall of thirsty revelers, three-deep at the bar. Hopping and waving, she caught Soheil's eye. He smiled and nodded toward the end of the bar.

Jack lost sight of her in the bustle. The place was tight, as were most of the guests, and the smoke hung heavy like a fog. He decided to get some air. Exchanging pleasantries on his way out, he escaped to the front stoop, where he stretched and took a deep breath of the night air.

Three meteorites crossed the sky in quick succession. The picket fence was lined with cars and rickshaws. "People can't walk three blocks?"

"Leaving so soon?" Emma shook a fresh glass at him. "One ice large cube for Jack Benoit."

"No, thanks," he said, yawning. "Gettin' a little crowded in there. Think I'll call it a night."

She lost her footing on the flagstone path, splashing both glasses. She threw back what remained of each and nearly toppled over when she bent to set the empties on the lawn. She'd clearly had her limit and then some. He looked at the row of vehicles.

"Is one of them yours?"

She raised an eyebrow at him.

"I didn't mean anything by it. Just thought maybe one of them was waitin' for you."

"I'd prefer you did."

"Did what?"

"Mean anything by it."

Jack wanted to fuck her.

"I think I should sit." She dropped onto the steps. He watched her sway and figured this wasn't the night.

"Okay, so we need to get you home."

Emma shook her head slowly and poked a thumb over her shoulder. She began to hiccup.

"You're stayin' here?"

She shot a finger gun at him and winked.

"How 'bout we get you upstairs?"

She giggled as he pulled her to her feet. "I thought you'd never ask, Jack Benoit, of the . . . *hic* . . . Louisiana Benoits."

It took some doing, but he got her up the stairs, where she pushed open the door to a small room papered in yellow with a violet print. The room had a warm glow issued by a small ornate table lamp featuring gilded cherubs under a straw-colored shade. He scooped up the petite woman and placed her on the bed. He worked the covers out from underneath her as she kicked off her flats. Jack rolled the comforter to the foot of the bed and tucked her under the sheet and a thin, pearl-stitched blanket. She squeezed his forearm. The look in her eyes was half lust and half lost.

"I understand you . . . *hic* . . . Yanks find the hiccups quite . . . *hic* . . . alluring."

She closed her eyes.

Jack brushed her bangs to the side. He touched her cheek, tracing a line across Orion's belt. Emma took his hand and kissed his fingers, peering at him with one eye. "Does she . . . *hic* . . . does freckle girl write you letters? Wonderful, scented letters from . . . *hic* . . . Louisiana?"

"Not for a while."

"Hmmm . . . *hic* . . . bitch."

"She's at college." He lied.

"*Hic* . . . Well, then . . . *hic* . . . smart bitch."

He kissed her forehead. "Sweet dreams, Emma." When he reached the door, he spun on his heels. "Alabama!"

Emma's eyes were closed. "*Hic* . . . Pardon?"

"Where I've seen this place before. In Montgomery. I remember my daddy walking up to a house. I stayed in the truck. But the front of the house, it looked just like this one, with the tower and all."

"Turret."

"You sure are a stickler for words, Emma Simpson." He returned to her. "When I talk, I figure if people get my meaning, the job's done. Seems expectations among RAF wives are somethin' higher."

"*Amongst* the wives." She snorted when she laughed. "Seems you're just cursed with cheeky . . . *hic* . . . freckled bitches, Jack Benoit."

She snorted again, triggering even more hiccups. "Freckled cheekies . . . *hic* . . . tell me, does Miss Louisiana correct your grammar . . . *hic* . . . , too?"

"No. But she uses big words like you do."

Emma curled up as the hiccups overwhelmed her.

"I prom . . . *hic* . . . promise to use . . . *hic* . . . just little words from . . . *hic* . . . here on out . . . *hic*. Agreed . . . *hic*?"

Jack tugged the brass chain hanging under the table lamp, and Emma let out a long sigh, interrupted by a sole hiccup. Then it was just deep breathing and muffled party noise through the floor. He closed the door, winnowed his way through the action downstairs, and slipped out front to find the briefest of showers had cleared the air. The damp flora shimmered in the moonlight, the scent of jasmine rising. He couldn't remember the last time his nose was filled with something entirely pleasant. Emma's neck smelled of lavender, like Chloe's, but that pleasure had been overwhelmed by smoke and alcohol as the night wore on.

The street was tight, both sides filled with cars and rickshaws. Down a ways from the gate, a handful of drivers were heads-down over a lively game of liar's dice they were shaking onto the hood of a deep red Austin Ten sedan.

But for a half dozen trucks and a few small dog packs, none of which paid him any mind, Jack biked back to Kyedaw by himself. Half an hour later, he slipped under the mosquito netting and into his cot, thinking about freckles, big words, lavender, and hazel eyes. "Good grief." Lying there, he missed Chloe something awful. The more he missed her, the more he drove his thoughts to the little one back at Fulton's place.

22

IT AIN'T SANTA CLAUS

DECEMBER 1941

Back in July, the Japanese Army established military airfields in French Indochina over weak Vichy French objection. In response, the United States government expanded its embargo of war materiel to Japan to include oil. There's no oil under the islands of Japan, and prior to the embargo, American supply had constituted nearly all of Japan's imports, and the emperor and his military leadership clearly understood the drastic implications. If their diplomats in Washington, D.C., failed to negotiate a lift of the oil embargo, the Empire would be left with a hard choice. First, they could expand the war with China to the north, attacking the oil-producing region of Siberia where the Soviets had stationed hundreds of thousand of troops in defense of that possibility. Second, they could invade the oil-rich Dutch East Indies. Because the Dutch had already capitulated to the Nazis in Europe, their eastern possessions would not be able to defend themselves for long. However, it was a near certainty the British would step in to defend the Dutch to deter direct Japanese action against the British possessions of Malaya and Burma. Any direct conflict with the Brits could trigger a hostile reaction by the United States, perhaps even its entry into the Pacific war. Lastly, the Japanese could negotiate for peace with China in attempt to hold gains made during the past four years of war. But suing for peace would mean a loss of face, inconceivable in the minds of army leadership. So, in the event of failed diplomacy in Washington, expansion of the war was inevitable, in one direction or the other.

An attack against the Soviets might bring the British into the fight anyway. But the Japanese military leadership rightly believed that the reverse was not true. They believed Joseph Stalin would not come to the aid of the Western defenders if the Empire attacked Dutch and British possessions to the south. The Japanese also believed the Americans would soon support their British allies by declaring war against the Germans and the Italians, which meant that it was only a matter of time before they would face conflict with the United States vis-à-vis the Tripartite Pact regardless of the path they chose.

The US had recently relocated its entire Pacific aircraft carrier force from California to Hawaii, and this meant the US fleet was within reach of a sneak attack. If the Imperial Navy could destroy the bulk of the American aircraft carrier force while in port, the victory would buy time to conquer, then stabilize their positions from Korea to Fiji, from Hong Kong to Burma.

In the north of China, supplies from the Soviet Union had dwindled to meaningless levels since the Nazis' springtime invasion of Russia. Cutting off the Burma Road would halt all supply from the south, so the Imperial Army could expect to overwhelm the Chinese Nationalist defenses within months. With the British struggling in Europe and Africa, and no other support available in the Pacific region, the Brits would be hard-pressed to defend colonial Australia and New Zealand. The Japanese could then leverage the growing Indian independence movement by turning Indian colonial prisoners of war captured in British Malaya back to fight against the Brits in their Indian homeland. If they could catch the US fleet in Pearl Harbor, it would not be unreasonable to envision the Japanese Empire encompassing the entire Pacific Rim and all of Asia below Russia. Then, if German efforts on Europe's Eastern Front entangled the Russians for much longer, the Japanese could invade Siberia to solidify the largest empire in the history of human civilization.

And so, it was decided. The Japanese would target the Dutch East Indies and act to prevent interference by the British and the Americans.

On the first Sunday of December, the Japanese launched its massive coordinated naval and army actions against their rivals all along the Pacific Rim. The hostilities commenced with dawn bombing raids on the defenses in the British and Dutch colonies and across multiple American possessions, and, by the next evening, Imperial

Army units had established beachheads on the Dutch East Indies, the northeast coast of British Malaya, and the southern coast of Thailand.

The West's reaction to the surprise attacks was both swift and momentous. The British and the Americans immediately declared war on Japan. Pursuant to the Tripartite Pact, Germany then declared war on the United States with Italy quickly following suit. Within forty-eight hours, the United States was at war and facing active hostility on three continents.

* * *

At Kyedaw Airfield outside Toungoo, most of the men were eating breakfast when a radio operator burst into the mess hall. "They bombed Hawaii! Those sneaking Jap monkeys fucking bombed Pearl Harbor!"

Jack, Sal, Shu Hao, and Toby ran to the briefing room where a radio was playing loud. Connecting the dots from a Radio Hong Kong broadcast with information sent to the Brits from their regional commands, they pieced together the details of the attack.

That morning the Imperial Navy bombed the British possessions of Hong Kong and Singapore, as well as the Dutch East Indies. In addition to Hawaii, they bombed three other American territories, the Philippines, Guam, and Wake Island. "Everywhere but Burma," Shu Hao noted. "And they will be here any moment now."

AVG Command posted the Hell's Angels as the initial assault echelon out of Kyedaw, with equipment fueled, armed, and ready for takeoff. The Panda Bears and the Adam and Eves would stand in reserve. Chennault issued a blackout order for the base and set up decoy lights at a dispersal field north of the main runways.

War had arrived, and everyone was on pins and needles. Still, for the next few days, the air above Kyedaw remained free of enemy activity. The quiet before the storm made the Old Man nervous, and he ordered reconnaissance flights over Thailand. Nothing was found to the north at Chiang Mai, but between eighty and a hundred Japanese attack planes were spotted on the ground at Don Mueang Airport near Bangkok.

Chennault was concerned these numbers might quickly grow to an overwhelming force that could crush his entire operation. He discussed the matter with the Generalissimo, who had just been petitioned by British Air Marshal Brooke-Popham to dedicate the entirety of the AVG to aiding in his defense of Rangoon Harbor. As he often did, Chiang split the baby, attempting to support both commanders with customized orders. The AVG would be repositioned to defend southern China from Wujiaba Airport in Kunming, save for eighteen Tomahawks that would be sent south, down to Mingaladon Aerodrome on the outskirts of Rangoon along with the RAF 67 Squadron to defend the harbor and the Syriam oil refinery. The latter duty fell to the Hell's Angels.

"Looks like we're heading south!" Sal posed like he was holding a baseball bat, a Lucky Strike dangling from his lips. "Spring training's over, boys. We're in the big leagues, now." He took a powerful swing and shaded his eyes as he watched the imaginary ball leave the imaginary ballpark.

Jack lay in his bed with a fever coming on. "Damn, Sal. I think I'm gettin' sick."

"No time for that! Wheels up in an hour, Captain Jack. If it hits you hard on the way down to Mingaladon, you go see the doc." Sal flicked his butt into the fire can. "Lots of pretty Britty nurses down there, no doubt." He stumbled around, imitating Frankenstein. "Rrrr! Britty boobies! Rrrrr!"

The flight was uneventful, but when Jack stepped onto the tarmac, he was hot and dizzy. "You look like hell, my friend. Let's get you to the infirmary." Sal asked for directions, and they climbed into a Jeep. Intake escorted Jack to a bed and handed him some pajamas. His head hit the pillow hard.

"Did someone here order a freckled bitch?"

He opened his eyes to a vision in white, her pink lips curled in a smile.

"Buy you a drink?" he joked.

She stuck a thermometer in his mouth and took his pulse. "I understand you just got into town. Couldn't wait to see me, Jack Benoit?"

He rolled his eyes.

"Vomiting? Diarrhea? Abdominal pain?"

"No, thank you."

She sat down next to him and pulled down an eyelid, looking closely. He looked closely, too, into those sunshine eyes. An erection started without him.

"Headache?"

Jack shook his head. Emma jotted some notes on a clipboard and caught a glimpse of the bulge under the sheet. "Why, Captain, you *are* happy to see me." Jack would have blushed if he wasn't so flushed from the fever. "When did you start feeling hot?"

"Just this morning."

"Well, it's still early. Hopefully we're not looking at malaria or dengue. Rest and liquids. If someone brings you something to drink, you drink it. If someone brings you something to eat, you eat it. That's an order."

"Yes, your majesty."

She pulled the drapes closed and positioned a privacy screen next to his bed. Jack rubbed a hand along her hip. "It's good to see you, Emma."

She stuck a needle in his buttocks. "This will help you sleep. My shift ends soon, so you might not see me when you wake. I'll check on you in the morning." She stroked his cheek and walked off, whispering to herself. "Goodness."

* * *

As the Hell's Angels settled into Mingaladon, 3rd Squadron Leader Oley Olson coordinated with the British brass and squad leaders. The base had two white crushed gravel runways that formed a large cross. RAF Group Captain Manning assigned the AVG to the east–west runway, and his Brewster Buffalos and Bristol Blenheims would use the north–south crossway. The runways were wide enough to allow traffic in both directions, so from ground level, scrambles looked like complete chaos. There was a riot of activity those first couple of days, while the Brit and American crews blended into concerted motion.

"Good morning, Jack Benoit." Emma pointed a thermometer at his mouth.

"She just did tha . . ."

Emma held his wrist and looked at her watch. She looked in his eyes, this time holding a small flashlight.

"How much time I got left, doc?"

She shook the mercury down and wiped the thermometer with alcohol-soaked cotton. "I'm happy to report your fever is down." She smiled. "It's still there, but directionally correct. We'll keep you here a while longer to make sure we're not dealing with something more than a common cold."

"You know I got a job to do."

"As do I, Captain Benoit."

"Oh, so now I'm *Captain*. Getting military on me? Ok then, I'm pullin' rank. Nurse, get me the doc. He'll see it my way."

Emma raised an eyebrow. "In your present condition, Captain Benoit, *I* am your doctor, and until *I* write the magic word on this piece of paper, *you* will stay right where you are."

"I don't need pamperin', I need to . . ."

She put a finger to his lips. "We need you healthy up there." She became very serious. "All of us. We all need you up there. So the moment your fever's gone is the moment you leave here and go do your job."

He listened as her heels clicked down the ward and felt awful for letting down his pals. They were so busy running drills and scrambling to false alarms, no one had come by to check on him. Finally, his fever broke, and he was released.

"You've been missing all the fun." Sal flicked a smoldering butt into the fire pail. "You're over there." He pointed to the next bunk, where Jack's duffle was waiting.

"No netting?"

"No mosquitos, really."

"Fill me in." He learned that even though the contingent from Kyedaw had been in Mingaladon just two days, everything was already running smoothly, from scramble practice to scouting, chow to leave rotations.

Sal was impressed. "I'd heard the Brits were all about protocol, but I gotta say, they sure did work their tails off to get us singing from the same hymnal."

Toby added his take. "Oley's been great getting things done with the RAF brass. I wouldn't say we're a well-oiled machine, but I think when the shit comes, we'll be ready for it."

Over the next week, Jack worked into the rhythm of the place. Briefings, patrols, and scrambling on false alarms, air-raid warnings without the air raids. Much of the civilian support for their operations disappeared as thousands of locals evacuated the city every day.

The Hell's Angels had just sixteen flyers in the rotation. They coordinated with RAF 67 Squadron, which was composed of thirty-six Brewster Buffalos, a slow, tubby US Navy relic relegated to the New Zealander "Kiwis" in the Asian theater to free up the higher-performing Spitfires, Tomahawks, and Hurricanes for the European and African theaters. RAF 60 Squadron, a bomber group stationed at Mingaladon, was down to four functional Bristol Blenheims, a correspondingly slow and thinly armored light bomber. "Airborne shit wagons." Sal shook his head. The more he learned about the Brits' equipment, the more Jack appreciated the P-40Bs. The Tomahawks had speed, firepower, armored cockpits, and self-sealing fuel tanks.

The colonials were sticklers for rank, and officers never fraternized with the enlisted men. Olson's team was the most relaxed about rank of the three American squadrons, and some of the Hell's Angels flyers and crewmen had become good friends up in Kyedaw. Here at Mingaladon, when an AVG flyer joined a Brit card game, it was understood that crewmen weren't welcome. But if a Brit officer wanted to join a Hell's Angel game, he'd better get comfortable socializing with ground crew.

Meanwhile, the bulk of the AVG made their way seven hundred miles north from Kyedaw to Kunming. By mid-December, they were settled in and ready for action, and none too soon because on the 20th, the AVG saw their first combat over the capital city. The results were announced in the Mingaladon ready room the following morning.

```
At 1030 Saturday, 20 December, AVG 2nd Squadron
engaged an enemy bomber group composed of Kawasaki
Ki-48 Lilys, which had circled the city to approach
from the west. The Panda Bears engaged, forcing
enemy aircraft to dump payloads outside the city.
Four confirmed enemy kills. No losses.
```

The room erupted with cheers. It was the first successful defense of Chinese airspace since the war had begun back in 1937. Squadron Leader Olson took the opportunity to reinforce Chennault's tactics. "The dual-engine Lily's primary defense is speed, but our dives are powerful enough to catch them. We'll have our chance to shine soon enough, so when you're up there, stick to the training. Hit and run. Show 'em who's boss."

During the two weeks following the December 7 sneak attack, the Japs continued to bomb Hong Kong, Manila, and Singapore, and to strengthen their beachheads in British Malaya and the Dutch East Indies. Rangoon was next.

* * *

Jack led the Hell's Angels' third flight group, which was on leave Monday, December 22. Four of his group's six pilots and most of their ground crew headed into Rangoon for an overnight of liquor and intimate interactions.

After lunch, the gang headed to the brothels, but Jack told them he wanted to keep walking, to take a look around before it all got bombed. A knapsack slung over his shoulder, he unfolded a piece of paper and showed it to a rickshaw driver.

"This way. Not far."

"Not far" did not mean "not long." The ride was slow as thousands of Burmese and Indians with bundles on their backs pushed top-heavy carts packed with their possessions and children along the clogged thoroughfares, some breaking off to scurry up alleys and down sidestreets in futile attempts to speed their exodus.

The jewelry store was set within a row of reputable looking shops. He handed the driver a wad of rupees and stepped into the chaotic street. The British expats that remained were engaged in bidding wars to keep or acquire replacement native help. Some shops were boarded up, and others that had been abandoned were now ravaged shells, stripped by looters. The few shop owners that were still in business sold essentials at exorbitant prices and everything else at fire-sale discounts.

"Hey, hot stuff!" The shout came from above, and he spotted her in a window over the jeweler's sign. She was resting an elbow on a crossed arm, a smoldering cigarette dangling between her fingers.

"Like in the turret," he laughed to himself.

"The blue door, down there past the tailor." She met him at the top of the stairs, took his face between her hands, and kissed him deeply.

The place was nice enough. A deep, narrow room split in the middle by a brass-frame bed. Near the door, a hot plate sat atop a cracked ancient icebox that wet his khakis with cool water as he brushed against it. "The boy Jitan Ram performed a miracle and found ice." Inside the front window, two wooden chairs were tucked under a small table, which held a bowl of fruit, some crisps, and a glass vase, all illuminated by the rectangular glow that seeped through the thin ivory curtain Emma had pulled across the window. The waterworks sat behind a flowered curtain in the back of the room, where pipes from the rooftop cistern led to a heating basin, which branched off to the sink and a claw-foot tub. "No fuel. We'll have to do with room temperature. The loo sticks open, so I stop it like this." She took the top off the tank and showed him the trick.

With the curtain closed, the room quickly grew stuffy, so Emma moved it aside and lit incense to cover the stench of the garbage piled on the street below. "We have tea and bourbon. Oh, and these." She pulled two bottles from the ice chest.

"Holy cow! Where'd you find Co-Cola?"

"You Yanks aren't the only ones who can go Churchill."

Jack laughed. *Churchill* was AVG code for pilfering British supplies.

For the remainder of the day, and throughout the night, Jack and Emma laughed, fucked, showered, talked, kissed, and slept. It was easy together, natural. Jack got along with most everyone, but Emma *fit*. She teased him about his legs. "This one looks like Popeye's arm," she said, rubbing his left calf. "From the flap pedal, to counter the yaw?"

He patted her bottom. "You've got the sweetest cheeks."

It was nearing dawn, and she watched Jack sleep while smoking at the window. She poured a drink and scooched onto the table to dangle her legs out the window. The cotton nightie she'd sheered at the upper thigh stuck to the sweating cracked paint of the window frame. She listened to bickering Burmese couples as they pulled overflowing ox carts toward the unknown.

"Crikey!" she screamed and spilled bourbon when Jack had snuck his arms around her from behind.

"Emma, you don't need me telling you what to do . . ."

"Then don't," she snapped. They'd already been through this.

"The shit's comin', and it's comin' hard." He pried the glass from her hand and set it on the table.

"Instead of getting on me about leaving, wouldn't you rather spend the next few hours feeling like you did during the past few hours?" She tickled his chin and looked into his blue eyes.

"Damn." It just popped out of him.

She asked why he was always cursing her eyes, so he told her.

"So that's why you're with me?" She looked steamed. "Because I remind you of *her?*"

"No. Y'all just happen to have the similar eyes."

"And freckles."

"Yes."

"And big words."

Jack pulled a soda from the icebox. It fizzed over on the floor when he popped the top. "Look, Emma. I can't help it, that y'all have things in common. What's so wrong with that?"

"Did you think of her, over there?" She pointed at the bed.

"Good grief. You *asked* me about her, alright?"

"I *asked* why you cursed my eyes." She went back to the window and lit a cigarette.

"You ain't so much alike."

Emma scoffed.

"Chloe's black."

She swung around, eyes wide. Jack reached for her hand. "Come to bed, Sweet Cheeks."

* * *

The morning was bright, and Emma rubbed slow circles on Jack's chest. "So, you learned that with Chloe?"

"It wasn't divine inspiration."

"Ha! It certainly was *inspired*. I've never, really. No one has ever . . ."

"Well, now someone has." He tickled her. "What can I say? I like the sweet stuff."

"There's more where that came from, in case you were wondering," she teased.

"Good to know. How 'bout somethin' to eat first? I'm starvin'."

"Help yourself. I'm going to wash." They washed and ate and crawled back into bed. She ran a finger down his cheek, down his neck. "Tell me more."

"I don't think so."

"I'm not jealous. I'm curious. And not because you told me she was black."

"Uh huh."

"I was surprised you left someone you loved, to fight Japs. I suppose . . . *I don't know* . . . the possibility just never crossed my mind."

Eventually, he did open up. He described the day they'd met on the coulee.

"You had both just arrived there, in Abbeville, within days of each other?"

He gave her a squeeze.

"But she's black."

"Yeah."

"In America."

"Yeah. It's illegal. Well, it's illegal to get married for sure. I didn't give it any thought, really, except when creeps were bustin' my chops. Then we just kept things quiet, snuck around." He took a pull of warm soda. "My daddy was friendly with Negroes in Texas. I s'pose in Alabama, too, but I was too little to know."

"What did your mother think of it?"

"About Daddy? I don't know. She was a drunk, Southern white woman. She hated everybody who wasn't like her. I s'pose she prob'ly just hated everybody, when you get down to it."

"So, she's at university?" A siren wailed, and Emma shrieked, jumping to her feet. "A frigging air raid!"

"It ain't Santa Claus."

* * *

They pushed their way through the mass of bodies, looking to hire a ride back to base. The traffic was gridlocked, so Jack yanked a teenaged boy off a bicycle, pressed a hundred rupees into his hand, and straddled the bike, steadying it so Emma could settle on the seat. They traveled slowly, making it just a dozen blocks or so before he stopped. "Here, get off." He walked the bike toward a tidy brick building where a motorbike leaned against a post. It was chained. "Dammit!" he kicked the ground. Hands on his hips, he scanned the street.

"Hey, genius." Emma was swinging the chain like Charlie Chaplin's police baton. "No lock."

He kick-started the bike as a middle-aged Indian man sprinted out the door, screaming curses and swinging a cricket bat. Jack tossed bills, fifty American, at the man's feet, pointed to the bicycle and told him he could collect the motorcycle at the aerodrome in Mingaladon. The owner wasn't having any of it and continued yelling, creeping closer. Emma stepped between the two men. "Look, we're RAF. He's a flyer, and the Japs are on their way to bomb us, so stand down!" Jack revved the engine. The man looked terrified, but he wasn't backing off. He pushed past Emma and straddled the motorcycle's front wheel, threatening Jack with the bat. Emma grabbed Jack's shoulder. "You go. I'll manage this." With that, she body slammed the man and tripped him to the ground. Jack put the motorbike in gear started down the street gutter.

It took him nearly half an hour to weave through the jammed-up traffic and reach the base. The ground crew had his flight group's planes positioned at the end of the runway, gassed and loaded, but no one else from the group had made it back to base. Jack was wearing sandals, short pants and short sleeves, and McClintock met him at No. 91 with his helmet and oxygen mask. No jacket and no sunglasses. He climbed in, ran through the fourteen-point pre-flight routine and the six-point ignition sequence, firing up his shark-toothed beast. The required four-minute engine warm-up felt like an eternity, and damn if he didn't have to pee. Finally, he was off the ground gaining altitude. Ground control filled him in on the situation.

Twelve Tomahawks and twelve Buffalos launched a half hour earlier to intercept the Japanese approaching the Gulf of Martaban from Thailand. The size of the attacking force wasn't known, but estimates from two different spotters were fifty planes and a hundred planes. What was actually on the way was a composite from four Japanese Army units, launched in two waves.

The 62nd Sentai consisted of fifteen early-model Mitsubishi Ki-21 Sallys. The Sally was the standard Imperial Army heavy bomber, defended by gunners positioned under the nose, in a round greenhouse mounted on top of the fuselage, and under the tail in the *dust bin*, a metal shoot that dropped from under the plane where a gunner lying on his belly could defend the rear from below the tail. Five gunners in all. Also incoming were the 31st Sentai, which consisted of nine Mitsubishi Ki-30 Anns. The Ki-30 was a light bomber defended by a single gunner at the back of a long greenhouse canopy that included the cockpit. So, twenty-four bombers in total, protected by a dozen Nakajima Ki-27 Nate fighter planes. Thirty-six planes heading straight toward Mingaladon Aerodrome. Behind them, launched thirty minutes later, a second wave approached on the same line. Twenty-seven late-model Sallys from the 60th Sentai, whose targets included the harbor and the oil refinery. Because the defenders would be busy with the first wave over Mingaladon, the second wave's commander expected no resistance, so his bomber flight approached without fighter cover.

The initial engagement took place forty miles out over the Gulf of Martaban, where six Buffalos attacked the fifteen Sallys of the 62nd Sentai that approached in a Porcupine formation, a tight-knit, multi-V configuration of aircraft painted in brown-and-green camouflage with a bright red ball on each wing. The Brits flamed two of the heavy bombers, both of which crashed on the shoreline. They smoked two more, forcing those to peel off from the attack and head back to Thailand. Due to tactical errors the Nates had been lagging behind but arrived in time to distress the Buffalos, which enabled the remainder of the Japanese bomber group to proceed toward Mingaladon.

The Tomahawks engaged just as the heavy bombers sighted the airfield. Flight Leaders George McMillan and Parker Dupouy split their ten flyers into two trios and two pairs and prepared to attack the reshaped Porcupine of Sallys. The Japanese Anns and Nates had caught up and were swarming above. A trio of Buffalos climbed to engage them while the last three followed the Tomahawks into the Sallys.

The Tomahawks rolled into dives, gaining speed as they screamed toward the three modified Vs below. The eleven bombers opened up the twenty-two machine guns poking out their greenhouses, lining the sky with streams of dull-yellow tracers. The first of the AVG trios dove from ten o'clock high, opening fire on the bombers in the rightmost V. Within seconds, the Tomahawk had blown past the Porcupine, and in his rearview mirror, McMillan saw streams of black smoke trailing from two of the bombers. The Hell's Angels regrouped and regained altitude for another run. But the Japanese fighters had dropped into the lower altitude fray, and the battle became fast and furious.

"Enemy sighted! Enemy sighted! Mingaladon under attack!" This was the last communication Jack heard before the channel filled with a mad, incomprehensible scramble of warnings and reports.

In twelve minutes, he was at the gulf coast cruising due east at twenty-one thousand feet. He was on oxygen, squinting in the bright sunlight with goosebumps on his bare arms and legs. He banked south hoping to intercept the second incoming formation or pick off a crippled straggler from the first wave. He caught a metallic reflection at ten o'clock below, some twenty miles out.

"Tower, this is Benoit. I've spotted . . . looks like . . . eighteen planes. Confirmed. A six-V Porcupine at twelve thousand feet heading west–northwest from the gulf. I'm engaging the second wave. Over."

He pulled hard on the T-grips at each side of his seat to charge the wing guns, then reached for the instrument panel to charge the nose guns. His rearview mirror was clear.

Two deep breaths, and he banked left. Two more deep breaths, and he set the propeller in coarse pitch, flicked the trigger switch on the control stick, and squinted hard at the shiny objects below.

The roar from No. 91's 1,040 horsepower Allison engine grew steadily louder as he closed distance on the enemy formation. At 16,000 feet, he was hard on the left pedal to counter the torque, and the speedometer needle was pointing at 440, an actual airspeed over 500 miles per hour. He was expecting to take fire, but there was nothing but sky between him and the planes below. He had surprise and targeted the closest plane on the nearest edge of the formation. Closing, he found his line was off, so he opened his .50-cal nose guns on the Sally positioned immediately to the lead ship's left. His tracers looked like a red ribbon lagging behind his target's tail fin. Standing on the left pedal now, he pulled up, and squeezed a second burst, dragging the red line up like a pen on paper to scribble on his target. The Sally's right wing burst into flame, and the plane tipped hard to the right and started down. Jack steered slightly to the right while switching to his wing guns. Two streams of red tracers crisscrossed with eight, maybe ten, yellow streams now rising from the Porcupine just two hundred yards below him. His tracers crossed the lead plane at the wings and fell off behind it as he punched the stick down to dive behind the broken V. Passing just of his target's tail, he was looking the basket gunner straight in the eyes when he was blinded by a flash of light. The Sally exploded and splattered No. 91 with shrapnel, rocking it hard. He was blinking, trying to regain his sight when he heard pounding behind him, the *thunk, thunk, thunk* of bullets piercing No. 91's fuselage. His eyes cleared, and he could see yellow streaks wavered just outside both side windows as he pressed toward the sea. Seconds later, everything was calm. He was out of range. He pulled off his oxygen and pulled out of the dive.

The smell of burnt cordite from his nose guns was stuck in his nose, and he could feel it scratching at his lungs as adrenaline coursed through his body. He squinted into the rearview mirror, then scanned the air over both his shoulders. No Nates. Two deep breaths, and he was climbing again.

He climbed to the south, intending to turn and reengage the enemy from out of the sun, but checking his instruments, he found the fuel gauge needle on E. That couldn't be right if the crew had topped off the tank, but he had to trust the instrument. Banking to port, he got a better look at the Japs that had turned for home. One Sally was lagging, trailing a thin line of black smoke from its port engine. Another plane had dropped to the floor and was practically skimming the waves of the gulf, trailing thick black smoke from both engines. Two other planes were falling back to escort the smoking laggard, which was struggling to maintain altitude. He so badly wanted another pass at the straggler and its escort, but hearing the Old Man's voice in his head, he thought better of it. *Live to fight another day.* The skimmer was bouncing just above the waves, trying to gain altitude. Jack watched as the Japanese bomber dipped, the water snagging a wingtip. The machine tripped, spinning into a ferocious cartwheel. Jack gained altitude and headed back to base.

* * *

He landed right behind Sal, both skirting two large craters in the runway. No. 91 hit some debris and blew a tire. The friends parked side by side at the end of the runway. Jack stepped out and slid off his wing.

"This Angel is one tough bitch!" Sal nodded patted his No. 82 on the belly. "Thank God Almighty." His hands shook some as he lit a Lucky Strike. Snapping his Zippo, he looked around. "This place is a fucking disaster."

"So you got in it? Where's Toby?"

"He's in. Got the runs bad and ran off to those trees. Oley told us you got up about ten minutes before we got to base. We connected with Dupouy just in time to chase the last wave out. I tangled with some Nates. It was nuts. Didn't get nothing. Toby smoked one of the Anns, but it didn't drop."

"How'd she do, Cap'n Short Pants?" McClintock trotted past Jack to check on his No. 91. Jack looked down at his own sandaled feet. He looked ridiculous.

"Yeah, how'd you do, Captain Jack?" Sal was sucking on that cigarette like it was oxygen.

"Two Sallys down, one more trailing smoke back to Thailand. It coulda been more, but my fuel gauge said I was on fumes just thirty minutes in." McClintock gave him a look. "That's right. Figure it out." Jack kicked the dirt and yelled. "Dammit, Scratchy! They didn't have any friggin' cover!" He'd never snapped at his crew chief like that.

McClintock rubbed his flattop like he did when he bluffed at poker. "And these?" He pointed at a line of punctures across the fuselage behind the cockpit. The jack of clubs sported a hole right between the eyes.

"Better him than me. How's everyone else? They all in?"

"Most everybody. I heard we did better than the Japs did."

"Who ain't in?"

"Gilbert and Martin."

Eleven of the thirteen Hell's Angels that got up had returned safely. Near the smoldering aerodrome, a crowd had gathered around Toby's plane. His tailfin was bent from an air-to-air collision.

"Crippled the Ann. The sorry Jap couldn't keep up with the other monkeys, and we jumped him again. Tore that sonuvabitch to pieces. Watched him burn and crash in the gulf."

At the debrief, Jack was credited for his kills. A British destroyer heading out to sea radioed in confirmation of both the fireball and the cartwheel. But there was still no word from the missing Hell's Angels. Surveying the damage on the ground, Jack's anger rose. The airfield was a mess. The aerodrome took numerous hits, and the runway was pocked with craters blown out by two-hundred pounders. He took on a squadron of Japanese bombers alone, and it could have been a much better outcome if he'd had even one from his group diving into that formation. With hindsight he knew they never should have gone on leave.

Three American Tomahawks and two British Buffalos had been destroyed on the ground, and death was a multinational affair. An Indian antiaircraft battery crew. A handful of pilots from the Burmese Volunteer Air Force. A couple British mechanics. All told, seventeen dead and another two dozen wounded on the ground. In the air, the Brits lost three pilots and their wings. The Hell's Angels' Neil Martin and Hank Gilbert were also shot down and killed. The AVG's first combat casualties.

A clerk found Jack in the ready room and handed him two envelopes, each postmarked Lafayette, Louisiana.

* * *

His head was pounding from dehydration when he hopped out of a jeep onto Thudhamma Road in Okkalapa where he kept a room in the home of British expats, the Addertons. He lay down while the number-one boy, Shaurya, boiled drinking water. Jack couldn't sleep for the headache, but fell into a hazy daydream of Emma, standing in her little white nightie, hands on her hips like she'd do.

Shaurya's knock on the door snapped him to attention. He drank like a fish, ate four sliced mangoes, and started feeling better. He lay back on the bed and tried to stop his heart from racing, to block out the fighting, to picture her asleep. Her soft breathing, and the way she twitched a little when she was dreaming. The smell of her, the lavender, like Chloe. The taste of her skin. He smiled through the headache, imagining the whispery squeaks she made when she came. How her leg would stiffen, just the one. Worry jumped him. He told himself she made it through the raid all right. Exhaustion rolled over the worry, and he fell into a deep sleep.

* * *

October 31, 1941

Dear PJ,

It has been so long since we heard word from you, nearly three months now. We pray for you every night and will pray for you at tonight's Mass at the cemetery. Everybody is wondering if we will join the war in Europe. Frank says it's inevitable.

The children are growing so fast. Junior is a handful. Frank says he takes after his uncle. Molly is a dear and so curious. She wants to know everything. She has started writing poems, and I have enclosed one for you that she wrote about China. What imagination!

Daddy's lumber business is struggling. I know Frank is worried, but of course he never says anything. There's a man Daddy knows who is talking to the army about making canvas for tents. There may be a place for Frank if it works out. He's such a good man. I'm sure the good Lord will provide.

I bought a pie today at the Music Box and talked with Menta and Chloe. Chloe said she wanted to write to you, so I told her if she wrote a letter, Frank could mail it from Lafayette with my own. I am sure Chloe will tell you about her situation with the college. I hope you receive both of our letters. We know you must be terribly busy. But if you can find time to write a few lines, we would love to hear you are safe. God bless you.

Love,

Odette

1 November 1941

Dearest PJ,

I understand from your letter you are now known as Jack. But you will always be my PJ, and so you must tolerate this from me.

I hope you receive this letter safe and well in China. It is hard to believe you will read its contents halfway around the world.

Menta and Francie both send their regards. Menta asked me to tell you she prays for you every night. Francie asked me to pose a question: "Do they have apple pie in China?"

I have reengaged my studies with Dr. Herod, but not so often as when I was younger. He graciously lends me books—his own, and books circulated among his learned colleagues and himself—and then we have discussions. As you know, President Reverend Johnson of Howard University extended my deferral of enrollment from the 1940 school year to this fall. However, further deterioration in Menta's health required me to remain in Abbeville to continue nursing her and to run the café. I was terribly angry with the reverend, blaming him for keeping me here. I remain convinced he did keep me here, but Menta is always saying, "Forgive and forget." I cannot say I have forgiven him, but I have taken it upon myself to forget. This will be my last mention of it.

Francie is a big help at the café. She can prepare all of our dishes now, and her diction is so much improved. She is more independent than before but still not capable of caring for Menta or the Music Box without me. I am hopeful Menta's health will return, for her sake and for mine.

You may be surprised to learn I attended a hootenanny in Opelousas just last weekend. It was quite an experience, surpassing my memories of the revelry at my Uncle Paul's nightclub in Paris. There was an extraordinary amount of alcohol involved and a terrible fight by two men with knives. Despite these and other depravities, I felt quite safe and enjoyed the music immensely. The bandleader's name is Milt Larkin, and I never before experienced such enthusiasm. The audience's reception would put Dr. Herod's congregation to shame, even on his best day. (Of course, I have not made the reverend aware of my attendance at the hootenanny. Will you keep my secret?) I believe you would have enjoyed yourself very much had you been present. But perhaps even your history as the sole white patron of the Music Box would have left you unprepared for this raucous black party. I am very excited because I may have the opportunity to see Lil Green in New Orleans in the coming weeks. I love jazz music and find the live performance of it exhilarating.

As for you, I am confident your disciplined self will ensure appropriate precautions to stay safe despite your courage. The war news here is mostly about Europe and Africa. (Your Odette sometimes kindly brings me Mr. Benoit's newspapers to read.) The few reports from China all describe Japanese successes, and I fear they will work hard to overwhelm you and your fellow warriors.

Please be safe, as safe as you can be given your undertaking. I think of you often and revisit warm memories of our childhood together.

Sincerely,

Chloe Boisvert

23

CHRISTMAS IN BURMA

DECEMBER 1941

The initial air defense of Rangoon was a success, with the Allies scoring ten Sallys down and sending three more bombers trailing smoke back to Thailand. With Toby's downed Ann, a total of eleven kills. This against two Tomahawks and two Buffalos downed, with three of the four pilots killed. The Japanese lost nearly ninety flight crewmen, and likely others lay dead in the smokers that made their way back to Bangkok. But factoring in the damage the Allies suffered on the ground, the score was pretty even on equipment lost, with the Americans and Brits losing a combined total of nine planes.

Christmas Eve at the base was a muddle. The entire ground crew had spent the night on the floor at the Rangoon Country Club because their barracks were flattened during the air raid. The common mess hall was also blown to bits, and the men made it through the day on cold bread and warm beer. The entire store of .30 caliber ammunition had exploded, a complete loss, so a truck was sent north to Kyedaw for resupply. Around the clock, Hell's Angels circled the airfield with empty wing guns and crossed fingers, hoping the Japanese would take the day off to lick their wounds. Fortunately, the Japanese Army Air Command at Don Mueang decided to regroup. They would attack Mingaladon on the twenty-fifth of December, sending up sixty-three bombers protected by twenty-five fighters, who together would annihilate the air defense of Rangoon.

Jack patrolled twice with Toby and Sal, midday and midafternoon. No. 91's fuel gauge had been replaced with one from a wrecked plane, and it seemed to be in working order. Without enough time to repair the holes in the fuselage, McClintock taped them over to reduce drag. He had the beast purring like a lioness.

The infirmary had been hit hard. A canister bomb tore off a whole corner of building. Jack entered the ward to find Emma tending to a wounded soldier. Bed sheets that had been nailed over the blown-out windows rippled in the soft breeze and glowed white, backlit by the hazy afternoon sun. Emma glowed in white, too, with a blue bandana around her neck. She smiled. "I heard you did well."

"Broke even, I s'pose."

She nodded while tucking in the bed covers. "Rest now." She touched the patient's cheek below a bandage wrap that looked something like a white version of Sergeant Major Dahrala's turban. He wondered how the Sikh warrior was faring in Malaya.

Emma wrapped her arms around him and squeezed tight, letting out a long sigh. She pushed him off and wiped a tear from her cheek. "They got Scotty." John *Scotty* McGowan had been the RAF's chief medical officer at Mingaladon. "C'est la guerre."

"I didn't want to leave you there."

"You did what you had to do."

"I'm off tonight." He phrased it like a question.

Emma took his hand and walked him toward the door. "I'm staying here."

"Have you slept?"

"Not since Rangoon."

Jack looked down the ward. "Got any bad ones?"

"Just him." She motioned to the head injury. "He's done tonight, I think."

"Then they won't need you here. The night shift's got it." He squeezed her hand. "Come stay with me."

"Jack . . ."

"Dammit, Emma. You said it yourself. It's a war." He raised his voice. "Those sons-a-bitches are coming back, and when they do, they'll come to finish it. But it ain't tonight. They won't make a night raid when we're such easy pickings in the daylight." He kissed her forehead. "Come with me tonight. My next patrol ain't 'til 1000 tomorrow. You leave me in the morning when you gotta leave, but come sleep with me."

She was exhausted, and he was right. The Japs weren't coming on a night raid, and it wasn't her shift. Hellfire was on hold, and she'd be needed most when it came. "Yes."

* * *

In his room at the Addertons, he ate some fruit and cheese, drank a warm beer, and took a bath. He instructed Shaurya to drain the tub and refill it with fresh steaming water. He lit rose-scented oil and sat on the bed, trying hard not to think. She was late. The bath water cooled, but the room smelled good. He woke when she crawled into bed.

"I'll get the boy to warm the tub."

"Please don't. All I want to do is sleep."

"That's all you want to do?"

Emma spooned into him, kissed his arm and tucked it under her own. She was out.

* * *

The sheer curtain over the window glowed sherbet orange with the dawn. Jack had neglected to pull the shade, and he was half asleep in a cloudy dream that felt like sex.

She rolled to face him. "Are you awake?" His eyes were crossing under heavy lids. He felt movement between his legs. "I woke up and the fella here was standing at attention." She slowly stroked him and whispered, "Let's make love." Jack had pins and needles in a numb arm. He flexed until it came back to life. Rolling on top, he kissed her neck and ear and quickly worked his way down her chest. He was kissing and licking her belly when she squeezed his shoulder. "Put him in me."

Jack eased in and started slowly. He cradled her leg in the crook of his arm. "Slow, please," she said, eyes closed. "Mmmmm. Thank you."

Jack obliged, and they blended into one. He was doing the best he could to last when Emma moaned. Her leg stiffened. She curled into him, convulsing, and he lost it. They finished together, kissing hard on the mouth. She wrapped her arm over his and took his hand, interlocking their fingers and kissing the tip of each one of his. She unwrapped herself from his embrace and popped off the bed. "I have to get back to the hospital."

"C'mon..."

"They need me."

Jack wanted to say that *he* needed her, but it sounded corny in his head. He caught her up and rubbed her arms, hugging her from behind. "No doubt the shit's comin' today, Emma. Comin' hard."

She spun and wrapped her arms around his neck. "Thank you for inviting me last night. "This meant a lot to me. *Means* a lot." While she dressed, she made an offer. "We spend time together when we can, whenever possible. What I mean is, when we're both not working, we're together. That's what we can have, so we take it. We take every minute of it." They shook on it, grinning. "Happy Christmas, Jack Benoit." Emma blew him a kiss and closed the door behind her.

* * *

He checked in at 0930 hours to learn his patrol had been rescheduled for 1100 hours.

To everyone's relief, the truck sent to Kyedaw had returned at half past dawn loaded with rations, spare parts, and fifty cases of .30-cal ammunition. No. 91 was gassed, loaded, and tested.

Jack led the patrol of three, with Sal and Toby on his wings. They climbed and had just settled in at twenty thousand feet when the tower broke in. "Japanese assault group approaching Rangoon. A hundred planes sighted. Scramble all available aircraft."

On the ground, it was scripted chaos as the RAF launched all twelve of their serviceable Buffalos. The AVG sent up the remaining Tomahawks, completing the defense with twenty-six fighters.

George McMillan took his flight over the Syriam oil refinery, and Parker Dupouy's flight joined Jack above the airfield. The Buffalos headed toward the harbor, and the Brits sent their handful of Blenheim bombers northwest, out of harm's way.

"Sal, Toby, chalk fuel and time. I ain't trustin' these gauges. We're gonna get busy in a hurry, so know your assets. The Japs'll be thick as gnats, so keep your cool and stick to the tactics. Don't take the bait and start turning with 'em. We fill 'em with lead and get the hell out. Clear?"

"Clear."

"Clear."

They gained altitude to the north, leveling at twenty-four thousand feet. Banking clockwise, they came around south and caught sight of an approaching enemy formation. Toby yelled. "God Almighty!"

"It's Christmastime, boys. Let's start tearing into them presents," Sal roared.

"Target and position. Stay on the edges, watch each other's backs. When you dive out, get clear, check guns, check fuel. Focus. Let's pound these little shits."

A Porcupine of twenty-one Sallys were approaching the airfield at seventeen thousand feet with support from a dozen Hayabusa fighters, trailing a couple miles back at twenty-one thousand feet.

"Let's get a clean run on the Sallys before the fighters have time to drop in. Concentrate on the right edge. Toby, it's you, then Sal. I'll cover on top. Prime guns. Trigger switch. Let's do this." Jack took two slow, deep breaths, and the three Tomahawks half-rolled in line to dive into the Japanese bomber formation below. Jack watched yellow tracers from the Sallys' forty-two greenhouse machine guns stream past Toby and Sal. Seconds later, almost all of those lines swung to their right. Dupouy's flight was attacking the bomber group from the south and was now taking the brunt of the defensive fire.

Sal opened up on the rightmost bomber with his nose guns, and a ball of fire burst from its left wing. Toby moved his fire into the V, spraying the lead plane with his wing guns. As he passed through, the second target was trailing smoke from its starboard engine.

Now it was Jack's turn. He checked the rearview and made out four small dots, a flight of Hayabusa fighters in the distance. They were on him but too far back to be of immediate concern. Three hundred yards out, he squeezed a short burst from his nose guns, and red tracers wavered just off the tail of the smoking Sally. He eased upward and squeezed a second burst on target. At a hundred yards, sparks and a cloud of black smoke shot out of the starboard engine. He was pounding .50-cal rounds into the fuselage when the Sally tipped out and fell hard. Jack was driving under the enemy formation when he heard a series of thuds. In the rearview mirror the four small dots had been replaced by two fully formed fighters. Full throttle, he rolled right and ran as fast as he could. The Hayabusas couldn't keep up.

The AVG communication frequencies were filled with chatter. Dupouy's flight group, six strong, had pulled up from the Sallys and were in a fierce tangle with Jap fighters. Jack broke in. "Sal, Toby. Status? Over."

It took a while for Sal to get the channel. "We're together, Captain Jack, climbing north. Over."

Jack searched the air through the canopy and scanned his rearview for the enemy. He spotted the chasers climbing to rejoin their group, up where Dupouy was wreaking havoc. "Two Sallys down, boys. Good work. But we're just getting started. I'm comin' to join you. Check guns and fuel."

Sal and Toby were both chomping at the bit. "It's a free-for-all over there. Let's get in it!"

Jack felt the pull, too. His comrades were mixing it up, circling with the fighters, but his discipline held up. "We're killin' today, not dyin'. Stick to the tactics. That's an order." They lined up again at eighteen thousand feet as the first wave of Japanese bombers dropped their payloads over the airfield. "We'll catch 'em turning out. Keep altitude and take a line west of the airfield."

"Prime and trigger." Jack inhaled deeply and led the dive to intercept the enemy bombers that were banking toward home.

"The Jap fighters, they bugged out!" Toby cried.

"Probably goin' up to cover a second wave. Focus, and let's light up these bastards. They're a little loose on the left side. Target the V that's laggin' there, see it?"

Sal opened his .30s and shot out the canopy on the outermost bomber. Toby pounded the lead plane, killing everyone in the cockpit, and it fell straight over its nose. Jack came in against only one machine gun from the greenhouse on the innermost bomber. He opened his wing guns on the outside plane. A long burst, and it was smoking badly, so he turned to spray the last of the three bombers in that lagging V. It exploded, and he passed under shredded metal, fire, and smoke. All three bombers dropped from the sky. As the second enemy wave neared Mingaladon, Dupouy and his two remaining wingmen were still duking it out with the Hayabusas east of the airfield.

"Guns and fuel, boys."

"Yes, Daddy," Sal laughed.

"My guns are good, but I'm showing near empty on fuel." Jack pulled off his oxygen.

"To altitude?"

"Negative. Let's catch these bastards before they get too far off. Don't approach from underneath. The dust binners'll cook you. We'll come in just above level from late afternoon, out of the sun, if we can manage it. Over."

The trio formed a V and climbed a line east–southeast to catch the retreating Sallys. Their wings were all in good shape. Toby piped in, "There they are."

"Roger that. I'll lead. Toby, you tail and keep an eye out for fighter cover."

The bulk of the Sallys had tightened their formation, but three planes were each trailing light smoke, and their V was slowly losing altitude. Jack decided they'd climb a little higher to add dive speed, then jump the stragglers. His fuel gauge was bouncing on E. "Good grief! I'm out of fuel. Let's make this run count."

Jack readied his weapons. T-grips. Nose guns. Trigger switch. Two deep breaths as No. 91 roared through a dozen yellow tracer streams at four hundred miles per hour. Sighting behind the rightmost plane, Jack triggered his wing guns and eased red tracers across the tail, into the fuselage and across the Sally's greenhouse, painting the canopy red with a gunner's blood. Sal followed and blew the cripple from the sky. There were no fighters to be seen, so Toby dove in and flamed yet another bomber. The team regrouped near the deck. In the distance, lines of smoke rose from the airfield. Jack was flying on fumes and Sal and Toby were in only slightly better shape. "Let's head to the dummy field. Hopefully, we can set down there without too much trouble."

All three pilots successfully skirted the half dozen bomb craters that pocked the dummy field runway.

"Seven of those bastards!" Sal did a little jig. Toby snatched the Lucky Strike smoldering between Sal's fingers and took a long drag.

"Oh boy, Jack." Sal punched him in the arm. "We really gave them what for." Jack just grinned, admiring their Tomahawks. They looked like strong, proud animals, like Criquette and Max resting in the flatbed after a fine hunt.

"Oh, shit!"

"What?"

"Look!"

They'd nestled their planes in a tight cluster. "We gotta split 'em up. Toby, move yours down there." Jack climbed back into No. 91. It fired, and he wheeled it some forty yards before it coughed, sputtered, and quit. The fuel tank was bone dry.

"Feel better, Cap'n Jack?" Sal flicked his butt into a high arch.

The bombing had ceased. The raiders were gone. Toby and Sal were wild with excitement, celebrating their victory as they walked back to base. Toby thought out loud, "I wonder how the other guys fared?"

"What's your hurry?" Sal complained as Jack double-timed them to the base.

"That's a helluva lot of smoke," he said, walking even faster.

They reported in and told the ground crew where the Tomahawks were parked. The last of the AVG flights were landing, as were the returning RAF. "I'll be right back." Jack ran to the infirmary. Craters, debris, fires, and smoke were everywhere. He stepped around a line of nine blankets, with nine pairs of boots sticking out the bottom. There were two massive craters near the infirmary entrance. The building was pocked with shrapnel but remained intact. Inside, it was a crazy mess. The beds were full, and dozens of casualties lay on makeshift pallets or leaned against the walls. The place was covered in dirt and debris, and two Burmese boys were mopping blood off the floor. He found Emma kneeling over one of the Burmese cooks, tending to the man's badly burned arm.

The cook managed a smile for the American flyer who'd always treated him kindly. Emma turned, and there he was, wearing the same crooked grin she left him with that morning. She laughed as tears welled in her eyes. He nodded and turned away to let her work.

"Captain Jack is a kind man."

"What?"

"I think you like Captain Jack."

Emma smiled and started dressing the cook's wound. "Yes. I think I do, too."

"Good choice."

Jack returned to the ready room for debrief. "Captain Benoit, good show!" The hand extended was that of General Sir Archibald Wavell, Commander-in-Chief India, who had landed at Mingaladon with US General George Brett, Deputy Commander of Allied Forces for the South East Asia theater, just as the raid began.

"Thank you, sir." He looked over the general's shoulder. "How'd we do? How'd *they* do?"

"What was it, George? Twenty-one kills, to our eight losses?"

General Brett nodded. "We lost eight planes. Six pilots."

"Some of our chaps were jumped by a swarm of Nates before they reached altitude. We lost five to four in that tussle, I'm afraid. Otherwise, it was a bang-up job. Splendid work, Captain."

Jack saluted. "General. General."

Sal lit a fresh Lucky Strike as they walked out of command.

"You looking to get inducted, Captain Jack?"

"Knock it off, Sal."

"Yes, sir, flight leader, sir. General, General, sir."

They found John McClintock at the rubble where the AVG hangar used to be. "We're tanking fuel to your landing site, Cap'n. You gentlemen want a ride over there to collect your wings?" McClintock reminded him, "You're up next, Cap'n. Patrol at 1500 hours."

"I think I have a fuel leak, Scratchy. Check it out."

* * *

Fortunately, most of the rations survived the raid. Beef stew, potatoes, carrots, and onions for Christmas dinner, with sweet mangoes for dessert. Rejuvenated, Jack returned to the infirmary, where he found Emma, ragged from hours of triage and surgery.

"Have you eaten?"

She just sighed.

"You need food. It'll give you energy." He opened his satchel and pulled out a tin of stew. He pointed a spoon at her, but she just kept hanging the wet washed bandages. "Let me do that." Jack snatched the roll from her hands. "Sit."

Surprising herself, Emma complied, then scolded him, "Disinfect your hands before you touch any more of those, Captain Benoit."

"When do you get off tonight, doll?" He did his best James Cagney.

"This is good. Thank you."

The place was beat to hell, full of pain and sorrow, and he knew he wouldn't be seeing her tonight. "Y'all need some help here?"

She emptied the tin and licked the spoon. "You need your rest, Captain Benoit." She tucked the empty tin into the satchel and returned to her bandages.

"Unless there's a raid, I'm off until 1400 tomorrow. I *promise* I'll let you sleep."

"Thanks, Jack." She tried to smile. "You know, I might. Later, if that's okay."

"Anytime."

* * *

He woke when the door clicked shut. The room was well lit by the thin rectangle of sunlight that snuck in aside the window shade.

"Going on a trip?"

She set the small leather case next to the chair. "Just a few essentials. Do you mind?"

"How could I object to essentials?"

She smiled an exhausted smile.

"A bath first?"

"Sure."

Jack hopped out of bed, poked his head out the door, and hollered for Shaurya. He had to go find the boy. When he returned, Emma was passed out, facedown on the bed.

It was close to noon when she shot up, disoriented. Jack was reading in the rattan chair in the corner.

She rubbed her eyes. "What is that?"

Jack flipped it to look at the cover. "Letters to a Young Poet, by Rainer . . ."

"Maria Rilke. In English?"

"Not a lot of big words," he grinned.

She shook her head, stretching her arms. "Who gave you Rilke?"

"Did you eat?"

"Stew."

"Okay, we're gonna to get you cleaned and fed." He walked to the door.

She called after him, "So you can properly seduce me?"

* * *

"I have patrol now."

She startled awake.

"Shaurya'll make sure no one bothers you." Jack began to dress.

"And the Addertons? What must they be *thinking*? She feigned concern."

"The Addertons? Ha! I already paid 'em for January. Hell, they'll bug out any minute, and I'm the one keepin' 'em alive 'til they do. So fuck what the Addertons must be thinking."

She smirked, then remembered and thought out loud, "Did I ever tell you? No, I think I didn't. After you left on the motorbike, downtown. Did I tell you what I saw?" Jack shook his head. "The streets were filled with people, remember? Terrified people, everyone running willy-nilly, trying to find shelter this way or that. A flight of Tomahawks passed overhead. I suppose it was McMillan's squad. Anyway, Jitan Ram comes running up the street, pointing and yelling, 'The enemy! The enemy!' I thought he'd left with his mother the day before. Anyway, I figured he was confused, right? But then a flight of Japanese fighters swooped down on the Tomahawks. Jitan Ram starts jumping up and down, waving his arms. He's shouting at the sky, 'Strike them! Strike them hard! Kill the oppressors!'"

"*Kill the oppressors?*"

"Who knew my water boy could be so eloquent, or so political?" Emma lazily stretched herself across the bed.

He eyed her breasts and gave her a wink. "Are you trying to make me late for duty?"

Emma rolled her eyes and continued. "But, Jack, even I hadn't thought of it that way, you know? There he was, cheering the frigging Japs, and he wasn't the only one. There were plenty of others, here and there, craning their necks over this chaotic scene, their hands pressed against the sky. Brown smiling faces welcoming the Japanese to Rangoon." She sighed. "These people have no idea how bad it's going to be for them when the Japs run this place. We Brits make a hash of it, there's no denying it. It's a colony, for crikey. But the Japanese, all they'll make are slaves and corpses."

Jack tried to picture Jitan Ram, but he'd never met the boy. He considered Shaurya.

"Are you thinking about Shaurya?"

Jack raised his eyebrows.

"Well," she continued, "if you were in his shoes, in his *chappels*, what would you think? Shaurya wasn't in Nanking. He doesn't know what those monsters do. They'll enslave his Indian father, kill his Burmese mother, and rape his sisters. Some infantry officer will make him a houseboy or slit his throat, just for fun. Maybe he'll toss a coin to decide which. But everything Shaurya's heard about them, he's heard from us Brits. So why would he believe any of it, given the way we treat these people? I wouldn't believe a word of it if I were him, you wouldn't, either." She searched for her cigarettes. "We're half the people fighting over who runs the darkies on this side of the world. White Brits. Yellow Japs." She was making herself melancholy.

Jack mused, "Is it really that simple?"

"Look where the Japanese attacked, Jack. All the Pacific colonies, Western colonies."

"Yeah, they bombed all of 'em."

"Exactly."

That's when he first understood. The only countries over here that weren't controlled by Western powers were Japan and China, where all of this started four years ago, when the Japanese invaded Manchuria.

"Don't misunderstand me," Emma spoke forcefully. "These thugs, butchers and rapists, they must be stopped. The Imperial Army? They're the worst of humanity. They go on about honor and duty. Rubbish. What they did in Nanking, they'll do everywhere they please."

"Worse than Hitler?"

She gave a cynical laugh. "True, Hirohito has nothing on that devil. But the best way this could end, when it's all sorted, is a free Burma. An independent Malaya. Just look at the Philippines. It's named for a Spanish king and run by Yanks. The Japanese bombed Pearl Harbor because they want to replace you. They want to replace all of us. *Meet the new boss*. Maybe they'll rename the Philippines. How does *Tojoshire* sound?" Emma's cheeks were pink. Her hands trembled as she lit a cigarette. Jack stayed quiet, trying to digest it all. She inhaled soothing nicotine. "Sorry. Got a little riled up. So, I'll finish the story." Her eyes were wet.

"So, there he was, Jitan Ram, jumping and waving. You'd think it was his birthday." She paused to take a long drag, then laughed nervously. "Then I heard the whistling. Bombs coming. I ducked under an ox cart, dragged an old woman under there with me, the best I could do, just before the first one exploded. It landed so close that debris blasted the cart. The old woman caught a piece of hot shrapnel in her side. She was screaming, her coat smoking. Three more explosions followed in quick succession, thankfully, moving up the road."

She was shaking now, and Jack took her in his arms, but she pushed him away and jumped off the bed. Pacing by the window, her arms crossed, cigarette up, like their first encounter but nude. "People were screaming, crying. Running this way and that. It was absurd. I saw a woman holding a screaming baby. The child's mouth was propped open by a shard of wood that impaled his face. Corpses in the street. Wounded civilians, crawling, wailing. And then I saw it, lying next to us in that garbage-choked gutter." Jack waited as she blew a large plume of smoke out the window. "It was his head." She took another drag. "Well, that, and his neck. A shoulder, and arm to the elbow." She turned to him, tears trickling. "Yes. The Japs sure liberated little Jitan Ram. Liberated his frigging head right off his frigging body."

Jack thought of the people he'd killed. Eight bombers, ten crew members each. Eighty Japs. He wondered if they were thugs, butchers and rapists. They bombed civilians. That was part of their strategy. He wondered about their families. They had parents, siblings. Maybe a wife, kids. Emma walked to the bed and extended her hand. He kissed it.

"Kill those arrogant bastards," she said. "Send them to their graves, so they can't do this anymore."

He lay back, pulling her down with him, and she closed her eyes, sobbing. She cried herself to sleep on his chest. So many thoughts swirled in his head. On Radio Tokyo, Orphan Ann was always talking about how the Japs were going to liberate everybody. Back in the States, people were always talking about liberty, too. How the Founding Fathers had liberated America from the British. Chloe had told him how the French made that possible. A guy named Lafayette, the town right up Highway 167 was named for him. She had talked about Paris, about how wonderful it was there. He knew how awful it was for her in Abbeville. Awful just south of Lafayette. He could hear Davey Johnson spit out *Coonsville* like he spat out tobacco juice. But the French still ran a colony in Indochina. They ran Hanoi and all the plantations, like the Brits used to run America. Now the Nazis ran France, and the Japs attacked China and Burma from Vichy French Indochina. "Too goddamn much liberatin' goin' on."

24

RELIEF

DECEMBER 1941

No. 91's steady rumble felt reassuring as a pale orange line sprouted on the eastern horizon. December 26. Boxing Day. It was his first combined offensive mission with the Brits in their Buffalos, and it wasn't his show. The attack group was crossing the Thai border to strafe the Japanese airfield under construction at Mae Sot, taking a northern route to avoid detection over the Gulf of Martaban. As they approached the Moei River, Cassiopeia was sitting low to the northeast, outshining all her competitors. They banked south to follow the river, and there was Orion, straddling Jack's right shoulder.

"Gentlemen, 100 kilometers to target." Newly promoted RAF Major Phillip Edwards's calm demeanor was even more reassuring at 20,000 feet over enemy territory. "Captain Benoit, it looks like our path is clear, so we'll engage as planned. Take your Angels in. If you get jumped, we'll support from above. If not, we'll follow directly with a second wave. Radio silence until go time. Over."

There was no distinguishing Burma from Thailand from the handful of crooked brown ribbons of river running through the otherwise seamless, smoky-green jungle canopy that covered the mountain gorges.

The radio crackled. "Flight Leader to Angel One. Come in Angel One."

Jack answered, "I hear you, Flight Leader. Over."

"Target eighty miles. Angel One, hold course, steady drop to eight thousand feet. When you have identified the target, commence your run at your discretion. Over."

"Roger, Flight Leader. Let's go, boys." The rising sun was growing on the edge of the world, just moments from escaping the horizon's grasp. Jack slid on his Ray-Bans. "Angels, prime guns, set triggers. Toby, your honor today. Sal, you're on his right. I'll hang behind you. Eddy, good hunting to you and your boys. Over."

"Godspeed, Angel One."

Not ten seconds passed before the major was back on the channel. "Flight leader to Angel One. Flight leader to Angel One. Enemy fighters closing on you, three o'clock high. I count three, yes, three Nates. Angel One, do you copy?"

"Flight Leader, we see the incoming. Three fighters, starboard high. Nothing below. Over."

"Very well, Angel One. Buffalos, let's join the dance. Two and two, on the Nates, now. Angel One, we're on our way. Over." Jack hung back to give Toby and Sal some distance. If the enemy fighters closed fast enough to tangle, he'd roll then and dive to pull as many away from the attack run as he could.

At four thousand feet, Toby was on the radio. "Looks like two Jap fighters approaching the deck. Hopefully they won't hear about us in time to pull out, and we can catch them on the runway."

Edwards broke in. "Angel One, we have a line on the Jap fighters. We'll give them a good blast and see if we can turn them. Over."

Over his shoulder, Jack could see the enemy planes at ten o'clock high, their blue-gray underbellies shimmering in the morning light as they closed fast. "The Nates are 'bout here, boys. Get down there and give 'em what for."

Two of the Nates opened up on No. 91, and all four Buffalos opened up on the Nates. Toby and Sal trained their sights on the runway. On the ground, enemy soldiers were taking a knee to sight their rifles on the pair of screaming Tomahawks. In a sandbag bunker off the far end of the runway, three soldiers frantically worked to ready a machine gun. Sal took the airwave. "Toby, I'll take the fighters that just landed. You hit that bunch on the left."

They couldn't believe their luck. The runway was lined on each side with enemy planes, standing wing to wing in tidy rows. To the left, the big bombers. To the right, the smaller fighters. A fuel truck was nestled between bombers, and the truck's crew was scrambling for cover, leaving the fuel line dangling from one of the Sallys. It seemed the fighters that had just landed got wind of the attack, because both planes were circling tightly on the runway, positioning for takeoff back directly into the attackers' path.

Sal and Toby opened their nose guns on the field. The nearest taxiing Nate exploded and crumpled, engulfed in flame. Sal followed through with a burst on the second fighter but to no visible effect. Toby focused on the nearest of the succulent string of Sallys on their left. The first bomber, just topped off with fuel, exploded into a massive fireball. Toby drove straight through the expanding cloud of black smoke, blindly spraying the row as he went. The pair made it through the run completely unscathed.

"Glad they couldn't get that machine gun to cooperate," Sal laughed. "Looks like we got two, Captain Jack. What's your position? Do you need help?"

Yellow tracers flashed over No. 91's canopy, but the Buffalo drivers gave the Nates all they had, scattering the three of them, one of which trailed smoke. This cleared Jack for a solo run on the airfield. "I'm on my approach, boys. Thoughts?"

Sal yelled, "It's stacked up like a parade ground! Target the fuel truck behind the fire. You'll blow those devils back to hell!"

Toby cut in, "Watch out for the machine gun at the end of the runway on the right. We'll come around behind you and take another pass."

Jack checked the trigger one more time. Behind the smoke, the tarmac looked like a car park, and Japanese pilots were scrambling to their wings. Ground crewmen were pulling tire blocks. On the runway, the intact Nate was trying to maneuver around his fiery wingman, looking for room to take off. Through the dark air, Jack could just make out the fuel truck and the five Sallys lined up behind it. His beast growled as he pulled her into a strafing angle. A single line of yellow tracers rose from the machine gun nest, but the stream lagged harmlessly behind him. A dozen riflemen were doing their best with carbines when he opened his .50s on the fuel truck, which erupted, shredding in a sphere of flame that shot a hundred feet into the air. In a split second, the planes on each side of the fiery truck exploded, and a breath later, a third victim blew. He kept pounding with his .50s, and as he entered the churning black cloud. He drained them into the last two planes in the row, which both burst into flame.

He rolled No. 91 out to the right, directly over the machine gun nest to protect his belly.

"Goddamn, Jack!" It was Sal. "Look at that beautiful sight. The whole row is on fire!" The base was engulfed in churning smoke from the fuel truck's inferno, the six destroyed Sallys, and the fiery Nate crumpled at the end of runway. "Let's take the fighters before they can get up!"

"Angel One to Flight Leader. Angel One to Flight Leader. Can you use some help? Over."

No response.

"Boys, get some altitude. We got at least three Nates in the air, and I'm checkin' on the Brits." He tried again to reach Major Edwards and this time received a response.

"Flight leader to Angel One. Two Buffalos down. A third smoking and heading home. I'm in the thick with a couple sticky Japs. Over."

"Where are you? We're comin' to help."

No answer.

"Climb, boys."

"But the airfield, Jack. It's ripe for the picking!"

"Shut up, Toby. The Brits have been takin' it hard while we've had a turkey shoot. We're gonna help Eddy, so punch it!"

Sal yelled, "I see them." The Buffalo was twisting with two Nates on his tail just a couple miles to the west.

"I see you, Eddy. Bring 'em toward the base if you can. We'll get . . ."

The Buffalo popped with a flash of light. A wing fluttered away as the remainder of the plane spun tightly toward the ground, engine aflame. Jack's gut wrenched as he watched his friend die.

"Fucking bastards!" Toby was hot. "Let's get those brown-eared monkeys!"

"Negative." Jack rubbed his eyes under his sunglasses. "Check for other fighters. We're climbing north and going around."

"No, Jack! They . . ."

"That's an order, Lieutenant. Shut your trap and follow me. We're gonna make sure one of 'em gets home."

Crossing the tip of the Gulf of Martaban, Jack thought back to the major playing piano at Fulton's place the night he'd met Emma. *A good egg.*

They caught up to the Buffalo and escorted the crippled beast into Mingaladon. Jack brought him down, then circled to land. When he came in, he found Toby and Sal on the tarmac lighting up and laughing with some of the other AVG pilots. Captain Thompson's Buffalo looked like a colander. Firemen's foam dripped from its smoking engine.

At the briefing, there was a lot of backslapping. With his share of his flight's combined success, Jack now had six and two-thirds kills. Squad Leader Olson congratulated him. "You're an ace!."

But with Eddy and Clarke dead, and Tommy burned up who knew how bad, he didn't feel like celebrating.

"Look, seven kills, three losses. We beat those goggle-eyed monkeys and good." Olson slapped Toby's back. "Get some grub and take some rest. You're on another combined strafing run with the 67th tomorrow."

Jack walked alone to the infirmary, mumbling to himself. "The 67th. What's left, a half dozen of 'em? It's criminal, puttin' good men in those flying coffins." His head ached, and he felt nauseated. Sinus pain from the altitude, dehydration. He kept forgetting to drink.

Emma was sitting on the first bed, leaning over Tommy. The side of his neck, and all the way down his arm, was a black, oozing crust. The fingers on that hand were fused together. Tommy's eyes were wrapped, and he was emitting a low morphine moan.

"You made it." She didn't look up.

"Eddy and Clarke didn't. Tilson, either."

Emma bowed her head and whispered, "All of them." She kept at Tommy's wounds. "And your boys?"

"We made it all right. Did a lot of damage."

Emma pursed her lips and nodded.

"I'm gonna get some sleep." He stopped short of the door. "I love you, Emma."

She didn't look up. A tear hung from her nose.

* * *

Oley Olson sent his status report to Chennault.

```
Eight flight worthy aircraft. Short on parts.
Sufficient stores of other supplies. Local
population fleeing north. RAF down to four
serviceable fighters. Recommend repositioning
squadron to Kunming. Require more planes,
```

ammunition, and critical parts to stay in business here. Please advise.

The consensus among the Hell's Angels was that they would have to absorb one more pounding, then evacuate by the end of the week. By now, the Japs must have an accurate assessment of the Allied air strength over Burma, and they would soon come to finish off the base. The Brits and Kiwis of the 67th were licking their wounds, but the pilots were the bravest men Jack had ever met. Standup guys, to a man. Eddy was the only other flyer at Mingaladon who didn't drink most every night. Jack preferred his conversation, talking about things besides Japs, whores and contraband. Shu Hao was away in China, and now Eddy was even further away. He still had Emma and was grateful.

* * *

"They're planning the evacuation." She plopped down on the bed.

"Makes sense. When do you leave?"

"They're airlifting the wounded out this afternoon."

"The way I see it, we'll bug out soon." Jack placed his hand on her thigh as she lit a cigarette.

"But your orders? I heard you AVG are staying to help the 67th strafe the airfields in Thailand."

"It won't last. With eight planes? Twelve all told, with them broken down Buffalos." He shook his head. "What are your orders?"

"I don't have orders."

"Well, the only way out is China, and now the Americans are taking over China air command. I suppose the RAF finds its way back to India, over The Hump outta Kunming."

"I'm not RAF."

"What?"

"I'm not RAF. I'm a volunteer. I came here on my own terms. I'll leave on my own terms."

She told him how she'd left India to nurse civilians in China and did that for a couple of years before coming down to Rangoon, with details she hadn't shared before. "I knew some of these men back in Delhi, before they shipped to Egypt. When I heard they got stationed in Burma to help the New Zealanders, I thought I'd come down to help. I suppose I missed it some."

"Missed it?"

"The life." Her laugh was low and cynical, and she took a deep drag. "I was so done with the whole Colonial thing. So damn British, I just couldn't stand it anymore. So I went to China to help people. To forget, and to help people." She looked confused, feeling around the covers for her cigarette case. "Anyway, I came to miss it. I missed the conversation, really."

"So you knew these guys back in India."

She nodded. "Like I said, some. Clarke. Johnny Boy. Tommy."

Jack tipped his head.

"No, Jack, I didn't *know* any of them like that. We were familiar, and after what seemed like an eternity soaked in Chinese blood, I made a change. Came down here to see if I might be of some help. Left the helpless to help the helpers. Yes, that's about it."

"So, you don't hafta go where the RAF tells you?"

Emma found her cigarettes.

"Then where are you gonna go?"

She couldn't find her holder and fired it unfiltered. Jack rolled his eyes.

"The Japs are going to start hitting Kunming hard again, that's a certainty." She took a long drag. "Maybe I'll work in a hospital up there. Start patching up civvies again."

Jack liked the answer. "You got money for a place?"

Emma squinted at him.

"Look, I didn't mean anything by it. You just told me you're on your own. It's not like the RAF is gonna put you up somewhere, right?"

She softened and put her hand on his chest. "I'll be fine, Jack Benoit. Really."

The answer unnerved him, and she hadn't called him by his full name since she'd moved into his room. He regretted saying what he had said earlier at the infirmary.

It turned out they were both wrong about the plans for the defense of Rangoon. Chennault agreed that Burma couldn't be protected with the air power on hand, and he reached out to the Generalissimo, proposing to bring the Hell's Angels back to Kunming. But Chiang was adamant about defending Rangoon Harbor and the Burma Road, and he ordered Chennault to reinforce Mingaladon to a total strength of eighteen operational Tomahawks. The following morning, after returning from an unproductive strafing mission on the Japanese airfield at Chiang Mai, they received orders from Olson.

"We're being relieved. The Old Man's sending down a mixed bunch of Panda Bears and Adam and Eves. Transports are already on their way with ground crew and gear, and the Tomahawks come in this evening. We're bugging out first thing tomorrow. Be in the ready room with your gear by 0700. Wheels up at 0730." He addressed Jack directly. "Your group is off tonight. I suggest you get packed before you take advantage of it."

Toby punched Sal in the shoulder. "Let's go!"

Olsen warned them, "Show up a minute late tomorrow, and there'll be hell to pay."

* * *

Emma wasn't at the infirmary, so Jack walked home. He found her lying in bed. "Are you okay?"

She lay quiet, sweating. He felt her forehead. "You're burning up. Let's get you back to the infirmary, and not to work this time."

"I just need a little rest," she protested.

Jack poured himself a glass of water, then refilled it and brought it to her. She looked awful.

"I have some news." When he told her was flying out in the morning, she curled herself into a ball. "Both the AVG and the RAF are sending reinforcements. Oley says the Brits are bringing medical, so you don't hafta stay. They'll be fine here without you. Come to China with me."

Emma just lay there, curled and shivering.

He tried again. "Look, the Japs are going to invade. Maybe in a couple of weeks, or hell, maybe tomorrow. Everyone's gonna bug out soon, and it'll be a goat rodeo at the end. So, since the RAF has the infirmary covered, let's get you on a transport tomorrow. We'll get you in a hospital bed in Kunming, and when you feel better, you just pop up and start your nursin'."

Not even a smile.

Shaurya heated water for Jack's shave and bath, and brought mango, cheese, and cured meats. Jack tried to get her to eat some fruit. "*Feed a fever*, right?"

The alarm clock rattled at 0500, and Emma slept through it. Jack dressed and buckled his duffle. He gently shook Emma awake. She opened her eyes and touched his hand.

"Please don't wait for the invasion. You want to help people, right Sweet Cheeks? What's it matter if they're Burmese, Brits, Indians, or

Chinese? You gotta get on a transport today. There's a couple scheduled for early afternoon, okay?"

She closed her eyes. "I love you, too."

"I'm gonna talk to Newkirk."

Jack Newkirk had brought his Adam and Eves into Rangoon late last night and had assumed command of the AVG at Mingaladon.

* * *

"Hey, Cap'n Blackjack!" It was Sal. He pulled a flat box out of a satchel. "Here, this is for you. It's Neil's 1911. We divvyed up the stuff in his locker, and Henry's, too. Since you missed out, I figured why not the pistol?"

With so many deaths the past week, the men stopped bothering with auctions. They just split up the newly departed's possessions, flipping coins to settle debates. Jack hadn't fired his own sidearm during the five months he'd been in Asia. "What the hell am I gonna do with this thing?" Distracted, craning his neck to see if that was Newkirk across the tarmac, he snatched the box and stuffed it in his duffle.

"We got her patched up pretty good." McClintock puffed on a stogie. "Still some tape jobs along this side and the wing. We'll fix her up right when we settle in Kunming."

Jack tipped his head at the new war paint.

"How about that?" McClintock blew out a scruffy ring of smoke. "Looks like a winning hand." The word *Black* had been painted in front of his name, and in a line underneath *BlackJack Benoit* were six bright red balls painted over six white rectangles. Japanese flags representing his kills. An ace of clubs had been painted behind the jack of clubs, who still had a black X of tape on his forehead. "Blackjack Benoit." McClintock chuckled. "Like when we were on the ship. I don't think you're gonna be able to shake it this time, Cap'n."

"A little . . . *ostentatious*, don'tcha think, *Scratchy?*" He could hear Emma enunciating the word, and he smiled.

"C'mon, Cap'n." McClintock toed an old butt on the tarmac. He wasn't fond of the nickname he'd earned from his record-breaking case of crabs.

Newkirk told Jack he'd have someone from the infirmary look in on Emma, and later that morning, an RAF nurse who'd just arrived from Singapore found her at the Addertons in a bad way. She was in the infirmary on liquids before Jack landed at Wujiaba Airport in Kunming, but he was pondering something other than her health during his flight north. Oley Olson had overheard Jack making the arrangements with Newkirk and bent his ear. "There's something you should know about your girlfriend."

25

MISTIGRI

FEBRUARY 1942

But for the hum of the struggling light bulb that dangled over the aisle, and a gentle snoring a few beds down, the ward was silent. She grazed his neck with her fingertips and caressed his cheek with the back of her hand. She gave it a light poke. "Not as pale today." She had a listen to his chest. No wheezing. After two hard weeks, his breathing was easy again, the rhythm reminding her of their first night together, how she'd woken in the dark, her head cradled in his arm, her cheek damp with sweat on his chest.

* * *

Fifty miles east of Kunming, the enemy bomber group had tightened their formation as the trio of Hell's Angels approached head-on.

"They know we're here, boys. Let's get at it."

Jack led the attack with Sal on his right wing, Toby on his left. None of them spotted the half dozen Nates dropping from above, and well behind, the bomber group. The Tomahawks rapidly closed distance on a collision course with the lightly gunned Anns, their drivers excited for what looked to be easy pickings. The leader of the Japanese fighter echelon, Lieutenant Suzuki, had rightly gauged he would not reach the Americans before they engaged his charge, so he directed his flight to lay in on the level behind the bombers and intercept the attackers head-on as the enemy completed its pass.

Suzuki's calculation was precise. When Jack cut loose the first barrage at the rightmost Ann, Suzuki and his wingmen were still a thousand yards behind the bomber formation. The Nates had closed to three hundred yards behind the Anns when Jack crossed directly over the burning Ann. Suzuki and two wingmen opened guns on the lead enemy fighter as it flew straight into their line of fire. The combatants had closed to sixty yards when Suzuki jerked his plane's throttle back. He was rocked in his seat when the rear wheel was torn from his plane by No. 91's tail fin.

The Japanese trio rolled out to reengage the Americans. As he came full around, Suzuki saw the lead enemy plane some three thousand feet below, slowly spinning in a nosedive and trailing a corkscrew of black smoke. A wingman reported that the other two enemy fighters were climbing, so Suzuki counted one kill and reformed his group more tightly above the surviving Anns.

Hell's Angel No. 91 was beaten and battered, the fuselage pocked with holes, the engine smoking and spraying the left side of the aircraft with coolant. A single 7.7mm round had pierced Jack's windshield at the seam and ripped through the side of his helmet. His Ray-Bans shattered, sending shards of glass into his left eye, and the bullet grazed his temple. It felt like someone stabbed his face with a filet knife. The bullet scooped a crescent of bone from his eye socket, and the concussion fractured the orbital structure on the left side of his face. It was the only round to enter the cockpit, and the bullet flattened against the thick, armored plate behind his seat. A half inch to the left, and he would have escaped unscathed. A half inch to the right, and he would've been instantly killed. Disoriented, and his eye pulsing with fiery pain, he somehow managed to pull his wounded beast out of the spin and crash-land in a field of cut wheat. On impact, his shoulder dislocated, and the collarbone snapped. Broken ribs smashed and collapsed a lung. Farmers pulled him out before the fire reached the cockpit.

* * *

The morning nurse released the window shade, and a trapezoid of white light bounced off the bleached-white bed sheet and stabbed his good eye. Groaning, Jack raised his good arm over his face. "Can we put that down, miss?" This was the longest he'd sat up in bed. He couldn't shake the smell of cordite, like the inside of his nose was scorched.

Dr. Lian told him the smell was stuck in his brain, not his nose.

"I'm all right, doc. Really."

The conversation was about morphine, three weeks since the crash.

"How 'bout we cut back some?"

Dr. Lian pushed his brown tortoiseshell glasses up the bridge of his nose. "Captain, there is no hurry. War for you is finish. So only concern is get better. And pain, instead of comfort, you see this will not make better, faster. Okay?"

Jack shook his head. "I know, doc. I ain't lookin' for punishment. I just don't like feelin' wacky. I like knowing what's going on, and that stuff makes everything . . . I don't know. It's like everything's out of reach, out there, somewhere. You know what I mean?"

"This simple. Your brain swollen. Smashing against the skull. You have much pain until swelling down. So when nurse brings you medicine, you take medicine. Do we understand?"

It was agreed the morphine dosage would be cut by half. As Dr. Lian and the nurse walked off, Jack tried to spot Emma down the ward. He'd been awake all of twenty minutes and missed her something awful. He thought of Chloe, too, and the morphine had him talking to himself.

"It's what, eight o'clock at night over there? Somethin' like that. Probably got her nose in a book." He pictured her eyes, like a bottle of cream soda in the sun.

"A yuan for your thoughts?"

Jack jerked his head at the voice and grimaced in pain. Emma frowned and took his hand.

"I understand you're being obstinate with Dr. Lian."

"It's my body." He shifted, trying his best to sit up straight. "And who are you to talk about being a bad patient? You were a damn pill in Rangoon."

"Jack, you remembered!" She sat next to him and stroked his hair. "See, they're coming back, your memories. So come on now."

He remembered most things. At least he thought he did. But things from just before the crash, not so much. She fluffed his pillows. "The morphine will relax you and decrease the likelihood of you . . ."

He glared at her with his bloodshot eye.

"Yes, *you,* aggravating your situation."

"But . . ."

Emma held a finger to his lips. "I don't tell you how to fight, Captain. You don't tell me how to heal." She brought his hand to her lips. "Do we have an understanding?"

As she stood, the sliver of white light skirting the window shade reflected off the side of her crisp white dress. Jack followed the thin radiance up to her cheek, her freckles. It was bright enough to see the flecks of pepper in her golden eyes. He leaned back into the pillows and sighed, mumbling through the morphine. "What are the friggin' odds?"

***

The Japanese had their way with the Allies for the three months following their surprise attacks. Hong Kong fell on Christmas Day. Singapore fell on February 15. Thailand fully capitulated by treaty, giving the Japanese bases from where they would mount the ground invasion of Burma. When the Japanese did invade, thousands of native Burmese formed the Burmese Liberation Army and turned on the British. Others who had worked in service to the Colonials became refugees, and hundreds of thousands of them streamed north on the Burma Road alongside the expat Brits and the Indians who were loyal to them.

Back in the States, it was bad news from overseas. The US territory of Guam had been overrun just two days after the attack on Pearl Harbor. Wake Island fell later in December, and the Japanese were still pounding American forces in the Philippines. It seemed only a matter of time before the Empire would consolidate land, naval, and air power from Korea to Indonesia.

But by sheer luck, the Allies had some reason to hope. The US Pacific aircraft carrier flotilla was not anchored in Pearl Harbor on December 7, and so escaped the attack. If the carrier groups could somehow counter Japanese naval air superiority, the Allies stood a chance. Meanwhile, since they were relieved from Rangoon in late December, the Hell's Angels had been fighting in the skies over China.

***

It was noon when he woke to warm lips on his cool forehead.

Emma whispered, "Happy Birthday, *Petit Jacques* Benoit."

He got a kiss and no knife in the eye.

"How'd you find out?" He pinched her forearm. "My birthday, *and* what they used to call me?"

"A little birdie told me. Actually, a rather big birdie." She tipped her head toward the door. "A bird colonel."

Jack was a little fuzzy, but he heard heels clicking along the corridor toward them. It was the Old Man and Harvey Greenlaw.

"Colonel." Jack saluted over his good eye.

Smiling, Chennault returned it. "Tell me, nurse. How's my boy doing?"

"Very well, Colonel. Thankfully, we skirted pneumonia, and we're in a very good position regarding infection. He just needs to rest." She leaned toward the patient. "*And* to heed his doctor's advice."

"Well, son, you gave us quite a scare." The Old Man's eyes were moist, his tone gentle. "It's good to see you're on the road to recovery." Chennault's soothing drawl took Jack right back to Texas and into the great room at the King Ranch.

"PJ . . ." Chennault caught himself. "Captain. We have a special guest today, who has asked to see you. You look fit enough for a visitor."

"Yes, sir."

Greenlaw waved at the backlit doorway, and a small, tight-knit group of people shuffled into the recovery room. Jack could make out Olga Greenlaw towering over four Chinese Army brass, all walking behind a Chinese woman, resplendent in a sky-blue silk suit. Chennault bowed slightly toward the woman, with Greenlaw next to him making a production of it.

Chennault cleared his throat. "Madame, may I introduce to you Captain Jack Benoit, flight leader of the 3rd Squadron, American Volunteer Group. Captain, Madame Chiang Kai-shek."

Jack noted what he'd heard was true. Madame was a beautiful woman who exuded confidence, elegance and grace.

"It's an honor to meet you, Madame Chiang."

The Generalissimo's wife stepped forward and offered her hand. "The honor is mine, Captain Benoit. To visit here, with one of our bravest Angels. The doctor tells me you are healing very well, and that you will have your strength again very soon. I am so happy to have heard this news."

He was puzzled by her accent. She sounded like she was from Georgia. They shook hands. "That's what I hear, too, ma'am. Excuse me, *Madame*." He smiled at Emma, who was standing to the side. The radiance of her smile struck him. This didn't seem the kind of event she would appreciate. *Rewarding carnage.*

"Jack? Jack!" It was Harvey Greenlaw, his voice booming.

"What?" He scanned their faces.

Emma stepped past Madame Chiang. "It's the morphine, Madame," she offered, as she fluffed the pillows that were propping up Jack. "One tends to drift off a bit."

"Yes, of course." Madame Chiang nodded with an understanding smile. "Captain Benoit, in honor of your dedication to the protection of the Chinese people, your outstanding bravery in action, and your success as a flying ace against the barbarous Japanese invader, it is with my humblest respect and gratitude, on behalf of President Chiang Kai-shek, the Chinese people, and honorable peoples everywhere fighting the terrible Japanese aggressor, I present you with this, the Order of Renaissance and Honour."

One of the Chinese brass held out a box to Madame Chiang and opened the lid. He detected a hint of jasmine as she tucked the ribbon over his head.

He picked it up and squinted. "It's pretty."

Madame Chiang laughed politely, and her entourage followed suit. "Thank you." She leaned forward and kissed his cheek.

Jack blushed and caught Emma's eye.

"Now, we must give my dear Angel time to rest. Good day, Captain."

Jack watched Madame and her entourage walk toward the bright doorway. Stabbed by pain behind his eye, he turned away as they exited the ward.

"PJ." The Old Man saluted and bit his lip.

"Sir." Jack returned the salute.

Chennault leaned in close. "Your daddy would be proud of you, son. I'm proud of you." He and the Greenlaws turned and followed the Chinese group out of the recovery room. Emma stayed behind.

"Well, how about that?" She injected seven milligrams of morphine.

Jack sank into his pillows as the drug dulled his senses and fogged his mind. "Think I'll take a nap, Sweet Cheeks."

It would be another five weeks, well into April, before Captain Jack Benoit was cleared to leave the hospital.

* * *

5 February 1942

Dearest PJ,

We were thrilled to receive your letter dated 4 January this afternoon and are so thankful you are well! I could not wait to write to you.

Here I sit, in the corner booth near the Victrola. It is quite a thought that my father had this machine delivered to our home in New Orleans so long ago, nearly fifteen years to this day. But now we often listen to the radio instead of records. Aunt Menta does not like to hear the war reports, but I try to keep up with happenings in the Pacific.

I think of you often. In the sky. In the clouds. Sometimes I think of you on the ground. I wonder about you with friends. Do you play cards, like we did when you were here? I like very much that your plane sports the jack of clubs. Do you remember how I debated Francie and Aunt Menta about the word "Mistigri?" In French, this is the jack of clubs. With the Creole here, this is the one-eyed jack, the jack of hearts. Perhaps you can favor my argument and name your plane Mistigri? (Francie just asked to read this start of a letter. She pounded the table, "No!" Squeezing an eye shut, she pointed at it and said, "Mistigri!" before running off. I believe if you were here, I might have heard a "Good grief.")

Returning to friends, I wonder about yours. I wonder about girls, and if you have one. I like to believe I would not be jealous to hear you have someone special in your life, but my heart aches when I think of it. So I try to be my best, to think only about your safety and your happiness. The world did not favor us, so I wish you joy without me. Yes. I do. I hope you can wish me joy without you.

Please write again as soon as you have extra time. My tummy tingles whenever there is an envelope in the mail.

Although he will never replace Louis in my heart, Count Basie has become a favorite. What The Count is doing with boogie woogie — so much enrichment with orchestral texture. I adore it.
Sincerely,

Chloe Boisvert

P.S. We all wish you the happiest of birthdays! I would send you a tart if I could.
P.P.S. I will never forget our special friendship.

***

The medical staff thrilled to his recovery.

"Other than missing eye, all right as rain," Dr. Lian joked. "No headache?"

"Not really."

"Shoulder?"

"It's fine."

"Not stiff?"

A shake of the head.

Jack had started up his calisthenics a couple of weeks earlier, despite the admonishments of the entire medical staff, including Emma. He couldn't stand lying there all day and night, feeling his muscles atrophy. He'd lost nearly twenty pounds and was disgusted by his ribbed chest and spindly limbs. So, he traded pain for improvement. The nurses worried about infection, and his shoulder retained some swelling, but his lung was healthy, and the break in his collarbone had set well.

"I see no reason to keep here anymore, Captain. We clear you today."

Jack stuck his hand out. "Thanks, doc. I know I was a pain in the butt. Thanks for everything."

The doctor and nurse left, and Emma came by soon after. "I hear you're a free man."

"One could say that."

She touched his cheek and ran her fingers along his eyepatch. "Hmm. So, what's next for Captain Blackjack? Search for Treasure Island?"

Jack touched the patch and took Emma's hand. "I had visitors last night."

She looked worried for his tone.

"You know how they ran that story on us a few weeks back, the magazine back in the States?"

"*Time* magazine. Yes, I do. They called you the Flying Tigers. And?" Emma's tone betrayed her.

"Well, back home, back in the States, I mean, they ain't got a lot of good news coming in, right?"

"I would think not."

"Right. So the Army brass wants to get me in the papers back there. Make a show of it, you know, about what we did in Burma. Here in China. The AVG."

Emma waited.

"So someone from *The New York Times* is gonna interview me."

She waited.

"So I'm going to New York."

Emma stood and straightened his sheet. "Makes perfect sense."

He felt awful, to see it in her face. "That's the start of it. After that, I'm going on a train tour across the country. Whistle-stop tour, they call it. Try to help sell war bonds."

Emma looked him in the eye. Hers were moist, about to spill. "When are you leaving?"

"Right away."

"I see." A tear trickled down her cheek. "Right thing to do. No use for you here." She turned and briskly exited the recovery room, bumping shoulders with an attendant from the AVG offices.

"Captain Benoit, you got a couple more letters."

* * *

February 26, 1942

Dear PJ,

We received your letter dated January 30 and were so relieved to hear from you. Frank and I have been terribly troubled since the papers announced the Japanese ground invasion of Burma.

I am collecting news accounts of the Flying Tigers. What an exciting name! But I cannot know what I do not have. Your name was in a syndicated article from the San Francisco Chronicle. They called you Jack Benoit and said you are nicknamed Blackjack because you are also an ace. Frank thinks that is very clever.

The children continue to grow and to grow unruly. I wish I knew what to do about the unruly part. Frank is gone so much of the time, sometimes I worry I may not be up to the task. But everyone is healthy, praise the Lord.

Frank sends his regards. He wants me to say, "Kill the ——— Japs." I suppose I just did, Lord forgive me.

We all wish you the happiest twentieth birthday, and the children just sang for you!

We are praying for you.

With love,

Odette

I had a nice visit with Chloe at the Music Box, and Frank will take our letters up to the post office in Lafayette when he drives to work tomorrow. She seems quite happy, and I hope you can be happy for her, too.

25 February 1942

Dear PJ,

Odette visited the Music Box and read me the letter you sent to her dated 30 January. It was a relief to know you are still safe in China. She also informed me of what she has learned from the papers.

We looked at a clipping of the San Francisco article. It was like a wild dream to see the photograph of the airplanes you fly, the Flying Tigers. They look so fierce with the shark teeth. I am certain the Japanese are very afraid when they see you in the sky. She told me they call you "Blackjack." This tickled me as I remember teaching you vingt-et-un so long ago. I shared that story with Odette, and I think she enjoyed it.

The café is doing better now that more people are working. We also have some more recent records to play on the Victrola, by the best musicians. Louis Armstrong and Count Basie remain my favorites.

Menta is up and walking, but it remains difficult for her. For some time she relied upon crutches, then Dr. Herod read about a new instrument called a walker. She cannot move quickly or carry things, but she recently started cutting vegetables and making gumbo with Francie's help.

I have exciting news to share. Arrangements are being made so I may start college in the fall. Dr. Herod is confirming the opportunity with the Dean of Arts and Sciences at the University of Chicago. It is an integrated school, if you can believe it! The idea was initially unfathomable, and I am still uncertain how I will fare. The arrangements include my teaching introductory French in exchange for tuition. I hope you can be happy for me. I am bringing Francie, and we will move in the summer.

You are in our thoughts always, and Menta has the whole church praying for you.

There is no doubt you must focus on the task at hand, but if you can spare any time to write to me, I would cherish your response.

Please stay safe in your courage.
Sincerely,
Chloe

He closed his eye and sank back into the pillow. The piercing pulse stabbed at the back of his empty eye socket. "Chicago. With Francie."

* * *

At dawn, a thoroughly saturated Toby Gyer plopped down on Jack's bunk.

"All packed, Cap'n?" He belched.

"You look nice and loose, my friend."

Toby chuckled and took the last pull off a fifth of Jim Beam. "Gil's dead."

Jack tipped his head. "How'd he get it?"

Toby teetered as he tipped the empty bottle over Jack's bunk.

"How'd he get it?"

"Fucking monkey blew him out of the sky. *Ka-boom!* Some Chink farmers saw him go down next to a pig barn. Nothing left but twisted metal and charred bones." He fumbled a pint of Jack Daniels out of his cargo shorts. It was early April and freezing outside, but Toby clearly wasn't feeling it. He took a long pull, then held the pint out to his friend.

Jack never liked Gil Weathers but took the drink for Toby, and for all the volunteers. "To Gil. Helluva guy." He threw back a shot and counted on his fingers. "Gil . . . Sal . . . Buster . . . Ebbe." Jack held out the pint, and his drunk friend snatched it, struggled to his feet, and drained what was left. He tossed the empty on Jack's bed and leaned a hand on each of his friend's shoulders, looking him in the eye.

"Go bang a truckload of pretty white New York girls for me, will ya?" Toby slapped the cheek under Jack's good eye, which sent a shock of pain through his face. He belched again and stumbled out of the barracks.

Jack hadn't seen Toby like this for weeks. All the Hell's Angels had straightened up since coming north. Patrols and sorties layered on each other, dawn to dusk. The ground crew was all business. Quite a few AVG had started up relationships with local girls, and most of the men regularly gave rations to hungry locals. There just wasn't much time for carousing and causing trouble anymore.

That evening, Emma opened her door. "*Yes?*"

"Don't, all right?" He slipped past her into the room.

"Make yourself at home, dear." There was a bottle on the nightstand, half-empty, and a glass in her hand, half-full. Wet brown stains of spilled bourbon dotted her nightie between her breasts.

"Goddamn, Emma." He turned to her. "What do you expect me to do? Sit around here, shufflin' paper for Harvey Greenlaw? I'm a one-eyed flyer. Means I'm good for nothin' here."

"Nothing?" she screamed, sneering over the rim of her glass, huffing with intoxicated frustration. She stumbled around the room, looking for her cigarettes.

"Here they are." He handed her the crumpled pack and Zippo that had fallen behind the Philco tabletop radio he'd picked up on the black market.

```
If I have to walk down
Them railroad track
```

She went to the window and fired a smoke as the radio transitioned from Cab's "Geechy Joe" to the Duke's "C Jam Blues."

"I hate this."

"*The Duke?*"

Nothing.

"Come with me."

Three little words, hanging in the air like a cartoon balloon.

He seized her shoulders and turned her around. She looked him in the eye, her head bobbing. He answered the question she hadn't yet asked.

"Yes, I *have* thought it through." He kissed her forehead. "Come with me. Get out of this damn war. Leave the *carnage*, as you call it. Let's just leave all this shit! We'll go to the States and make a life. The war's done for me. It can be done for you, too. Done for *us*."

His stomach tightened as his good eye did its best to discern her kaleidoscope of emotions. Surprise and confusion, wonder and hope, panic, all soaked in drunk. She dropped to the bed, stupefied. Forgetting her cigarette, she scorched the sheet. He plucked the smoke from her fingers and tamped down the smoldering blanket. Leaning against the window frame, he crossed his arms.

"Well, what do you say, Sweet Cheeks? Do you want to make an honest man of me?" He paused. "Or not. Either way."

She crinkled her nose and giggled. He felt self-conscious and straightened up. She broke into a smile and leaped into his arms, throwing hers around his neck. She laughed and cried on his chest. He blurted out, "Chicago," startling himself.

"What?" She wiped her eyes. "*Chicago?* Are you saying you want to live in Chicago?"

They agreed to leave Asia for the States. Surely the Americans would need nurses at home, with so many casualties returning from the Pacific. They could live in California. San Francisco, maybe San Diego, near a navy hospital. Jack would be leaving China with close to four thousand dollars in his pocket. A pretty good stake, even if he never saw the seven grand in kill bonuses he was owed. He'd figure out something to do. Emma was a volunteer here, held in China by her personal commitment and nothing more. All they needed to do was get on a plane.

* * *

Emma wanted to make her goodbyes, so they agreed to meet in the AVG offices at Wujiaba Airport. Jack had procured two jump seats on a CNAC C-47 Dakota cargo plane to be flown over The Hump to Dinjan, India, piloted by none other than Shu Hao. From Dinjan, they would catch a transport to Calcutta. Another flight to Bombay, then a steamer around Cape Good Hope and up the Atlantic to New York.

Jack pawed at the pavement. "Goddamn." It wasn't like her to be late, but then with the air raid that morning . . .

Emma had taken a rickshaw north to the French hospital to wish a couple of friends well, and the roads were a mess. Clouds of dust over rubble. Ravenous rats over garbage. Wailing mourners over corpses.

He raised his wristwatch and waved at Shu Hao, who had finished his equipment check and was firing the engines. The cargo door was rising, and a corporal with a clipboard was frantically waving Jack toward the air stairs. Emma came running. His heart soared. But her hands were empty, and his head spun, his cheeks flushed.

"What the . . ."

She was breathing hard, hands on her knees. He pulled up her chin and found bloodshot eyes and cheeks streaked red from tears.

"I can't leave them."

"What? Who? *Them who?*"

Trying to catch her breath, she stepped back and opened her arms. "Them. All of them. *This!* This is where I'm meant to be. This! Them! This!" Her eyes were pleading. "*This* . . . this is *me*."

His chest pounded. His eye throbbed and stabbed his brain. "This?" he yelled, spreading his arms. "Emma, *this* is a friggin' airport!"

* * *

While the Dakota climbed to the west, Jack rode a carousel of emotions. Shock to sadness. Longing to anger. Fiery daggers stabbed through his missing eye and into his brain.

"Fuck!" He unbuckled his harness and pressed his forehead against the cold window glass. It was a bright, cloudless sky over northern Yunnan Province. He squinted to study the contours of the fields and pastures, the hamlets and rivers, forcing his mind off the tarmac at Wujiaba Airport. The two-dimensional picture distracted him. The Dakota's engines droned.

"Captain?" It was the copilot, saluting. "It's an honor to be flying you home, sir. May I shake your hand?"

"Not sure I'm callin' Dinjan home, but I appreciate the sentiment." He gripped the lieutenant's hand. "Call me Jack."

"Lieutenant Sam Miller, sir, from Albuquerque."

"Glad to meet you, Sam. You been flyin' The Hump a while?"

"No, sir. To tell the truth, this is my first trip."

Jack slapped him on the shoulder, and the jarring motion spiked his phantom eye. "The first of many."

"Yes, sir."

The boy's eagerness cheered him some.

"Well, Sam, you couldn't be in better hands than with Shu Hao. He's the pick of the litter."

"Yes, sir, Jack, sir. Would you like to sit up front with the captain? He asked me to ask you. Here, take these." He handed Jack his own sunglasses and stepped aside.

The Himalayas were just sprouting on the western horizon. "Quite a view."

"My good friend, Captain Jack Benoit. Have a seat."

"I'm headin' home, Shu."

The pilot nodded. "At university in England, I knew a Yank. He had a saying about home. What was it, exactly? Yes. I remember. 'Home is where the heart is.'" Shu Hao looked at his friend's face. "So, Jack, are you going home, or are you leaving home?"

Sweet Cheeks. Honeybee. He mumbled, "Goddamn."

"What was that?"

Jack shook his head and scoffed. "Seems I'm a citizen of the world, Shu."

"*Casablanca!*" Shu Hao belly-laughed. "Yes, I saw that movie at the Metro Cinema, in Calcutta."

Jack didn't know what he was talking about and was eager to change the subject, regardless.

"How many hops've you made, Shu? *Shu Hao*." He just remembered what Emma told him about how to properly address his Chinese friend.

"This is my nineteenth trip. The lieutenant's first. He's a good man, Lieutenant Miller. I'm confident he has the stuff."

"Tell me what you've been doin'. Last we talked was in Kyedaw, damn, November, right?"

"Not quite, Jack. I came to see you in the hospital in Kunming." Shu Hao laughed. "We talked then, but you weren't all there." He spun a figure at his temple.

"The morphine."

So Shu Hao caught him up. He'd been one of the Generalissimo's personal pilots during the first two months of the year. "A lot of hurry up and wait. British brass to and from India."

"Didn't you help evacuate Hong Kong?"

Shu Hao nodded.

"So you just rotate from cartin' bigwigs to cartin' crates."

Shu Hao laughed again. "Yes, it seems so. Recently, a lot of crates and a few Americans. Sometimes the army can't get them over The Hump, so I do it. The Yanks are coming fast to take the lead on the China defense."

"I'm not sure the Generalissimo would agree."

Shu Hao shook his head. "The Japanese will tidy up the Rim soon enough, then they'll come at China full force. They'll work to disrupt India, too. I've heard ten thousand captured Indian colonial troops have already turned. Five gets you ten the Japs will turn that many again by summer. What would happen in Bengal if twenty thousand Indian soldiers showed up with as many Japanese regulars and uncontested air cover? The Brits would face rebellion across India. If the Yanks don't solidify here quickly, all may be lost. We can't get it done in China without American air support. I'm certain the Generalissimo understands that clearly."

Jack looked out the window, noting the weather to the northwest. "Have you heard from your sister? Is she still with the Communists?"

"I received a letter from my father in February. He sent it from Nanchong. He informed me that he was heading north to join her. He would be searching for my sister in Yan'an."

"Your father? The industrialist?" Jack couldn't believe it. "Is your mother with him?"

"My mother passed in December. She was very ill. I learned of her passing from my father's letter."

"I'm sorry, Shu. Damn. I am sorry." Jack touched his eyepatch. "And your father's a Communist now?"

"It is not unheard of for the headstrong daughter of a capitalist to travel north. Certainly, it is less common for her capitalist father to follow her."

Jack considered what he was hearing. "So your family's all Commies now, but you fly the Generalissimo and Madame Chiang here and there. Do I have that right?"

"I can't say my father is a communist, no. He has a need to see his daughter. What may happen, I may only guess. As for the Chiangs, they've never questioned my loyalty." He paused. "But it is clear the Generalissimo has advisors who are not so certain."

"That level of trust says something about you, Shu. *Shu Hao*. Fuck."

Shu Hao gave him a quizzical look and continued. "I am Chinese first, Jack. There is no doubt that once we have repelled the Japanese invaders, China will struggle for a new identify. There is a great deal of bad blood between the Nationalists and the Communists. The Generalissimos actions of the April 12 Incident is still bright in the Communists' minds, though fourteen years past. *The Feast of the Heads*, as it is known by some, for all of the decapitations. It was a mistake, and the Communists remain correct that China must have land reform. After the war, we cannot continue to run our country in a feudal manner. But still, the Generalissimo is a fierce leader fighting for a strong, independent China, and he has a fierce partner in Madame Chiang. No, it will not be easy to become one China."

"So after you finish kickin' the Japs outta here, what are *you* gonna do?"

"I will fight for peace for China, in China. There will be a struggle for power, but I will fight for peace among the Chinese. We have had too much suffering and death. There are years more to come, more suffering and death, to rid ourselves of the imperialist aggressor. When the Japanese have been repelled, I will fight to end violence in my homeland."

Shu Hao pointed at the saw teeth forming on the horizon. "Look. The Himalayas. They are beautiful and ruthless. The weather is entirely unpredictable. We will ice completely and fly on instruments, bounced by storms between the peaks. These are the few hours of flight I have never enjoyed. It was more comfortable taking flak while evacuating Hong Kong. But, Jack, the crew at Dinjan is brilliant. First-rate to a man. Chinese nationals up and down the ranks. I'll introduce you around. There's not much to the base, but given what they have to work with, they do spectacular work." As the mountains grew on the horizon, Shu Hao said, apologetically, "I will need Lieutenant Miller in a few minutes, Jack. Shall we continue our conversation on the ground, over tea?"

The ride over The Hump was turbulent, but not violent, and when they landed, Jack's legs were so numb from the cold, he had trouble standing. He hadn't dressed warm enough for the duration of the flight at altitude in a C-47 Dakota with a malfunctioning heater.

Shu Hao summoned ground crew to help his friend regain his legs. Jack's head throbbed, his missing eye the eye of the hurricane swirling in his brain. "My first altitude since the surgery," he managed, then crumpled on the tarmac and vomited.

"Let's get you warmed up. A nice cup of tea to wash down some aspirin powder, right?"

Jack finished the last drop of a large bowl of vegetable red curry with jasmine rice and mint. He was feeling better, warm and hydrated. It was eighty degrees Fahrenheit in Dinjan, fifty degrees warmer than when he'd turned away from Emma that morning.

"The color is back in your face."

Jack was reminded how observant his friend was, so perceptive during their training at Kyedaw. Nothing escaped him. "So, Shu, Shu Hao, how long do you think you'll fly The Hump?"

"I don't know, Jack. I prefer supplying our men to . . . how did you say it? Carting bigwigs. Of course, when we have bomber strength, I want to be over Tokyo." Shu Hao nodded to himself. "Madame once asked if I was eager to bomb the Japanese."

"What did you say?"

Shu Hao laughed. "I wasn't shy in my answer. I'm hopeful the Generalissimo will insist on including Chinese crews in the first wave of attack over Japan, but I fear the Americans will press that effort without us."

"Why's that?"

"How many Chinese flew Tomahawks over Rangoon, Jack?" He finished his tea. "It is the Western way. You don't believe natives are capable beings. Whether those natives are Burmese, Chinese, or even American."

"I know you're capable, Shu!" Jack was indignant.

Shu Hao laughed and shook his friend's arm. "I was referring to the collective *you*." He laughed harder. "We have known each other for only a short time, you and I. But I can see you embody *wu wei*, and that is extraordinary, especially for a Westerner."

"What the hell is woo wee? Sounds like some cracker callin' hogs."

"My friend, I mustn't be late for my briefing. Let's get you introduced to the commander, so you can work out arrangements for your trip home. We'll have dinner together tonight at the tea plantation, and I'll introduce you to the men at the hostel. And I warn you, I'm going to convince you to return to Dinjan to fly with us, once your head heals."

* * *

After a long nap, Jack read through the notes from his meeting with the base commander's chief of staff. Transport to Dum Dum Airport in Calcutta. Calcutta to Bombay, where he'd catch a steamer to New York. He'd be in the States in four weeks' time.

26

THE BIG APPLE

JUNE 1942

She wriggled and giggled as he gently traced lines from freckle to freckle across her torso. She lifted his chin to look into his eyes. "I love you."

There was a banging at the door. Jack climbed out of bed and crossed the room, rubbing his eye. He wasn't clear who it was he'd been dreaming about when he cracked open the door.

"Captain Benoit?"

"Yeah? Whaddya want?"

"Truly sorry to disturb you, Captain. You requested a wake-up call for nine o'clock, sir. I'm afraid it's approaching nine ten. I've been knocking, sir."

Jack pulled open the door. "C'mon in."

Distracted from the guest's nudity, the bellman's gaze locked on the pink-and-blue mess where an eye should have been, then went straight down to his own shoes. "Sir, may I fetch your robe?"

Jack looked down. "Ha! Yeah, a robe would do, wouldn't it? Sorry 'bout that. I'll put somethin' on."

"If I may, sir." The bellman slipped past him and pulled from the closet a luxurious cotton robe with a blue letter A embroidered over the left breast. He held it open as Jack slid his arms inside.

"Well, there we go. All right, what can I do for you?"

"Captain Benoit, you requested a wake-up call. My understanding is you have a breakfast meeting scheduled this morning with a member of the press, sir."

"Yeah, yeah. I remember now. Thanks. And can we turn off the *sirs*? Name's Jack."

The bellman accepted his hand. "Milton Wills at your service, sir."

"There you go again, Milton."

The young man walked to the door and turned. "May I be of further service, Captain Benoit? Is there anything you need? Anything at all."

Jack pulled an American five spot from the wad on the nightstand and pressed it into the bellman's hand. "Seriously, it's Jack, Milton."

"Sorry, sir. *Jack*. It won't happen again."

"See to it, Milton."

"I'm on duty until six this evening, and the management here at the Astor has assigned me to you. Whatever you want, I will ensure arrangements are made to your satisfaction."

Jack cocked his head. "You sure talk smart. Someone'd think you owned the place."

Milton smiled. "Thank you kindly . . . um . . . Jack, sir. If you need anything, just ring on the house phone, and I'll be here in a jiffy."

Jack swung the door closed and headed to the bath. That was when it struck him. His head didn't hurt, not a bit. He looked close in the mirror, into his eye. It was clear. His head had pounded for so much of the past few weeks, and that damned stabbing behind his eye, coming and going. The up and down from Kunming to Dinjan had him crumpled on the tarmac, but the landing in Calcutta wasn't bad. Bombay was rough going again, with pain and nausea. Then, for much of the steamer trip around Africa and up the Atlantic, all the way into Chelsea Piers, his skull had squeezed his brain, a strobe light pulsing whenever he closed his eye.

The absence of pain was bliss. In good light for the first time, Jack leaned into the mirror over the sink and studied the pink mess on his face. "Under the circumstances, Milton held up pretty good."

Shaved and bathed, he was feeling good. He was glad he'd kept up his calisthenics on the ship despite the headaches they triggered. He adjusted his patch and tucked a clean white shirt into freshly pressed khaki pants. His boots were polished over the scuffs, and he looked himself up and down in a full-length mirror for the first time in over a year. Checking his backside, he muttered, "I don't have a butt!" He scraped the room key off the dresser and headed to the elevator.

He was so tired when he arrived that he hadn't really taken in the lobby. Now he spun under the high ceiling, which featured a circular mosaic of stained glass. The hotel interior was gorgeous, fancier even than the Raffles back in Singapore. He strode toward the Indian Grill Room and heard someone behind him call out his name. He turned to find a very large man under a curious gray Homburg, a small green feather tucked into the hatband. The color of those little butterflies in Toungoo.

"Captain Benoit?"

"How'd you guess?"

"The eyepatch is kinda a giveaway."

Jack laughed at the guy's brass. "What can I do for you, pal?"

"I represent a gentleman here in the city, someone who's a great admirer of yours. A word, please." The bruiser, who wore an immaculate navy-blue suit, beckoned him to the side. Jack could hear Sal in the man's accent.

"And you are?"

"Tony Campisi. Pleasure." He pulled off the Homburg and stuck out a hairy bear paw, squeezing Jack's thin hand.

Tony Campisi was a bulky fellow with an even larger presence, this morning sporting a fresh haircut, manicured nails, and too much cologne. A thin, faded scar ran down his face, starting mid-forehead, jumping an eye, and picking up again on his cheek to finish at his chin. A white dot from a styptic pencil secured a small dome of blood on that chin, confirming his five o'clock shadow wasn't from lack of effort.

Campisi told a crisp story, direct yet polite, then offered his services and asked that Jack call the number on the back of the calling card he presented. The big man replaced his Homburg and exited the hotel, followed by another serious-looking man who'd been hovering near the revolving doors.

"Captain Benoit!" The maître d' had been waiting at a comfortable distance. "If I may have the extraordinary pleasure."

Jack shook the man's pale, thin hand and chuckled, thinking about his own wasted grip. He mumbled, "Shoulda been squeezing a ball or something."

"Right this way, Captain Benoit. Your party is waiting."

They crossed a packed dining room, and as they reached the table, both occupants stood. The entire room followed suit and broke into applause. Jack looked around. They were applauding *him*. A "Bravo!" rose from the crowd, then another, and another. Jack gave them a relaxed, two-finger salute and slapped the maître d' on the arm.

"Helluva diner you got here, friend."

He bowed. "If I may be of service."

Jack guffawed. It seemed everyone in New York wanted to be of service. The taller man at the table stabbed out his hand. "Joel Silverman. Assistant Managing Editor for *The New York Times*."

"And I'm Bob Schneider. I write." Jack felt the callouses on the tips of this guy's fingers.

"Jack Benoit. Currently between engagements," he said with an easy smile. "Call me *Jack*, right?"

The men sat, and Silverman thanked him for coming.

He hadn't given much thought to what folks would be like in New York. If he had, this guy might have come to mind, based on what little he'd seen in magazine ads. The neat, angular cut of his gray, double-breasted suit. A tie populated with dandelion-yellow stars that seemed to pulse against a ruby-red landscape. Gold cufflinks shaped like fat babies. "Cherubs, crafted in Czarist Russia. A gift from a dear friend in Vienna." His jet-black hair, slicked tightly to his head, accented above each ear by white-gray streaks, the color of which perfectly matched his razor-sharp pocket square. Jack figured this guy had spent more time in the mirror that morning than Emma did in a month. The only thing he seemed to be missing was a chin.

Silverman recommended the Eggs Benedict and ordered for the table. "A stockbroker named Benedict invented the dish in the 1890s. A bartender at the Ritz invented the mimosa in the twenties. Undoubtedly, you'll love them both."

The first round of libations arrived in short order, and Schneider, seeing his superior's cosmopolitan air wasn't making the desired impression on their guest, interjected, "I'm confident we won't have to be nearly as *inventive* with your story, Jack. I understand you've had quite the adventure."

The room was buzzing, heads swiveling, necks straining to better see the man with the eyepatch. Jack hadn't expected public attention. He hadn't really thought that through. It was an interview, a few bucks. Help the War Department shill bonds. He decided to put the breakfast crowd out of his mind, grabbed the champagne flute, and tipped it toward Schneider. "To good eggs." In his head, he toasted Eddy.

Schneider was chomping at the bit. "So we can start the interview as soon as you'd like, Jack. I was thinking a couple sessions, a couple hours each, if you're up for it. Maybe start tomorrow morning?"

Jack took a bite of the Benedict. Silverman hadn't exaggerated.

The editor interrupted his reporter to explain it was all up to Jack. "Bob can take notes in a quiet room here at the hotel, in a restaurant, in a bar. Whatever you please. We want to make sure you're comfortable, Jack, to ensure we capture the essence of your story." He reiterated the deal. The War Department had asked the *Times* to put the pilot up in a nice place.

Silverman excused himself early. He had another commitment and explained again that Jack's hotel bill would be taken care of, including all expenses. "Meals, drinks, laundry. Whatever you need here at the Astor, Jack. Welcome to New York, The Wonder City."

As the editor left, Jack leaned over his food. "So you ask questions. I answer 'em."

Schneider laughed. "That's pretty much it. I'll take notes, then I'll write something up. We'll go through it together, to make sure you're good with it, then Mr. Silverman has a staff of editors, but I think he's planning to touch this one up personally."

"So, editing. That's spelling, punctuation, stuff like that?"

"It's a bit more. Pace. Style. Joel likes things to flow a certain way. So, I'll put it together the way he likes it. Get it close. It's not just reporting what happened. It'll be a story. My goal is twofold. Get it right, and give the people reason to believe."

Jack nodded. He took another drink and studied Schneider's face. Bear-fur eyebrows under thick, dark hair, dry and a little mussed. He had missed a good-sized spot on his chin. Dusty-blue eyes in a boyish face. Brown corduroy sports coat with faded maroon patches on the elbows. After a year of khaki and olive, Jack had been noticing folks' clothes here at the Astor.

Schneider looked eager to please and leaned in. "May I ask you a question?"

"I thought that was half the deal?" Jack drained his mimosa. The empty was immediately swept up and replaced with a fresh one. He remembered Soheil's attentiveness at the party where he met Emma.

"No, I mean, before we get started. Off the record."

"Why not?" He thought Silverman was right about the mimosas, too.

"What does it feel like? Being a hero?" Schneider tipped his head toward the next table, where three sets of curious eyes were focused on the man wearing the eyepatch. Jack held his glass up by the stem to study the bits of orange pulp stuck inside. Into the silence, Schneider explained, "I'm not sure you're aware of just how famous the Flying Tigers are here in the States, Jack. We haven't had a lot of good news from the wars, in Europe or in Asia. Nothing at all, really, except about the Flying Tigers. Since Pearl Harbor, everything has been . . . well, everything's just been about fear. People have decided to live in fear." He continued, "And the powers that be understand fear isn't especially productive. So, when you boys started downing Japanese planes, well, it was like a ray of sunshine poking through a dark and gloomy sky. These people," he tipped his head back toward the gawkers, "they're looking for hope. And Jack, right now, in this room, they're looking *at* hope."

He scanned the room and returned nodded greetings to some of the gawkers.

"You boys are bigger than the Yankees, Jack. As you might guess, word's spread that you're in the city."

"Silverman?"

"Now who doesn't want to be associated with heroism?" Schneider asked, rhetorically. "Of course he let it slip about the meeting. Wouldn't you?"

Jack thought back to Gil Weathers and the others, letting it slip to Orphan Ann. "It ain't like tipping off the Japs or something."

Schneider was confused.

"Say, Bob, does the name Meyer Lansky mean anything to you?"

Schneider looked surprised, then answered in a low voice. "Yes, I know of Mr. Lansky. Why do you ask?"

Jack handed the writer Tony Campisi's calling card and related the story from the lobby. Schneider studied the card.

"My understanding is Meyer Lansky is something of a patriot." He paused. "He's known to particularly hate Nazis."

Jack looked puzzled.

"He's Jewish, Jack."

Jack didn't know what being Jewish had to do with anything. The news about the Nazis that made it to China was mostly about Brits taking it on the chin in Africa, and though he'd heard a little of

European politics back in Texas, he barely remembered any of it. He shrugged.

Though Schneider was on world desk at the *Times*, he palled around with the city writers and knew the scuttlebutt. He explained how Lansky was a leader in the New York syndicate, along with Lucky Luciano. Gambling, prostitution. The mob controlled vice all down the Eastern Seaboard. They had a lot of influence with the Teamsters union, too, and they controlled labor on the docks. "There's a rumor the Feds cut Lansky a deal. The FBI would look the other way on smuggling in the harbors in exchange for the syndicate's assurance on two matters. First, there's a lot of Italians working the docks, and the Feds don't want trouble from any Mussolini sympathizers. They're also worried about Nazi sabotage in the shipyards where naval vessels are built and repaired. In Brooklyn. In Jersey. For the government, turning a blind eye to some vice seems a small trade for secure harbors."

Schneider presented a pack of Camel filters, which Jack declined. The writer pulled out a pocket lighter and flamed his smoke. "*So?*" He flicked the brass Zippo shut.

Jack smiled, picked the card off the tablecloth, and tucked it into his shirt pocket. The men made arrangements to get started the following morning at a diner on Fortieth Street. They talked for another half hour, and Schneider tried again, "*So*, are you going to call Lansky?"

"Off the record?"

Schneider grinned. "Sure."

"Yeah, I'm gonna call him." Jack nodded and downed his coffee. "I'm curious."

"So am I."

"You wanna come?"

Schneider chuckled. "I don't think that would be wise."

The men changed plans, agreeing to meet the following evening to talk over a drink or two. Schneider looked thrilled. "I'll be your Silverman, introduce you to some of the more *inventive* areas of New York."

They shook on it.

* * *

The midday sun was roasting the caverns of Midtown Manhattan while Jack walked with Big Tony Campisi to Broadway and 43rd

Street, where they entered a kosher deli and crossed to a door in the back. The men descended a steep set of concrete steps. It was cool down in the dimly lit, nondescript passage, and they made their way through three or four sharp turns. Jack figured they must have walked at least a hundred yards and were probably under a different building by now. Campisi stopped in front of a dark, oak-paneled door and pressed the ivory buzzer. Standing behind the muscle, it occurred to Jack he'd never seen such a wide man, and in another impeccably tailored suit to boot. A latch snapped, and the door swung open to reveal another large man in a dark suit, this guy was taller but not nearly as thick as his escort. Jack squinted as his eye made the transition from the dark hallway to a well-lit office.

"Welcome, Captain Benoit. Please come in." Standing behind a large, wooden desk, Meyer Lansky beckoned for him to approach, then motioned for the tall man to leave the room. Campisi closed the door behind them and took a seat in the corner. "Please." Lansky indicated two cordovan-leather chairs at the side of the room. "Captain Benoit, let's sit and talk." Jack accepted Lansky's hand, then the seat.

"You can call me Jack."

Lansky smiled. "Thank you, and please, call me Meyer. May I offer you something? A drink? A cigar?"

Tony grunted involuntarily as he started to stand.

"No, thank you, Meyer. I'm just fine. Had a big breakfast at the hotel this mornin'."

Lansky laughed heartily. "Wonderful! Thank you so much for coming, Jack." He walked to the desk and picked up something. "I've been reading about the Flying Tigers and of your own personal accomplishments." He handed Jack a newspaper. It was a recent copy of the *San Francisco Chronicle*. The right column headline read: "Flying Tigers to Join Army, Navy, Will Continue Fight in the Pacific."

"You have every right to be proud, Jack. You and all the AVG boys. What you've accomplished, and under such challenging circumstances. Truly remarkable, and truly honorable, in the name of freedom and all that is good."

Jack wondered if this guy went to school in Europe, too. "Thanks."

"Are you sure you wouldn't like something? Anything?"

"A Co-Cola with ice, if you got one."

Lansky gave Campisi a look, and the big man was out the door. The other, taller man stepped inside and pulled the door closed and locked it. For a moment, the room was uncomfortably quiet. "So, Mr. Lansky . . ."

"Please, call me Meyer."

"Right. Meyer. I'm not sure why I'm here."

Lansky chortled. "Yes, you're right, Jack. I'm so glad we have this chance to meet. So let's get down to business, shall we?"

The leather chair was slippery in the cool room. Jack straightened up and noted the table lamp with its large, Tiffany-style shade. The green-and-yellow stained glass was shaped into long, narrow leaves, like the one over Olga Greenlaw at the Fulton place in Toungoo. "I know a guy with one of these." He pictured Emma. He was tucking her in with her hiccups.

"Jack, I don't know what you know of me, or what you've heard." He paused, but Jack refused to take the bait. "My partners and I, we have varied business interests in New York and other localities down the Atlantic coast. Here, one of our major interests is in the docks. New York Harbor, Brooklyn Yards, and across the river in New Jersey."

Jack listened.

"Well, after the attack on Pearl Harbor, and we entered the war, the government became concerned, and rightly so, that these harbors might be susceptible to attack, to acts of sabotage. So, they came to me. They asked if my business associates and I might keep an eye on the goings-on out on the docks, *look out for trouble*, if you will."

"And you said?"

"I said, 'Of course!'" Lansky leaned forward, looking Jack in the eye. "And do you know why I did this?"

He shrugged. Didn't seem like a big deal, helping out like that. Not like it makes you a hero because you chose to not be a jackass. "Because you're a patriot?"

"Precisely!" Lansky exclaimed. "This country, it gave me nothing, nothing except the chance to be *something*. The land of opportunity. That's what America is." He was smiling, nearly giddy, until his mood turned on a dime. "Then there's the Nazis, those soulless bastards. The lowest form of scum on earth, a Nazi. Hitler. Himmler. Goebbels. Pasty little shits who look in the mirror and see a grand Nordic god, all hell-bent on taking everything and killing everyone they think is beneath them. *Parasitic vermin*. That's what they call Jews and others they believe are beneath them. Can you believe that?" Lansky's face was red, his piercing eyes hot. "They intend to enslave or kill every Jew in Europe, and they'll take their pogrom, their *Abrechnung mit den Juden*, to every land they occupy."

Jack didn't know what to say. Schneider had told him the Nazis had been rounding up Jews and putting them in concentration camps for years. But then the States had just rounded up all the Japs and put them in concentration camps. This was the first he'd heard of slavery, though, and he figured it was probably so. The Japanese were doing it, so the Germans and the Italians were probably doing the same.

After a pause, Lansky continued, his mood sly. "Did I mention I'm Jewish?"

They both laughed.

"You don't say."

"Okay. So, here I said to you we'll get down to business and then I get all long-winded about fucking Hitler."

Jack shrugged again.

"I asked you to meet me so I might convey my gratitude, personally and on behalf of this great country of ours. Despite our faults, which are many, America is a shining light, a beacon, leading the world toward freedom and opportunity. I truly believe that, Jack. And so, the business I wish to conduct with you may be summed up simply. May I be of service?"

Jack snorted. He flushed. "Sorry, Meyer. I've just been hearing that an awful lot since I got to New York."

"And rightly so, Jack. You are a genuine hero of these United States, and it's not everyday a man in my position can offer his gratitude to a hero. So I want to thank you for your time, and I want to offer you my service, whatever that may be, to help you now that you're back home." Lansky unconsciously raised his nose toward Jack's eyepatch. "If you need any assistance getting situated, finding a good living. If you need a doctor, I know the best in New York. The best in the country! Anything at all. Please, reach out to me anytime."

As Lansky handed Jack another calling card, there was a knock on the door. It was Big Tony with a chilled bottle of Coca-Cola and a glass of ice. Jack stood and accepted the glass. Lansky poured the liquid into it, ice cubes crackling. He snatched a tired glass of scotch off his desk.

"Wherever fate may take you, Jack, know that I am your friend," Lansky said. They clinked glasses and drank. Jack wiped his mouth on his sleeve. Lansky grinned.

"Thank you, Meyer." He held up the card. "I appreciate the offer."

Lansky retrieved his smoldering cigarette from the smoke stand at his desk, took a drag, then stubbed it out. The lighter on the stand caught Jack's attention. He picked it up to take a look.

Lansky smiled. "An oil barrel. A friend at the Magnolia Oil Company made a present of it to me."

"Gold?"

Lansky nodded, grinning.

The men shook hands, and Tony escorted Jack from the room. They headed out a different way than they'd come, walking a short, dark, and cool distance to a staircase where a door entered the back of a smoke shop. They exited the shop, and Jack found himself next to a wooden Indian on Sixth Avenue off Bryant Park. He squinted against the bright afternoon light. The old, piercing pain pulsed, and he fumbled the aviator shades from his breast pocket.

"So, that's it?"

Big Tony Campisi nodded. "I'll pick you up tonight."

They shook on it, the muscle's huge paw engulfing Jack's hand once again. Campisi pulled a cigar out of his pocket and stopped short of his lips. He held it out to Jack.

"See you tonight, Tony."

***

It was approaching eight o'clock when Jack stepped from the taxi onto East Seventh Street and entered McSorley's, one of the city's oldest pubs and Schneider's favorite joint. Its walls were covered with a sundry collection of framed photographs, sketches, news articles, posters, and cartoons. A ninety-year potpourri of New York history.

"See that light hanging over the bar?" Schneider pointed to a fixture shaped like a sideshow strongman's barbell with a big glass ball of light at each end. "See those old turkey wishbones hanging on that crossbar? During the Great War, each doughboy from this neighborhood hung one up there before packing out. The ones who made it home came by and picked theirs up."

Jack counted seventeen dusty wishbones.

"Mr. Benoit." It was Big Tony Campisi.

"Tony, meet my friend, Bob Schneider. Bob, Tony Campisi. Tony's takin' us out tonight."

Schneider's eyes widened and his bushy brown eyebrows climbed up forehead.

"Taking us somewhere . . . a little livelier?" Jack raised his glass to the wishbones and drained what was left of his Coca-Cola with lemon.

Campisi slapped a ten spot on the table. "After you, gentlemen."

Schneider eyeballed Jack, who threw his arm over the surprised and worried writer's shoulder. "Ready for a little adventure?"

Big Tony's driver dropped the trio in Harlem near the corner of 124th and Lenox, where they were met by an eager young black man in a cherry-red tuxedo. He escorted the party into the Lenox Lounge and across a packed house to the lone open table at the foot of the stage.

"Dis place ain't nothin' like da Cotton Club was, but it's got the best jazz in the city tonight," Campisi assured them.

They sat down and Cherry Tux introduced them to Billy, their waiter. "Champagne's on the house tonight, Mr. Campisi." He placed an ice bucket at the table and twisted the 1938 Dom Perignon.

"What'cha think, gents?"

Jack asked for a Coca-Cola and a rye, both with ice. Schneider followed suit. Tony eyeballed the writer. "Yeah, why not? Make it three, boy, but no soda for me, and leave dat bottle ah fizz here."

Jack surveyed the room. Except for a corner booth where a couple of goombahs were canoodling a trio of blonds under a thundercloud of cigar smoke, everybody in the place was black, and not a one was paying him any mind. For the first time since he stepped into The Astor, he didn't feel people staring at him.

"And these?" Jack asked about the three empty chairs at their table.

Big Tony grinned. "Dat's what the champagne's for."

The stage door opened as their drinks were served, and the room erupted with shouts and whistles. "Satchmo! Lou-eee!" Louis Armstrong led his five-piece band onto the stage. The leader sat on a stool, dabbing his forehead with a kerchief as the other players settled in. He held the white cloth in his palm while his fingers lightly drummed the trumpet valves. He counted off.

```
'Cause my hair is curly
Just because my teeth are pearly
Just because I always wear a smile
Like to dress up, in the latest style
```

The second song into the set, and the joint was jumping when Cherry Tux reappeared with three white dollies in tow. The men stood. Tony spread his arms wide. "Girls, dese are da boys. Boys, da girls. Introduce you'selves."

The evening's company was composed of two attractive brunettes, Lucy and Liz, and an auburn-haired beauty named Molly. Lucy, wearing a sprayed-on black cocktail dress, shimmied up close to Jack.

"You look good tonight, babydoll," Campisi complimented the gorgeous redhead, attired in hunter-green silk and sparkling, cut-glass earrings. She applied red lipstick to his cheek.

Schneider pulled out a chair for Liz, who was sporting a black-sequined cocktail dress over maroon fishnet stockings and pumps. The girls took little time with the champagne, then asked for Green Dragons. Molly was on Big Tony like ham on rye until he slapped her on the thigh, telling her to hold her horses. She huffed and pulled out a silver cigarette case. Tony was squinting at the hoods across the room and didn't notice. Jack wasn't carrying his pocket lighter, so he knocked knees with Schneider, who reached across the table with his torch. Molly leaned back as she took a long drag, eye to eye with Jack. She held the cigarette up, elbow leaning on a crossed arm as she blew smoke across the table. He shook Emma out of his head. Lucy ran her fingertips up his thigh, her dark eyes made more mysterious by smoky eye shadow and thick mascara. Her heavy perfume was fruity, a little off for her look.

"So you're the flyboy, huh? The one they call Blackjack. You killed all them Japs in Asia, right?"

"That sums it up." Emma wouldn't leave his head.

"Bombing Pearl Harbor like that, right out of the blue," Lucy continued. "The nerve of them sneaky Japs."

Jack threw back his rye. Billy showed in a flash with a fresh glass. Lucy stubbed a butt into the camel-shaped ashtray on the table, and Big Tony opened his cigarette case. Jack noticed how Lucy eyed the tough as he lit her smoke. Seemed *Red* over there might be in for some competition.

Lucy surveyed the room as she slowly exhaled a gray-blue fog. She made what Odette would call a *stink face* and caught Jack's eye. The band was on a break, and the conversation on his side of the table was failing. "It's too *dark* in here, for my taste." She took another drag. "The way they're locking up the Jap monkeys in California, you'd think they'd do something about these damn chimps here in New York."

Jack couldn't place her accent. "Where are you from?"

"I came to New York from Cincinnati, if that's what you're getting at."

"Hey, Luce!" It was Big Tony. "How 'bout a smile or somethin'? You look like someone just stole your purse. Lighten up already, it's a party for Chrissakes."

"Work's work," she mumbled. "Liz, darling, would you come with me? I need to powder my nose." The men stood as the two brunettes left for the toilet.

Jack studied the side of Molly's face while she flirted with the big man. It was too dim and smoky to see if she had freckles, and her face was probably covered in paste anyway.

"Dammit, Tony!" The brunettes were back.

"What's your problem, Luce?"

"They only got colored toilets in this joint. Liz and I need to powder our noses. We need to find a place."

"Shit," Tony groused and slid out of his chair. "You comin', dammit?" Molly stubbed a butt and got up, taking Tony's arm.

"Quite an evening," Schneider offered, almost a question. Jack nodded. He was watching Tony talking at Cherry Tux, who escorted the ladies through the stage door.

"You all right?" Schneider asked.

"Sure. It's been a hoot."

Tony plopped back down. "They got a white toilet in the back. We's got an interest in this joint." He winked.

Armstrong and his band returned to the stage.

```
Meet me in the bottom, bring my boots and shoes
I've got to leave this town, I got no time to lose
```

Jack drank a lot. They all drank a lot. The crowd was in a frenzy when the band finished its last set, and Cherry Tux approached their table. "Mr. Campisi, I hope you enjoyed your evening."

"It was tops, Willy. No complaints."

"Willy and Billy," Jack snorted.

"I got a treat for you guys. C'mon." Tony stood and lit a cigarette.

Molly was pouting. "What about us?"

"You wait here, toots."

Willy escorted the three men backstage. "Mr. Armstrong, some gentlemen to see you."

Big Tony elbowed past the manager and into the tiny room.

"Mr. Campisi, greetings." Armstrong stood and gave him a little bow.

Jack, thoroughly inebriated, reached past his host. "Jack Benoit. My pleasure, Mr. Armstrong." He was vigorously shaking the musician's hand. "I enjoyed tonight very much."

Armstrong, soaked in sweat, replied with a bleached-white toothy grin. "Thank you, sir! Yes, thank you very much. And may I ask, do I hear some Louisiana there, some *down home* in your accent, sir?"

Jack grinned and staggered, looking at Schneider. "How 'bout that?" He turned back to Armstrong. "You're from N'Orleans, am I right?"

"Yessiree. Born and raised down New Orleans way. A lot of water under the bridge since then, but yes, yessir. And might I ask whereabouts you from, Mr. Benoit?"

"Call me Jack."

Big Tony mumbled, "Fuck."

"I lived in Perry for a while. Vermilion Parish."

Armstrong lit up, his eyes round and wide. "No kiddin'! I thought I heard a little Creole vibe rollin' 'round in here. You know, Missah Benoit, the prettiest little girl I ever did see's from li'l ol' Abbeville, Louisiana, right there in Vermilion Parish, yessiree. Name's Chloe. Chloe Boisvert."

Jack froze, his chest tight.

"Yessiree. Met Mademoiselle Chloe when she was jus' a sweet li'l thing, about so tall. Back in my days in gay Paris."

Tony mumbled again.

Armstrong continued as though he didn't hear. "Knew her daddy well, I did. Monsieur Paul Boisvert. Owned a beautiful club, La Pomme d'Or. Played there a ton when I lived overseas. Quite the place, yessiree. In fact, my former spouse, Miss Lil Hardin, she the one who brought the mademoiselle back here, back to the States after her daddy died, poor li'l thing." Louis shook his head. "Sad, sad story, yessiree."

Jack was sweating, his chest pounding. He leaned on Schneider.

Armstrong sighed. "Well, well. I'll be. Haven't thought of that sweet chile for the longest time. She really was the bee's knees."

"Yeah, that's all just peachy," Campisi blurted. "Dis here's Captain Jack Benoit. A fuckin' bona fide war hero! Killed Japs in China. Blew dem yellow bastards right outta da sky. How many was it?" He poked Jack's arm. "Somethin' like a dozen ah those little fuckers."

Schneider interjected, "Fourteen and a third kills."

"Yeah, whatever. He's a goddamn fighter ace. An ace! And not the *ace of spades*. Thought he'd like to meet Satchmo, here, and that's what we's doin'."

Big Tony's voice was scornful. Disgusted. It was bad enough sitting out there in a mixed club, but tight quarters backstage with this sweaty nigger, with all his smiles and sass, it was too much to bear. Campisi liked playing the big man in the room, and most often he *was* the big man in the room. This uppity nigger was playing *Old Home Week* with this hick flyer, and he'd had enough.

Schneider watched the mobster turning red and the flyer turning green, both looking like they might pop. "Pleasure to meet you, Mr. Armstrong, but we've got some girls waiting, right, Tony?" Schneider winked at the tough and steadied Jack by the arm.

Campisi tipped his head at the door. "Let's dust dis place."

"Thank y'all for comin' by!" Armstrong was smiling so big you'd think he just hit the numbers.

Campisi's surly disposition reached the table before he did, and Molly straightened up and stopped her pouting quick. The Lenox Lounge had emptied out, save for a half dozen thoroughly soused revelers propped up by the bar.

Schneider was looking to change the mood. "A shot for the road?"

"Why not?" Campisi put his fingers to the corners of his mouth and whistled. In no time, the whole table was throwing back shots of smooth Cuban spiced rum. Five of six spirits improved, but Jack was still quiet.

"So, some show," Schneider offered.

Jack nodded.

"You ready to call it a night?"

He nodded again.

"Hey, Tony." Schneider reached out to shake his hand. "Great night. Very magnanimous of you, really." He stuck his thumb at the door. "I'm gonna get outta here. I need to hit the sack. Thanks for everything."

Molly and Lucy had the big man sandwiched, so he was understandably distracted.

"Look, I can give Jack a lift back to the Astor. Not a problem."

Molly was practically in Big Tony's lap, blowing in his ear. Campisi squinted at the reporter. "Yeah, right. Jack, you good wit dat?"

Schneider tugged Jack's coat sleeve. "Let's hit the road, Jack."

"Hey, Schneider, you best see my man to the hotel, you hear me?" Tony hollered as the men approached the door. "Up to his room!" Schneider touched the brim of his hat and pushed Jack out the door.

The night air had cooled, and it straightened Jack up some. A black cab stopped at the curb, but he kept stumbling uptown. Schneider offered a cigarette. Receiving no acknowledgment, he lit one for himself. They were slowly making their way north, and Schneider was getting nervous. A lot of liquor flowed in Harlem on Saturday nights, and there was plenty of trouble to be had walking past the Apollo at three in the morning. Jack seemed oblivious. Schneider waved in another cab and shoved his charge into the back. As they rolled south on Central Park West, Schneider broke the silence.

"Good show."

Nothing.

The reporter figured he'd make a go while Jack was still drunk. "You've seemed down since we met Louis Armstrong."

Jack rolled the window down to half and laid his cheek on it. The air whipped his sandy locks and made a little whistling noise under the lip of his eyepatch.

"Chloe."

"What?" The girl Armstrong was talking about? You know her, this Chloe Boisvert?"

Jack let out a sigh, and Schneider was stunned by the tear rolling down his cheek.

It was approaching four o'clock when they reached Jack's room at the Astor, and they agreed to meet later that day. The reporter figured

Jack wouldn't remember, so he tore a page out of his pocket notebook and jotted a message, which he left on the nightstand.

Jack slept restlessly until early afternoon. He cleaned up, wolfed three hot dogs on the street corner, and grabbed a cab downtown to the Battery, where he boarded a tour boat to the Statue of Liberty. Standing at the rail, he remembered the whale. The peaceful calm in her bright eye. Chloe's honey eyes. A torn muddy dress off Coulee Galleque. Emma's golden eyes. A torn muddy dress in downtown Rangoon. That story Emma told him about the bombing. Some little shit puni wallah he'd never met, cheering as bombs rained down on his oppressors. Cheering until the yellow bastards in the sky blew his body to pieces. He wondered how many little shit black boys in Harlem would cheer yellow bastards dropping bombs on the Upper West Side. He doubted the Japs would even bother to fake it for the Negroes here like they were doing with the Burmese and Indians over there. The sound of children shrieking interrupted his thoughts. A small group of kids were cheering the Statue of Liberty as she grew off the starboard bow.

* * *

"Really great material to work with, Jack. You've been incredibly patient and so generous with your time and answers. Thank you very much." The men shook hands and parted ways. Schneider hadn't probed any further on the Chloe story. "If you ever need anything in New York."

"You'll be of service?" They both had a good laugh.

Jack was running late for his meeting with the war bond people. When he found the offices off Seventh Avenue, he was swarmed at the door by glad-handing suits and fawning secretaries. A crowded room, but not a lot of uniforms. Just a ruggedly handsome one-armed bird colonel named Kurtz, a sickly-looking lieutenant with a stutter, and a wide-eyed corporal standing at a typewriter. All three wore US Cavalry insignia.

The meeting was pleasant. A green-eyed brunette scribbled rapidly in a notebook while Colonel Kurtz framed up the program for him. The brunette blushed and stroked her ponytail the few times Jack caught her eye, and after the meeting, he wandered over to her desk. "What's this?"

"That's an advertisement, Captain Benoit." Her face was beet red.

Centered on the eighteen by twenty-four inch poster was a photo of him standing on the wing of No. 91. He couldn't remember the photo being taken, but he was leaning next to nine kill flags, so he figured it was from January. The photo was set inside a jack of clubs with an ace of clubs behind it, like his war paint. Above this collage was a title:

Jack "Blackjack" Benoit
Double Ace over the Pacific

The girl rocked her shoulders and giggled. One of the suits slid a document in front of him and said, "Sign here." Jack signed the document without reading it, and the man handed Jack an envelope, which he figured was a confirmation of logistics. He stuffed it in his pocket. "We'll have your uniforms delivered to the Astor."

This particular program of the War Loan Drive was called the *Whistle-Stop Tours*. Multiple train tours across America, stopping in big cities and small towns to pitch war bonds, and Jack's tour would kick off with a rally in Central Park in front of an estimated fifteen thousand enthusiastic New Yorkers. He would be the last featured speaker before the mayor directed the crowd to dozens of tables lining the park at which clerks from city banks would process bond sales on the spot.

The emcee introduced him as Captain Blackjack Benoit, and Jack stumbled through the short script with a mumbling, stilted cadence. He finished quickly to hearty applause. Rather dazed there at the microphone, the slew of politicians perched nearby rushed in to shake his hand, preening and posturing for the official photographer and the newspapermen. Jack was disappointed in his performance and embarrassed by the whole display. As he made his way out of the park, he must have shaken at least three hundred hands. He still wasn't used to people staring at his patch, and it unnerved him.

He snaked through the dispersing crowd as quickly as he could and headed south on Broadway. Tired and hungry, he found the Astor's dining room populated with mid-afternoon lingerers, spun on his heels and found the bar.

A single bartender in a crisp white jacket and bowtie approached as he took a stool at the large empty black oval bar. Steak and potatoes, chocolate cake and a cream soda. He heard laughing over his shoulder and spotted a couple of dapper-looking fellas enter the room. To his relief, they paid him no mind and made their way to the other end of the bar.

Two in the afternoon, and it was so quiet. No traffic noise. No trains. No ship engines. No blathering people. No one grabbing at him. No mosquitos. No puddle of sweat forming on his lower back. No stench in his nose. Just blissful silence, interrupted only by a handful of giggles emanating from the end of the bar where the two sharp men whispered over martini glasses.

"Fairies." The bartender set down the slice of cake and cleared his plate. "We keep 'em down at the end. They botherin' you?"

Jack watched the men talk. They didn't look different to him. "How'd you know that?"

"I work here, bud." He wiped the bar. "So, you good? Another cream soda?"

"Water with lemon." Jack couldn't take his eye off the couple at the end of the bar. The only fairy he'd known was Richard Sizemore, the clerk with the AVG who got sent home in a hurry. He remembered thinking at the time the guy worked hard, did his job. Who cares what a man does when he's off duty? The guys who drank until they puked their guts out, they were hungover on duty. It impacted their work. Sizemore didn't come in hungover after blowing some guy. So he was a little swishy, so what? It was war. Whatever gets you through the night, just do your friggin' job. All he could make from the guys at the end of the bar was they looked pretty damn happy. He envied them.

He opened the envelope the suit had handed him back at the War Loan Drive office. It was a check for fifty dollars made payable to Jack Benoit. A grin spread across his face as he dipped a finger in the chocolate frosting. "Y'ain't in China anymore." Three days ago, he'd deposited $4,068 into a new bank account.

* * *

The day before the Central Park rally, *The New York Times* published its feature on Jack and included a list of the cities scheduled for the Whistle Stop Tour. They were off to Newark, then into Pennsylvania with stops in Philadelphia, Harrisburg, and Pittsburgh. Three more stops across Ohio, then turning south toward Louisville, Nashville, and Memphis. The last leg included Greenville and Jackson, Mississippi, terminating in New Orleans, Louisiana.

The Associated Press wire service picked up the story for distribution in local papers, and local volunteers coordinated the distribution of fliers, posters and print ads, as well as logistics. Jack's tour was one of a half dozen that would cross the country, all similarly structured with a core team of brass from each branch of service and their support staff. The War Department created spots for local radio and scripted a newsreel for national distribution using stock footage of the heroes going on tour and some scenes from the Central Park event. By week's end, Jack would be in movie theatres all across the country.

Jack looked down at the brown water as the train crossed the Hudson River into New Jersey. It wouldn't be long before he'd be back in Louisiana.

27

HAMILTON

JULY 1942

He was as disappointed with his performance in Newark as he was in New York. But behind the microphone in Philadelphia, he met eyes with a young boy holding a small flag on a short stick. A man Jack figured to be the boy's grandfather stood behind him, holding him by the shoulders. He wondered if the kid's daddy had shipped out. He tucked the script back into his pocket and looked over the crowd. He took two deep breaths.

"This ain't about Pearl Harbor. You know, when I was over there, fighting for the Chinese, the Japs attacked every military force in the Pacific. Americans. Brits. Dutch. Everybody who could stand up to them, who could stand up for China, they attacked." He looked the old man in the eye. "Hirohito. Hitler. Mussolini. They wanna take over the world. All of it. And we gotta stop 'em." A tall dark-haired woman in red polka dots nodded, dabbing her cheek with a handkerchief. "There ain't no glory in it. To tell you the truth, I was scared. All of us were scared. But we worked hard to prepare and did our jobs the best we could. We had great training. The colonel. Colonel Claire Chennault. He taught us how to beat the Japs in the air. And we did. But all that time, we were short on equipment. The goods we had worked great. Our Tomahawks. They're the tops. Real beasts. But we didn't have enough of 'em. Didn't have the parts." He met Polka Dots' eyes. "Simple as that."

"The Japs had it easy before we got there, but we gave 'em what for. But if we'd got more planes, more parts, we coulda sent even more of 'em to hell." He panned the silent audience. "So that's it, folks. Equipment, gear, rations. It's gonna take a lot of money. And that's what the president's been talkin' about, right? We need money to save the whole damn world from these butchers. *Your* money."

Jack nodded and turned to walk away. He stopped himself as scattered applause started to grow. As he stepped back up to the microphone, *shhhhs* rose throughout the crowd, and it fell silent again.

"I can't fight anymore because of my eye, but there's good men over there, still doin' their part. You probably got men over there, or goin' soon, right? So if y'all have some money, and I s'pose you probably do if you're here today, buy a bond. Thanks." He walked off the platform.

Back on the train, he revisited some thoughts he'd had on the way down from Newark. He figured it'd take something like two or three grand to get Chloe through school and keep Menta going while she was studying. He watched as the ponytail girl from the New York office hustled up the Thirtieth Street Station platform with an armful of notebooks, her hair swinging with each set. He had his own compartment, with heroism came rewards, and from it he watched her step up to Colonel Kurtz, who had just exited the station office. He was hollering something at her, shaking a handful of papers at the sky with his one arm. He made a beeline for Jack's car, and Jack figured he was in for a busting over what he said at the rally.

"That was quite a speech you gave back there."

Jack didn't respond.

"Just a little off script."

"Yup."

"The brass and the politicians were none too pleased."

"You know . . ."

The colonel raised his hand. "So, would you care to guess how many bonds have been sold since the rally ended, less than an hour ago?"

"Couldn't say, Colonel."

"More than what we sold in Newark the whole day." Kurtz grinned. "We're on pace with New York, from a crowd a third the size. Hell, people are still lined up a hundred deep at the tables!" Kurtz put his hand on Jack's shoulder. "Not everyone was pleased with what you did back there, Jack. In fact, *no one* was pleased, and the big brass wants you off this train." The colonel adroitly single-handed a cigarette and leaned back. Jack wondered if Norah made it out of Singapore. "My mission is to sell bonds." The colonel took a long draw.

Jack clicked the window and let it drop fully open.

"This bothering you?" The colonel flicked his smoke out the window and slid open the compartment door to let the air flow through. "Jack, what I saw today, well, I'll tell you straight. I think you're the best goddamn thing to happen to this program. The people need to feel connected to what's going on over there. It's important. The brass can peacock around with ribbons on their chests, and the politicians can bluster on about the land of the free and the home of the brave. But I'm telling you, when you were up at that microphone, you were speaking from the heart. It was genuine. So, you say whatever you damn well feel like saying. It's important for the drive. It's important for the country. And if the brass gets a stick up their ass, I'll be the one to pull it out, understand? You be Captain Jack Benoit, Blackjack Benoit, whatever the hell you want to be. You say whatever you're feeling, and we'll get the money for the equipment our boys need."

* * *

The program was producing results, and Jack's tour had attracted hundreds of thousands of people. Memphis wasn't great because the train pulled in under a torrential downpour. It was still raining, but easier, when they reached Greenville, Mississippi. The crowd cheered wildly for Senator Theodore Bilbo while the famous segregationist waxed poetic about American virtue on the same train platform where National Guardsman Curly Wilson put a bullet in the back of Theo Chantale's head. Steaming south from Jackson, Jack's thoughts turned to family. Frank and Odette would be at the rally. He started missing Pumpkin. He started missing Chloe.

As the train slowed, pulling into the Crescent City, Colonel Kurtz tried one last time to convince Jack to sign up, to join his team. Jack had other plans swirling in his head, but they agreed a compromise. He would do a couple weeks out west. "Fantastic! I'll take what I can get."

Jack couldn't spot Frank or Odette in the crowd, but they found him at the side of the stage before Governor Long hit his stride.

"How long can that man talk?" Jack mused as Odette squeezed him tight.

"Mais, you so skinny, Sha!" she exclaimed. "I gonna put some meat on those bones. Bon Dieu!" She touched his cheek. "It hurt you, Sha?"

Frank grabbed his brother's duffle. "Let's get out of here, *Blackjack*."

Jack punched his brother's arm.

* * *

He stared out his window as they crossed the Huey P. Long Bridge.

"So Menta's still sick?"

"Sumpin wrong wit her feet. I think she got the gout. But, Sha, poor thing, she sick in da lungs, too. It's bad. They thought she what-in gonna make it. Mais, then at Christmas, she got up and was helpin in the café. Then back down. It were hard on Chloe."

"The Good Samaritan here chipped in by buying two pies a week. *Two!* That's why my wallet's so thin, yeah, Bebe?"

"An why ya belly hangin on ya belt like that? Nobody else here complaining, Mr. Benoit."

"We have an oven, Mrs. Benoit."

Odette stuck her tongue out at him. "Afta Menta got up, it all starts agin. She was thin, thin cause she was sick so long and her wrist was staying stuck. Ooh, her fingas were hurtin, and those ankles swelled like sun muss melons! Mais, she's back off her feet agin like before."

"Then is she leaving this fall, Chloe? She wrote something about Chicago. What happened to Howard University?"

Sitting between the brothers, Odette nervously bounced her legs, staring through the windshield.

"So, what then, she's just stuck there, slinging grits, nursing Menta, herding Francie?" He shook his head. "Dumb fuckin' luck."

"PJ!" Odette scolded.

Jack rolled down the window and stretched his arm against the air.

"It's all working out," Frank interjected.

Odette shushed him.

"What? You think the boy ain't gonna find out?"

"Find out what, Frank?" Jack asked.

"Chloe's got a beau from up in Chicago. Some music man she met. Came 'round this way, looking for musicians to play in mobster clubs up north."

"Frank!"

"It's true, dammit. She's moving to Chicago and taking her sister with her. She's engaged to the guy."

Jack was dumbstruck. He tried to shrug it off, Odette even noticed the shrug. He heard clearly now what Louis Armstrong had said at the Lenox Lounge. *Mademoiselle Chloe when she was just a sweet li'l thing.* He thought about their last night together. That freckled nose crinkling over her wet lips. Her smooth cinnamon skin and soft pink tongue.

"So what happens to Menta?"

As best Odette knew, Menta was going to live with a cousin's family upstate, near Shreveport. They'd agreed to take her in so long as Francie wasn't part of the package. Chloe's fiancé told her Francie could come live with them in Chicago, and she'd have a job in the kitchen at one of the clubs. Chloe would marry, and she'd study at the University of Chicago.

Jack's mind raced. She's in love with another guy. She was leaving Abbeville. She was finally getting what she'd always wanted. He just wasn't the one giving it to her. He never could have. The car was silent the rest of the way home.

It was after seven when Frank pulled the Ford onto their crushed stone drive. Jack lit up when Pumpkin trotted off the porch. But when he stepped out of the car, she greeted him with a low growl and raised hackles. When he spoke her name, she jumped to him, pressing into his legs, yelping ecstatically. He knelt to wrap himself around her.

"I'll make suppa when I come back." Odette waved as she walked off to pick up the kids from the neighbors.

"Remember, it gets pretty stuffy in the attic. I opened the windows this morning to air it out." Frank reached for his brother's duffle.

"Thanks, I got it." Jack rubbed Pumpkin's ears. "Think I'll take a walk."

"Just leave it be, PJ," Frank gruffed, certain his kid brother was heading to the Music Box Café.

Instead, Jack and Pumpkin crossed the Vermilion River at the railroad bridge under a radiant half moon that illuminated the tracks and the path along Coulee Galleque. The Big Tree had changed some, thick with undergrowth. The rope still hung there, frayed and slick with moss. Jack gave it a tug and swung it out over the water, which was down, green and stagnant. Nothing like his first time he came here. Below the lip, the bowed roots tucked back into the ground a couple of feet above the still waterline. He kicked at the dirt where Chloe had spit up the brown water. He buried the thought behind a closed eye and chose instead to remember her first orgasm. A breeze gusted with pungent honeysuckle. He smashed a mosquito against his neck and pictured Coonsville, muttering, "She deserves better than this shithole." Pumpkin grazed the stick in her mouth across his shin. Jack gave it a toss and watched the Lab gleefully bound after it.

He'd never been to Chicago and figured it was probably like Philadelphia, maybe even New York. This guy was in the music business, running nightclubs. *Could be worse.* He tossed the stick again, and Pumpkin's joy made him smile. "At least she'll have things, and Francie'll be okay." He slapped a couple mosquitoes on his forearm. "Like friggin' Kyedaw. One more toss, and we're headin' out, Pumpkin."

By the time they made it back to the house, Odette was in bed, having left him a plate of quarter chicken with spiced red potatoes.

"You shoulda been here. It's been a damn year, PJ," Frank snapped at him from behind the *Times-Picayune* he'd picked up in New Orleans.

"You're right, Frank. I wasn't thinkin'."

Pumpkin whined from the front porch, her nose pressed against the screen door. Frank shook the paper and folded it back on the crease. He squinted to read the financial section as Jack made his way to the attic ladder. The breeze was done, and the air in the attic just crouched there, thick and wet.

He unpacked, tucking his clothes and the few souvenirs he kept into the chest of drawers. A small silken bag holding tiny, cut rubies. A dark jade Buddha crowned with the ushnisha, the size of his open hand. Neil Martin's .45 caliber Colt 1911, still fresh in the box. He set the foot-tall, green-and-gold cloisonné vase atop the chest. He'd give it to Odette in the morning, tell her he was sorry he missed her dinner. In the time it took to empty the duffle, his T-shirt was soaked. He chuckled at the cowboy scene painted on the shade of the small table lamp and pulled the chain.

The clear night's moon reflected a rectangle of sunlight onto his old bed. Window screens kept the mosquitos at bay, and it was quiet, just a few crickets. It was hot but didn't feel Burma hot. He appreciated the absence of stench – jungle rot, Flit, smudge pots. Still, he couldn't sleep. He tossed the thin blanket down the hole and descended the ladder into the dark house. He grabbed an embroidered throw pillow off the parlor sofa and settled himself on the front porch. Thrilled, Pumpkin curled up next to him. Crickets spreadin' rumors. He tried imitating the tree frogs that croaked outside his window on Thudhamma Road, and Pumpkin excitedly licked his face for the strange noises. She curled herself up again and sighed deeply before falling asleep.

* * *

There he was, standing in the dining room, which was silent but for the tick-tock of the Regulator wall clock.

"Chloe?"

She burst through the swinging doors and sprinted across the room, practically tackling him as she threw her arms around his neck and squeezed hard. "Mon Dieu!" Her tears dampened his shirt. He took her by the waist and rubbed the small of her back.

She led him to a booth where she covered his hands with her own and studied his thin face. She touched the patch and ran a finger down his cheek to his chin. The whole time, tears were trickling from both of her eyes. "It is you." She was giddy, laughing, crying, covering her mouth.

"It is me."

"Oh, I am so happy to see you, dear PJ. You are here!"

"I'm here. So are you."

"Yes, but I am always here."

"Not for long." His tone wasn't pleasant. "What I mean is, congratulations. Odette told me you're getting married and moving to Chicago."

Chloe's hands slid off his. She'd no idea he would come. Odette told her that she and Frank were driving down to New Orleans. She'd hoped.

Francie plopped down next to him and scooted him over with her butt. "Are we having pie, PJ?"

Jack laughed and rubbed her back. "Anything you want, Francie. I'm buying."

"People call you *Blackjack*. It's in the newspaper. Chloe showed me," Francie said, matter-of-factly.

"Do they now?"

"Yes. Everyone has seen da paper and talks about da hero from Abbeville. Menta calls you *Petit Mistigri*." She poked at his patch and ran the tip of her finger under the band to his ear where she snapped it. She pinched his cheek hard and giggled. They ate strawberry-rhubarb pie with whipped cream, and when Pumpkin started whining through the screen door, Francie brought out her dirty plate for Pumpkin to lick clean.

"Does it hurt? Your eye?"

He lied, "Sometimes there's a little . . . just an annoyance."

"*Annoyance?*" Chloe giggled. "Did you find a dictionary in China, PJ Benoit?"

He fidgeted. "In a way, I s'pose I did. Sorry you didn't get to go to Howard, that you've been stuck here all this time. The reverend, and all that."

She waved it off, smiling. "No, no. It is nothing. Dr. Herod was quite helpful, really, and yes, I was accepted to Howard University some time ago. But that was impossible, and, yes, I became terribly angry . . ." Her eyes glazed over, but for just a moment. "But it was for the best! If I had gone to Howard, I would not have what I have now."

He wanted her to feel bad for going to Chicago with another man.

"It is quite all right. You see, I will attend university. I will study at the University of Chicago. I wrote that to you, PJ, yes? Dr. Herod corresponds with many professors and administrators and knows the Dean of the College of Arts and Sciences there. I will study in the languages department and assist a professor with first-quarter and second-quarter French. In a way, it will be a continuation of my schooling in Paris, with Dr. Montessori, but with teaching, too." She laughed and tapped her fork on the table. "I will continue with my education after finishing my relaxing sabbatical here in Abbeville, Louisiana!" Chloe laughed harder than Jack had ever seen. "Yes, me, in my paper bag." She pressed her hands to her cheeks. "Off to university in Chicago!"

He muttered, "Paper bag?"

"I will talk to white people without *yessah* or *yessam* in every sentence." Her eyes grew hot. "Imagine, *I* will be teaching *white* people." She leaned back, wearing a determined scowl.

Francie returned from washing the plates and pulled on Chloe's sleeve. "We must cook for the lunch."

Chloe popped out of her seat. "No, Francie. We will not be serving lunch today. We are taking a holiday." She left the room and returned with a paper sign that read *Will Open for Dinner*. Pumpkin sat up, panting, and watched as she flipped the sign in the window to *Closed* and draped the note over it. "PJ Benoit, let us go for a walk. I want to hear all about my childhood friend's adventures and heroism."

As they walked down to Railroad Avenue for the first time in years, they were met with disgusted looks, no different than when they were children. If people had acknowledged Jack as the war hero he was, it might have been enough to temper the slurs. Still, the streets were fairly empty, so they were subjected to only one ugly episode. In what seemed no time at all, they were back at the coulee under the Big Tree, Pumpkin's tail wagging hard as she pressed the stick in her mouth against Jack's calf.

"I love this place." He tossed the stick.

"Not everything that happened here was happy."

"Is that a requirement to love somethin'? It's all gotta be happy? Besides, it's just a figure of speech."

"Here is Mr. Dictionary again," she teased.

He tossed the stick into the coulee. "That's *Captain Dictionary* to you, *Miss University*." Pumpkin searched the bank for a way down.

"Ah, yes! Perhaps I shall not take Hamilton Jones' name after all."

That hit like a punch to his gut.

"You know, Chloe." He paused, snapping off a willow whip. He started stripping the bark, the stickiness on his fingers raised pleasant childhood memories. "I'm happy you're happy. I am."

"Thank you, PJ. Hearing that from you, it means very much to me."

He knew he shouldn't say what he wanted to say.

"What is it, PJ?" Chloe took his hands. "I think I know."

Jack looked into her eyes. "Honeybee."

"Yes, PJ. I will always love you, too."

They embraced. Jack wanted to kiss her, desperately. But he rattled his head and let her go.

"Francie is talking real good. Clear, I mean."

Chloe beamed. "Yes, she has worked diligently on her grammar. Her speech is much improved, and she is calmer, too. Not so quick to anger. I have enjoyed helping her."

It was noon and sweltering. He asked her about Hamilton.

James Hamilton Jones, born and raised in Chicago, Illinois. Manager of two successful Negro clubs on Chicago's South Side. All kinds of music: swing, blues, big band. A couple times a year, he would hop into a roadster and head east to New York, or south to Georgia, Louisiana, all over, and seek out new talent.

"Like your Uncle Paul."

"Exactly!"

"So, you met him in New Orleans?"

"No, Hamilton came here, to Abbeville."

"Who did he come to see in Abbeville?"

"Me."

"*You?*"

"Yes, me."

"For playing piano?"

Chloe giggled and covered her mouth. "No, that was not it. I had met Hamilton when I was young. While traveling from Paris to here."

"You met him . . . *what?*" Jack was baffled. "You were what, eleven years old? You mean to tell me you were with this guy when you were eleven years old?"

"Do not be stupid, PJ Benoit. I was not *with him* when I was traveling from Paris. But we did first meet when I was there, in Chicago." She had never said a word to anybody about the incident at the Chicago Theatre.

"He was kind to me. He helped me. It was he who delivered me to Abbeville. He escorted me on the train trip to Lafayette." She continued, "Years passed, yes. But he remembered the little Chloe Boisvert he once brought to Louisiana. So from New Orleans, he drove here and walked into the Music Box. I did not recognize him at first, but he knew it was me."

Chloe glowed, swinging her shoulders as they walked. "We talked and talked and talked. He told me he never forgot me." She smiled softly. "He wanted to see what I was like all grown up."

Jack's face hardened. "So, love at first sight. Like in a movie." The words dripped with sarcasm.

Chloe poked him in the arm. "Hamilton couldn't get a room in town, so he stayed in Lafayette." She couldn't contain her excitement. "For four days he stayed, can you believe that? Four whole days, just for me. We agreed he would visit again, so corresponding with his visits to St. Louis, *ahh*, Tulsa, yes, and down in Texas. He came through Abbeville on his return trip and stayed seven days that time."

"Who's counting?" He knelt and took Pumpkin's ears in his hands. Her smiling face tempered his unease.

"On the fifth day, he asked me to marry him. On the sixth day, I said yes. Dr. Herod kindly offered his connections at the University of Chicago, and I informed Hamilton of my desire to go to college."

Jack pawed at some gravel between railroad ties.

"And he was immediately agreeable. So, yes, I will be a university student in Chicago next fall." Her cinnamon cheeks sparkled with sprinkled sugar in the sunlight.

His heart ached.

"Francie is coming with me. Hamilton has a job for her. Menta will sell the restaurant and go to live with her cousin up in Shreveport."

They neared the café.

"I've heard some stories, Honeybee." He kissed her on the cheek. "And that was a good one."

Chloe blushed, then shrieked when a siren blasted directly behind them. The patrol car stopped, and two doors swung wide, presenting identical crests. A gold star with the words *Vermilion Parish Sheriff* printed underneath. Standing behind the passenger door was none other than Deputy Davey Johnson. Jack hushed Pumpkin, who'd started barking.

"Well, well. Ain this a pitchur?" Johnson slammed the door and sauntered toward the pair. "Homecomen for Li'l PJ Benoit. You gonna cook up sompin nice an hot for yo nigga-loven white boy, huh, girl?"

"What can I do for you, Davey?"

"Do ma eyes deceive me?" Johnson asked the driver, Deputy Jimmy Sweeney. "Or did I jes see dis heah man kiss dis heah nigga on dis heah street ah mine?"

Sweeney hesitated.

"Think I'm gonna hafta run you in foe public lewdness, Benoit."

"Chrise, Davey," Sweeney interjected.

"Wha?" Johnson snapped.

Sweeney fidgeted, talking under his breath, "He's a goddamn war hero."

"And it's the fucken law, deh-poo-tee!" Johnson was incensed. He shook out his handcuffs and strode forward.

Jack stepped in front of Chloe. "You're right, Jimmy. This keeps goin', and it ain't gonna end well for you, or for your partner here." He stared down Johnson, dead-eyed, and the lawman balked. "So me and my friend here are gonna go get a piece of pie over at the Music

Box Café." He took Chloe's arm. "Y'all're welcome to join us. My treat."

"You ain *ma* war hero, Benoit! An you sure ain't welcome heah! I say you finish whateva business you got an get cho ass outta heah righ quick, or they's goan be hell to pay, boy."

Jack escorted a trembling Chloe to her porch.

"I don't know how you can do that," she whispered.

"What?"

"Antagonize the law like that."

"Haw!" Jack fell back, laughing. "Davey Johnson ain't the law, Honeybee. He's a piss-ant piece a shit hidin' behind a badge. A scared little bully who needs a crack upside the head every now and then to learn what's what, that's all."

Chloe shook her head, squinting. "To you, yes." Her face grew angry. "But to me, to us . . ." She nodded toward the restaurant's door. "He can do anything he wants to us. Here, there is no law other than Johnson law." She pinched her forearm. "Not with *this*. He does not call *this* cinnamon." She turned to leave him.

"Please." He pulled her close. "Don't get angry." He was trying to think of the words to say. "Look, Chloe, I've seen . . . dammit, I've seen horror. All colors of people, all butchering each other. A complete friggin' mess. And I've seen love. White, black, yellow, brown, it don't matter. If I've learned anything since I saw you last, it's that you can't have love without a fight. They just don't let you have it. They . . . them butchers over there, and these jackasses over here, they ain't gonna get outta your life, so you gotta push 'em out."

"Oh, I see." Chloe crossed her arms. "The big war hero, he returns to Abbeville, and *he* will protect us all, yes? You will push out Davey Johnson, and the rest of them. No! You will leave, PJ Benoit. You will leave them to do as they please. You always leave."

"Well you're getting out of here, too. You're going to Chicago. What do you care?"

Chloe looked him in the eye, seething. They stood, staring at each other. Her eyes moistened, and she lowered her head. "Sometimes I don't know why I love you, PJ Benoit." She opened the screen door and went inside. Pumpkin looked up at him from a lowered head. He bent to rub her ear. They walked back to Frank and Odette's.

* * *

Before dinner, the little ones wouldn't leave their uncle alone. He wasn't in the mood, but their enthusiasm finally won him over, and over shrimp and grits he told them stories about Asia. Odette was entranced by his descriptions of the mountainous jungles, the flowers, the insects, the dogs. The endless line of trucks, carts, and people on the Burma Road. Looking down from ten thousand feet over monsoon-swollen rivers angrily churning through the deep green gorges, their rocky cliffs thick with exotic plants, vines, and trees.

"The colors," Odette pondered. "All we seen are a couple grainy black an white pichas in the paper. Maybe three of em, right, Beb? Now I see tha colors. Tha life."

"You should write a book," Frank added.

"Mais yeh!" Odette cried, excitedly. "An with you bein a war hero and all, it's gonna do really good. That, I'm sure."

Jack laughed. One of the children poked at him with a fork under the table, and Jack teasingly scowled and barked. "I wouldn't know what I'd write, really."

"So, then what's next?" Frank asked, reaching for the last biscuit. "What's *Blackjack Benoit* gonna do?"

"Good question. I met a guy in New York who has some businesses. Thought I'd give him a call, see what's what." He didn't mention the guy was Meyer Lansky, or that Meyer's partner, Lucky Luciano, was newly released from federal prison.

"Well, whateva you do, you gonna do good." Odette stood to clear the dishes. "But me, I think you oughta write a book."

"Help your mother." Frank flicked his finger at the children. "Take a walk?"

Jack nodded.

"Thanks, sweetie." Frank's pat on her bottom brought a flush to Odette's cheeks.

"Out uh my kitchen, Beb."

They moseyed down the street. Frank stopped to fire his pipe. The struck match returned Jack to the hospital in Kunming. Burnt cordite. That smell was in his nose for months. He searched the sky for Cassiopeia.

"It's good to have you home, PJ."

"I'll be leaving soon."

"Where you headed?"

"The War Loan Drive wants me to make a swing through California. A couple weeks, then a couple rallies in Texas."

"Good for you." Frank puffed a lazy smoke ring into the night air.

"Yeah, the patch sells."

Frank popped a smoke ring at his brother. "I heard you up there. You're good at it, 'specially compared to all of them blowhard politicians. The people in the crowd got excited when you were talking, not them. More like, agitated, even. You stirred 'em up. That's the trick, I think."

Jack was searched the sky for Orion.

"So, after seeing that, I can't say I can picture you living here. After all you've done and seen, Vermilion Parish just ain't gonna do it for you."

Jack found Scorpius in the southern sky. "Havana."

"Havana? What, in *Cuba?* What the hell are you gonna do in Cuba?"

"I told you, this guy I met in New York has a bunch of businesses. Some up there, some in Miami and Havana. A rich guy. Real money, you know, Frank? I'm gonna fly his plane." He found Orion and murmured. "Shan? Shen?"

"No Japs up there, PJ."

"Yeah." He sighed. "It's peaceful here. For some folks, anyway."

"You talking about Chloe now?" Frank probed.

"This Hamilton guy. S'pose he sounds alright."

"And?"

"Shit, Frank. I know you don't want to hear it."

"That's exactly right," Frank agreed. "I *don't* want to hear it. But I want you to say it. Get it out of your system and move on."

Jack smiled, trying to remember what Shu Hao said about some old man stumbling over wisdom. So he started talking. He talked a long time. Frank puffed and listened. He bit his tongue. Then they called it a night.

* * *

Odette handed him a glass of sweet tea. A beautiful summer morning on the front porch. They watched the kids play in the yard, taking turns on the tree swing Jack had hung for them. "Think I'll take 'em up to the Big Tree."

Odette scowled at him.

"Okay, okay, settle down, sister."

A Checker Cab with a New Orleans phone number on the door pulled up in front of the house. The cabbie strode up the walk, holding a yellow envelope.

"Mr. Jack Benoit?"

Jack signed for the delivery. "What's this?"

"It came in a few days ago. They said to tell you they tried to find you at the rally, but you must have already left."

Jack asked about the expense.

"Taken care of, sir."

Jack pressed a fiver into his palm.

"What it say?" Odette was on the edge of her seat.

```
Getting the band back together.
Need you to fly The Hump.
Am in the States.
Please call WAS dc 4402.
WL Bond
```

Jack rubbed Pumpkin's head. "It says I'm going back to China."

28

REUNION

AUGUST 1942

He woke to a knocking on the compartment door. "Grand Central Terminal, Mr. Benoit. End of the line." He had dozed off outside Philadelphia and slept hard while the train rolled through New Jersey. He scooped up his shaving kit and headed to the toilet to freshen up.

An hour later in the lobby of the Astor Hotel, he asked to use the house phone. The man on the other end of the line told him to hold and didn't return until a good five minutes later, when he had Jack take down an address.

"It's good to see you, Jack," Meyer Lansky said. "Or should I call you *Blackjack* like all the papers do?"

Jack rolled his eye. They shook hands, and he passed on the drink Lansky offered. "That's right, clean-cut, All-American boy. Well, it's really too early for me to imbibe as well, so we'll have some coffee. Tony, have Bill bring two cappuccinos. Have one yourself, if you'd like."

The men sat in the same chairs, under the same stained-glass lamp.

"So, you're ready to come work for me."

Jack grimaced. "Meyer, I do want to work for you. But I got an offer I can't refuse."

Lansky sat back.

"They reached out to me. Bondy, from CNAC." Noting his blank face, Jack realized Lansky didn't know the players. "Anyway, I'm going back. Gonna fly the Hump."

"The Hump?"

"Right. Transport from India to China. They need pilots to fly war materiel into Kunming."

Lansky nodded. "The Himalayas. Yes, I remember reading something about that. Very dangerous work."

"Kinda surprised myself, Meyer. But when I got the telegram, it felt like . . . I don't know. Like I wasn't done yet. Do you know what I mean?"

Lansky smiled. "I understand perfectly, Jack."

Big Tony Campisi opened the door for a young man who set down a tray holding three cappuccinos. He handed one to Lansky, who furrowed his brow and tipped his head to Jack. When the boy left, Lansky apologized for the slight. "Bill's new. So, Tony, our hero hasn't had enough of the war. He's going back."

"How you gonna shoot Japs wit jus' one eye?"

The other two laughed.

"I'm haulin' equipment, Tony. Easy like. Easy like Campisi."

Tony chuckled. "So you doan wanna work here?" The muscle looked sheepishly at Lansky, knowing he'd just put his foot in it.

Jack threw back the last of his cappuccino and stood. "I'll come back when I'm done, Meyer, if you'll still have me."

Lansky stood, and Jack stuck out his hand again. The boss pushed it aside and went in for a hug. "When you've finished off the damn Japs, you come back here, and we'll have a helluva party. Hopefully we'll be done with those sons-a-bitches Hitler and Mussolini, too!"

He gave Jack a new card. This one had six different phone numbers on it. Two each with New York, Miami, and Havana exchanges. "Anytime, my friend."

Campisi walked him out. "Can I take you somewheres?"

Jack wanted to walk, and Big Tony looked like he'd gotten even bigger over the summer. "Not right now, Tony."

Jack meandered north and into the park, where he grabbed a pretzel from a vendor off Central Park West. It was a glorious summer day, and two women passed by, complaining about the city heat. "If only they knew," he said to the pretzel guy.

Like during his last visit to the city, people stared at the eyepatch. No one in China would have even noticed. They dressed pretty snazzy in New York, and a lady he was walking behind looked like a taller Madame Chiang in her blue suit and was trailing jasmine. He was back in the hospital bed in Kunming when the traffic signal gonged, snapping him back to the present. He gulped down the last of the pretzel and headed to the Astor.

* * *

Campisi rose from a chair in the lobby. "Mr. Lansky gave me the day off in case you wanted to do somethin' in the city. Whatcha say we go find some action. I'll get us a couple girls."

"Yeah? What're you thinking, Tony?"

"Your black pal's playin' in the Village tonight. I know a nice Chelsea girl, and she's gotta friend. We're pickin' 'em up on the way. Already arranged."

Jack agreed. He didn't want to be alone.

Bonnie and Rachel, factory girls, were waiting outside a tobacco shop on West Twenty-First. As soon as she got in the car, Bonnie Wilson started in on Big Tony with the baby talk, and he was eating it up. Bonnie's friend, Rachel Applebaum was more reserved, shy even, and certainly not what Jack had been expecting. A small but sturdy girl in her early twenties, Rachel had dark eyes and full, dark lips under a slightly hooked nose. Her olive face was framed by dark curls that cascaded over her shoulders. Her horn-rimmed glasses reflected the streetlamps as they passed, making it difficult for Jack to read her eyes.

Louis Armstrong was scheduled to headline that night at the Village Vanguard, but he was ill and didn't show. Instead, Clark Terry fronted his sextet. Management apologized to Big Tony and set them up with a complimentary bottle of their best champagne.

"I've never heard of this happening," Rachel offered as she declined Campisi's cigarettes.

"What's that?"

"Mr. Armstrong. I understand he is very resilient. He will play through anything. I have seen him play just once, at the Famous Door, and we were fortunate to be close to the stage, like here. I could see him so clearly. His lips were cracked and bleeding. He kept dabbing them with his kerchief. By the end of the show, the cloth was covered with red spots." Rachel took a sip of wine. Jack liked her soft voice. She was looking at him, too, and when her lips curled into a curious smile, Jack realized that she wasn't wearing lipstick. She leaned closer. "I closed my eyes to listen, and he was perfect. *Perfect!* Can you imagine? Caring for your craft so much, loving it so very much that you could do something like *that*, playing beautifully through such pain?"

The bottle was empty and a round of drinks arrived. Campisi had a hand up Bonnie's dress, caressing a thigh. The big man was fidgeting, like he couldn't get comfortable. Thinking he was being discreet, he elbowed Jack, then unzipped his fly and clumsily extracted a small gun.

"Nickel-plated thirty-two." He flashed it low at Jack before stuffing it in a front pocket of his suit jacket. "They never check the crotch. Worried about comin' off as fairies, you know? It ain't got a lotta umph, but hollow points do the trick."

Jack turned back to his date. "What's your accent? If you don't mind me asking."

"German."

"When did you come to the States?"

A sadness washed over her enthusiasm.

"Sorry, I didn't mean to pry."

"No, no. It is quite fine. I escaped in 1937. My father's sister and her husband lived here." She took a sip of wine. "My parents, they could not get out at the time."

"Where are they now?"

"We do not know. They were ordered to a concentration camp soon after they sent me here."

Rachel was misting up when a band member bumped their table while retaking the stage, leaving behind a trail of reefer. Jack handed her his kerchief, and she dabbed the corners of her eyes. Tony pulled hard on his cigarette. Tipping his head back, he exhaled a slow-moving ring, followed in rapid succession by two smaller donuts that pierced the first one, a trick perfected by someone who had spent a lot of time waiting.

"How 'bout we get some air?" Jack offered. Rachel nodded and pushed her seat back. He was surprised when she thanked her host and said goodbye to her friend. He nodded to Bonnie and shook Big Tony's hand.

"See ya 'round, Blackjack!"

As they climbed to street level, the band started its second set.

```
My poor heart is sentimental, not made of wood
I got it bad and that ain't good
```

He stopped at the top of the stairs, envisioning Norah, sparkling onstage in that green dress.

The streets were wet from a brief shower, and the night air hit his face like a refreshing splash of cool water. Rachel took his arm as they started up Seventh Avenue. Three blocks up, and he noticed she was limping. He asked about her shoes.

"I borrowed them from Bonnie. They are a little tight, but I am fine, really."

"Tight and tall. I'll get us a cab." He stepped into the street.

"No, no, that is not necessary."

"You ain't makin' it to Twenty-First Street in those, girlie."

Rachel agreed and walked over to a bench. "If you do not mind." She extracted a pair of thin leather slippers from her bag and struggled the pumps off her feet.

As she pulled the slippers over her stockings, it occurred to him that neither Chloe nor Emma wore stockings. Emma, even when she was working in the hospital. How did she get away with that?

"Better?" he asked.

"Much better. Thank you." She smiled. "It is a little chilly. Maybe we walk briskly?"

Rachel was a seamstress who worked on Thirty-Seventh Street, just a mile from her aunt and uncle's apartment. Jack enjoyed the cadence of her speech. "I used to work for my uncle. But last year, my cousin became old enough to help in his store, so I took a job sewing military insignia for the soldier uniforms. It is good work. My uncle could not pay me very much, and with their kindness in letting me stay with them all these years, I could not ask for much. But now I can help out. I also save a little something for myself. It is a good arrangement."

Jack wondered how long it would take Rachel to save forty-seven hundred bucks.

"My aunt's birthday is in September. I will buy her new gloves with fur wrist collars for the winter. I have nearly enough money saved."

He liked her smile.

"This is my building." She turned to him. "I had a wonderful time, Jack. Thank you for the conversation, and for the escort home."

He leaned in for a kiss, but she turned her head. He gave her a peck on the cheek. "My pleasure, Rachel. Good night."

He caught a cab on Ninth Avenue. Humming the tune to "I Got It Bad," his mind wandered. Norah. Concentration camps. Was Norah in a concentration camp? Maybe she made it to Australia. What about Major Whatshisname and Dahrala? The Sikh didn't seem the kind to go over to the Japs. He figured they were both slaving for the Japs, cuttin' some stinkin' jungle road somewhere. Sick on the way to dead.

"Friggin' Japs."

"What's that, sir?" The cabbie's question snapped him out of it. "Here we are. The Astor Hotel. That'll be two bits." Jack peeled off a five spot. "Gee, thanks, mister! That's awful generous!"

Jack didn't know why he kept peeling off fivers, but it felt good.

* * *

The monsoon weather departed Upper Assam earlier than usual, so this mid-October afternoon in Dinjan was bearable. As Jack strode down the cargo door of the new C-47 Skytrain transport he'd ridden all the way from Norfolk. He heard a familiar voice.

"Well, I'll be a monkey's uncle! I sure never figured on seeing you again, Cap'n Blackjack." It was Carl Jones. He pointed at the patch. "How's the eye?"

"Couldn't tell you, Carl. It's been a while since we were last together."

Jones guffawed and clapped. "So you're gonna fly for CNAC?"

"That's the plan."

"Couldn't get me over those damn things again." Jones pointed to the Himalayas. "Not after the flight I had coming here from Kunming."

"How many of our guys are here?"

"We have a dozen old AVG ground personnel here in Dinjan and twenty some in Kunming. Pilots? Let's see, with you it'll make six Flying Tigers. Most of the pilots are Chinks from the Old Man's CNAC crew. More army comes in everyday, but they can't seem to get their shit together. The army just sits out the storms, which is most of the time. Except for a couple Yanks, the CNAC bosses here are all Chink. But they get things done." Jones caught him up on the whereabouts of the other AVG guys as best he knew. The ones who'd signed with the army, and the guys who'd gone commercial with Pan Am. "This place ain't nearly as shitty as Burma, and Calcutta's a great place to get your kicks, if you know what I mean." Jack swatted a pair of mosquitoes on his forearm. His khaki shirt was already spotted with sweat. "You're looking like you might got a fever, Cap'n. I'd check out the infirmary if I were you."

Jack settled in at the tea plantation hostel and woke the next day after a solid night's sleep, relieved his forehead was cool. He found the base well organized. CNAC had started flying materiel from the States over The Hump in early summer, and things were running smoothly despite shortages of just about everything. CNAC shared this converted RAF base with US Army operations. Since the Japanese took Burma and shut down the road, the only substantial aid and materiel making it into China flew out of Dinjan, and the Americans were keen to keep the Chinese front viable. It was thought a trickle of supplies still made its way in from Russia to the Communists in the northern mountains, but the fighting was in the south, so that's where the bulk of the refugees were, too. In September, at the height of monsoon season, CNAC flew 136 tons into Kunming with just nine planes, a mix of C-53 Dakotas and C-47 Skytrains. The US Army's operations delivered just half that tonnage with thirty-five of the larger capacity Skytrains.

In three weeks time, Jack would be worked into the rotation as a pilot. But first, he was required to copilot on training flights while taking classroom instruction on both of the transport aircraft models. He figured hauling crates would be a piece of cake compared to combat, but crossing The Hump was extremely dangerous. Massive electrical storms, pounding hail, horrifying turbulence. Typically, the windows iced thick, leaving the crew to fly for hours on instruments over craggy mountains that peaked at sixteen thousand feet. Both the pilot and copilot used handheld compasses to verify the navigator's instrument readings. Navigating The Hump was a craft. Flying it, an art.

* * *

4 August 1942

Dearest PJ,

Odette provided me with the address for the base in India, so I am hopeful this letter will make it to you.

In a few days, I will leave Abbeville to start a new life in Chicago. Hamilton will arrive on Monday to collect Francie and me. We are to be married on 21 August.

I wanted to write to tell you how much your good wishes meant to me. It was lovely to see you here, and I wish you every happiness.

I am happy you will no longer be fighting the Japanese, but sometimes I worry about you flying into China with no guns to defend yourself. Then I remember how brave you were the first time we met, jumping into the coulee like that with three bullies hovering over the bank. You were my hero then, and you are my hero now.

For me, leaving Abbeville is like escaping bondage. Every day I have felt like a bird living in a cage, except for the time I spent with you, PJ. I will cherish our time together for the rest of my life. I have found a path to a happy future, and I wish the same for you, including someone for whom you can truly be her Mistigri, her jack of hearts.

I will remember you forever.

With love,

Chloe

29

THE HUMP

OCTOBER 1942

The hostel was situated a couple miles from the base, on a picturesque tea plantation with terraced rows of tall green tea plants swirled across the mountain gorges. Jack quickly settled into his routine, waking early for calisthenics before a shower and a shave. The houseboy, Suko, took such care pouring his cups of green tea. *One must let the water calm so as to prevent scorching the leaves.*

The weather was no less comfortable than Louisiana. The insects were not overwhelming, merely bothersome, but the kerosene smell of Flit was still everywhere. All in, Dinjan was an absolute pleasure when compared to Toungoo, and Jack much preferred the quiet of the tea plantation to the bustle of Kunming.

Sipping tea, he ran the numbers on a piece of paper again. Scale pay for the minimum flight time of sixty hours per month was 800 US dollars. Add twenty hours overtime, and he'd collect 1,010 US dollars each month. He figured in six months time he'd have banked another five grand, give or take, making about ten grand total. That would be the start of the next monsoon season, and he'd consider then whether he would stay or cut loose.

The friendliest Americans he met at Dinjan were Pete Goutiere, Jimmy Fox, and Charles Sharkey, who referred to themselves as *The Boys*. Each of The Boys flew as often as they could to reach a hundred flight hours, the minimum required to qualify for leave in

Calcutta. Jack heard their stories and figured it to be the same for most of the guys. Work what you had to, to get out of there, then downcountry for liquor and whores. Same as how it started in Burma, just longer stretches of on and off. Maybe he'd find something worth doing in a big city like Calcutta.

Sharkey was the youngest flyer in CNAC and a real piece of work. He was reputed to spend every nickel to his name and then some, leaving massive tabs at the clubs in Calcutta. A couple times he was simply lucky to have made it back from leave alive. Jimmy once crowed, "When we're not humpin' it to China, we're humpin' it on Kariah Road," Calcutta's red-light district. Jack's favorite Yank was a guy named Hugh Woods, a solid guy with a good head on his shoulders.

* * *

Shu Hao entered the classroom. "Welcome back, my friend."

Jack cheered and hugged his friend. "You're a sight for sore eyes." He absentmindedly touched his patch.

"You've returned to us. Good show."

Jack asked if he was teaching.

"Not today. I just came by to welcome you. After you finish with classroom and local flights, you'll complete training by copiloting four rounds over The Hump. I have asked for the privilege of piloting you on those runs."

Classroom instruction was similar to training back at Randolph. They learned features and performance standards for the C-47 Skytrain and C-53 Dakota equipment according to US Army protocols. Then, there were discussions of the hazards involved in traversing the Himalayas.

The route to Kunming started from Dinjan with an immediate climb over the twelve-thousand-foot Patkai mountain range to reach the northern Burmese jungle, followed by a second climb to clear the sixteen-thousand-foot Three Gorges mountains in western China, where the weather was ferocious, unforgiving. During the winter, they could expect to fly four to five hours on instruments with iced windows. Massive downdrafts would drive a plane thousands of feet down in just seconds, requiring a cruising altitude well over twenty thousand feet where the cabin temperature would drop to minus twenty Farhenheit, with frost threatening to lock up the engines' carburetors. At times, the jet stream over the range was so strong it would push a plane backwards. Jack imagined what it would be like to pilot a plane backwards through a two-thousand-foot downdraft, blinded by ice. He was relieved that Shu Hao would be training him.

* * *

He often took tea with Shu Hao after evening mess, and he enjoyed these opportunities to get to know his friend better.

Before the war, Shu Hao's father had owned a short-haul shipping company that did very well serving routes to Japan. He'd sent Shu Hao, his only son, to university in England, expecting the boy to help run the business. But as tensions escalated with the Japanese, the business struggled, and Shu Hao's father shifted his focus to the British ports at Hong Kong and Singapore. In May of 1938, when the Japanese amassed forces in occupied Xuzhou, young Shu Hao disobeyed his father's instructions to stay put in England and returned home to fight. He'd intended to be a soldier, but his father fiercely objected. "When he resigned himself to my involvement in the war, he was adamant it would not be as a foot soldier."

Through his father's connections, Shu Hao met T. V. Soong, Madame Chiang's brother and the Kuomintang government's finance minister. Soong was instrumental in the creation of the CNAC, the China National Aviation Corporation. So, Shu Hao became a pilot, eventually training at Yunnan-yi under Claire Chennault in 1940. Jack asked what equipment he'd flown.

"I count fourteen different planes. Twenty-three if we include model upgrades. And how about you, Jack?"

Jack thought back to his time at Randolph and counted on his fingers. "With upgrade models, twenty-three. How 'bout that?"

They laughed at the coincidence, and Shu Hao asked about Jack's family.

Jack stretched the truth and told him both of his parents were dead, and Shu Hao looked embarrassed. "I should not have assumed they were alive. Sometimes I forget that tragedy is not limited to war zones." He paused. "My mother died recently from illness, and my father struggles still. But he counsels me, 'With so much suffering in the world, there is little time to pity oneself, and no value in it. We will grieve when the war is over.'"

Jack had been in the hold as they crossed the mountains during his flight out from China some six months ago, so this was his first view of The Hump from a cockpit. They were fortunate to have good weather, which provided excellent visibility to study the mountain formations. When they reached Yunnan Province, the flight's radio operator connected with ground control at Wujiaba Airport in Kunming. Good news. No Japanese in the skies between their C-47 Skytrain and the base. "You will see more of your AVG friends soon."

"My brother, Frank . . ." Jack started out of the blue. "He's a good egg. Married a sweet girl named Odette. They have a couple little ones."

"Your brother, he's at home?"

"Yeah. He's 4-F." Jack thumped his chest. "Seems he's got a bum ticker. Who knew?" He scanned the horizon. "It's good to know he ain't in this shit, know what I mean?"

Shu Hao nodded. "Like my sister. Shu Ai, who is with the Communists in the north."

"But your sister's a soldier."

"Yes. However, it's unlikely she's fighting. There's very little action up north. In April, when the Russians signed the Japanese–Soviet Nonaggression Pact, the Russians ceased shipping significant armaments to the Communists. At least that's the official story. Also, it's very difficult for the Japanese to make progress in the mountainous terrain. So long as the invaders focus on the Nationalists in the south, perhaps Shu Ai will stay out of harm's way."

Jack looked down on the pastures, the cut wheat and the pig farms. "What's she like, your sister?"

"It's been seven years since I've seen Shu Ai. She is older than I."

"*Shu Ai*. What does it mean?"

Shu Hao laughed hard. "Ai means love, or loving."

"So, your sister's not so loving?"

"No, no. It's not that. Ai is a name of Japanese derivation. I only just saw the irony." Shu Hao continued, "I remember Shu Ai as beautiful and delicate. The young men in the city were always interested in Shu Ai." He surprised Jack by pulling a cracked and frayed photograph from his bomber jacket. It showed a smiling teenaged girl sitting on a smooth boulder near a stream and holding a white linen umbrella. "I was very young then, but I thought of myself as her protector." Shu Hao tucked the photo back into his jacket. "She has a soft voice, which is deceiving." He laughed. "Ai was terribly headstrong, even so with our father. But compassionate. Very compassionate. I think that's why she was attracted to the

Communists. She disliked our family having money when the peasants had very little, with coolies starving. My parents loved her dearly, but there would be embarrassing arguments. She left home to join the Communists soon after I departed for England. We corresponded by letter while I was in school but lost touch when I returned home. I believe she would like to write, but the tension between the Nationalists and the Communists has not dissipated. To communicate is difficult at best."

The mountains sunk into the horizon behind them, and the sun was following the mountains down as Shu Hao landed the Skytrain at Wujiaba Airport. Jack felt anxious.

"The landing was not to your satisfaction?"

"I'm just thinkin'. There's someone here I'd like to see."

"A woman named Emma?"

Jack grimaced. "Not sure where she is."

"I don't know either, Jack. But let me know if I might help. Of course, I know people here. If you wish, I could make inquiries."

He thanked Shu Hao for the offer. "If I strike out, I might take you up on that."

He bumped into a few people from his AVG days, ground crew working the Kunming side for CNAC. Most of what was left of the AVG had joined the army or shipped out. Late in the summer, Toby rejoined the service, but switched branches. He was somewhere in the Pacific, a marine flight leader for Boyington, who it seemed had turned into a real fighter pilot and reentered service as a major. No one could say where Emma was. Jack took a rickshaw to the Chinese hospital and asked around, but no one recognized her name. So during the return flight, he asked Shu Hao to make inquiries next time.

He and his friend shared more about their upbringings. Jack spoke of his father, telling stories about the Three Musketeers, starting with when he first met Chennault in Alabama.

"You've known the general since 1927? Fifteen years."

Jack was all smiles as he recalled the King Ranch hunt, reminiscing about Criquette and Max, how the trip led to his brother getting hitched, then Jack moving to Louisiana.

"It seems General Chennault has had a great deal of influence on your life, my friend."

Jack never really thought about it, but he might not have wound up at Randolph if Chennault hadn't written that letter of recommendation to General Briscoe. He wouldn't have met Chloe, that's for sure, because Frank wouldn't have met Matt Sweetwater then married Odette. Probably wouldn't have become a Flying Tiger, so wouldn't have met Emma, either. Maybe he'd still have two eyes, or maybe instead he'd just be a corpse somewhere in a North African desert.

"My dad was dead when I was ready to enter the service, and the colonel wrote a letter for me, making sure I got to fly. I lied about my age, but he was in China and had no reason to remember how old I was."

"You are how old?"

"Twenty."

"Ha!" Shu Hao doubled over. "By three methods we may achieve wisdom. By reflection, which is the noblest means. By imitation, which is the easiest way. By experience, which is the bitterest. At just twenty years of age, you have had some experiences, my friend."

Jack never thought of himself as having any wisdom. He told Shu Hao the story of his first time in an airplane, sitting with Frank on life preservers in the back of that PT-3 over the Great Flood of 1927. About how the blacks were made to work the levee while the whites were evacuated to Red Cross shelters. Shu Hao followed with the story of the Yellow River Flood. How in 1938, Generalissimo Chiang ordered the destruction of levees on the Yellow River to flood Hunan and delay the Japanese invasion.

"What happened?"

"The tactic was effective. The Japanese were delayed. But hundreds of thousands of our people died. Millions became refugees, forced from their homes, their farms, never to return, because when the water receded, much of the land lay under a deep layer of silt. Millions of hectares of productive farmland were ruined. Chiang never admitted to ordering the demolition, but of course that is what he did." Shu Hao paused, thinking. "I often consider the Yellow River Flood. If we say, 'Yes, this was done to protect us,' then we must answer the question, 'Who is us?' Because if this was done to protect *us*, then *us* cannot include those who were killed. It follows then that whoever issued the order is the man who defined *us* at the time." He sighed. "In a just world, this would not be accepted."

Shu Hao surveyed Chinese history for his friend. The dynasties. The Great Wall. The Opium Wars. The First Sino-Japanese War. "It has been so long since the Chinese people have had peace, and we have never had freedom. Never. We moved from warlords and emperors to suffer Western colonialism under the gunboats, then into conflict between the Nationalists and the Communists, and now another war with Japan. I am hopeful that after we remove the invaders, we will settle our internal differences peacefully and move forward for our people." He drank from his canteen. "China is a land rich in resources and populated with honorable, hardworking people. The foreigners have always taken from China for themselves. Even some people in CNAC." He flicked his thumb toward the American navigator. "Even they want to take from China for themselves."

Smuggling was rampant on the airlift, no different than on the Burma Road. War creates opportunity for geographic arbitrage, and corruption and smuggling always follow. With China, smugglers would bring in gold or hard currency to buy rubies and sapphires at depressed, war zone prices. By releasing the gems from the hyperinflationary Chinese war economy, a buyer could double his investment just by selling the stones in Calcutta. Early during the airlift, an aircrew was caught smuggling a large haul of gold into Kunming, so CNAC assigned inspection crews to check both incoming and outgoing flights. The effort stemmed the tide for a short while, but it really just drove the men to concoct more creative schemes. "Just before you arrived in Dinjan, a Dakota was boarded by the authorities. They'd received a tip that the plane was smuggling gold into China, and they found more than twenty-five pounds."

The smugglers had intended to sell the gold for Chinese yuan, then trade the yuan for Indian rupees, cash the rupees in Calcutta for US dollars and net a 125% profit.

"Had the transaction not been foiled, it would have yielded a profit of fifteen thousand US dollars."

"Holy cow! Someone could make as much as Hank Greenberg in a couple trips."

"Who is Hank Greenberg?"

"Only the best baseball player ever. He makes thirty-five thousand a year."

Shu Hao nodded.

Jack didn't understand the economics of gold and the currencies, so Shu Hao explained that taking wealth out of China at a discount hurt the country, and dealing in foreign currency undermined the Chinese yuan at home.

"So that's why all the lectures about smuggling. We can wear one watch. No fountain pens. It's so we can't bring in gold."

"Precisely."

"Yeah, but if inflation makes the yuan not worth much, doesn't it make sense to get people in China different money that works better? Or something that's actually worth something, like gold? Why's that so bad?"

Shu Hao tried again to explain, but Jack couldn't see it. He figured if most everyone in China was hurting, then it must be a good thing when at least some people got help. Wasn't that the whole point of the airlift? He wondered why all his favorite people were smarter than him.

"I don't get it, Shu Hao," Jack confessed. "I just don't see a problem with making a little money by helpin' people out."

* * *

During their next outbound flight, the C-47 Skytrain had engine trouble, but nevertheless Shu Hao brought them into Wujiaba safely. The problem would take some time to repair, so the flight crew got an extra day in Kunming, and Jack decided to take advantage of the downtime to reconnect with some former AVG at the training center out at Yunnan-yi. He borrowed a Jeep and headed west.

John McClintock flicked his Lucky Strike butt into the gutter. "The key is to keep it small and light." They were meandering along Wenhua Road, lost, looking down side streets. Jack asked directions from a street vendor who ignored what he was saying and kept hawking his own pancakes and dumplings until Jack produced a coin and asked again. The vendor motioned left at the next corner, and Jack flipped him the silver. They picked up the pace and quickly found the joint. Jack peered through the dusty window at the dangling roast ducks. McClintock waved him in. "The dim sum's good."

It was warm near the kitchen. McClintock, who'd gained a good bit of weight, wobbled on a rickety chair.

"You know, Scratchy, I'm just not interested."

"Dammit, Captain Jack!" McClintock whined, his head on a swivel. "Nobody here calls me that, and I'd rather they didn't start, so cut it out."

"They're called rubbers, John."

"Is that right? Well, you know rubbers don't do a damn thing for crabs!"

Jack pointed at McClintock's closely cropped scalp. "Maybe that's your solution."

The men ordered from the proprietor, a handsome youngish man with a long black ponytail wagging under his red-and-black silk dǒulì. Dim sum, two ducks, and beers. He returned quickly with room-temperature cans of Schlitz. McClintock toasted, "Here's to the good ol' US of A!"

Jack took a sip and watched McClintock drain his can, then squash the empty between his meaty fingers and thumb.

"There'll always be room for you in the circus back home." Jack teased.

The duck was tender, and the dim sum was superb. McClintock had a few more beers. Jack followed his Schlitz with a green tea.

"Seriously, Captain Jack, I've figured it out." McClintock's head was on a swivel again. "Chinese bonds."

"What are you talking about?"

Many of the Chinese people held yuan-based bonds issued before or during the war, and hyperinflation had dramatically devalued them. The ones dating from the mid-1930s were worth one-sixtieth of face value in the current local market. But outside China, the banks that underwrote the bonds stood by their value at politically agreed-upon exchange rates. Rates that were much higher than local market rates. So, trading Chinese bonds for foreign currency somewhere outside the war zone would result in a fantastic return.

"Think about it. Five, ten thousand yuan on just a single piece of paper. Hell, in one trip we could move fifty thousand yuan folded up in your wallet!" McClintock continued. "We can buy the bonds here with dollars for, on average, 30% of face value. That would mean a 200% return, after expenses. It's nuts, Captain Jack. Crackers!"

Jack sipped his tea. He knew Shu Hao disapproved, but he still didn't understand why. He played it back for clarity. "So we buy these bonds here, then I trade them in at a bank in Calcutta for dollars?"

"No, you cash them for yuan at the bank in Calcutta. Remember, out there, the exchange rate for yuan is much higher than here. You get the yuan, then make a second trade for dollars."

Jack shook his head. "Smugglin' hurts the economy here, doesn't it? Look at these people." He pointed out the dusty window at two emaciated coolies. "They need us to make it better, not worse."

"I think that line is all wet, Captain." McClintock sat back, the rickety chair struggling to sustain him. "I don't know nothin' about economics. All I know is the people here want gold, and the next best thing is good ol' US greenbacks. A sawbuck keeps its value, while yuan are worth less and less every damn day. People do business with dollars, British pounds, Mexican pesos. Pretty much anything *but* yuan. I think we'd be doing these people a favor getting them real money, and from the conversations I've had, they think so, too."

McClintock told Jack about the discussions he'd had with some Australian expats who claimed to know some big bondholders. "These Chinamen used to be rolling in the dough. Manufacturing. Shipping. The industrialists that made China run before the invasion, before they lost their factories in the east, over in Nanking and Shanghai, you know? Now, they don't got any chips, so they can't rebuild here in Kunming, up in Chongqing."

Jack still didn't get it.

"Look, we know who it helps. These guys who want to build factories. And who else does it help? Us, that's who. And who does it hurt? I don't see nobody getting hurt, Captain. I think whoever's telling you that just wants to grab the wad himself."

Jack pictured Shu Hao's earnest face. Shu Hao believed what he was saying, and he was educated. He'd studied economics in London. But what Scratchy was saying made a lot more sense.

"Meet these guys. You'll see. They know the bondholders. We all put in money. I collect the paper and get it to you. You fly it out and cash the bonds at the Bank of China in Calcutta. You bring the dollars back next time, and we do it again. A few rounds like that, and boy, oh boy, pennies from heaven, Captain. A monsoon of pennies from heaven."

Shu Hao greeted Jack outside the motor pool wearing a forlorn expression.

"What is it? Trouble getting the parts?"

"No, Jack. It's Emma Simpson."

Midsummer, Emma had been working at the French hospital when Japanese raiders rained hell, a massive daylight bombing raid on the center of town. It was devastating, killing thousands of civilians. They destroyed the city's largest brickworks, along with noodle factories, silk filatures, tea shops, and markets. Emma was rushing patients to less exposed internal corridors when a two hundred pound bomb crashed into the burn ward next to the blackened and oozing Chinese Army sergeant she and another nurse were placing on a gurney. Nothing remained of the sergeant, or the nurses who'd been trying to save him.

Jack's legs buckled.

30

THE RAJ

DECEMBER 1942

Jack didn't recognize the maître d' and wondered if Naresh had taken the day off or if he had taken ill. He didn't ask.

"How about over there?" Jack pointed toward the southern end of the Great Eastern Hotel's second-story veranda, where the perimeter's wrought-iron railing curved around the corner of Old Court House Street to Waterloo Road. He pulled up a chair at the last table and took in the morning light that was stretching westward, illuminating the tops of the tall, manicured trees that lined Government Place Boulevard and setting aglow the fearsome white lion poised atop the pale yellow North Gate entry to the Government House grounds, home of the British Viceroy.

Seven days into his first leave, he'd learned to avoid outdoor dining due to the stench off the streets. But after last night's rain, the early morning air was clean and the sweet blended scent of petunia, marigold, cineraria, and violet wafted over his table from the large clay pots that lined the railing. Al fresco breakfast under a pure cobalt sky, he picked up a buzzing from the pots during the quiet between rumblings that rose from the street as the trolleys rolled past.

"Honeybees."

"Sir?" Tea, biscuits, and berries served with milk, cream, and a yellow ceramic beehive filled with gooey sweetness. He twirled the wooden dripper over his teacup, and the viscous amber liquid took its sweet time. He asked after Naresh, the regular waiter, and learned the man's daughter was to marry that afternoon.

While downcountry, his American colleagues split their time between drunk and hungover. Jack paced himself with The Boys, joining them for a rowdy dinner and an early show every other night. Otherwise he stepped out on his own to enjoy jazz ensembles over ginger beer at the Bengal Club or to catch a movie, nibbling a bag of fresh warmed cashews at the Roxy Cinema.

He befriended the wealthy White Russian couple who lived in the corner suite situated behind his new breakfast spot on the veranda. They taught him chess and cribbage, which he always lost. The wife was more adept at the games than the husband, a rotund gentleman with long meticulously coiffed gray hair styled in a swirl atop his balding pate, his thick handlebar mustache tipped with black dye and curled with wax over his jowly cheeks. Late evenings he held court in the library over a cadre of the bored, never seeming to notice his pale and powdered wife, a Rubenesque woman wrapped in silk and sporting one of variety of crystal tiaras, motioning Jack from across the room to unabashedly propose a mid-morning rendezvous.

At the gymnasium, he met a Brit named Danny who'd beaten the Nazis at the 1936 Olympics five years to the day before he lost a leg them in Tunisia. Danny worked in Colonial Army administration, swam regularly in the Great Eastern's pool, and was happy to teach Jack proper form. He joined Jack in the gymnasium for calisthenics, claiming exercise helped clear his mind. Danny explained his stutter. "Something I pih . . . pih . . . pih-icked up in Tu . . . Tunisia in trade for the leh . . . leh . . . leg." Predawn, they had the pool to themselves, and Jack swam without his patch. The mess above his eye seemed to put Danny more at ease with his own stutter.

Jack tried morning walks to explore the city, but each time he was assaulted by a confluence of abject poverty, garbage, carcasses, and incessant begging. After lunch, he practiced in one of the C-47 Skytrain flight simulators the US Army kept in a suite at the hotel, sometimes alongside a bleary-eyed colleague who'd just rolled out of bed. In the afternoons he'd read over green tea, newspapers and books he remembered Chloe talking about. He liked Ernest Hemingway the best. When he tried *Don Quixote* and thumbed through *Les Misérables*, he figured she must have been pulling his leg.

It was the twenty-first of December, Saint Thomas Day in the colony, and Jack tried a walk under a bright morning sun. In Dalhousie Square, he stopped to admire a massive red-and-white,

Byzantine-style building. The Charted Bank of India, Australia, and China. On a whim, he stepped inside and wired some money to Frank. As the clerk performed the transaction, Jack answered a question no one asked. "If I get whacked, the crows'll just divvy up my stuff, so why not keep it in the family, like them fat Russians?"

He grabbed the receipt, and as he was walking out, an idea struck like lightning. "S'cuse me. Can I get some paper and a pen?" He sat down and started a letter.

Dear Meyer . . .

* * *

At the 300 Club that evening, during the band's first break, the patrons broke out in song. "Silent Night." "Come All Ye Faithful." Jack nursed a pint while the packed house joined in the Christmas carols. Boris Lissanevitch, the White Russian owner of the nightclub, took to the microphone and announced that printed lyrics to a brand new song were being delivered to each table. A boy in a black fez bowed as he set a textured manila card next to Jack's ale. "White Christmas" was embossed in gold. Jack flipped the card to find verses penned in calligraphy with Indian ink.

The band settled in for the second set, and the leader grabbed the room's attention by rapidly tapping his microphone with a conductor's baton. He raised his arms, and on his first downstroke the entire room joined in song. The effect was marvelous. Jack closed his eyes and imagined Chloe in a crisp white dress, singing over the piano, but he couldn't get the image to fully form.

There was Emma, sitting on the edge of their bed at the Adderton place, sexy in her customized white nightie, a cigarette glowing on the end of that stupid art deco holder as she swirled ice in bourbon and recited a naughty limerick. The roar of the Dakota. Her puffy eyes filling with tears. If he'd stayed, would she have moved to the damn French hospital? If she did anyway, would she have been on duty that day? Would she be dead if he'd stayed? The chewy ale was buzzing his head, swirling melancholy between his ears. He tipped his head back to watch smoke spin into the ceiling fan turning slowly above him as the song entered its final verse.

It started snowing. A dozen of the black-fez boys were skipping between the tables, throwing white confetti into the air.

May your days be merry and bright

Someone nudged his foot.

"I see you've met Sasha!" Sharkey crashed into the empty chair next to him.

Jack peered under the table to find a six-foot snake slithering between his legs. It was Boris Lissanevitch's pet python.

Sharkey was blitzed, liquid. "Blackjack, I want you to meet someone." Standing over Sharkey's shoulder was a serious-looking Indian gentleman clad in a pristine, blue-silk ssherwani with gold buttons, over a pure-white dhoti trimmed in gold. On his head sat a golden peta adorned with stark-white ostrich feathers. "The maharaja." Sharkey bowed and stumbled.

Jack stood. "Glad to meet you."

"I have heard a great deal of your bravery and success over Burma and China, Captain Benoit. It is wonderful to have such formidable allies."

"Call me Jack."

The maharaja invited him to join his table.

"C'mon, Blackjack! Don't be a stick in the mud, like your usual . . . mud stick." Sharkey popped him in the shoulder, belched, and met the maharaja's eyes. "Certified . . . stick . . . in . . . mud."

Jack sat next to the host at the maharaja's table. Lieutenant His Highness Sri Sri Maharaja Jagatdipendra Narayan Bhup Bahadur, Maharaja of Cooch Behar, or *the Raj,* as the Boys called him. Under the British Suzerainty, he was the ruler of a princely estate that stretched more than four hundred miles from the Nepalese and Bhutanese borders in the north down below Calcutta, all the way to the Bay of Bengal. The Raj had held his reign since he was seven years old, when his father died. Educated at Cambridge, he cut a dashing and confident figure, pleasant to look at and charming in conversation.

"So you're a lieutenant and a prince." Jack sipped at a fresh pint. "How d'y'all make that work?" By the table's reaction, Jack figured his question was inappropriate, but he didn't care, and the Raj just laughed.

"It is a struggle, really, Captain. I wish to fight, but my duties in Cooch Behar pull me away from any sustained action."

An attendant offered Jack a cigarette.

"I served for some time in North Africa but was kept from the front lines. I'm sure you can understand."

Jack nodded over his pint.

"Under the circumstances, I felt it would be more productive, and more sincere, to shed the pretense and return to Behar to support the war locally, rather than push paper around a desk in Cairo."

"Makes sense to be where you can be the most use."

"Exactly, Captain Benoit." The Raj smiled. "I thought you might agree. Now that the Japanese have found success in Burma, we can expect more direct action against India. Calcutta, where we sit this very evening, is at risk. Calcutta supports the airlift from Upper Assam, and the loss of either position would mean the end for China, freeing the Japanese Army to engage India en masse."

Jack finished his ale, and a fresh pint appeared in its place. He was thinking about Sergeant Major Dahrala, that first night at the Lagoon Club. With the Japanese capture and occupation of Hong Kong, Malaya, and the Dutch East Indies, nearly thirty thousand Indian colonial regulars had been captured. He asked his host what he thought would happen, what the colonial prisoners would do, if the Japanese invaded India. The Raj was taken aback by the question, as this topic was never raised in public. Jack sensed his princely irritation, but the alcohol in his bloodstream prompted him to probe.

"I'm asking because from what I saw in Burma, the British brass tends to think pretty damn highly of their capabilities. No matter what the local people think or want, the Brits are gonna stay in control, just 'cause that's how it is. But they didn't, did they? Stay in control." Jack glugged beer and measured the Raj's reaction, which was silence. "Up in Dinjan, the US Army thinks pretty damn highly of itself, too. But what's happening is, CNAC, the *Chinese* company, is moving six times the tonnage into Kunming. Six friggin' times the Yanks, and with less equipment. Seems to me the *big brass*, whether they're here or in China or back in the States, they all might start considerin' what the locals think, and what the locals can do. What the locals *will* do."

The Raj narrowed his eyes, studying the brash American while his attendants fidgeted in their seats. He leaned in close. "We tend not to discuss the possibility of insurrection and rebellion in public, Captain

Benoit. An unswerving show of strength and resolve is necessary to maintain order. It is true, the independence movement may attempt to turn the circumstances of global war to its advantage. But there is no doubt in my mind that India would suffer greatly under Japanese influence, and even more so under Japanese control, whether it were to take the form of rule or protectorate. This is why the airlift is so critically important. We must keep China in play until the Americans can gather the strength necessary to threaten Japan from the east. If we do not keep China supplied, we must then imagine the possibility of a world in which the Japanese have enslaved everyone from Seoul to Karachi."

The Raj sipped his cocktail. "But enough of politics. For the next few hours there is nothing for us to do to support the Allied effort. Let us enjoy the remainder of the evening." He raised his glass. "To the Allies."

"To the Allies!"

"To India."

"To India!"

Jack clinked glasses with the Raj. He was imbibing significantly more than usual and feeling no pain. Here he was in India, approaching his twenty-first birthday and singing Christmas carols with a prince. He felt good, truly good, for the first time since he could remember. Sitting back behind a crooked grin, he soaked it all in. The gilded ornamentation, the white tablecloths, the crisply starched server under his velvet fez. The slow fans blended countless streams of smoke into a blue-gray mist that hung over the room. The band sounded great. He closed his eye and let his mind wander. The Raj was speaking, but Jack didn't hear the words, only the accent. A little bit Emma, a little bit Shu Hao. He opened his eye grinning, bringing the half-empty pint to his lips. Three people born thousands of miles apart. One white, one yellow, one brown. "Y'all sound the same."

The rest of the party was drinking Bengals, a lovely sunset of a drink that blended curacao, brandy, bitters, and pineapple juice. Jack tried one, but its subtleties were lost to his inebriation. "Tastes like sugar."

"Speaking of Bengals . . ." The Raj invited Jack and The Boys up north for a tiger hunt, and within minutes, it was decided they would all fly to Cooch Behar the following afternoon. Sharkey let out a whoop and ordered shots of rye for the table. The party agreed to meet at Dum Dum Airport, and one of the Raj's men excused himself to commence preparations. Around midnight, Jack stumbled out of the 300 Club, his head swimming. The air was cool, and he waved off the doorman, waved off the taxis, and headed toward the Maidan for a walk back to the hotel.

The Maidan, the massive park that held Calcutta's major cricket field and horse track, was glutted with policemen at night, so it was possible to traverse the grounds without interference from beggars. This was his first drunk in the city, and a few of the police officers he'd befriended during previous outings offered him assistance. Eventually he made it to the Great Eastern and plopped facedown on his bed.

The Raj and the bulk of his entourage departed for Cooch Behar early. That afternoon, two members of his staff accompanied Jack and The Boys on a Skytrain that would make a detour on its way to supply Dinjan, and the Americans suffered their hangovers during the turbulent two-hour flight. At Cooch Behar they were whisked to the palace in identical spotless Rolls Royce Wraiths, both sporting angelic hood ornaments made of solid gold. At the palace, each pilot was escorted to his own opulent guest room adorned with extravagant frescoes depicting Bengalese fauna and flora. Still hurting, Jack curled himself onto the massive down comforter and surveyed the ceiling with his good eye. In each corner, a ferocious tiger struck a different pose.

The evening's festivities commenced with the Gambhira and other traditional West Bengali dances, followed by a sumptuous feast of unimaginable proportions. Luscious fruits, curried fish and vegetables, lamb biryani, and other delicacies covered tables adorned with exotic flowers.

A young girl with a drop nose ring presented Jack with a small bowl. "Violet, if you please, sir."
He picked out the delicate flower and placed it on his tongue, just as she had pantomimed. It was sweet and floral, as though he was tasting a scent.

"Candied." She held a small vacant space between her thumb and forefinger. "Just a little."

"Thank you."

"The sandesh is something to try after the meal," she recommended. "I hope it will please you."

The best aged French wines flowed, and The Boys' behavior flowed with it. Jack was embarrassed by the way they harassed the female attendants and dancing girls. The Raj wasn't drinking, and when Jack asked him why not, the maharaja laughed, explaining he never consumed alcohol and was a strict vegetarian. The Bengals that he and his entourage consumed at Boris Lissanevitch's 300 Club were free of alcohol.

The following day the flyers were taken on a two-hour drive west to the hunt's base camp, and the party settled in for dinner. It was clear to Jack that all of this couldn't have just started up the day before. In fact, preparations had begun a full week earlier, well before the palace received word there would be visitors arriving from Calcutta. The Raj had hoped to invite some flyers up for a hunt, so the plan had been set in motion in anticipation of acceptance.

Tigers hunt for prey across vast territories, prowling in long, circuitous routes through jungle terrain and tall grasses. Tiger hunters locate their prey by using live bait tied to trees near the big cats' suspected routes. A bait kill signals close proximity of a tiger, and hundreds of people who participate in the hunt quickly converge on the location. As luck would have it, two of the six baited bison were killed. One of the slain beasts lay eight miles west of the base camp. The other, another two miles further west.

The hunt commenced at daybreak on a scale of endeavor that dwarfed the spectacle of the welcome-feast at the palace. With bellies full from a predawn breakfast, the Americans were taken west.

Centered on the site of the west-most bait kill, a mass of *beaters* formed a bowed line, a crescent moon of men and boys that stretched north-to-south for more than a quarter mile. Just past dawn, they began a steady march into browning grass that was taller than the tallest man, most of them banging wood blocks with sticks, and some carrying spears and shouting. They paced forward, maintaining the crescent moon formation in an effort to drive two tigers due east toward a wide nala, a river wash that was mostly dry this time of year.

Along the eastern bank of the nala stood dozens of *stoppers*, beaters who would bang on logs and drums to turn an on-coming beast either upstream or downstream along the wash. Cow bells would signal a tiger sighting at the turn.

The flyers rode Asiatic elephants from base camp to the nala, straddling each graceful beast behind her mahout. Three miles trekked, and they were split into two pairs along the wash. Jack and

Hugh took a left turn to head south along the bank. Pete and Sharkey, both terribly hungover and barely functioning, headed north. A quarter mile downstream, Hugh hopped off with his gun bearer at the first tree stand. Jack continued and took his perch some two hundred yards further downstream. As he climbed a banyan tree to the stand, he heard the beaters in the distance, perhaps only a mile or so to the northwest.

Jack stood with his gun bearer, each of them holding one of two loaded .45 caliber double-barrel rifles. Bolt-action carbines were too slow for tigers. In the time it would take to reload, a missed shot could quickly turn the tables on the hunter. Jack had his Colt 1911 holstered on his hip.

The beaters were closing the distance. "About a half mile, sir." Jack figured the bearer was around fifteen years old, so he had maybe five years on the boy.

The racket from the west grew steadily louder, then a slow beat started in the north. Moments later, they heard a cow bell. A tiger was in the nala.

Jack's adrenaline rose in a way he hadn't felt since combat, and he eased it down just the same with a couple deep breaths. A bit of the Raj's speech at the banquet raced through his mind. How these man-eaters would attack villagers and wreak havoc on their herds of goats and sheep. A shot rang out. It was close. The gun bearer pointed. "From your partner's tree stand."

Jack checked the gun's load, snapped it closed, and cocked both hammers. He and the bearer focused on the nala to the north, searching for movement. The bearer tapped his arm and pointed to the far bank some eighty yards upstream. He whispered, "There!"

It was the most stirring sight Jack had ever witnessed, this magnificent orange and black tiger cantering across his field of vision. As he trained the gun's notch sight on his target, he was struck by just how fast this massive beast was moving, even at a canter. Instinctively, he swung the barrel like a shotgun on a wood duck and gently squeezed the trigger. The recoil was unexpectedly violent. He regained his footing as the tiger fell and rolled, raising a cloud of dust. It climbed to its feet and shook its coat.

"Again! Again!" the bearer pleaded. "Shoot!"

The tiger turned his head in the direction of the voice. Panting hard, he stared directly at them, snarled and charged as Jack struggled to get the bead on the beast. His line was nearly head-on and down, and he gave it his best. The tiger lost his footing in the sandy wash some forty yards out, tumbling headfirst into a shallow waterhole.

The bearer pressed the second rifle against his arm. "Please, sir. Please!" The wet, muddy cat rose instantly and scrambled out of the hole to bound toward the tree with a noticeable limp. He closed to the east embankment in just a half dozen jumps where he leaped and clawed his way over the lip. Just two more bounds brought him to the base of the tree, where he leapt at his antagonists. Jack had cocked the second weapon, but there was no time to shoulder it properly. As the massive cat stretched toward him, Jack shot from the hip. The recoil tore the gun from his hands, propelling it back and out of the tree stand, and dislocating his trigger finger as it went.

The bearer had been frantically reloading the first rifle when the tiger's face slammed into the branch that supported the platform, rocking its occupants. He cried out as the beast's claws sliced into the platform as he fell backward, sliding off to land on his back with a thud.

Jack's heart raced as he unholstered his sidearm and took a deep breath. With shaking hands, the bearer reloaded the first rifle, its companion lying twelve feet below. He hurriedly finished and pressed it toward Jack, who was leaning over the edge, the Colt in his left hand and trained on the menace. He marveled at the beauty of this animal. It looked nothing like the frescoes painted on the palace walls, and he couldn't have invented this sight, not in his wildest dreams. He flashed back to Coulee Galleque, in a different grand tree, looking down on the most beautiful creature he'd ever seen. That day, he'd saved it. Today, he killed it.

"Shoot, sir, shoot!" It took some effort to convince the bearer that the tiger was no longer a threat, and they climbed down to survey the prize. Jack raised the tiger's heavy head. He'd shot it directly in the eye. A tear welled in his own as he laid the big cat's head down.

Back at the base camp, there was a massive celebration. This tiger was the oldest male in the region, and a known man-killer. He'd recently run through a village, snatched a toddler by the shoulder and disappeared into the jungle without breaking stride. He was so large, it took fourteen men to pole him back to camp. A second tiger had run up the nala northward, but neither Pete nor Sharkey were quick enough to trigger a shot on that speedy, fortunate cat.

Jack was of two minds regarding the tiger. He'd needed to be stopped, to be sure. But tigers had lived in the jungle long before people started burning it down to grow crops and graze livestock. The tiger was the menace because that's where people placed the blame, and people could enforce their opinion with more powerful weapons.

Jack had learned something of the Indian caste system from Shu Hao, and now he could really see it in action, the physical divides between people in camp. Here in West Bengal it wasn't white over black like in the States, or yellow or white over brown, like in Burma. It was brown over brown. He wasn't feeling the joy, and at the dinner he snapped at the Raj. "People just make up whatever shit they want. Race. Religion. Just spout some bullshit to justify taking whatever they damn well want from other people, from nature."

He started off on a walk, but his bearer quickly caught him, pulling on his sleeve. "Too dangerous."

Jack took a series of deep breaths. "I never asked your name."

"Shudra."

"What's it mean?"

The boy looked at his feet. "It means lowest caste . . . but for na chhoone yogy."

"What the hell is that?"

"The untouchables."

Jack reached into a cargo pocket. He pulled out a wad of rupees and slapped the whole mess into the boy's hand. "So, Shudra, how 'bout you jump a train and get the hell outta here?"

The boy's eyes were wide as saucers as he stared at the cash. "I cannot . . ."

"And get yourself a new friggin' name while you're at it."

As they returned to the Raj's campfire, he tried to put on a good face as thanks and adulation streamed from the natives. They were extremely grateful, and proud to have helped. They chanted.

Mahaan shikaaree
Andhere baagh ka hatyaara

In song, Jack was now a great tiger hunter, having killed the terrible *Dark One,* as this cat was known from Cooch Behar to Siliguri, for both his ferocity and his extraordinary, thick black stripes. It was a grand party. The Boys were the only imbibers, but they did their best to pick up the Hindus' slack.

* * *

Back at the Great Eastern swimming pool, Danny had Jack executing a passable double flip off the high platform. Jack pulled himself up the pool ladder, pleased with himself. The pair agreed to visit the 300 Club that evening. Danny was engaged to a local girl, a sweet nurse named Rohini who bore a large birthmark on her left cheek and wore a tiny diamond stud in her nose, a gift from her fiancé. The couple had been conspiring to set Jack up with Rohini's friend, Christie, a South African nurse. When presented with this idea, Jack found himself enveloped by such a fog of melancholy that he declined. "Maybe next time."

* * *

Jack hugged his friend. "You look well rested."

Shu Hao had spent his leave in China. "I was in the country, up a ways north with my aunt and cousins. The country is good for one's spirit. Turning the soil. Feeding the pigs. It had been such a long time." He smiled under a faraway look. "We raised a community barn. Yes, I *am* refreshed and ready for business."

When Shu Hao asked Jack about his leave, he related only the story of "White Christmas" at the 300 Club.

Jack was assigned a newbie copilot, James Christopher Swenson, who was even smaller than Jack and had a high-pitched voice. Swenson wore an outsized golden crucifix around his thin neck and introduced himself by his initials, so The Boys tagged him with the obvious nickname.

During their first layover in Kunming, Jack pulled a Jeep from the motor pool and drove to Yunnan-yi, where he handed John McClintock two thousand US dollars. "Test it out. You get the bonds, I'll collect them next trip."

McClintock thumbed the cash, his bushy eyebrows pushing altitude. "You trust me with all this?"

"It's not like there's somewhere you can hide."

Back in Dinjan, Jack stitched a cloth pouch inside the back of his bomber jacket. He'd earned a hero's status and a reputation at CNAC for clean flights, so the inspectors who boarded his planes always left him alone. The next time he was in Kunming, he headed to the motor pool.

"Hey, Captain, do you mind if I tag along?" It was JC, double-timing to keep up.

"I don't think where I'm goin' is where you want to be."

"Don't be too sure. C'mon, show me around some, sir."

"I'm going to a whorehouse, JC." That freed up his day.

He and McClintock went to the same duck joint, and McClintock pushed an envelope across the table, which Jack tucked into his jacket's pouch. "Aren't you gonna count 'em?"

Jack figured no one would screw him on the first round. It would threaten the whole scheme. "Next time."

Stuffed with dumplings and duck, McClintock lit a cigarette and slid the pack across the table. "Oh, yeah. So still don't smoke?"

"Never developed a taste for it."

"Keeps the stench out of my nose. At least some of it. Remember Toungoo?"

"At least some of it."

"Foul place. Like living in shit. Seems like a long time ago, and it's been what, just about a year now? Crazy."

"Crazy."

Jack dropped McClintock at the hostel near Yunnan-yi and ground the Jeep into gear to head back to Wujiaba. McClintock shouted. "Almost forgot. Colonel Moreland wants to see you."

"Moreland? What the hell does the army want to see me for?"

"He has your kill bonuses, from Chiang."

"I have contraband on my back, Scratchy."

"You think they're gonna pat you down, Captain? The colonel'll make you listen to some blowhard speech, then he'll hand you a check. You'll be outta there lickety-split."

McClintock was right about Moreland. After thanking Jack *on behalf of the American people*, the colonel waxed poetic for a quarter hour on the efficiency and effectiveness of the army operations at Yunnan-yi. "But I digress." The colonel snapped his fingers, and a lieutenant crossed the room carrying two boxes. "Fetch Major Broomfield." He opened the larger of the two boxes and extracted three medals, each attached to a different-colored ribbon. He laid them in a row on a small table.

"The Generalissimo and Madame Chiang asked that we ensure you receive these, along with this letter." He placed a faint-pink envelope next to the medals and cleared his throat, silently reading something scrawled on an index card. "Make yourself comfortable. Take off your jacket."

"Thanks, I'm good."

"Okay, then. This award on the left is the Chinese General Air Force Medal. In the middle here is a Ten Star Wing, presented by the Chinese Air Force to you as a double ace, for your eleven confirmed air combat kills in the Second Sino-Japanese War." The colonel set the index card on the table and raised each of the first two medals over Jack's head. He picked the card up and resumed.

"This third award is rarely bestowed and has, for the first time, been awarded by China to foreign military support, including Colonel Chennault and select members of the American Volunteer Group." He picked up the third medal by its red-and-white ribbon. A white, eight-point star was set atop a gold, eight-point star background. The colonel hung it around Jack's neck and returned to his index card. "On behalf of the Chinese people, and in the interest of freedom from aggression and oppression everywhere, Generalissimo Chiang Kai-shek is pleased to present Captain Jack Benoit of the American Volunteer Group with this highest of honors, the Order of Cloud and Banner with Grand Cordon."

He picked up the pink envelope. "May I?" He pulled out the letter to read aloud.

Dear Flight Leader Benoit,

I had the privilege to present you with the Order of Renaissance and Honour following the unhappy circumstance of your crash while protecting Kunming. On the 4th of July, we held a banquet in honor of the AVG, known now to all the world as the Flying Tigers, and to be forever remembered by me as my Angels. To my sadness, you were unable to attend this event. Therefore, I have entrusted the enclosures to the US Commandant of the Yunnan-yi Airfield, so that they may be delivered to you safely and as soon as possible.

The entirety of the AVG has been awarded the General Air Force Medal, an expression of Generalissimo Chiang Kai-shek's appreciation for your gallant efforts in defense of our beloved China.

You are one of only six pilots in the history of our great nation to be awarded the Ten Star Wing Medal.

Nine foreigners have been presented with the Order of the Cloud and Banner, and you are one of two members of the AVG to receive the Order 2nd Grade, Grand Cordon.

We hope you will accept these tokens of our esteem with pride and the knowledge that China and its people will be forever in your debt.

We have also included payment of your bonuses. As a double ace with fourteen confirmed enemy aircraft destroyed, please accept this check for seven thousand United States dollars and our enduring gratitude.

Go well my Angel, Captain Benoit.

Respectfully yours,

Madame Chiang Kai-shek

Moreland tucked the letter and the check back into the envelope and set it on the table. He lifted the lid of the second, smaller box, and extracted its contents. "This is the Medal of Merit." As he placed the award around Jack's neck, the four medals clanked. "Chief of Staff, General George C. Marshall made the recommendation himself, and President Roosevelt signed the proclamation in September. Congratulations, Mr. Benoit. You have just received the highest honor that may be bestowed upon an American civilian." Moreland stepped back and saluted. Jack returned it. He plucked up the medal and held it away for a good look. A golden eagle perched on a pedestal inscribed with the words *Novus ordo seclorum* set atop a blue ring filled with white stars.

"You did a fantastic job, Jack, and now, the US Army has the matter in hand. Tell me, how do you like flying The Hump?"

They were discussing the recent Japanese attacks on Dinjan when a British major entered the room. With some ceremony, this Major Broomfield presented Jack with the Distinguished Flying Cross, an ornate silver medallion on a purple-and-white striped ribbon that clanked against the others already piled on his chest. "For valor, courage, and devotion to duty with the American Volunteer Group in the Burma theatre, alongside 67 Squadron and 113 Squadron of the Royal Air Force. The major clicked his heels and saluted. Jack returned the salute, clickless.

Colonel Moreland lit his pipe. "You're quite a sight, Mister Benoit."

Jack ignored the inherent slight in the colonel's manner of addressing him and shook off the struck-match reminder of his crash. He tucked the medals back into their boxes.

"Would make for a pretty successful Mardi Gras."

There was hand-shaking, back-slapping, congratulations, and, "Good shows!" as he traversed the hallways with three boxes, five medals, a thank-you note from Madame Chiang, a check for seven grand, and close to four thousand dollars of contraband Chinese bonds stuffed down the back of his jacket.

* * *

Jack took the same room at the Great Eastern and proceeded with haste to the Bank of China, where he was escorted into a small private room. The banker deposited Chiang's check, then completed the bond transaction. Jack asked the banker to exchange the yuan for US dollars, so he walked out the door with a new bankbook, the ledger reading 10,628.43 USD.

The next morning, he found a card under his door announcing he had mail at the front desk. There was both a large box postmarked Cooch Behar and a letter postmarked New York. He slid the letter into a pocket and asked the bellman to deliver the box to his room. Later, he opened the box to find the Dark One's skin. The tiger's eyes had been replaced with large polished carnelians, painted with black, cat-eye pupils. The pelt was accompanied by two gold-embossed envelopes and a wooden plaque featuring a photo of the American flyers, the Raj and members of his staff, and Jack's bearer, Shudra. Behind them, the Dark One hung from a pole, stretching nearly the width of the photo. A golden tag on the plaque read:

The Dark One
taken by
Captain Jack "Blackjack" Benoit
23 December 1942

Inside an envelope was a handwritten note.

Dear Captain Benoit,

The enclosures are sent to you in appreciation of your heroic taking of the Dark One, the fierce tiger that had ravaged the villages of northern West Bengal for so many years.

Sincerely, and with the utmost gratitude,

His Highness Sri Sri Maharaja Jagatdipendra Narayan Bhup Bahadur, Maharaja of Cooch Behar

The other envelope held the photograph he'd requested before leaving Cooch Behar, a snapshot of him and Shudra. He regretted what he'd said to the boy and tucked the snapshot into his breast pocket. He regretted how rude he was to the Raj. He penciled Frank and Odette's address on a slip of paper and dialed the front desk.

The letter from New York confirmed Meyer Lansky's enthusiasm for the bonds. He proposed they continue their communications by telegraph instead of letter to expedite discussions. Because the contents of their telegraphs would be exposed to outsiders, it would be necessary to speak in code, and he proposed a cipher. Kunming would be Kalamazoo. Dinjan would be Denver. Calcutta would be California. Dollar amounts would be represented by silverware, a steak knife representing a thousand dollars, and so on. It seemed a little overdone to Jack, but he could write in code. He'd just have to make sure he wrote it down right, and Lansky had even thought of that, recommending Jack decipher his own messages to check the accuracy before sending them.

He and Lansky swapped telegrams during the remainder of Jack's leave, Lansky asking questions and Jack answering the best he could. Lansky was thrilled to hear of the successful test run. Still, he wanted to engage a test run with his own money in advance of a large transaction. Jack had hoped for a quicker turnaround, but he knew he'd have to work the China side in conversations with McClintock anyway. Lansky wasn't so concerned about the nature of the transaction. He trusted Jack's word and understood a larger sum would work no differently than the successful test run. What he didn't trust was the Australian and Chinese involvement in the supply. If Jack was tricked into buying forged documents, he'd be arrested at the bank in Calcutta, and Lansky would be out a lot of money.

31

THE LAST RUN

JANUARY 1943

Four hard weeks later and Jack was downcountry again, swimming with Danny, playing chess with the fat Russians, enjoying jazz at the 300 Club and the Bengal Club, and trading telegrams with his friend in New York. As requested, he provided Lansky with the names of the bondholders, along with other identifying information. The best Lansky could do was try to verify the accuracy of business and educational claims, this one had owned a factory in Shanghai, that one had sent a child to Princeton. The sketchy details checked out, but that didn't preclude the risk of fraud.

Jack tired of the handwringing and called an end to the discussion.

```
Either do it or don't. I will sell 15 steak knives
in Kalamazoo. Buyer needs more. In or out?
```

The morning of his return to Dinjan, he received another telegram.

```
My other suppliers will not ship stock. I have
shipped 120 steak knives from my inventory to
California warehouse. M.L.
```

Jack made a stop at the bank on his way to Dum Dum Airport then hopped a transport north.

* * *

The Japanese had raided the base at Dinjan twice during his leave. Dozens were killed and more were injured, with two administrative buildings and a hangar damaged. Four C-47s were destroyed on the ground, but US Army Warhawk drivers downed three Japanese Nates and a Sally. The runways were badly beaten, and engineers were blading them smooth when Jack's transport landed.

He carried a hefty wad of cash, 135 US thousand-dollar bills and nine hundreds. He confirmed the deal with McClintock in Kunming during his next run, and McClintock assured him the bearer bonds would be delivered in ten-thousand-yuan denominations. At the agreed exchange rate, Jack would return to Dinjan with 189 of bonds, a stack of paper over an inch thick. If the bonds were delivered in smaller denominations, he wouldn't be able to fit them all in his pouch.

He was training a new copilot, an eager beaver named Billy Hebert. Jack noted his accent. "Do I hear the Delta in there? I knew some Heberts back in Louisiana."

"Yes, sir. Houma, sir."

"Why aren't you in the army?"

"I was, Captain. Flew recon over the Caribbean for 'bout a year. Then I busted up a knee somethin' awful, and they wouldn't let me fly no more. I caught wind of this slick operation, and here I am."

"How'd you bust up your knee?"

"Fell down some stairs, sir."

"Drunk?"

"No, sir, I don't drink."

Jack laughed as he pushed the throttle forward. "Well, Billy, you'll fit right in."

When they came down The Hump on the China side, ground control informed them that bogeys had been sighted along the gorges. Fortunately, they brought the C-53 Dakota in without incident. Jack had Billy land it, and the trainee did well.

He made an excuse for leaving in a hurry. Sweating into the money on his back, he was eager to get this done. The rendezvous was set at the home of a relative of one of the bondholders on the far west end of Kunming. Jack was the last to arrive and sensed some serious tension as he entered the house.

A small, older woman bowed low and waved for him to follow her as she limped on feet crippled from binding to the dining room where an older businessman in an impeccably tailored suit sat at the head of the table. A tough in aviator sunglasses and a fine dark suit stood over the businessman's shoulder, and a little man wearing thick round spectacles was seated to his right. McClintock sat between the bespectacled accountant and a rough-looking white guy with beard stubble who Jack figured was one of the Australian bond wranglers. A second white guy was off to the side, leaning on a buffet table. The room was thick with cigarette smoke. The Chinese tough sent the old woman to the kitchen for tea, and the men got down to business.

McClintock opened the dialogue. It was simple. All they needed to do was count. Jack pulled off his leather jacket and extracted the envelopes of cash. The accountant reached into his briefcase and placed the stack of bonds on the table. The guy at the buffet motioned to McClintock, and they both left the room. The Chinese tough shifted his weight.

McClintock had cut a deal with the Aussies for a 3% finder's fee on the gross investment and cut the same deal for himself with Jack. Jack had agreed a 10% fee with Lansky, so he, himself, would net a return of 4% off the mobster's stake. The Aussie's would get $4,300 off the total $135,000 investment, as would McClintock.

McClintock looked pale when he reentered the dining room and grabbed Jack's elbow. "A word, Captain." The Chinese muscle watched them walk into the kitchen. "The Aussies want 10%." Jack looked over his friend's shoulder into the dining room. "Look, they're saying they have a gang ready to jump the place if we don't cooperate." Jack stepped back, crossed his arms, and studied his friend, wondering, *Is Scratchy tryin' to fuck me?* He concluded that, no, he wasn't that stupid.

"Dammit, Captain. Let's just give it to 'em. There'll be plenty left over."

"They're bluffing."

"I don't know. These guys are big in town, you know? Smuggling. Opium. Girls. I think they mean it."

Jack nodded. "Let's find out."

He pulled his Colt from the back of his belt and handed it McClintock. "When I make the move, you put that on the Chinese tough. *Yes,* the bodyguard. And make sure he sees it." He pulled a second Colt from his belt and cocked it, grabbed the flatiron off the stove, and strode into the dining room where he smashed the iron against the back of the seated Aussie's skull. As the man' head hit the table, Jack trained his pistol on the other Aussie's chest. The businessman's bodyguard reached into his suit jacket.

McClintock yelled, pointing the gun at the Chinese tough. "Bié dòng! Bié dòng!"

"Scratchy, tell the businessman what's going on."

Using a hash of broken Mandarin and English, McClintock did his best to communicate the situation to the bondholder and his associates. The Aussies were working a double cross, but everything was under control. The businessman nodded and motioned for his bodyguard to stand down.

Jack motioned to McClintock. "Get his gun." McClintock crossed the room and patted down the second Aussie. He pulled a holstered revolver from under the man's jacket. The Aussie Jack had cracked in the skull was on the floor. He kicked the heap. "This one, too." Once the Aussies' guns were collected, Jack told McClintock to set them in front of the bodyguard. "Ask him if we're good."

The businessman raised a palm and answered in perfect English. "Yes, yes. We are fine. You handled the situation admirably. However, I must question your choice of business associates." The Aussie on the floor moaned and tried to sit up. Jack kicked him in the face, laying him out cold.

McClintock shared what the conscious Aussie had said in the kitchen. The businessman spoke in Mandarin to his bodyguard, who pulled a gun and pressed it against the Aussie's temple. "Let us hear your plan," the businessman said calmly. The Aussie was trembling, claiming it was all a bluff. The businessman continued. "Either you lied to Mr. McClintock earlier when you said there would be an ambush, or else you are lying to all of us right now. So all we know for certain is that you are a liar. Therefore, we know you do not value the truth. But we will find something you do value, so that we may have the truth." He nodded to the tough, who pistol-whipped the guy then pulled a straight razor, placing the blade under his nose. "We will remove appendages until we are satisfied you have overcome your propensity for dishonesty."

McClintock gaped at Jack. The Aussie with the knife to his nose pissed his pants. The businessman tsked. "Pity. Perhaps we will solve that problem in due time." He nodded to the goon, who promptly sliced off an earlobe.

The businessman instructed his accountant to recommence the count. Two sliced nostrils later, and the bondholder was satisfied the disruption to the meeting was in fact a bluff. He signaled his man to stand down. The small woman hobbled into the room to attend to the Aussie's bleeding parts, followed by a boy with a mop and bucket.

"You are fortunate to have retained your most valued appendages. There is a shelf in my office where your testicles would have resided in a jar." The accountant peeled off his glasses and nodded. The businessman rose from the table. "Mr. McClintock, it seems our business is concluded satisfactorily. We shall take our leave."

He made a slight bow toward Jack, who reciprocated. "You mind me askin', what're you gonna do with the money?"

"Build a grain mill."

* * *

In the Jeep, McClintock pounded the dash. "That was crazy! Hot damn! I need a drink."

"I'm droppin' you and drivin' back to Wujiaba to get some shut-eye. I gotta get out of here with this paper." He ground a gear as he shifted the Jeep. "It ain't done yet."

They rode for some time before McClintock broke the silence. "So, seems there's an extra 3% . . ."

"Don't go there."

"A two way spli . . ."

Jack cut him off. "Count yourself lucky I'm not cuttin' you out altogether! Do you have any idea how bad that could have gone back there?"

"No worse than what goes on up there!" McClintock pointed to the sky.

"We didn't invite the Japs, Scratchy. But you invited those dimwits. Be happy you're still getting anythin'." Jack ground the gears again and muttered under his breath.

* * *

He was sitting on the branch where the rope was tied, swinging his legs as the angel below raised a bourbon to her lips. She looked up with sunshine in her eyes, sunshine that turned a fiery red as she transformed into a snarling orange beast. Roaring, she lunged, baring shark teeth, yellow streams of light shooting out her mouth and eyes. He followed the streams into the sky where Orion held his bow. "Nutty dreams."

He and Billy got their preflight briefing in the Wujiaba ready room. "There's been a lot of Jap radio traffic. Likely to fill the skies either here or over there."

"Or both."

Billy looked nervous as they headed to the plane, and Jack wasn't thrilled with the payload they were carrying. In addition to three tons of tin, a half dozen British brass were bumming a ride, and here he had more than $200,000 of contraband stuffed down the back of his jacket. As the crew finished the instrument check, their passengers embarked.

"Well, gentlemen. It looks like we're in good hands this afternoon." It was Major Broomfield. Half an hour into the flight, the major approached the cockpit.

Jack gave Billy the thumb. "Have a seat."

"Appreciate it, really." The visitor gave the panel a once-over. "Never flown one of these. How do you like it?"

"It's not a Tomahawk, that's for sure. But it's solid equipment. A little sluggish haulin' anything over three tons. So, you fly?"

"Did do." The major scanned the horizon. "Drove Spitfires during the Blitz, then Tomahawks in North Africa. They dusted me off last summer for General Wavell's staff. I was his China liaison for the air wing but wasn't there long before Stillwell was handed the Asian theater in August. I've been the British attaché to Stillwell since then."

Jack figured he'd give it a shot. "When you were in Africa, did you know a flyer named Simpson? Alfred Simpson."

"Alfie! Did you know Alfie?"

"I don't. Someone . . . someone in Burma mentioned his name. Heard he flew in Africa. Just thought I'd ask."

* * *

When Emma had finally come north to Kunming, the pair picked up where they'd left things in Rangoon, and Jack asked about what Oley Olson had told him. That Emma was married.

"It's hard to divorce someone who's fighting in the desert while you're knee-deep in gore five thousand miles away. My husband, Major Alfred James Simpson III, was a chronic philanderer. He had a tidy little arrangement with another officer's wife in Delhi. Wasn't one to turn away the casual opportunities, either, which were plentiful." They'd grown apart. "Just as well. What romance we did have died early. Can't say I blame him for looking elsewhere, really. It was fine by me." She paused, looking a little misty. "But I was dead inside, there in Delhi. No true friends. Just going along, getting along. So, I thought to make a change, make myself useful. Hopped a transport to China."

"So no divorce."

"Didn't think about it, really. Still don't. What's the point? I have no intention of marrying again. God, why would I?" She lit a smoke and took a deep draw. "I suppose after the war, assuming everyone makes it to the end, we'll tidy things up." She looked sideways at him. "Would that work for you?"

Jack squinted at her. "You don't need to be . . ."

"Facetious?"

"Yeah."

"No, Jack, I don't." She snuffed the butt. "You don't deserve that."

"I think I deserve you."

"All of me?"

"Bits and pieces, anyway."

"See any bits or pieces you deserve right now?"

* * *

The major waxed nostalgic. "Alfie and I came up together. He was my best friend."

"Was?"

"Oh, I supposed you knew. Alfie was killed over Gazala, back in March."

Jack pictured Emma on the tarmac. Turns out she was single at the time. "So, Africa. What was it like, in a P-40 tangling with Messerschmitts?"

The major's gregarious nature wasn't a surprise. Ask brass a question, and you're guaranteed a good five to ten minutes of answer. "Men thoroughly enamored with their slight opinions," as Emma had put it.

"That afternoon we flew into a wasp nest. Must have been six to one against. We knocked down eight Kraut 109s during the tangle. Alfie scored three before they blew his wings out from under him. I had the bastard in my sight but lit him up too late to spare Alfie. I was his wingman, you know."

"No, I didn't."

"More often than not, I was his wingman on leave, too, if you catch my drift."

"What drift is that?"

"Alfie was quite popular with the ladies. I remember a particular leave in Cairo. Birds were lined up. Had him completely surrounded, entranced as he waxed poetic at the bar." Broomfield chuckled. "Alfie was tall, some six three. Could hardly squeeze into his Tomahawk. That night, I'll always remember it, from across the room he looked like an orchid in a flowerpot made of girls."

The major continued, but Jack drifted into Emma's eyes. Sweet Cheeks, blown to bits by a damn Jap. The Hump was growing on the horizon, and Billy tapped the major out of his seat. Jack mumbled, "Listening to that man is friggin' exhausting."

At altitude they iced up thick, but the turbulence was manageable. On the way down, the radioman opened a channel to base and learned it was under attack. They were instructed to divert to the north and circle.

The crew monitored the radio for close to an hour before the all-clear was given. Fuel was getting low, but they were only thirty minutes out. Jack was banking into approach when the ground operator shouted, "The Japs are back at it! A second wave is fifty miles out. Incoming traffic, divert. I repeat, incoming traffic, divert north!" They escaped detection by the approaching enemy and cleared the airspace with their fuel gauge bouncing on empty. Billy switched to auxiliary fuel, which was estimated to last thirty minutes.

Twenty minutes later, ground control confirmed the second wave of attack was still engaged. The sun had dropped behind the northwest mountain horizon, which meant two things. The Japs would bug out soon, and if the Dakota held this pattern much longer, they'd be ditching in the dark.

The successive raids had hit the base hard. As Jack banked the Dakota toward the runway, he and Billy saw the inferno that had been a fuel truck. The power station at the edge of the base was burning and throwing electrical sparks into the night sky. Ground crew lined the pocked runway with Jeeps, lighting it with headlamps. They had tossed flares into the bomb craters so Jack could pick a safe line. At 1500 feet the Dakota's port engine sputtered and quit. Billy grabbed the copilot's wheel to help combat the yaw. Then, just before the wheels touched down, the starboard engine died. The port landing gear clipped a crater, snapping like a toothpick, and the port wing sliced into the muddy ground, shearing it from the fuselage. The plane skated a hundred yards on its belly. Fortunately, no fuel meant no fire. The cargo held, but the passengers got pretty banged up. Whipsawed in their harnesses, three of the men suffered fractured clavicles, including the pilot. Adrenaline suppressed his pain until he stepped into a Jeep. Major Bloomfield reached in and shook his hand. "Thanks for the lift."

His shoulder ached, and the sharp pain in his neck was exceeded only by the stabbing behind his empty eye socket. It wasn't until he stepped into the infirmary that he remembered the inch-thick stack of paper stuffed down the back of his jacket. He shrugged off the nurse who proposed cutting him out of his bomber jacket. Peeling it off himself meant excruciating pain, then he refused to give it up to the nurse, keeping it next to him on the exam table. The infirmary didn't have an X-ray machine, but the doc surmised he'd fractured the same collarbone that had broken when he was shot down over Kunming, and he'd probably dislocated the same shoulder, but it had popped back into the socket.

The ride to the tea plantation was a lot bumpier with his arm in a sling. Plus, the aspirin powder he'd taken was doing nothing for his head. He was scheduled for a morning transport to the Calcutta hospital.

"Exciting day."

"Not sure I'm in the market for more excitement, Shu Hao. Did they kill anybody?"

"Not a one." Shu Hao studied his friend's face. "Perhaps it's time you had some peace."

"You mean quit?" Jack rolled to his side, grunting through the pain. Shu Hao propped his friend's arm up with a pillow. "I'll give it some thought downcountry."

Jack couldn't sleep for the pain behind his eye and the throbbing in his shoulder. He made tea and packed his duffle, cleaning out his footlocker. That morning, Shu Hao noted the overstuffed bag.

"Someone's made a decision."

"Maybe."

"A good traveler has no fixed plans and is not intent on arriving."

"Confucius?"

"Lao Tzu." Shu Hao smiled. "Breakfast?"

***

Jack set his duffle on the bed of Room 303 and looked out the window at the Government House grounds. His favorite view in Calcutta. The base doctor got it right. His collarbone suffered two fractures, and his shoulder joint was swollen stiff. He was to wear a sling that fastened to his torso for the next four weeks. The banks were closed for the day, so the transaction would have to wait. He winced as he unbuckled his duffle and was surprised to find a parcel wrapped in brown paper lying on top of his clothes. He unwrapped a homemade book, its pages bound with looped twine. The linen cover was decorated with flowers in watercolor. The title was painted in black ink.

Tao Te Ching

Inside he found the following inscription:

**Translated by Shu Hao
for his friend Jack Benoit
January 1943**

When he woke, the pain behind his eye socket was so bad that he skipped calisthenics and swimming, but the banking went smoothly. In a series of transactions, he cashed the bonds for yuan, converted the yuan to dollars, and wired Lansky's proceeds to an account at Chase National Bank in New York. Including the 3% windfall from what was supposed to have been the Aussies' fee, the deposit totaled $199,728.20, resulting in an 85% profit for Lansky. Having cleared his own transaction, including his fee, Jack's sixteen grand was now $32,490.10. The little bag of rupees he had stored in the Great Eastern safe was worth at least two grand, and he still had about six hundred bucks in his account back in New York. With the couple hundred folded in his pocket, Jack Benoit walked out of the Calcutta branch of the Bank of China worth nearly forty thousand dollars.

He telegraphed word of the wire transfer to Lansky, then lunched alone on the hotel's veranda, ordering a Bengal in hopes of easing the pain behind his eye. In Dinjan, he'd refused any painkillers stronger than aspirin powder, and the aspirin wasn't doing the trick. Two of the potent drinks and a belly full of bacon and eggs later, he felt some relief while pondering his future. Back home, he could buy a house for three or four grand. Another grand for a nice ride, maybe a motorcycle, too. He was flush. Buy a business? Frank could use some money.

32

EL HOTEL NACIONAL

MARCH 1943

At the head of the long table in the dining room of El Hotel Nacional, Meyer Lansky stood and tapped his wine glass with a teaspoon. "Gentlemen, may I have your attention, please?"

The conversations at the table came to an abrupt halt, as did the conversations at some of the nearby tables. "I asked each of you to join me tonight in celebration of our guest of honor. In these troubled times, all around the world, it has been difficult to find good news and reason to hope for the future. Here in Havana, we are just a stone's throw from the greatest country in the history of mankind. A country that provides opportunity for those willing to sacrifice and work hard. A country that rewards diligence, patience, and perseverance. We all must do what we can to defend and protect our country, and to ensure that opportunities for success and prosperity exist for those willing to do what it takes to achieve them." He asked Jack to stand. "Captain Jack Benoit, flight leader for the Flying Tigers, the first Americans to step up and fight for the preservation of freedom and opportunity in the face of violent aggression. He and his colleagues braved the most difficult circumstances and faced the most difficult odds to . . . well . . . plainly . . . to kick Jap bastard ass."

Whoops and hollers rose from Lansky's lieutenants and connections, who were smoking cigars and pouring drinks into bellies full of shrimp cocktail and marinated skirt steak.

Lansky raised his hands for quiet. "Yes. Yes. Captain Jack Benoit shot down fourteen enemy planes. One man, *fourteen* planes! A double ace is what they call it. An extraordinary feat equaled only by a handful of flyers in the entire history of warfare. Then, our friend himself was shot down in a battle over China. While healing from his wounds, he returned to our country to help raise money for the war effort, and he played an integral part in the most successful whistle-stop tour of the whole war bond program. Then, if that wasn't enough, he went back to Asia to fly supplies to China over the Himalayan Mountains. Imagine that, if you will. Flying over a stack of fifteen Empire State Buildings through the most horrific storms. How many times did you fly over those treacherous mountains? Twenty times, was it?"

"Twenty-seven round trips."

Lansky pulled a piece a paper from a pocket of his suit jacket and pulled his reading glasses from another. He cleared his throat. "I did a little calculation before dinner tonight. Let's see. Yes. *If my math is right* . . ." He paused, and the men, knowing their boss's scrupulous attention to all numbers in business, laughed heartily. "If my math is right, our friend Jack spent approximately 200 hours flying war materiel over the most difficult airspace on the planet. And this *after* shooting down fourteen planes over the damn jungle!"

Lansky pulled off his readers and returned them to his breast pocket. Picking up his wine glass, he continued, "You're looking at a man who volunteered to do what it takes to defend and preserve freedom. *Our freedom.* Then, when he got his ass kicked, no disrespect intended, Jack, what did he do? He went back and did it again! *Cojones de Latón*, gentlemen, is what they call that here in Cuba. Brass . . . fucking . . . balls. Now let's give Jack our thanks. If it wasn't for the brave men like him who are fighting over there, we wouldn't have the opportunities we have over here." Lansky waited for the applause to die down. "Now please provide your warmest welcome to our guest of honor, our friend. Because Jack has agreed to come work for me." More cheers. "He'll be flying my beautiful new Bellanca CH-400 Skyrocket airplane, transporting important business associates, guests, and celebrities from the States to our casino here in Havana, and he'll support other business arrangements by doing the same over Miami and New York. So, please welcome Havana's newest and most illustrious resident, Jack Benoit, our very own Flying Tiger!" The suits and mobsters all stood, clapping and cheering, taking turns introducing themselves and shaking his hand. Lansky motioned for everybody to sit. "Would you say a word, Jack?"

He stood with no idea what to say. Memories raced through his mind. Feral dogs fighting for scraps. Mosquitoes buzzing in his ear. His fingertip tracing dots across Emma's cheek. The smell of burnt cordite. Toothless sunburnt coolies bowing in thanks for the coins he pressed into their palms. The roasted hazelnut smell of Chennault's pipe. The Dark One sliding off the tree stand. The comfort of Shu Hao's voice. The puddle of sweat on his back under an inch of Chinese bonds.

"I met Meyer in New York. What, eight, nine months ago?"

Lansky nodded. "A lot of water fast under the bridge."

"From that first time, Meyer's always made it clear that he'd be there for me. He's a patriot, if anything, right?" Shouts of agreement rose from the table. "I suppose I did my part, and what's a little wear and tear?" He adjusted his eyepatch, and Campisi whistled and slapped the table.

"I appreciate the opportunity to work for Mr. Lansky, and I suppose I'll be seein' y'all around some. Thanks."

Tony gave him a big squeeze and threw his arm over his shoulders. "C'mon, somma da guys are goin' over to da Tropicana. We got some nice girls lined up, I mean *nice*, capisce? Come with."

Jack begged off. "I'm fishing early tomorrow, so I'll take a rain check, Tony."

Lansky lingered while the last of the party filed out. "I want thank you again for the action out of China. That was a brilliant transaction, flawlessly executed."

"My pleasure, Meyer."

"Walk with me, Jack. You know something? This past baseball season, Joltin' Joe DiMaggio, the best damn ballplayer ever, do you know how much he got paid?"

Jack shook his head. "I remember Greenberg making thirty-five grand last year."

"Of course." Lansky laughed. "You've had other things to think about. But all kidding aside Jack, DiMaggio, the very reason the Yankees won the World Series, made forty-two thousand last year." He winked at Jack's good eye. "I cleared over ninety grand on our little endeavor, Jack, on all of six days of worry. Now, I know you made a little for yourself, as we agreed, but I want to express how deeply I appreciate you bringing me the opportunity, and how I appreciate you being straight with me about the Australians. Mostly, I appreciate our friendship, Jack."

Lansky pulled an envelope from his jacket. "Let's call it profit sharing." He gave Jack a hug, patting him on the back. "And of course let's keep this between us, all of it. Good night, Jack. I hope the fishing is good for you tomorrow."

As Lansky walked away, Jack opened the envelope to find a stack of hundred-dollar bills. Thirty-six of them.

* * *

While returning alone to his apartment, a sight brought Jack to an abrupt halt outside the arches of the Gran Teatro de La Habana. It was an eight-foot movie poster glowing blue green under the tall streetlamp. Toby Gyer's doppelganger, cheek to cheek with Joan Fontaine.

"*Suspicion*. Ha, Toby's never looked that serious in his whole life." Lansky had mentioned that back in the summer the Bronx borough president presented Toby Gyer with a key to the city. Jack chuckled. "A key to the hearts of all those pretty white New York girls."

The following morning, Jack made his way along the walk edging Havana Port. Some hundred-fifty feet out, a husky man in a green guayabera shirt over khaki shorts stood atop a fishing boat, its hull painted black. The man waived, shouted and pointed. "Go to Javier! Over there!"

Jack found steep stone steps leading down to the water where a man sat in a white dingy, one hand holding a rope looped over a large cleat at the bottom of the stairs. "Señor Benoit, yes?" He raised his straw hat. Moments later, Jack stepped off the dingy and climbed a hook ladder up the side of the fishing boat. He was greeted with a robust handshake and a wide grin. "Hola, amigo!"

A week earlier, while sipping green tea at a table outside the Café Americano, a beefy, handsome, mustachioed American approached his table. "Forgive my forwardness, but am I correct in assuming you are Captain Jack Benoit?"

Jack touched his eyepatch. "Yup."

"Ernest Hemingway." The writer stuck out a large, calloused paw. "I'm a great admirer of yours, Captain Benoit." So, there he was, having tea with one of the greatest of all American writers, a man who could barely contain his eagerness to learn about the war in the Pacific.

Hemingway had a way about him, a respectful ease that felt good. It wasn't like talking with Lansky's guys, who always seemed to be looking for an angle, probing for weakness, like a subtle interrogation from a suspicious lover. Hemingway seemed like what you might get if you stirred Shu Hao and John McClintock in a mixing bowl. Observant, insightful, bursting with life.

"Looks like a beautiful day for fishing, Ernest."

"Winds under five knots, so it should be a comfortable morning. Hopefully, it will be productive, too. Please, this is Gregorio Fuentes, the Pilar's first mate. Gregorio, this is Jack Benoit, one of the bravest men you'll ever meet."

33

THE LETTER

MARCH 1943

The letter was postmarked Abbeville and addressed in Odette's indelible cursive. *Dinjan, Upper Assam* was stamped along one side, and the forwarding address he left with the base was hand-printed below. *Jack Benoit, Hotel Nacional de Cuba, La Habana, Cuba.* He'd moved out of the hotel a couple of weeks ago when he took the apartment.

Jack handed the boy a few pesos, swung his apartment door closed, and flipped the envelope over to find the little flowers Odette always drew on the back in colored pencil. Burgundy rosebuds this time. He grabbed his jacket, pocketed the letter and walked to La Palma for lunch.

November 10, 1942

"A lot of water under the bridge."

Dear Jack,

I hope this letter finds you well in India. I am sure you have been too busy to write. We pray for you every day.

Frank has been out to Lake Charles on business for the past week, and I don't expect him home for

another week. You would not believe your eyes to see our ragamuffins. They are getting so big!
I am sorry to tell you Pumpkin passed away four days ago. Frank took her for ducks just a week earlier, and she was a little stiff but according to Frank she still "got after it." We think maybe she got into something because she went quick.

His Café Americano arrived with a raspberry scone. "Gracias, Benita." He sniffed the pastry and took a sip of coffee, thinking about Pumpkin. Her napping on the Music Box porch on a hot afternoon, running aside the boxcar in the dark, curling up with him on Frank's porch during his last visit. The last time he saw her, she was sitting on the platform at the train station with a gray muzzle and worried brown eyes.

There's news about Chloe.

Jack set the letter on the table and slouched back in his chair. Gulping his Americano, he caught Benita's eye and pointed to his cup. "Uno más, por favor." He liked the language. A lot easier than Chinese.

Her beau Hamilton had some business in New Orleans and was supposed to come to collect Chloe and Francie for the drive to Chicago, but there was trouble in Baton Rouge.

He read on.
"Señor Benoit?" Benita was wearing a concerned expression when Jack met her dark round eyes. "You do not look well, Señor Benoit. I will bring you some water."
He set the letter aside and held his head in his hands. He couldn't sort through his emotions.
"Sons-a-bitches."
The waitress returned with a glass of water. "I added ice, Señor Benoit, to cool you. To make you feel better."

* * *

Hamilton Jones made multiple stops on his way to Abbeville. He heard a blues guitarist in Jonesboro, a gospel quartet and a saxophone player in Memphis. He couldn't locate the reputed twelve-year-old blues guitar prodigy outside Tuscaloosa. His last scheduled stop before collecting his fiancée was New Orleans, where he listened to a few bands. Up until his last night in the Crescent City, the trip had been a bust. He heard some good stuff, and he heard some not-so-good stuff, but nothing was worth bringing up to Chicago. Then, Saturday night on South Rampart Street, his luck changed. At the Eagle Saloon, Bunk Johnson was blowing hard, backed by a tight, swinging band. During a set break, Hamilton hooked the bandleader at the bar. Chicago sounded good to Bunk, and they agreed to talk through the particulars after the gig. During the second set, Hamilton relaxed on a stool and hit the bourbon.

"Gotta light?"

Here stood all kinds of fine, a pretty young blond in a tight black dress, not quite five feet of obvious trouble stilted on three-inch heels, a fresh Lucky Strike slotted between her fingers. Hamilton grinned and struck his Zippo. The Eagle was a black club, but as often as not, tables filled mixed or white. Hamilton's local connection had left the club to find a stick of tea, but an hour had passed, and Hamilton figured he was on his own for the remainder of the night.

"What's your name, handsome?" The blond took a long draw, looking him up and down. Hamilton introduced himself, and the girl leaned in to smell the red carnation tucked into his lapel.

Beatrice, Beattie to her friends, was a college girl visiting childhood friends in the city. After a day in parlors with parents, the girls slipped out in search of a little fun. Beattie was already pretty high, and Hamilton was feeling no pain. He joined the girls at their table. "This is Mary. That's Mary Pat."

"Ursuline grads. We're good girls." Mary threw back a shot and licked her lips. "But since Beattie's gone up to Louisiana State, we don't have nearly as much fun as we used to." Mary Pat winked at a young man in a cream-colored zoot suit sitting at the next table. A couple drinks later, Beattie whispered in Hamilton's ear. He called for the check, figuring he could track down Bunk tomorrow. He paid another round for Mary and Mary Pat, snuffed a butt, and pulled out Beattie's chair.

"*Be good!*" Mary and Mary Pat sing-songed, raising their glasses.

Hamilton woke to Beattie humming as she dressed. "Well, good morning. Did you enjoy your vanilla treat, my chocolate baby?"

"I liked the chocolate vanilla swirl just fine, thank you very much."

He walked her to the streetcar.

"I'm heading back to school today. If you're ever in Baton Rouge."

"You know, I just happen to be headin' through Baton Rouge on Sunday."

"Well, my, my. Isn't that . . . *advantageous?*" She suggested a segregated boarding house that a like-minded sorority sister had told her was discreet, and they made a date for Sunday night. He tracked down Bunk in the early afternoon and agreed to bring him to Chicago later in the year.

Hamilton was supposed to arrive in Abbeville on Sunday to start the drive to Chicago with Chloe and Francie the following day. But the sun set, and no Hamilton. Chloe was worried for him.

"He problee jus' hadda tie up some loose ends in N'Orleans," Menta offered. "Tha place full o' sound. Problee fown too much good stuff to get outta theyah on time."

Hamilton rolled into the outskirts of Baton Rouge late afternoon. He filled up with black gas, bought a Coca-Cola, and got directions to the Campbell Boarding House, where he took a private room with a full-size bed for just the night. The manager had a message for him.

Change of plans.
122 Sycamore.
Nine o'clock.
Come around the back.

He grabbed his lye soap, a washcloth and towel, and headed down the hallway to the bath.

He reread the note. "Just how someone would set me up on the South Side." He crumpled the paper and tossed it across the room and torched a cigarette. "That girl was all in, mmm-hmmm." He figured this was legit. He'd check it out, and if it didn't look right, he'd just keep on moving.

He cruised the street to find the house number then turned onto the boulevard where the car would be less conspicuous with others parked along the thoroughfare. There was a path in the back, and he found a gate under a trellis strewn with dormant rose vines. The backyard was dark, but across it a low light shone through curtains in the kitchen window. He approached the back stoop and found Beattie standing on the other side of the screen door wearing nothing but a smile.

"Hey, Mr. Hershey. Did you bring me something sweet?"

Hamilton stepped inside.

"My great aunt is out of town, so I thought this would be more comfortable and discreet.

Quickly it was all moans and groans, until they heard a noise.

Beattie sat up. "Oh my God!"

Someone was banging on the front door. Hamilton jumped from the bed to find his pants, and the banging continued.

"What're we gonna do?" Beattie's face was as pale white as the sheet she had pulled to her chin.

"Get dressed, fast." Hamilton pulled on his shirt. "Do it! Then go see who's at the door." He couldn't find a sock, so he pulled his shoe onto a bare foot. He hadn't finished buttoning his shirt when they heard noises from inside, back in the kitchen.

"Beattie? You here?"

"Oh my God! That's Bradley Whitten, from school!" she whispered.

"Where's the party, Beattie?" It was another voice, in singsong.

"The party's right here!" a third added. "See, someone brought beer. Oh, wait, that was me!" Boys laughed, girls giggled.

"Shit!" Beattie whispered. "Maybelle must have told them I came out here tonight. They've brought a party."

Hamilton grabbed his jacket and hat and double-timed from the bedroom. He made it through the parlor and to the front door fast. As he struggled with the lock, a voice rose behind him.

"Hey! Who the hell are you?"

He turned to find three white faces staring at him, mouths agape. He worked the lock and busted out onto the porch, hopped the side rail, and made a beeline across the lawns toward Signal Boulevard. His Chevy was refusing to turn over when two white boys came sprinting around the corner. They were at his back bumper when the engine fired, and were pounding on his windows when he peeled out. At the boarding house, he frantically packed his bag, dropped the key and a ten spot on the bed and dashed back to the car.

He'd put a few miles between his taillights and Baton Rouge. "It ain't nothing. Been closer calls." He lit a cigarette with a shaking hand and slapped the dash. "You jerk!" He found Highway 76 to Lafayette, thinking he'd drive through to Abbeville and sleep in the car there. Get Chloe and Francie early morning and drive straight through to Chicago.

He woke to a tapping on the rear window. He'd parked on Valerie Road, a couple blocks from the café. It was nearing dawn, and he raised a hand to shield his eyes from the blinding light. He could just make out the silhouette of a man under a campaign hat when the window shattered on him. Dragged from the car, he was pummeled with batons, losing consciousness within seconds.

It was Monday after the breakfast crowd, and Chloe was helping Francie bus tables when a neighbor lady burst through the front door, crying out, "Oh, dear chile!" That's when Chloe learned her Hamilton was locked up in the Abbeville jail.

"Dear Lore, whateva foe?" Menta asked. Chloe's heart raced.

"I'm sorry ta be ta one to tell you, deah. But dey says he rape a white girl over ta Baton Rouge."

Chloe fainted.

When her friends interrupted the interracial dalliance, Beattie had no choice but to cry rape. The boys got a decent look at the car, and the Baton Rouge police department issued a bulletin throughout central Louisiana for a Chevy coupe with Illinois plates. A second-shift Lafayette Parish deputy reported seeing a car fitting the description heading south on Highway 167 and called up the Vermilion Parish Sheriff, Bubba Johnson, who sent a deputy out to cruise Coonsville.

Menta fanned Chloe's face. "Francie, run get yo sista a glass ah watta. Git!" Chloe revived, sobbing.

"Oh deah Lore! Deah Lore!" Menta held her niece's head, gently rocking the girl. Francie came with the water, and Chloe pushed it away.

"I want to see him. I will go to the jail!"

The neighbor lady shook her head, severely. "No, deah, you do no such ting! They's ah mob ah white folk up theyah, yes, ma'am." She looked at Menta. "They's got ta blood up."

Chloe cried out and dissolved in her aunt's arms.

"Theyah, theyah, chile. We's goan go talk ta Dr. Herod. He'll know bess."

***

"Miss. Tah. Chicago." Deputy Davey Johnson punctuated each word. "You tink you ken come down heah, spreadin yo nigga filth round, rapen our women, yeah?" He dragged a baton across the cell bars. "Boy, you goan find out jus how we deal wit niggas like you heah in Louisiana, yeah." The deputy cut chew and plugged his cheek. "We goan haf a fine time wit you." He leaned against the bars. "Buh you ain goan haf a fine time wit us, no, boy. Taint how dis work."

They had removed the mattress from the wire cot, and Hamilton lay curled on the concrete in the corner of the cell. His cracked jaw throbbed, and the swollen-shut eye ached, but it was his busted ribs that hurt the most, with every breath and tremble.

The crowd outside was getting louder, the chatter rising to shouts every time the door to the station house opened. This time, he heard a new voice under the shouts. "Nine?" He couldn't see the door from his cell, but he did make out Johnson nodding while slapping the baton into the palm of his hand. The door closed and it quieted some. "You bess geh ready, boy," the deputy laughed. "You goan ta ah party tonight."

The whole mob dispersed for dinner and to put their little ones to bed, then started collecting again out front around eight o'clock. Only a few of the participants knew the particulars of the plan, and they were the calmer for knowing. The remainder, close to thirty men and women, were working themselves into a frenzy.

"Kill the damn nigga!"

"Drag him out!"

"String up the devil rapist!"

Deputy Davey was off duty but returned with his daddy, Sheriff Bubba, about a quarter of nine. A good number of the lynch party had arrived in flatbeds, carrying torches, shotguns, and ax handles. By midnight, the mob totaled sixty-plus, some having drove down from Lafayette Parish and another group had come all the way from East Baton Rouge Parish. A yell of "Burn Coonsville!" triggered a chorus of shouts in agreement and creative opinions regarding what to do to Abbeville's niggers. Sheriff Bubba raised his arms. "First things first. We got us a nigga rapist we gotta deal wit. Tha wha we doin heah, we doin no moe."

Sheriff Bubba approached the cell "Well, well." He tipped back his campaign hat. "Dis heah ta nigga tha rape one our girls, requiren me ta quit my hunten trip early, yeah." He saw the boy had been beaten good and tossed his son a look. "Lady justice got a start. Time we let her finish. Open it."

Deputy Jimmy Sweeney, in street clothes, unlocked the cell, and Hamilton pressed himself into the cinderblock corner. The deputies each took one of his arms. The handcuffs he'd been wearing since before dawn cut deeper into his swollen wrists as the deputies struggled the man to his feet. The Sheriff instructed his kid, "You go out theyah an make it plain. Nah tin town. Nah tin ta street. Make sure dey undastan."

The younger Johnson stepped outside and had a chat with Gene Blackmore, Sweeney's best bud from Lafayette. Close behind, Sweeney pushed Hamilton Jones through the doorway. He tumbled off the stoop and rolled on the pavement where he was swarmed by raging, screaming, kicking men and women. Sheriff Bubba came out and shot his pistol in the air. "Not heah!"

Sweeney and Blackmore dragged the prisoner into the street and shoved him in the back of a car. As the sedan eased through the crowd, folks jumped up on the flatbeds or ran to other vehicles. All in, more than two dozen men followed the sedan out of town with nearly as many wives in tow. A half dozen teenagers piled into a beater pickup truck, the driver grinding gears as he u-turned to follow the caravan.

A good five miles outside of town, they settled at the designated spot near the river. No Johnsons were in attendance. Sweeney and Blackmore dragged the accused under a large oak where a noose already dangled from a high branch. Hamilton struggled, trying to block the loop with his cuffed hands as the men forced it over his head. Sweeney cracked a wooden club against his skull. The noose was pulled tight and tied off. They cinched the handcuffs with a rope around his waist and slid a slipknot over one ankle. Blackmore tossed the rope over a branch, pulled it tight and anchored it around the tree truck, raising Hamilton's leg to spread him open like a pair of scissors. He struggled to balance on the one leg, the noose stretching his neck, but not enough to strangle him.

The spectators closed in, shouting racial epithets and more general slurs. A woman spat in Hamilton's face. Blackmore produced a long, heavy pig knife and sliced off his shirt, pants, and undergarments, etching the skin on his chest, torso and thighs where thin lines of blood started to ooze. The sun had finished its day, and tree canopy was lit from underneath by a dozen or so torches.

Sweeney smashed his club against Hamilton's face, shattering his nose. The loud crack and bloody mess raised cheers from the exuberant crowd. With that blow, Hamilton Jones stopped being the handsome rake he was just twenty-four hours earlier.

"Gimme a turn!" A man surged from the crowd swinging an ax handle like a baseball bat. He landed the hickory stick against Hamilton's rib cage. The man swung twice again before Sweeney and Blackmore pulled him off. The crowd was in rapturous rage as Hamilton coughed up blood and bile.

"Alrigh, who ess wanna crack at ta coon?" Blackmore was sweating like a stuck pig, the beer belly hanging over his belt straining his shirt buttons.

A man named Bobby Tilden kicked Hamilton square in the groin, a blow that surely would have doubled him over if he hadn't been strung up tight. Mabel Mayfield snatched a torch from her husband and placed the flame under Hamilton's elbow. She giggled while he howled in agony, his skin sizzling. Mabel slapped the torch against his torso. The flame scorched his underarm and melted flesh off his ribs. Terrible screams curdled under the oak as the smell of burning flesh wafted into the crowd.

"Burn da nigga rapist! Burn im!"

Sweeney took hold of Mabel's arm. "That's nuff now. We got plenny ah time." She stared at the deputy through crazy eyes as he pried the torch from her clenched fist.

"You hongry, boy? Hunh?" Gene Blackmore was yelling in Hamilton's face. He turned to the crowd. "He look a li'l hongry, doan he?" Blackmore twisted the pig knife over his head, the blade glimmering in the torchlight.

"Cut ta nigga!"

"Slice im up!"

Blackmore grabbed Hamilton's penis, lifted it and sliced off the scrotum. His sack and testicles dropped to the dirt.

"Fuck, Gene!" Sweeney punched him in the arm. "He goan bleed out now, and quick like!"

Blackmore paid his friend no mind. The crowd cheered his blade and jeered the nigger. He picked the filthy mess up off the ground and scooped out a testicle. Hamilton, his nose smashed and windpipe constricted by the noose, gasped for breath. Blackmore jammed the testicle into his mouth and pressed his jaw closed. "Chew, nigga! Chew it!" Hamilton, delirious from the pain, couldn't breathe at all.

His struggles were hardly noticeable with how tightly he was hogtied.

Sweeney was right. People knew you didn't cut off a nigger's dick, not until you were finishing up. Blackmore let go of Hamilton's chin and spat in his eye, enraptured in his rage. He screamed again, "I said chew, nigga!"

Hamilton coughed out the dirt-crusted bloody egg, which glanced off his tormentor's cheek and bounced back into the dirt and leaves. "Sheeeit!" Blackmore wiped his cheek and thrust the pig knife into Hamilton's abdomen, twisting it hard. He stuck it in again and again, screaming, "Fuck you!" with each thrust. He was stabbing a corpse. Hamilton had bled out in a hurry, just as Sweeney said he would. After ten or twelve thrusts, Gene Blackmore fell to his knees, hunched over, sweat dripping off his nose. The slurs, cheers and excitement were quickly replaced by mumbles, shuffling feet and disappointment. Everyone had expected the party to last longer. The crowd milled about for a few more minutes, then dispersed to their vehicles. Most left quietly, all but the few who were stinking drunk. They were still whooping and yelling. Sweeney put his hand on his exhausted friend's shoulder. "Big fun."

Blackmore was still breathing hard, his head hangin over his gut. "Goddamn."

Car doors slammed, truck engines turned over, and the people headed back to their homes. Some of the folks would show up late for work the next morning. Sweeney and his pal were climbing into the sedan when the deputy had an idea. "Less teach dem Coonsville niggas sumpin bout hidin a damn rapist." He popped open the trunk and pulled out a hatchet. Twisting it in the moonlight, he grinned. Blackmore grinned, too.

Chloe had gone to bed early, emotionally spent. Menta let her sleep late that morning, and she did, until she was awakened by her aunt's screams. Chloe snatched her robe and sprinted through the kitchen and dining room. She found Francie at the screen door, crying hard. Menta was on her knees on the porch, wailing with her head in her hands. Francie turned to hug her sister, and Chloe tried to settle her, bringing her to a booth. "I'll be right back." She hurried out onto the porch. "What is it? What is wrong, Menta?" Then she saw it. A leg, severed at the knee, lying there on a flagstone, swollen and blue, caked with dirt, leaves and dried blood. A short length of rope was tied around the ankle. A feral dog with its head low stared at her, baring its teeth and growling as he crept slowly forward from the street.

* * *

"Señor Benoit? *Señor?* I brought you another glass of water."

Jack snapped out of his daze. He'd figured Chloe was long gone to Chicago. He'd wired some money to Frank, but he hadn't reached out since leaving for India, and he realized now something like seven months had slipped by. The spoon jumped off the saucer when he slammed the table with his fist.

"Jack!" Hemingway shouted as he strode into the room. "I need to fish, and I need a companion!"

"Damn right. I'm your man."

"Brilliant! Let's do it. To the Pilar!"

Jack caught Benita's eye and winked over a forced smile. "Sorry, sweetie." He tossed some pesos on the table. "Para ti, señorita."

Jack landed a hearty tuna and a nice amberjack. He boated one white marlin with a little damage from the sharks. The host was disappointed he didn't find any Atlantic blues for his new friend to fight. He asked Jack to join him for dinner. "Fresh amberjack tonight!" Jack accepted the offer. The news of Hamilton's death wouldn't leave his head, and he really didn't want to be alone.

Hemingway and Fuentes cut up the fishes, and, as was his habit, Hemingway gave all but that night's dinner to the impoverished locals who took turns waiting on shore for the generous man to return. This day a grateful father presented him with a box of fresh fruit.

Jack sat with his host poolside under the large vine trellis and washed down fruit, corn tortillas and butter with chilled sangria. Hemingway unabashedly swam in the nude. Jack joined him.

Their conversations at Finca Vigía were always a wonderful blend of relaxation, entertainment, and education. Mostly the worldly writer probed for details about the war in the Pacific, but at times he would pontificate, going on at length with fascinating hypotheses for the end of all the wars, what collectively had became known as the Second World War. But Jack liked hearing Hemingway's stories best. The stories he told about Paris reminded Jack so much of Chloe and the stories she shared at the Music Box, and in the Hebert's barn loft. He whispered. "Y'all knew the same people." He must have chuckled to himself because Hemingway asked what was funny. Jack shrugged him off as a breeze rustled the leaves on the palms. That was when he noticed the activity over the flowerpots that lay behind their deck chairs.

"Monarchs!" Jack climbed out of the pool. "Monarch butterflies."

Hemingway smiled. "Yes. *Danaus plexippus*. More commonly known as the monarch butterfly. They migrate here from the northeastern States. Some come all the way from Canada."

Jack spun on his heels, "Canada?"

"Yes, my good man." Hemingway looked perplexed. "Quite a journey. Some two thousand miles, if I have that right. An admirable feat for any species, but especially so for these fragile, lovely creatures."

"So some of them go to Mexico, and some come here?"

"Yes, you can believe your eyes."

He grabbed a towel. "I gotta go."

"Where is it, you *gotta go*, Jack?"

"Louisiana."

Hemingway chuckled and wrapped himself in a robe. "That was sudden." He gave his friend a bear hug. "Jack Benoit, I'm happy to call you my friend. Ring me up when you return. The blues should be in our water any day now, and I'm looking forward to seeing your first battle."

Jack had no idea what he would say to her. He cabled Odette and Frank, letting them know he'd be stopping by. Then he went to see Meyer Lansky.

34

GONE FISHIN'

MARCH 1943

"Thanks, Meyer. I'll take real good care of her." Jack had taken some liberties with the truth when he asked to borrow Lansky's Bellanca Skyrocket.

"Family's the most important thing of all, Jack. Family and your health. Always remember that."

"Will do. I'll settle up the fuel cost when I get back. Don't worry, I'll be here in plenty of time to make the trip to Washington that's coming up."

Twelve hours later, he was at his brother's place in Perry.

"A motorcycle!" Odette exclaimed from the porch, hands on her aproned hips.

Jack pulled the goggles to his forehead. "Why not?"

He'd spotted the Indian in the hangar at New Orleans Airport and offered the owner, a young mechanic named Joey, fifty dollars to borrow it for a couple days. The wrench got comfortable only after Jack pointed out that Lansky's Skyrocket would be sitting right there until he returned.

"Do you wanna go for a spin?"

"Oh, no, no!" But she had a huge smile on her face. "Maybe tomorrow, when the sun shining."

"Frank home?"

Odette waved him in. "Tomorrow."

After getting his fill of chicken and dumplings, Jack started on the peanut butter cookies and furthered his inquiries. Odette cleared the dishes.

"It was just awful wha they did to that boy. Parts uh him all 'round town. An who knows wha really happen up ta Baton Rouge. Instead of takin the causeway heah, he go all the way 'round Baton Rouge to break into a house where that college girl sleepin ah lone, then some friends come save her from . . ."

Jack had no doubt that man had an invitation. He took his plate to the sink. "So, how's she doin', Chloe, now, that is?"

Odette sighed. "I went by the café couple uh days ago. Thought I'd get a pie, maybe heah sumpin. Chloe was quiet. Didn't say anything much. The whole place was . . ." He waited for it. "Solemn."

Odette washed. Jack dried.

"And?"

"Well . . . Chloe had a shiner."

"*A shiner*?"

"Yes. A black eye. Sah little green. She musta had it a while. Last week, Frank was in Lafayette foe some meetins. On the way home he stopped wit the domino boys at the fillin station in Abbeville like he do sometimes. It got late, so he drove by the café to see if they had any pies to sweeten me up for missin suppa. Anyway, he was real shook when he got home."

"Yeah, go on."

"He said I shouldn't pay him no mind. Said he was just worrin bout business. Mais Sha, Frank don't get like that bout business no more. He just don't get worked up like he used to."

Jack couldn't make anything of it. "What kind?"

"What kind what?"

"What kind of pie did he bring home?"

"He! Well that's the funny part. He dint even get one. Here he says he was goan sweeten me up, and he dint even get that right. Can you believe it?"

Jack couldn't.

He walked out back to where Odette told him. He crouched over the chunk of limestone and ran his hand across the scratches in it that spelled *Pumpkin*, working grit between his thumb and forefinger. He hoped the old girl was in a good place with lots of squirrels. A soft blanket on a porch in the sky and lots of squirrels and rabbits to chase. He figured he'd drop into the Music Box for lunch tomorrow.

CHLOE'S MISTIGRI

* * *

He woke early and did calisthenics out back near Pumpkin's grave. He thought better of lunchtime. She might feel awkward or self-conscious with a bunch of people there. *Awkward. Self-conscious.* He thanked Emma for the vocabulary lessons.

The café was empty but for a pair of women cackling over watery remnants of sweet tea.

"PJ! PJ! PJ!" Francie body-slammed him and squeezed tight. "Petit Mistigri!"

His heart leaped when Chloe followed from the kitchen. She was wearing a red bandana and twisting an ancient dishtowel. He closed the distance between them, dragging along Francie, who wouldn't give up on her hug.

"I heard about Hamilton. Sorry."

No tears. No honey. Her eyes were empty, nothing but a yellow tint under one of them.

"Pie! PJ needs pie!" Francie burst through the saloon doors into the kitchen.

"How 'bout we sit?" Jack waved to the corner booth. Chloe plopped into the nearest chair. Francie took a while, during which nothing was said. She brought three plates, sat herself down, and ate with gusto. Chloe just stared at the tabletop.

"So, Francie, what's new?"

"Ducks. We have really good gumbo, PJ."

Jack eyed Chloe, who hadn't moved. Francie scraped her plate with her fork. Jack took a bite, pointed his fork at the plate, and made a yummy noise.

"Yes!" Francie agreed. "Scuze me, please." She took her plate to the kitchen.

Jack leaned in. "You okay? Talk to me."

Chloe raised her eyes, which were dead as doornails. "What would you like to talk about, Captain Benoit?"

Jack's heart sank, and he got a little angry. "Hell, I don't know, Chloe. I wanna know you're doin' all right."

"*Doo-en* all right." She huffed out a laugh. "Yes, Captain Benoit. I am *doo-en* just fine. How are you *doo-en?*" She crossed her arms, and now her eyes were on fire, and Jack's anger rose. He was there to help.

"Okay, then." He stood to leave, and that's when he noticed the shelves. There was a big empty space. A good quarter or more of the records were gone. "What happened there? Where's all the records?"

Francie hollered from the kitchen. "Chloe smash them. Then we burn them."

"Huh?"

"Thieving white man music."

"Excuse me. I must return to work now." Chloe disappeared through the kitchen. Francie stood at the saloon doors.

"Chloe hates the mean white men. I hate them, too. But you're not mean." She hugged him tight.

Jack took the Indian for a spin west on Highway 14. When he hit the Coulee Galleque crossing on the way back, he angled the bike onto the footpath, motoring south to the Big Tree. A couple spots were overgrown with thorny vines that scraped his forearms along the way. He sat himself on the bank and watched the striders skate on glassy brown water. It was nearing dark when he pulled the motorcycle up front at Odette and Frank's place. His brother met him on the walk.

"Glad to have you back. Hope you'll stay a bit longer this time."

He peeled off the goggles, dislodging his eyepatch. Frank stiffened.

"Thanks. It's good to be here."

They settled on the porch.

"A tiger skin? Really? You shot that thing."

Jack nodded.

"I'm gonna need to hear that story."

Odette brought iced tea and joined them.

"The Dark One! That's straight out of a movie, like Tarzan or something, right Bebe? You know, PJ, I appreciate the thought, really I do. But what the hell am I gonna do with a tiger skin?"

Odette scolded her husband for his language.

"I don't know. Butter up Daddy Sweetwater, Mr. *Louisiana State Tigers* himself. Better yet, sell it to a fancy whorehouse down in N'Orleans. No doubt there's plenty of fat-cat politicians who'd like to go for a ride on a tiger skin."

"Jack!" Odette crossed herself. "Sha, bon Dieu!"

After dinner, the brothers sipped bourbon on the porch, where Jack learned most all the hardwood in Louisiana had been cut, and peckerwooding was going the way of the horse carriage. But Edward

Sweetwater had some investors and pitched a canvas manufacturing company to supply the army.

"He says I can have a job if they get the contract."

"And?"

"Not that I ain't grateful, but it's time I make my own. Just not sure how to go about it. But how 'bout you?"

Jack was evasive about his boss, but Frank was more interested in hearing about the fishing anyway.

"Ernest Hemingway! Jiminy Cricket, PJ!"

"Beb, you know he go by Jack now." Odette gave Jack a smile and sat with them.

"Fishing with Ernest Hemingway."

"He's a good egg," Jack deadpanned.

"Ha!" Frank slapped a thigh. "Do you hear that, Bebe? Ernest Hemingway's a good egg." He twisted a thumb at his wife. "Odette's read everything that man's written, I think. I liked, what was it, Bebe? *For Whom the Bell Tolls?* Jordash. A mercenary, like you, PJ."

"Jack." Odette raised an eyebrow.

"Yeah, Robert Jordash. He was a good egg, too. And this one's started scolding me for still calling you PJ. Says you've outgrown it."

"S'pose she has a point."

Frank laughed. "S'pose."

Odette returned for the dishes, and to put the kids to bed. The brothers sat quiet. But for a mockingbird on the corner electric pole and the occasional moth fluttering against the screen door, they enjoyed silence as the dusk went dark.

Jack decided to go fishing. "I went up to the Music Box."

Frank didn't bite.

Jack sucked on some ice. "Chloe's a bit of a mess."

Frank looked away, down the empty street.

"I said . . ."

"I heard you," he snapped, still staring down the street.

"Odette told me you saw her a couple weeks ago. Said you said she had a big ol' shiner."

Frank didn't budge.

Jack leaned back into his chair and studied his brother hard. Frank still wasn't much for hiding emotions.

"You talked to her, Frank. What'd she say?"

Still nothing.

"You're gonna tell me, so just do it now and get it over with. What'd she say? How'd Chloe get the shiner, Frank?"

Frank pulled out his handkerchief and leaned into it, covering his eyes. He turned away, looking about to cry. Jack had never seen his brother cry.

"Okay, goddammit. What happened with Chloe? You tell me now."

"Look," Frank cleared his throat, "you promise me you won't do anything stupid. No one needs more trouble around here, you understand? 'Specially not Chloe and hers. Get it?"

"I s'pose I will when I have somethin' to get."

Frank took a deep breath. "You stay cool now."

* * *

Frank stopped in Abbeville on his way back from Lafayette. He got to talking at the filling station and joined the dominos game. Before he knew it, it was dark outside, so he swung by the Music Box to pick up something sweet for Odette and the kids. It was Wednesday night, so Menta and Francie would be at church, but Chloe might be there. Sure enough, the lights were on in the dining room. Frank pulled open the screen door. He thought it odd that the main door was closed on that muggy night. As he pushed it open, he was greeted by Deputy Johnson.

"Davey Johnson?" Jack straightened up and cocked his head.

"Yes, Deputy Davey."

* * *

"Nutin ta see heah, Frank. Shop's closed, yeah." Johnson put a hand on Frank's chest, backing him out the door. Over the deputy's shoulder, Frank caught a glimpse of two men up near the kitchen doors.

"What's goin on, Deputy? Some kinda trouble?"

Johnson pulled the door closed behind him.

"Got evthin in hand heah. Nutin ta see. You jus go en home, now, ya heah?"

Frank walked back to his Ford and started the engine. It wasn't like Deputy Davey to shoo folks from his work. He loved a crowd. The deputy was still standing there, arms crossed in the doorway, and Frank's gut sank.

He drove down the street a couple blocks then circled back, stopping behind the patrol car he found parked on the residence side of the house. The front rooms were dark, but the door was unlocked. As he walked through the house and into the kitchen, he heard a ruckus coming from the dining room. At the swinging doors he yelled, "Stop!"

* * *

At the roadhouse south of Lafayette, Jimmy Sweeney and Gene Blackmore were reminiscing on the lynching a ways back. "Den you go an bleed im like dat." Sweeney punched his buddy in the arm. "I hadn gah mah fill, me. Sumpin missin."

Blackmore pounded his boilermaker and wiped his mouth on his sleeve. "Yeah? Like what?"

"Like dat nigga bitch he goan marry, yeah. Nigga come down ta Abbeville ta hide. Ta bitch was goan run wit im, damn black buck."

Blackmore flagged the barkeep. "Seems she need a lesson. You goan school eh?"

Sweeney tipped his deputy campaign hat back. "*We's* goan school eh."

Davey Johnson thought it was swell idea. "Wedsday nigh. Da otha ones go ta nigga church, she doan."

About the time Frank pulled his pocket watch and told the domino boys it had to be his last game, Jimmy Sweeney was steering the patrol car past the filling station. He cruised past the Music Box, and Gene Blackmore, sitting in back, spotted the girl through the front window. "Theyah's dat coon bitch!"

"Pull round ta da house side." Johnson instructed Sweeney. "Make sure no one ovah theyah."

When the two white men burst through the café door, Chloe tried to escape through the kitchen and ran smack into Deputy Davey Johnson. He grabbed her by both arms. "Pull dem shades. School's in session."

* * *

"Stop!"

Chloe was bent over the booth. Jimmy Sweeney was standing to the side, swaying drunk. Gene Blackmore stumbled as he turned to look, propping himself with the broom. Johnson, caught off guard, quickly raged.

"Frank? Goddamit. I toll ya ta git."

But Frank took the offensive. "I ain't having it, Davey!" he yelled, pushing him aside. "This stops! It stops, now!" He shoved the deputy twice more and pointed a finger in his face. "No! No more!"

He strode to the booth and slammed both palms against Blackmore's chest. The pot-bellied drunk fell hard. He was rubbing his head, "Still my turn." Frank swung a fierce uppercut that landed square on his chin.

Red as a beet, Frank jammed a finger in Johnson's face. "Don't fuck with me, Davey! Don't you fuck with me! It's time y'all leave. Go! Git!" Frank maneuvered himself between the booth and the two lawmen as Johnson and Sweeney stepped closer.

"I's done an way." Johnson forced a laugh. He poked Sweeney. "Get im up. Less get outta heyah."

Frank worked the girl off the table and into the booth seat where she collapsed, sobbing, head on her forearms. She recoiled at his touch.

He thought to get Odette, but that would mean leaving her alone. He didn't know any of the neighbors. He thought out loud. "Maybe Menta will come home soon." She did.

* * *

All Frank told Jack was the bit about the deputy out front, then how he cut through the kitchen.

Jack listened, stone-faced. "Who else?"

Frank shook his head.

"Who else was there, with Davey Johnson?"

Frank shook his head. "I told you, PJ. *Jack*. Nobody needs more trouble. I never shoulda told you any of it. Leave it be."

Jack stood.

"Where you going?"

"To see Deputy Davey. Got a crime to report."

"Goddammit, PJ. No kidding, you're gonna get yourself killed."

Jack stared down his brother with one cold blue eye. "Then tell me, Frank. Who else?"

Frank put his head in his hands. "Jimmy Sweeney and Gene Blackmore."

Jack wasn't surprised to hear the other deputy's name.

"Who's this Gene Blackmore?"

"Some pal of Sweeney's. Lives up in Lafayette."

Jack stood over his brother. "Forgettin' anyone?"

Frank got in his face. "There weren't nobody else, PJ! Goddammit, just leave it be. Done is done, and there ain't no good can come from you gettin' involved. Leave it be."

Jack was a cool as a cucumber. "No worries, Frank. I just wanted to know. What was it Mark Twain said? 'It's better to know than to s'pose.' Yeah, that's it." He patted his older brother on the shoulder and went inside.

The next morning, Frank found him in good spirits, breakfasting with Odette.

"Jack's goan fishin."

Frank narrowed his eyes.

"I pulled somma your gear out of the car barn. Hope you don't mind."

"I give him your sleeping bag, Beb."

"Too bad you can't join me, Frank, havin' to work and all."

"Where you goin'?" Frank asked, suspiciously.

Odette interjected, "*Lake Artur.*"

"Colonel Chennault has a place out that way. Said I could use it anytime. Thought I'd do some bass fishin'."

Frank started on his coffee.

Odette walked Jack out and kissed his cheek. "Have fun. Bring what ya catch, and I'll fry 'em up for us."

He jumped down on the bike, revved the engine, and threw some gravel as he hit the road.

* * *

"That it?" Odette stared down at the six filets. "You gone three day an bring me *tree* fish?"

Jack smiled a crooked smile. "I was hungry. I ate the rest." He put his arm around her as they walked inside.

* * *

"I won't be back for dinner," he hollered as the screen door slammed behind him. He took the Indian into Abbeville. As he entered the café, the half dozen patrons gazed in amazement, each black face betraying disgust behind his back.

Menta came by. "I gitcha some tea."

"Is Chloe here?"

"Chloe's nah worken tonigh."

He figured she was in the house. Francie sat herself across from him in the booth. He asked her.

"Chloe is always home. Doesn't go see ta Revernd anymore."

He pushed through the saloon doors and found her sitting out front on the house side.

"What do you want?" Her voice was empty.

"I want to talk to you."

"And what about what *I* want?"

Jack was at a loss. He didn't even know what he wanted to say. "Frank said . . ."

Chloe shot him a glance, her eyes narrow.

"He didn't tell me *what*."

Her eyes welled.

"He told me *who*. And you ain't gonna hafta worry 'bout them anymore."

A tear stream ran down her cheek. "Worry?" She stood and yelled, "Worry! Do you think that is what I am feeling, PJ Benoit? I am *worried*? You could not be any more of an imbecile."

"What I mean is, it's gonna be . . ."

Chloe shouted him down, shaking with rage. "What is it is going to be? What does this white man with the patch say it is going to be?" She crossed her arms and rocked from side to side, hovering there while Jack sat down on the porch step.

"You smashed all them records. The ones made by white people." He noted the dandelions in the yard sprung early this year. "I'm coming back here tomorrow, and we're gonna go out to have a little fun."

She eyeballed him like he was a crazy man, hollering on a street corner.

"Yeah, it'll be fun." He stood and flashed her a crooked grin. "You'll see."

Both of the Vermilion Parish patrol cars were sitting out front of Frank and Odette's place when he banked the rumbling Indian into the drive. Frank, Odette, Sheriff Bubba Johnson, and Deputy Davey Johnson filed out the kitchen door.

"Evenin', boys," Jack offered as he swung off the bike.

Frank started. "Jack, Sheriff Johnson here . . ."

"I'll handle it," the sheriff interrupted. "Weah you tree days ago, PJ?"

Davey Johnson cut and stuffed a big chunk of chew. Odette nervously kneaded a dishtowel.

"I s'pose they already told you, Bubba. I was fishin'."

The lawman scowled. Jack knew he didn't like being called Bubba. It was Sheriff Johnson, Sheriff Bubba to his friends. "You got people ta back ya story?"

Jack laughed. "Story? You think I'm tellin' a story, Bubba? I went fishin' over Lake Arthur way. Ain't no story. Odette here fried up my catch real nice."

The sheriff cleared his throat. At six foot two with a girth to match, he was an imposing figure. "Taint jus a story if some un comes ford ta say dey witchoo da whole time."

"*Comes forward?* So just what y'all talkin' about, Bubba? You got somethin' to accuse me of, then accuse me of it. Otherwise, get the hell outta my way so I can set down to whatever delicious dish Odette's servin' tonight."

"You watch yo mouth, son! Dep-tee Sweeney was las seen at ta Crossroad Bah en Monday. Dat is til he come up dead en Coulee Galleque."

"So, what then? You wanna know if I had some drinks at the Crossroad Bar with my old school pal, Jimmy Sweeney? Did I go skinny-dippin' with the little faggot? Is that it?"

The sheriff placed his hand on his revolver. "Weah you gun, Benoit?"

Jack waived his arms. "What friggin' gun?"

Frank chimed in. "Jack, just settle down and answer the sheriff's questions."

"No doubt you carry a .45, one ta army issue, yeah."

Jack looked at Odette and Frank, who were both staring at their feet.

"I wasn't in the army, Bubba. But yeah, I got a .45 caliber Model 1911 A1. You wanna see it?"

"Damn right!" Davey Johnson couldn't contain himself.

Jack started into the house.

"No." The sheriff stopped him. "You tell us weyah tis. Ta deputy heah'll go fetch it."

Jack told them to look in the old chest of drawers in the attic room. The younger Johnson spat a stream of tobacco juice and headed inside.

"Top drawer on the right, Deputy Davey!"

The sheriff was beet red.

"Deputy Sweeney." Jack kicked the dirt. "Tough findin' good help, ain't it Bubba?"

The sheriff's kid returned with a flat box tied with a string. He handed it to his daddy, who pulled a pocketknife and cut the string.

"Tis you gun?"

"Yup."

The sheriff removed the 1911 from the box and inspected it in the light streaming out the kitchen screen door. "Colt .45."

"Sure is."

The sheriff pulled out the clip. Cocked the gun. Thoroughly studied the sidearm. "Ain been shot."

"That's a fact."

"So you go fight a war, an you doan shoot you gun?"

Jack laughed. "I killed Japs with .50 cal machine guns drivin' a fighter plane 500 miles an hour, Bubba. Not sure I woulda had the same results swingin' a pistol 'round like Randolph Scott in some western."

"Geezus, Davey." The sheriff pushed the gun at Frank and shook his head.

Frank saw an opening. "So, Sheriff, what's all this about, anyway? Deputy Sweeney didn't drown? He got shot?"

"Bon Dieu!" Odette exclaimed.

The sheriff paused to light a cigarette. "Had tree hole en is head. Ta doc pull one um slugs out."

".45 caliber?" Frank asked.

"No sheeit." The sheriff had obviously had his fill. He shook a finger in Jack's direction. "We goan figure dis out. Meantime, you doan be goin no weah."

"Look, Bubba."

"Sheriff Johnson ta you, you leel fuck!"

"Look, *Sheriff Johnson*. I'm just finishing up a little visit with my brother and his family here, and I gotta get back to work. So, sorry to disappoint you, but I *will* be going somewhere." He stared down the big lawman. "I didn't kill Jimmy Sweeney, y'all's friggin' dumbass inbred deputy. So unless you're gonna arrest me for having a gun that ain't been shot, I suggest you get to work finding out who really killed Davey's li'l pal, 'cause it wasn't me."

Both squad cars sprayed gravel.

"Bebe, how about you get dinner ready?" Frank was seething, staring at his brother. After Odette went inside, he posed the question. "What the hell did you do, PJ?"

"Nothin', Frank. Nothin' at all. By the way, I'm heading out tomorrow. Should be back in a week or so, if that's okay with y'all."

Frank flicked a glowing butt high into the air, and they watched it arc toward the gravel drive. "Goddamit, PJ," he said in a hushed tone. "You can't just kill people, no matter what they done. This ain't China!"

Jack reassured his brother. "I ain't killed nobody, and I don't intend to. I gotta go down to N'Orleans for business, but I'll be back here in a week or so, if that's alright."

"This business have to do with Chloe?"

"I don't know who killed Jimmy Sweeney, Frank, and I don't care." He paused, searching the sky for Cassiopeia. "But the world's a better place without that piece of shit breathing out here."

"You're playing with fire, PJ."

Jack took a deep breath and hollered through the kitchen door. "Smells good, Odette! Shrimp and grits. Smells like home." He slapped his big brother on the back. "No worries, Frank. Look, I gotta adjust the bike. Tools in the car barn?"

Frank narrowed his eyes and shook the boxed pistol at his brother. "Think I'll keep an eye on this for you, if you don't mind." He yanked open the screen door and stepped inside. Jack shuffled around in the garage until he found some oil rags in a rusty, old bucket. He pulled his Colt out from the back of his belt, wrapped it in the rags, stuffed the bundle in the bucket, and slid the bucket onto a high shelf. "Yeah, shrimp and grits."

* * *

Sunday morning, he headed out early. He stopped and revved the rumbling Indian until Menta hobbled to the street in her worn pink housecoat and slippers. He cut the engine and stated his proposition, handing her the money. As he strode into the house, she counted the twenties and shrieked.

"Get dressed. We're going for a ride."

Caught off guard, Chloe asked, "Where?"

"Never you mind. You'll like it. Get dressed."

She surprised herself by doing just that. Twenty minutes later, he handed her the helmet.

"You ever ride a motorcycle?"

Chloe shook her head as he buckled the strap under her chin.

"Just wrap your arms 'round me."

She did as he said, and he jumped the kick pedal. The rumbling coursed through her body. As he accelerated east onto Highway 14, she felt alive.

35

REMINISCENCE

MARCH 1943

Her head was sweaty at the top of the helmet, and the air that snuck in along her temples cooled her in a way she never felt before. Loose strands of curly black hair whipped at her neck. The breeze tickled her bare arms and pressed into her short sleeves, puffing the back of her dress and tightening it against her breasts. She squeezed two handfuls of leather and studied the Chinese writing on his back of his bomber jacket as the morning sun flickered through the tips of the tall pines lining Highway 90. The steady rumble heightened all of her senses, the vibration resonating throughout her body. The rich pleasant scent of dewy-morning pine filled her nose, subject to an occasional interruption of pungent skunk or offensive pigsty. She rested her head on his leather clad back and felt only the moment, her head clear for the first time in months. They'd traveled some fifty miles when Jack slowed the machine and rolled it through a U-turn.

"Where are you taking me?" She shouted.

"To my favorite restaurant in the whole wide world!" He pulled off the road and shut down the bike. "And you know I've been around some."

Chloe stepped down and giggled as her legs wobbled beneath her. A bent old black man in a dirty apron walked toward them. "Kin I hepya, missah man?"

"You open?"

"All day, yessah." Chloe pulled off the helmet. The man's eyes widened. She looked past him toward an old shack and could barely make out the writing on the weather-worn sign. *Écrevisse Paradis*.

"How's the gumbo?"

"Bess in Saun Mar-ee Parish, yessah."

"Crawfish pie?"

"Yessah. Duck gumbo, if thas aright."

"Two and two, and a couple Dr. Nuts." He peeked at Chloe and found her smiling. "I need to find a toilet."

Chloe stretched her legs, dangling the helmet by its strap. She spun around, wondering what in the world was happening. Maybe he was taking her to New Orleans?

She was hungry, and the gumbo was delicious. Jack ravaged his bowl, wiping it clean with fresh-baked bread.

"Whaddya think 'bout Crawfish Heaven here?"

"It is quite good. So, this is your favorite restaurant?"

"Huh? Never been here in my life." He put his hand on hers, and she blushed.

"Anthen else, missah man?"

Jack pressed a ten spot into the old man's hand. "Y'all have a great day." He straddled the bike while Chloe buckled the helmet strap.

"So, we will return to Abbeville, now that you have shown me your favorite restaurant?" She hoped not.

"I have a better idea."

"Are you taking me to New Orleans, PJ?"

"That's exactly what I'm doin'."

It was nearly two more hours to the city, with nobody asking how she was. Nobody looking at her with pity in their eyes. Only the sounds of whistling wind and rumbling engine in her ears, the heat of the early spring sun on her shoulder, the steady tremor of the bike between her legs. When they crossed the Huey P. Long Bridge into New Orleans, she patted his arm and pointed off the road. They stepped off the cycle and stretched.

"What is your plan, PJ?"

"I have somethin' to show you, that's all. Once you've seen it, I'll take you home."

"I would like you to take me somewhere first."

He looked at his wristwatch. "Sure. You know how to get there?" She didn't. He picked up directions and chewing gum at the next gas.

As they approached the crypt, Jack slowed his walk to let her go on ahead. The box had grayed some, but she recognized the shape, and that odd step on the front. She ran her fingers along the chiseled dates, stepped back, and crossed herself, something she hadn't done since the last time she'd stood in that spot. She picked up Jack's hand and led him away.

They motored east along Lake Pontchartrain to New Orleans Airport, and he swung the bike into the hangar. The Skyrocket was resting right where he'd left it.

"Where the hell you been?" Wiping a wrench with a stained gray rag, the mechanic's tone signified both anger and relief. He was not at all pleased with the man who'd kept his bike a week longer than agreed. "Was wonderin' if I's ever goan see you again."

"I do love this bike, Joey. But not quite ready to trade the plane for it." When Chloe pulled off the helmet, the mechanic startled. "Here's the extra rent." Jack pressed two twenties and a ten into his grease-stained hand.

The mechanic's eyes lit up. "Zowee! You wanna keep it another week?"

"Maybe another time."

"Why are we here, PJ?"

"I told you I'd take you back after I showed you something."

"Yes?"

"Well, I'm gonna show you my home."

She looked puzzled. "Do you live in New Orleans? We are at the airport. Where do you live, PJ?" Chloe scrunched her face when he told her. "*Havana?* Havana, in *Cuba?*"

"Yeah, smart girl. That's where I live."

She was dumbstruck.

"Our ride." Jack thumbed over at the plane.

Chloe put her hand to her mouth. "Mon Dieu! An aeroplane?"

"It's a morning of firsts for the *mademoiselle*." He squeezed her hand, then shooed her to go see the plane. He lingered in the hangar with Joey, confirming maintenance and fuel. Everything seemed in order, but the mechanic's mood visibly soured.

"Where's the toilet?"

Joey pointed to the terminal door. "Just inside, near the ticket counter." As they approached the door, the young man yelled,

"Colored is down there!" They stopped, turning to look at him. "Down at the end, on the outside! Colored!"

They walked outside the length of the building. She tugged on his shirt. "I cannot leave, PJ. I cannot leave Menta and Francie. They cannot manage without me."

"Honeybee." He took up her hands and rubbed them with his thumbs. Chloe's knees weakened.

"The Music Box is closed. Menta and Francie are taking some time off. A little vacation."

"But . . ."

"I gave Menta some money and told her we'd be back in a couple weeks. They'll be fine. It's about time she had a little rest, right?"

"*A couple of weeks?* But . . ."

"You'll have a vacation, too! I wanna show you my new home, introduce you to some friends of mine." Above and between two metal doors hung a white metal sign with the word *Colored* painted in red letters. Jack winked and pushed through the door marked with an M.

* * *

"C'est magnifique!"

"What?"

Chloe leaned in, looking him in the eye. "It is so beautiful, PJ! The ocean. So blue, so green. The waves stretch out forever. Yes, it is magnificent!"

"You're gonna like Cuba."

"Why will I like Cuba, PJ Benoit?" she asked, playfully.

"You'll just hafta wait and see."

"The surprises today have been very nice. Like your favorite restaurant in all the world." Jack pointed to the horizon. "*Cuba?*" she asked excitedly.

He nodded, then pointed starboard. "Mexico over there. That's Yucatan." It was a little hazy, but Chloe thrilled to see the green peninsula on the western horizon.

When the cabbie tried to return his change, Jack held his hands up. "Quédatelo!" He tucked Chloe's arm through his. "We'll grab a bite here." They entered La Palma.

"Señor Benoit! So good to see you!"

"Two for dinner, Silvio."

Chloe quickly realized they were not properly dressed. She blushed deeply as they were seated, while Jack, oblivious, ordered two Coca-Colas with ice and lime.

"Silvio, bring somethin' special, please. This lady's never had Cuban food." Jack noticed Chloe was looking down into her lap, fidgeting. "What, don't you like Co-Cola anymore?"

"No. It is fine."

"For the señorita. May I?" The astute waiter draped a delicate green sweater embroidered with tiny white-and-yellow flowers over her shoulders. "Better, yes?"

Jack still didn't get it. "Silvio, this is Chloe. Chloe, Silvio. The best waiter in all of Havana."

Silvio bowed, then headed to the kitchen. As he walked away, it finally occurred to Jack how they looked. He was in his usual disheveled khaki, but Chloe's dress was pure Coonsville, worn damn near threadbare. He pushed his chair back. "Excuse me a minute."

Chloe watched from across the room as Jack chatted up Silvio and pressed something into the waiter's hand. He sat back down and tore off a piece of Cuban bread fresh from the oven, sputtering through a mouthful, "I forgot you didn't bring a bag."

Chloe glowered at him and whispered tersely, "Of course I did not bring a bag! When you kidnapped me, I did not know I would be traveling to another country."

Jack scraped the bread across the butter plate. Chloe shook her head and tried to suppress an insistent smile. He dusted off his hands. "No worries, Honeybee. Silvio is gonna get y'all set for tonight. Then tomorrow, we'll hit the shops." Chloe flushed and covered her mouth. Silvio returned alongside another server, who placed a steaming bowl in front of Chloe.

"Ropa vieja, for the señorita."

"Beef stew. It's delicious, really." Jack poked a fork at her dish. "Rice, black beans, and plantains. Here, try one." He stabbed a piece of the fruit and held it up to her. "They're sweet, and I tell you, this is the best damn meal in town." She pulled the plantain away with her lips, and Jack saluted Silvio with the empty fork. She watched, aghast, as Jack took no time at all to wolf down everything on his plate.

"Comment il est grossier." She laughed out loud.

"Wha?" he asked, mouth full.

"You are right, PJ. This is delicious." She tried more of the plantain and scanned the room. It housed a growing crowd, growing louder as the drinks freely flowed. It struck her, this scene. All of these brown people. Most were light brown, but the room held people of a variety of colors, and at mixed tables. Everyone seemed to be having a splendid time. She gasped, "Together."

She wondered. *Is this Havana like Paris? Could it be?* She locked her wide eyes on Jack, who responded by stopping mid-chew. He looked down at his shirt, self-conscious.

"Wha?"

Chloe beamed. It had crossed her mind numerous times during the flight, and again in the taxicab. *Where will I sleep tonight?* Now she knew she would sleep in his arms. They lingered over espresso and chocolates, which tugged on her sweet memories of Paris.

When they arrived at his apartment, they were greeted by a short stack of pink-striped boxes tied with ribbon. Silvio had arranged the after-hours delivery of a simple cotton nightgown, tasteful undergarments, and a cheery yellow sundress with sandals and hat. Chloe held the nightie against her chest and spun around. "It is so beautiful." Her eyes were moist.

Jack removed the garment from her hands and tossed it on a chair. "So are you."

Chloe luxuriated in a long bath with vanilla salts before they turned out the light.

They woke famished and walked the Paseo del Prado to have breakfast. Chloe twirled in the bright morning sunlight, her eyes sparkling. "Do you like it?"

"Si, señorita. Mucho!" Jack teased.

They enjoyed a leisurely meal before visiting the shops on San Rafael Avenue. Chloe couldn't stop giggling.

* * *

"I see somebody made the shopkeepers happy this morning." Hemingway drummed his fingers on the uppermost box of the tall stack resting near the couple's patio table at El Café al Atardecer.

Jack jumped from his seat. "Ernest!" The men hugged.

"So good to see you, my friend. I came searching for you the other day, and Silvio informed me you were gone, to the States, I presume." Hemingway gave Chloe the once-over. "And who might this be?"

"My . . . friend, Chloe Boisvert. Chloe, this is Mr. Ernest Hemingway." Chloe's mouth dropped. Without thinking she reverted to a habit long gone, dangling her hand over the table. Hemingway kissed and patted it.

She was blushing something awful. "I am pleased to make your acquaintance, Mr. Hemingway. I have so enjoyed reading your works."

"That is very kind of you to say, Miss Boisvert, and may I ask, do I detect a Parisian accent?"

Chloe glowed. "Perhaps. I was in France for some time, as a child."

Hemingway, grinning, shook Jack's shoulder. "I too spent some time in France, where I often *acted* like a child."

"Have lunch with us, Ernest, please." Jack caught the waiter's attention.

* * *

Hemingway raised his glass to Chloe and drained it.

"I knew a Boisvert in Paris. A very charming nightclub owner. Paul was his name. Yes, Paul Boisvert. He had the loveliest wife. Yvonne."

Chloe nearly fainted. She caught herself against the tabletop, and Hemingway shot up. "Dear girl, are you alright?" Jack reached for her, but Hemingway had her arm, and was flagging a waiter. "A cold, damp cloth. Quickly! Go!" Jack crouched next to his girl and rubbed her forearm.

"Paul Boisvert was Chloe's uncle. He raised her."

"Dear God!" Hemingway exclaimed. "This *is* a small world." He hesitated. "You said *was* her uncle. So, *the war?*"

"No. Before that."

Hemingway seemed beside himself. "Oh, dear girl, I am so sorry to have distressed you!" He yelled to the waiter. "The cloth, damn you! Ahora!" Help arrived, and Jack pressed the damp rag to her forehead. She took it from his hand and set it on the table.

"I am fine, just fine, thank you." Her head was swimming. "I remember my uncle telling me you were coming to Paris. We had been talking about your books."

Hemingway made a case to exit. "I've disturbed you enough."

"No, no! Please, sit with us, Mr. Hemingway," Chloe pleaded. "I am quite fine. This was just, just a surprise. This was a shock to hear my uncle's name after so many years."

Jack grinned. "Chloe's had a few surprises the past couple days." She rolled her eyes at him. Hemingway snapped his fingers at a waiter and ordered a plate of Torticas de Morón for the table.

"You'll love them. I guarantee they will soothe you. And a Cuba Libre for me."

Chloe and Jack ordered another round of lemonade, and Hemingway toasted, "To a gorgeous day with a beautiful woman. Welcome to Havana, Madmoiselle Boisvert!"

The conversation quickly grew comfortable as Ernest regaled the couple with stories of Paris in the twenties, spurring a series of vague remembrances for Chloe, some of which flowered into lovely, fully formed memories of happy people and gay parties.

"All the writers, the musicians, dancers and artists, of all of them the most intriguing, exotic, and charismatic was Josephine Baker."

"Auntie Josephine!"

"*Auntie* Josephine? Surely you jest."

"She was not really my aunt, but yes, that is what I called her." Her eyes misted over her smile. "I loved her very much and felt she loved me, and of course, there was Chiquita." A happy tear formed in the corner of her eye. Hemingway squinted at her over a sly grin. "Josephine's cheetah." Chloe giggled and dabbed her eyes. "Chiquita was quite gentle with me, yet not so much when she was in the club during Auntie Josephine's performances."

Hemingway laughed heartily. "When I knew Josephine, she wasn't exactly keen on children. But then she was still quite young. To be your auntie, you must have made some impression."

"We had so much fun together."

The two stunned each other with tales of Josephine Baker. Her stories were sweet and surprising. His bordered on raunchy. Jack just sat back quiet, a fascinated witness to this extraordinary meeting, and he'd never seen Chloe so full of life. The way Hemingway described his friends in Paris, all the particulars, the subtleties, so vividly. Styles, mannerisms, speech patterns. Although Chloe had never met most of them, she felt she recognized many from his descriptions.

"Did you know Marie Laurencin?"

Hemingway pounced. "Marie! That dear, dear soul! Her paintings were not so much my preference, but excellent in their way, quite so.

I remember her house teeming with tiny dancers. Lovely little ballerinas, and their White Russian patron, his name eludes me. After I left France so many years ago, Marie and I maintained a correspondence. Sadly, I haven't heard from her since before the Occupation. Nowadays one never knows what will get through the post with the damn Nazis reading everything and stealing what they wish. I must send Marie a note, informing her of this happy coincidence."

After the initial shock of hearing her uncle's name wore off, Chloe could not have enjoyed Hemingway's colorful conversation more than she did.

"Tell me, what do you think of the Torticas?"

"They were splendid, yes. Thank you for introducing me to them."

Jack chimed in, "Chloe here is an excellent baker."

"Is that right, dear girl?"

Chloe blushed yet again.

"She makes this apple pie. What's that cheese you put in it?"

"Gruyère."

"I remember that, indeed. Tarte aux pommes avec gruyère. You learned in Paris?"

"Oui."

"Then I must ask you this favor, Chloe. Please, would you make your tarte aux pommes and allow me a taste? I haven't experienced that treat in such a long time."

"Ça me ferait plaisir, Monsieur Hemingway."

The writer slapped the table. "You are one fortunate man, Jack Benoit." He let out a hearty laugh. "Such a fortunate man."

Hemingway telephoned his wife, Martha, to clear the way, and invited the couple to dinner the following evening. He received their acceptance with a hearty "Bravo!" then excused himself from their company. "Oh, one more thing. May I?" He pulled a Brownie out of his satchel. "May I take your photograph? I'll send one to Marie, to accompany the letter that informs her of this fantastic coincidence."

* * *

Chloe was perched on the edge of her seat as the hired car cruised through San Francisco de Paula. "Can you believe it, PJ? We are visiting the home of Ernest Hemingway and Martha Gellhorn!"

As they climbed the winding drive between rows of tall arched trees, slivers of light lanced the canopy and burst on the shoulder of her scarlet polka-dot dress. Jack tossed some bills on the front seat and confirmed that the driver would return for them in two hours' time. He slid his arm around his nervous girl's waist. "They're just people, Honeybee."

"I'm not accustomed to keeping company with whites. You know that."

He cupped her face in his hands. As he drew closer, she closed her eyes, and he kissed both of them. "How 'bout we consider that maybe, *just maybe*, Ernest and Martha don't come from the same barrel as them crackers you've been dealing with?"

"I'm fine." She exhaled. "I promise."

"You know," he began, as they climbed the stone steps to the doorway, "I'm not having any of your pie tonight."

She turned to him, crestfallen. "Why would you say something so cruel, PJ Benoit?"

"I'm going to save room for my *favorite* dessert." He winked his eye and pinched her bottom.

Martha threw open the door. "Oh, Jack, isn't she lovely!"

"Martha, this is Chloe Boisvert. Chloe, Martha Gellhorn."

"Really, Jack. You sound like a boy at cotillion." The hostess turned to the girl. "How about a drink, Chloe?"

She was surprised the house was so simple. A single story, just two rooms wide. Beautifully furnished, but not extravagantly.

"We're fortunate to have so much light, which allows for all the flora in the house. It's what I like best about Finca Vigía. Nature doesn't stop at the door."

"It is truly a lovely home, ma'am." Chloe presented Martha with two flat boxes. They were warm.

"My dear, do I smell apple?"

"Yes. Two pies. Mr. Hemingway requested."

"Ha! Mr. Hemingway *requested*. Leave it to my husband to ask a dinner guest bring him a stack of pies."

Chloe blushed. "I believe he intends to present one of them to someone else, ma'am."

"Well, I can't imagine. Let's interrogate the scoundrel, shall we? And please, dear girl, call me Martha."

As they walked along a lengthy path of white marble lined with palms, butterflies fluttered in her stomach. They found Ernest reclining near the pool under the trellis, thick with flowering vines.

He smiled over the reading glasses perched on the end of his nose and set down his book.

"Buenas noches, Jack and Chloe!" He squeezed Jack tightly then kissed Chloe's cheeks. "Come, sit. We have a fresh pitcher of sangria. Martha's *perfecto*. Try some." He poured three glasses and topped off his own.

"The baked goods you ordered arrived."

"What?"

"This angel brought pie! In fact, pies. I understand this was at your . . . *suggestion*?"

"Oh, yes! Thank you, dear, dear girl." He turned to Martha. "Jack told me I must taste one of Chloe's delectable treats. We'll have one this evening. The second is for Elisa. Fulgencio and I are shooting clays tomorrow. I'll drop it by the house."

"For gracious sakes, Ernest." Martha sighed rather dramatically. "This *Fulgencio* to whom my husband refers is none other than El Presidente Batista, the man who runs this country. Elisa is his charming wife, la Primera Dama de Cuba." She whispered to Chloe, "Elisa is known for her sweet tooth."

Chloe's eyes widened, and Jack doubled over, laughing. "Moving up in clientele some, huh, Chloe?" He picked up two glasses, handing one to his girl. "Here's to you, kid!"

"*Casablanca!*" Martha and Ernest howled together. Jack joined in the laughter. Chloe was beside herself, confused. She was trembling, certain they were laughing at her. Martha stepped forward to ease her discomfort.

"Dear, I understand Ernest placed his order just yesterday." She feigned a sneer at her husband. "How ever did you create such gorgeous treats so quickly?"

Jack took up Chloe's hand and explained how La Palma had let her use their kitchen that morning. He whispered in her ear, "It's all good, Honeybee. You ain't in Abbeville anymore." He kissed her cheek.

Hemingway issued a proclamation. "Tonight, we eat dessert first."

Chloe sputtered an uncomfortable laugh as she wiped the tear that was trickling down her cheek. She saw the pool and gasped. The inside walls were aqua, the bottom a rich blue. She looked into Jack's eye. Her heart soared, but she still couldn't stop the tears.

***

She had a morning soak with chamomile bath salts in Jack's tub. The profusion of Parisian memories stirred up by last night's conversation competed for her attention until they were interrupted by a knock at the door. "May I come in?"

"Of course not. I'm not decent." He entered just the same. Chloe covered her breasts with a washcloth.

"Yeah, like I ain't seen 'em before."

She splashed him, which raised a crooked smile. He sat down on the commode.

"I've been thinking. How'd you like to open a place here? A restaurant. A bakery. Whatever you want. You're really good at cookin', and I have some money. Between Meyer and Ernest, they know everyone in town. It'd be a smash. Whaddya think?"

What do I think? There was Francie rolling her chestnut on a booth table. The reverend waving the letter from Howard University. Menta soaking her swollen feet. The dog running off with Hamilton's leg. Davey Johnson's tobacco spit running down her back.

"Why do you . . ." She paused. He sat there in silence. She screamed at him. "I have a life, PJ Benoit!"

"In Abbeville? You call what you have in Abbeville a friggin' life?"

"I have a family! Obligations. Francie needs me. Menta needs me. And all you care about is keeping me here with you. You are selfish, PJ Benoit. You want me to yourself, doing whatever you want me to do. Well, I am my own person! I am black, but I am . . . I own my life." She splashed him and screamed, "Get out!"

***

He kicked at a flattened cigarette butt and stepped into La Palma, plopping himself down on a barstool. "Café Americano, por favor." The barkeep hopped to it. Jack caught his reflection in the aged mirror behind the bar. The expression on his face. It was his daddy's, across the kitchen table from his mama as she ragged on him for spending time with darkies. "If she could see me now."

"Perdón?" The bartender reached for Jack's empty cup. "Uno mas, Señor Benoit?" Jack held up a finger.

"Señor Benoit?" It was smaller voice, coming from behind him. He turned to find a boy in a blue uniform. "El porter del edificio del apartamento me envió aquí. El telegrama."

Jack. Trouble here. Music Box burned.
Menta and Francie safe but need help.
Please reply. Frank.

* * *

"You were just there." Lansky stated the obvious and waited for Jack to fill in the blanks.

"It's an emergency, Mr. Lansky."

"Another emergency?" Lansky was aware that Jack had a new roommate, the result of his last trip, but he didn't mention it. "Sure, Jack. Whatever you need. But first I need you to make the run to Washington on Wednesday. It's important."

His first request to use the plane had been much more casual, and he was obviously in distress this time. But Lansky pressed him. "Look, I need you to collect the senator. We have important business to discuss. I just don't see you flying off to Louisiana again and leaving me hanging here, when I need you to fly in three days' time."

Jack knew he couldn't get access to another plane in short order. It was the Skyrocket or nothing. "Lives are at stake, Meyer," he said, coolly.

Lansky pursed his lips, looking into Jack's eye. He placed a hand on the young man's shoulder. "I told you once, Jack. Anything I can do for you, and I'm a man of my word." He pointed at the big man in the corner. "Tony, you go with him."

"Really?" Big Tony pushed himself out of his chair while Lansky glared at him. Immediately contrite, Big Tony changed his tone. "Sure, boss."

"It's not my preference, Jack, but I'll fly the senator down here commercial. You straighten out your situation. I'd like you back here by Sunday to fly the senator and some of his friends back home. Can we agree to that?"

Jack shook Lansky's hand with both of his own. "Thanks, Meyer. Thanks a lot. I won't be long."

As Campisi turned to follow Jack out of the office, Lansky caught him. "Let me know."

Chloe was curled under a throw on the davenport. He walked to the bedroom and tossed a change of clothes into a small canvas duffle. He was packing his shaving kit when she appeared in the mirror.

"Where are you going?" Her voice was scratchy, her eyes puffy and red.

"I hafta fly today. Do a job for Meyer."

She sensed something off in his voice. "That is not why you are leaving."

"No? Why am I leaving, Chloe?" He tossed the kit into the duffle and buckled the bag.

"You are done with me." A tear rolled down her cheek.

Jack's shoulders drooped. "Gahdammit, Chloe, I'm not done with you. Do you really believe I brought you all the way here, to friggin' *Cuba*, just to fly off and leave you here, in friggin' *Cuba*?"

She shrieked, "I do not know why you brought me here at all!"

He took her by the shoulders. "Chloe. Honeybee! Look at me. Look at me, please."

Her eyes were wet and clouded, but she met his.

"I love you. I ain't goin' anywhere. Well, I am, but just for a couple days. I hafta do somethin', then I'll be right back."

She backed away. "So, when you return, then you take me back to Abbeville? Is that what happens?"

"Of course not. Just stay here until I get back."

Chloe's anger rose again. "But what about Francie? What about Menta? They cannot run the café. They cannot get along without me."

Jack snorted. "You ain't gotta worry about that anymore."

"What do you mean, that I need not worry?"

Jack stammered. He'd blown it.

"Well . . . tell me!" Her eyes were crazy.

Hands on his hips, he stood there, thinking. Chloe was about to burst. Biting her lip, she waited him out.

"Okay. There's been some trouble in Abbeville."

"What?" Her tone shifted from angry to concerned. "What happened in Abbeville?"

Jack sat her on the bed and took her hands. "They burned the café."

She squeezed her nails into his hands, horror on her face.

"Frank sent me a telegram. Francie and Menta are okay. They got out safe, and they're with friends. I'm goin' up there to get them out."

"Out? What do you mean, out?" Chloe pushed him away. "You will get them out of Abbeville? Where do you think they are going?"

Jack tried to calm her. "Look, I'm gonna get 'em out of there. I figure I'll take 'em down to N'Orleans and give 'em some money until I can figure out what to do next."

"You? *You* will figure out what is next?" She stared him in the eye, her eyelids quivering with rage. "You killed that man, that *Sweeney* man."

"Look . . ."

She slapped him hard. "Yes, oh yes. This is what my family needs, this white man to tell them what they will do. You will them where they will go." She pounded on his chest with her fists. "Damn you, PJ Benoit. Damn you to hell!" She pushed him and stomped across the room. She pulled a second duffle from the closet shelf and emptied the drawer holding her new clothes into the bag.

"I didn't want to put you in danger."

Her voice lowered to a growl. "You will return me to Abbeville, and *I* will take care of *my* family, damn you." Seething, she got up in his face and stared him down again. "*You* did this."

* * *

"Dis is da famous Chloe Boisvert." Campisi curled his lip, learning just now that Jack's new roommate was black.

She smirked at the big man and curtsied. "Oui, je m'appelle Chloe Boisvert. Enchanté, vous grosse bête Italien." She was still seething, with no idea why she spoke in French.

Jack saw this going nowhere good. "Let's just get on the plane and get this done, all right?" Tony entered the cockpit to take the copilot seat, but he was too wide to fit. "Back there." Jack thumbed him toward the passengers' compartment and commenced the ignition sequence.

"With the nigg . . ." Jack glared at the muscle, raising a finger in his face. Tony glared back. "Fuckin' dark meat."

He took a seat across the aisle from Chloe. She huffed, unclipped her seatbelt, and moved toward the cockpit. Big Tony grabbed her by the arm and yanked her back into the seat.

"Dere ain't no way you're gonna sit in front of me, blackie."

Chloe knew that if she tried again to stand, the big man would smack her. She took a deep breath and closed her eyes. *Francie and Menta. Francie and Menta.*

"Strap in!" Jack yelled over the roar of the engines.

36

TRADING RECIPES

MARCH 1943

Campisi lit up the dark passenger cabin when he fired his first Lucky Strike. He pocketed his silver Zippo and leaned across the aisle, mouthing something Chloe couldn't hear over the noise of the engines. She shrugged and watched him take a deep drag. This time he yelled, "I said, I met a friend of yours in New York!"

She glanced up at Jack, who was wearing headphones and focusing on the instruments. "Whom did you meet?"

Campisi smirked. "Louis Armstrong."

Astonishment overwhelmed animosity.

"Yeah, he was playing at a club up in Harlem." He pointed the glowing butt at the cockpit. "I introduced him to Blackjack there."

Chloe put a hand to her mouth. She leaned into the aisle. "I knew Louis when I was a child, in Paris. He is a fine musician and a wonderful man."

Campisi chain-lit another cigarette and flicked the spent butt to the floor, twisting it under his shoe. "Me, I'm more of a Harry James guy."

Chloe pictured the vinyl exploding into shards at her feet. She figured this lummox wouldn't know real music if it poked him in the eye. "But I like his stuff okay, Armstrong, dat is. My girl, Bella, she likes him. I take her to 52nd Street, not uptown with all them niggers."

Chloe's rage coursed back through her veins, but she gave it a moment of thought. *Why not?* She took a deep breath. "You have a girl in New York?"

"Yeah."

"And you live in Cuba?"

"I go where Mr. Lansky goes. He's in Havana, I'm in Havana. He's in Manhattan, dat's where you kin find me." The gorilla pulled a silver flask out of his coat and took a swig.

"You are fortunate," Chloe offered.

"Yeah? How's dat?" Campisi kept squirming. Too much ass, not enough seat.

"I have not heard Monsieur Pops play for many years, and you can see him most anytime when you are in New York. That is why you are fortunate." Campisi squinted at her as he took a long draw from his cigarette. "I traveled across the Atlantic with his wife, Lil Hardin Armstrong. She was his wife then. She wrote many of the songs he made famous."

"Dat right? A woman writin' songs."

"Yes. Much of today's music comes from songs written by women, back in the twenties and thirties."

"You don't say?" He opened the flask again and pointed it at her. "And I suppose women invented booze, too, huh?" He belly-laughed and took another pull.

"No, I am quite certain a man invented alcohol, vice being an inherently male characteristic."

Campisi guffawed and coughed. "Well, ain't you jus' the philosophical nigger."

Chloe bristled. "I am a lady, *Mr.* Campisi."

Big Tony flushed with anger. He dropped the butt to the floor with the other, ground it the same, flamed another Lucky Strike and snapped his pocket lighter hard. He looked across her seat, out the window at the burnt orange glow on the western horizon.

"Mr. Lansky told me to watch out for the both a youse," he said, shaking the Zippo at the cockpit. "But that don't mean I gotta take no lip from you, capisce?"

"Qualsiasi cosa tu dica, Il Duce!" She surprised both of them.

"What'd you say to me? Il Duce? You callin' me Mussolini?"

Chloe snapped back. "You would prefer El Duse?"

Campisi's eyes widened, incredulous. He worked to parse what she'd said. Eleanor Duse was Italy's most famous stage actress. Chloe sat back with a smirk. Something had come over her. Something she hadn't felt since Paris. Confidence. She whispered to herself, "I'm done living in fear of these white men." She glared at Campisi. "To hell with all of you!"

Big Tony Campisi was laughing hard so didn't hear her. "El Duse. I get it!" He had worked out the pun. "Youse full of surprises, ain't choo, kid?"

Chloe studied him. "What happened to *nigger?*"

Campisi drew hard on the cig and took another pull off the flask, pocketed it, and tapped the lapel of his overcoat. Then he leaned back easy and started rambling.

In a blend of English and Italian, he talked at her about food. Where to find the best imported tomatoes in New York. His mother's cannoli. How he liked the thick spaghetti best. Chloe just sat there, flabbergasted. After a lengthy session on olives, he paused to flame another cigarette, so she joined in. Her Italian was rusty, but just last year the reverend had loaned her a copy of *Orlando Furioso*, which she read through twice.

She told him how Miss Sophie would have her name ingredients in different languages while they baked at the apartment on Rue de l'Odéon, and she listed all she could remember in Italian. He recited his mother's recipe for manicotti. She recited Sophie's recipe for spinach ravioli. They laughed to learn that Carli olive oil had been ever-present in both of their childhood kitchens. Chloe closed her eyes and pictured the bottle on the counter. She could feel the warmth of the stove, the smell of provolone, parmesan, and garlic as Sophie tossed tortellini and pine nuts in a cast-iron skillet.

Jack set the autopilot and climbed back. He found his passengers laughing and cackling in Italian like a couple of old ladies walking up Mulberry Street. Campisi was beet red, laughing so hard he had started tearing up. He honked into his kerchief. "Da kid here's a hoot!" Jack was speechless.

"Who is flying the plane, PJ?" Chloe asked, nervously.

"Yeah . . . so we're approaching N'Orleans. We'll be down in about twenty minutes. Make sure you're buckled in." Campisi lit another cigarette. Jack waved his hand through the fog hanging in the cabin. "You keep that up, and I'm gonna hafta crack a window so I can see the damn runway." He eyeballed Campisi. "It'll get a little cold." Big Tony grunted and snuffed the butt.

As Jack taxied to the hangar, Joey flagged the plane to the same spot it had sat just days ago. Jack spun it toward the runway. A tall white man in a brown overcoat and tweed cap greeted Campisi and leaned into his ear, pointing to two black sedans outside the fence. He handed Big Tony a key and left in one of the sedans.

"Good to see you again, Captain Benoit." Joey shook Jack's hand.

"I'd love to borrow the Indian again, Joey, but I have guests this time." After sizing up the mobster, the mechanic grew sheepish. "Check it out and fuel it tonight," Jack told him. "Not sure how long we'll be in town."

"Tonight? It's almost midnight! They told me I had to stay until . . ."

"You heard da man." Big Tony got in the mechanic's face. "You make sure dat everything checks out." He pressed a Ben Franklin into the mechanic's greasy palm. "You're gonna stay here, right here, until we get back. You ain't goin' home tonight, capisce?"

Jack smiled at the young man. "I'm not sure when we'll be back, sometime tomorrow. What my friend is asking is for you to stay here until we show up. It's important, Joey, and it'll pay." The boy looked confused, and he wouldn't look the massive hood in the eyes. He nodded.

"Yes, sir. I'll stay right here until you get back."

Jack snatched the key from Campisi. "You don't know these roads." He winked at Chloe. "Wouldn't do to skid into a swamp and end up gator bait, now would it?"

Chloe smiled. "No, it would not do."

Campisi was down from his high and getting grumpy. "Let's get somethin' to eat. They got any decent places here?"

Chloe and Jack looked at each other and grinned.

It had been far too long between meals for the muscle when they pulled off the side of Highway 90 at Écrevisse Paradis, and Big Tony was angry. Three feral cats were tearing at something on the roadside, and he growled, "What's dis dump?"

"Crawfish Heaven. A good friend of mine here makes the best damn gumbo in St. Mary's Parish!"

Chloe leaned forward from the backseat. "Il miglior gumbo, El Duse!"

"Fuckin' hicks." Campisi shook his head. "I'm not eating in dat outhouse." Chloe and Jack both climbed out of the car, and Campisi shouted out the window, "What the fuck is gumbo?"

A barefoot kid ran out from the shack. He turned and yelled, "Dat white man's back!"

The old man came out, barefoot and rubbing his eyes. It was something past two in the morning. Jack shook the old man's hand.

"Clarence. Not sure you remember us. I'm Jack, this is Chloe."

"I sho do! Eh's good to haff you back, Missah Benoit. Youse wanten mo gumbo? Eh's pretty late fo suppa, ain't it?"

"Three bowls, Clarence. You got any gator?"

"Sho do. Yessah. Fry some up fresh jes foe you."

"That's great, Clarence. And three cold Dr. Nuts."

"Yessah. Right away. Boy, go teh deh icebox."

Campisi joined them at the picnic table, grumbling in the dark, he was swinging at a mosquito. "I'm so damn hungry. Can't believe you brought me to dis dump, you sonuvabitch." He looked around. "I don't know how you people live way the fuck out here. Christ Almighty."

Clarence and the boy arrived with three steaming bowls of gumbo, a plate of fried alligator, fried pickles, and bread.

"The rice been sittin', Missah Benoit. Hope dat okay. These heah sawses, the red one hot, oooooweee boy. Northern folk needs be careful. The brown one sweet. Youse enjoy."

Jack dipped a piece of fried gator in the red sauce and popped it in his mouth. He pushed the plate to Campisi. "Try some."

Campisi pinched a fried pickle chip and tossed it back, dry. He dipped one in the sweet sauce, then another. He wolfed down the gator bits. "Not bad."

"Try the gumbo," Chloe offered. "There is rice on the bottom of the bowl. You mix it on the spoon."

"Like Chink food." Big Tony dug in.

The boy brought a loaf of bread with butter. Jack twirled his empty Dr. Nut. "Another round." As Campisi wiped his bowl clean with a piece of bread, Jack finished his second soda.

"You ate up like a right ol' coonass, my Italian friend."

Campisi smirked, wiped his mouth with brown paper, and looked around. "Can't say I 'preciate the ambience, but the food was damn good." He started walking toward the woods.

"Where you goin'?"

Campisi hollered back without turning around. "I ain't gonna piss in no nigger shack, now is I?"

Chloe laughed, and Jack looked at her, puzzled. "Your mobster friend is a jackass, PJ Benoit. L'âne extraordinaire."

"Let's go." He took her arm. "You know, that jackass is here to make sure your family's safe, and he didn't know y'all are black. You might want to remember that."

It was after four when Jack cut the sedan's engine on the street outside Frank and Odette's place. The windows were dark. "I'll go wake my brother. Y'all stay here."

A light appeared inside the house. The front door opened, and two shapes moved onto the porch. "Let's go." Campisi pulled his door handle.

As the girl and her protection approached the Benoit brothers, the screen door burst open. Wrapped in a robe, Odette bumped into her husband as she ran to throw her arms around Chloe. Odette was sobbing, and Frank had to pry her off the startled girl. Chloe looked up at him, but Frank averted his eyes.

"We don't need a show, Bebe." He extended his hand to the big man. "Frank Benoit."

"Tony Campisi. Pleasure."

Frank turned to Jack. "Let's have a chat. Odette, take Chloe inside, please." The men walked around to the drive. "How was your trip?"

"Really, Frank?" Jack said, dryly. "What's the situation? Where are they?"

Frank explained how Menta and Francie were still in Abbeville, staying with friends. Odette had brought them lunch and found Menta scared to death. Francie was terribly upset about the Music Box. They'd escaped with nothing but their nightclothes.

"The people they're staying with are afraid. All Coonsville is. The lynchin', the Jones man's parts, the fire. They want Menta and Francie gone, but they got nowhere to go."

Jack told Frank he'd find them a place down in New Orleans, figure out what to do more permanently once things cooled off. Frank shuffled the dirt with his feet and shook his head.

"I don't know if things are ever gonna cool off, Jack. Deputy Davey came by here last week. He told me if he finds you in Vermilion Parish, it ain't gonna be pretty."

Jack laughed.

"Dammit, Jack, he means to kill you."

"Well, big brother, that's somethin' you might've told me before we showed up."

Frank was incensed. "You think I'm going to send you a telegram saying the law wants you dead? You didn't even tell me you were coming! You just show up here in the middle of the night. Goddamn, PJ."

"I'm Jack, remember?" He joked.

Big Tony raised his meaty chin and blew a slow fat smoke ring into the night, then popped a smaller one through it before they both dissipated over Frank's head. Frank looked at the two of them like they were out of their minds.

"Okay, Frank, okay. I get it." Jack said calmly. "Look, we're just gonna go pick 'em up and get the hell out of here. No one's even gonna know we were in town."

"You best watch it," Frank warned. "Don't you go strolling into Coonsville thinking it's a piece of cake. It ain't. If Johnson gets wind you're in town, it's gonna get ugly and fast."

Jack asked, "What do you think, Tony?"

Frank studied the mobster. By the look of him, the guy had skills, but he didn't know Louisiana. The Johnsons would cut this dago to shreds and feed him to the gators.

"Waiting 'til daylight don't get us nutin'. If dey're watchin' the place, dey ain't gonna take a break, whether the sun's shinin' or not." He flashed the Zippo and flamed another smoke. "If dey're watchin' the place, we'll need a diversion. Something dat'll pull 'em outta dere long enough for us to get in, get out." He snapped his fingers.

As the plan was hatched, Frank's blood boiled. "You're proposing to start a fire, as a *diversion?*"

Campisi asked if anyone on the other side had a property nearby. "It's the last thing they'd expect. And fuck 'em. They deserve it. Am I right, or am I right?"

Frank couldn't believe what he was hearing and started yelling at the tough. Jack stepped between them.

"Settle down, Frank. We don't want to wake the neighbors. We ain't gonna burn nothin' down. Look, Tony. First off, let's just drive by there. We just cruise through easy, see? See if anyone's keepin' an eye out. This ain't New York, and it ain't likely they're gonna have someone sittin' there in Coonsville at what . . ." He checked his wristwatch. "At four in the mornin'. And if anyone is there, they'll be in a car where they can see the house, right?" Jack turned to Frank. "No car, no diversion. No need to get worked up about a plan we don't know we need. Most likely there ain't gonna be anyone 'round to bother with."

Campisi agreed. "Yeah, I can't see no coppers losin' sleep to make sure a cripple nigger woman don't slip away in the night. We'll be in and out, *zip zip.*"

"I gotta pee." Jack walked off toward the car barn and disappeared into the darkness. He didn't bother with the drop lamp and fumbled for the old bucket on the high shelf. The .45's clip still held seven rounds.

The women joined the men in the drive, and Campisi went around back to relieve himself.

"What is going to happen, PJ?" Surprisingly, Chloe sounded calm.

"We're gonna pick up Menta and Francie. Simple. We're doin' it now."

Chloe shivered.

Odette started. "PJ, you think . . ."

Frank interrupted her, "It's the best way, Odette. There ain't no other choice. Now get inside."

"Wha?"

"You shouldn't hear any of this. Just go inside, please."

Odette huffed and stormed into the kitchen.

Jack explained to Chloe that she would hide in the backseat as they cruised past the house. If they didn't see anyone suspicious, she would get out and wake the people inside. He and Tony would circle the block so as not to draw any suspicion or frighten anyone. They'd park a few doors up the street and wait for her to come out with Menta and Francie. "We pull up to the house, y'all hop in, and we're off to N'Orleans."

"And what if someone is watching?"

Jack looked at his brother. "No one'll be watchin'. It's all gonna work out fine."

Chloe looked at Frank, who caught her gaze. He quickly looked away, then at his feet. Chloe took three big steps and threw her arms around him. As she squeezed tight, Frank's face flushed and his arms spread wide, like wings on a totem pole. Chloe sniffled, patted him on the back and whispered, "Thank you." Frank released the breath he'd been holding and wrapped his arms around the girl. She pushed off him and ran to the car.

Jack gave his brother a lazy salute. "I'll give y'all a holler when it's settled." They shook hands, and Jack pulled him close and whispered, "I left you a little something. It's in the seat of your truck."

"What's that smell?" Chloe asked as they climbed into the sedan.

Campisi answered, "Dat's Plan B."

In the trunk sat a can of kerosene Tony had found in the car barn. As they pulled away, Odette hollered for them to wait. She ran over to Jack's window. "This come for you." She handed him an envelope and took his hand. "Be careful, Sha."

Frank opened the door to his truck. Patting the seat in the dark, he felt a piece of paper. It was a check made payable to Frank Benoit for fifteen thousand dollars. The scribble on the note line read, "*Start a business t-boy.*"

37

THIRTY-TWO

MARCH 1943

A chill ran down her spine as the car moved up Louisiana Street, and she gasped when they rolled past the remains of the café. The tallest bits standing were a blackened stove and the charred pile that had been the Victrola. "Mon Dieu."

Tony flamed a smoke and exhaled the plume out the window. "What's done is done. Cut the lights." They headed east and circled the block of the house where Menta and Francie were hiding. "I don't see nothin'." His eyes darted like a fox on the hunt. "One more time around."

He had Jack pull over just up the block. Chloe jumped out, and Jack pulled away, his expression betraying his anxiety. Tony filled the front seat with blue-gray smoke.

"Hold it together, my friend. Can't be any worse than them Japs, am I right, or am I right?"

Jack let out a nervous laugh and, following orders, circled a couple blocks and pulled the dark car to a stop three doors up from the house, which was now lit from the inside. He didn't get anxious in the sky over Burma, over China, over the Hump. But this was clawing at his gut.

"Dumb niggers got the lights on," Tony fumed. "Don't know nothin' from nothin'."

Five minutes passed, then ten. "Dis is taking too long, and the goddamn lights are still on. If anyone comes 'round, it's gonna draw attention."

CHLOE'S MISTIGRI

"What do you want to do about it?"

"We'll give 'em a couple more minutes, den we'll go in dere and move dere black asses."

A couple minutes later, an eternity for Jack, the house went dark. Shapes appeared in the front yard. Jack started the car and pulled up to the house.

"Get your sorry black asses in here, now!" Big Tony slapped the car door.

Francie climbed in. Chloe helped Menta. She closed the door and ran around the back to get in on the other side. Francie pushed by her and ran back into the house.

"What's going on?" Tony was incensed.

Chloe ran after her sister. The lights came up in the house again, and from the car, they could hear commotion from inside.

Jack asked Menta, "Do you know what's happening?"

She was shaking. "Francie musta lef sompin, I doan know."

A light flashed in the sedan's rearview mirror. A vehicle had turned onto the street two blocks back and was heading their way. The girls were still in the house, and Jack could see movement through the curtains in the windows. The headlamps were closing in.

"What do we do, Tony?"

The mobster slid a hand under his coat. "Jus' be still." As a dilapidated green Ford flatbed slowly rolled past, Jack met eyes with the driver, who was holding a pint bottle against the steering wheel. He'd never seen the Lafayette man named Gene Blackmore, so he didn't recognize the face. A single brake light flashed as the truck stopped in the road ahead. Just then the sisters came running out of the house and jumped in the car.

"He's pullin' out." Tony pointed as the truck turned at the next corner. "We've been made. Let's get outta here."

As Jack turned from the muddy streets of Coonsville onto the highway, he caught a glimpse of the three terrified faces in the rearview. Campisi pulled a cigarette and tossed the empty pack out the window. He flamed the smoke and slammed his silver pocket lighter closed. "Goddammit." He turned to face Chloe. "Didjou tell 'em like I said?" Chloe nodded.

She explained again to Menta what they were doing. At least what the story was. "We're going to New Orleans. There's a place where you can stay. Everything's going to be all right."

"Where I kin stay? What dat mean, I kin stay? Mean you ain't stayin' wit me? Wit us?" Menta was crying hard.

"Of course I will. Everything is going to be fine."

Big Tony was seething. "What the fuck was dat about, anyways?" the mobster shouted at the windshield. Francie started to wail, and Campisi pounded his fist on the dashboard.

"Look, Tony, it's done," Jack said. He raised his voice to be heard in the backseat. "We're outta there. Never goin' back. It's done."

Francie was rocking over her cupped hands.

"Was it the chestnut, Francie?" Chloe asked. "Is that why you went back into the house?"

Francie, crying softly, nodded. Chloe cradled her sister, rocking with her as the car raced east on Highway 14.

* * *

It took all of twenty minutes to make Highway 90 at New Iberia. It would be three more hours to the airport. "PJ, we need to pull over."

Tony jerked around. "What? Are you crazy?"

Chloe continued, "Menta can't hold it. She has a condition."

Tony fumed, "Goddamn circus!"

"We'll figure it out," Jack said, calmly. "We'll pull off outside town." Ten minutes later, he steered the sedan onto a dirt road.

"Make a three-point and get us facin' the highway," Tony ordered. When Jack shifted the car into neutral, Chloe and Francie helped Menta out of the car. Jack tossed Chloe his handkerchief, and Tony mumbled something under his breath, then threw open his door. "I'm gonna take a piss." He'd settled down some by the time he crawled back into the car. He lit another cigarette. "Dis'll work out. If dey ask dem niggers back at the house, dey'll hear we headed north."

Dawn was a short time off when they cruised through Amelia. "Best joint in Mary's Place," Tony chuckled as they passed Écrevisse Paradis on the outskirts. All three women were asleep in the back. Tony tuned the radio. Peggy Lee was belting out, "Why Don't You Do Right?" It woke Chloe.

"Great song. Dame's got pipes." Tony drummed the dash along with Benny Goodman's band.

"This is 'Weed Smoker's Dream.'"

"Wha'd you say?"

Chloe repeated herself, informing the men in the front that Joe McCoy wrote and recorded the song back in 1936. She leaned over the bench. "It was originally called 'Weed Smoker's Dream.' *White thieves.*"

Dawn was breaking, and the snoring in back had settled, leaving nothing to compete with Alice Faye's torching rendition of "A Journey to a Star."

This journey that we're on
Where both of us grow strong

"Shit." Tony reached out the window and adjusted the side mirror. "Coppers." Sure enough, back in the distance, a pair of bright white lights framed a flashing red one. The lights were closing fast.

Jack straightened up. "What do we do?"

Tony took a drag and flicked the butt out the window. "Jus' keep cruisin'. It might be somethin' else. If it is, pullin' off would jus' draw attention." He flared another cigarette, pocketed the lighter, then patted his lapel. "If dey pull us over, you follow my lead." Jack retrieved his Colt from under the seat. He cocked a round into the chamber and tucked the handgun under his thigh.

The squad car was on his bumper, and Jack struggled to see the road past the glare in the rearview. The cops hit the siren, and Tony pointed to a dirt turnoff up ahead. "Here. Take 'em down a ways, get 'em off the highway." As they bounced onto the muddy side road, all three women woke with a start.

"What is it, PJ?" Chloe touched his neck.

Tony answered her, "Dey're onto us, kid."

Tony reached back to her, and Jack caught a flash of silver. "What, are you givin' her your lighter? The kerosene?"

Menta moaned. She was breathing hard and began to wail.

"Shut up, woman!" Tony barked. "We'll handle dis. Youse jus' keep your yaps shut! Youse don't say nothin', capisce?" Jack stopped the car, and the men rolled their windows down all the way.

"Turn off the car," the order blasted from a bullhorn. Beyond the patrol car's headlamps, Jack could make out the silhouette of a figure standing behind the open driver's door.

He cut the engine and turned off the headlamps. He grabbed the door handle.

"Stay in the fuckin' car," Tony ordered. But Jack stepped out.

He tried to shade his eye from the squad car's headlights. "What's the problem, officer?"

"I'll tell you what ta problem is." Jack could now see that the silhouette was holding a shotgun. It was Davey Johnson.

"Are my eyes foolin me, oh ain dat Li'l PJ Benoit." The deputy approached slowly, followed by Gene Blackmore. "Gene, once again I fine mahsef in ta comp nee of ta famous war hero." He circled around Jack. "Jap killah. Flyin Tigah. Mah ass." In a flash, he cracked the butt of his shotgun against Jack's skull, dropping him to his knees. He brought the butt down hard on the back of the dazed man's neck, then took another crack at his skull. "A nigga-loven murderer! Keep yo eye en im."

Blackmore stepped forward, cocking the deputy's .38 revolver, pointing it at Jack's head as he lay motionless, face in the dirt.

Johnson poked the shotgun barrel through the driver's window and jabbed the mobster's chest.

"Wha we have heah?" he said, looking back and forth between Tony and the terrified women in the backseat. Menta whimpered while Chloe stroked Francie's hair. "Seem deez white boys transpoatin' Abbeville's celebrity niggas down tah N'Orleans, yeah. Toll jah theyah be headen dis way." He poked Tony in the shoulder with the shotgun barrel. "Who dat?"

"Name's Campisi. What the fuck is it to you?"

Johnson screamed, "Get yo fat ass outta theyah! Now!" He yanked the driver's door open. "Slide ovah heah and keep yo hands weah I can see im." As Tony struggled his large frame across the seat, Johnson told Blackmore to get the women out of the back. "If any dem niggas even twitch, you shoot im in dah head, you heah?"

"Should I call ta sheriff, Davey? On da radio? Get some backup?"

"We doan need no backup."

"Well, how we gonna git im back ta town? They's too many of im."

"Tain goan back ta town, fool!" Davey Johnson's eyes flared with rage. "We goan finish it righ heah. Ain't no one goan no weah but in da ditch!"

Jack moaned and rolled in the dirt, trying to sit up. His ears were ringing, and his head throbbed. Everything was blurred, and all he could hear past the ringing was Menta moaning, "Les diables. Les diables."

Johnson screamed at the broken-down woman, "You goan mee tah tie!"

Tony was standing at the driver's door. "How much?"

"Wha? Whadya say ta me, you stin ken dago wop?"

"My employer is a very powerful, very rich man. I'm sure we can make an arrangement dat makes everyone happy."

"Ya heah dat, Gene? Dirty Italian pig sa goan make us rich men, yeah." He turned back to Tony. "Ya know, I tink en steah, maybe we jus skin ya an sell ta hides. Wouldn get nuttin foe dem niggas but . . ." That's when he saw the smallest of the three silhouettes behind Blackmore reaching out. "Da bitch gah ta gun!"

Chloe's entire body was shaking as she worked to steady Big Tony's nickel-plated .32 on Davey Johnson's chest. Blackmore raised the .38 special. Chloe got there first, squeezing a round into the man's neck. As Blackmore dropped to his knees, gurgling with both hands on his throat, Johnson swung the shotgun, but Campisi deflected the barrel. The blast tore through the side of the big man's overcoat, spraying buckshot into the sedan.

Jack writhed in the dirt as the blast stabbed his brain behind his empty eye socket. Everything was distorted and slow.

Big Tony fell against the sedan and slumped to the ground. Johnson pumped a fresh shell into the chamber of the shotgun. Jack was trying to stand when another blast rattled his head, and he reeled and dropped to all fours. Johnson buckled, tumbling over the shotgun, his heavy frame smashing Jack into the dirt.

His brain muddled, Jack felt someone tugging on his arm. Still, all he could hear over the ringing in his ears was Menta wailing. His sight was blurred, but he could make out the silhouette of a man, backlit by the squad car's headlamps. He was on his knees, his hands around his throat.

Blood spurted through Gene Blackmore's fat stubby fingers, trickled down his arms and dripped off his elbows, dappling the legs of his bib overalls. From beneath Davey Johnson's corpse, Jack watched as Blackmore tipped forward, his face smashing into the dirt road.

Chloe dropped the .32 and ran to Jack. She cradled his head and caressed his bloody hair. "PJ? Can you hear me? PJ?" Francie was crying, pulling on his arm.

He tried to focus his eye on Chloe's face. "Honeybee? What happened? Where's Tony?" The big man was right there next to him, propped against the car door, coughing.

"Voilà, he is here." Chloe touched her love's forehead. Jack struggled to his feet and studied the lawman and his cohort, two blurry heaps on the road. With his foot, he lifted Johnson's head and found a bloody mess where the deputy's right eye used to be.

"They're all done, Honeybee."

Chloe squeezed him tight.

"Your girl shot them sons-a-bitches." Tony winked at Chloe and coughed again. "Saved all our sorry asses." The coughing wouldn't stop.

Jack dropped to his knees, his ears still ringing. "Let me take a look." He tugged on the big man's overcoat. It was shredded on the one side, smelled of gunpowder and was wet with blood. He peered inside and was relieved to find the buckshot had just grazed the side of his friend's ample belly.

Tony friendly-slapped Jack's face. "Nothin' to see here, Cap'n Blackjack." He motioned Chloe closer. "C'mere, kid. Here's da plan."

Chloe extracted the wallet from his suit coat and found the calling card. "Address. Right dere. If more coppers show, I'll take care of 'em while youse keep goin'. At da garage, you ask for Vinnie. He'll work it all out."

Jack nodded, but he still wasn't right in the head. He couldn't focus, and the terrible piercing pain behind his empty eye socket was making him nauseated. Chloe was trembling.

"Look, youse jus' follow me. Dat plan's jus' for if tings don't work out so good." They struggled the big man to his feet, but he wouldn't let either of them tend to his wound. "Leave it. We's got work to do." They eased him behind the wheel of the squad car.

He asked Jack, "Sure you're okay to drive?" They laughed, and Tony entered a coughing fit. "Dem stiffs in da trunk?"

Chloe nodded, tears streaming down her cheeks. Tony pulled out his handkerchief. She took it with a sad smile.

"Shut the door, kid. It's all good."

Chloe closed the car door and leaned in the window. The tough pointed at her. "Take care of that boy, capisce?" As the big man started up the squad car, she reached in and touched his sweaty head. "Put that copper hat on me, will ya?"

Jack dropped in behind the wheel of the sedan and promptly vomited. Chloe helped Menta and Francie get settled in the back. Both women were in shock. Chloe slid into the front on the driver's side, nudging Jack from behind the wheel with her bottom. "I will drive."

Jack chuckled, his head bobbing. "You don't know how to drive."

Chloe pressed the sedan's clutch and turned the key. The engine fired. "I watched Hamilton do it, and it did not look difficult to me. Instruct me." Moments later, she was in second gear, following close as Big Tony steered the Vermilion Parish Sheriff's car east on Highway 90. She ground it into third gear and soon was cruising along to the Ink Spots' "Don't Get Around Much Anymore." Her exhausted and concussed passengers snored heavily. Campisi's passengers didn't make a sound.

As the sun cleared the trees, Chloe knew it was shining down on New Orleans. *Not far now.* She pictured her papa dancing to the new Victrola in the parlor. It wasn't a memory, just a thought. She pictured his rain-soaked corpse on the train platform in Greenville, Mississippi. Her mommy singing and cutting carrots over the sink. Her pale, withered body in the casket at St. Augustine's. Uncle Paul smiling in the deck chair, scanning the horizon for whales. His ashen arm dangling off the stretcher. Hamilton jitterbugging at the hootenanny in Opelousas. That mangy dog dragging his severed leg down Louisiana Street. The booze-soaked rapists, sweating, grunting, laughing over her in the café. Their lifeless bodies marinating in blood, piss and shit in the trunk of the car she was following. She could see Big Tony's head bobble under that ridiculous campaign hat. It happened every time he coughed blood into his lap. She was trembling again and wished her PJ was awake. She stroked his crusty hair, matted with dried blood and dirt. His cheek was warm in her lap.

An hour later, Jack was still out cold. Francie was sporting drool. Menta jerked and snorted as they crossed the Huey P. Long Bridge and rolled into the Crescent City.

Chloe stopped behind the idling patrol car and shut down the sedan. The address on the door was the one on the card Tony had given her. She shook Jack awake. "We're here." She pointed at the patrol car. "He's just sitting up there." Jack approached the driver's side and found Big Tony with his head drooped under the campaign hat, his chin stained with blood. Chloe told Menta and Francie to stay in the car, hopped out and banged on the garage bay door. A man threw it open from the inside. It was the man named Vinnie, and Chloe explained about Campisi. She took the wheel of the patrol car through the window while Vinnie and Jack pushed it into the garage.

They worked the big man out from behind the wheel and got him on a cot. Vinnie made some phone calls, then informed Jack he had the situation in hand. They were to drive to the airport and fly out.

"What about Big Tony?" Jack asked.

"Nothing here for you to do. Mr. Lansky wants you to fly the plane out as soon as possible. We'll handle Big Tony."

With his head clearing, Jack could now see that Campisi was a lot worse off than he'd first thought. "Get better. I'll see you soon."

Tony opened his eyes. "We'll take da girls uptown to see your horn player." He winked at Chloe. "You're some tough cookie, kid."

In less than an hour, Jack had the Skyrocket climbing over the Delta, and Francie had her nose pressed against the window, amazed by the morning sun sparkling on the green water below. Menta was still moaning some, and she kept asking Chloe the same question, "Weah we goan agin?"

"We're going home." She kissed her aunt's cheek and moved up to the copilot's seat, where she took Jack's hand. He smiled under his Ray-Bans, which sat crooked over the patch. He tried to speak in a squeaky falsetto, like some cheesy damsel-in-distress in the movies. "You're my hero."

Chloe leaned over his seat and kissed him on the cheek. "Yes. Yes, I am."

38

SHINE

JULY 1943

The *Pilar* rocked on a mellow swell off Cayo Cruz del Padre.

"Cuba Libre?" Hemingway held out the icy highball, sweat trickling down the glass.

"Thanks, no."

"You choose to forego some fine opportunities for pleasure, my friend." Hemingway took a swig from the glass. "Mmm. Love the mint." Jack kept fiddling with his reel. "That's quite a story."

Jack nodded. He'd recollected the trip with unflinching candor, save for just one nickel-plated omission. Hemingway continued, "But that was Campisi's way, wasn't it? He lived by violence, he died by violence. The man met his maker the way he was meant to, protecting his charge." Jack said nothing. "So, no one knew they were chasing you? Nobody else knows what happened to them?"

"Best part of the story."

Hemingway was astonished. "I wish I could write it, Jack. I surely do. But, of course, I'll respect your wishes." While Jack tugged at the tangled fishing line, Hemingway laughed. "Are you about done yanking on that rat's nest? She's a goner, my friend. Toss it and grab another reel. Let's get some bait in the water."

For another hour and a half, they trolled for blues with no luck, which irritated Hemingway, who felt he was letting down his guest. But Jack didn't mind. It was a beautiful day to be on the water. Peaceful. The drone of the engine was comforting, the salt air felt good in his lungs.

"I heard Elisa verily enjoyed having Chloe for tea."

"Yeah, Chloe said she liked the pies so much she wants to set up a regular delivery to the presidential palace."

"That's grand!" Hemingway exclaimed. "An excellent foundation for the restaurant's success."

"Maybe so. They talked mostly about books and things. That's what Chloe said. La Primera Dama asked her if she's considering the university here."

"And?"

"And that's all she's been talkin' about since."

"And the restaurant?"

Jack smirked. "Maybe *I'll* be bakin' pies."

Hemingway cut loose with a hearty laugh. "Honest work! But I can't picture you standing in a kitchen all day."

They decided to call it a day.

Jack roped the buoy and tied off the boat.

"Just three days out. Are you ready?" Hemingway touched his shoulder.

Jack tucked his hands in his pockets and shrugged, but the crooked smile betrayed him. He fumbled in his back pocket and pulled out the envelope Odette had handed him that night in Abbeville. It had been there all this time, a letter postmarked Kunming, China.

```
8 March 1942

Dear Jack,

I hope this letter finds you fully healed and well
in America. We could use you here, but it's best for
you to remain healthy.

In February, I left CNAC to join the Kōngjūn. Our
operations have benefited from the US naval
victories at Midway Island and Coral Sea as the
Imperial Navy struggles to support the army's
efforts led from Indochina and Burma. We still meet
stiff resistance in the air and from the ground but
have had good success bombing Japanese bases and
```

harassing their ground forces. I lead the 5th Squadron of the Chinese American Composite Wing, all Warhawk drivers, and we are coordinated with the US 14th Air Force under the Generalissimo's command. Much hope for continued success against the aggressors.

I had a headstone made for Emma's grave. She rests in the cemetery at Changchun Mountain. I thought you should know.

With kindest regards,

舒浩

Shu Hao
Major, 5th Squadron

P.S. Wheresoever you go, go with all your heart.

    Jack folded the letter and rubbed his eye. He shook his host's hand. "I'll see y'all this weekend. This is very kind of you and Martha."

* * *

He hadn't been downtown for a couple days, and the kitchen looked fantastic. Beautiful stainless steel and iron. Shiny new pots, pans, and utensils hung from a large wire rack above the center island that divided the run. Opening wasn't for a couple weeks, but things were taking shape. Menta was mixing shrimp and grits, and something sweet was baking in the oven. Francie sliced fruit as Chloe stirred pork sausage in a sauté pan with onions, peppers, tomatoes, and spices. Amrita was organizing the spice rack, and Rodolfo and Cedro were overdue to practice recipes.
    "Smells wonderful." He kissed the back of her neck.
    "The sign man is coming at noon."
    "Sure he his." He snagged a slice of mango from Francie's pile and popped it in his mouth.
    She waved her knife. "No picking, PJ! You wait like the rest of us."

"You're the boss, Francie."

The sign man was late, but Jack had nowhere else to be. All the equipment was in. The chairs weren't right and had to be sent back, but that would be resolved in a few days. The electricity, the gas, the water. Everything else was set.

"Easy now." An old man and two young ones struggled with ropes and ladders to raise the sign above the entryway. They finished midafternoon. The women joined Jack on the street, along with Rodolfo, Cedro and Amrita. There it was, spelled out in red neon cursive over a large acrylic jack of hearts. *Café du Mistigri.*

"I like him," Chloe cooed, rubbing circles on his back.

"He doan look like you," Francie deadpanned. "He has a beard."

"I still think we shoulda named it the Honey Pot."

Chloe wrapped her arms around his waist. "I told you, everyone would think we sold honey."

"Or that we ran a whorehouse."

She huffed and pinched his bottom. Francie pulled them together for a tight, three-way hug. Chloe peeked again at the sign.

"It's beautiful. Menta, are you excited?"

Menta, leaning on her walker, just glowed.

***

Jack found his razor in the tub again. "*Really?* This is my last blade, and I gotta get to the airport."

"Just stop." Chloe put up a hand. "PJ, it is so close. Can this not wait until afterward?"

"I told you, Meyer insists."

Jack knew he wouldn't be able to placate her, no matter what he said. "Look, it's my job. No different than if I had a job that took me down to Santiago for a couple days."

He stood there.

She stood there.

"I told you, Honeybee, I'll be talkin' to Meyer about makin' a change. But I gotta make this run. It's important to him, and I made a commitment."

She turned her back to him. "Don't you *Honeybee* me."

He moved in behind her and caressed her shoulders. Touching her neck, he ran his fingers up to tweak her earlobe. The smoothness of her skin triggered his adrenaline. He closed his eye and savored the scent of the arm she raised to cradle his head, lavender mingled with musky almond. He flicked her ear with his tongue until she got the chills and curled around into him. With her eyes closed she took his tongue into her mouth.

In the taxi, it occurred to him this was the first time he'd lied to her. At a stoplight, he watched two little ones on the corner play cup-the-ball.

An hour hadn't passed when she heard the apartment buzzer. The letter was special delivery, addressed to Señorita Chloe Boisvert. She tipped the boy and curiously, furiously, tore open the envelope. It was her acceptance to La Universidad de la Habana. She would start in September. An ecstatic thrill pulsed through her body, then she cursed him for not being there.

* * *

On Saturday, he hired a car to Finca Vigía, and they arrived just past six o'clock. A party server answered the door. Martha burst forward and greeted them all with hugs and smiles.

"Hello! Come in! Justice Valdez is in the parlor. Don't you look lovely, Miss Francie!" Francie blushed and skipped into the house in her new blue linen dress.

"They say it makes one an honest man." Hemingway threw his arm over Jack's shoulders.

"I think they say a lot of things, Ernest. I say I'm lucky to have her."

Hemingway shook him hard as they hugged. "I'd offer you a drink, but I know the answer."

A gravelly voice carried into the entryway from the landing behind them. "Is that you, Miss Chloe?"

"Monsieur Pops! Mon Dieu!" She ran through the door and threw her arms around the man.

"Oh, my, my!" Armstrong belly-laughed.

She inquired breathlessly, "Comment allez-vous venu ici?"

"Cap'n Jack, here, mademoiselle. Yessiree! He come to get me in New York jus' yesterday. Fly down here in that fancy airplane. I been bustin' to see you, chile, but we thought surprise might be the way to go."

"Le coquin! Why did you not tell me?"

Jack absorbed her drumming on his chest. "That's how surprises work. If you tell someone, it's not a surprise anymore."

"Did someone say *surprise?*"

"Odette! Mon Dieu!" Chloe covered her cheeks, shocked.

"Did you think I was gonna miss my baby brother's wedding?" Frank stuck out his hand.

Chloe squeezed it with both of her own. Frank raised hers and topped them with a kiss.

"Sha Bebe, Chloe!" Odette hugged her tight, then held her out at arm's length. "You so beautiful. Sha, you really are." She lost a tear, and Frank pressed his handkerchief into her palm.

"My little brother flew us all the way here from Dallas, Texas."

Chloe was welling up. "Yes, so I see. And how is the tent business, your factory in Texas?"

"Actually, I'm making canvas knapsacks. Got two production lines up and . . ."

"Frank Benoit!" Odette scolded him and blew her nose. "Nobody here wanta talk bout yo work."

Chloe squeezed Jack's arm. "So, this is, *these are*, what Meyer needed flown into Cuba, yes?" She laughed through her tears.

Hemingway burst into the group. "Louis Armstrong!" He took up the horn player's hand, shaking it vigorously. "I'm a big fan of your music. Hear you on the radio all the time when we're out on the water. Brilliant!"

"Thank you, sir, thank you. And might I say, Mr. Hemingway, I enjoy your stories very much, yessiree."

Martha slid her arm under Chloe's and pulled her into the house. "Welcome, all of you! Please, come in and make yourselves at home." Francie returned and helped Menta with her walker.

* * *

The ceremony started promptly at seven. A simple civil affair with few words spoken. Jack slipped a narrow band of platinum onto Chloe's finger. They kissed.

The dinner was delicious, the conversation lively. Two dozen guests mingled on the patio under strings of Chinese lanterns. Jack pictured Emma in the corner, raising a bourbon. Stars sparkled in the sky, and fireflies danced among the begonias. Francie caught one, cupping it in her hands. She watched it flash through a hole between her thumbs until the critter crawled out the back and joined her kind among the trees. Menta was still on a comfy down cushion in a white wicker chair, smiling and nodding at the pleasantries directed her way. Hemingway poked Jack in the arm. "I understand you're married to a college girl."

"It is a dream." Chloe joined them, taking up Jack's hand.

"No. It's your life." He kissed her forehead.

"Choices." Hemingway interjected.

"Huh?"

"Chloe. This dear girl has choices." He motioned to one of the party staff, then tapped a wine glass with his pipe. "If I may have your attention, we have a little something for the newlyweds."

The guests turned their attention to the server, who brought in a thin, rectangular something wrapped in brown paper. Hemingway directed Chloe to a chair and set the package in front of the stunned, blushing bride. She tore the paper and gasped. Jumping to her feet, she threw her arms around the famous host.

"Merci! Merci! Merci beaucoup!" She kissed each of his hairy cheeks twice. Jack took up the lithograph, a young girl standing in a blue-and-white dress. In was inscribed with pencil in the bottom corners.

73/75   Laurencin 33

"For those who may not know, the wonderful French artist Marie Laurencin is a dear old friend of mine, and we have continued our correspondence despite the current conditions in Europe, where Marie lives in the dire state of Nazi occupation and oppression. Marie knew our beautiful bride during her childhood years in Paris, and she was thrilled to hear Chloe had come to be with us here in Havana. She asked me to pass along this portrait, made when the bride was just a child. Marie informed me she had made an oil of the portrait, too, which she sold some years ago. She made inquiries and learned some Nazi son of a bitch stole it from its Jewish owner. Nevertheless, this is a doubly happy occasion. A wedding *and* a reunion. A reunion of Mrs. Chloe Benoit with la petite jeune française, Chloe Boisvert."

Jack studied the print, an impression captured just months before he caught his first glimpse of this angel on the bank of Coulee Galleque.

"In her letter, Marie obliged me to look out for her *jolie jeune fille*." Hemingway raised his glass. The server carried away the print, and Chloe took Jack's hand. Hemingway blew her a kiss. "In no way shall I consider Marie's charge any manner of obligation. It will be an honor and a privilege, if Jack will humor me, and both Martha and I will engage our charge with vigor."

Jack snatched a glass of champagne from a server's tray as the room drank to Hemingway's toast. "I'd like to say somethin'."

"I can't imagine . . ." He turned to face his hosts. "Ernest and Martha, thanks loads for hosting our wedding. Y'all've been so kind to me and Chloe here." He scanned the room, all smiles and silence but for the leaves rustling in the gentle breeze beyond the veranda doors. "I've been around some. You know, I've seen some things, including a lot of folks who seem more caught up in the color of folks' skin than what's inside. And those folks ain't so kind. Hell, lots of 'em kill for it. Back home, we weren't even s'posed to talk to each other. Had to fly to Cuba, like the butterflies."

He met Meyer Lansky's eyes. "People back home call it the land of the free and the home of the brave, right? Seems to me there's some work to do on that first bit. Yeah, work to do on that first bit everywhere I've been." He paused in the silence. "So, anyway, thank all y'all for comin'. It means a lot to us. It does." Without a word, the room drank the toast.

Hemingway patted his back. "Well said, my friend. You are truly a citizen of the world, and you really should consider writing your story." He leaned toward the bride and whispered, "Chloe, we have yet one more wedding surprise for you." He handed her an envelope. "You might want to read this in private."

Martha led her to Hemingway's study. She motioned Chloe to his desk chair and exited the room, closing the door behind her.

Chloe sat down with the envelope. It was addressed to Madame Chloe Benoit, postmarked Marrakesh, French Morocco. In the desk drawer, she found a letter opener with some kind of antler for a handle. She sliced open the envelope and extracted a folded sheet of pink stationery.

15 June 1943

Chloe, my sweet Créole princess,

When word of you reached me from my dear friend Ernest, my heart leaped with joy and my eyes wept with relief. You cannot know the intensity of regret I have felt all these years for putting you on that ship. I should have kept you with me and raised you as my own. I shudder to think what you may have experienced in the south of the United States and will always hold myself accountable for any and all trouble that may have befallen you there.

In his letter to me, Ernest expressed his immense admiration and respect for your groom, Captain Jack Benoit. I trust my friend's judgment without reservation, and I sincerely hope the happiness you feel on your wedding day only grows over time. I will never forgive myself for sending you off, but with comforting the thought of you in love, in safety, health and happiness, my sleep last night was restful for the first time in ages.

I am in North Africa entertaining the Allied troops, doing what little I can to help them turn back the Nazi's and Fascist's abhorrent aggression. If I could be there with you, I would beg your forgiveness and hold you tightly, if you would let me. My immense love for you will never, ever leave my heart.

With deepest sincerity,

Auntie Josephine

A tear dripped off her nose and onto the pink page.

Meyer Lansky motioned Jack aside. "I've always admired your courage, Jack, and or course I appreciate the business we conducted overseas." He glanced over at Menta. "We've never had occasion to discuss it, Jack, but I will speak plainly. I don't approve of race mixing, and I must say that what I've learned today, I find disappointing, disturbing, to be honest. It's best if we agree to part ways. Thank you for inviting me, but I must take my leave now."

Lansky crossed the room to Ernest. "Thank you for having me in your charming home." He retrieved his hat and headed to the door.

It hadn't occurred to Jack that Meyer didn't know Chloe was black. The two hadn't met, and after learning it on the Skyrocket, Tony took it to his grave.

"Are you okay?" Hemingway looked concerned.

"With everything going on . . . a friggin' racist Jew. You believe that?" His head was on a swivel. "To hell with him. Where's my girl?"

Francie tugged on his sleeve. "I got a prezen for you." Pinched between her finger and thumb was a tiny white box tied with a thin yellow ribbon.

"For me?"

She helped him pull the ribbon.

"Francie!" Jack tipped the old chestnut into his palm. It had been rubbed clean of all but a few flakes of gold paint stuck in the crevices. Francie hugged him, laying her head on his chest. "Now you are one of us, PJ."

Chloe reappeared with Martha, who had waited for her outside Ernest's study. Her eyes were puffy and bloodshot. Armstrong dabbed her cheeks with his hankie. "Jus' look at you, chile." He raised her hand and kissed it. "Cap'n Jack, you one fortunate man, yessiree. This here Chloe was the sweetest little thing in all of *Gay Paris*. And now, looky you. A grown woman, an' a heavenly sight."

"Merci, Monsieur Pops. And thank you, Ernest, Martha, for acquiring Marie's painting, the print . . . the *Parisian Chloe*, and for allowing us to be married in your beautiful home. Seeing this picture, it fills me with such wonderful memories. C'est extraordinaire! And this letter . . . Mon Dieu." She held the envelope to her heart. "This is so . . . lovely. All of you are so kind. I cannot express my happiness, my gratitude."

Hemingway grinned. "You just did." He raised his voice to recapture the room's attention. "Everyone, please! Eat, drink, and be merry! Nuestra casa es vuestra casa!"

Chloe asked Armstrong if he'd sing a song. "Anything for you! What would you like to hear?"

"Whatever you wish, Monsieur Pops."

He whispered in her ear, and she nodded. The whole party squeezed into the parlor where Armstrong pulled the bench out from under the Steinway baby grand. Chloe sat and stretched her fingers.

"This is somethin' you mighta heard before, but I'm gonna start it up with how it was original, way back in 1910, I do believe. And the lovely bride, *Madame Benoit*, has graciously agreed to accompany me. I hope you enjoy it."

When I was born they christened me
Plain Samuel Johnson Brown
But I hadn't grown so very big
'Fore some folks in this town
Had changed it 'round to "Sambo"
I was "Rastus" to a few
Then "Chocolate Drop" was added
By some others that I knew

And then to cap the climax
I was strolling down the line
When someone shouted, "Fellas, hey!
Come on and pipe the shine!"
But I don't care a bit
Here's how I figure it

It had been years since Chloe last played "Shine."

Well, just because my hair is curly
And just because my teeth are pearly
Just because I always wear a smile
Like to dress up in the latest style

Her eyes locked on her PJ, so handsome in his wedding coat. Before this afternoon, she'd never seen him in a tie.

Just because I'm glad I'm livin'
Takes trouble smilin', never whine

PJ was looking at something outside, through the veranda doors.

Just because my color's shady
Slightly different maybe
That's why they call me Shine

Amid the applause and cheers, Chloe hugged her Monsieur Pops and crossed the room to her PJ, where he kissed her forehead and whispered in her ear.

"Honeybee."

PJ adjusted his eyepatch over a crooked grin and held his wife's hand.

ACKNOWLEDGEMENTS

My heartfelt gratitude and thanks to the inspirations and support for this story:

Terese, who one Thanksgiving during college brought me to her parents' home where I met her uncle, a Flying Tiger from the Second Sino-Japanese War. I regret I cannot recall his name, but he could tell a story.

My college roommate Bill, who turned me on to the Chicago blues. Koko Taylor, who performed at The Joynt in Eau Claire, my first blues show. The Blackcat Lounge, which for years served as my blues heaven in Austin. The Elephant Room in Austin, the Village Vanguard in New York, and le Caveau du Hauchette in Paris, where jazz took meaning for me. Bessie, Ma, Sippy, Lil and the other wild women who invented the blues. Louis, for decades of joy. Josephine, for her courage.

The wonderful historical writer John M. Barry for his insight and work. Ernest Hemingway for his written art.

The Flying Tigers, for their courage. Brad Smith, son of Flying Tiger ace Robert T. Smith, for the usage of the iconic aerial photography incorporated in the cover art.

All who fought and continue to fight aggression and injustice, including those who fight against the scourge of Jim Crow that still lives, breathes and thrives through greed and ignorance today.

My appreciation and thanks go out to those who assisted this project, including Suzanne Blankenship, Audrey Doidge, Lisa Leach, and Kimberly McPherson for their alpha reads and the care with which they delivered guidance regarding the manuscript. Adam Coffey for his counsel. Connie Herrman, Maya Smith, Monika Smith, Elijah Forzani Garrison, Jill Pellerin, and Sandy Termato, for their assistance with the cover art. The fine baristas at Dazbog, Alley Cat, and Genoa in Fort Collins, A Cup of Common Wealth in Lexington, and Ground Central on Manhattan's East Side where much of this book was written, for their cheer and great coffee. Laurie Chittenden and Constance Renfrow for editing, and Danielle Mazzella di Bosco for the cover design.

A very special thank you to Teresa Simoneaux, for her love and protection of Louisiana Creole language as expressed through my Odette's voice.

Please nurture love, craft peace, and never, ever relent in the fight against oppression and fascism.

PRIMARY CHARACTERS

Louis Armstrong	Songwriter, musician, bandleader
Lil Hardin Armstrong	Songwriter, musician, bandleader
Sri Sri Maharaja Bahadur	Maharaja of Cooch Behar, West Bengal, India
Josephine Baker	Entertainer
Jacques (Big Jack) Benoit	PJ's father
Elaine Benoit	PJ's mother
Frank Benoit	PJ's brother
Odette Benoit	PJ's sister-in-law
Petit Jacques (PJ) Benoit	Big Jack and Elaine Benoit's youngest son
Gene Blackmore	Jimmy Sweeney's friend from Lafayette
Chloe Chantale Boisvert	Theo and Pascale Chantale's youngest daughter
Paul Boisvert	Chloe's maternal uncle
Yvonne Boisvert	Chloe's maternal aunt
Sarah Brown	Lil Hardin Armstrong's assistant
Tony Campisi	Meyer Lansky's employee
Sal Capone	Flying Tiger pilot
Francie Chantale	Chloe's sister
Theo Chantale	Chloe's father
Pascale Chantale	Chloe's mother
Claire Chennault	Leader of the Flying Tigers
John James Clarke	British Royal Air Force pilot
Abhaijeet Dahrala	Indian Colonial Army sergeant major
Norah Davies	Jazz singer
Phillip (Eddy) Edwards	British Royal Air Force pilot
Martha Gellhorn	Writer and wife of Ernest Hemingway
Toby Gyer	Flying Tiger pilot
Shu Hao	CNAC and Chinese Air Force pilot
Ernest Hemingway	Writer
Doctor James Herod	Reverend of St. Mary's Congregational Church
Josephine Herod	Wife of Doctor James Herod
Bubba Johnson	Vermilion Parish sheriff
Davey Johnson	PJ's schoolmate
James Hamilton Jones	Chicago jazz club manager
Carl Jones	Flying Tiger ground crew chief
Sophie Landren	Chloe's nanny
Meyer Lansky	Mafia leader
Marie Laurencin	Painter
John McClintock	Flying Tiger ground crew chief
Manuel Molero	Boss of Plaquemines Parish
Maria Montessori	Founder of Montessori schools
Archibald Mountbatten	British Army major
Hank Novak	Army Air Corps sergeant
Leander Perez	Boss of St. Bernard's Parish

Sanda	Burmese prostitute
Bob Schneider	New York Times writer
Charles Sharkey	CNAC pilot
Shudra	Gun bearer
Emma Simpson	Nurse
Jimmy Sweeney	Davey Johnson's sidekick
Edward Sweetwater	Odette's father
Rob Talent	Davey Johnson's sidekick
Charles Thompson	British Royal Air Force pilot
Gil Weathers	Flying Tiger pilot
Armintha (Menta) Williams	Chloe's fraternal aunt

SONG BIBLIOGRAPHY

Chapter	Song
2	Atlanta Black Bottom *Discography of American Historical Recordings*, s.v. "Vocalion matrix E4094-E4095. Atlanta Black Bottom / Royal Flush Orchestra; Fess Williams," accessed April 24, 2020, https://adp.library.ucsb.edu/index.php/matrix/detail/2000222632/E4094-E4095-Atlanta_Black_Bottom.
2	Irish Black Bottom *Discography of American Historical Recordings*, s.v. "OKeh matrix 9981. Irish black bottom / Louis Armstrong; Hot Five," accessed April 23, 2020 https://adp.library.ucsb.edu/index.php/matrix/detail/2000202117/9981-Irish_black_bottom.
2	I'm a Mighty Tight Woman *Discography of American Historical Recordings*, s.v. "OKeh matrix 9929. I'm a mighty tight woman / Sippie Wallace," accessed April 24, 2020, https://adp.library.ucsb.edu/index.php/matrix/detail/2000202065/9929-Im_a_mighty_tight_woman.
2	Big Butter and Egg Man *Discography of American Historical Recordings*, s.v. "Columbia matrix W141238. Big butter and egg man / Phil Baker," accessed April 24, 2020, https://adp.library.ucsb.edu/index.php/matrix/detail/2000031002/W141238-Big_butter_and_egg_man.
2	The King of the Zulus (at a chit'lin rag) *Discography of American Historical Recordings*, s.v. "OKeh matrix 9776. The king of the Zulus (At a chit'lin' rag) / Louis Armstrong; Hot Five," accessed April 24, 2020, https://adp.library.ucsb.edu/index.php/matrix/detail/2000201912/9776-The_king_of_the_Zulus_At_a_chitlin_rag.
2	Dusty Bottom Blues *Discography of American Historical Recordings*, s.v. "OKeh matrix 9960. Dusty bottom blues / Richard M. Jones' Jazz Wizards," accessed April 24, 2020, https://adp.library.ucsb.edu/index.php/matrix/detail/2000202096/9960-Dusty_bottom_blues.

3   Down on the Levee Blues
        Discography of American Historical Recordings, s.v. "OKeh matrix S-71945. Down on the levee blues / Rosetta Crawford," accessed April 24, 2020, https://adp.library.ucsb.edu/index.php/matrix/detail/2000204095/S-71945-Down_on_the_levee_blues.

3   Broken Levee Blues
        Discography of American Historical Recordings, s.v. "OKeh matrix W400492. Broken levee blues / Lonnie Johnson," accessed April 24, 2020, https://adp.library.ucsb.edu/index.php/matrix/detail/2000209263/W400492-Broken_levee_blues.

5   Candy Lips (I'm stuck on you)
        Discography of American Historical Recordings, s.v. "OKeh matrix W80214. Candy lips (I'm stuck on you) / Clarence Williams' Blue Seven; Eva Taylor," accessed April 24, 2020, https://adp.library.ucsb.edu/index.php/matrix/detail/2000206843/W80214-Candy_lips_Im_stuck_on_you.

5   You Made Me Love You
        Discography of American Historical Recordings, s.v. "OKeh matrix 9980. You made me love you / Louis Armstrong; Hot Five," accessed April 24, 2020, https://adp.library.ucsb.edu/index.php/matrix/detail/2000202116/9980-You_made_me_love_you.

5   Red Hot Flo (From Ko-ko-mo)
        Discography of American Historical Recordings, s.v. "OKeh matrix W80740. Red hot Flo (From Ko-ko-mo) / Eva Taylor," accessed April 24, 2020, https://adp.library.ucsb.edu/index.php/matrix/detail/2000207383/W80740-Red_hot_Flo_From_Ko-ko-mo.

7   Chanson creole de La creole
        Fry, Andy. "'Du Jazz Hot à "La Créole"': Josephine Baker Sings Offenbach." *Cambridge Opera Journal* 16, no. 1 (2004): 43-75. http://www.jstor.org/stable/3878304.

9   If You Don't Want Me Please Don't Dog Me 'Round
        Discography of American Historical Recordings, s.v. "OKeh matrix S-70353. If you don't want me (please don't dog me 'round) / Daisy Martin; Tampa Blue Jazz Band," accessed April 24, 2020, https://adp.library.ucsb.edu/index.php/matrix/detail/2000202480/S-70353-If_you_dont_want_me_please_dont_dog_me_round.

10   Cocktails for Two
Discography of American Historical Recordings, s.v. "Victor matrix PBS-79156. Cocktails for two / Duke Ellington Orchestra," accessed April 24, 2020, https://adp.library.ucsb.edu/index.php/matrix/detail/200060960/PBS-79156-Cocktails_for_two.

10   Tomorrow Night
Discography of American Historical Recordings, s.v. "Victor matrix BS-75423. Tomorrow night / Louis Armstrong Orchestra," accessed April 24, 2020, https://adp.library.ucsb.edu/index.php/matrix/detail/800040708/BS-75423-Tomorrow_night.

10   Night and Day
Discography of American Historical Recordings, s.v. "Victor matrix CS-75028. Night and day / Phil Dewey; Paul Whiteman Orchestra; Pickens Sisters," accessed April 24, 2020, https://adp.library.ucsb.edu/index.php/matrix/detail/800040322/CS-75028-Night_and_day.

10   Honeysuckle Rose
Discography of American Historical Recordings, s.v. "Victor matrix BVE-58546. Honeysuckle rose / McKinney's Cotton Pickers," accessed April 24, 2020, https://adp.library.ucsb.edu/index.php/matrix/detail/800029270/BVE-58546-Honeysuckle_rose.

13   You're Next
Discography of American Historical Recordings, s.v. "OKeh matrix 9537. You're next / Louis Armstrong; Hot Five," accessed April 24, 2020, https://adp.library.ucsb.edu/index.php/matrix/detail/2000201673/9537-Youre_next.

15   Good Morning, School Girl
Discography of American Historical Recordings, s.v. "Victor matrix BS-07649. Good morning, school girl / Sonny Boy Williamson," accessed April 24, 2020, https://adp.library.ucsb.edu/index.php/matrix/detail/200027355/BS-07649-Good_morning_school_girl.

16   The New San Antonio Rose
Discography of American Historical Recordings, s.v. "Victor matrix BS-063739. San Antonio Rose / Tito Guizar," accessed April 24, 2020, https://adp.library.ucsb.edu/index.php/matrix/detail/200050059/BS-063739-San_Antonio_Rose.

17   Dinah
Discography of American Historical Recordings, s.v. "Victor matrix CS-74877. Medley of Armstrong hits / Louis Armstrong Orchestra," accessed April 24, 2020, https://adp.library.ucsb.edu/index.php/matrix/detail/800040171/CS-74877-Medley_of_Armstrong_hits.

17   Louisiana Swing
Discography of American Historical Recordings, s.v. "OKeh matrix W404047. Louisiana swing / Luis Russell Orchestra," accessed April 24, 2020, https://adp.library.ucsb.edu/index.php/matrix/detail/2000212974/W404047-Louisiana_swing.

17   Chlo-e (song of the swamp)
Discography of American Historical Recordings, s.v. "Victor matrix BS-053580. Chlo-e / Duke Ellington Famous Orchestra," accessed April 24, 2020, https://adp.library.ucsb.edu/index.php/matrix/detail/200045453/BS-053580-Chlo-e.

19, 28   I Got It Bad and That Ain't Good
Discography of American Historical Recordings, s.v. "Victor matrix PBS-061319. I got it bad and that ain't good / Ivie Anderson; Duke Ellington Famous Orchestra," accessed April 24, 2020, https://adp.library.ucsb.edu/index.php/matrix/detail/200049146/PBS-061319-I_got_it_bad_and_that_aint_good.

19   Oh Johnny, Oh Johnny Oh
Discography of American Historical Recordings, s.v. "Victor matrix B-19378. Oh Johnny, oh Johnny, oh! / American Quartet," accessed April 24, 2020, https://adp.library.ucsb.edu/index.php/matrix/detail/700004454/B-19378-Oh_Johnny_oh_Johnny_oh.

25   C Jam Blues
Discography of American Historical Recordings, s.v. "Victor matrix BS-070683. The "C" jam blues / Duke Ellington Famous Orchestra," accessed September 29, 2020, https://adp.library.ucsb.edu/index.php/matrix/detail/200053345/BS-070683-The_C_jam_blues.

26, 38   Shine
Discography of American Historical Recordings, s.v. "OKeh matrix W404421. Shine / Louis Armstrong; Sebastian New Cotton Club Orchestra," accessed April 24, 2020, https://adp.library.ucsb.edu/index.php/matrix/detail/2000213412/W404421-Shine.

26   Hey Lawdy Mama
Discography of American Historical Recordings, s.v. "Decca matrix 64733. Hey! Lawdy Mama / Count Basie ; Freddie Green ; Jo Jones ; Walter Page," accessed April 24, 2020, https://adp.library.ucsb.edu/index.php/matrix/detail/2000292846/64733-Hey_Lawdy_Mama.

30   White Christmas
Discography of American Historical Recordings, s.v. "Victor matrix PBS-072435. White Christmas / Freddy Martin Orchestra ; Clyde Rogers," accessed April 24, 2020, https://adp.library.ucsb.edu/index.php/matrix/detail/200054421/PBS-072435-White_Christmas.

37   Why Don't You Do Right?
Discography of American Historical Recordings, s.v. "Decca matrix 69743. Why don't you do right / Nora Lee King," accessed April 24, 2020, https://adp.library.ucsb.edu/index.php/matrix/detail/2000297856/69743-Why_dont_you_do_right.

37   A Journey to the Stars
Discography of American Historical Recordings, s.v. "Decca matrix L 3265. A journey to a star / Judy Garland," accessed April 23, 2020 https://adp.library.ucsb.edu/index.php/matrix/detail/2000269688/L_3265-A_journey_to_a_star.

37   Don't Get Around Much Anymore
Discography of American Historical Recordings, s.v. "Victor matrix PBS-049656. Don't get around much anymore / Duke Ellington Famous Orchestra," accessed April 24, 2020, https://adp.library.ucsb.edu/index.php/matrix/detail/200043943/PBS-049656-Dont_get_around_much_anymore.

SELECT BIBLIOGRAPHY

Austin, Jane, 1775-1817. *Pride and Prejudice*. New York: Modern Library, 1995.

Barry, John M. *Rising Tide: The Great Flood of 1927 and How It Changed America*. New York: Simon & Schuster, 1997.

Bishop, Chris, General Editor. *The Illustrated Encyclopedia of Weapons of World War II*. New York: Metro Books, 2014.

Brasseaux, Carl A. *French, Cajun, Creole, Houma, A Primer on Francophone Louisiana*. Baton Rouge, LA: Louisiana State University Press, 2005.

Clements, Terrill. *American Volunteer Group "Flying Tigers" Aces*. Oxford, London: Osprey, 2001.

Colette, Sidonie-Gabrielle, 1873-1954. *Duo*. Translated into English by Peter Owen Publishers. London: Peter Owen Publishers, 2000.

Crouch, Gregory. *China's Wings*. New York: Bantam Books, 2012.

de Maupassant, Guy,1850-1893. *Le Maison Tellier,* from *The Works of Guy de Maupassant* by Garstin Quesada, Louise Charlotee. Mishawaka, IN: Palala Press, 2015.

de Stendhal, M. (Marie-Henri Beyle), 1783-1842. *Le Rouge et Le Noir, chronique de XIX siègle*. Paris: A. Levavassuer, Libraire, Palais-Royale, 1831.

Dibbs, John M. and Holmes, Tony. *Flying Legends*. New York: Crestline, 2015.

Dumas, Alexandre. 1802-1870. *La Reine Margot*. Preface by Jean Tullard, edited by Gallimard. Paris: Folio Classique, 1973.

Ford, Daniel. *Flying Tigers, Claire Chennault and His American Volunteers, 1941-42*. Revised edition, New York: Harper Collins/Smithsonian Books, 2007.

Fry, Andy. "'Du Jazz Hot à "La Créole'": Josephine Baker Sings Offenbach." *Cambridge Opera Journal* 16, no. 1 (2004): 43-75. http://www.jstor.org/stable/3878304.

Greenlaw, Olga. 1908-1983. *The Lady and the Tigers. The Story of the remarkable woman who served with the Flying Tigers in Burma and China, 1941-1942.* New York: E.P. Dutton Books, 1943. Edited with notes and additional material by Daniel Ford. Warbird Books, 2012.

Hemingway, Ernest. 1899-1961. *For Whom the Bell Tolls.* New York: Charles Scribner's Sons, 1940.

James, C.L.R. *The Black Jacobins, Toussaint L'Ouverture and the San Domingo Revolution.* New York: Vintage Books of Random House, Second Edition Revised, 1989.

Lao Tzu. *Tao te Ching.* Translated to English by Witter Bynner (*The Way of Life According to Lao Tzu*). New York: Perigee, 1944.

Larsen, Nella.1891-1964. *Passing.* First published in the United States by Alfred A. Knopf, Inc., 1929. Edited and with an introduction and notes by Thadious M. Davis, 1997. New York: Penguin Books.

Mitter, Rana. *Forgotten Ally, China's World War II, 1937-1945.* Boston: Houghton Mifflin Harcourt, 2013.

Rilke, Rainer Maria, 1875-1926. *Letters to a Young Poet.* Translated to English with a forward by Stephen Mitchell. New York: The Modern Library, 1984.

Samson, Jack. *The Flying Tiger. The True Story of General Claire Chennault and the U.S. 14th Air Force in China.* Guilford, CT: Lyons Press, 2011.

The Holy Bible: King James Version. Dallas: Brown Books Publishing, 2004.

Valdman, Albert, Senior Editor. *Dictionary of Louisiana French, As Spoken in Cajun, Creole and American Indian Communities.* Jackson, MS: University Press of Mississippi, 2010.

Van Vechten, Carl, 1880-1964. *Nigger Heaven.* New York: Alfred A. Knopf, 1926.

Wright, Richard, 1908-1960. *Native Son.* New York: Harper Perennial Modern Classics, 2005.

FOR BOOK CLUBS

If your book club is interested in suggested questions for discussion, you may find a list on the publisher's website. If you wish to contact the author, please make your inquiry at www.nocopublishing.com.